# A
# CAVERN
## OF BLACK ICE

## Prophecy of the Reach

Once in 1,000 years an innocent is born with the uncontrollable power and need to reach across the barrier of worlds, into the realm of the dead—an release the Endlords from their eternal prison, to annihilate *all* life . . .

Ash March is an innocent. She is also a Reach. And her time is now . . .

## Praise for *A Cavern of Black Ice*

## Books by J. V. Jones

### THE BOOK OF WORDS TRILOGY:

*The Baker's Boy*
*A Man Betrayed*
*Master and Fool*

### THE SWORD OF SHADOWS SERIES:

*\*A Cavern of Black Ice*
*\*A Fortress of Grey Ice*
*†\*A Sword from Red Ice*

*The Barbed Coil*

\*A Tor Book
†forthcoming

# J. V. JONES

# A CAVERN

# OF BLACK ICE

TOR®
fantasy

A TOM DOHERTY ASSOCIATES BOOK
NEW YORK

This is a work of fiction. All the characters and events portrayed in this book are either products of the author's imagination or are used fictitiously.

A CAVERN OF BLACK ICE

Copyright © 1999, 2005 by J. V. Jones

All rights reserved, including the right to reproduce this book, or portions thereof, in any form.

Edited by James Frenkel
Cover art by Jean-Pierre Targete

A Tor Book
Published by Tom Doherty Associates, LLC
175 Fifth Avenue
New York, NY 10010

www.tor.com

Tor® is a registered trademark of Tom Doherty Associates, LLC.

ISBN 0-765-34551-X
EAN 978-0765-34551-6

First edition: March 2005

Printed in the United States of America

0 9 8 7 6 5 4 3 2 1

*To Paul,*
*who, on the far side of the Atlantic,*
*keeps hours every bit*
*as strange as mine*

# ACKNOWLEDGMENTS

With a book as large as this one a lot of help is needed to pound it into shape. My thanks and gratitude are owed to Betsy Mitchell, Tim Holman, and Russell Galen. Thanks also to James Frenkel and the staff at Tor, who worked on this new edition and did some pounding of their own.

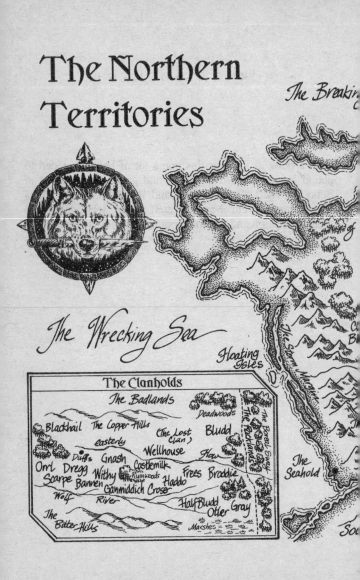

# The Northern Territories

The Breaki...

The Wrecking Sea

Floating
Isles

## The Clanholds

The Badlands

Deadwoods

Blackhail   The Copper Hills   (The Lost Clan)   Bludd

easterly   Wellhouse

Dhoone   Gnash   Castlemilk   Haw

Orrl   Dregg   Withy   Rumwoods   Frees   Broddie

Scarpe   Bannen   Haddo

Ganmiddich   Croser

Wolf   River   Half Bludd   Otter Gray

The   Bitter Hills   Marshes

The Storm Margin

The Boreal Sway   The Racklands

The
Seahold

The Bitter Hills

# CONTENTS

# —A—
# CAVERN
## OF BLACK ICE

# PROLOGUE

## A Birth, a Death, and a Binding

TARISSA WHISPERED A HOPE out loud before looking up at the sky. "Please make it lighter than before. *Please*." As her lips came together she looked up past the wind-twisted pines and the ridge of frost-riven granite, up toward the position of the sun. Only the sun wasn't there. Stormheads rolled across the sky, cutting out the sunlight, massing, churning, driven by winds that snapped and circled like pack wolves around sheep. Tarissa made a small gesture with her hand. The storm wasn't passing overhead. It had come to the mountain to stay.

Dropping her gaze, she took a steadying breath. She couldn't afford to panic. The city lay a thousand feet below her, rising from the shadow of the mountain like a second, lesser peak. She could see the ring towers clearly now, four of them, two built hard against the wall, the tallest piercing the storm with its iron stake. It was a long way down. Hours of walk, even. And she had to be careful.

Resting her hand on her swollen stomach, she forced herself to smile. *Storms?* They were nothing.

She moved quickly. Loose scree, bird skeletons, and snags of wind-blasted wood tripped her feet. It was hard to walk, even harder to keep her balance on the ever sharpening slope. Steep draws and creases forced her sideways instead of down. The temperature was falling, and for the first time all day Tarissa noticed her breath came out white. Her left glove had been gone for days—lost somewhere on the far side of the mountain—and she stripped off her right glove, turned it inside out, and pulled it onto her left hand. The fingers there had started to grow numb.

Dead trees blocked her path. Some of their trunks were so smooth they looked polished. As she reached out to steady herself against one of the hard black limbs, she felt a sharp pain in her lower abdomen. Something shifted. Wetness spilled down her thighs. A soft sting sounded in her lower back, and a wave of sickness washed up her gullet, depositing the taste of sour milk in her mouth. Tarissa closed her eyes. This time she kept her hopes to herself.

Wet snow began to fall as she pushed herself off from the dead tree. Her glove was sticky with sap, and bits of pine needles were glued to the fingers. Underfoot the granite ledge was unstable; gravel spilled from deep gashes, and husks of failed saplings crumbled to nothing the instant they took her weight. Despite the cold, Tarissa started to sweat. The pain in her back chewed inward, and although she didn't want to admit it, didn't even want to acknowledge it, her lower abdomen began contracting in rhythmic waves.

*No. No. NO.* Her baby wasn't due yet. Two weeks more— it *had* to be. She needed to make it to the city, to find shelter. She'd even held back enough coins for a midwife and a room.

Finding a lead through the rocks, she picked up her pace. A lone raven, its plumage dark and oily as a scorched liver, watched her in silence from the distorted upper branch of a blackstone pine. Spying it, Tarissa was conscious of how ridiculous she must look: fat bellied, wild haired, scrambling down a mountainside in a race against a storm. Grimacing, she looked away from the bird. She didn't like how it made her feel.

Contractions were coming faster now, and Tarissa found that it helped if she kept on the move. Stopping made the suffering linger, gave her seconds to count and think.

Mist rose from crevices. Snow flew in Tarissa's face, and the wind lifted the cloak from her back. Overhead, the clouds mimicked her descent, following her down the mountain as if she were showing them the way. Tarissa walked with her gloved hand cradling her belly. The fluid between her legs had dried to a sticky film that sucked her thighs together as she moved. Heat pumped up through the arteries in her neck, flushing her cheeks and the bridge of her nose.

Faster. She had to move faster.

Spotting a clear run between boulders, Tarissa switched

her path farther to her right. Thorns snagged her skirt, and she yanked on the fabric, losing patience. As she turned back to face the path, the raven took flight. Its black wings beat against the storm current, snapping and tearing like teeth.

The instant Tarissa stepped forward, gravel and rocks began running beneath her feet. She felt herself falling, and she flung out her arms to grab at something, *anything*, to hold her. The mist hid everything at ground level, and Tarissa's hands found only loose stones and twigs. Pain exploded in her shoulder as she was thrown against a rock. Pinecones and rocks bounced overhead as she tried desperately to break her fall. Her bare hand grasped at a tussock of wolfgrass, but her body kept sliding downward and the roots pulled free in her hand. Her hip bashed against a granite ridge, something sharp shaved skin from the back of her knee, and when she opened her mouth to scream, snow flew between her lips, freezing the cry on her tongue.

She came to. There was no pain, just a fog of ragged light lying between her and the outside world. Above her, as far as her eyes could see, stretched walls of hand-polished limestone, mason cut and smooth as bone. She'd finally made it to the city with the Iron Spire.

Dimly she was aware of something pushing far below her. Minutes passed before she realized that it was her body working to expel the child. She swallowed hard. Suddenly she missed all the people she had run from. Leaving home had been a mistake.

*Kaaw!*

Tarissa tried to shift her head toward the sound. A hot needle of pain jabbed at the vertebrae in the base of her neck. She blacked out. When she came to again she saw the raven sitting on a rock before her. Black-and-gold eyes pinned her with a look that was devoid of pity. Bobbing its head and raising its scaly yellow claws, it danced a little jig of damnation. When it was done it made a soft *clucking* noise that sounded just like a mother scolding a child and then flung itself to the mercy of the storm. Cold currents bore it swiftly away.

*Pushing.* Her body kept pushing.

Tarissa felt herself drifting . . . she was so tired . . . so very, very tired. If only she could find a way through the fog . . . if only her eyes could show her more.

As her eyelids closed for the last time and her ribs pressed an unused breath from her lungs, she saw a pair of booted feet walking toward her. The tar-blackened leather melted snowflakes on contact.

\* \* \*

THEY APPLIED THE LEECHES to him in rings of six. His body was crusted with sweat and rock dust and dirt, and the first man scraped the skin clean with deer tallow and a cedarwood wedge, while the second worked in his shadow with metal pincers, a pitchpine bucket, and heavy buckskin gloves.

The man who no longer knew his name strained against his bindings, testing. Thick coils of rope pressed into his neck, upper arms, wrists, thighs, and ankles. He could shudder and breathe and blink. Nothing more.

He could barely feel the leeches. One settled in the fold between his inner thigh and groin, and he tensed for a moment. Pincer took a pinch of white powder from a pouch around his neck and applied it to the leech. Salt. The leech dropped away. A fresh leech was applied, higher this time so it couldn't attach itself to skin that wasn't fit.

That done, Pincer stripped off his gloves and spoke a word that sent Accomplice to the far side of the cell. A moment later Accomplice returned with a tray and a soapstone lamp. A single red flame burned within the lamp, heating the contents of the crucible above. When he saw the flame, the man with no name flinched so hard that the rope binding his wrists split his skin. Flames were all he had now. Memories of flames. He hated the flames and feared them, yet he needed them, too. Familiarity bred contempt, they said. But the man with no name knew that was only half of it. Familiarity bred dependence as well.

Thoughts lost in the dance of flames, he didn't see Pincer kneading an oakum wad in his fist. He was aware only of Accomplice's hands on his jaw, repositioning his head, brushing his hair to one side, and pushing his skull hard against the bench. The man with no name felt the frayed rope and beeswax wad thrust into his left ear. Ship's caulking. They were shoring him up like a storm-battered hull. A second wad was thrust into his right ear, and then Accomplice held the nameless man's jaws wide while Pincer thrust a third wad into the back of his throat. The desire to vomit was sudden and overpowering, but Pincer slapped one large hand on the nameless man's chest and another on his belly and pressed hard against the contracting muscles, forcing them flat. A minute later the urge had passed.

Still Accomplice held on to his jaw. Pincer paid attention to the tray, his hands casting claw shadows against the cell wall as he worked. Seconds later he turned about. A thread of animal sinew was stretched between his thumbs. Seeing it, Accomplice shifted his grip, opening the nameless man's jaws wider, pulling back lip tissue along with bone. The man with no name felt thick fingers in his mouth. He tasted urine and salt and leech water. His tongue was pressed to the base of his mouth, and then sinew was woven across his bottom teeth, binding his tongue in place.

Fear came alive in the nameless man's chest. Perhaps flames weren't the only things that could harm him.

"He's done," said Pincer, drawing back.

"What about the wax?" breathed a third voice from the shadows near the door. It was the One Who Issued Orders. "You are supposed to seal his eyes shut."

"Wax is too hot. It could blind him if we use it now."

"Use it."

The flame in the soapstone lamp wavered as Accomplice drew the crucible away. The man with no name smelled smoke given off from the impurities in the wax. When the burning came it shocked him. After everything he had been through, all the suffering he had borne, he imagined he had outlived pain. He was wrong. And as the hours wore on and his bones were broken methodically by Pincer wielding a goosedown padded mallet, Accomplice following after to ensure the splintered ends were pulled apart, and his internal organs were manipulated with needles so long and fine that they could puncture specific chambers in his lungs and heart while leaving the surrounding tissue intact, he began to realize that pain—and the ability to feel it—was the last sense to go.

When the One Who Issued Orders stepped close and began breathing words of binding older than the city he currently stood in, the man with no name no longer cared. His mind had returned to the flames. There, at least, was a pain that he knew.

# ONE

## *The Badlands*

RAIF SEVRANCE SET HIS sights on the target and *called* the ice hare to him. A moment of disorientation followed, where the world dropped out of focus like a great dark stone sinking to the bottom of a lake; then, in the shortest space that a moment could be, he perceived the animal's heart. The light, sounds, and odors of the badlands slid away, leaving nothing but the weight of blood in the ice hare's chest and the hummingbird flutter of its heart. Slowly, deliberately, Raif angled his bow away from the target. The arrow cracked the freezing air like a word spoken out loud. As its iron blade shot past the hare, the creature's head came up and it sprang for cover in a cushion of black sedge.

"Take the shot again," Drey said. "You sent that wide on purpose."

Raif lowered his bow and glanced over at his older brother. Drey's face was partially shaded by his fox hood, but the firm set of his mouth was clear. Raif paused, considered arguing, then shrugged and reset his footing on the tundra. It never felt good deceiving Drey.

Fingers smoothing down the backing of his horn-and-sinew bow, Raif looked over the windblown flats of the badlands. Panes of ice already lay thick over melt ponds. In the flattened colt grass beneath Raif's feet hoarfrost grew as silently and insidiously as mold on second-day bread. The few trees that managed to survive in the gravelly floodplain were wind-crippled blackstone pines and prostrate hemlock. Directly ahead lay a shallow draw filled with loose rocks and scrubby bushes that looked as tough and bony as moose antlers. Raif dipped his gaze a fraction lower to the brown lichen mat surrounding a pile of wet rocks. Even on a morning as cold as this, the lick was still running.

As Raif watched, another ice hare popped up its head. Cheeks puffing, ears trembling, it held its position, listening for danger. It wanted the salt in the lick. Game animals came from leagues around to drink at the trickle of salt water that bled across the rocks in the draw. Tem said the lick welled up from an underground stream.

Raif raised his bow, slid an arrow from the quiver at his waist. In one smooth motion he nocked the iron arrowhead against the plate and drew the bowstring back to his chest. The hare swiveled its head. Its dark eyes looked straight at Raif. Too late. Raif already had the creature's heart in his sights. Kissing the string, Raif let the arrow fly. Fingers of ice mist parted, a faint hiss sounded, and the arrowhead shot straight into the hare's rib cage. If the creature made a sound, Raif didn't hear it. Carried back by the force of the blow, it collapsed into the lick.

"That's three to you. None to me." Drey's voice sounded flat, resigned.

Raif pretended to check his bow for hairpin cracks.

"Come on. Let's shoot at targets. No more hares are going to show now you've sent a live one into the lick." Drey reached out and touched Raif's bow. "You could have used a smaller head on that arrow, you know. You're supposed to *kill* the hare, not disembowel it."

Raif looked up. Drey was grinning, just a bit. Relieved, Raif grinned back at him. Drey was two years older than he, better at everything an older brother should be better at. Up until this winter he had been better at shooting, too. A lot better.

Abruptly Raif tucked his bow into his belt and ran for the draw. Tem never let them shoot anything purely for sport, and the hares had to be taken back to camp, skinned, and roasted. The pelts were Raif's. Another couple more and he'd have enough for a winter coat for Effie. Not that Effie had much use for a coat. She was the only eight-year-old in Clan Blackhail who didn't enjoy running around in the snow. Frowning, Raif twisted the arrows free from the twig-thin bones of the hare's rib cage, careful not to break the shafts. Timber straight enough for arrows was rare in the badlands.

As he sealed the carcass in his game pouch, Raif checked the position of the sun. Nearly noon now. A storm heading elsewhere blew eastward in the far north. Dark gray clouds rolled across the horizon like smoke from a distant fire. Raif shivered. The Great Want lay to the north. Tem said that if a storm didn't begin in the Want, then it sure as stone would end there.

"Hey! Rough Jaw! Get your bow over here and let's shred some wood." Drey sent an expertly pitched stone skittering off rocks and hummocks, to land with a devilish skip precisely at Raif's feet. "Or are you scared your lucky streak just ended?"

Almost against his will, Raif's hand rose to his chin. His skin felt as bristly as a frozen pinecone. He was Rough Jaw all right. No argument there. "Paint the target, Sevrance Cur. Then I'll let you take a hand's worth of practice shots while I restring my bow for wood."

Even a hundred paces in the distance, Raif saw Drey's jaw drop. *Restring my bow for wood* was exactly the sort of high-blown thing a master bowman would say. Raif could hardly keep from laughing out loud. Ignoring the insult and the boasting, Drey snorted loudly and began plucking fistfuls of grass from the tundra. By the time Raif caught up with him, Drey had smeared the grass over the trunk of a frost-killed pine, forming a roughly circular target, wet with snowmelt and grass sap.

Drey shot first. Stepping back one hundred and fifty paces, he held his bow at arm's length. Drey's bow was a recurve made of winter-cut yew, dried over two full years, and hand-tillered to reduce shock. Raif envied him for it. His own bow was a clan hand-down, used by anyone who had the string to brace it.

Drey took his time sighting his bow. He had a sure, unshakable grip and the strength to hold the string for as long as his ungloved fingers could bear. Just when Raif was set to call "Shot due," his brother released the string. The arrow landed with a dull *thunk*, dead center of the smeared-on target. Turning, Drey inclined his head at his younger brother. He did not smile.

Raif's bow was already in hand, his arrow already chosen.

With Drey's arrow shaft still quivering in the target, Raif sighted his bow. The pine was long dead. Cold. When Raif tried to *call* it to him as he had with the ice hare, it wouldn't come. The wood stood its distance. Raif felt nothing: no quickening of his pulse, no dull pain behind his eyes, no metal tang in his mouth. Nothing. The target was just a target. Unsettled, Raif centered his bow and searched for the still line that would lead his arrow home. Seeing nothing but a faraway tree, Raif released his string. Straightaway he knew the shot was bad. He'd been gripping the handle too tightly, and his fingertips had grazed the string on release. The bow shot back with a *thwack*, and Raif's shoulder took a bad recoil. The arrow landed a good two hands lower than the target.

"Shoot again." Drey's voice was cold.

Raif massaged his shoulder, then selected a second arrow. For luck, he brushed the fletchings against the raven lore he wore on a cord around his neck. The second shot was better, but it still hit a thumb's length short of dead center. Raif turned to look at his brother. It was his shot.

Drey made a small motion with his bow. "Again."

Raif shook his head. "No. It's your turn."

Drey shook his own head right back. "You sent those two wide on purpose. Now shoot."

"No, I didn't. It was a true shot. I—"

"No one heart-kills three hares on the run, then misses a target as big as a man's chest. No one." Drey pushed back his fox hood. His eyes were dark. He spat out the wad of black curd he'd been chewing. "I don't need mercy shots. Either shoot with me fair, or not at all."

Looking at his brother, seeing his big hands pressing hard into the wood of his bow and the whiteness of his thumbs as he worked on an imagined imperfection, Raif knew words would get him nowhere. Drey Sevrance was eighteen years old, a yearman in the clan. This past summer he'd taken to braiding his hair with black leather strips and wearing a silver earring in his ear. Last night around the firepit, when Dagro Blackhail had burned the scum off an old malt and dropped his earring into the clear liquor remaining, Drey had done the same. All the sworn clansmen had. Metal next to the skin attracted frostbite. And everyone in the clan had seen the black nubs of unidentifiable flesh that the 'bite left behind. You could find many willing to tell the story of how Jon Marrow's member had frozen solid when he was jumped by Dhoonesmen while he was relieving himself in the brack. By the time he had seen the Dhoonesmen off and pulled himself up from the nail-hard tundra, his manhood was frozen like a cache of winter meat. By all accounts he hadn't felt a thing until he was brought into the warmth of the roundhouse and the stretched and shiny flesh began to thaw. His screams had kept the clan awake all night.

Raif ran his hand along his bowstring, warming the wax. If Drey needed to see him take a third shot to prove he wasn't shamming, then take another shot he would. He'd lost the desire to fight.

Again Raif tried to call the dead tree to him, searching for the still line that would guide his arrow to the heart. Although the blackstone pine had perished ten hunting seasons earlier, it had hardly withered at all. Only the needles were missing. The pitch in the trunk preserved the crown, and the cold dryness of the badlands hindered the growth of fungus beneath the bark. Tem said that in the Great Want trees took hundreds, sometimes thousands, of years to decay.

Seconds passed as Raif concentrated on the target. The longer he held his sights, the deader the tree seemed. Something was missing. Ice hares were real living things. Raif felt their warmth in the space between his eyes. He imagined the lode of hot pulsing blood in their hearts and saw the still line that linked those hearts to his arrowhead as clearly as a dog sees his leash. Slowly Raif was coming to realize that still line meant death.

Frustration finally got the better of him, and he stopped searching for the inner heart of the target and centered his sights on the *visual* heart instead. With the fletchings of Drey's arrow in his eyeline, Raif released the shot.

The moment his thumb lifted from the string, a raven *kaaw*ed High and shrill, the carrion feeder's cry seemed to split the very substance of time. Raif felt a finger of ice tap his spine. His vision blurred. Saliva jetted into his mouth, thick and hot and tasting of metal. Stumbling back, he lost his grip on the bow and it fell to the ground point first. A crack sounded as it landed. The arrow hit the tree with a dull thud, placing a knuckle short of Drey's own shot. Raif didn't care. Black points raced across his vision, scorching like soot belched from a fire.

"Raif! Raif!"

Raif felt Drey's huge, muscular arms clamp around his shoulders, smelled his brother's scent of neat's-foot oil, tanned leather, horses, and sweat. Glancing up, Raif saw Drey's brown eyes staring into his. He looked worried. His prized yewbow lay flat on the ground.

"Here, sit." Not waiting for any compliance on Raif's part, Drey forced his younger brother onto the tundra floor. The frozen earth bit into Raif's buckskin pants. Turning away from his brother, Raif cleared his mouth of the metal-tasting saliva. His eyes stung. A sickening pain in his forehead made him retch. He clenched his jaw until bone clicked.

Seconds passed. Drey said nothing, just held his brother as tightly as he could. Part of Raif wanted to smile; the last time Drey had crushed him like this was after he fell twenty feet from a foxtail pine three springs back. The fall only broke an ankle. Drey's subsequent bear hug had succeeded in breaking two ribs.

Strangely, the memory had a calming effect on Raif, and the pain slowly subsided. Raif's vision blurred sharply and then reset itself. A feeling of badness grew in him. Swiveling around in his brother's grip, Raif looked in the direction of the camp. The stench of metal washed over him, as thick as grease smoke from the rendering pits.

Drey followed his gaze. "What's the matter?" His voice was tight, strained.

"Don't you feel it?"

Drey shook his head.

The camp was five leagues to the south, hidden in the shelter of the flood basin. All Raif could see was the rapidly darkening sky and the low ridges and rocky flats of the badlands. Yet he felt something. Something unspeakable, as when nightmares jolted him awake in pitch darkness or when he thought back to the day Tem had shut him in the guidehouse with his mother's corpse. He had been eight at the time, old enough to pay due respect to the dead. The guidehouse was dark and filled with smoke. The hollowed-out basswood where his mother lay smelled of wet earth and rotten things. Sulfur had been rubbed into the carved inner trunk to keep insects and carrion feeders away from the body when it was laid upon the ground.

Raif smelled badness now. He smelled stinking metal and sulfur and death. Fighting against Drey's grip, he cried, "We have to go back."

Drey released his grip on Raif and pulled himself to his feet. He plucked his dogskin gloves from his belt and pulled them on with two violent movements. "Why?"

Raif shook his head. The pain and nausea had gone, but something else had come in its place. A tight shivering fear. "The camp."

Drey nodded. He took a deep breath and looked set to speak, then abruptly stopped himself. Offering Raif his hand, he heaved his brother off the ground with a single tug. By the time Raif had brushed the frost from his buckskins, Drey had collected both bows and was pulling the arrow shafts from the dead tree. As he turned away from the black-stone pine, Raif noticed the fletchings in Drey's grip were shaking. This one small sign of his brother's fear worried Raif more than anything else. Drey was his older brother by two years. Drey was afraid of nothing.

They had left the camp before dawn, before even the embers on the firepit had burned cold. No one except Tem knew they had gone. It was their last chance to shoot game before they broke camp and returned to the roundhouse for winter. The previous night Tem had warned them about going off on their own in the badlands, though he knew well enough that nothing he said would stop them.

"Sons!" he had said, shaking his large, grizzled head. "I might as well spend my days picking ticks from the dogs as tell you two what you should and shouldn't do. At least come sundown I'd have a deloused pup to show for my trouble." Tem would glower as he spoke, and the skin above his eyebrows would bunch into knots, yet his eyes always gave him away.

Just this morning as Raif pulled back the hide fastening on the tent he shared with his father and brother, he noticed a small bundle set upon the warming stone. It was food. Hunters' food. Tem had packed two whole smoke-cured ptarmigan, a brace of hard-boiled eggs, and enough strips of hung mutton to mend an elk-size hole in a tent. All this for his sons to eat on a hunting trip he had expressly forbidden them to take.

Raif smiled. Tem Sevrance knew his sons well.

"Put on your gloves." It was Drey, acting just like an older brother. "And pull up your hood. Temperature's dropping fast."

Raif did what he was told, struggling to put on gloves with hands that felt big and slow. Drey was right: It was getting colder. Another shiver worked its way up Raif's spine, making his shoulders jerk awkwardly. "Let's go." Drey's thoroughness was beginning to nettle him. They had to get back to the camp. Now. Something wasn't right.

Although Tem warned them constantly about the danger of using up all their energy by running in the cold, Raif couldn't stop himself. Despite spitting profusely, he couldn't remove the taste of metal from his mouth. The air smelled bad, and the clouds overhead seemed darker, lower, *closer*. To the south lay a line of bald, featureless hills, and west of them lay the Coastal Ranges. Tem said that the Ranges were the reason why the Want and the badlands were so dry. He said their peaks milked every last drop of moisture from passing storms.

The three hares Raif had shot earlier thumped up and down in his pack as he ran. Raif hated their warmth against his thigh, was sickened by their fresh-kill smell. When the two brothers came upon Old Hoopers Lake, Raif tore the pack from his belt and threw it into the center of the dull black water. Old Hoopers wasn't frozen yet. River fed, it would take a full week of frost before its current-driven waters plated. Still, the lake had the greasy look of imminent ice about it. As Raif's pack sank to the bottom, swirls of vegetable oils and tufts of elk hair bobbed up and down on the surface.

Drey swore. Raif didn't catch what he said, but he imagined the words *waste of fine game* in their place.

As the brothers ran south, the landscape gradually changed. Trees grew straighter and taller, and there were more of them. Beds of lichen were replaced by long grasses, bushes, and sedge. Horse and game tracks formed paths through the frozen foliage, and fat grouse flew up from the undergrowth, all flying feathers and spitting beaks.

Raif barely noticed. Close to the camp perimeter now, they should have been able to see smoke, hear the sound of metal rasping against metal, raised voices, laughter. Dagro Blackhail's foster son, Mace, should be riding to greet them on his fat-necked cob.

Drey swore again. Quietly, to himself.

Raif resisted the urge to glance over at his brother's face. He was frightened of what he might see.

A powerful horseman, archer, and hammerman, Drey pulled ahead of Raif as he charged down the slope to the camp. Raif pushed himself harder, balling his fists and thrusting out his chin. He didn't want to lose sight of his brother, hated the thought of Drey arriving at the tent circle alone.

Fear stretched over Raif's body like a drying hide, pulling at his skin and gut. They had left thirteen men standing by at the camp: Dagro Blackhail and his son, Mace; Tem; Chad and Jorry Shank; Mallon Clayhorn and his son, Darri, whom everyone called Halfmast . . .

Raif shook his head softly. Thirteen men alone on the badlands plains suddenly seemed unbelievably easy prey. Dhoonesmen, Bluddsmen, and Maimed Men were out there. Raif's stomach clenched. And the Sull. The Sull were out there, too.

The dark, weather-stained tents came into view. All was quiet. There were no horses or dogs in sight. The firepit was a dark gaping hole in the center of the cleared space. Loose tent flaps ripped in the wind like banners at battle's end. Drey had broken ahead, but now he stopped and waited for Raif to join him. His breath came hard and fast, and spent air vented from his nose and mouth in great white streams. He did not look round as Raif approached.

"Draw your weapon," he hissed.

Raif already had, but he scored the blade of his halfsword against its boiled-leather scabbard, mimicking the noise of drawing. Drey moved forward when he heard it.

They came upon Jorry Shank's body first. It was lying in a feed ditch close to the horse posts. Drey had to turn the body to find the deathwound. The portion of Jorry's face that had been lying against the earth had taken on the yellow bloom of frozen flesh. The wound was as big as a fist, heart deep, made with a greatsword, and for some reason there was hardly any blood.

"Maybe the blood froze as it left him," Drey murmured, settling the body back in place. The words sounded like a prayer.

"He never got chance to draw his weapon. Look." Raif was surprised at how calm his voice sounded.

Drey nodded. He patted Jorry's shoulder and then stood away.

"There's horse tracks. See." Raif kicked the ground near the first post. He found it easier to concentrate on what he could see here, on the camp perimeter, than turn his sights toward the tent circle and the one shabby, oft repaired, hide-and-moose-felt tent that belonged to Tem Sevrance. "Those shoemarks weren't made by Blackhail horses."

"Bluddsmen use a grooved shoe."

So did other clans and even some city men, yet Raif had no desire to contradict his brother. Clan Bludd's numbers were swelling, and border and cattle raids had become more frequent. Vaylo Bludd had seven sons, and it was rumored he wanted a separate clanhold for each of them. Mace Blackhail said that Vaylo Bludd killed and ate his own dogs, even when he had elk and bear meat turning on the spit above his fire. Raif didn't believe the story for a moment—to eat one's own dogs was considered a kind of cannibalism to a clansman, justifiable only in the event of ice-bound starvation and imminent death—but others, including Drey, did. Mace Blackhail was three years older than Drey: when he spoke, Drey took heed.

As Drey and Raif approached the tent circle, their pace slowed. Dead dogs lay in the dirt, saliva frozen around their blunted fangs, their coats shaggy with ice. Fixed yellow eyes stared from massive gray heads. Glacial winds had set rising hackles in place, giving the dogs' corpses the bunched-neck look of buffalo. As with Jorry Shank's body, there was little blood.

Raif smelled stinking, smelted metal everywhere. The air around the camp seemed different, yet he didn't have the words to describe it. It reminded him of the slowly congealing surface water on Old Hoopers Lake. Something had caused the very air to thicken and change. Something with the force of winter itself.

"Raif! Here!"

Drey had crossed into the tent circle and was kneeling close to the firepit. Raif saw the usual line of pots and drying hides suspended on spruce branches over the pit, and the load of timber waiting to be quartered for firewood. He even saw the partially butchered black bear carcass that Dagro Blackhail had brought down yesterday in the sedge meadow to the east. The bearskin, which he had been so proud of, had been set to dry on a nearby rack. Dagro had planned to present it as a gift to his wife, Raina, when the hunt party returned to the roundhouse.

But Dagro Blackhail, chief of Clan Blackhail, would never return home.

Drey knelt over his partially frozen corpse. Dagro had taken a massive broadsword stroke from behind. His hands were speckled with blood, and the thick-bladed cleaver he still held in his grip was similarly marked. The blood was neither his nor his attackers'. It came from the skinned and eviscerated bear carcass lying at his feet; Dagro must have been finishing the butchering when he was jumped from behind.

Raif took a quick unsteady breath and sank down by his brother's side. Something was blocking his throat. Dagro Blackhail's great bear of a face looked up at him. The clan chief did not look at peace. Fury was frozen in his eyes. Glaciated ice in his beard and mustache framed a mouth pressed hard in anger. Raif thanked the Stone Gods that his brother wasn't the kind of man to speak needlessly, and the two sat in silence, shoulders touching, as they paid due respect to the man who had led Clan Blackhail for twenty-nine years and was loved and honored by all in the clan.

"He's a fair man," Tem had said once about the clan chief in a rare moment when he was inclined to speak about matters other than hunting and dogs. "It may seem like small purchase, and you'll find others in the clan willing to heap all manner of praise upon Dagro Blackhail's head, but fairness is the hardest thing for a man to practice day to day. A chief can find himself having to speak up against his sworn brothers and his kin. And that's not easy for anyone to do."

It was, Raif thought, one of the longest speeches he'd ever heard his father make.

"It's not right, Raif." Drey said only that as he raised himself clear of Dagro Blackhail's body, but Raif knew what he meant. It *wasn't* right.

Mounted men had been here; broadswords and greatswords had been used; clan horses were gone, stolen. Dogs were slaughtered. The camp lay in open ground, Mace Blackhail was standing dogwatch: a raiding party should not have been able to approach unheeded. Mounted men made noise, especially here in the badlands, where the bone-hard tundra dealt harshly with anything traveling upon it. And then there was the lack of blood . . .

Raif pushed back his hood and ran a gloved hand through the tangle of his dark hair. Drey was making his way toward Tem's tent. Raif wanted to call him back, to tell him that they should check the other tents first, the rendering pits, the stream bank, the far perimeter, *anywhere* except that tent. Drey, as if sensing some small portion of his younger brother's thoughts, turned. He made a small beckoning gesture with his hand and then waited. Two bright points of pain prickled directly behind Raif's eyes. Drey always waited.

Together the sons of Tem Sevrance entered their father's tent. The body was just a few paces short of the entrance. Tem looked as if he had been on his way out when the broadsword cracked his sternum and clavicle, sending splinters of bone into his windpipe, lungs, and heart. He had fallen with his halfsword in his hand, but as with Jorry Shank, the weapon was unbloodied.

"Broadsword again," Drey said, his voice high and then rough as he sought to control it. "Bludd favors them."

Raif didn't acknowledge the words. It took all he had just to stand and look upon his father's body. Suddenly there was too much hollow space in his chest. Tem didn't seem as stiff as the others, and Raif stripped off his right glove and bent to touch what was visible of his father's cheek. Cold, dead flesh. Not frozen, but utterly cold, absent.

Pulling back as if he had touched something scorching hot rather than just plain cold, Raif rubbed his hand on his buckskins, wiping off whatever he imagined to be upon it.

Tem was gone.

Gone.

Without waiting for Drey, Raif pushed aside the tent flap and struck out into the rapidly darkening camp. His heart was beating in wild, irregular beats, and taking action seemed the only way to stop it.

WHEN DREY FOUND HIM a quarter later, Raif's right arm was stripped to the shoulder and blood from three separate cuts was pouring along his forearm and down to his wrist. Drey understood immediately. Tearing at his own sleeve, he joined his brother as he went among the slain men. All had died without blood on their weapons. To a clansman there was no honor in dying with a clean blade, so Raif was taking up their weapons one by one, drawing their blades across his skin, and spilling his own blood as a substitute. It was the one thing the two brothers could give to their clan. When they returned home to the roundhouse and someone asked, as someone always did, if the men had died fighting, Raif and Drey could now reply, "Their weapons ran with blood."

To a clansman those words mattered dear.

So the two brothers moved around the camp, discovering bodies in and out of tents, some with pale icicles of urine frozen to their legs, others with hair set in spiky mats where they had been caught bathing, a few with frozen wads of black curds still in their mouths, and one man—Meth Ganlow—with his beefy arms fixed around his favorite dog, protecting the wolfing even in death. A single swordstroke had killed both man and beast.

It was only later, when moonlight formed silver pools in the hard earth, and Tem's body was lying beside the firepit, close to the others but set apart, that Raif suddenly stopped in his tracks. "We never found Mace Blackhail," he said.

# T W O

## *Days Darker Than Night*

ASH MARCH SHOT AWAKE. Sitting up in bed, she dragged the heavy silk sheets up over her arms and shoulders and clutched them tight. She had been dreaming of ice again.

Taking deep breaths to calm herself, she looked around her chamber, checking. Of the two amber lamps on the mantel, only one was still burning. Good. That meant Katia had not been in to refuel it. The small ball of Ash's silver blond hair that she had pulled from her hairbrush before she slept still lay fast against the door. So no one else had entered her chamber, either.

Ash relaxed just a little. Her toes formed two knobby lumps beneath the covers, and as they looked a ridiculously long distance from her body, she wiggled them just to check that they were hers. She smiled when they wiggled right back at her. Toes were funny things.

The smile didn't quite take. As soon as Ash's face muscles relaxed, the *fact* of her dream came back to her. The sheets were twisted around her waist and they were sticky with sweat, and the yeasty smell of fear was upon them. She'd had another bad dream and another bad night, and it was the second in less than a week.

Without thinking Ash brought her hand to her mouth, almost as if she were trying to hold something in. Despite the warmth of the chamber—the charcoal smoking in the brazier beneath a layer of oil-soaked felt, and the hot water pipes so diligently tended by a furnaceman and his team working three stories below—her fingers felt icy cold. Against her will and her very best efforts, images from the dream came back to her. She saw a cavern with walls of black ice. A burned hand reaching toward her, cracks between its fingers oozing blood. Dark eyes watching, waiting . . .

Ash shivered. Swinging her hand down onto the bed, she beat the images back by pummeling the mattress as hard as she could. She wouldn't think about the dream. Didn't want to know what those cold eyes wanted.

*Thht. Thht. Thht.* Three knocks rang lightly against the fossilwood door.

Something deep inside Ash's chest, a band of muscle connecting her lungs to her heart, stiffened. Although breathless from beating the pillow, she didn't take a breath or even blink. Silent as settling dust, she told herself as her eyes focused on the door.

Finely grained and hard as nails, the door's perfect gray surface was marred by three black thumb-size pits: bolt holes. Six months earlier Ash had paid her maidservant, Katia, four halfsilvers to go down to the metalworkers' market near Almsgate and purchase a bolt and socket for the chamber door. Katia had done her bidding, returning with an iron bar big enough to secure a fort. Ash had fixed the metal plate and socket in place herself. She had blackened a fingernail in the process and broken the backs of two silver brushes, but the bolt pins had gone in and the fastening mechanism had worked smoothly, and for a week Ash had slept more soundly than she could ever remember sleeping.

Until . . .

*Thht. Thht. Thht.*

Ash stared at the empty bolt holes. She made no motion to answer the second round of knocking.

"Asarhia." A pause. "Almost-daughter, I will have no games played with me."

Tilting her body minutely, Ash slid down amid the covers. One hand stole beneath her head to turn the sweat-stained pillow facedown upon mattress, while her other hand smoothed her hair. Just as she closed her eyes, the door creaked open.

Penthero Iss had brought his own lamp, and the fierce blue glow of burning kerosene put Ash's own resin lamp in the shade. Iss stood in the doorway and looked at Ash. Even with her eyes closed she knew what he was about.

He made her wait before he spoke. "Almost-daughter, don't you think I know when I'm being deceived?"

Ash kept her eyelids closed, but not tightly—he had caught her on that in the past. In no way did she respond to his words, simply concentrated on keeping her breathing low and metered.

"*Asarhia!*"

It was hard not to flinch. Mimicking a kind of dazed surprise, she opened her eyes and rubbed them vigorously. "Oh," she said. "It's you."

Ignoring her show of bafflement, Penthero Iss walked into the room proper, set his lamp on the rootwood prayer ledge next to the offering bowls of dried fruits and pieces of myrrh, brought his long-fingered hands together, and shook his head. "The cushions, almost-daughter." The index finger on his left hand circled, indicating the foot of the bed. "A sound night's sleep seldom includes kicking cushions so hard that the impression of one's foot stays upon them till dawn."

Ash cursed all the cushions in Mask Fortress. She cursed Katia for piling the silly, fluffy, useless bags of goosedown high on her bed each night.

Penthero Iss crossed over to Ash's bed. Fine gold chains woven into the fabric of his heavy silk coat chinked softly as he moved. Although not muscular, he carried something hard within him, as if his skeleton were made out of stone. His face had the shape and smoothness of a skinned hare. Holding out a long, carefully manicured, completely hairless hand, he asked, "How much do I love you, almost-daughter?" Untaken, the hand moved away to carve a circle in the air. "Look at all I give you: dresses, silver brushes, perfumed oils—"

"You are my father who loves me more than any real father ever could." Ash spoke Iss' own words back to him. She had lost count of how many times he had said them to her over the past sixteen years.

Penthero Iss, Surlord of Spire Vanis, Lord Commander of the Rive Watch, Keeper of Mask Fortress, and Master of the Four Gates, shook his head with disappointment. "You would mock me, almost-daughter?"

Feeling a bite of guilt, Ash slid her hand over his. She owed love and respect to the man who was her foster father and surlord.

Sixteen years ago, before he took the title of surlord for his own, Penthero Iss had found her outside Vaingate. She was a newborn, a foundling abandoned within ten paces of the city gate. All such foundlings were considered Protector's Trove. Iss had been Protector General at the time, in charge of city security and defenses. He had patrolled the Four Gates, led his red-bladed brothers-in-the-watch, and commanded the forces that manned the walls.

Ever since Thomas Mar had forged the first Rive Sword with the steel and rendered blood of the men who had betrayed him at Hove Hill, no protector general had ever been paid for his work. For centuries protector generals lived off income from their grangeholds, inheritances, and land grants. Today there was no land left to grant, and more and more baseborn men were joining the Watch, and protector generals now gained income by other, less noble means. Contraband goods; swords of illegal length or blade curvature, arrows with barbed tips; prohibited substances such as sulfur, resins, and saltpeter that could be used in making siege powders; unlawfully produced liquor, poisons, sleeping drafts and pain dullers; ill-gotten gains; anything found in the possession of known criminals; and all goods abandoned within the city—whether they be crates of rotting cabbages, fat pigs broken loose from their tethers, or newborns left to die in the snow—were the protector general's to do with as he saw fit.

Protector's Trove had made Penthero Iss a rich man.

As if guessing her thoughts, Iss brought his lips close to Ash's ear. "Never forget, almost-daughter, that during my commission I came upon dozens of foundling babies, yet you were the only one I chose to raise as my own."

Ash tried, but she couldn't quite stifle the shiver that worked its way down her spine. He had sold the other babies to the dark-skinned priests in the Bone Temple.

"You are cold, almost-daughter." Penthero Iss' hand, with its hairless knuckles that never cracked, glided up Ash's arm and along her shoulder. His fingers prodded the flesh of Ash's neck, testing for warmth, blood pulse, and swollen glands.

The urge to shrink away from his touch was overwhelming, but Ash fought it. She didn't want to provoke Iss in any way. If she needed any proof of that, all she had to do was look at the three blind bolt holes in the fossilwood door.

"Your blood is racing, Asarhia." Iss' hand moved lower. "And your heart . . ."

Unable to stand it any longer, Ash jerked back. Iss grabbed hold of her nightgown and twisted the fabric in his fist. "You've been having the dream again, haven't you?" She didn't answer. Threads of muslin in her nightgown were laddering under the pressure of his grip. "I said *haven't you?*"

Still Ash made no reply, but she knew, she just *knew*, that her face gave her away. Her skin flushed with every lie.

"What did you see? Was it the gray land? The cavern? Where were you? Think. *Think.*"

Shaking her head, Ash cried, "I don't know. I don't know. There was a cavern lined with ice . . . it could be anywhere."

"Did you see what lay beyond?" The words left Iss' mouth like frost smoke, sparkling blue and utterly cold. They hung in the air, cooling the space between Ash and her foster father, making it difficult for Ash to breathe. Ash saw Iss' lower jaw come to rest. She heard saliva smack inside his mouth.

"Father, I don't understand what you mean. The dream was over so quickly; I hardly remember what I saw."

Penthero Iss blinked at Ash's use of the word *Father*. Sadness flitted across his face so quickly, she doubted she'd seen it at all. Slowly, intentionally, he showed his gray-cast teeth. "So it has come to this? Lies from the foundling I raised as my own."

Rare were the times when Iss showed his teeth. They were small and positioned well above his lip line. Rumor had it that a sorcerous healing practiced upon him when he was just a boy had burned the enamel from them. Whatever the cause, Iss made it his habit to speak, smile, eat, and drink without ever drawing back his lips.

With one quick movement Iss found and pressed the curve of Ash's left breast. He weighed the small globe of flesh and then pinched it. "You can't stay a child forever, Asarhia. The old blood will show soon enough."

Ash felt her cheeks burn. She didn't understand what he meant.

Iss regarded Ash for a long moment, his green silk robe switching colors in the fierce light of burning kerosene, before releasing his hold on her nightgown and standing. "Tidy yourself up, child. Do not force me to lay hands on you again."

Ash kept her breath steady and tried not to let her fear show. Questions piled on her tongue, but she knew better than to ask them. Iss had a way with answers. He gave them, they sounded perfectly logical, but then later when you were alone and had time to think, you realized he had told you nothing at all.

As Iss moved away, Ash got a whiff of the smell that sometimes clung to her foster father. The smell of old, old things locked away so tightly that they dried to brittle husks. Something shifted at the edge of Ash's vision. All the hairs on her body bristled, and against her will she was drawn back to her dream . . .

*Reaching, she was reaching in the darkness.*

"Asarhia?"

Ash snapped back. Penthero Iss was looking at her, his long, skinned-man's face showing the faintest sheen of excitement. Light from his lamp sent his shadow flickering across the watered-silk panels on the walls. Ash could still remember the soft marten and sable furs that had once hung in their stead. Iss had sent a brother-in-the-watch to tear them down and replace them with smooth, bloodless silk. Furs and animal hides were distasteful to him; he called them barbaric and would have none hung in any chamber he might chance to enter in the massive, sprawling, four-towered fortress that formed the heart of Spire Vanis.

Ash missed the furs. Her chamber seemed cold and bare without them.

"You are not well, almost-daughter." As Iss spoke, his hands came together in a smooth knot of knuckle and flesh that was peculiar to him alone. "I will sit with you through the last hour of night."

"Please. I need to rest." Ash rubbed her forehead, struggling to keep her mind in the now. What was wrong with her? Raising her voice, she said, "Go. Just go. I have to use the chamber pot. I drank too much wine at dinner."

Iss remained calm. "Yes, wine . . . and to think Katia informed me that you refused both the pewter containing the red and the silver she brought later with the white." A dull metal tap sounded: Iss kicking the empty chamber pot that lay at the foot of Ash's bed in the center of a hill of cushions. "And somehow you managed to wait until now to relieve yourself."

Katia. Always Katia. Ash scowled. Her head ached, and her body felt as tired and shaky as if she'd spent the night running uphill rather than sleeping in her bed. She desperately wanted to be alone.

Surprisingly, Iss crossed over to the door. Fingers slipping into the vacant bolt holes, he turned to face Ash and said, "I will have my Knife stay outside your door tonight. You are not well, almost-daughter. I worry."

The idea of having the Knife camped outside her chamber frightened Ash nearly as much as her dream. Marafice Eye scared her—he scared a lot of people in Mask Fortress. That was, she supposed, the main reason her foster father kept him around. "Can't we call Katia instead?"

Iss began shaking his head before Ash finished speaking. "I think our little Katia might not be a wholly reliable guardian. Take tonight: *You* said you drank wine, yet she swore you didn't, and of course I must take my daughter's word over that of a common servant. So I have no choice but to conclude the girl reported wrongly and might easily do so again." A cold smile. "You are not well, Asarhia. Ill dreams trouble you, headaches plague you. What sort of a father could I call myself if I did not watch my daughter closely?"

Ash bent her head. She wanted to sleep, close her eyes, and not have to dream. Her foster father was too clever for her. Lies, even small ones, were as silken rope in his hands.

He could pull and distort them, use them to tie their speaker up in knots. She had gotten herself into enough trouble tonight. The best thing to do would be to say nothing more, nod her head meekly, and let her foster father bid her good night. He was already making his way toward the door; another minute and he would be gone.

*Yet. . . .*

She was Ash March, Foundling, left outside Vaingate to die. She had been abandoned in two feet of snow, wrapped in a blanket stiff with womb blood, beneath a sky as dark as night in the twelfth storm of winter. She had been forsaken, yet somehow she had lived. She had been weak, yet some tiny spark of life within her had proven strong. Straightening her spine, she looked her foster father straight in the eyes and said, "I want to know what's happening to me."

Holding her gaze, Iss reached for the kerosene lamp. The iron base was stamped with the Surlord's seal: the Killhound rampant, the great smoke gray bird of prey sinking claws the size of meat hooks into the tip of the Iron Spire. Ash remembered her foster father telling her that although killhounds fed on spring lambs, bear cubs, and elk calves, they were known for killing hunting dogs that ranged too close to their aeries. "They never feed upon the hounds they kill," Iss had said, a gleam of fascination firing his normally cold eyes. "Though they do make sport with the carcasses."

Ash shivered.

Iss closed the spillhole, snuffing the lamp. Holding open the fossilwood door, he stepped into the column of cold air that rushed in from the corridor beyond. "There's nothing for you to be worried about, almost-daughter. You're just catching up, that's all. Surely Katia must have told you that most girls your age are women in *all* senses of the word? Your body is simply doing those things that theirs have already done. One would hardly expect such changes to occur without some small measure of pain."

With that he moved into the shadows of the corridor, swiftly becoming one himself. The metal chains sewn into his coat chimed softly like faraway bells, and then the door clicked shut and there was silence.

Ash fell back onto the bed. Shaking and strangely excited,

she pulled the covers over her chest and set her mind to thinking of ways she could find answers for herself. Her foster father's words only *sounded* like the truth. She knew she wouldn't sleep, could absolutely *swear* she wouldn't sleep, yet somehow, unbelievably, she did.

Her dreams, when they came, were all of ice.

* * *

THE LISTENER COULD NOT sleep. His ears—what were left of them—pained him like two rotting teeth. Nolo had brought him fresh bear tallow from the rendering pit, and it was good and white and looked creamy enough to eat, so the Listener had done just that. Waste of good tallow—using it to plug up two old black holes that had once been ears. Waste of good muskox hair to warm them, too. But there was little to be done about that: Nothing needed warming as much as an old scar.

Nolo's footprints formed a visible line to and from the rendering pit and then over to the meat rack in the center of the cleared space. Looking at them, the Listener made a mental note to have a talk with Nolo's wife, Sila: She wasn't filling her husband's mukluks with enough dried grass. Nolo's booted feet had melted snow! Sila would have to get chewing.

The Listener spent an idle moment imagining Sila's plump lips chewing on a tuft of colt grass to make it soft enough for stuffing into the space between her husband's outer and inner boots. It was a very pleasant moment. Sila had unusually fine lips.

Still, he was old and had no ears, and Sila was young and had a husband, and together they had four good ears between them, so the Listener nudged aside the image of Sila and turned to the matter at hand: his dream.

Sitting on a stool carved out of whalebone, with his old brain-tanned bear's hide around his shoulders, the Listener sat at the entrance to his ground and looked out at the night. Heat from his two soapstone lamps warmed his back, and cold from the still, freezing air chilled his front: that was the way he liked it when he was listening to his dreams.

Lootavek, the one who listened before him, swore that a man could only hear his dreams *as* he was having them, yet the Listener thought him mistaken. Much like Nolo's boot lining, dreams needed to be chewed on.

The Listener listened. In his lap he held the hollow tip of a narwhal's tusk, a little silver knife that had once been used to kill a starving child, and a chunk of sea salt-hardened driftwood from a wrecked ship that had been beset then stoved in by the cold blue ice of Endsea. Like all good talismans, they felt right in the hand, and as the Listener's body heat warmed them in varying degrees, they released his mind into the halfworld that was part darkness and part light.

Fear gripped at the Listener's belly as he fell into his dreams.

*Hands reached. Loss wept. A man with an impossible choice made the best decision he could . . .*

"Sadaluk! Sadaluk! You must awaken before the cold burns your skin."

The Listener opened his eyes. Nolo was standing above him. The small, dark-skinned man had his prized squirrel coat tucked under his arm and a bowl of something hot and steaming in his hand.

The Listener shifted his gaze from Nolo to the night sky. The pale glow of dawn could clearly be seen across the Bay of Auks. Stars faded even as the Listener looked away. He had been listening to his dream for half the night.

Nolo tucked the squirrel coat around the Listener's shoulders and then held out the steaming bowl. "Bear soup, Sadaluk. Sila made me swear to watch you drink it."

The Listener nodded gruffly, though in truth he was quite pleased—not about the bear soup, which he could get from any fire around the rendering pit, but for the fact of Sila's attention.

The bear soup was hot, dark, and strong, and bits of sinew, bear fat, and marrow bobbed upon the surface. The Listener enjoyed the feel of steam on his face as he drank. The warmth of the bone bowl soothed the joints in his black, hard-as-wood hands. When he had finished he held out the empty bowl for Nolo to take. "Go now. I will return the squirrel coat to you when I am rested."

Nolo took the bowl with all the usual carefulness of a husband handling one of his wife's best dishes and made his way back to his ground.

The Listener envied him.

After what his dreams had shown him this night, the Listener knew that such a base and mortal emotion should be beneath him. But it wasn't, and that was the way of the world.

The Listener had seen the One with Reaching Arms reach out and beckon the darkness. And that meant only one thing.

Days darker than night lay ahead.

Pulling hides across his doorway, the Listener retreated into the warmth and golden light of his ground. His bench was thick with animal skins heaped high with fresh white heather, and he lay down upon it and closed his eyes. He had no wish to dream and sleep, so he turned his thoughts to Sila and imagined her and Nolo sledding across the frozen margins of Endsea. He imagined the rime of ice beneath the sled runners wearing thin and Nolo calling a halt so that his wife could make new ice by the quickest way she could.

This pleasant image held the Listener's attention for only a short spell. There was work to be done. Messages had to be sent. Days darker than night lay ahead, and those who lived to know such things needed to be told. Let no one say that Sadaluk, Listener of the Ice Trapper tribe, was not the first to know.

# THREE

### *A Circle of Dust*

ARE YOU SURE YOU checked the rear of the horse corral?" The freezing wind made Drey Sevrance squint as he spoke. Ice crystals glittered in the fox fur of his hood, and pine needles clung like matted hair to his shoulders, arms, and back.

Raif thought his brother looked tired, and older than he had ever looked before. Dawn light was showing yellow on the horizon, and it cast pits of sulfur shadow on his face. "I checked," Raif said. "No sign of Mace."

"What about the alder swamp and the stream?"

"Swamp's frozen. I walked along the stream bank. Nothing."

Drey stripped off his gloves and ran his bare hands over his face. "The current might have carried the body downstream."

Raif shook his head. "There's not enough water to carry a bloated fox from one bend to another, let alone a full-grown man clear from the camp."

"It would have been running faster yesterday at noon."

Raif took a breath to speak, then thought better of it. The only time that stream would ever be strong enough to carry a body was during the second week of spring thaw when the runoff from the balds and Coastal Ranges was at its height—Drey knew that. Suddenly uneasy but not sure why, Raif reached out and touched Drey's sleeve. "Come on. Let's get back to the firepit."

"Mace Blackhail is out here somewhere, Raif." Drey pushed a hand through the frozen air. "I know he's more than likely dead, but what if he isn't? What if he's wounded and fallen?"

"There were those tracks—"

"I don't want to hear about those tracks again. Is that clear? They could have been left by anyone at any time. Mace was standing dogwatch—he could have been anywhere when the raid came. Now either the raiders got to him first and he's lying frozen in some draw on the floodplain, or he made it back to the camp, warned the others, and we just haven't found him yet."

Raif hung his head. He didn't know how to reply. How could he tell his brother he had a feeling that no matter how long and carefully they searched, they would still find no sign of Mace Blackhail? Shrugging heavily, he decided to say nothing. He was dead tired, and he didn't want to argue with Drey.

Drey's face softened a fraction. Frozen colt grass cracked

beneath his feet as he shifted his weight from left to right. "All right. We'll head back to the firepit. We'll search wider for Mace come full daylight."

Too exhausted to hide his relief, Raif followed Drey back to the tent circle. Wind-twisted hemlocks and blackstone pines thrashed against the sky like chained beasts. Somewhere close by, water trickled over loose shale, and far beyond the horizon a raven screamed at the dawn. Hearing the rough and angry cry of the bird the clan called Watcher of the Dead, Raif raised his hand to his throat. With his thick dogskin gloves on he could barely feel the hard hook of the raven's bill he wore suspended on a length of retted flax. The raven was his lore, chosen for him at birth by the clan guide.

The guide who had given Raif the raven lore was five years dead now. No one had been more deeply honored in the clan. He was ancient and he'd stunk of pigs and Raif had hated him with a vengeance. He had saved the worst possible lore for Tem Sevrance's second son. No one before or after had ever been given the raven. Ravens were scavengers, carrion feeders; they could kill, but they preferred to steal. Raif had seen how they followed a lone wolf for days, hoping to snatch a meal from an opened carcass. Everyone else in the clan, men and women alike, had fared better with their lores. Drey had been given a bear claw, like Tem before him. Dagro Blackhail's lore was an elk stag, Jorry Shank's a river pike, Mallon Clayhorn's a badger. Shor Gormalin was an eagle, like Raina Blackhail. As for Dagro's foster son, Mace . . . Raif thought for a moment. What was his lore? Then it came to him: Mace Blackhail was a wolf.

The only person in the entire clan who had a lore stranger than a raven was Effie. The guide had given her nothing but an ear-shaped piece of stone. Raif grew angry just thinking about it. What had the Sevrances ever done to the old bastard to deserve such short shrift?

Raif tugged at the raven's lore, testing its oiled binding. When he was younger he had thrown the thing away more times than he could recount, yet somehow the guide always found it and brought it back. "It's yours, Raif

Sevrance," he would say, holding out the black piece of horn in his scarred filthy palm. "And one day you may be glad of it."

All thoughts of ravens flew from Raif's mind as he and Drey approached the tent circle. The first rays of sunlight slid across the frozen tundra, illuminating the campsite with long threads of morning light. Already the six hide-and-moose-felt tents, the horse posts, the firepit, the drying racks, and the chopping stump had the look of ruins about them. Tem had once told Raif a story about a great dark deathship that mariners swore guarded the entrance to Endsea, keeping all but the blind and insane away. That was what the tents looked like now: the sails of a dead ship.

Raif shivered. His hand dropped from his neck to the hollowed-out antler tine that was attached to his gear belt by a ring of tar-blackened brass. Sealed inside the tine was hallowed earth: dust ground from the guidestone that formed the Heart of Clan. Every clan had a guidestone, and every clansman carried a portion of it with him until he died.

The Clan Blackhail guidestone was a massive slab of folded granite as big as a stable block, shot with veins of black graphite and slick with grease. Clan Bludd's guidestone was also folded granite, but it was studded with seams of red garnets that shone like drying blood. Raif had never seen the powder that came from the Bluddstone, but he thought it must look pretty much the same as that ground from the Hailstone: smooth gray powder that ran through the hand like liquid smoke.

As he neared the firepit, he plucked the tine from his belt, breaking the brass ring. The tine was sealed closed with a cap of beaten silver, and Raif ran his thumb along the tine's length, feeling for the edge. Twelve men had died here, and only two remained. And two men without horses, carts, or sleds could never hope to bring back the dead. The round-house lay five days' hard travel south, and that was more than time enough for scavengers to tear the bodies to shreds.

Raif wouldn't have it. Ravens were in the sky already, turning circles a league across, and soon wolves, coyotes, bears, and tundra cats would harken to the sound of their *kaaw*ing. All beasts that fed upon dead things would be drawn to the camp, in search of one final meal to gorge on before winter started true.

Shaking his head with a single savage blow, Raif flicked the cap from the tine. It popped open with a small hiss. Fine powder from the guidestone streamed in the wind like a comet's tail, bringing the taste of granite to Raif's lips. After a moment of utter silence, he began walking the circle. Around the firepit, the drying racks, the tents, and the bodies he moved, carving a path of air and dust. The gray powder sailed long on winter's breath, riding the cold eddies and swirling updrafts before sinking to its frozen bed.

Nothing was ever going to take Tem Sevrance. Ever. No ravens would pick at his eyes and his lips, no wolves would sink their fangs into his belly and his rump, no bears would suck the marrow from his bones, and no dogs would fight over scraps. He'd be damned to the darkest pits in hell if they would.

"Raif?"

Looking round, Raif saw Drey standing at the entrance to their father's tent, carrying a bundle of supplies pressed hard against his chest. "What are you doing?"

"I'm drawing a guide circle. We're going to burn the camp." Raif hardly recognized his own voice as he spoke. He sounded cold, and there was a challenge in his words he had not originally intended.

Drey looked at him a long while. His normally light brown eyes were as dark as the walls of the firepit. He knew Raif's reasons—they were too close as brothers not to know each other's minds—but Raif could tell he was not pleased. He'd had plans of his own for the bodies.

Finally the muscles in Drey's neck began to work, and after a moment he spoke, his voice hard. "Finish the circle. I'll load these supplies by the horse posts, then find what oil and pitch I can."

A deep band of muscle in Raif's chest relaxed. His mouth was dry—too dry to speak. So he nodded once and continued walking. Raif felt Drey's gaze upon his back until the moment the circle was joined. And he knew with utter certainty that he had taken something precious from his brother. Drey was eldest. He should have had first say with the dead.

Drey Sevrance did what was needed to start a good fire. He worked thoroughly and tirelessly; chipping and shredding firewood, stripping nearby trees of their needles to kindle the bare ground between the tents and the pit, spreading great heaps of moss around the bodies, and lacing everything with wads of rendered elk fat and ribbons of oil and pitch. The tent hides he doused with the hard liquor that was always to be found in Meth Ganlow's pack.

Through all the preparations, Raif did only those things Drey asked of him, nothing more; suggesting nothing, saying nothing. Giving Drey his due.

Ravens circled closer as they worked, their long black wings casting knife shadows on the snow, their harsh carrion calls a constant reminder to Raif of the thing he wore at his throat. *Watcher of the Dead.*

When it was all done and the two brothers stood outside the guide circle, looking in at the primed firetrap they had created, Drey took out his flint and striker. The circle Raif had drawn was not visible to the eye. The powder was fine and the colt grass thick, and the wind had carried much of it away. But it was there. Both Raif and Drey knew it was there. A guide circle carried all the power of the guidestone it had been drawn with. It was Heart of Clan, here, on the frozen tundra of the badlands. All those within it lay upon hallowed ground.

Tem had once told Raif that far to the south in the Soft Lands of flat-roofed cities, grassy plains, and warm seas, there were others who used guide circles to protect them. Knights, they were called. And Tem said they burned their circles into their flesh.

Raif didn't know about that, but he knew a clansman would sooner leave the roundhouse without his sword than without a flask, pouch, antler tine, or horn containing his measure of powdered guidestone. With a sword, a man could only fight. Within the hallowed ground of a guide circle, he could speak with the Stone Gods, ask for deliverance, absolution, or a swift and merciful death.

A wolf howled in the distance, and as if its call had woken him from a trance, Drey pushed back his hood and stripped off his gloves. Raif did the same. All was still and quiet. The wind had died, the ravens landed, the wolf silent, perhaps scenting prey. Neither brother spoke. Words had never been the Sevrances' way.

Drey struck the flint. The kindling caught, flaring fiercely in Drey's hand. Drey stepped forward, knelt on one knee, and lit the run of alcohol-laced moss he had laid.

Raif forced himself to watch. It was hard, but he was clan, and his chief and his father lay here, and he would not look away. Flames raced toward Tem Sevrance, eager yellow fingers, sharp red claws. Hellfire. And it would eat him as surely as any beast.

*Tem. . . .*

Suddenly Raif could think of nothing but stamping the blaze out. He stepped forward, but even as he did so, liquid fire found the first tent, and the primed elkhide burst into a sheet of flames. Sparks flew upward with a great gasp of smoke, and a thunderous roar of destruction shook the badlands to its core. Flames so hot they burned white danced in the rising wind. Pockets of ground ice melted with animal hisses, and then the stench of burning men rose from the pyre. Rippling air pushed against Raif's cheek. His eyes burned, and salt water streamed from them, running down his cheeks. He continued to look straight ahead. The exact piece of ground Tem lay on was etched upon his soul, and it was his Stone God—given duty to watch it until it had burned to dust.

Finally there came a time when he could look away. Turning, he looked to his brother. Drey would not meet his eyes. Drey's hand was bunched so tightly into a fist it caused his chest to shake. After a moment he spoke. "Let's go."

Without glancing up to check his brother's reaction, Drey crossed over to the horse posts, picked up his share of the supplies, and hefted them over his back. From the bulky look of the packs, Raif guessed Drey had chosen to carry the heaviest bundles himself.

Drey waited by the post. He would not look at his brother, but he would wait for him.

Raif walked to meet him. As he suspected, the packs Drey had left were light, and Raif shrugged them on his back like a coat. He wanted to say something to Drey, but nothing seemed right, so he kept his silence instead.

The fire roared at their backs as they left the badlands campsite and headed south. Smoke followed them, fire stench sickened them, and ashes settled on their shoulders like the first shadows of night. They crossed the floodplain and the sedge meadow and headed over the great grasslands that led home. The sun set slow but early, lighting the sky behind them with a lingering bloody light.

Drey never mentioned continuing the search for Mace Blackhail, and Raif was glad. Glad because it meant his brother saw the same things he did along the way: a broken pane of ice on a melt pond, a horse's hoof clearly stamped in the lichen, a ptarmigan bone, its end black from the roast-fire, picked clean.

When exhaustion finally got the better of them, they halted. An island of blackstone pines formed their shelter for the night. The great centuries-old trees had grown in a pro-tective ring, originally seeded from a single mother tree that had matured in the center, then later died. Raif liked being there. It was like camping within a guide circle.

Drey lit a dry fire and pulled an elkhide over his shoulders to keep warm. Raif did the same, and the two brothers sat close around the flames and ate strips of hung mutton and boiled eggs gone black. They drank Tem's dark, virtually undrinkable homebrew, and the sour taste and tarlike smell reminded Raif so strongly of his father it made him smile. Tem Sevrance's homebrew was the worst in the entire clan; everyone said so, no one would drink it, and it was rumored to have killed a dog. Yet Tem never changed his brew. Much like heroes in stories who poisoned themselves a little each day to protect against attacks from artful assassins, Tem had become immune to it.

Drey smiled, too. It was impossible not to smile when faced with the very real possibility of death by beer. A soreness came to Raif's throat. There was just three of them now: he, Drey, and Effie.

*Effie.* The smile drained from Raif's face. How would they tell Effie her da had gone? She had never known their mother. Meg had died on the birthing table in a pool of her own blood, and Tem had reared Effie on his own. Many clansmen and more than a few clanswomen had told Tem he should remarry to provide his sons and daughter with a mother, yet Tem had flatly refused. "I have loved once, completely," he would say. "And that's blessing enough for me."

Suddenly Drey reached over and cuffed Raif lightly on the cheek. "Don't worry," he said. "We'll be all right."

Raif nodded, glad to his heart that Drey had spoken and comforted by the realization that the same thoughts sifting through his mind were sifting through Drey's as well.

Sitting back, Drey adjusted the fire with a stick. Red-and-blue flames danced close to his gloved hand as he turned out charred logs. "We'll make Clan Bludd pay for what they did, Raif. I swear it."

A hand of pure ice gripped Raif's gut. Clan Bludd? Drey had no proof of what he said. The raid could have been mounted by any number of parties: Clan Dhoone, Clan Croser, Clan Gnash, a band of Maimed Men. The Sull. And then there was the nature of the wounds, the stench of badness, the feeling that something more than death had taken place. The warriors of Clan Bludd were fierce beyond telling, with their spiked and lead-weighted hammers, their case-hardened spears, their partly shorn heads, and their greatswords cut with deep center grooves for channeling their enemies' blood; yet Raif had never once heard either Tem or Dagro Blackhail say that Clan Bludd was involved in . . .

Raif shook his head. He had no words for what had happened at the campground. He just knew that any clansman worth his lore would turn his back on such a thing.

Glancing over at Drey, Raif took a breath to speak. Then, seeing how viciously Drey poked at the fire and how the stick he held was bent close to breaking, he let the breath out, unused. In five days they would be back home. All truths would come out then.

# FOUR

## *A Raven Has Come*

ANGUS LOK WAS RECEIVING kisses. Fourteen of them, to be exact, one for each halfpenny that Beth and Little Moo would cost him. It was Beth's idea, of course; she wanted new ribbons for her hair, and she was prepared to do any-thing—kissing included—to get them. Little Moo was far too young to have formed any opinion on ribbons other than that they were good to chew on; yet she was kissing her fa-ther anyway, giggling wildly and wetting Angus' face with sticky, ever-so-slightly gritty kisses that tasted of oatcakes.

"Please, Father. *Please*," Beth said. "You promised."

"Pweez, Papa," echoed Little Moo.

Angus Lok groaned. He knew when he was beaten. Slap-ping a hand on his chest, he cried, "All right! All right! You've torn your poor father's heart out along wi' his purse! Ribbons it is! I suppose I should ask what colors you'll both be wanting?"

"Pink," said Beth.

"Noos," said Little Moo.

Angus Lok picked up Little Moo, lifted her from his lap, and planted her gently on the fox pelt rug at his feet. "Pink and noos it is, then."

Beth giggled as she laid one last kiss on her father's cheek and stood. "*Blue*, Father. Little Moo wants blue."

"Noos. Noos," echoed Little Moo happily.

"Angus."

Angus looked up at the sound of his wife's voice. Two syllables, yet straightaway he knew something was wrong. "What is it, love?"

Darra Lok hesitated a moment in the doorway, as if reluc-tant to move forward, then took a small, resigned breath and walked into the farmhouse kitchen. Coming to join Angus by the fire, she paused to push a stray strand of hair from Beth's face and deprive Little Moo of a hairy bit of oatcake that the child had just plucked from the depths of the fox pelt rug.

Sitting down on the oakwood bench that her father's steward had made for her as a wedding gift eighteen years earlier, Darra Lok took her husband's hand in hers. Checking first that the two youngest of her three daughters were caught up in their own worlds of ribbons and oatcakes, she leaned close to Angus and said, "A raven has come."

Angus Lok took a deep breath and held it. Closing his eyes, he spoke a silent prayer to any and all gods who might be listening. *Please let it not be a raven. Please let Darra be mistaken and it be a rook, a jackdaw, or a hooded crow.* Even as he wished it, he knew he was wrong. Darra Lok knew a raven when she saw one.

Angus raised his wife's hand to his lips and kissed it. He knew the gods didn't like it if a man asked for one thing straight after another, so he didn't pray that his fear wasn't showing on his face. He simply hid it as well as he could.

Darra's dark blue eyes looked into his. Her normally lovely face was pale, and little lines Angus had barely noticed before were etched deep into her brow. "Cassy spotted it this morning, circling the house. It didn't come to land until now."

"Take me to it."

Darra Lok let go of her husband's hand and nodded. She stood slowly, reluctantly, brushing imaginary dirt from her apron. "Beth. Watch your sister. See she doesn't get too close to the fire. I'll be back in just a minute."

Beth nodded in a movement that was so similar to the one Darra had just made, it turned Angus' heart to lead. A raven had come to his house, and although the massive blue black birds with their long knife wings, powerful jaws, and human voices meant many different things to many different people, to Angus Lok they meant just one: leaving home.

Darra walked ahead of him out of the kitchen, and Angus paused a moment to run his hand over Beth's cheek. "Pink and blue," he mouthed as he left, so she knew he wouldn't forget about the ribbons.

It was raining outside, a steady drizzle that had begun just before dawn, and the grounds around the Lok farm were turning to mud. Darra had spent most of the morning harvesting the last of her herb garden before first frost, and the small patch of ground just below the kitchen window was stripped bare. To the side of the herb garden, the chickens clucked nervously in the coop, built in a lean-to against the kitchen chimney. They knew all about ravens.

"Father!"

Angus Lok turned toward the voice of his eldest daughter. Cassy Lok had dirt smeared on her face, her hair was plastered to the sides of her head in two wet sheets, and she was wearing an ancient oilskin cape that had come with the farm together with a milk churn and two rotting plows. Yet to Angus she looked perfectly beautiful. High spots of color glowed in her cheeks, and her hazel eyes were as bright as raindrops glistening on amber. Sixteen, she was. Old enough to be wed and have children of her own. Angus frowned. How was she ever going to meet a young man, hidden out here in the farm and woodlands two days' northeast of Ille Glaive? She wasn't. And that was one reason Angus Lok didn't sleep well at night.

"Have you come to take a look at the raven?" Cassy said, excitement spilling into her voice as she ran to join her father. "It's a messenger, like the rooks that sometimes come. Only bigger. There's something tied to its leg."

Darra and Angus Lok exchanged a glance. "Cassy, go inside and warm yourself. Your father and I will see to the bird."

"But—"

"Inside, Casilyn."

Cassy brought her lips together, made a small huffing sound, then turned and made her way inside the house. Darra seldom used her full name.

Angus ran a hand over his face, brushing the rain from his eyebrows and beard. He watched as Cassy closed the kitchen door behind her. She was a good girl. He'd talk to her later, explain what he could.

"This way. The bird has no liking for the rookery like the rest. It's perched itself in the old elm around the back." Without waiting for her husband to acknowledge what she said, Darra cut across the yard and down along the side of the house. Angus had lived with his wife too long not to know that her briskness was a cover. Darra was nervous and trying not to show it.

To the rear of the Lok farmhouse lay open woodland. Great old oaks, elms, and basswoods grew tall and spread wide over a rich damp underwood of lichen, dead leaves, loam, and ferns. In spring Cassy and Beth would search for blue duck eggs, wood frogs, and wild mint, and in summer they'd spend entire days in the woods, picking cloudberries, blackberries, gooseberries, and black plums, coming home after sundown with sticky faces and baskets crammed with dark mushy fruits that would have to be soaked in water to drown the maggots out. In autumn they would hunt for field mushrooms and milk caps, and in winter, during those times when Angus' work took him away, Darra would set traps to catch small game.

*Kaaw! Kaaw!*

The raven announced its presence with two short, angry notes, drawing Angus Lok's gaze skyward, up through the branches of the great white elm that provided summer shade for the entire house. Even surrounded by branches as thick as arms, the raven's form was unmistakable. It perched in the tree with all the arrogance of a panther resting after an easy kill. Black and still, it watched Angus Lok with eyes of liquid gold.

Angus' gaze shifted from the creature's eyes to its legs. A marked thickening directly above its left claw was clearly visible: pikeskin, sinew bound, then painted with a resin seal.

*Kaaw! Kaaw!*

*Look, I dare you.*

Angus heard the raven's call as a challenge. Only two people in the Northern Territories used ravens to carry their messages, and Angus knew in the soft marrow of his bones that he didn't want to hear from either of them. The past lay within that pikeskin pouch, and he and the raven knew it.

"Call it down." Darra's voice was low, her hands twisted at the fabric of her apron.

Nodding softly, Angus whistled as he had once been taught nearly twenty years earlier: two short chirrs followed by a single long note.

The raven bobbed its head and shook out its wings. Gold eyes appraised Angus Lok. Seconds passed, and then, making a noise that sounded just like human laughter, the raven flew down from the branch.

Darra stepped back as the huge bird landed. Angus had to fight the urge to step back himself. The raven's bill was as big as a spearhead, sharp and hooked like the shredder on a plow. Apparently delighted by Darra's fear, the bird danced toward her, bobbing its head and calling softly.

"Nay, yer little beastie." Angus grabbed at the raven, one hand circling its belly, the other clamping down on its bill. Pulling the bird from the ground, he hefted it fast against his chest. The raven jerked its wings and clawed its feet, but Angus held it firm, increasing his pressure on its bill. "Darra. Take the knife from my belt and cut the message."

Darra did as she was asked, though her knifehand shook so much as she broke the seal that she nearly bled the bird. With the sinew and resin bindings broken, the small package, no bigger than a child's little finger, fell into Darra's left palm.

Angus turned away from his wife and threw the raven from him. The bird spread its wings and soared into the air, laughing, laughing, as it disappeared into the blade-metal sky.

"Here. Take it." Darra Lok held out the package. The pikeskin wrapping was badly stained by rain, resin, and bird lime, but small silvery green patches of skin were still visible along its length. Pikeskin was light, strong, and waterproof and could be molded in place when wet. A useful material, yet Angus couldn't recall the last time he'd received a message so wrapped. The moment Angus' fingers closed around the soft, damp package, Darra took a step back. Angus sent his wife a glance. *Stay.*

Darra shook her head. "No, my husband. I've been married to you for eighteen years, and I have never once looked upon any message they have sent. I do not think it would be a good time to break my tally now." With that Darra Lok ran a hand over her husband's right cheek and turned and walked away.

Angus cupped his hand to his face where his wife had touched him, holding on to her warmth as he watched her disappear behind the corner of the house. He didn't deserve her. She was a Ross of Clad Hill, and her father was a grangelord, and nineteen years ago when they'd first met, she could have had any man she chose. Angus Lok never forgot that. It ran through his mind now as he unraveled the roll of pikeskin and pulled out the length of saliva-softened whitespruce bark.

Sliced so thinly that Angus could see his thumb through the fibers, the soft strip of inner bark carried a border of seals chasing quarter moons burned into the wood. The message was also burned in, painstakingly pricked out with the tip of a red-hot needle:

*The One with Reaching Arms Beckons*

*Days Darker Than Night Lie Ahead*

*Sadaluk*

Angus stepped toward the great old elm and leaned heavily against its trunk. Rain dripped around him, forming a curtain of beaded light. Many things he had been prepared for, many terrible, terrible things. But this . . . A bitter smile flashed across Angus' face. This was something he had thought well behind him. They all had.

*It's your choice, Angus Lok. Make of it what you will.* The past pulled like a much used muscle within Angus' chest. It shortened his breath, making it difficult to breathe. He would have to leave. Tonight. Head for Ille Glaive, meet with those who needed to be told. It never occurred to him to doubt the message. Sadaluk of the Ice Trapper tribe was not the sort of man given to rash communication. Twenty years, and this was the first time Angus had ever heard from him.

Beneath Angus' feet, the bald earth around the elm turned to mud. The raven's laughter echoed in the last of the tree's attached leaves. Angus glanced at his house. Inside Cassy would be helping Darra stack the fire before supper, Beth would be rolling dough for the sweet, sticky unnameable pastries that she and Little Moo loved to eat. As for Little Moo . . . well, she had probably keeled over on the rug and was currently fast asleep. That child could sleep anywhere.

Pain, which had never quite left Angus' chest, reasserted

itself with a single, soft stab. How safe were all his children tonight?

Tucking the message in a slip inside his waistcoat, Angus pushed himself off from the elm and headed for the warmth of his house. No. He wouldn't leave his home, not in darkness. Those who sent messages could go to the deepest spiraling hell. He had promised Beth and Little Moo ribbons, and by all the gods, they were going to get them. Yet even as Angus Lok found some satisfaction in defiance, fear settled like dust within his bones. A raven had come, and a message had been received, and the past was now a tightly held fist knocking at his door.

\* \* \*

As QUIET AS SETTLING dust, Ash March told herself as she slipped through her chamber door. Cool air from the corridor brushed against her nightdress, and Ash had to bite the inside of her mouth to stop herself from shivering. Why did it have to be so cold? She glanced back at the door. Should she have brought an outer robe after all? Suddenly the idea of wandering around Mask Fortress wearing little but a nightdress and a wool tunic didn't seem nearly as clever as it had earlier. Still, this way, if she were caught, she could at least claim sleepwalking and have a chance of being believed. Wearing a cloak would make things harder. Did sleepwalkers dress before they went outside? Ash didn't know.

Looking ahead at what she could see of the gently spiraling corridor of cut and angled stone, Ash listened for the sound of Marafice Eye. The Knife had moved from his post by Ash's door some minutes earlier, probably assuming his charge was fast asleep. Ash didn't know where he had gone, had no idea when and if he would return. She just knew that he was sick of spending his nights camped outside her door. She didn't blame him. It was cold enough to turn breath white, and, discounting watching dust settle and greenwood torches burn out one by one, there was nothing to do.

Laughter. Ash tensed. The sound came again, down the corridor and off to the right. Katia's room. Yet that wasn't

Katia laughing. Not unless she'd spent the night swilling hot tar and chewing on gravel.

"I said blow out the light."

Immediately Ash recognized the cold, imperative tones of Marafice Eye. He was in Katia's room . . . *with Katia.* Ash shuddered; she didn't like the thought of that one bit. Katia was so small, dark and tiny like a doll. And Marafice Eye was a huge bull of a man, with arms that took the sleeves of four men to cover them and wrists like iron bars. Slipping into the shadows against the opposite wall, Ash walked quickly ahead.

The limestone walls were bitterly cold, and Ash avoided touching them as she moved. Both her own and Katia's chambers were situated in the shortest and thickest of the four towers in Mask Fortress: the Cask. The Cask was the principal fortified structure in Spire Vanis, and its walls were twenty feet thick. A series of spiraling corridors and winding staircases led from its base like a path weaving around a hill, breaking occasionally for defensive bastions, archers' roosts, chambers, walled-in snugs, and recessed alcoves with cut stone benches known as graymeets.

Ash's chamber formed the heart of the Cask. Directly below her floor, the tower wall was spiked with a ring of fortifications so thick that from outside they looked like a massive limestone bird's nest clustered around a tree. The Cask was not a pretty sight. Of the three towers that were livable within the fortress, it was the least graciously set, having none of the wrought ironwork and lead cladding found in the Horn or the crow-step gables and black marble eyelets of the Bight.

As for the Splinter, the tallest tower in Mask Fortress, capped with the Iron Spire, where high traitors were once impaled at a height of six hundred feet so that everyone within the city could see them and know fear . . . Ash shook her head. No one had been there for years. The Splinter was unstable, uninhabitable, freezing, damp, broken. It was a wonder the whole thing didn't collapse. One end was said to be embedded so deeply within the frozen bedrock of Mount Slain that the tower shuddered along with the mountain. And the other end soared so high into the clouds that moisture continually ran in rivulets down its walls whether it was raining or not. In winter the entire structure was encased within a layer of rime ice a knuckle thick. Pale, narrow, and twisting, the ice-bound tower had been called by many names: the Winter Spire, the White Thorn, Penthero Iss' Bloodless Prick. Ash frowned. Katia was always passing along such nonsense.

Reaching the first set of steps, Ash risked looking back. Katia must have blown out the light as Marafice Eye had bidden, for the space beneath the little maid's door was now dark. That was good, Ash told herself, moving her mind away from the subject. She didn't want to think about what might be happening within.

Solid limestone steps muffled her footfalls as she descended the stairs. Iron hooks, mottled brown and orange with rot and rust, jutted from the stairwall like bird claws, forcing her to walk dead center. Once they had been used to suspend great fire-blackened chains that linked all the Cask's portcullises to a single lever in the strongroom below. Now they were just one more hazard to avoid, like servants, brothers-in-the-watch, and the raw mountain air.

Ash rubbed her arms. She was so cold. Freezing. Yet she had thought to wear her thickest nightgown, and her feet were slippered in moleskin. It wasn't even winter yet, not properly, so why could she never get warm?

*You are not well, almost-daughter. I worry.*

Ash shook her foster father's voice from her head. She wasn't unwell in the way he meant. Katia had told her all about what happened to girls when they came into their blood, and nightmares and cold sweats formed no part of it. "You get stomach cramps," Katia had said, an air of vast superiority warming her voice. "And your mind starts turning to men." Ash blew air through her nostrils. Men. No, that definitely wasn't happening to her.

Something else was. Ten nights in a row she had dreamed of ice. Always she awoke to find sheets damp with sweat twisted around her arms like rope. The dreams were so *real*, and the voices of the creatures who spoke to her were like nothing she had ever heard before. *Mistressss,* they murmured, as sickly pleasing as sweet rolls spread with honey and jam, *come for us, stretch toward us, reach . . .*

Ash took a deep breath to stop herself from shivering. The thought of returning to her bedchamber was suddenly *there* in her mind, and it was hard to keep moving forward. Her foster father knew what was wrong with her, she was sure of it. She was also sure he would never tell her the truth.

He watched her constantly; stealing into her room when she was sleeping, examining her breasts, her hair, her teeth, questioning Katia about the tiniest details of her life. Nothing was too insignificant for him: the contents of her chamber pot, the amount of goose fat left on her plate after dinner, the changing dimensions of her corselet and small linens. What did he want with her? Wasn't being his almost-daughter enough?

Ash pushed the hurt away before it reached her. He wasn't her real father, she had to remember that. He never called her daughter without speaking the word *almost* first.

The stairs came to an abrupt halt between stories to allow access to the battlements, then resumed after a short ramp. Ash increased her speed. The light level was rising, and shouted orders and the clatter of steel on steel began to filter up from the Red Forge below.

Penthero Iss *knew* something, something about her, her parents, or the circumstances of her birth. Something that made him guard her closely at all times, set his Knife outside her door, and call upon her day and night unannounced, hoping to catch her . . . doing what? Ash shook her head. She might find the answer to that tonight.

Every evening in the hour before midnight, Iss left his private chambers in the base of the Cask and went elsewhere. Ash had seen him leave and return countless times over the years, yet she did not know where he went. According to Katia, he seldom locked the chamber door behind him. It was late, and the Cask was secure, and only Ash, Katia, and a handful of trusted servants were allowed access during the night. The Rive Watch garrison, the mighty Red Forge where brothers-in-the-watch struck and cooled their blood-red swords, was situated adjacent to the Cask. No one could enter the tower unchallenged. Iss' chamber was secure against intruders, but not against someone who was already within the tower.

All her foster father's private papers were held within his chamber. If there was any record of the day he had found and claimed her, it would be buried somewhere deep beneath his slate books and ledgers, his onionskin atlases and manifests and lists.

Ash began her descent of the second flight of stairs, her hand trailing from hook to hook along the stairwall. Iss' voice followed her like smoke from the greenwood torches. *Is this how you repay me, almost-daughter? I clothe you and feed you, and then as soon as my back is turned you betray me like this. You disappoint me, Asarhia. I thought you loved your father more.*

*Asarhia.* Ash bristled. She was Ash, just Ash, yet no one within Mask Fortress would acknowledge it. Everyone called her Asarhia or Lady Asarhia or mistress. It was yet another thing she owed to Penthero Iss. He had found and then named her: Asarhia because it was a fashionable name given to ladies of high birth, and March because of where she was found: on the very border of the city itself. *Five paces farther south of Vaingate, almost-daughter, and you would not have been mine to keep. Protector's Trove ends within a shadow's fall of the gate.*

Ash breathed in cold air from the shadows as she paused upon the final landing to listen for sounds of brothers-in-the-watch.

Vaingate. Why Vaingate? Spire Vanis had four gates, each one facing a cardinal point. Vaingate faced south. *South.* No roads led from it, no brothers-in-the-watch patrolled it, no carts loaded with wares ever trundled past its posts. Vaingate opened onto the north face of Mount Slain! It had been built purely for show, satisfying some ancient masonic code of order that demanded a walled city have four gates. Who would leave a baby outside a gate that was never used?

The answer came to Ash with the same sickening pull as always: Someone who wanted their baby dead.

Once, just once, she would like her foster father to answer her questions. Had she been left with linens and spare clothes? In a basket or a blanket? Had she been wiped clean and suckled? Or left bloody and thirsty and exposed? Yet always when she asked, Iss would shake his head. "You were abandoned, almost-daughter. Surely that's all you need to know?"

Voices. Close by.

Ash stilled herself. She spent hours each day watching fortress cats chase mice and birds in the quadrangle, and one thing she knew for sure was that a cat never pounced unless it saw something move. The trick was keeping your nerve. Mice didn't, birds didn't, but some old hares did. Ash had seen them, sitting perfectly still on the archers' block as brazen as you like. The shadows on the stairwell were deep, slanting, and Ash leaned into them, pressing her shoulders against the limestone wall. The voices grew louder. Footsteps clicked over tile, *click, click, click.*

"Don't hold the bowl out at arm's length like a used chamber pot, you great moose. It'll cool in no time that way. Hold it against your chest. Can't have His Coldness complaining about lukewarm beans—not with them being late and all."

"And why not? It's certainly not him that eats them. Beans is common fare, and we all know how high and mighty the Killhound is. Wouldn't eat a pork sausage if his life depended on it."

"I don't know nothing about that. Beans in soft butter he's asked for, and beans he's going to get. Now deliver 'em sharpish—they're long past due as it is. And be sure to let him know that no one in the kitchen's to blame. Furnacemen! Hmph! When I find which of those dog-faced devils killed my stove, I swear I'll . . ."

The voices trailed off as the two figures disappeared along the corridor, and Ash pulled back from the wall. It was just Mistress Wence and a manservant. They hadn't even glanced up as they passed. From the sound of things, they were late delivering food to her foster father. Which meant that Iss was still in his chamber. Annoyed, Ash brushed lime dust from her shoulders. What was she going to do now?

Matters were decided for her by the sound of booted feet descending the stairs. A brother-in-the-watch, judging from the faint jingle of metal that accompanied each step, so there was no going back. Leaving the safe haven of the shadows, Ash took the last of the steps and moved into the corridor below. The entrance to the Red Forge lay on the south side of the tower, so she took the way north instead, following Mistress Wence and the manservant toward Iss' chamber.

At ground level the curvature of the Cask's corridors was so slight, it was easy to forget they ran in a circuit around the base of the tower. Only a quarter of the rotunda was given over to Iss' private rooms. The remaining space was taken by state rooms: the Hall of Trials, the Blackvault, and the main entrances to the quadrangle and the Red Forge. Along the entire length of the circuit ran a series of life-size statues hewn from marble the color of smoke: the Founding Quarterlords and Impaled Beasts of Spire Vanis.

Ash shivered hard as she heard the brother-in-the-watch open the main rotunda door behind her. Cold air pushed against the backs of her legs. She was beginning to wish she hadn't started this. But then, doing anything these days was preferable to sleeping.

Dreams woke her every night. Her mind drifted . . . she saw the ice cave, felt the terrible cold breath that steamed from its shining walls . . .

Another door banged closed, bringing Ash back. Voices again. Mistress Wence and the servant returning from Iss' chamber. They would be here any moment.

Panicking, Ash wheeled around. Smooth walls, an iron-plated door that led to the unused east gallery and was kept locked at all times, a lit greenwood torch, and a recess housing a statue of Torny Fyfe, Bastard Lord, swordsman and glutton, and least highly regarded of the Founding Quarterlords were the only things in sight.

Mistress Wence's heels tapped a march against the limestone floor. Her thin nasal voice piped in displeasure.

Ash ran for the greenwood torch, tugged it from its pewter casing, and rammed the burning end against the wall. The flames died instantly, killing the light. Thick smoke from the charred end curled toward the ceiling as Ash recouched the torch. The smell of burned resin helped clear her head. Turning about, she ran for the statue of Torny Fyfe, squeezing herself behind his great marble thighs and thanking the

Maker for every eight-course meal the Quarterlord had ever eaten. The shadow cast by his overhanging belly was enough to provide a team of dogs with shade.

"Really! Between you and furnacemen I don't know who's the dimmest. You were supposed to tell Iss that it *wasn't* the kitchen staff's fault. Not just stand there mumbling a lot of old nonsense about the lumber and the fire."

Rounding the curve, Mistress Wence and the manservant came to an abrupt halt several paces short of Torny Fyfe's likeness. Although light in the corridor was now limited, it was far from dark, and Ash could clearly see Mistress Wence's sharp nose quiver.

"Torch has gone out. Take a flint to it, Grice. We don't want to give His Coldness anything else to find fault with."

As Grice slapped his tunic looking for a flint, Ash felt a trickle of cold sweat slide past her ear. Dream or no dream, she was returning to her chamber as soon as this pair was gone. She should never have come here. The whole idea had been a mistake from the start. She'd rather be lying in bed dreaming of ice than wedged behind a marble backside, hiding from the fortress staff.

Realizing Grice was flintless, Mistress Wence sniffed with venom. "Really! How can you call yourself a man and not carry a flint?"

"I can relight it from one of the torches, mistress."

To Ash's very great relief, Mistress Wence shook her head, shoulders, and chest. "You will do no such thing, you great oaf. What if Iss came from his chamber and saw you hulking around with a smoking torch in your hand at this time of night?" Three sniffs followed in rapid succession. "He'd think you were a hideclad come to finish him off, that's what. And sure as rotten apples bring flies, he'd make you pay for it. You're coming to the kitchen with me and pick up a flint this minute. Move sharpish, now!" With that Mistress Wence and the manservant resumed their journey along the corridor.

Slumping forward against Torny Fyfe's shoulder, Ash exhaled softly. A wisp of marble dust spilled down her neck, cold and grainy like powdered snow. Ash shook it away. She was stiff, half-frozen, and her nightgown was plastered to her back with icy sweat. Sucking in her chest and stomach, she squeezed herself free of Torny Fyfe's shoulders and shuffled her ankles clear of his blocky, basestone feet. As she stepped into the open corridor, her head jerked back painfully. Turning about, she saw where a lock of her hair had snagged in the Quarterlord's elaborately worked scabbard. Cursing all fat men with swords, Ash edged back to release it.

Besides arming Torny Fyfe with a sword long enough to impale a horse, the sculptor had also conceived of a brisk wind to blow at his cape, and sharp folds of marble shaved Ash's shins as she moved. Letting out a sound halfway between a squeak and a sob, Ash vowed to run back to her chamber and never, ever, venture out again.

*Sss*. A door whirred open in the distance, making a faint hissing sound. Ash looked up. The noise came from the direction of Penthero Iss' private chamber. Even before she could decide what to do, she heard softly soled feet slapping stone. Iss was coming this way.

Wrenching her trapped hair free, Ash drew herself into the deepest shadows of the recess. Iss would be furious if he found her here. Furious. The time she fixed the bolt on her door was nothing compared to this.

Before she had chance to settle herself into a position she could comfortably hold, her foster father rounded the corner. Thin, pale, and hairless except for his closely shorn scalp, Penthero Iss had the look of something drowned and then pulled up a week later from a lake. Everything about him was pallid, smooth, and bloodless. His eyes were green, but barely so; his lips and cheeks had the color and texture of cooked veal; and the skin on his earlobes let through light.

Carrying a covered bundle in his left arm, Iss walked faster than was normally his wont. Blue silk, heavily embroidered with metal chains and pieces of agate, thrashed against his thighs as he moved.

Ash held her breath. All of her shrank back, away from her foster father. She closed her eyes as he passed.

Only he didn't pass. Not completely. He walked to a point and then stopped. All was silent. Realizing she had been discovered, Ash opened her eyes. The sleepwalking excuse was a dead dog now.

Ash blinked. Fully expecting her foster father's pale green gaze to be upon her, she was surprised to see that he wasn't even looking her way. His back was toward her, and he was standing in front of the iron door. Ash saw the tendons in his wrist rise and fall, and then a muffled *clunk* sounded as lock and key turned.

In all her years of living within Mask Fortress, Ash had never once seen the iron door opened. It led through to the unused east gallery and then to the Splinter beyond. No one ever visited the Splinter. It was forbidden by rule of law. Workmen had died there, people said, plunging to their deaths through gaps in rotten timbers, crushed by falling masonry, and impaled upon the banister of spikes that wove around the main stairway like a handrail to hell.

Ash inched forward, resting her hand on Torny Fyfe's smoothly chiseled rear.

The door swung back as Penthero Iss pushed against the metal plating. Stale air breathed into the corridor like fine mist. Ash smelled the dry, itchy odor of old stone and withered things. It was the same smell—part of it—that clung to Iss sometimes when he visited her chambers in the middle of the night. Ash trembled, not sure if she was excited or afraid. The lock had turned with barely a sound! The door hinges glided as smoothly as a pat of butter running down a roast. Everything had been oiled. Recently. There was no rust, no rot.

Iss slid into the darkness on the far side of the door. All previous vows about returning to her room forgotten, Ash *willed* her foster father not to lock the door behind him. He was in a hurry, she knew that. Would he pause to lock the door?

The iron door closed as easily as something a quarter of its size. Switching air caused one of the iron plates to jiggle in its frame. Ash listened for the sound of Iss inserting his key. She heard something, a click or tap, and then everything was quiet.

Ash waited. Her heart was pumping fast and hard, and she was ready to run for the door. She forced herself to count seconds. Her foster father had gone to the Splinter. The *Splinter*.

Minutes passed. Beneath Ash's hand, Torny Fyfe's backside warmed to a toasty glow. Ash patted the marble. She was growing rather fond of the old Quarterlord.

This time she slipped smoothly from the recess, tucking her hair beneath her nightdress and lifting her ankles high to avoid sharp edges. Working the stiffness from her legs and back, she crossed to the door. Seen up close, the metal plates were scored and then case hardened to form a rigid skin of steel. The mark of the Killhound standing high atop the Iron Spire was stamped upon each one.

Unsettled, Ash pushed against the door. The cool metal gave, sweeping back beneath her palm. Shadows and old air stole across Ash's fingers and up along her arm. Iss had not locked the door. It seemed mad, impossible. Doubt spiked in her stomach like a violent cramp. Still she kept pushing, forcing the door back into the corridor beyond. Secrets lay ahead, she was sure of it. And she had to know if those secrets involved her.

Stepping into the shadows, she let the door fall shut behind her. A different kind of coldness from that present in the rotunda gripped at her chest: dry, bitter, and weighted, as if the air were thick with particles of freezing dust. Ash stilled herself for a moment, giving her eyes time to adjust to the darkness.

The east gallery was a long arcade of limestone arches roofed with slate—she knew that because the structure formed the massive east wall of the quadrangle—yet the shadows surrounding her gave little of that away. Dark gashes of open space, pale glimmering edges, and hoods of matted stone were all she could see. Soft warbling sounds came from somewhere high above, and Ash guessed that pigeons had found their way in to roost.

Hoping they were the only living things she would encounter, she began to walk in the direction she imagined was forward. Stone dust crunched beneath her slippers with each step. Icy fingers of frost tugged at her arms and ankles. The odor of dry decay sharpened. Suddenly nervous, she picked up her pace, striding into the tunneling darkness. *I can turn back at any time*, she told herself, trying to sound strong.

The gallery stretched on and on, and except for occasional

chinks in boarded-up windows where single beams of moonlight shone through, there was no increase in light. Ash glanced into the shadows pooled to either side of the walkway. What could a man see in such darkness? She slowed. What could he *do*?

Ash halted and peered into the distance. A curving endwall, black yet planed smooth enough to reflect some measure of light, blocked the way ahead. Just visible against the dark stonework was the outline of a heavily carved door. Ash recognized it instantly. Another identical door, locked, barred, and boarded, stood outside against the fortress wall. The wood had been worked in such a way to fool the eyes into thinking that the door was already open and Robb Claw, great-grandson of the Bastard Lord Glamis Claw, was on his way through.

The second entrance to the Splinter.

Even as Ash tensed muscles to step toward it, the ground beneath her feet shuddered. Overhead beams creaked. Dust sifted to the floor like fine rain. Tiny hairs along her arms lifted. Everything stilled, yet something within the air and shadows continued to change. Ahead the endwall seemed to grow darker, blacker, deeper, siphoning substance from the night. The air temperature dropped so quickly it felt like liquid against Ash's skin. Shadows bled. Bearings shifted. Everything became somehow *less* than it was.

And then Ash felt it.

Something evil and wanting and broken. Something trapped in the darkness, drying slowly to a scaly husk. Something nameless and full of hate, driven by loneliness and terror and savage, blinding, unspeakable pain. Malice filled it, fear consumed it, need pumped like blood through its dark, voided heart. It wanted, *wanted*. It hardly knew what, but it wanted. And hated. And was utterly alone.

Dread stole over Ash like deep cold. All the breath rushed from her body, leaving her lungs hanging dead in her chest. An instant floated in the air like dust too fine to settle. Ash felt as if she were sinking in ice cold water. She couldn't breathe, move, think.

Slowly, slowly, and at terrible cost, the nameless wanting thing turned its mind toward Ash March. Ash felt the great millwheel of its awareness pass over her, and in those seconds she came to know the full burden of its existence. It made her mouth go dry.

The creature reached.

It wasn't there, wasn't beside, above, or beneath her. But it reached.

Ash shrank back. She sucked in breath, turned on her heel and ran.

Fists beating air, hair streaming loose, moleskin slippers smacking against stone, Ash raced along the east gallery, back toward the iron door. Walls, arches, and openings blurred into a single streak. Ash's heart beat in her throat. When she came upon the iron-plated door, she blasted through it like a bear through sheet ice. The rotunda corridor was warm and full of light. The torch she had extinguished had been relit and burned with a crackling yellow flame. Part of her wanted to rip it from the wall and throw it into the darkness beyond the door and burn whatever lived there.

The desire to flee was greater. Not stopping to watch the door swing shut behind her, or check if anyone was coming, Ash dashed along the rotunda toward the stairs. Limestone walls that earlier had felt as cold as gravestones now seemed as warm as sun-baked clay.

Ash shook her head as she took the stairs two and three at a time. She had been a fool. A fool. Everyone knew there was no such thing as good secrets. She should have kept away, not looked, not dared. Even if she had gone to her foster father's private chambers instead of heading for the Splinter, the story would have been the same. She wasn't really going to find some magical slip of paper that told of how she was more than just a foundling, how Penthero Iss had robbed and tricked her real parents into giving her up. There *were* no good secrets. And she was a fool for believing otherwise.

Ash let out a hysterical sob.

She was Ash March, Foundling, left outside Vaingate to die.

Tears stung her eyes as she climbed the last stairs to her chamber. She didn't want to think about the nameless creature in the Splinter, didn't want to know what it was.

"What have we here?"

Ash rounded the final turn in the staircase and came face-to-face with Marafice Eye. The Knife moved directly into her path, preventing her from taking another step. The bow curve of his chest forced her to edge back. Marafice Eye had small eyes and a small mouth and hands as big as dogs. Ash was scared of his hands. She had seen him break iron chains with them.

"Where have you been? Sick of pissing in a pot? Thought you might get up and use the jacks instead?"

Ash made no reply. Marafice Eye liked to use obscenities around women. He took pleasure in it.

Holding her gaze down, refusing to meet his eyes, Ash stepped to the side, meaning to pass the Knife. She didn't want him to know she was upset.

Marafice Eye stepped with her, barring her way once more. The block of purple flesh that formed the Knife's left fist swung up to Ash's chin. The fist barely touched flesh, grazing the underside of her jaw with a knuckle the size of a bird's skull, yet it was enough to make Ash look up.

The Knife's lips twisted into a smile. "What's upset our little girly, then? Did she see something she wasn't supposed to, or did the frost just bite?"

"Leave me alone!" Ash exploded forward, pushing against Marafice Eye's chest with all that was in her. The Knife barely swayed. His oxblood leather tunic creaked as he leaned forward to absorb the blow. Ash fell back on her heels, jolted and off balance as if she had walked straight into a door.

Smile twisting to its narrow limits, the Knife resettled his fist under Ash's jawline, pushing his knuckles into the soft hollow where her neck and jaw met. "I've killed women for less," he said, small eyes glinting. "What makes you so sure I wouldn't kill you?"

Ash's legs felt like straw sticks. She could feel the nameless creature's presence like greasy residue against her skin. Her chest was shaking with exhaustion, and despite running through the fortress at full speed, she felt as cold as if she had been standing still.

Raising her head clear of Marafice Eye's fist, she took a deep breath and said, "Iss set you to *watch*, not touch me. Now step aside and leave me be, and perhaps, just perhaps, come tomorrow I won't tell him how easy it was to slip through your guard."

The Knife's eyes narrowed to two dark slits. The slabs of flesh on his face stiffened. He looked at Ash, breathed on Ash, and then, in his own good time, stood aside and let her pass.

Ash felt malice on her back for the second time that night as she climbed the last three steps and took the short walk back to her chamber. Marafice Eye watched her all the way. As her hand reached for the chamber door, he spoke. "Push me again, Asarhia March, and you *will* end up dead."

Ash closed her eyes, shutting out the words. Her knees buckled and she had to lean into the door to stop herself from falling. Although she didn't look around, she knew Marafice Eye had seen her collapse. She hated him for it.

With all the strength she could muster, she pushed against the door. It opened and she half staggered, half fell, into her chamber. Even though she could barely stand, the first thing she did was pull the chair from her dresser and jam it against the door. It wasn't enough. Ash looked wildly around the room. Settling on her cedarwood clothes chest, she dragged it from its warm, dry place by the charcoal brazier and set it in place next to the chair. That done, she picked up her three-legged nightstool and added that to the pile. Still not satisfied, she went to work on the dresser itself, shouldering and then kicking the wood until it slid along the floor. She moved slowly, methodically, dazed with exhaustion, piling things high against the fossilwood door.

# FIVE

## *Homecoming*

SLEET FELL IN GRAY sheets as they entered the clanhold. Raif hated sleet—rather rain or snow or hailstones. Something that *knew* what it was.

It was bitterly cold. Not freezing, but the wind made it

seem so, blowing and switching, making it impossible to feel warm. Everything in sight was gray. The oldgrowth forest in the Wedge, the pines on top of Pikes Peak, the stream that led into Cold Lake, and Mad Binny's crannog that was built on stilts over the water's edge: all as gray as slate. Raif kicked at a sod of dirt and grass. A sense of wrongness itched at his gut.

Drey jabbed his arm. "Smoke. Over there."

Raif looked where his brother pointed. Ragged gusts of smoke blew above the line of oaks and basswoods that spread across the rise. Seeing them made muscles in Raif's throat tighten. The roundhouse lay in the valley beyond. Home was nearer than he thought.

"Be there soon." Drey made a point of moving into Raif's line of view as he spoke. Both of them had their fox hoods pulled close around their faces, and unless they faced each other head-on, they couldn't see each other's eyes. Sleet hung in Drey's eyelashes and the bristles of his six-day beard. "Be there soon," he repeated. "Warm fire, warm food. Home."

Raif knew Drey wanted him to say something, to reminisce out loud about sleeping around the Great Hearth, or sitting at table and eating Anwyn Bird's fine mint-wrapped lamb and roasted onions, or standing beside the guidestone and singing to the Stone Gods. Yet words wouldn't come. Raif tried, but they wouldn't.

After a moment Drey moved ahead, shoulders stiffening beneath his oilskins, gloved hands running along his elkhide pack to brush off sleet. Raif knew he was disappointed. "Drey."

"What?"

Raif took a breath. It suddenly seemed important to say something, *now*, before they reached the roundhouse. Only he wasn't sure what, or why. "The raid."

"What of it?" Drey didn't look up. Thick tufts of grass hid ankle-breaking boulders, bog holes, and snags of long-gone trees, and Drey suddenly seemed engrossed in choosing his steps.

"We can't say who attacked the camp." Raif struggled for the right words. "We just need to be . . . careful, that's all.

You and me. Careful." The wind picked up as he spoke, howling through the trees on the slope, thrashing grass flat against the earth and driving sleet into their faces. Raif shivered. He glanced at Drey.

His brother's hood now pointed ahead. After a moment Drey pushed it back, exposing his face. He stopped in his tracks. "There's Corbie Meese. Up on the rise, by the old black oak."

A muscle in Raif's stomach pulled with a soft, sickening twist. Hadn't Drey heard what he said? Raif opened his mouth to speak again, but Drey's arm came up and he began shouting.

"Corbie! Corbie! Over here!"

Raif pushed back his own hood and ran his hand through his hair. He watched as the gray figure on the slope raised a hand in acknowledgment, then slipped back a few paces and trotted his horse into view. It was Corbie Meese all right. Even from this distance his stocky hammerman's body with its disproportionately muscular arms and neck was clearly identifiable. Even the slight flattening on the left side of his head above his ear, where a training hammer had clipped his skull when he was just a boy, showed up against the light gray sky. Corbie's hammer was strapped to his back, as always. Raif noticed that its iron head reflected no light as Corbie swung up to mount his horse. Which meant the normally smooth metal had been laid upon an anvil and chisel scored.

"He's riding back," Drey said. After a moment he spoke again, his voice soft. "He must be meaning to gather the clan."

Raif sucked in breath. A hammerman scored his hammer only in times of war. Smooth metal reflected light and could give away a position, plus a glancing blow with smooth metal was just that—a glancing blow—but with metal raised in jagged ridges a glancing blow could tear the skin from a man's face.

Raif's hand came up to his neck to search for the reassuring smoothness of his raven lore. Clan preparing for war? Had they already received word of the raid?

Five days he and Drey had been traveling on foot. Five

days of freezing nights, bitterly cold days, and driving
winds. Raif was tired beyond knowing. He couldn't recall
the last time he had felt warm or completely dry. They had
run out of ale on the second day, and Raif's lips were
cracked from sucking on ice. It was only yesterday morning,
when they'd finally crossed over the balds and into the clanholds, that the temperature had begun to rise above freezing.
Yet that was when the sleet started, so there was little reward
for leaving the badlands behind.

Through it all Raif had felt a deep sense of unease.
Freshly broken twigs, sap frozen around the break, hoofprints stamped in hoarfrost, and broken ice over melt ponds
kept catching his eye. Elks and bears could break surface ice
and twigs, he told himself, and lone hunters from Clan Orrl
often used Blackhail's hunting paths. Yet Raif felt no better
for telling himself such things. They sounded reasonable,
but they didn't stick.

"Come on, Raif. Race you to the rise." Drey grabbed
Raif's arm and yanked it hard as he ran ahead. Raif grinned.
Not wanting to disappoint his brother again, he tore after
him, crashing through tangles of ground birch and alder, his
pack slamming against his side as he ran.

Drey was the stronger runner, and even sweeping in wide
arcs and topping every rock and fallen log he encountered,
he reached the slope well before Raif. Climbing halfway to
the rise, Drey turned, grinned, and waited for his brother to
catch up.

Raif was breathless by the time he reached him. Blisters
on his heels rubbed raw by days of walking throbbed like
burned skin. Raif found comfort in the fact that Drey was
clearly favoring his right foot, and his face was as red as beet
water.

"We're home, Raif," Drey said, punching Raif's pack.
"Home!"

Raif swung a punch at Drey's ribs, then took off at full
speed toward the rise. Drey yelled after him to wait, called
him a devil's cur and a moose stag in rut, and then started
running himself.

Laughing, whooping, and wrestling, the two brothers

reached the rise. They stopped dead when they saw the meet party riding up the leeward slope toward them.

Corbie Meese, Shor Gormalin, Orwin Shank and his two middle sons, Will Hawk, Ballic the Red, a dozen yearmen and tied clansmen, Raina Blackhail, Merritt Ganlow, and the clan guide Inigar Stoop. All including the women and Inigar Stoop were heavily armed. Spears bristled in their couchings, and greatswords, hammers, and more than a few war axes weighed across backs. Ballic the Red's great yew longbow was braced and ready in its case, his side quiver fat with the red arrows that gave him his name. Shor Gormalin carried only a shortsword. It was all the soft-spoken swordsman ever needed.

Then, as Raif and Drey stood on the ridge, side by side, breathless, their exposed faces cooling in the sleety air, the troop of two dozen parted and through their midst, wearing a cloak made of black wolf fur that rippled in the wind like a living, breathing thing, rode Mace Blackhail high atop Dagro Blackhail's blue roan.

Drey gasped.

Raif looked hard into Mace Blackhail's face. And didn't stop looking until Mace met his eyes. *"Traitor."*

The word brought the meet party to a halt.

At his side, Raif heard Drey inhale sharply.

Mace Blackhail didn't blink. Bringing up a hand gloved in the finest lamb's leather and dyed three times until it was the perfect shade of black, he made a settling motion to those behind him. He held Raif's gaze for a time, sleet collecting in his oiled braids and sliding down his narrow nose and cheeks. When he spoke it was to Drey.

"Where were you when the attack came?"

Drey straightened his shoulders. "Raif and I were out at the lick, shooting hares."

"Where were *you*?" The rawness of Raif's voice caused some in the party to draw breath. Raif hardly cared. Mace Blackhail was standing before him, mounted on Dagro Blackhail's horse, unharmed, well fed, and acting like lord of the clan. Raif's lore burned like a hot coal around his neck. While he and Drey had stayed at the camp taking care of the dead, Mace Blackhail had ridden back to the round-house in haste. It was the blue roan that had stamped its hooves in mud and hoarfrost and broken ice in newly set ponds, not some daring Maimed Raider or a lone Orrlsman tracking game.

"I," Mace Blackhail said, his voice hard, "was seeing off a bear at Old Hoopers Lake. The beast broke bounds at first light, spooked the horses. Killed two dogs. I headed it off, chased it east along the rush, and speared its neck. Just as I was set to finish the kill, I heard sounds of fighting from the west. I rode back to the camp at full gallop, but it was too late. The last of the Clan Bludd raiders were already riding away."

As he spoke the last sentence, Mace looked down and touched the pouch containing ground guidestone that hung from one of the many leather belts around his waist. Others in the party did likewise.

After a moment Drey did the same. The muscles in his throat worked a moment, and then he repeated softly, "Clan Bludd?"

Mace nodded. His wolf cloak gleamed like oil floating on the surface of a lake. "I saw the last of them. Caught sight of their spiked hammers and the red felt laid over their horses' docks."

Ballic the Red shook his head gently, his callused archer's hands caressing the red-tailed hawk fletchings on his arrows. "'Tis a bad thing for a clansman to do: make raid on another's camp at first light."

Corbie Meese, Will Hawk, and others grunted in agreement.

Raif spoke up to silence them. "The raid didn't take place at first light. It happened at noon. I didn't feel anything until—"

Raif felt Drey's fist hit the small of his back. Not an all-out punch, but enough to knock some wind from his lungs.

"We don't know when the raid took place, Raif," Drey said overloudly, clearly unhappy at having to speak out. "You got a bad notion in the pit of your stomach at noon, but who's to say the raid didn't happen before then?"

"But, Drey—"

"*Raif!*"

In all his life Raif had never heard Drey speak his name with such harshness. Raif pressed his lips to a line. Heat flared in his cheeks.

"Drey." Raina Blackhail trotted her filly forward, coming to a halt a few paces ahead of her foster son, Mace. White smoke streamed from the filly's nostrils. "What did you see when you came upon the campsite?"

Raif watched Raina's face as he waited for his brother to reply. Raina Blackhail's gray eyes gave little away. Dagro Blackhail's first wife, Norala, had died of lump fever, and Raina was his second wife, taken in the hope that she would provide the clan chief with a son to carry his name. After the second year of marriage, when Raina's belly had failed to quicken, Dagro Blackhail had reluctantly taken a foster son, a child of his sister's from Clan Scarpe. Mace had been eleven when he was brought to the Blackhail roundhouse, just eight years younger than his foster mother, Raina.

Drey glanced at Raif before he answered Raina's question. "We reached the camp about an hour before dark. We saw the dogs first, then Jorry Shank . . ." Drey hesitated. Orwin Shank, Jorry's father, leaned forward in his saddle, his normally ruddy face as pale as if it were covered by a sheet of rime ice. "I don't know how long he'd been there, lying in the scrub, but he was part frozen. And there wasn't a lot of blood."

Mace Blackhail kicked the roan's flank, then quickly pulled the reins, causing the gelding to stamp its feet and shake its head. "It's just as I said," he cried, easily controlling the agitated roan. "The Bluddsmen are arming themselves with hell-forged swords. They slip into a man's gut as smooth as a spoon scooping bacon fat, then burn his insides hot and fast, roasting his flesh around the blade."

Merritt Ganlow swayed in her saddle. White-haired Inigar Stoop leaned over and steadied her, his pouches, horns, and slices of bone tinkling like shells as he moved.

Raina Blackhail shot a warning glance to her foster son. "Drey hasn't finished yet."

Drey shifted his weight. He wasn't comfortable being the center of attention. "Well . . . I don't know about hell-forged blades. I didn't see any signs of burnt flesh. . . ."

"Go on." Raina Blackhail's voice, while not gentle, was no longer as severe as it had been.

"Raif and I went around the camp. We tended the bodies: Meth Ganlow, Halfmast—I mean Darri—Mallon Clayhorn, Chad . . . all the others." Drey swallowed hard. Raif saw where his brother had gripped his oilskin so tight, the hide had split along the seam. "All the wounds looked the same: clean, not much blood, swiftly done. Broadswords or greatswords looked to have been used."

"It's as Mace says," murmured Ballic the Red. "Clan Bludd."

Many in the party nodded and murmured, "Aye."

Noticing that Raina Blackhail was one of the few who remained silent, Raif spoke up, addressing his words to her alone. "Clan Bludd aren't the only ones who use greatswords. Clan Dhoone, Clan Croser, Clan Gnash"—Raif stopped himself from naming Clan Scarpe, Mace Blackhail's birth clan—"Maimed Men: All use swords as their second weapons."

Mace Blackhail kicked the roan forward, coming to rest mere paces in front of Raif. "I said I saw Bluddsmen fleeing from the camp. Are you calling me a liar, Sevrance?"

Out of the corner of his eye, Raif saw Drey's hand come up, meaning to pull back. Raif stepped away, out of his brother's reach. He would not be silenced in this. Gaze fixed firmly on Mace Blackhail's narrow, gray-skinned face, Raif said, "Drey and I saw to our clansmen. We didn't leave them out on the tundra for the carrion beasts to take them. We gave them blood rites, drew a guide circle around them. Paid them due respect. What I *am* saying is that perhaps you were in too much of a hurry to get back to the roundhouse to pay retreating raiders fair due."

Drey swore, softly to himself.

Everyone in the meet party had some reaction. Ballic the Red snorted, Merritt Ganlow let out a high, wailing cry, Corbie Meese sucked air between his wind-cracked lips, and the color returned to Orwin Shank's face as quickly as if he had been sprayed with paint. Shor Gormalin moved his head in what might have been a nod of agreement.

Raina Blackhail, almost as if she were afraid of showing any reaction, raised a gloved hand to her shoulders and pulled up her sable hood. Even though he was aware it was ridiculous to think of such a thing at such a time, Raif couldn't help but be struck by Raina Blackhail's beauty. She wasn't pretty, not in the way that young girls like Lansa and Hailly Tanner were, but a kind of clear strength shone in her eyes that made everyone who saw her look twice. Raif wondered if she would ever marry again.

Mace Blackhail waited until everyone was quiet before he spoke his reply. His eyes were as hard and bloody as frozen meat. A small movement sent his wolf fur rippling and served to expose the sword at his thigh. Ignoring Raif completely, he turned to face the meet party. "I won't deny that I rode back as fast as I could—the boy has the truth of it there." Mace paused, allowing a moment for the slight emphasis he had placed on the word *boy* to sink in.

"I wasn't thinking of the dead, I admit that. And I look back now and I'm ashamed of what I did. But when I saw my father's body lying on the ground near the posts, his eyes frosting over even as I looked, all I could think of were the people at home. The Bluddsmen were heading east, yet what if they turned at the Muzzle and headed south instead? What if, whilst I stood there deciding whether to pull my father's body from the cold or hold blood rites where it lay, a second, greater party descended on the roundhouse itself? What if I returned to find that the same thing that had happened to my father and his camp had happened *here* in the Heart of Clan?"

Mace Blackhail met the eyes of all who counted one by one. No one spoke, but some of the yearmen, including Orwin Shank's two middle sons, shifted restlessly in their saddles.

Sleet flew into the faces of the meet party, melting against the hot, flushed skins of Orwin Shank and his sons, Ballic the Red, Corbie Meese, and Merritt Ganlow, while clinging and staying partially frozen against the paler skins of Shor Gormalin, Raina Blackhail, and Will Hawk. All sleet that fell on Mace Blackhail turned to ice.

Finally, after he had forced many in the meet party to look away, Mace Blackhail spoke again. "I am sorry for what I did, but I would not change it. I believe my father would have done the same. It was a choice between the living and the dead, and everyone here who knew and loved Dagro Blackhail must allow that his first thoughts would have been for his wife and his clan."

Ballic the Red nodded. Others followed. The tendons to either side of Corbie Meese's powerful hammerman's neck strained against his skin, and after a moment he looked down and murmured, "That's the truth of it." Raina Blackhail edged her filly round, so that her face was not visible to anyone in the party, including her foster son.

Raif stood at Mace's back. The bristling anger he had felt at being called a boy was now mixed with something else: a kind of slow-setting fear. Mace Blackhail was going to get away with it. Raif could see it on the faces of the meet party. Even Shor Gormalin, who never rushed to judgment on anything and was as careful about all decisions he made as he was with his blade around children, was nodding along with the rest. Didn't he see? Didn't he realize?

And then there was Drey. Raif glanced over his shoulder, where Drey stood only a pace behind him, a handful of Raif's oilskin twisting in his fist. If Raif meant to move forward to speak, Drey meant to pull him back.

"Dagro's body," Raif hissed for Drey's ears alone. "It wasn't—"

"What's that you say, boy?" Mace Blackhail spun the roan around. Brass bow and hammer hooks jangled like bells. "Speak up. We are all clan here. What you say to one you must say to all."

Anger made Raif slam his elbow into Drey's first to free himself from his brother's hold. Blood pumped into his temples as he spoke. "I said that Dagro Blackhail didn't fall by the posts. We found him by the rack. He was butchering the black bear carcass when he was taken."

Mace Blackhail's eyes darkened. His lips curled, and for half an instant Raif thought he was about to smile. Then just as quickly he wheeled back to face the meet party, stopping all hushed mutterings dead. "I moved the body from the

posts to the drying rack. I didn't want to leave my father outside the tent circle, exposed. It may have been foolish, but I
wanted him close to the fire."

"But the bear's blood—"

Drey grabbed Raif's wrist with such force that bones
cracked. "Enough, Raif. You're hounding the wrong person.
It's the Dog Lord and his clan that we should be attacking.
We both saw the grooved hoofprints made by the Bluddsmen, you can't deny that. What else *didn't* we see? In our
way we acted just like Mace—doing things foolishly without thinking. We weren't there, remember. We weren't there.
While we crept away in the dark to shoot ice hares, Mace
was standing dogwatch over the camp. We can't blame him
for slipping bounds to see off a bear. Either one of us would
have done the same."

Releasing his hold on Raif's wrist, Drey turned and faced
his brother full on. Although his expression was tense, there
was an unmistakable appeal in his eyes. "Mace did the right
thing coming back, Raif. He acted like clan, doing what any
experienced clansman would have done. We acted like"—
Drey hesitated, searching for the right words—"two brothers
who had just lost their da."

Raif looked down, away from his brother's gaze and the
sharp looks of the meet party. Drey had just won himself a
lot of respect in the eyes of the clan; Raif saw it in their eyes
as they listened to him speak. Drey was the voice of reason,
humbling himself, speaking with the same weighted reluc-
tance that his father had before him. Raif swallowed, his
throat suddenly sore. For a moment it had been just like listening to Tem.

Glancing up, Raif saw Mace Blackhail watching him.
His face was fixed in lines of concern, in keeping with the
new mood Drey had set, in keeping also with rest of the
meet party, who waited quietly, gravely, to see what Drey
Sevrance's troublesome younger brother would do. Raif's
gaze descended from Mace Blackhail's face to his gloved
hands, which flicked at the roan's mane with all the satisfaction of a wolf switching its tail. Drey had done his work
for him.

Mace Blackhail's gaze met Raif's, and in that instant Raif

knew he was dealing with something worse than a craven. Mace Blackhail had ridden to the badlands on a stocky, fat-necked cob, one of twenty dozen other yearmen, a fosterling from another, lesser clan. Now he sat on his foster father's blue smoke roan, wearing a wolf cloak that reflected only rich shades of black, speaking with a newly modulated voice and manner, and adopting the clan chief's authority along with his clothes and his horse.

Raif massaged his wrist where Drey had gripped it. It wasn't even worth asking how Mace had come to ride home upon his foster father's gelding. Mace Blackhail wasn't going to be caught out this late in the game.

"Raif."

Drey's voice brought Raif back to the meet. Looking into his brother's face, Raif saw how tired his brother looked. It had been a long six days for both of them, yet it was Drey who had carried a greater portion of the weight on the journey back, Drey who had spent an extra hour each night stripping logs down to the heartwood so the fire wouldn't burn out while they slept.

"You two lads need to come inside." It was Shor Gormalin, speaking in his soft burr. The small, fair-haired man, whose quiet ways disguised the fiercest swordsman in the clan, looked from Drey to Raif as he spoke. "You've walked a long way, and had a hard journey, and seen things that none here would wish to see. And no matter what was the right and wrong of what you did, you stayed and saw to our dead. For that alone we owe you more than any here can repay."

Shor paused. Everyone in the meet party either nodded or murmured, "Aye." A muffled sob escaped from Merritt Ganlow's lips.

"So come wi' me now. Let Inigar grind some guidestone for your tines, and let us warm you and feed you and welcome you home. You are clan, and you are needed, and you must tell us of our kin."

The swordsman's words had a profound effect on the faces of the meet party. Orwin Shank closed his eyes and held a fist to his heart. Seeing their father's actions, the two Shank yearmen did likewise. Other yearmen followed, and within seconds the entire meet party sat high on their saddles, eyes closed or cast down, paying due respect to those who were dead. Raina Blackhail trotted her horse over to Shor Gormalin's side and laid her hand on the swordsman's arm.

Out of the corner of his eye, Raif saw Mace Blackhail look up and take note of the contact. His eyes caught and reflected a thin break of sunlight, and for an instant they shone yellow like a wolf's.

Forcing aside his unease, Raif stepped toward his brother. Drey was waiting for him and brought up his arm straightaway, wrapping it around Raif's shoulder. He didn't speak, and Raif was glad of it. There was little choice here: Raif loved his brother and respected Shor Gormalin too much to hold out against them.

Shor Gormalin vaulted from his horse with the speed and agility that never failed to surprise Raif, even though he had seen the swordsman do so many times before. A moment later Corbie Meese also dismounted, and the two clansmen came forward, offering Drey and Raif their mounts. Mace Blackhail trotted his horse down the slope, positioning himself to be head rider when the meet party turned for home.

Shor Gormalin's blue eyes looked straight at Raif as he handed him his reins. "'Tis a good thing you did, lad, you and your brother. We are Blackhail, the first of all clans. We must be and act as one in this."

Raif took the reins. Although he didn't say it outright, Shor Gormalin spoke of war.

The party of twenty-six rode in single and double file down the slope toward the roundhouse. As the wind had turned and quickened, they were forced to ride through the roundhouse's smoke. Raif didn't mind. The smoke was warm and smelled of good, honest things like resinous wood, charred mutton, and shale oil. The darkness it created hid his face.

Below lay the roundhouse. Home. Raif remembered how it had felt to see it in the past. His mood blackened.

From above, the roundhouse looked like a massive island of gray white stone set in a frozen sea. Sunk a hundred feet deep into the ground to protect from the fierce winds, blinding snows, and crippling frosts of winter, the stronghold was invisible from outside but for the upper quarter of its curtain wall and its heavily barricaded stone roof. Windows cut tall to let in light, yet kept narrow enough so that no man could ever force his way through them, were set into the stonework like slits. Over the years mud and dirt had built up around the base, mounding against the outer wall, burying even more of the roundhouse beneath the earth. Every autumn Longhead and his crew spent two weeks digging away the excess dirt. It took them a whole day just to root out rogue saplings that had seeded on the roof.

Some clans let the dirt build so high around their round-houses that eventually even the roof grew over, and plants and grasses hooked their roots into the stone. Clan Bannen's roundhouse didn't even *look* like a building from the outside, just a perfectly formed hill.

That wasn't Blackhail's way. *We protect ourselves against the cold and our enemies, but would sooner face death than hide.* Raif had heard those words and others like them said a thousand times. Every clansman repeated them, and what had started out as an idle boast from one clan chief to another had become a way of life. Now even clan dead were left out in the open. Laid in hollowed-out basswoods in clear sight of wagon trails, passes, and streams, Blackhail corpses scorned hiding until the very last.

Raif shook his head violently. He had seen the bodies. Sulfur and other washes kept the feeders away for only so long. After a good rainfall or a hard frost the ravens always came.

"Raif."

Raina Blackhail's voice snapped Raif back. He watched as she turned her smart chestnut filly on a hairpin and rode along the ranks toward him. The fur of her hood and cloak gleamed like sealskin. In the few minutes they had been riding, the temperature had dropped and the sleet was turning grainy like snow. Raina's breath purled white as she rode.

Raif watched as others made way to let her pass. Even though her husband was now dead, Raina retained her standing in the clan. Dagro Blackhail's wealth and respect were her due. A new clan chief would have to be chosen, and although Raif knew Mace Blackhail would try to take his foster father's place, he also knew that if Raina decided to marry again, the man she chose as her husband had a good chance of becoming chief. Raina's decisions were always well heeded. Whenever Dagro Blackhail was away from the roundhouse and problems arose that needed handling, the clan would look to his wife. "Raina knows her husband's mind," they would say, meaning they trusted her judgment completely. Breech births, bad omens, blood rites, wife beatings, drunken brawls, border and damming disputes, cattle raids, and matters of clan pride: Raina Blackhail had seen to them all.

*And Effie . . .*

Raif took a deep breath and held it in. Raina Blackhail had been as good as a mother to Effie.

"Days are failing," Raina said, glancing at the sky as she fell in by Raif's side. "Soon there'll be scarce enough light to aim an arrow by." She smiled briefly. "But then again Tem was telling me just before he left how you could find a target in the dark."

That made him turn and pay her heed.

Raina Blackhail didn't permit herself a second smile. "It wasn't your fault, you know. Yours or Drey's. Just about every man in this clan has slipped bounds at some time or other to run off and shoot game at the lick."

Raif wound his reins around his fist. "Is that what you came here to say?" As he spoke he spied Mace Blackhail at the head of the party, pointing to the far pasture and saying something to Will Hawk and Ballic the Red that caused both clansmen to nod in agreement. Raif drew the reins tighter, stopping the blood from flowing to his fingers.

The small display of Mace Blackhail's authority did not go unnoticed by Raina. She made a minute movement with her shoulders, squaring them and causing her sable cloak to resettle on the dock of her filly. "I came here to talk about Effie. You must be gentle with her, Raif. She's such a quiet child. It's hard to tell what she's thinking."

"What has she been told?"

Raina hesitated. "Mace spoke to her before I had chance to. He told her that you and Drey had died along with her da."

Raif exhaled with a soft hiss. "How did she take it?"

"Not well. She seemed . . ." Raina shook her head,

searched for the right word. "Angry. She ran away, and for the longest time no one could find her. We tore the round-house apart looking. Corbie Meese and Longhead arranged a search party. Letty and the girls lit torches and walked the length of the graze. Orwin Shank's two eldest rode as far as the Wedge. It was Shor Gormalin who found her in the end—tucked in the corner of the little dog cote, stiff with cold and covered in dirt. Had that blessed stone of hers in her hand. Rocking back and forth with it, she was. Made herself so sick she could barely stand." Raina clicked her tongue. "How she managed not to get eaten by those wolfhounds the Shanks keep, I'll never know. Orwin feeds them but twice a week, I swear."

Relaxing his grip on his reins, Raif guided Shor Gormalin's gelding around a bank of loose shale. His own anger suddenly didn't seem important anymore. "How's she been since?"

"Well, that's what I came to warn you about. She's lost a bit of weight. And she keeps so much to herself. . . ." Raina's words trailed away as a small figure stepped out from the roundhouse below.

As Raif and Raina trotted their horses down into the valley, and Mace Blackhail and his lead riders drew close to the roundhouse, the figure took hesitant, child-size steps forward. It was Effie. Her dark auburn hair gave her away. Raif leaned forward in his saddle. She was so *thin*.

"Just you be careful with her, Raif Sevrance," Raina Blackhail said, kicking her horse forward. "You and Drey are all she has."

Raif barely acknowledged what Raina said. He glanced two riders ahead, where Drey was riding at Orwin Shank's side. Drey looked back. His fox hood was up again, and the sky was nearly black, but the expression on his face was clear. *What has happened to Effie?*

Feeling a stab of unease in his chest, Raif kicked Shor Gormalin's gelding into a canter and raced along the file. Drey came seconds behind.

The beaten clay court outside the roundhouse greatdoor was filling rapidly with people. Some carried pitch-soaked torches, others smoking racks of charred mutton and spits of rabbits roasted in their skins. A few brought feed and blankets for the horses. One figure, Anwyn Bird by the looks of her round belly, rolled a keg of hearth-warmed beer before her that belched steam into the freezing air.

Effie stood ahead of everyone, her shoulders hunched together, shivering and clutching her blue woolen dress. No one had thought to throw a cloak over her shoulders or push mitts on her hands. As Raif approached, he saw where his sister's cheeks had sunk away, leaving little pits beneath her eyes and around her jaw. His heart ached to see them.

He slid from his horse and ran to her. Effie took a small step forward. Her grave little face was turned up toward his, and after a moment she held out her arms and waited to be taken. Raif scooped her up and brought her to his chest. Pushing her body against his, he drew her within the folds of his oilskin to protect her from the cold. She was so light. It was like picking up a blanket stuffed with straw. Raif hugged her harder, wanting to give her his heat and his strength.

Then Drey was there, and Effie shifted in Raif's arms and Raif released her to his brother. Drey's big arms enveloped Effie completely, and his head came down to hers, and he nuzzled her hair and her temples and the bridge of her nose. "It's all right, little one. We're back now. Raif and I are back."

Effie snuggled against Drey's chest. "I knew," she said quietly, seriously, glancing from Drey to Raif, then over to Mace Blackhail, who was busy hefting the saddle from the roan. "He said you were dead, but I *knew* it wasn't so."

## S I X

### *The Inverted Spire*

ASH MARCH TWISTED THE sheets around herself as she turned in her sleep. Linen spun so smoothly by the old women of Maker's Isle that it felt as cool as glass rode up between her thighs, wound around her belly, and coiled about her wrists.

Ash dreamed she was enclosed within a womb of ice. Blue white light shone on her arms and legs, making them gleam like smooth metal. The icewall was slick where she had touched it, skin warmed and dripping. Ice squeaked and cracked as she moved. Frost fumes filled her mouth like milk.

If she could just push further, *deeper*.

Something shifted. The massive lode of ice above her juddered, and freezing splinters rained on her face and chest. Spiky and hard as needles, they punctured the skin on her arms and her breasts, drawing tiny drops of blood. Even as Ash brushed away the splinters, the ice ceiling dropped. A blizzard of cold air pumped against her face, and then the ice ceiling slammed into her chest. Ice shattered against her skin with a crack of white light, and a spume of sleet and smoke filled the air.

Ash screamed.

Suddenly there was nothing below her, and she fell and fell and fell.

Voices whispered to her, coaxed and pleaded like starving men. *Reach, mistressss. So cold here, so dark. Reach.*

Ash shook her head. She tried to move, but her body was numb. Frozen.

No longer falling, she stood in the center of a cavern of black ice. All was dark except for the glimmer of smoothly frozen things. Even the breath that steamed from the walls was dark and dense, like smoke from a poorly aired fire. Fear gnawed at the edges of Ash's thoughts. When she breathed she took in the smell of cold things. She was not alone. Something within the cavern stirred. It made no move toward her, but it shifted its weight so that its presence would be known.

*We have waited such a long time, mistressss: a thousand years in our chains of blood. Dare you make us wait a thousand more?*

Ash felt her knees buckle. The voice *pulled*.

In the distance, beyond where she could see, beyond even the walls of the cave, creatures with muzzles howled. Shadows flickered upon the surface of the ice, man shapes and beasts and demon horses. And then suddenly there was no

ice at all, just darkness that stretched toward a place where
Ash knew in the deepest depths of her soul that she did not
want to be.

*Reach, mistressss. Pretty mistressss. Reach.*

At her side, the bones in her wrists twisted. Saddles of
muscle in her chest and back tensed, ready to pull weight.
Tendons strained. Fingers uncurled, forcing a closed fist into
an open hand as knuckles cracked like wet sticks.

*Reach for us. Reach for us. REACH.*

Bones glided in their sockets as Ash's arms began to rise.

*Kaaw!* A raven's cry pierced the darkness, jolting Ash's
body like a needle in her spine.

Her eyes sprang open. The darkness sped away in a long
blurred streak. She was in her chamber. The embers in the
brazier glowed with a faint orange light. Both amber lamps
were dead.

Knocking.

Ash's head spun around toward the source of the sound.
Not the door, but the tiny shuttered window on the opposite
side of the room. She waited. The noise didn't come again,
but a soft tearing sound, like the flap of wings beating air,
faded into the distance. A bird. Ash shuddered. A raven.

Suddenly aware of how cold and wet the sheets were, she
tugged them from her body. Her nightdress was soaking, so
she pulled it over her head and threw it the way of the sheets.
Freezing and naked, she ran over to the charcoal brazier and
knelt in its warm glow. Using the little copper tongs that
were hooked at its base, she stirred the embers within. The
oil-soaked felt had long since burned away, taking the odor
of almonds and sandalwood with it. Ash was glad. She was
in no mood to breathe in rich and sickly scents.

Her hands shook as she replaced the tongs. A haze of cold
sweat covered her skin, and her knees felt as shaky as if she
had run up all the stairs in the Cask without pausing to rest
halfway. With a small sigh, she pulled at the corners of the
needlepoint rug she was kneeling on, drawing the soft green
wool around shoulders and making a little pocket for herself
in the center. She was so tired. All she wanted to do was
sleep.

Feeling a bit better for being wrapped up, she glanced

over to the door. The empty bolt holes stood as a reminder that either Marafice Eye or Penthero Iss could enter her chamber any time they pleased. Not that Marafice Eye ever had, but Ash knew he was out there, sitting on a graymeet bench, big hands testing the give of the leather bindings on his tunic or pushing against the bench's armrests, bringing the entire weight of his body to bear upon any flaws he found in the stone. He was always testing things to see what it took to break them.

Ash pulled the rug closer. She had tried to avoid Marafice Eye for the past week, ever since the night he had first blocked her way on the steps. The Knife didn't like to be avoided, though, and had now taken to blocking her way whenever he safely could. If he met Ash alone in a corridor or on the stairs, he would step directly in front of her and wait, forcing her to walk around him. He never touched her, never spoke, but his small lips would twist with pleasure and his small eyes would look beyond her as if she weren't there at all. Like the armrests on the bench and the leather of his tunic, she had become yet another thing to push to breaking.

Ash tugged a hand through her hair. She was a foundling, alive only because Penthero Iss had chosen to save her. She wasn't a noblewoman and she wasn't a servant, so where did she fit in? Marafice Eye didn't know; that was why he was testing her: to see just how far he could go before Iss stopped him.

"Miss." A soft voice whispered through the door. "Can I enter, miss?"

Ash didn't want to see anyone. Not now, not like this. "Go away," she mumbled. Disgusted by how weak her voice sounded, she tried again. "I'm tired, Katia. Let me sleep."

"I've brought some hot milk and rose cakes."

So Iss had sent her. Ash stood, allowing the rug to drop flat on the floor. "Wait a moment while I dress." There was no point in sending Katia away, not when she was under orders from Iss; the girl would just stand outside the door all night, calling every few minutes for permission to enter until she wore Ash down. Penthero Iss never raised his voice, never threatened violence, but he had a way of getting people to do exactly as he wished.

Wrapping a fresh linen robe around her shoulders, Ash took a few deep breaths and tried to settle herself back to normal. More and more these days it was harder to remember what normal was, though. She never felt like herself, she was always tired and sweating and cold. Then there was her body. . . . Ash glanced down. That definitely wasn't normal anymore. Breasts had come from nowhere in just two months.

"You can come in now." Ash stepped into the corner as she spoke. She didn't want Marafice Eye to see her as Katia opened the door.

Katia was small and olive skinned, with dark eyes and dark lips and black curls that spat out pins. Ash could never look at the girl without feeling a stab of envy. Katia made her feel pale and bony and *straight*. Everything of Katia's curved: her lips, her cheeks, her hips, her hair. Ash's own hair fell as sheer as water, pale and silver blond, down past her waist. Ash had tried hot irons, damp rags, pins, and nightly braiding, yet her hair would have none of it, defying her every time by unraveling straight.

"Put the tray on the stand, Katia."

Katia jumped at the sound of Ash's voice. "There you are, miss. Gave me such a fright hiding behind the door."

Ash ignored Katia's statement. The girl was always claiming fright over something.

Having placed the copper tray on the stand, Katia moved over to the mantel to relight the lamps. Briefly Ash considered speaking up to stop her, then decided against it. Penthero Iss had doubtless given Katia orders to take a good look at her mistress, and the fastest way to get the whole thing over and done with was to let her go right ahead. As Katia refilled the lamp with the small pieces of amber that she kept in a cloth bag around her waist, Ash took the opportunity to smooth down her hair and rub her face. She wished she didn't feel so shaky. But there was nothing to be done about that.

"One should be enough," Ash said after the wick thrust into the oil-and-amber mixture took the spark. "Come here, and let's have it over and done with."

"Have what done with, miss?"

Ash smiled. Katia was a terrible liar. "Well, my foster father obviously sent you to check up on me, so go right ahead and check." She held out her arms, letting her robe fall open around her breasts. "Should I strip naked, or will this be enough?"

Katia shook her head, black curls bouncing. "Why, you're wicked, miss! Plain wicked. His Lordship never said such a thing. I came here to bring you a late supper out of the goodness of my own heart, and this is what I get for my trouble!" She nodded in the direction of Ash's silver-banded dressing table, where an untidy stack of books and folded manuscripts looked set to topple over. "Been reading too much for your own good, if you ask me. A hot supper's just a hot supper, you know. Nothing's attached but the skin on the milk."

Suddenly glad Katia was there, Ash pulled her robe together. Katia had been with her for fourteen months now—longer than any other maid she'd ever had—and it felt good to know someone well enough to tease them. "I'm sorry, Katia. But the rose cakes always give Iss away. They're quite tasteless, smell like old roses, and cost a small fortune to prepare."

Katia snorted, but quietly. "Well, if you don't want them . . ."

"Take them. In future, if you must interrupt me in the middle of the night, bring me fresh bread, salt butter and lots of it, and beer instead of milk. A dark brew, mind. One that's thick enough to float a spoon and has to be sieved through a cheesecloth to remove the hops." Ash tried to keep her face straight as she spoke, but the word *cheesecloth* proved too much, and she burst out laughing.

"Oh, miss! You are wicked."

Katia's laugh was just a little too loud to be considered feminine, and Ash loved to hear it. Sometimes it was hard to remember that Katia was a full year younger than she was. Katia was so grown-up, so . . . well . . . *rounded*, yet whenever she laughed she became a child again.

Abruptly, the smile slid from Ash's face. "Katia."

"Yes, miss?"

Ash struggled to find words. "Are you still"—seeing the

servant girl's large dark eyes looking straight into hers, Ash hesitated, wishing she had never started—*"friendly* with Marafice Eye?"

Katia's expression changed. "And if I am? 'Taint nothing to do with you."

Ash took a breath, decided not to say any more, then went right ahead and spoke anyway. "He's such a big and powerful man. Like an ox. You should be careful, that's all."

With a forceful shake of her head, Katia said, "What I do in my own good time is my business. Unlike some around here, I'm a full-grown woman, and those that aren't and hain't ever so much as kissed a man should keep their opinions to themselves."

Blood flushed Ash's cheeks. She didn't speak. Stupidly, ridiculously, she felt her eyes stinging.

After a moment Katia's expression changed right back again, and she crossed the room and put her hand on Ash's arm. "I'm sorry, miss. Truly I am. You made me speak a stock of nonsense that I surely didn't mean. You'll come to your blood any day now, I'm certain of that." She drew Ash over to the bed as she spoke. "And as soon as that happens you'll have fine, proper dresses, a ladies' maid to preen your hair, and suitors lining up from Hoargate to the Red Forge, all begging for the priv'lege of your hand."

Katia placed a hand on Ash's shoulder, gently pressing her to sit. A second hand flitted to her brow. "Why, you're shaking, miss. And hot and cold all in one."

"I'm fine, Katia, really. Carry on telling me what will happen when my blood comes." Ash didn't much care for the idea of suitors lining up from one end of the city to the other, and she knew that any ladies' maid worth her salt would end up storming off in frustration within a week, muttering to herself about hair that *refused* to take a curl. Yet she liked to hear about them anyway. When Katia spoke of such things, Ash could almost believe that everything was normal and would continue to be normal, and that the strange, almost hungry look she saw in her foster father's eyes when he studied her these past few months was nothing more than a trick of the light.

Katia reached for a brush and started working on Ash's hair. "Well, miss, let me see. There'll be new shoes, of course, a dozen of them: lamb's hide for day and embroidered silk and stiff lace for night. You'll have to have a new riding habit—trimmed with black fox, no matter what His Lordship says—and you'll need a proper lady's filly, not that old cob Master Haysticks lets you ride around the quad. His Lordship might even bring in some old cloistress t'elp with your manners and table 'port. Though there's no need to teach you how to read and write, His Lordship's done that himself. . . ."

Ash nodded, enjoying the sensation of Katia's capable hands brushing her hair and letting her mind slip away as the little maid chattered on.

Too much had changed this last year. There had been a time when her foster father was different, when he sent for her each day and spent his own time teaching her how to read and write. Any number of priests and scribes could have done the work for him, yet Penthero Iss had chosen to do it himself. And it wasn't just because he liked to keep her away from anyone who might befriend her—though Ash had recognized that possessiveness in him early on, as time after time maidservants and fortress children whom she became close to were routinely sent away. No. Her foster father had genuinely enjoyed instructing her. Knowledge was one of his joys.

". . . and of course there'll be a new chamber, one with proper isinglass windows and—"

Ash blinked back, suddenly interested in what Katia was saying. "A new chamber?"

"Why, yes, miss. That much is certain as ice on the Splinter."

"I don't understand. Why?"

Katia put down her brush. Eyes darting in quick glances as if she suspected people could be hiding and listening, she lowered her voice and said, "Oh yes. There's been talk of it already. Just the other day when I was . . . er . . . *visiting* with the Knife in the Forge, His Lordship came in and told him that he needs to be ready to move you on his say. 'Course when old Vealskin saw me he stopped dead, gave me one of his looks—you know the sort, all pale and scary like a frosted-over corpse—and sent me running out of the room without so much as a spoken word." Katia beamed. She loved telling secrets.

Ash swallowed. She was glad she was sitting. "Move me on his say?"

Nodding, Katia crossed to the dresser and popped one of the precious rose cakes in her mouth. Chewing, she spoke. "That's what was said. If you ask me, it'll be to one of those fancy upper chambers in the Bight, with all the black marble and dark glass cut into the floors. Might even have a private entrance and a staircase all your own." Katia took a second rose cake, looked at it, then set it down. "You must swear to take me with you, miss. Wherever you go. I couldn't stand going back to the kitchens and scrubbing pots again. Couldn't stand being made to—"

"Hush, Katia." The servant girl's chatter was beginning to irritate Ash.

Katia's mouth closed with a squeak. Skirts whipping air, she moved around the chamber and began checking shutters, stirring the brazier and making preparations for the night.

Ash barely noticed. A move away from the Cask? It was unthinkable. This chamber had been her home for as long as she could remember. Of all the four towers in Mask Fortress, the Cask was the only one she knew. She had broken her arm here, climbing the outer battlements when she was six; when she was eight she had been confined to her room for two months because of blood fever, and her foster father had visited her every day, bringing iced honey and yellow pears; and when she was eleven her caged bird had grown sick in this very chamber and had started pulling out its own flight feathers and chewing on its claws, and to please her Iss had performed a little ceremony by the door before sending it to Caydis for a mercy killing. All her life was here. All of it.

Distressed, Ash drew her feet off the floor and hugged her knees to her chest. No one had mentioned a move to her. Nothing had been planned; no workmen or carpenters called. Surely someone should have told her something? She rubbed her bare shins. The sheets beneath her feet were damp with sweat. Icy.

No. Ash shook her head. She wouldn't think about the dream. It was nothing. Nothing.

Katia popped the remaining two rose cakes into her amber pouch. "Will you be wanting anything else, miss, 'fore I go?"

"No." Something about the sight of Katia walking toward the door made Ash change her mind. "I mean yes. One more thing."

"What?" Katia's full lips were made more so by an exaggerated pout.

"I know you're going to see my foster father now—" Seeing Katia ready to protest, Ash held out her hand. "No, don't deny it. I don't blame you. It's what you have to do to keep out of the kitchen. I'd do the same if I were you." Katia remained sullen, yet Ash carried on. "I don't mind you telling him that I don't feel well and don't look well, and even that the bed is messed. But please don't tell him that I know he's planning to move me. *Please.*"

Katia looked at her mistress. Ash knew that the servant girl was envious of her and coveted all the clothes and pretty things in her chamber like silver brushes and tortoiseshell combs. Yet she also knew that Katia could be kind when it suited her. She had once walked all the way to Almsgate and back to purchase a bolt and plate for the door.

Sighing with exaggerated force, Katia sent her curls dancing. "All right. I'll do my best—but only for my own sake, mind. If old Vealskin finds I've been blabbing about things I overheard and wasn't supposed to, he'll have me downstairs in no time. And it won't be in the kitchens scrubbing pots."

"Thank you, Katia."

Katia harrumphed as she stepped toward the door. "I still have to tell him how you are, though. There's no getting round that. You know how he is."

Ash nodded as she snuffed out the lamp. She knew exactly how Iss was.

*   *   *

THE CAUL FLIES HUMMED within their netting, black translucent wings beating faster than the eye could see. Four winged, lean bodied, and with the long, double-jointed legs of flesh settlers, the creatures flew slowly despite their efforts, swinging clumsily from side to side to side. These were females, of course. The shiny green black sacs around their abdomens were bloated with hundreds of eggs. Penthero Iss, Surlord of Spire Vanis, Lord Commander of the Rive Watch, Keeper of Mask Fortress, and Master of the Four Gates, preferred not to hold the netting too close. The caul flies were past due and were desperate to lay, and their serrated chitinous mouthparts were quite capable of breaking through gauze. Especially if the females smelled blood.

Iss watched with fascination as one female flew to where his pale hand gripped the netting. The skin was clean and unbroken, not what the creature wanted at all, but Iss had seen some caul flies capable of causing the wounds they needed. This one, however, would not get that chance. With his free hand, Iss pulled a cloth of blue felt from around his waist and laid it over the top portion of the netting. He would arrive at his destination within the quarter, and a short period of darkness would not make the females drowsy. Iss had made a study of their weaknesses. It was the cold, not the dark, that slowed them.

As he walked through the deserted east gallery toward the Splinter, Iss counted days. Six. He kept records, of course, but he trusted the thoroughness of his own mind more than any scribbles on a page. He didn't want to risk weakening the Bound One too soon after the previous drawing. Thoroughness in all things, most especially the use of power.

Six was enough, though. Six was well and good.

Winter came early to the mountains and the city of Spire Vanis, and the temperature in the east gallery was currently just below freezing. Iss fought the desire to shiver. He had grown up hating the cold. Cold meant too little wood on the fire and not enough blankets for the bed, and Iss knew all about that. As a child he had dreamed of glowing hearths and crackling flames and layer upon layer of goosedown piled high upon his chest. Forty years later he had all that, yet he could not say it was enough.

He was surlord, not king, and although he might rule for twenty years or more, a violent death would be his in the end. It was the way of things in Spire Vanis. Historians might speak the names of Uron the Pure and Rhees Gryphon and a handful of other men who had ruled the city and died in their sleep. Yet Iss had stood in the shadows and watched as five sworn brothers cut Borhis Horgo to strips. Old he was, dry and shriveled; Iss could hardly believe how much he bled. Sometimes he saw the blood in his dreams. Sometimes the blood was his.

So many surlords. Borhis Horgo, Rannock Hews, Theric Hews, Connad Hews, Lewick Crieff, who was called the Halfking, Garath Lors, Stornoway the Bold . . . and so the list went on, back and back, to Theron Pengaron, who was slain by his nephew's hideclads on ground where the Splinter lay today. All had died a surlord's death: knifed in the back, shot at distance, poisoned, bludgeoned, betrayed. The only law of succession in Spire Vanis was the law of superior might. Once a rival smelled weakness, he drew his conspirators about him and plotted his surlord's death. Iss knew his likely fate. He knew and refused to accept it.

It wasn't enough to be surlord. He must make himself something else.

Cold air settled in Iss' lungs as he neared the Splinter. Limestone as pale and smooth as lake ice stole the warmth from the soles of his feet. Heavy things swung from his belt nestling against the double-woven silk of his robes. The little stone lamp so ingeniously crafted by the barbarians who lived in the north along the coast, with its baleen guards and shaved horn covering, gave off heat and light more safely than any other lamp. It could be knocked over, and still the flame would stay inside the central chamber. Even now bumping lightly against his thigh, it was a benign and pleasing warmth to enjoy. As for the other two packages that hung from the belt, Mistress Wence had better hope she wrapped them securely. Pan-heated honey and mashed then strained yellowbeans could both leak juices that a man wearing silk had no use for.

Iss had found the caul flies liked to feed after they had laid their eggs. It was a common misconception that mature females fed off blood. Iss had observed them and knew they did not. Honey was what they liked best, preferably warm. The flies had been fortress bred in the cold climes of the

Northern Territories, yet they still retained memories of the Far South where they belonged.

As for the yellowbeans, they were to feed the Bound One. Iss had asked Mistress Wence to enrich them with butter and egg yolks and salt them as mildly as she would food for a child.

Holding the partially covered netting out before him, Iss approached the Splinter. As always, the temperature dropped the nearer one drew to the door. In just the past few days water weeping from the stonework had quickened to form a skin of blue ice above the arch. Iss took out the key. Impaled beasts with many heads and the thick muscular tails of serpents watched the lock turn from their position at the spire's base. The oil lamp flickered, making the relief carvings dance upon their poles. Iss adjusted the lamp, the light dimmed, and the creatures stilled to stone.

The door opened with a small hiss. Frost smoke writhed through the opening, like the tissue of a newly risen ghost. Within the netting, the caul flies drew in their wings and dropped to the bottom of the makeshift bag.

First frost was always the worst in the Splinter. The outer stonework ran with moisture year-round, and every arch, ledge, and cornerstone let in rain. The interior walls bled. Rivulets ran in thin lines, following the curves of bias-cut stone and the edges of steps. Drips gained mass on overhangs, pools collected in ruts and trenches, and entire walls glistened with damp. First frost turned it all to freezing mist. As the weeks passed and the days shortened and rime ice formed on the exterior walls, the water would cool, then freeze. Expanding as it quickened, the ice split rock as surely as a mason with a mallet. Each mild spell and subsequent thawing pushed the Splinter one step closer to collapse. The entire structure was flawed, crumbling, broken. The only thing that kept it standing was the precision cut and placement of each stone.

And the foundations, of course, Iss thought with a quick humorless smile. No building in the Northern Territories had foundations to compare with the Splinter.

The light from the stone lamp did little but reflect back in Iss' face as he stepped through the smoke into the tower's lower rotunda. Cracked tiles rocked beneath his feet as he moved. Whole sections of the original flooring were missing, either torn up by greedy workmen or destroyed by frosts and falling stones. Iss didn't care. The Splinter's staircase spiraled through the tower's heart, stopping off at thirty-nine successive stories before reaching its apex in the spire that pierced storms, yet Iss had little but a passing interest in any of it. Aboveground the Splinter's stone was as dead and worthless as a foot black with frostbite. It was belowground, in the Inverted Spire, that the stone became a vital, living thing.

Iss crossed to the base of the spiral stair, to the dark shadows and awkwardly shaped space that lay beneath the first flight of steps. Bending his back as needed, he followed the crook of the stairs until his body was tucked against the endwall.

Tensing his jaw and his fists, he spoke a word. It weakened him more severely than he anticipated, and drops of urine splashed against his thigh. The pain was sharp but fleeting, and a powerful contraction of his stomach wall flooded his mouth with the taste of salt.

Even before he could spit it away, the stairwell rumbled and began to swing inward like a gate. The grinding of iron wheels and chains was muffled by walls three feet thick. Above Iss' head, the great stone staircase shuddered, its blocks shifting minutely in their beds of rotten mortar. Limestone dust sifted onto his shoulders as the wall completed its movement, revealing a cavity not much larger than the size of a crouching man.

This was the part Iss hated. Still shaken from the drawing, his knee joints as weak as green timber, and urine still wet upon his thigh, he forced himself through the breach. No frost smoke rose from the void to greet him. The coldness here had a different, more permanent quality, and all mist had long since settled and froze. Deep down at the apex of the Inverted Spire the air was different, warmer, but ice seams remained year-round at the rim.

Like the cold, the darkness was also more concentrated, and Iss was forced to unhook the stone lamp from his belt and adjust the baleen fibers to let in greater amounts of air.

He didn't care much for darkness, though he was willing to allow it had its uses. Things kept within it usually broke down given time.

Spitting to clean the last traces of metal from his mouth, he edged forward in small, toe-size movements until his feet found the lip of the first stair. Unlike the tower above, the Inverted Spire did not boast a central staircase; rather the steps ran along the outer wall, gradually spiraling downward in a great winding arc. A gaping many-storied trough lay in its center. Black as night, colder than pack ice, fed by self-generating winds, and subject to each shift and roll of the mountain it bored down through, the Inverted Spire was a force unto itself. As deep as the Splinter was tall, narrowing to a nail-hard point, it pierced the bedrock of Mount Slain like a stake in its heart.

Its frost-riven walls glittered in the light of Iss' lamp. The farther the Surlord descended, the clearer and harder the ice became. Ground to lenses by the weight and compression of Mount Slain, the ice found colors in the lamplight that no eye could see. Not for the first time, Iss resisted the urge to reach out and touch it. Once, nearly eight years ago now, he had lost the skin on his middle finger that way.

The mountain fought the Inverted Spire, chewing through whole sections of granite facing like oak roots through earth. Even breached as they were by the white knuckles and bones of Mount Slain, the walls remained intact. The facing had been mined from the Towerlode at Linn, and there were said to be blood spells and sorcerers' curses set deep into the stone. Robb Claw, great-grandson of Glamis Claw and builder of Mask Fortress, had once claimed that it would take an act of God to break the Spire.

Shivering, Iss drew the netting to his chest. The cold had made the caul flies torpid, and not one of the dozen females now moved. A few would die; he was prepared for that. Once, several years earlier, in the middle of one of the coldest winters Spire Vanis had ever known, all of the laying females had died. It had been messy, but he *had* managed to extricate their eggs. Though regrettably a much smaller portion than normal had gone on to hatch and survive.

With one hand holding the lamp and the other clutching

the netting, he found the descent slow and difficult. Iss had long since mastered the art of *not* looking down, yet the knowledge of the deep chasm below lay like clothing next to his skin. Each stair was three feet wide—a goodly length— yet the steps began in pressure-formed granite as slick as glass and ended in fresh air, and a man couldn't be too careful where he stepped. Iss kept to dead center and turned his mind to matters he found pleasing.

Take the servant girl Katia, for instance. Such a sly, bright girl. Too good by far to be penetrated by the Knife. Iss had no interest in bedding her himself, though it would be interesting to see just how far she would go, just what she would *do* to free herself from the threat of the kitchens.

Iss smiled with all the satisfaction of a jeweler setting a gem. That was Katia's weakness: her fear of ending up in the kitchens, broken veined and red faced, her once high breasts resting like drained waterskins upon her belly, her once bright hair turned to gray. Fortress born and bred, Katia had grown up seeing the exact same thing happen to every other woman who worked there: Mask Fortress took and took but seldom gave. Now the sharp little minx was afraid that the same thing would happen to her.

Once Iss discovered a person's fears they were his. Katia was his now. The girl loved Asarhia March, admired and protected her. Yet she was also envious of Asarhia. Deeply so. Envy and love warred within her heart, yet the fear of returning to the kitchens always won the day. Take tonight. The girl had clearly not wanted to tell him that her mistress's chamber, bedclothes, and hair were in disarray; that Asarhia's skin was hot, yet the sweat that lay upon it was as cold as water wept from ice. Yet Katia had told all that and more. Her mistress wasn't the one who could save her from a life in the kitchens. Iss made sure the girl knew that.

As for the other matter—the possibility that the girl had told Asarhia what she had overheard the other day in the Red Forge—well, that really didn't matter at all. The Knife watched Asarhia day and night, even when she left her chambers and didn't realize she was being watched. Iss' steps slowed for just a moment. He did not relish taking such measures against his almost-daughter. Asarhia was normally such a sweet and trusting girl, yet she was beginning to get frightened. And Iss knew from experience that people who were frightened did foolish things.

Feeling a gust of warmer air puff against his cheeks, Iss made his final adjustment of the lamp. The first chamber couldn't be much farther down now. The Inverted Spire had only three chambers, all lying close to or just above apex. By the time one descended to the first of them, the spire had narrowed to the width of a bullpen. The second chamber was smaller still, and the final chamber was barely the size of a well shaft. Cupped within a seam of black rock, its base ended in a needlepoint of steel.

Not for the first time, Penthero Iss found himself wishing the stone lamp could better light his way. The curve of the stairs was more pronounced lower down and the gradient sharper. Stepping from one worn and sloping step to another was a danger of the worst kind. Iss knew he could use sorcery to draw forth light, yet he also knew it wasn't a cost he cared to pay. The speck of frozen urine currently thawing against his thigh was reminder enough of that. He was not a man of great ability, like some. He had enough. Only enough. His strengths lay elsewhere . . . as in his ability to choose men.

Marafice Eye was one of his chosen. The Protector General of the Rive Watch was dangerous; he could inspire loyalty in fighting men. Iss had realized this early on, in the days when Marafice Eye was a lowly brother-in-the-watch, with a new-made sword at his thigh and the muck of Hoargate still caked upon his boots. Iss had been protector general then, always on the watch for rivals. Another man might have made it his business to destroy Marafice Eye, slay him before he grew into a threat. Iss had made it his business to draw him close. He saw a man who could be useful to him, one who had qualities of dominance and brutality he lacked. When the time came to storm the fortress and overthrow the aging and sickly Borhis Horgo, it had been Marafice Eye who had commanded the Rive Watch; Marafice Eye who'd slain a dozen grangelords and Forsworn on the Horn's icy steps.

It had been a bloody ten days. The Forsworn had been expelled from the city; and their walled keeps, which they called Shrineholds, had been stormed and broken. When it was done, Penthero Iss, kinsman to lord of the Sundered Granges, had taken the title of surlord for himself. Marafice Eye has stood at his side, his protector general and Knife.

Fifteen years later, and they were still surlord and Knife. Iss had little cause to regret his choice. With Marafice Eye at his back, keeping the Rive Watch loyal, his hands were free to deal with the grangelords.

The great houses of Spire Vanis were a thorn in his side, braying constantly for land and titles and gold. Thirteen years ago a bargain had been struck, and the grangelords never let Iss forget it. "You promised us the chance to win land and glory," the Whitehog had said just six days ago in Iss' private chamber. "That's the only reason why you're surlord today. Forget that, and *we* just might forget that we spoke oaths in the Blackvault to protect you."

Iss had almost smiled as the Whitehog spoke. Threats from seventeen-year-old boys had that effect on him. Still, he had seen enough to realize that the young and ambitious grangeling who stood before him, wearing the white and gold of Hews and carrying a five-foot greatsword on his back, might one day make a bid for his place. The boy had already taken to calling himself the Whitehog, in honor of his great-grandfather who had led the Rive Watch to victory at High Rood. It didn't take a seer to know that he held similar dreams of glory for himself.

*Well,* Iss thought, peering into the darkness below, *perhaps the Whitehog might get the chance to lead a force sooner than he thinks. Perhaps he just might find a clansman's ax thrust into his porcine heart.*

Spying the top of the first stone ceiling beneath him, Iss allowed himself to relax a little. Now if he fell, he wouldn't break his neck.

The ceiling stretched across the Inverted Spire like a great stone valve across a pipe. Over the centuries debris had collected on the topside, shaken down from the walls above. Rock fragments, facing tiles, and odd pieces of masonry lay in disjointed heaps amid the yellowing bones of rats, pigeons, and bats that had gained entry to the spire by means

Iss couldn't guess. Human bones were down there, too. Two rib cages could clearly be seen peeking through mounds of rock dust like spiders hiding in sand. Iss had made it his business to search once, yet he'd only ever found one skull.

Bits of food, strips of netting, and a few other scraps had fallen from the Surlord's own hands. Last summer during Almsfest, he had brought a basket of soft strawberries with him, only to find they had slipped from his hand halfway through the descent. They were still there now, spread across the stonework like spattered blood. Red and glistening and smelling like perfume on a filthy whore, they were only just beginning to turn. This deep within the mountain's core, things took years to decay.

Ahead, the staircase ducked below the stone platform and into the chamber below. Iss minded his head. The air stilled immediately, no longer subject to the chasm's winds. Increased warmth came with the calm. The flame within the stone lamp shivered and darted, lighting a circular chamber with polished walls. Dog hooks and metal rings had been hammered into the stone. Chains ran through a series of loops and then ended abruptly, hacked off in midlink. If one looked closely, one could see scraps of brown fabric caught within the chains. Untanned leather, it might be, yet if Iss had to put money on it he'd guess human skin.

Descending on a curving slant along the perimeter of the chamber, he barely spared a passing glance for the chamber's contents. Soon, very soon, he would have Caydis remove the wire cage and the weightstone and the cracked and greasy wheel. Pretty things would be brought in their place: plump cushions, silkwood chests, and tapestries woven with blue and gold thread. Things that would please a girl.

Descending into the apex chamber, Iss shrugged away all thoughts but those he needed. The air down here was as thick and heavy as still water at the bottom of a lake. No matter how many times he neared the final chamber, the sudden change always took him by surprise. His lungs had difficulty expelling air, and deep within his ears two sharp points of pain pushed inward. The Surlord swallowed hard, prayed that his ears wouldn't pick this time to bleed.

The stone facing here was thicker than anywhere else in

the Spire. Pressure-formed granite, whorly and knotted like the bark of a tree, defied breaking by all but the most violent convulsions of Mount Slain. Flecks of bastard's gold shone within the stone.

Unhooking the packs containing honey and yellowbeans from his belt, Iss took the final seventeen steps and descended into the apex chamber. The Bound One waited there: hungry, broken, desperate for light, perfectly insulated from the outside world by the structure and peculiar properties of the Inverted Spire.

Iss took out his silver tweezers and uncovered the caul flies. He would draw power beyond his means tonight.

# SEVEN

## *The Great Hearth*

EFFIE, YOU KNOW WHAT you said the other day when Drey and I came home, when we first met you outside the roundhouse?" Raif waited until his sister nodded. "Remember what you said?"

"Yes. I said I knew you and Drey would come back." Effie Sevrance regarded her older brother with serious blue eyes. "I tried to tell the others, but no one would listen."

Raif shifted his weight from one leg to another. He was crouching in the shadow of the clan guidestone, in the dark and smoke-filled structure of the guidehouse. A full twelve tapers were lit, but the guidestone soaked up light and heat like a black body of trees at the center of a snowmelt. The stone's granite surface was rough and unfinished, and only jagged edges shone. Sometimes the chiseled edges looked like ears, sometimes like chips of bone and teeth. Veins of graphite formed bruises around the newer chisel marks, forcing beads of greasy ink to the surface. No guidestone liked to be cut.

No matter what time of day he came to the guidehouse,

Raif always thought it felt like night. Built adjacent to the roundhouse, the guidehouse was not as well protected or insulated from the cold. Some clans kept their guidestones inside the main building, fearing that raiding clans might make off with them under cover of darkness. Looking up at the massive slab of folded granite that was the size of a one-room cottage, Raif couldn't see how any but a band of giants equipped with rollers, pulleys, and levers could ever hope to steal it away within the space of a single night. And Blackhail's stone was only half the size of some.

Still, thirty-six years earlier Clan Bludd *had* managed to steal Dhoone's guidestone, forcing the mightiest of the clans to send their guide south to the stonefields of Trance Vor in search of a replacement. Raif had heard many of his own clansmen speak about the incident, talking in the hushed voices they normally used around bloodshed. All of them held that Clan Dhoone had never been the same since.

Clan Bludd had broken the Dhoonestone down into rocks and built an outhouse from it. The entire operation—the raid, the movement of the stone, and its subsequent breaking and rebuilding—had been planned by the Dog Lord, Vaylo Bludd. A yearman at the time, Vaylo Bludd had been a bastard son of the clan chief, Gullit Bludd. Within that same year Vaylo killed his two half-brothers, married his half-sister, and usurped his father's place. To this day it was said that Vaylo Bludd made it his business to use the outhouse every night before he slept.

Raif frowned. Sometimes he didn't know what to make of all the stories surrounding the Dog Lord. Mace Blackhail came up with new ones by the day.

Feeling a hot sting of anger in his chest, Raif pushed aside all thoughts of Mace Blackhail. Now wasn't the time for them. Effie was sitting cross-legged before him, her pale face made old by shadows, her lovely auburn hair tangled, her skirt damp from sitting beneath the stone bench where he had found her. In her hands and littered across her lap were her collection of rocks and stones. She played with them while she waited for him to speak, moving one piece and then another in sequence. For some reason Raif found himself wishing he could brush away the entire collection.

"What made you so sure Drey and I would come back, Effie?" he asked softly. "Did you feel something bad"—Raif jabbed his stomach—"here, inside?"

Effie thought about the question. She pushed out her bottom lip, fixed her gaze in midair, then slowly shook her head. "No, Raif."

Raif looked at Effie a long moment, then breathed a sigh of relief. Effie hadn't felt anything similar to the sensation he'd experienced the day of the raid. That was good. One outsider in the family was enough. Effie's words had been on Raif's mind for days. He had been meaning to talk to her about them ever since he'd returned from the badlands, but the first night hadn't been a good time, as the clan wanted nothing more than to hear the story of what he and Drey had done to the bodies of their kin. The day after was given over to mourning. Inigar Stoop had split a heart-size chunk from the guidestone, cracked it into twelve pieces—one for each man who had died at the camp—and then laid them upon the earth in place of bodies.

It had gone hard on everyone. When Corbie Meese and Shor Gormalin had sung deathsongs in their fine low voices, and all the women who had lost husbands, including Merritt Ganlow and Raina Blackhail, cut widow's weals around their wrists, Raif had not been able to think of anyone except Tem. The only time the silence was broken that night was by Mace Blackhail swearing vengeance against Clan Bludd.

The following day Raif had looked for Effie but found her only when it was too late for anything except sleep. Now, finally, he had her here. Shor Gormalin had told him how he often saw Effie slipping out to play in the guidehouse when it wasn't in use. And sure enough Effie had been here, sitting in almost-darkness, hiding beneath the bench where Inigar Stoop normally sat grinding stone, playing with her bits of rock.

Raif looked at Effie. She had lost a shocking amount of weight while he and Drey were away. Her eyes were huge and dark, blue as their mother's had been before her. Such a serious little girl, she never smiled, never played with other children. It was easy to forget she was only eight years old.

Raif held out his arms. "Come here and give your old brother a hug."

Effie thought a moment. "You won't be wanting to kiss me, will you?"

It was a serious question, and Raif treated it as such. He thought a moment. "No. Just a hug will do."

"Very well." With great care Effie laid her collection of rocks on the packed earth floor, then shuffled over to Raif. "No kiss, mind," she repeated as she let herself be hugged.

Raif grinned as he held her in his arms. Effie had reached the age when she didn't care to be kissed by any men, even her brothers. Still, she made no move to pull away from him and nestled close to his chest, resting her head on his shoulder. "Da will never come back," she said. "I knew that all along."

The grin slid from Raif's face. Effie spoke with such quiet certainty it chilled him. Unconsciously he hugged her closer. As he did so, he felt something hard press against his ribs. Gently he edged Effie back. "What have you got there?" he asked, nodding toward her neck.

Effie looked down. "My lore." Small hands fished inside the neck of her dress and pulled out the plum-size stone. It was gray, featureless, by far the plainest rock in Effie's collection. A tiny hole had been bored close to the edge, and a strand of coarse twine had been threaded through. "Inigar made a hole for me last spring," she said. "So I could wear it next to my skin like everyone else."

Raif took Effie's lore from her hand. It wasn't unusually heavy or cool to the touch. Just plain stone. Abruptly he let it go. Easing Effie from his lap, he stood. "I say we go and find ourselves some supper. Anwyn Bird has been boiling bacon all day, and unless someone stops her soon we'll never get rid of the smell."

Effie began gathering her rock collection into a pile. The bones in her arms showed through her skin as she reached forward to scoop up a handful of pebbles. Raif hated to see them. He'd make sure she ate well from now on.

With her rocks in her little rabbit pouch, Effie took Raif's hand and together they left the guidehouse. It was good to get out of the smoke. The short tunnel that led through to the roundhouse was lit by a series of overhead slits. The sky outside was turning dark. Noon had passed less than two hours earlier, yet that never mattered much in winter. Within a month there would hardly be any daylight at all, and everyone who lived on the clanhold in crofts, strongwalls, farms, or woodsmen's huts would come to the roundhouse to sit out winter's worst. Numbers had already begun to swell, yet Raif didn't think it had much to do with the season.

Even as he and Effie walked through to the main entrance hall, a group of crofters were being greeted by Anwyn Bird. The stout-bellied matron wasted no time in ordering the men to strip down to their softskins and felt boots. Raif took note of the snow on the crofters' shoulders and hoods. He also noticed that all three men had their bows braced and ready. The oldest man, a great red-haired giant who Raif recalled was named Paille Trotter, had a donkey basket on his back crammed with arrow and spear shafts and a bucket of neat's-foot oil hanging on a rope around his neck. It was a point of honor among all tied clansmen that they never came to the roundhouse empty-handed.

Suddenly uneasy, Raif raised his hand to his neck and searched out the hard smoothness of his raven lore. This was the first year he had ever known a crofter to bring weapons, not food, to pay for his winter keep.

"Now go and warm yi'selves by the small hearth and I'll send a girl in with some peas and bacon. There's no blackening left, mind, only meat and soft lard." Anwyn Bird's tone dared any of the crofters to find fault with the offered fare. None, including Paille Trotter, who was twice Anwyn's size and had a face fierce enough to scare bears, had the nerve for it. Anwyn Bird nodded, well used to cowing all who stood before her. "Go on with you, then. You'll find a skin of good ale warming by the fire."

The crofters, looking slightly embarrassed in their softskins and felt boots, were quick to do Anwyn's bidding.

Anwyn Bird, grand matron of the roundhouse, head cook and brewer, expert on all things including childbirth and bowmaking, turned the considerable force of her attention upon Raif and Effie Sevrance. "And where might you two have been?"

Seldom asking a question that she wasn't prepared to answer for herself, Anwyn Bird gave neither of them the chance to speak. "Been dawdling in the guidehouse, I'll swear!" She nodded at Effie. "You, my girl, are coming with me. Everyone else round here might dither about, 'fraid that you'll run off again and never be found. But I for one intend to see that you get a good hot supper, some oatcakes, and a sop full of butter. If you get any thinner, I swear Longhead'll mistake you for a sapling and plant you in the graze."

"Longhead plants the saplings in the rise, not the graze," Effie said matter-of-factly. "And it isn't the season for them anyway."

The loose skin under Anwyn Bird's chin wobbled in indignation.

Raif bit his lip to stop himself from smiling. Raina Blackhail and Effie Sevrance were the only two people in the guidehouse who could render Anwyn speechless.

Muttering to herself about young girls today, Anwyn Bird grabbed Effie by the collar and marched her toward the kitchen. Effie's rock collection knocked together as she moved, and just before Anwyn passed out of earshot, Raif caught the phrases "lot of nonsense" and "fuss about old rocks" puffing from her lips.

Glad that Effie had fallen into the hands of someone who would see her fed, Raif let out a breath of relief. At least for tonight that was one less thing to worry about.

Spinning around, he took a moment to think where Mace Blackhail would likely be at this hour. Despite the eleven-day mourning set by Inigar Stoop, events were moving fast. Crofters were coming early to the roundhouse, bringing arms and bow grease, the guidehouse windows had been boarded up and barricaded with pullstones, and just this morning Raif had woken to the clang and shudder of the clan forge—and it hadn't even been dawn. Clan Blackhail was preparing for war, and they were doing so under Mace Blackhail's orders and supervision.

Raif pressed his lips into a white line. The man was worse

than a murderer. He had ridden home from a killing field with his mouth full of lies. Even before he had made a decision where to go, Raif exited the entrance hall. He had to find Mace Blackhail, see for himself what the man who would be clan chief planned next.

The interior of the roundhouse was a vast warren of stone. Tunnels, ramps, and dug steps led down to windowless chambers, grain cells, root cellars, arms locks, and vaults where enemy bones had once been laid facing north to rot. Way down, two full stories belowground, Longhead kept a wet cell and grew mushrooms year-round. All chambers were stone walled and barrel ceilinged, supported by massive bloodwood stangs sealed with pitch.

Nothing was locked, not even the strongroom. A clansman who stole from his own was considered as good as a traitor and promptly staved and skin hung. Raif had seen it happen only once, to a soft-spoken luntman named Wennil Drook. Wennil's job as luntman was to keep all torches lit in the roundhouse. He had access to all chambers, could go wherever he chose, unnoticed and unquestioned. When Corbie Meese's fine silver handknife went missing one night after supper, the entire roundhouse was searched. Mace Blackhail found the knife a week later wrapped in dockleaves at the bottom of the luntman's pack.

Raif ran down a series of short ramps. Early the next morning Wennil Drook was taken onto the court and laid facedown upon the clay. One sharp pole was inserted under his skin from shoulder to shoulder and a second from hip to hip. Wennil Drook was then lifted by the staves and suspended between two horses. The horses were ridden by their riders over the fellfields and onto the Wedge. Wennil Drook only made it halfway. The skin on his back tore off in a single piece, and he fell to the ground and was dead before dark.

Corbie Meese was given the skin off Wennil Drook's back. He had used it once to clean his hammer, then thrown it away.

Frowning, Raif took the steps down to the fold, the great chamber that lay directly beneath the entrance, where all horses and livestock were held during hard frosts and sieges.

It was empty. Not one clansman stood in the center, training his dogs, nor one clanswoman leaned against the enclosure wall, letting her children run and play. Raif halted by the entrance. The fold was the largest cleared space in the roundhouse. On days as cold as this it was usually heavily used.

Coming to a halt, Raif made a decision. It was time he paid a visit to the Great Hearth. How long had he been in the guidehouse with Effie? Less than an hour?

The tunnels and ramps of the roundhouse were built narrow and winding so they could be easily defended if the main gate was breached. Raif found himself cursing every twist and curve as he ran. A man could get nowhere fast. Passing alongside the kitchen wall, he heard children's laughter bubbling against the other side. The sound did little to settle his mind. Children playing in Anwyn Bird's kitchen? Wasn't the deepest spiraling hell supposed to freeze over first?

The Great Hearth was the roundhouse's primary chamber aboveground. Yearmen, visitors, and all male children old enough to find food and beds for themselves slept there each night around the fire. Most clansfolk ate supper at the curved stone benches lining the chamber's east wall. In the evenings everyone gathered about the fire to keep warm, tell tales, sample one another's homebrew, smoke pipes packed with dried heather, court, sing, dice, and dance swords. It was the Heart of Clan; all decisions of weight were made there.

Even as he rounded the last of the steps, Raif knew something was wrong. The Great Hearth's oak doors were closed. Not pausing to smooth his hair or brush down his coat, he pushed against the oak planking, forcing his way through.

Five hundred faces turned to look at him. Corbie Meese, Shor Gormalin, Will Hawk, Orwin Shank, and dozens of other full clansmen were gathered around the vast sandstone hearth. Raina Blackhail, Merritt Ganlow, and a score of other women with due respect also had places close to the fire. Sitting around the edge of the room on curved benches were the yearmen: the two middle Shank brothers, the Lyes, Bullhammer, Craw Bannering, Rob Ure, who was fostered from Clan Dregg, and dozens of others.

Raif felt a hard lump rise to his throat. Drey was there too, sitting beside blue-eyed Rory Cleet, his hands resting upon the newly scored hammer in his lap. Raif looked and looked, but his brother wouldn't meet his eyes.

"You weren't called to this meeting, boy." Mace Blackhail stepped out from behind a bloodwood stang and walked five paces forward before coming to a halt. "You won't be made yearman till next spring."

Raif didn't care for the tone of Mace Blackhail's voice. He also didn't care for the fact that Mace Blackhail was wearing his foster father's Clansword. Steel skinned, black as midnight, and hilted with human bone packed with lead, it was kept in the roundhouse at all times and worn only by the clan chief when he was called upon to pass judgments of death and war.

Glancing around the Great Hearth, Raif took full count of the group. More clansmen than he had seen together in one place since spring Godsfest had gathered for a meet. Even a few tied clansmen—crofters, pig farmers, and woodsmen—had been given places near the door. The only full-sworn clansmen who weren't present were those manning the strongwalls and borderholds, the hundred or so standing nightwatch, and those away on longhunts in the far northern reaches of the clan.

Raif's eyes narrowed. "If you have met to speak of war," he said, glancing from face to face and ignoring Mace Blackhail completely, "then I demand to be present. Before the first battle is joined, Inigar Stoop *will* hear my oath."

Corbie Meese's large head, with its hammer dent, scar, and bald spot, was the first to nod. "He's right, you know. We're gonna need to bind as many yearmen as we can, as soon as we can. And that's no mistake." Ballic the Red and several others nodded right along with him.

Mace Blackhail cut the nodding short before it had chance to spread. "We must decide upon a clan chief before we speak of war."

Raif shot Drey a hard glance, boring through his brother's skull until Drey was forced to look up. Mace Blackhail had called a meeting to decide on the next clan chief, and his own brother hadn't even told him. Raif scowled at Drey.

Didn't he realize he was playing right into Mace Blackhail's hands?

"So," Mace Blackhail said, taking the last few steps toward the door and pausing before he opened it. "As war isn't our main purpose here, I say we let this boy go." He smiled almost sweetly. "Delicate matters such as these would more than likely bore him."

Raif stared at Drey's bent head. This time his brother refused to look up.

Mace held open the door. With his back turned to the clan, he sent Raif a look filled with malice. *Go*, he mouthed, his eyes shrinking to two black-and-yellow strips.

"I say he stays." It was Raina Blackhail, standing as she spoke. "Despite what you say, Mace Blackhail, Raif Sevrance is hardly a boy. If he wants to have his say along with the rest, I for one won't stop him." She looked her foster son straight in the eyes. "Would you?"

In the seconds it took Raina to speak, Mace Blackhail's face changed twice. By the time he had turned back to the clan, the only trace of the anger her words had caused him was the rapidly diminishing lines around his mouth. He let the door fall closed. "Very well. Let the boy find a place at the back."

Raif held his position a moment longer, then edged sideways, joining a group of crofters behind the door. His gaze did not leave Mace Blackhail for a moment.

"I warn you, boy," Mace said softly, weighing his words. "We're not here to rake over what happened at the badlands camp. You're upset about the loss of your da—we all saw that the other day. But we're in mourning for others besides Tem Sevrance, and you'd do well to remember that. You weren't the only one who lost kin." Mace made a swallowing motion with his throat. "Others did, too. And every time you speak up rashly without thinking, you injure their memories and wound the grieving."

Mace Blackhail's words stilled the clan. Many looked down, at the floor, at their hands, at their laps. Several of the older clansmen, including Orwin Shank and Will Hawk, nodded. The tied clansman by Raif's side, a pig farmer named Hissip Gluff, edged minutely away.

"Let's get back to the matter in hand." Shor Gormalin spoke in an even tone. He was standing by the hearth, his fair hair and beard smoothly cut and tended, his swordarm resting on the mantel. "I daresay the lad knows himself when's right and proper to speak."

As always when the small swordsman spoke, people agreed. And those men and women who had given Raif sharp glances seconds earlier now found other things to look at. Raif said nothing. He was beginning to realize just how clever Mace Blackhail was with words.

"Well," Ballic the Red said, stepping forward into the cleared space in the center of the room. "Mace is right. We must decide upon a clan chief and quickly. Dhoone is weak, and its sworn clans are suffering from want of protection. We all know the Dog Lord's been sniffing around the Dhoonehouse like the hound that he is—the man has seven sons, and each one of them craves a clanhold of his own. Yet now it seems to me as if the Bludd chief craves more. I think the man has each and every one of us in his sights. I think he has a fancy to call himself Lord of the Clans. And if we sit on arses and do nothing, then it'll only be a matter of time before his Bluddsmen come calling with swords."

Shouts of "Aye!" chorused around the Great Hearth. Corbie Meese took his hammer from his back and pounded the wooden butt against the floor. Several yearmen, Drey included, began pummeling their fists against the bench. Many clansmen stamped their feet or hammered ale jugs against the walls. Mace Blackhail waited until the noise was at its greatest before speaking.

Raising an open hand, he shouted over the clamor, "Aye! Ballic has the right of it! The Dog Lord would have our land, our women, and our roundhouse. And when he's done he'd turn around and shatter our guidestone to dust. He slaughtered our chief in cold blood, in the no-man's-land of the camp. What worse will he do when he comes west to raid our clan?"

Mace Blackhail curled his hand to a fist. The noise had died now, and the only person moving was the luntwoman Nellie Moss, who was busy carrying shredded sprucebark from torch to torch. The fire in the Great Hearth roared like wind from the north, and all around the room bloodwood beams creaked and shuddered like timbers in a storm.

Raif felt the heat leave his face. The world was shifting beneath everyone's feet on the word of just one man. He couldn't believe how quickly it was happening. It was like watching a dog round up a herd.

"My father died at Vaylo Bludd's hand," Mace Blackhail said, letting his voice tremble along with his fist, "killed by a hell-forged sword, left to rot on frozen earth. I say the Dog Lord must pay long and hard for what he did. We are not Clan Dhoone to stand by and let someone steal our guide-stone while we lie in bed with our women atop us. We are Clan Blackhail, the first of all clans. We do not hide and we do not cower. And we *will* have our revenge."

The clan thundered to life. Everyone stood. Axmen and hammermen pounded their weapons against the stone floor, yearmen began chanting *"Kill Bludd! Kill Bludd!"* and those standing by tables took out their handswords and thrust the blades into the wood. The women tore the sleeves from their dresses, baring their widow's weals for all to see. Corbie Meese hefted a skin of hard liquor over his head and sent it crashing into the fire. The skin exploded in a ball of pure white flame, scorching the hair of all who stood close and sending out a wave of heat that hit everyone in the room.

As smoke rolled from the hearth in black storm clouds, Ballic the Red aimed his bow. Shaped from a single piece of heartwood yew, strengthened with plates of horn, then curve-dried over sinew, the longbow drew as smoothly as the setting sun. Ballic held the string to his cheek, kissed his arrow's fletchings, and let it fly. The arrow parted smoke like a knife slitting throats. Shooting into the red heart of the fire, it severed the tops of flames and shattered the glowing embers like a rock smashed into ice. Hot coals rained onto the hearthstone, dark and ashy, their red eyes flashing.

"That's for the Dog Lord," Ballic the Red shouted above the uproar, tapping imagined dust from his bow.

Even as Raif found himself envying the sheer force of Ballic's shot, his gaze was drawn away to the opposite end of the chamber, where Drey stood chanting at the top of his voice. He and smooth-cheeked Rory Cleet were shouldering

and pushing each other, seeing who could shout the loudest.
Drey had his hammer in his hand and kept turning to pound
the bench behind him. Briefly he met Raif's gaze, then
quickly looked away. A muscle twisted in Raif's gut. That
wasn't Drey. His face was so red, it didn't even look like him.

*Kill Bludd! Kill Bludd!*

Edging back against the door frame for support, Raif
looked away. He felt physically sick. Noises pushed against
his face like blows. *We don't know Clan Bludd did it*, he
wanted to shout. But Mace Blackhail had ensured that anything he said would be dismissed as the immature rantings
of a boy who had lost his da. Raif punched his fist against
the door frame. Why couldn't anyone see Mace Blackhail
for the wolf that he was?

As he raised his hand from the wood, he was aware of
someone's gaze upon his back. Assuming it was Mace
Blackhail, he spun around to face him. But it wasn't Mace; it
was his foster mother, Raina. Raif let his fist fall to his side.
In a roomful of people straining, shouting, and clamoring to
be heard, Raina Blackhail was an island of quiet calm. The
bandages around her widow's weals had been torn away, revealing the fierce red flesh of new wounds. No scabs would
be allowed to form over the cuts as they healed. Instead her
skin would be held together by tightly bound sinew, until
bands of hard flesh had been raised around her wrists. These
she would carry with her until death.

For the first time, Raif realized what Raina was wearing
over her shoulders: the black bear pelt that Dagro Blackhail
had died scraping. Yet the pelt looked clean and newly
washed, and the flesh side was creamy and bloodless. Raif
felt the ground shift beneath his feet one more time. Drey
must have carried it back. He must have bundled it into his
pack, brought it home from the badlands, finished scraping
the flesh, then lime-washed and softened the inner hide. All
done quietly and without fuss, so Raina Blackhail could
have her husband's last token.

Sobered, Raif unclenched his fist. Sometimes he hardly
knew his brother at all.

As if aware of Raif's thoughts, Raina Blackhail pulled the
bear pelt close around her shoulders. Tears shone in her

eyes. She made no motion to speak, made no gestures with her hand or head, simply held Raif's gaze as surely as if she were holding his arm. Her husband was dead, and she meant for him to remember that fact.

*Kill Bludd! Kill Bludd!*

"Hold your cries!" Mace Blackhail cried, raising the Clansword above his head as he stepped upon a table close to the center of the room. His black dogskin pants and tunic had been slashed by his own hand, and his wolf lore lay on the outside for all to see. With his dark hair, dark clothes, and yellow wolf tooth shining against his skin, he looked fierce and full of rage. The Clansword fit his grip perfectly, and already he had its weight and balance judged.

The clan quieted. Thanks to Ballic the Red's arrow, the fire now gave off a flickering uneven light. Dark smoke vented from the cooling embers in thin plumes. Around the walls of the Great Hearth, torches burned with the crackle and putter of things just lit.

Mace Blackhail waited for perfect silence. The Clansword gleamed like black ice as he spoke. "We must make raids and make war—we know that now. Our warriors must ride east and meet the Bluddsmen full on. Now more than ever we need a strong man to lead us. War is never solely about battle. We must make alliances, mass ourselves, know our weaknesses and use our strengths. We can never replace Dagro Blackhail, and I for one will fight anyone here and now who claims otherwise." Mace brought the Clansword down and swept it in a half circle around his chest. For a fraction of a second his gaze rested on Raif, then his lips twisted minutely and he looked away.

Finding none who would speak up against the dead, he continued. "Yet choose a leader we must. All here have the right to draw the Clansword and claim the Blackhail name. As a Blackhail by fosterage, I have more rights than some, but that's not what I called you here to say. What I mean to state here, before all clansmen and yearmen and women with due respect, is that I will pledge myself to any man who is named clan chief and follow him until I die."

Mace Blackhail's words stunned the clan. Mouths fell open, breath was inhaled. Old Turby Flapp lost his grip on

his spear, and it went clattering to the floor. The crofter to
Raif's side pulled up his chin and whispered to his companion that it was "a fine thing for Mace Blackhail to do." Raif
waited. Like everyone else he was surprised by Mace Blackhail's words, yet he knew it wasn't the end. Even as Mace
Blackhail lowered the sword, the chorus began.

"A Blackhail is as a Blackhail does." Corbie Meese
stepped into the center of the room, the boiled hide of his
coat armor embellished only by his hammerman's chains.
"Mace has shown himself to be a true clansman like his father before him, and I for one would be proud to follow his
banns into battle." With that, Corbie laid his great iron-
headed hammer on the ground beneath Mace Blackhail's
feet.

"I'll second that." It was Ballic the Red, stepping forward
with his braced yewwood bow. "The moment the badlands
raid happened, Mace Blackhail's first thoughts were for
those who were left at home. Now I don't mean to speak ill
of the two Sevrance lads—all here agree that what they did
was right and fitting—but to my mind Mace Blackhail acted
like a clan chief from the start."

Raif closed his eyes as calls of "Aye!" circled the room.
He heard Ballic the Red lay his bow by Corbie Meese's
hammer, and when he opened his eyes again Orwin Shank
and thin-bearded Will Hawk were doing likewise with their
axes and swords. Along the east wall, yearmen shifted restlessly against their benches. It wasn't their place to move before full clansmen and women with due respect.

Other clansmen came and laid their weapons by Mace
Blackhail's feet. The twins Cull and Arlec Byce crossed
their matching limewood axes on top of the growing pile.
Still, some men held back. Shor Gormalin was the most no-
table. Standing close to Raina Blackhail, he watched the
proceedings with glinting eyes, not a muscle on his lean face
moving. Others, many older clansmen like Gat Murdock and
the fierce little bowman whom everyone called the Low-
draw, took his lead and did the same. Raif noticed several
clansmen and most of the clanswomen looking to Raina
Blackhail.

When it was obvious that all the full clansmen who were

prepared to come forward had done so, Mace Blackhail pressed the flat edge of the Clansword to his heart. His black hair and close-trimmed beard made his skin look as pale as ice formed around a window at night. His teeth were strong and white. A few had the sharp-edged look of fangs.

Turning, he addressed his words to Raina alone. "What say you, Foster Mother? I did not ask for this, and in truth I am not sure that I want it. And no matter how much my fellow clansmen's support stirs my heart, what you think matters more."

Raif ground his teeth together to stop himself from crying out. Mace Blackhail wasn't even a full clansman! He was a yearman, like Drey, pledging himself one year at a time to his clan, until he married or settled and was ready to commit himself wholly and for life. Most yearmen pledged to their birthclans, but some married elsewhere, or fostered elsewhere, or found themselves better needed and more valued at a foreign roundhouse far from home.

Raif sucked in breath. His gaze flicked to Raina Blackhail, who stood in her own space, slightly apart from the other women. Mace Blackhail had put her in a difficult position; to speak against blood or fosterkin in front of clan was unthinkable. Most especially against a foster son who had just paid his foster mother a compliment far greater than due respect.

Mace Blackhail maneuvered like the wolf he was: isolating his target, then forcing it to run alone.

Raina Blackhail was not the sort of woman to be hurried, though, and with a slow shrug of her shoulders she let the black bear pelt fall to the floor. Everyone in the Great Hearth watched as she deliberately stepped upon it. Her lips and cheeks were pale, her dress of housespun wool dyed a subtle shade of gray. The only bright spots on her entire body were the blood seeping from her widow's weals and the film of unshed tears across her eyes.

"Foster son," she said, placing a slight but unmistakable emphasis on the word *foster*. "Like my husband before me I am a person rarely given to hasty judgment. You have spoken well, and humbly, and have gained the support of many of the clansmen who lie above you in rank." A pause followed, where Raina let the clansmen remember for themselves that her foster son was but a yearman.

For the first time since he had entered the chamber Raif felt a spark of hope. No one in the clan was respected as highly as Raina Blackhail.

"I believe you are a strong man, Mace Blackhail," Raina continued, "with a strong will and a strong arm and the ability to make others do your bidding. I have seen you on the practice court and know you wield both the ax and the greatsword deftly. You are clever with words—as the men from Clan Scarpe so often are—and I suspect you will be clever at battle as well. Given these qualities, you may indeed make an excellent clan chief. However, I am Dagro Blackhail's widow, and his respect is my due, and as such I demand that no decision be made tonight."

As the last words left Raina Blackhail's lips and the clan responded to the mettle in her voice, Raif heard the pounding of footsteps on the outer stairs. Even as he gave silent thanks for Raina Blackhail's caution and saw for himself that no man or woman present would dare defy her on this matter, the double doors of the Great Hearth burst open.

A clansman, his forehead and cheeks red with sudden exposure to heat, his nose and eyes running, and his oilskins shedding snow, dashed into the room, stumbling forward in his haste. Breathless, his hair damp with sweat and his boots lip high in mud, he stood a moment, gulping great mouthfuls of air to still himself. Raif recognized him after a moment as Will Hawk's son, Bron. A yearman, fostered to Dhoone.

Raif felt his skin cool as surely as if Bron Hawk had brought the cold from outside with him. His stomach knotted, and beneath his buckskin tunic and wool shirt, his raven lore cooled to ice.

All gathered held their breath as they waited for Bron Hawk to speak. Mace Blackhail and the pile of pledged weapons standing below him were forgotten. Raina Blackhail's words and her husband's final token lying beneath her feet slid from the clan's minds like runoff down a slope. Five hundred pairs of eyes focused with blind intent toward the door.

Bron Hawk pushed the fair hair from his face. After a

brief glance around the chamber, his gaze finally rested upon Raina Blackhail and the small swordsman Shor Gormalin, who stood at her back. "Clan Bludd has taken the Dhoonehouse," he said. "Five nights ago. They slaughtered three hundred Dhoonesmen with weapons that drew no blood."

A single hiss of shock and anger united the room. Raif felt the knot in his stomach unfold with soft liquid slowness. No one would ever question Mace Blackhail's story about the badlands raid again.

# EIGHT

## Trapping in the Oldwood

COME ON. PUT ON your coat and oilskin. You're coming with me." Raina Blackhail grabbed the corner of Effie's blanket and heaved it from the pallet.

Effie Sevrance blinked. The lamplight hurt her eyes, and she didn't much like the idea of going outside. The land beyond the roundhouse was big and open and cold. A person could get lost on the fellfields and never be found. "Please, Raina, I don't want—"

"No, my girl," Raina said, cutting her short. "I don't care what you say. You need some fresh air on that pale face of yours, and sure as the Stone Gods created the clanholds, I'm going to see you get it." She patted Effie's thigh. "Come on now. We're going to the Oldwood to check my traps, and I want to be there and back before morning's end."

Moving around the small cell where Effie slept alone, Raina Blackhail plucked oilskin, dog mitts, and a wool coat from the chair and the dog hook where they had been neatly hung or folded. Effie told herself she didn't mind Raina being here, not really. She wasn't like some people who just wanted to be nosy and make fun. Letty Shank was always here, stealing stones, scattering them around the chamber, snatching the lore from Effie's neck and wearing it herself. "Look at me," she'd call to Mog Wiley and all the others. "As dim as the rock the clan guide gave me."

Effie bit her lip. Everyone would laugh as if it were the funniest thing they'd ever heard. Crowding around Letty Shank, they would try to take the lore from her, anxious to wear it themselves.

Rising from the box pallet, Effie frowned at Raina. Raina wanted to put on the coat and mitts for her, but Effie preferred to do it herself.

This made Raina smile. "There's some good rocks out on the west side of Oldwood, you know, by Hissip Gluff's place. You might be able to find something new for your collection."

"They're sandstone," Effie said. "Like the roundhouse."

"Oh, I don't know about that, Effie Sevrance. When I was up there last I could swear I saw something shining beneath my fox trap."

"You did?" Effie was instantly interested. She knew Raina Blackhail wasn't the sort of woman to lie about anything, most especially rocks.

Raina bent and kissed the top of Effie's head. "Yes. Hurry now. If your oilskins and boots aren't on in the next minute, I'll have Longhead come down here and plant mushrooms over your bed. I swear it's wet enough to grow them here." She shivered. "I really do."

Effie almost laughed at the idea of mushrooms growing on her bed, but she didn't like the way Raina had turned up her pitch lamp and was now looking around the little stone cell with a disapproving air. Effie spoke to head her off. "I don't want to go and sleep with the other girls. Please. Anwyn has given me her best goatswool blanket. And I keep a torch burning most of the night."

The worried look that always made Effie feel bad appeared on Raina's face. "Bind your mitts tightly," was all she said. "It's white weather outside."

Effie liked the roundhouse best in early morning. Few people were around, mouthwatering smells of bacon and scorched onions wafted up from the kitchen, and light pouring through the high windows promised good things to come. It was as if whatever had gone on the day before was completely canceled out. As they walked up the ramp to the entrance hall, the only person they encountered was the luntwoman Nellie Moss. The skin on Nellie's hands was red and shiny with old scars from torch burns, and all the other children including Letty Shank and Mog Wiley were afraid of her. Effie wasn't . . . not *quite*. Nellie Moss got to move about the roundhouse unheeded and did most of her work in the dark. Effie rather liked the idea of that.

Raina Blackhail stopped Nellie from walking straight past by putting a hand on the luntwoman's arm. "Any sign of their return?"

Nellie shook her head. "Nay. None's come back this night."

Raina nodded. The worried look crossed her face again. "If they do come back, be sure to let them know I'm in the Oldwood with my traps. I'll be back before noon."

"In the Oldwood with yer traps," repeated Nellie in her low mannish voice.

Effie thought she saw something unpleasant in Nellie Moss' face, but when she blinked it was gone. Briefly Effie remembered the little luntman Wennil Drook, who had lit the torches before Nellie. Effie didn't believe what anyone said about him stealing Corbie Meese's knife. Wennil had known things about rocks. Hardly a week went by in summer when he didn't bring her some new bit of stone for her collection.

"Effie. Pull up your hood."

Effie did as Raina said, and together they left the roundhouse by the side door that led out past the guidehouse to the stables. Everything, the stables, the graze, the clay court, and the gray slate roof of the guidehouse, was covered in a thick layer of snow. Even the little stream that ran behind the birches—the one Orwin Shank called the Leak on account of its yellowy green water—was now running beneath a sheet of snow-covered ice. It had been snowing on and off for seven days now, ever since Bron Hawk had returned from Dhoone.

The clan had split up the following morning. Mace Blackhail and his pledged men had ridden east to scout the Dhoonehouse. Drey was in the party. . . . Effie worried about that. Raif had gone with Shor Gormalin and others to Clan Gnash, to learn what they could from the Gnash chief, who shared borders with Blackhail and Dhoone. More men still had been put on east- and southwatch, and all tied clansmen had been ordered to the roundhouse to defend it in case of raids. Mace's and Shor's parties were due back any day. Then there would be a big meet where only the sworn clansmen were allowed.

Effie supposed they would make Mace Blackhail chief. Finally.

"Don't just stand there, Effie Sevrance," Raina said, following the much trodden path toward the stables. "You must help me kit and saddle Mercy."

Glancing over the graze to the low sandstone ridge that lay beyond, Effie chewed on her lip. The snow made everything seem wide open. Vast. The countryside stopped being identifiable parts, like the sheep graze and the cow graze and Longhead's apple orchard and the Wedge, and became one whole thing instead.

Inside her chest, Effie's heart began to beat a little faster. The land was a big white nothingness, like the spaces in dreams that stretched on and on and on. . . .

"Oh no you don't, Effie Sevrance," Raina said, tugging on her arm. "You're not bolting on me this time. There's nothing to be afraid of, only fresh air and snow. I won't leave you. I promise."

Effie let herself be dragged into the stables. She liked the stables, but not as much as the dog cotes. The stables were enclosed by thick stone walls, but they were large and high roofed, and there was too much space above a person's head. Not like the cotes. The little dog cote was so low that no grown man could stand in it. Effie grinned at the memory of Shor Gormalin's bent back as he'd come to drag her from it two weeks ago. He was nice, Shor Gormalin. He'd understood when she'd told him that she hadn't really run away at all. "Just finding a fair spot to think," he had said with a thoughtful nod of his head. "I can see that. Do it myself from time to time. Though I daresay I'm inclined to pick somewhere warmer and less chancy than the dog cotes. Those shankshounds could tear off a man's head."

*Shankshounds.* Effie's grin widened. Orwin Shank's dogs were as soft as puppies around her.

Seeing Effie smile, Raina smiled. "It'll be nice, you know. I've grilled us some apple slices wrapped in bacon."

Suddenly feeling a lot better, Effie began buckling Mercy's bridle. She loved it when Raina smiled.

When the filly was saddled and two empty leather saddlebags were laid over her docks, Raina trotted her onto the court. The Oldwood lay to the west of the roundhouse, past the graze and up over the north ridge. Tall spires of paper birch and black spruce broke the skyline, and high overhead a line of geese flew south. Fresh snow crackled beneath Effie's boots, its surface hardened by overnight frost. It was bitterly cold, and Effie could feel her cheeks burning beneath her fox hood. Ice crystals glittered on the branches of Longhead's saplings.

Effie crossed her arms over her chest and walked with her mitted hands thrust under her armpits. Winter always came fast to Clan Blackhail. Da said it was because . . .

Effie stopped dead.

There was no Da.

Da had gone.

"Effie." Raina spoke softly, her voice sounding very far away. "It's all right, little one. You'll be safe with me. I swear it."

Something hurt at the back of Effie's eyes. She blinked, but it wouldn't go away. Raina said things and squeezed her shoulder, but Effie barely felt or heard. Her lore pressed against her collarbone like a poking finger. Da was gone. And she had known something wasn't right from the very first morning he'd ridden away. Her lore had told her so.

"Come on, Effie Sevrance. Up on Mercy." Effie felt Raina's hands slip under her arms and lift her clear off the ground. She saw the sky come closer, white and choked with snow clouds, then felt her bottom come down on the hard leather saddle. "There. Take the reins. Mercy will treat you well. Won't you, Mercy?" Raina patted her filly's neck.

Effie took the reins and let Raina adjust the stirrups to her feet. Beneath her oilskins and wool coat, Effie was aware of her lore pushing, *pushing*, against her skin. It wanted to tell her something . . . like the day Da had ridden north to the badlands.

Effie shook her head. She didn't want to know. Her lore told bad things. It made her feel queasy inside. Clutching the reins in her left hand, she reached down inside her oilskin and pulled out the little rock given to her by the clan guide at birth. One sharp tug was all it took to snap the twine. Even through her dogskin mitts the rock felt alive. It wasn't warm and it didn't move, but somehow it *pushed*.

"What's the matter, Effie? Has the rock scratched your skin?" Raina was walking alongside Mercy, looking up at Effie, her face all creased and pale.

Leaning back in the saddle, Effie reached back with her hand to feel for one of the saddlebags. When her mitt slipped under the leather lid, she released her grip on the lore and let it fall to the bottom of the bag. A tight itchiness prickled through her stomach as it dropped. She took a breath, told herself it was silly to be afraid of a rock no bigger than her nose. "I'm fine, Raina. Just . . . cold. The rock felt cold against my skin."

Raina nodded her head in a way that made Effie feel bad. She hated to lie.

They walked in silence after that. Raina led Mercy over the ridge and into the bottomlands beyond. Old elms, basswoods, oaks, and dog birches began to spike the path, their bare limbs clutching at the sky with every gust of wind. Gobs of frozen sap shone like eyes in the places where branches split into twigs, and deep within their hollowed-out boles, wet ice glittered like teeth.

Effie shivered. Normally she liked old trees, yet today she found herself seeing only the bad things: the wood ear fungus eating into the bark, the slimy green moss growing on south-facing trunks, and the tubes of rootwood poking through the earth around the bases of the old oaks. Surely roots weren't meant to be seen? Just looking at them made Effie feel queer, as if she were catching a glimpse of hidden things, like the pale wingless insects that lived under the roundhouse floorboards and deep within its walls.

Feeling her heart begin to patter again, Effie looked away. Fixing her gaze on the space between Mercy's ears, she tried not to think of her lore lying at the bottom of Raina's saddlebag or the roots of the old oaks. She wished she didn't have her mitts on and could touch Mercy's neck. She knew it would be warm and soft and nice. "Good girl," she whispered, needing to hear the plain sound of her own voice. "Good Mercy."

The Oldwood crept up on one slowly. First there was just a softening of the ground underfoot, a few bushy birches and alders, and a string of old elms. Then the ground snow thinned, revealing the broad leaves of winter ferns and stripped shoots of milkweed. A little later there were rounded boulders speckled white with bird lime and yellow with withered moss. Then every time you took a step, *years* of dead and frozen matter crackled beneath your feet. The light dropped, then later the wind. The smell of damp earth and slowly decaying things sharpened. And finally, after you walked a while longer past rotten stumps and needle-thin streams, you were there, surrounded by a shuddering, creaking forest of basswood, elm, and oak. The Oldwood.

Effie was glad to get out of the open spaces of the valley, pleased that she could no longer see more than a short walk ahead. Still, it was very quiet and the wind didn't quite blow through the trees: It hissed. Effie glanced at Raina, wishing she would speak. Raina was quiet, though, her face tilted down toward the path. There was a ring of mud and snowmelt around the hem of her woolen skirt, and ice crystals had formed along the breathline of her hood.

Effie dearly wanted to say something to Raina, something funny or interesting or clever, but she wasn't very good at talking. Not like Letty Shank and Mog Wiley.

In silence, Raina led them through the south corner of the Oldwood and onto the west fringe. The temperature had risen slightly, and the snow underfoot was no longer as brittle as it had been. A few winter birds, mostly robins and grouse, called to each other from places Effie couldn't see. Every now and then she felt something *push* against the base of her spine. It was a metal buckle or a hard lump of leather in the saddle. It had to be. Her lore couldn't push right through the saddlebags *and* Mercy's rump. It couldn't.

The east fringe of the Oldwood was best for traps. Many clans-women trapped animals here, and all had their own territories and secret places. Effie knew Raina's places well.

Raina had exclusive rights to the stream between the two sister willows and the bluff, and to the bluff itself, where bearberries and blackberries grew high atop the ridge. Effie didn't know much about trapping game, but she knew that the berry bushes were a good thing. All sorts of creatures came to eat the fruit.

They arrived at Raina's trapping ground while the sun was still rising. Effie slid down from the filly's back as Raina hiked up the bluff. Reaching the top of the bank, Raina ducked beneath a bearberry bush to inspect one of her traps. After a moment she made a pleased sound. "I've got one, Effie. A fox. A big one with a beautiful coat. It's still warm."

Effie walked a little way up the ridge, deliberately putting some distance between herself and the saddlebag containing her lore. She wished the fox hadn't been warm. That meant Raina would stop and skin it before it froze. You couldn't skin a frozen fox.

Raina emerged from the bush holding a blue fox by the scruff of its neck. Its yellow eyes were still open, but there was no fox cunning spilling out. "Effie. Fetch the skinning knife from my left saddlebag."

Effie wasn't very good at her left and rights. She needed to have both her hands in front of her to work it out. Making a little weighing movement with her mitted fingers, she frowned. The left bag was the one containing her lore. Heart beating just a little bit quicker than moments earlier, she weighed her left and rights again.

"Effie! Hurry now! I want to be back by noon."

Raina's voice was sharper than normal, and Effie ran the short distance back to Mercy. Eyes closed, lips pressed firmly together, she thrust a mitted hand into the saddlebag. Even as her fingers found and closed around the cool metal of the skinning knife, her lore *pushed* against the back of her hand. Effie jumped. Her lore wanted to be picked up and held . . . like the time in the small dog cote just before Shor Gormalin came.

"No," Effie whispered. "Please. I don't want to *know*."

"Effie, the knife!"

Grabbing tight hold of the knife, Effie yanked her arm free of the saddlebag. She spent the next moment standing perfectly still, her face all scrunched, the knife held out at arm's length, waiting to see if anything terrible would happen. Only nothing did. Trees creaked. An owl that didn't know what time of day it was hooted. Breathing a sigh of relief, Effie ran up the slope and joined Raina.

Raina had already cut the trap wire from the fox's snout and was busy brushing away bits of leaves and snow from its coat. Effie handed her the knife, but as she did so the temptation to lean in close and hug Raina was overpowering, and she wrapped her arms around Raina's waist.

"Little one. Little one." Raina pulled down Effie's hood and stroked her hair. "I shouldn't have brought you all this way. It was wrong of me."

Effie didn't much care that Raina had misunderstood things. The sound of Raina's voice, gentle, good, and completely familiar, was all that counted. Just to hear it made Effie feel better. She hugged her for a bit longer and then pulled away. Raina let her go. The fox hung by its brush from her free hand, and Effie could tell she was eager to skin it and be gone.

"I know," Raina said, making a small gesture indicating that Effie should pull up her hood against the cold, "why don't you go and check on the other side of the bushes for those shiny stones we were talking about? Right between the two oaks, under the bearberry."

As Effie nodded, snow and earth crackled in the bushes below. Branches moved. A jackdaw took to the air, screaming at the sky as it flew. Metal jingled softly.

Raina beckoned Effie to her. She had already made the first incision along the fox's snout, and there was a film of blood on her blade. As Effie came forward, she let the fox drop to the ground.

Mace Blackhail emerged from the bushes below them, leading his blue roan by the reins. The gelding was lathered, its coat steaming in the cold air and its nostrils frothing with mucus. Mud was sprayed over its belly and legs, and the skin around its saddle was patchy and chaffed. Mace Blackhail looked little better. His fox hood was matted with muck and ice, and his cheeks were burned red by snow glare.

"Foster Mother!" he called. "I arrived back at the roundhouse a quarter after you left."

Raina made no reply. Her fingers dug into Effie's shoulders.

Mace Blackhail shrugged. Coming to a halt, he tied the roan's reins to a whip-thin birch. Effie heard metal things—weapons, she supposed—clink beneath his oilskins.

"We need to talk, you and I, Foster Mother." Mace shot a glance Effie's way. "Alone and in private."

Not releasing her grip on Effie's shoulder or the skinning knife, Raina began to descend the slope. "Effie's but a child. She won't—"

"She's a Sevrance," cut in Mace Blackhail. "She'll go running back to that sneak-eyed brother of hers, sniveling and telling tales."

"You mean Raif?" Raina's voice had a catch to it that Effie didn't understand. "As you and Drey seem to get along well enough. He seemed eager enough to pledge his hammer to you the same night Bron came from Dhoone."

Mace Blackhail pulled down his hood. His face was dark, thin from long days in the saddle. "Get rid of the child, Raina."

Effie kept herself still. She imagined she could still feel her lore pressing against her mitted hand.

Raina took a small breath and patted Effie's shoulder. Lowering her head, she spoke words for Effie's ears alone. "Run along and find those stones behind the bushes like we talked about. I'll keep watch. I won't leave without you. I promise."

Effie twisted her head around so she could look at Raina's face. What she saw frightened her. "Raina?"

"Go, Effie." Raina patted her shoulder—harder this time. "Go. Everything will be fine here. There's nothing to worry about. It's just me and Mace."

Effie scrambled down the slope. Mace Blackhail watched her descend. When she drew level with the horses, Mercy whickered, and Effie reached out to touch her neck.

*Push.*

Snapping her hand back, Effie bit hard on her lip to stop any noise from leaving her mouth. It couldn't be her lore. It *couldn't*. Turning on her heel, she found herself face-to-face with Mace Blackhail. Before she could move away, Mace grabbed her chin with a gloved hand.

His hair dripped snowmelt onto his cheeks as he angled her face one way and then the other. He smelled of skinned animals. His voice when it came was as smooth and cold as ice. "As it is you'll be no great beauty. Though you're liable to end up looking worse if you go telling tales."

"Leave her alone!" It was Raina, coming down the slope. Effie noticed she still had the skinning knife in her hand.

Mace Blackhail smacked Effie's buttocks. "Don't come back until I'm gone."

Effie dashed away into the bushes, hardly caring where she was headed. She heard Raina call out to her, some sort of warning about not going too far, yet Effie could barely hear it over the fast beating of her heart. A finger of oak scraped along her cheek. Ferns slapped at her boots and skirt, and snow and twigs crackled beneath her feet. She hardly knew if she was running from Mace Blackhail or her lore.

When the ground finally steepened, Effie slowed. Her hood was down, but her face didn't feel cold at all. Breath fogged as it left her mouth. She glanced over her shoulder, but all she saw were oaks and elms barricading the way. Oak roots peeped out above the snow line, pale and fat like worms.

Effie looked away. Up the slope and off to the left lay the backs of the bearberry bushes where Raina kept her traps. Effie frowned. Going that way would almost be the same as going back to the clearing. But Raina had told her not to go far. Unsure of what to do, she hesitated; her hand stole up to her neck, searching for the lore that wasn't there. Funny how she always held it when she had decisions to make. Laying her mitted palm flat on her chest, she tried to still her heart instead. She wished Raina were here.

A light wind blew through the trees and up the slope, making topsnow ruffle like an animal's coat. Effie chewed on her lip. She didn't like Mace Blackhail, and it made her stomach go all tight to think of him alone with Raina.

With a small flick of her head, she started up the slope. She didn't need an old piece of rock to make decisions for her. She was old enough to make them herself.

The back of the bluff was harder to climb than the front.

Littered with loose rocks and fallen logs all slippery and green, the south slope was normally used by foxes and Hissip Gluff's goats. The snow made everything worse, hiding brambles, sinkholes, and rootwood. Effie plucked up her skirt and held it high above her knees. Somewhere below she could hear the willow stream running over sandstone. She didn't look down. By the time she reached the top of the slope her skirt was black with snow and mud. Ahead she saw the line of bearberries and the two oaks Raina had mentioned earlier. Although she didn't much feel like it, Effie turned her mind to stones. Shiny ones, Raina had said. Beneath the bushes.

*"Get away from me!"*

Effie stopped dead at the sound of Raina's voice. She wondered if snow hadn't worked its way inside her collar, for something liquid and icy slid down her spine. *Raina.*

Thrashing through snow and ferns, Effie dashed to the far side of the ridge where the bushes grew. One of Raina's traps could clearly be seen on the ground beneath the densest cluster of stems, its lip open, waiting to be sprung. Swinging away from it, Effie fell to her knees and crawled the rest of the way.

No more words came from below, but she could hear twigs snapping and oilskins creaking. One of the horses stamped its hooves. A breath was sharply taken, then the clear sound of a belt buckle unsnapping chimed through the air like a bell.

Down on her belly in the snow, Effie pushed herself along by her knees and feet. Her heart thumped against the ground. She was listening so hard her jaw ached.

More sounds. Oilskins, mostly, and crunching snow. Someone or something grunted: Effie couldn't tell whether it was Mace Blackhail or one of the horses.

Easing her head into the tangle of stems and leaves that marked the edge of the ridge, she peered into the clearing below. She saw Mace Blackhail's roan first, then Mercy. Red bearberries, cold and almost frozen, tapped against her cheeks like glass beads.

Hard breaths sounded, and Effie's gaze found Mace Blackhail's back. It was moving up and down. Effie frowned. Where was Raina? That was when she noticed Mace Blackhail's hand; it was pressed hard against Raina's mouth. Raina was beneath him. On the ground. In the snow. Her oilskin was spread open about her.

Effie's chest tightened. What was he doing to her? Even as she looked, she saw Mace Blackhail lean forward and *kiss* Raina's face. Raina jerked her head back. Mace continued moving up and down. He was breathing very hard now.

A glint of silver on the ground near the horses caught Effie's eye. Raina's knife. From where she lay, Effie could just make out three blotches of blood sunk deep into the surrounding snow. Her gaze was drawn back to Mace Blackhail. He shuddered, issued a hard cry like a cough, then slumped onto Raina's chest. Raina's eyes were closed. Mace no longer had his hand over her mouth, but she made no move to cry out, simply lay there with her eyes closed, perfectly still.

Mace said something to her that Effie didn't catch, then he rolled to the side and picked himself off the ground. Still Raina did not move. Her skirt was hitched up about her waist and her tunic was open, revealing her linen under-bodice beneath. Effie averted her eyes: like the oak roots, they were things not meant to be seen.

Mace Blackhail belted and fastened himself up. His sword swung at his waist, held in place by a doeskin scabbard dyed black. As he returned to his horse, Effie saw a line of bright blood on his cheek and a second on his neck. When he approached Raina's skinning knife, he kicked it hard, sending the silver blade shooting into a tangle of snowy gorse. He spat, smoothed back his hair, and then mounted the blue roan. The gelding shook its mane and switched its tail, but Mace pulled hard on the bit, taking command of its head.

Turning the gelding, Mace Blackhail took a moment to regard Raina as she lay on the ground. Raina still had not moved. Effie could just see the rise and fall of her chest. Her eyes were closed, but as Mace looked on she opened them.

Mace's mouth twisted. "Tidy yourself before you return," he said. "If we are to be wed—as this surely means we must—then I will not have my wife arrayed like a coarse-house wench for all to see." With that, he kicked the roan into a trot and rode from the clearing.

Effie watched him go. The left side of her face was numb, and her entire body was colder than she could ever remember it being before. Even her heart felt cold. For a reason she didn't understand, she began naming the Stone Gods. Inigar Stoop said they were hard gods and they answered no small prayers. *Never ask anything for yourself, Effie Sevrance,* Inigar's dry old voice reminded her. *Ask only that they watch over the clan.* To Effie, Raina Blackhail *was* the clan, so she spoke the nine sacred names of the gods.

As she named Behathmus, who was called the Dark God and was said to have eyes of black iron, Raina began to stir in the clearing below. Her legs came upward and her arms slid inward and her chin came down to her chest. She shrank as Effie watched, her body closing around itself like a dead and curling leaf. No noise left her lips, no tears spilled from her eyes, she just drew herself smaller and smaller until Effie thought her back would break.

Effie cried for her. She didn't know that she was crying until the wetness reached her mouth and she tasted salt. Something bad had happened. And Effie wasn't sure what it was, but she knew two things without question:

Raina was hurt.

And she, Effie Sevrance, could have stopped it.

Her lore had known. It had wanted to tell her. It had *tried* to tell her. It had pushed and pushed, but she'd refused to listen.

Scrambling free of the bushes, she brushed snow and ice from her oilskin, hood, and skirt. She didn't know if she was still crying; her cheeks were too numb to feel tears.

She could have stopped Mace Blackhail from hurting Raina. She could have taken the lore in her fist and held it until she saw the bad thing. It had happened like that with Da. . . .

A deep shiver worked its way up her spine. Suddenly anxious to be away, back inside the small enclosed space of her cell, she ran along the ridge and down the slope.

She didn't know how long it took her to get back to Raina—a quarter, perhaps; no longer—but by the time she reached the clearing Raina had become herself. Her hair was newly smoothed, her skirt free of ice, and her oilskin fastened tightly all the way down to her knees. She smiled briefly as Effie approached.

"I was just about to come looking for you. It's time we were home. Come on. I'll put you on Mercy's back." Her voice was level with just a slight strain to it. Her eyes were dead.

Effie didn't speak. A lump had come to her throat.

# NINE

## *The Dhooneseat*

VAYLO BLUDD SPAT AT his dog. He would have preferred to spit at his second son, but he didn't. The dog, a hunter and wolf mix with a neck as wide as a door, bared its teeth and snarled at his master. Other dogs leashed behind it made low growling noises in the backs of their throats. The wad of black curd spat by Vaylo Bludd landed on the first dog's foreleg, and the dog chewed at its own fur and skin to get it off. Vaylo didn't smile, but he was pleased. That one definitely owed more to the wolf.

"So, son," he said, still looking at the dog, "what would *you* have me do next, seems you ill like the plans made by your father?"

Vaylo Bludd's second son, Pengo Bludd, grunted. He was standing too close to the fire, and his already red face now glowed like something baked in an oven. His spiked hammer trailed on the floor behind him like a dog on a leash. "We must attack Blackhail while the win is still upon us. If we sit on our arses now, we miss our chance to take the clanholds in a single strike."

Sitting back on the great stone Dhooneseat that formed the center of the mightiest and best fortified roundhouse in the clanholds, Vaylo Bludd considered spitting again. With no black curd in his mouth, he worked up a dose of saliva by jabbing his tongue against his teeth. Stone Gods! But his teeth ached! One of these days he was going to find a man to pull them out. Find a man, then kill him.

Vaylo Bludd swallowed the spit. He took a moment to look at his second son. Pengo Bludd had not shaved back his hairline in days, and a bristling band of hair framed his face. The longer hair at the back, with its braids and twists, was similarly ill tended. Bits of goosedown and hay were caught in the matted strands. Vaylo Bludd made a hard sound in his throat. Legitimate offspring were born to complacency and arrogance. You wouldn't see such sloth on a bastard!

"Son," he said, his voice as low as a dog growl, "I have lorded this clan for thirty-five years—a good five of that before you were born. Now I daresay you'd think it boastful of me to point out just how far Bludd has come under my lording, but *I* say I don't care. I am clan chief. Me, the Dog Lord. Not You, Lord of Nothing but What I Choose to Give you."

Pengo's eyes narrowed. The hand that held his leather hammer loop cracked as it curled to a fist. "We have Dhoone. We can have Blackhail as well. The Hailsmen—"

Vaylo Bludd kicked out at the wolf dog, making it jump back and yowl. "The Hailsmen will be expecting us to attack. They'll have that roundhouse of theirs sealed as tight as a virgin's arse the minute we break their bounds. Hailsmen aren't fools. They won't be found slacking like Dhoones."

"But—"

"*Enough!*" The Dog Lord stood. All the dogs leashed to the rat hooks skittered back. "What advantages we had here will not be easily got again. They come with a price, as such things do. And it will be for me to say when and if we use such means again. We have Dhoone. Make use of it. Go, take Drybone and as many of those useless brothers of yours as you can muster afore noon, and ride out to the Gnash border and secure it. All the Dhoonesmen that rode away are likely there, and if an attack is going to come, then it will more than likely start at Gnash." Vaylo smiled, showing black aching teeth. "While you're out there mayhap you can claim what land you see fit for your steading. I heard it said once that a chief should always house his sons on his borders."

Pengo Bludd snarled. Tugging on his hammer loop, he raised his hammer from the floor and weighed its limewood handle across his chest. The spiked hammer head bristled like a basket of knives. Eyes the same color as his father's burned coldly like the blue inner tongue of flames. Without a word he turned on his heel, his braids and twists swinging out from his skull as he moved.

When he reached the chamber door, Vaylo stopped him with one word. "Son."

*"What?"* Pengo did not turn around.

"Send the bairns to me afore you leave."

Pengo Bludd snapped his head, then continued his journey from the door. He slammed it with all his might behind him.

The Dog Lord took a long breath when he was gone. The dogs, all five of them including the wolf dog, were quiet. After a moment Vaylo bent on one knee and beckoned them as near as their various leashes would allow. He tousled them and slapped their bellies and tested their speed by grabbing their tails. They snarled and snapped and nipped him, wetting his hands and wrists with their frothy saliva. They were good dogs, all of them.

Unlike most hunters and sled dogs, whose fangs were filed to stop them chewing through leashes and ruining pelts by tearing at game, Vaylo's own dogs still had fangs of full length and sharpness. They could rip out a man's throat on his say. None of them had names. Vaylo had long ago stopped keeping track of all the names of those around him. A man with seven sons who all had wives and in-laws and children of their own soon gave up keeping tally on what people were called. What they *were* was the only thing that counted.

Feeling separate pangs of pain in each of his remaining seventeen teeth, the Dog Lord stood. Bones in his knees cracked as they dealt with his weight. The Dhooneseat, carved from a single slab of bluestone as tall as a horse, beckoned him back. Vaylo moved away from it, picking a plain oakwood stool close to the hearth. He was too old for stone thrones and too wary of growing used to them. A bastard learned early that he always had to be ready to give up his place.

Glancing toward the door that his second son had slammed moments earlier, Vaylo frowned. That was the problem with all of his sons: None of them knew what it was to give up their place to another. They knew only the politics of take.

Behind his back, Vaylo could hear the dogs scrapping among themselves. He heard the wolf dog's low distinctive growl, and he knew without turning to look that the dog was being attacked by the others because of the favor its master had showed it. Vaylo made no move to interfere. Such was the way of life.

*So*, he thought, stretching out his legs before the fire as he looked around the room, *this is the great Dhoone round-house*. Men calling themselves kings had lived here once. Now there were only chiefs.

A smile spread across Vaylo's face as he remembered the last time he was here. He had not been invited that time either. Thirty-six years ago it was now, in the dead of night while Airy Dhoone, the clan chief at the time, and his sixty best men were away. Vaylo slapped his thigh. That bloody guidestone had been murder to move! Old Ockish Bull had ended up with a hernia as big as a fist! And of the other four dozen clansmen who had helped pull it free from the guide-house, only two were able to move the next day, and none could mount their horses for a week.

Vaylo chuckled. The whole operation had been without a doubt the most misguided, ill-planned, fool-stupid thing fifty grown men had ever conspired to do. They never did get the guidestone farther than Blue Dhoone Lake. It was still there today, at the bottom of the copper-tinted lake, resting amid the silt and the sandstone, sunk within three hundred paces of the Dhoonehouse itself.

None but the fifty knew that, of course. When they returned to the Bludd roundhouse twenty days later, all swore blind that the collection of rocks they arrived with, pulled by a team of mules in a war cart, was none other than the broken-down guidestone itself. Not some quarry-purchased rubble and a bucket of ground glass. And it *had* made such an excellent outhouse. . . .

Vaylo Bludd leaned forward on his stool. Those were the

days! Jaw was all that counted. Jaw had taken him, a bastard son with only half a name and enemies for brothers, to the chiefship he held today. Take, he had. But it wasn't an assuming, born-to-expect-it kind of take. It was take hard learned and hard won. He hadn't gone to his father for a handout. Gullit Bludd had said but a handful of words to his bastard son from the moment he'd acknowledged him as his own. And a good half of them were curses.

Knocking.

The Dog Lord looked to the door. He had been too long alone and his mind had got thinking, and that was never what a Bluddsman was about.

"Enter."

Expecting his second son's children, who had arrived from the Bluddhouse that morning, Vaylo had his gaze focused halfway down the door when it opened. A man's waist met his eyes. Seeing the long white robe and smooth, almost womanish hands, the Dog Lord let out a hard sigh. If you dealt with the devil, his helpers always arrived soon enough.

"Sarga Veys. When did you get here?"

A tall man with a sallow complexion and womanish eyes entered the room. Although dressed in the plain white robe of a cleric, Sarga Veys was no man of God. "In my own small way, Lord Bludd, I have been here all along."

Vaylo hated the man's high voice and the overly fine shape of his lips. He hated being called Lord Bludd too. He was nothing but the Dog Lord, and both he and his enemies knew it. Suddenly angry, he cried, "Close the door behind you, man!"

Sarga Veys was quick to do his bidding, moving in the loose-jointed way of a man possessing little physical strength. The dogs growled behind his back. Sarga Veys didn't like the dogs, and when he was finished with the door, he moved as far away from them as possible. When he spoke, a tremor that may have been fear, yet Vaylo Bludd suspected was anger, showed itself in his voice. "I see you're making yourself at home, Lord Bludd. The Dhooneseat quite suits you."

A small nod on Sarga Veys' part led the Dog Lord's gaze to the foot of the Dhooneseat, where a thin strip of leather lay on the stone. Vaylo's eyes narrowed. Such a tiny thing, a bit of leather fallen from his braids, yet the devil's helper had picked up on it straightaway. Not for the first time, Vaylo reminded himself to be cautious of this man.

"So," he said, hands patting his belt for his pouch of black curd. "You've been within the clanholds all along. Tell me, did you stay in the safe refuge of a stovehouse? Or did your master want you closer for the show?"

"I don't think," Sarga Veys said, color rising to his cheeks, "that where I stay is any business of yours."

The dogs found much to dislike in Sarga Veys' tone of voice. Snarling and snapping, they tested their leashes in his direction. The wolf dog began worrying at its tether.

Sarga Veys' mouth shrank. His violet eyes darkened.

*"Dogs!"* called Vaylo Bludd. *"Quiet!"*

The dogs became silent immediately, dropping their heads and tails and slumping down onto the cut stone floor.

The Dog Lord watched Sarga Veys closely. Wondered, for a brief moment, if he hadn't seen the man's throat working along with his violet eyes. That was another thing to remember about devil's helpers: No matter how weak they looked they were seldom defenseless. Sarga Veys was a magic user, Vaylo was sure of it.

"Did you ride here alone, or with a sept?"

"I head a sept as always."

*Head?* Vaylo doubted that. Protected by one, more like it. Seven fully trained, fighting-fit swordsmen would hardly allow a man like Sarga Veys to lead them. Hard campaigners couldn't stand his type.

"I shall be riding south to meet my master after I've left here." Sarga Veys seemed more at ease now the dogs were quiet. He took a moment to smooth back his fine hair. "I shall tell him, of course, of your great success. Assure him that everything went smoothly, and report that you are well on your way to becoming Lord of the Clans." Sarga Veys smiled, showing small, white, but ever so slightly inward-slanting teeth. "My master will be pleased. He has done his part. Now it's up to you to do—"

Vaylo Bludd spat out the wad of black curd he'd been

chewing, silencing Sarga Veys as effectively as his dogs. "Your master wasn't the one who planned the raid and took the risks. He didn't cut through the darkness and smoke not knowing what each new step would bring him. His blade wasn't bloodied. His sons weren't risked. His balls weren't froze with the waiting."

"Thanks to my master," Sarga Veys said, his voice dropping a tone lower, "*your* blades weren't as bloodied as they might have been."

*Crack!*

The Dog Lord smashed his foot down on the hearth stool, breaking its carved legs like sticks. Across the hearthwell, the dogs shrank back against the wall. Sarga Veys flinched. A muscle in his throat quivered.

"Try any of your foul magics upon me," Vaylo roared, "and as the dogs are my witness you will not leave this roundhouse alive."

Hearing their name spoken, the dogs thrashed their muzzles and snarled, spraying the surrounding stone with drops of urine.

Unable to take a farther step back as his heels were already pushing against the door, Sarga Veys pinched in his lips. "Yes. I see now why they call you the Dog Lord."

Vaylo nodded. "That's me." With the side of his foot, he shoved away the broken stool.

"Well, Lord of Dogs, or whatever else you choose to call yourself, you took my master's help quick enough when it suited you. I don't believe your anger caused you to break any stools then. Yet now you stand here at the very hearth he helped you win, issuing physical threats to his envoy in the manner of some common stovehouse brawler." Sarga Veys stepped forward. "Well let me tell you—"

Vaylo cut him short with a fierce shake of his head. "Tell me what you came to say. Then be gone. Your voice grates on my dogs. If your master has brought a message, speak it. If he has named a price, then name it." As he spoke, Vaylo watched Sarga Veys' face. It wasn't right that a man have violet eyes.

Sarga Veys made a small shrugging motion. He brought his facial features under control, yet it took him a long moment to do so. When he spoke there was still a residue of anger in his voice. "Very well. I bring you no message from my master. When the deal was struck he asked for nothing in return, and continues to do so now. As he said at the time, he wishes only to see the clanholds under a single firm leadership, and he believes that you are the man to do it. I cannot say when and if he will offer his help again. He is a man with many claims upon his time and resources. I do know, however, that he will be watching your progress with interest. I should imagine he would be quite upset if after all the trouble he has taken, you find the Dhooneseat as comfortable as a padded cot and decide to bed down upon it. There are many clanholds yet to be taken."

The Dog Lord sucked on his aching teeth. Glancing around the old Dhoone chief's chamber with its huge blue sandstone hearth, its comfortable animal-hide rugs and wall coverings, and its smoky isinglass windows, he thought hard upon Sarga Veys' words. They weren't truthful, Vaylo was sure of that, yet there *was* truth in them.

"I have plans of my own for Blackhail and the rest," he said. "And will move upon them in my own good time. I must secure the Dhoonehold first."

A quick smile flitted across Sarga Veys' face. "But of course. My master places great store in your judgment."

Frowning, the Dog Lord crossed toward the door. He had the satisfaction of seeing Sarga Veys shrink away from him, but the pleasure was only fleeting. He really didn't like the man at all. Veys was dangerous. He had a temper better suited to a man with the muscle to use it.

"You'll be on your way now," Vaylo said, reaching for the door. "Be sure to tell your master that the message you came expressly *not* to deliver was heard well and good."

Sarga Veys inclined his head. As he did so, Vaylo realized that the skin on the man's face wasn't as smooth and hairless as he had first thought, just razored with an expert hand.

"I shall tell my master you find the Dhooneseat to your

liking," Veys said. "And that you have—how should I put it?—*long-term* plans to take the Hailhold as well."

Vaylo Bludd came close to hitting Veys then. His face flushed and his fist curled and the bones in his jaw and neck cracked all at once. Smashing the heel of his hand down upon the door handle, he fractured the oak lintel beneath. "Leave!" he cried. "Take your sly half-truths and your mincing Halfman ways and get your bony, well-shaved arse off my land."

Sarga Veys' violet eyes darkened to the color of midnight. His face twisted and hardened. "You," he said, his voice rising as he lost control of it, "should watch that dog-muzzle mouth of yours. You're not talking to one of your animal-skinned clansmen now. I came here as a visitor and envoy, and at very least should receive due respect." Veys stepped over the threshold and then turned to face Vaylo Bludd one last time. "I wouldn't get too comfortable on the Dhooneseat if I were you, Dog Lord. One day you just might turn around and find it gone."

With that Sarga Veys clutched at the sides of his robe, lifting the fabric clear of his ankles, and stalked away.

The Dog Lord watched him go. After a length of time he let out a heavy breath and closed the door. The last thing to remember about devil's helpers was that they were often more trouble than the devil himself.

Crossing to his dogs, Vaylo slapped his thigh. "What do you think, eh?" he murmured, bending to rub throats and cuff ears. "What do you make of the Halfman Sarga Veys?"

The dogs yelped and growled, tussling for attention and nipping his fingers. Only the wolf dog stood his distance. Sitting close to the wall, its massive shoulders twitching in readiness, it watched the door with orange eyes.

"You're right, my beauty," Vaylo said to it. "The Halfman has told me nothing I don't already know: Only fools and children never watch their backs."

"Granda! Granda!" Tiny feet pattered against stone, and then the door burst open once more. "Granda!" Two small children appeared in the doorway, smiling, giggling, and shrieking loudly.

The Dog Lord thrust out his arms toward his grandchildren. "Come and give your old granda a hug and help him with these uppity dogs."

The dogs managed something close to a collective groan as the two children raced across the room to Vaylo Bludd. The eldest child, a bright beauty with the dark skin and dark eyes of her mother, giggled madly as she hugged her grandfather with two arms and pestered the huge pony-size dogs with her feet.

The dogs knew better than to growl at Vaylo Bludd's grandchildren and allowed themselves to be vigorously petted, teased, and called by ignoble names. The children called the wolf dog Fluff! And he answered to it! It was the funniest thing Vaylo Bludd had ever witnessed, and it never failed to make him laugh out loud. He loved only two things in life: his grandchildren and his dogs, and when he had both together in one room he was as content as a man could be. Within a month he would have all his grandchildren here, in the Dhoonehouse safe and sound, where he and his dogs could watch over them.

As he tousled the hair of the youngest grandchild, a fine black-haired boy who Vaylo secretly thought looked much like himself, Sarga Veys' words prayed upon his mind. *One day you just might turn around and find it gone.*

Vaylo glanced around the chief's chamber, his eyes picking out the details of defense: the glint of spiked gratings blocking the chimney flue, the iron clamps punched into the stonework around the windows, and the pullstone lying flat against the wall beside the door—all emblazoned with the Bloody Blue Thistle of Dhoone. Would his grandchildren be safe here? It was the finest roundhouse ever built, ten times more defendable than the Bluddhouse, yet it was the only thing the Dog Lord had ever taken without jaw. There was shame in that, and Vaylo knew it. The Stone Gods would rather a man win an oatfield with blood and fury than take a continent with tricks and schemes.

Seventeen teeth ached with a fierce splitting pain as for the first time in his life Vaylo Bludd found himself wondering if he had done the right thing.

# TEN

## *Return*

RAIF TENDED TO HIS horse in the stables before he stepped foot inside the roundhouse. Shor Gormalin and the others had gone on ahead of him, leaving their mounts to the excited crew of children who had gathered at their return. Raif's horse was not his own, though. It had been lent to him by Orwin Shank. Orwin bred dogs, horses, and sons, and now with two of his sons dead, he claimed to have more horses than he needed. Chad and Jorry were gone, but whoever had killed them had stolen their horses as well, so Raif didn't see how Orwin Shank had any extra to spare. Yet somehow he had laid his hands upon a pair, and the day after Bron Hawk returned with news from the Dhoone roundhouse, he had offered one to Raif.

"'Tis nothing," the red-faced axman said. "I want you to have it. And if it suits you to call it a loan, then it suits me also, but I tell you now, Raif Sevrance, I shall not ask for it back. You and your brother took care of my boys, you drew a guide circle for them, and it eases a father's mind at night to think of them resting within it."

Later, Raif learned that Orwin Shank had *lent* one to Drey, too.

Raif scratched the gray gelding's neck. Orwin Shank was a good man, just like Corbie Meese and Ballic the Red, yet why did he allow himself to be led by Mace Blackhail? Raif let out a long breath, determined to control his emotions. There was no easy answer. Mace Blackhail was persuasive, he lied well, his stories fell upon eager ears.

Raif dropped the latch on the horse stall. What next? That was the question that really counted. Seven days was a long time. What else had Mace Blackhail managed to manipulate during his absence from the roundhouse? He was back, that much Raif knew. The children were full of the tale of how he'd come galloping up to the roundhouse early that morning, stepped inside for just one moment, and then gone galloping back out to the Oldwood. While he was absent the others in his party returned.

It was dark now, a full four hours past noon. Mace Blackhail had had plenty of time to regain charge of the roundhouse. Raif really didn't see how rushing from the stables to hear what the self-appointed clan chief had to say would make one whit of difference to anything and anybody. Whatever new schemes Mace Blackhail had conceived were doubtless well under way by now.

Kicking hay from his path, Raif walked along the stable's central aisle. Drey would be inside with Mace Blackhail. Drey, who, if Raina Blackhail hadn't spoken up at the meeting before the yearmen had had chance to pledge their weapons, would have gladly laid his hammer at Mace Blackhail's feet. Raif could still see the eagerness in his older brother's face. It sickened him. It tainted everything they'd gone through together at the camp.

Raif tasted bitterness in his mouth as he worked the bolts on the stable door. Now that Drey had spent the past seven days riding out with Mace Blackhail, he would be completely under the Wolf's control. Another member of his pack. Nothing drew men closer than shared danger. Mace Blackhail had personally asked Drey to accompany him on the ranging to Dhoone.

A sound not much like laughter escaped from Raif's throat. At the same time he was hand-picking one brother, Mace Blackhail was trying his damnedest to get the other brother sent away on westwatch. Westwatch, a hundred leagues west of the roundhouse in the cold blue shadows of the Coastal Ranges, where old clansmen who wanted nothing more out of life than to fish, hunt goats, smoke heatherweed, and sing the old songs of how Ayan Blackhail killed the last Dhoone King went to end their days.

Shor Gormalin had stepped in to stop it, though. "I'll take the Sevrance lad wi' me to Gnash," he had said. "By all accounts he's handy with a bow, and we canna afford to waste even one able man in times such as these. I'll keep my eye on him, make sure he doesna stray."

No one, not even Mace Blackhail, could argue with the most respected swordsman in the clan, so Raif had found himself one of a party of ten riding out to gather intelligence from Gnash.

It had been a hard seven days. They had ridden day and night. One man's horse had collapsed beneath him, and all mounts had to be changed at Duff's Stovehouse halfway. On the return journey they had changed their horses back. Shor Gormalin had said nothing about speed or haste, driven no man into the saddle before he had taken his black beer and larded bread in the morning, yet somehow he had created in everyone a burning desire to get back. More than once Raif found himself wondering if it had been Shor Gormalin's intent to return to the roundhouse before Mace Blackhail. Raif shrugged, but not lightly. If it was, the small fair-haired swordsman had failed by half a day.

Done with the final iron bolt, Raif drew up his fox hood and braced himself for the short run to the roundhouse. It could not be put off any longer; his borrowed horse was brushed down and fed, and it was getting to the point where his absence would be missed. It was time to face Mace Blackhail once more.

The air outside was cold and still. Raif hardly seemed to be in it a moment before he was shouting his name through the heavily tarred oak of the roundhouse greatdoor and gaining access to the warmth and the light.

The roundhouse was crowded and noisy. Tied clansfolk stood in groups, clogging passageways, stairwells, and halls. Dressed in brain-tanned hides and roughspun woolens, they worried out loud about their crofts, their ewes, their children, and their future. Raif had never seen so many farmers and crofters in the roundhouse at one time before, not even in the heart of winter. Whoever had been sent out to the far reaches of the clanhold to bring them in had done a fine job. Raif couldn't put names to a good third of the people he passed.

Fewer full clansmen and yearmen crowded the halls, but

that didn't mean anything. Mace Blackhail probably had them gathered in the Great Hearth for a meet.

"Raif! Over here!"

Raif recognized his brother's voice before he saw him. Hiking himself up on a luntstone, he peered over the crowd in the entrance hall. Although he had planned to be distant with his brother, the minute he saw Drey standing by the far wall, the muck and grease of the road still upon him and the shadow of a seven-day beard darkening his jaw, he breathed a sigh of relief. Drey was home. He looked tired. His braid was matted with fox fur, and the hammerman's chains that stretched across his boiled leather armor looked as if they'd been blackened in a fire. Apart from a few broken veins across the bridge of his nose, his face looked unchanged.

Keeping his place across the hall, Drey waited for his brother to join him.

The two clasped hands. "Have you seen Effie?" were Raif's first words.

Drey shook his head. "No, but others have. She was out in the Oldwood with Raina. Anwyn saw her return. Said she was as quiet as a mouse and slipped off to her cell. Anwyn sent Letty Shank down with some milk and bannock."

Raif nodded. A long moment of silence passed.

"So," Drey said, speaking to break it, "you and the others returned safely?"

"Yes. The Gnash roundhouse is full to bursting with Dhoonesmen. All those who escaped or were away from the roundhouse when it was taken are gathering at the old strongwall there." As Raif spoke he noticed Drey glance at the stairs that led up to the Great Hearth. "Another meeting?" he said, his voice hardening.

Drey looked down.

Raif breathed before he spoke. It was hard to keep the hurt from his voice. "When were you going to tell me, Drey? Once it was over and done?"

Drey shook his head. "No. It's not what you think. Mace Blackhail wants to marry Raina and he—"

"*Raina?*" Raif inhaled sharply. He felt as if he'd been thrown into the middle of a game that made no sense. "She'd never marry Mace Blackhail. She's his foster mother . . . she spoke up against him at the last meet . . ." Raif shook his head savagely. "She hates him."

Drey swore. "Don't start that again, Raif."

"Start what?" To Raif's ears his voice sounded sullen.

"Twisting the truth. Making up things. Embarrassing us." Drey ran a hand over his beard. "You're not the only one who has to live with the consequences of what you say. If you don't care about me and my standing in the clan, I understand that, but at least think about Effie. She's young. Now Da's gone she needs the clan to look after her. And every time you open your mouth and say something bad about Mace Blackhail, you hurt her as well as yourself." Drey reached out to touch Raif's arm, but Raif pulled away. With a small, unconvincing shrug, Drey let his hand fall to his side. "Mace Blackhail *is* going to be clan chief, Raif. And you're going to have to accept that—for all our sakes."

Raif looked at his brother carefully. He had a suspicion that Drey had been practicing his piece about family and clan loyalty for quite some time. The words had a stilted, preprepared feel to them, and they didn't sound right for Drey. They sounded more like something Mace Blackhail would say. "How long have you been waiting for me, Drey? Did Mace Blackhail make you stand watch, here, in the hall? Did he tell you that I couldn't be allowed into the Great Hearth until I'd listened to what you had to say, then nodded like a good brother should?"

The color in Drey's face rose as Raif spoke. "It wasn't like that, Raif. I was worried that the clan might turn against you . . . and Mace said that a man never listens to reason about himself, but when he's made to think of his family he'll—"

Raif grabbed his brother by the shoulders. He needed to make him *see*. "Drey. Listen to me. I'm not going to do anything to harm you and Effie. Mace Blackhail's putting words in your mouth. It was you and me who were together at the badlands camp. You and me. We saw what we saw, and while we kept to our story, Mace Blackhail kept switching his."

Drey pulled himself free of Raif's grip. "Stop it, Raif! Just stop it! Mace warned me you were too young to listen." With a disgusted shake of his head, Drey turned and made his way to the stairs.

Raif watched his brother go. After a time his hand rose to
his lore and his fist closed around the hard piece of horn.
Mace Blackhail was tearing the Sevrances apart.

Aware that people were looking at him, Raif let his lore
fall to his chest. He was shaking, and it took an effort to
bring his body under control. Smoothing his hair and
clothes, he followed Drey's path to the Great Hearth. Deliberately, he kept his thoughts away from his brother. He
wouldn't think about Drey now.

The stairs were crowded with people. Children raced up
and down, shrieking and giggling wildly. Groups of women
sat on steps, talking in quiet voices, chewing on slices of
dried fruit, and mending bits of cloth and leather harnesses.
Twice as many torches were burning as normal, and bands
of greasy black smoke choked the air. Raif resisted the desire to push people out of his way. Didn't they have anywhere else to go? Why hadn't Anwyn Bird moved them to
cells of their own?

He came to a halt by the Great Hearth door. Two clansmen stood guard before it. They crossed spears the moment
they saw him.

Rory Cleet, golden haired, blue eyed, and the object of
much excited interest on the part of the maidens of Clan
Blackhail, was the first to speak. "Can't come in, Raif.
Sorry. Mace Blackhail's orders. Sworn clansmen and yearmen only."

Bev Shank, the youngest of the Shank boys and not even a
yearman himself, nodded. "Sorry, Raif. Nothing personal."

"Mace Blackhail isn't chief yet. He's got no right to give
orders." Raif stepped forward. "Besides, when was the last
time either of you can remember armed guards being posted
outside the Great Hearth?" Bev and Rory exchanged a
glance.

Rory Cleet sucked in his lips, lowered his black steel
spearhead a fraction. "Look, Raif. This is nothing to do with
me. Mace Blackhail says watch that none but sworn clansmen enter, so that's what I'm doing. It's only fitting that
those who have spoken oaths have the right to speak clan
business in private." Rory's blue eyes looked straight into
Raif's. "There's talk of Inigar hearing oaths next week, and

mayhap you and Bev can step forward and become yearmen along with the rest. Then when you come to me demanding entry, I'll be more than happy to let you pass."

Raif shook his head. He liked Rory—he was a friend of Drey's and wasn't a bit full of himself despite his good looks—but he was in no mood to have anyone prevent him from entering the Great Hearth. Shouldering closer to the door, he said, "Let me pass."

"Can't do it, Raif." Rory Cleet pressed the flat of his spear against Raif's arm. Raif grabbed the spear shaft and pulled forward hard. As Rory stumbled forward, Raif smashed his fist into Rory's fingers. Rory's fingers sprang apart and he lost his top grip on the spear. Furious, Rory swung a punch, clipping Raif's ear and making him fall forward against the door. Wood cracked. Even before Raif could take a breath, he felt the point of Bev Shank's spear on his kidney.

"Step away, Raif," he said, his red Shank's cheeks flushed with excitement.

Raif felt the door behind him open. He stumbled back. Warm, smokeless air breathed along the back of his neck. Someone stepped forward from inside the room.

"What have we here?" It was Mace Blackhail. Fingers tapped against leather as he spoke. "The Sevrance lad causing trouble again, I see." Raif twisted his neck around in time to see Mace Blackhail shake his head at someone in the room. "I thought you were going to take your brother in hand, Drey?"

Raif winced. Grabbing the shaft of Bev Shank's spear, he pushed the tip away from him. Things were going from bad to worse. He couldn't hear all of Drey's reply, but the words *Sorry, Mace* came through clearly.

"By the weight of the Stone Gods, Mace, what did you expect? Keeping a guard outside the door." Orwin Shank came forward and grabbed Raif's arm. "Got yourself in the middle of it again, eh, lad?" He winked at his son. "Good job wi' that spear, Bev."

Bev grinned at his da.

Rory Cleet stood back, his eyes not leaving Raif for a second. The fingers on his right hand were already beginning to blacken and swell.

Raif went to say something to him, but Orwin Shank hauled him through to the Great Hearth before he had chance to speak. "No sense in leaving the lad out there," he said, shutting the door behind them. "He rode out to Gnash with Shor Gormalin. His report will be as good as any."

"Aye," Shor Gormalin said from his place near the fire. "Bring the lad over to me. I'll vouch for him."

Raif glanced around the room. Three hundred clansmen and yearmen were gathered, backs bristling with case-hardened arms and strung bows, boiled hides and blue steel strapped across their chests. Not one woman was present. Not even Raina Blackhail.

Mace Blackhail took a thin breath, clearly displeased. Raif thought it highly likely that Bev and Rory had been set outside the door solely to keep him out. "This is men's parley tonight," Mace said, extending his arm to block Raif's path. "Anyone who doesn't know what it feels like to thrust a hand up a girl's skirt has no business being present."

Along the east wall of the room, two dozen yearmen found something interesting to look at on the floor. Some coughed nervously, others blushed. Huge hound-headed Banron Lye, who had turned yearman only last spring but looked a good ten years older than his age, cracked his knuckles one by one. Raif glanced at Drey, who was standing close to a bloodwood stang. Although he made a point of not meeting his brother's eyes, he noticed that Drey wasn't among those who looked down at his feet while Mace spoke. Raif ran a hand over his roughly shaved chin. He knew less about his brother than he thought.

"Mace Blackhail," Shor Gormalin said softly, turning so the torchlight fell upon the short unassuming sword at his waist. "If having a hand up a girl's skirt is test of a man, then there's a good fifty in this room tonight who you'll be needing to see to the door."

The room rang with laughter. Most full clansmen laughed with genuine amusement. A good portion of the yearmen laughed with relief.

Without waiting for a reply, Shor Gormalin beckoned to Raif. "Over here wi' me, lad, and quick about it."

Mace Blackhail did not drop his arm as Raif approached,

and Raif was forced to push past him to join Shor Gormalin by the hearth. Dirt and soil were lodged beneath Mace Blackhail's fingertips, and his clothes carried the damp, rotting leaf odor of the Oldwood. "Easy with me, boy," he murmured as Raif shoved against him. "You'll push me too far one of these days, I can tell."

Raif tried to avoid Mace Blackhail's eyes, but somehow he found himself looking into them. The irises were dark and shifting like the surface of a lake by night. When Mace blinked, the water deposited over them had a greasy, reflective quality that gave his irises a yellow cast. Quickly Raif looked away.

Shor Gormalin patted Raif's shoulder as he came to stand beside him. The heat from the fire was hot on the backs of his legs, and despite the chimney and several open windows, Raif found it difficult to breathe. The air seemed thick and poisoned. Out of the corner of his eye, he was aware of Drey staring at him from across the room. He had taken his hammer from the leather cradle at his back, and his fingers pressed hard against the varnished limewood handle.

"So, Mace," Orwin Shank said, dabbing his red and sweating cheeks with a shammy, "what's this rumor that's spreading about you and Raina?"

Mace Blackhail smiled a fraction. He shrugged and looked down at his hands. His boiled leather coat was inlaid with disks of sliced and blackened wolf bone. The Clansword was couched in a newly worked scabbard at his thigh. "Normally I would be reluctant to talk about such things—what's between a man and woman is their affair and no one else's." He paused to give clansmen time to nod. "But a certain lady and myself find ourselves in a difficult position; one which, if things aren't explained good and early to as many ears as possible, could easily be misunderstood." A pause. "I will not let that happen. I will hear no bad words spoken against Raina. If either of us must take blame, let it be me." With that, Mace Blackhail brought his hand to rest on the lead-and-bone hilt of the sword.

Raif felt sweat trickle down his neck as flames roared away against his back. Where was Nellie Moss or Anwyn Bird? Couldn't someone dampen the fire?

"So," Mace Blackhail said with a heavy sigh, "I must say what I must say. Early today when I returned to the round-house, I got word that Raina was in the Oldwood tending her traps. Naturally, as she is first respected in the clan as well as my own beloved foster kin, I rode out to greet her and give her my news." Mace rubbed a gloved hand over the pale skin on his face. Once again he looked down. "This is not easy for me. A man does not like to talk of such things . . ." His voice trailed away, inviting someone to speak up and encourage him.

Corbie Meese cleared his throat with a rough hacking sound. Standing where he was, directly in front of a brightly burning greenwood torch, the hammer dent in his head showed up more clearly than ever. "Tell us your story, Mace. 'Tis obvious you are reluctant to speak—no one here can fault you for that—but if it concerns the clan, we must know."

Mace Blackhail nodded along with a hundred others. He took a step forward, then another back, looking for all intents and purposes like a man hardly knowing what to say or where to begin. The lines around Raif's mouth hardened. He didn't believe Mace Blackhail capable of faltering for a moment. The Wolf knew exactly what he meant to say right from the start.

Finally Mace looked up. "Well, I rode to the Oldwood and came upon Raina sitting on a fallen basswood. She was in a bad way. I think everyone here knows just how much she loved her husband, and when I found her it was obvious she had come to the Oldwood to be alone with her grief. She's a proud woman—we all know that—and she didn't want anyone to know how deeply Dagro's death had cut her."

Mace Blackhail had nearly everyone in the room with him. Raina *was* proud, even Raif had to admit that. And it sounded true enough that she would go off alone before giving in to her grief . . . but then Drey had said Effie was there with her. The skin on Raif's face slowly switched from hot to cold as Mace Blackhail continued speaking.

"Of course I went to comfort her. We share a man's loss and are close bound by it, and we wept upon one another's shoulders and swapped our grief. Raina was understanding and gentle, and, as women often tend to, helped me more than I helped her." Mace made a minute gesture with his hand. He swallowed hard. "I . . . I must own up to what happened next. I would not be a man if I didn't. Our closeness drew us closer, and we fell into each other's arms and came together as man and woman."

The clan was silent. Breath hung in three hundred throats. The light in the room dimmed as one of the central torches burned out. At his side, Raif was aware of a muscle pumping in Shor Gormalin's cheek.

Mace Blackhail continued speaking, his voice low and halting. "I will make no excuses for my actions. It was wrong of me to take advantage of the situation. As an elder yearman and Dagro Blackhail's foster son, I should have known better. I should have pushed Raina from me and walked away. Yet I didn't. I let the moment get the better of me, we both did, and if I could reclaim the past five hours and undo what has been done, I would. By all the gods watching from their Stone Havens tonight, I wish I had never ridden to the Oldwood.

"Raina is no blood kin to me, but she has cared for me as family, and I owe her respect. Now I have wronged her—and deeply. It matters not that she was willing. One of the first things my foster father taught me is that a man should always take responsibility for his actions, most especially when those actions concern women."

Although Raif saw looks of condemnation and disapproval on many faces, especially those of the older clansmen, he also saw a good few men nodding and sighing along with the Wolf. Ballic the Red had an arrow in his cracked and calloused bowhand and was stroking the fletching feathers, nodding almost continually. Nearly all the yearmen showed small signs of sympathy, pulling on their chins, pressing their lips together, and exchanging small knowing glances. Raif couldn't bear to watch them. How could they stand by and listen to the lies?

"Second, I want to say before all here and now that I will make amends for what I have done. Raina is older than me and her womb has proven barren, yet I could not live with myself unless I took her for my wife. We sinned in the eyes of nine gods, and I cannot call myself a man unless I put it right." Finished, Mace Blackhail stood in the center of the room and waited.

All stood or sat without movement. No matter if they sympathized with Mace Blackhail or not, they were wary. Marriage between a clan chief's widow and his fostered son was serious business. Most especially when it came a mere fourteen days after the chief's death. After a long moment, Orwin Shank made a smacking sound with his lips. "Well, you've certainly landed in the bloody flux this time, Mace. Good and proper. What were you thinking, lad? Wi' *Raina*?"

Mace Blackhail shook his head. "I wasn't thinking, that was the problem."

"Thinking wi' your balls, more like," said Ballic the Red, slipping the last of his arrows into his bowcase. "O' course you'll damn well have to marry her now. You're right about that. You can't have the ladle without taking the pot. By the Stone Gods, man! What a damn fool thing to do!"

"Aye," cried Corbie Meese. "You'll feel my hammer up your arse if you don't wed her good and proper. And prompt at that. Barren she may have proven in the past, but there's still a chance a bairn may come from the joining, and I for one won't stand by and watch as Raina's good name is dragged through the muck."

"Aye!" shouted a dozen others.

Raif listened as Will Hawk, Arlec Byce, and even tiny liver-spotted Gat Murdock agreed vigorously with Corbie Meese. Fierce and highly specific threats were issued concerning the future of Mace Blackhail's manhood if he failed to do his duty by Raina. Clansmen were always fiercely protective of their women, and it seemed as if the Wolf had walked himself straight into a trap. Raif couldn't shake off the feeling that the clan was responding exactly how Mace Blackhail wanted them to. There were lies here, clever ones. Yet Raif couldn't guess what they were. Had Mace Blackhail and Raina been planning to marry all along? Raif shook his head. He couldn't believe that.

Looking up, he locked gazes with his brother. Surprisingly, Drey had taken no part in demanding that Mace should marry Raina. Raif remembered how Drey had carried the black bearskin from the badlands camp . . . all that way without saying a word.

The stone flag Raif stood upon rocked beneath him as Shor Gormalin stepped forward to speak. "Has anyone thought to ask what Raina cares to do? I for one would like to hear what she has to say on this matter." The small swordsman was not as soft-spoken as normal, and his blue eyes were hard as they regarded Mace Blackhail. "It's *her* future we're discussing here."

Mace nodded so quickly, Raif knew he had been expecting such a demand all along. "Drey," he said, his gaze not leaving Shor Gormalin for an instant, "run down to the underspace and fetch Raina. Tell her all that has happened so she comes upon us at no disadvantage."

Before Drey could move from his place near the stang, Gat Murdock spoke up. The ancient turkey-necked bowman shook his head. "It isn't right and proper to drag Raina before us just so we can have the satisfaction of seeing her admit to her mistake. By the hells! What sort of men are we if we allow such thing?"

Ballic the Red was quick to back up his fellow bowman. "Gat's right. It's not fitting to shame Raina in such a way. It's one thing for a man to steal sauce when he can, quite another for a woman."

Mace looked regretfully from bowman to bowman. "Aye, you're right. But there's some here"—sharp glances at Shor Gormalin and Raif—"who need to hear the truth of it for themselves. Drey, fetch Raina and do as I say."

Drey left the room. Raif listened as he pounded down the stairs, eager to do Mace's bidding. Mace Blackhail had manipulated another situation, and Raif was just beginning to work out how he did it. He had a way of admitting to his own faults, robbing others of the satisfaction of pointing them out or using them against him. And his lies were always mixed with the truth.

After a few minutes of silence, Mace Blackhail sighed. The wolf bones on his coat chimed like shells. "Gat and Ballic are right. Bringing Raina here to face the clan is ill use. It's a woman's right to pick and choose what she tells of her private affairs. I for one wouldn't blame her if she denies the whole thing ever happened, or even went so far as to claim she'd been taken by force. It's her privilege to keep such things to herself, and by bringing her here before us, we rob that from her. And who amongst us can blame her for protecting her modesty by any means she can?"

Raif frowned. He didn't understand what Mace was getting at.

Others seemed to, though, and many men, mostly full clansmen in their thirties and older, nodded softly at Mace's words. One or two muttered *Aye, 'tis so.* Ballic the Red glowered at Shor Gormalin.

More torches went out during the wait. Raif wondered where Nellie Moss could be. She was a strange woman with the voice and hard chest of a man, yet she never missed her rounds.

Finally the doors opened. Raina Blackhail walked in wearing a plain blue dress, thickly stained around the hem and cuffs. The bandages covering her widow's weals were not fresh, and dried blood and mud were caked upon the linen. Drey came to rest a few paces behind her, and then a moment later Nellie Moss entered the room, carrying bundles of greenwood and a skin of wick oil.

Raina stood in the entry space, head held high, not saying a word. Raif thought he saw her hands trembling, but she quickly grasped at the fabric of her skirt and he couldn't be sure.

An awkward moment passed, where everyone assumed that someone else would be the first to speak. Everyone except Mace Blackhail, that was, who leaned against a blood-wood stang, seemingly in no hurry to do or say anything.

Finally Orwin Shank spoke. "Thank you for coming before us, Raina." The red-cheeked axman was clearly unhappy, and the shammy he held in his hands was dark with sweat. "Mace has told us . . . well . . . about what happened in the Oldwood . . . and we wanted to let you know that no one here blames you for the incident."

Ignoring Orwin Shank completely, Raina addressed her words to Mace Blackhail. "So, you have told all here you took me freely?"

Mace shot a quick glance toward where Corbie Meese,

Ballic the Red, and others were gathered. He let out the smallest possible sigh. "I told them the truth, Raina. If it saves your pride to present it in a different light, I for one won't stop you. I own to knowing little about women, but I hope I learned enough from Dagro to treat all with due respect."

Raina winced at the mention of her husband's name. Her gray eyes were dull, and for the first time in all the years he had known her, Raif thought she looked her age.

"He'll marry you, Raina. You have my word on it." It was Ballic the Red, his normally fierce voice soft enough to calm a frightened child. "I'd have his balls for my waxing pouch if he didn't."

A tear slid down Raina's cheek.

"Raina." Shor Gormalin came forward. He tried to touch her arm, but she pulled back. The swordsman frowned. Holding up his hands for her to see, so that she knew he would not touch her again, he said, "Raina, you know I will stand beside you whatever you decide, but I must know the truth of it. Did you join with Mace in the Oldwood?"

Raina made no reply. The room was quiet except for the sound of Nellie Moss tending the torches. Raif watched the expression on Mace Blackhail's face; the Wolf's eyes were narrow, and inside his mouth he was sucking on his cheeks. Slowly Mace turned his head toward Raif. As his gaze met Raif's, his jaws sprang apart, revealing strands of saliva quivering between his teeth. Raif had to stop himself from stepping back. In the space of an eyeblink Mace was himself once more, and Raif knew without looking that no one else had seen his wolf face.

"Raina?" Shor Gormalin's voice broke the silence. "You have nothing to fear by speaking the—"

"Yes," Raina snapped, cutting him short. "Yes, we joined in the Oldwood, if you can call it that. Yes. Yes. *Yes.*"

The small fair-haired swordsman closed his eyes. A muscle in his cheek pumped once, then was still.

"That's settled, then," Orwin Shank said with obvious relief. "You must marry Mace."

"Aye," cried Ballic the Red, hands slipping beneath his boiled leather breastplate to find his supply of chewing curd.

"And we'll have an end of this scandal before it has chance to smirch the clan."

"And if I choose not to marry?" Raina asked, looking straight at Mace Blackhail.

Gat Murdock shook his head heavily, blowing air between his toothless gums. Orwin Shank wrung sweat from his shammy, and Ballic the Red took a handful of black curd between his calloused hands and squeezed them flat.

Mace Blackhail sent a small look their way. *What am I to do with this woman?* it seemed to say. He sighed. "Raina, you have been first woman in this clan for ten years. You know more than anyone what becomes of a woman who allows herself to be ill used by a man and then cast aside. All due respect is lost. Ofttimes the woman is shunned or reviled, and judges it best to leave the clan in order to escape the bad name she has bought herself." Mace thought a moment. "And then there's the question of a woman's possessions and wealth. All here have known instances when a woman's own family have stripped the fine furs and cut stones from her back."

Clansmen nodded gravely. Raif had heard such stories himself, stories of women cast from the roundhouse wearing only rough pigskins on their backs and boasting nothing more than a week's worth of bread and mutton to their names.

"I'd try to do what I could, of course. . . ." Mace Blackhail dragged his words. "But even I must bow to clan custom."

Raina smiled in such a way, it made Raif's chest ache. "You are a Scarpe through and through. You can take the truth and twist it into any basket you choose to shape. If you were to cut me down with the Clansword here and now, within the hour you'd have everyone nodding and patting your shoulder and telling you how they'd known all along such a thing had to be done. Well I shall marry you, Mace Blackhail of Clan Scarpe. I will not give up my due respect and my position in the clan. And even though this is what you counted on all along, it doesn't mean you won't live to regret it in the end."

Shaking with anger, Raina looked around the room. No clansman would meet her eyes. "You have chosen both your chief and his wife in one night, and I will leave you well alone now so you can slap each other on the backs and drink yourselves sodden." With that she turned and began the short walk out of the room. It was Drey who ran ahead of her to open the door, Drey who closed it gently when she was gone.

Raif, along with dozens of others, stared at the space Raina Blackhail had just vacated. The silence she left pressed against his skin. No one wanted to be the first to speak into it. After a long moment, Shor Gormalin hooked his great elk cloak across his chest and walked from the room. As he passed close to Mace Blackhail, Raif saw the swordsman's knuckles whiten upon the hilt of his sword.

Mace Blackhail's thin-cheeked face was pale. He no longer leaned casually against a stang, and for once the Wolf was at a loss for words. After watching him for a minute or so, Raif decided it was time to go. He had been right from the start: Nothing he could do would make one whit of difference to anyone or anybody. Mace Blackhail had it all in hand.

Even as he strode across the room and Drey moved to open the great metal-girded door, Mace Blackhail cleared his throat to speak. Raif passed from the room and didn't hear what he said, but a few seconds later the voices of three or four dozen clansmen filtered down along the stairs. Raif wasn't surprised when the word they spoke was *Aye*.

Down Raif went, following a path cleared by Raina Blackhail and Shor Gormalin before him. Crofters and their families were silent as he passed. Those who had children with them held them close, and Raif could only guess what had been showing on Shor Gormalin's face to make them so afraid.

Raif made good time as he traced his steps back to the stables. His chest was tight and his heart was beating fast, and something sour burned in his throat. He needed to get away. He wouldn't sleep tonight; the memory of Raina Blackhail's face wouldn't let him. *What had Mace Blackhail done to her?*

The raven lore lay like ice against his chest as he picked up his pack and bow from the horse stall where he'd left them. Orwin Shank's horse whickered softly as he saddled it, then sniffed his hands for treats. Raif found a couple of frost-split apples in his pack and fed them to the gelding. It was a good horse, with sturdy legs and a broad back. Orwin said its name was Moose on account of it being surefooted on snow and ice.

Raif led his borrowed horse onto the clay court, strung his borrowed horn and sinew bow, and strapped it to his back. A pale moon rode low in the sky. The wind was rising and from the north; it tasted of the badlands. Iced-over puddles crunched beneath his boots. As he mounted the gelding, he noticed a second horse's tracks freshly stamped on the court. *Shor Gormalin*, he thought, kicking the gelding into a trot.

The land directly surrounding the roundhouse was set aside for grazing sheep and cattle and was kept free of all game by Longhead and his crew. If a man wanted to hunt he had to ride northwest to the Wedge or south to the hemlock woods beyond the ridge. The Oldwood was closer, but that was set aside for trapping, not hunting. And trapping was for women, not men.

Raif rode south. Moose was not a swift horse, but he gave a steady ride. Moonlight reflecting off the snow made it easy to find a path, and horse and rider made good time. As soon as he was free of the valley and onto the wooded slopes, ridges, and grassy draws of the southern taiga, Raif began to search for game. Frozen ponds with surface ice broken, tufts of hair snagged on ground birch, hemlock girdled by wild boars and goats, and fresh tracks stamped in the snow were signs he looked for. He didn't much care what he brought down. He just needed to turn his mind from the roundhouse and the people in it.

A hawk owl soared overhead, a mouse or vole twitching in its claws. Raif watched as the bird flew down into the cavity of a broken top snag. At the base of the lightning-blasted tree, two eyes glowed golden for a instant and then winked out, leaving darkness. Fox. One hand reining Moose, another reaching for the bow at his back, Raif held his gaze on the-fox space. The bowstring was cold and stiff, but he didn't have time to run a finger over it and warm the wax. He could no longer see the fox, but he knew it was there, withdrawing slowly into the tangle of gorse and dogwood beyond. Like most clansmen, Raif kept his arrows in a buckskin case at his side to cut down on the sort of motion that sent game running, and he slid an arrow from his pack and nocked it against the plate all with a single movement. The bow ticked as he drew it.

Raif *called* the fox to him. The space separating them condensed, and almost immediately he felt the heat of the creature's blood against his cheek. He tasted its fear. Everything sloughed away, leaving only him, the fox, and the still line that lay between them. The raven lore itched against his skin. This was what he wanted. Here at least he had some control.

Releasing the string was little more than an afterthought. Although he could no longer see the fox, he had its heart in his sights, and when his fingers lifted and the arrow streaked forward, Raif knew without a shadow of a doubt that the shot would find its mark.

The fox fell with barely a sound. A few leaves rustled, fox weight thudded onto hard snow. Raif peered into the killing ground beyond the base of the old snag. He wanted more.

Heart racing, he slid down from Moose, bow in hand. Even as he took his first step upon the ice-crusted snow, his breath crystallizing in the freezing air, he became aware of another creature hiding far on the other side of the bluff, fast against a year-old hemlock. As he raised his bow and sighted it, Raif couldn't say if he had seen the animal's eyes, caught a glimpse of its cowering form, or simply heard it move. It didn't matter. He sensed it, that was all he knew.

The flight feathers on the arrow kissed his cheek as he called the creature to him. It was a weasel, tick infested and thick jointed with age. Its heart beat too fast in its chest. Raif's hand was steady on the belly of his bow as he released the string. By the time the twine came back, Raif was already looking for something new to kill. His lore hummed against his chest, and his bow sang in his hand. The night was alive, his senses were sharp, and every pair of eyes shining in the darkness had Mace Blackhail's name upon them.

# ELEVEN

## *Oaths and Dreams*

WATCHER OF THE DEAD was out tonight. The Listener knew because his dreams told him it was so. The Watcher was a long way away, how far the Listener did not know. Dreams could tell a man with no ears only so much.

"Sadaluk! Sadaluk! You must wake and come inside. An ice storm is on the way, Nolo says so."

The Listener was not happy at being wakened. Although his dreams had gone, he was still listening to the echoes they left behind. He opened one eye and then the other. Bala, Sila's unwed sister, stood before him. She was dressed in fitted sealskin pants and an otter coat. Her hood was framed with muskox underfur, warm and golden as the setting sun. Very rare. Bala always dressed nicely. Young men lined up from the smoking rack to the dog posts for the privilege of gifting her with skins.

"Sadaluk. Nolo says you must join us in our house. You have sat with your door open for so long that your own house is too cold for waiting out a storm." Bala looked over the Listener's shoulder as she spoke, peeking into his ground beyond.

Sadaluk knew what she was after. "Have you brought me a hot drink?" he asked, knowing well enough she had not, as her hands were empty. "Bear soup? Boil-off from the auks Sila caught and fermented?"

Bala looked down. "No, Sadaluk. I am sorry. I did not think."

Sadaluk made a *tsk*ing sound. "Your sister, Sila, would not have forgotten. Whenever she comes she brings me soup."

"Yes, Sadaluk."

Bala looked so pretty looking down that the Listener was inclined toward forgiveness. She didn't have Sila's plump, pot-shaped lips, but her nose was the flattest in the tribe. A man could run his hand from cheek to cheek and hardly feel the bump in between. And Bala's hands were small as a baby's, made for slipping down a man's pants without him ever having to unlace a strap. The Listener sighed. The man who wedded Bala would be fortunate indeed.

"Please, Sadaluk," Bala said, tugging on his coat. "The storm will be here before we have chance to seal the doors."

The Listener knew storms better than he knew dreams, and although one was indeed on its way, it would not arrive before dawn. "I shall not move from my seat," he said. "My dreams call me back. Now run along and return home, and be sure to tell Nolo that you did not think to bring me soup."

"Yes, Sadaluk." Again, Bala glanced over his shoulder into his ground. She bit her lip. "Sadaluk. Nolo also asked me if you could return his wound pin to him. The seal carcass must be frozen by now."

The Listener *tsked*. The black scars where his ears had once been ached with the kind of hollow pain that only lost ears could. Nolo's wound pin was very old. It had been made by the Old Blood far to the east and was beautiful beyond imagining. Nolo was very proud of it, so much so that he was torn between his desire to use it for what it was made for—fastening seal wounds closed so blood didn't drain from carcasses before they were brought home—and keeping it purely for show. Those times when he did use it, he was always anxious to have it back.

The Listener stood. Bones cracked as he moved, and the necklace of owl beaks he wore at his throat tinkled like breaking ice. His boots needed tending, and want of blubber and saliva made them stiff. They cracked and flaked like tree bark when he moved. His ground was lit and heated by two soapstone lamps, yet as the door had been open for several hours, it was as cold outside as within. Frost crystals glistened on the caribou skin-covered walls and floor.

The young seal Nolo had brought this morning as tribute for the good luck he had received while hunting was indeed frozen, and its sleek cat face had lost its oily sheen. The wound pin was fastened just above its hind flipper, its purpose now made obsolete by flesh that had frozen fast. With hands that had not stretched flat for twenty years and were so black and scarred by chilblains and hard wear that they seemed more like wood than flesh, the Listener unhooked the pin. Made of no animal bone he could identify, diamond hard and diamond smooth, it belonged to an older time and place. The Listener sighed as he handed it over to Bala. It would be a fine talisman to hold in his hand when he listened to his dreams.

"Now go back to Nolo," he said. "Tell him I will come and knock on his door just before the ice storm hits, and no sooner."

Bala opened her mouth to speak, then closed it. She nodded. Her small hands slipped the wound pin into a fold in her otter coat. Pulling her hood close around her face against the rising wind, she cut across the cleared space to Nolo and Sila's house.

The Listener returned to his seat. Snow swirled like murky water before him, but it wasn't cold, not really. Winter had only just begun. The bear coat was enough to keep his body warm, and the thick guard hairs at his collar allowed no drafts. His head, he chose to leave uncovered. The Ice God had eaten his ears thirty years ago. If he'd had a fancy for his nose and cheeks, he would have taken them by now.

Fishing in his pike pouch, the Listener searched for his talismans: the narwhal tusk, the silver knife, and the driftwood. Sea, earth, and that which grew to the sky. *Now. Where was I?* Sadaluk shuffled the talismans in his lap, trying to recapture the images of his last dream. The two kidney-size scars on either side of his head burned beneath their bear tallow plugs. Briefly he thought back to Nolo's wound pin. He would have dearly liked to hold it in his hands. The Old Blood knew much about dreams . . . and even more about Watcher of the Dead.

*Show me the one who will bear Loss*, the Listener asked for the second time that night. *The one named Watcher of the Dead.*

Time passed. The talismans grew warm in his hands. Then suddenly, abruptly, the ground slipped from beneath his feet and he fell into his dreams. Lootavek had once said dreams were a tunnel to pass through; to Sadaluk they were a pit. Always he felt as if he had been swallowed and was falling down a great bear's throat. Voices spoke to him as he descended, so he did what he had been taught: He *listened*.

The dream place was dark, and there were things within it that knew and did not fear him, and unless he listened carefully, he might lose his way. Lootavek had lost his way only once, yet it had been enough to lure him out of his house and onto the sea ice, to the soft dripping edges where white floe and black water met. It was enough to make him take a step onto the colorless grease ice beyond.

The Listener closed his fist around the narwhal tusk. All those who listened to their dreams were eventually led to their deaths. Each time he listened, Sadaluk asked himself, *Will this time be my last?*

As the meat of his thumb pushed against the smooth ivory of the tusk, the Listener saw Watcher of the Dead. He was hunting as before, ranging over a land fat with game, Death running like a hound at his heels. Yet even as the Listener looked on, Death departed. There was someone else close by whom she must attend to this night.

\* \* \*

MOOSE'S RUMP WAS AWASH with blood. A pair of foxes, a weasel, a marmot, a side of jackrabbits, three minks, and a snagcat bounced up and down across the gelding's back. Moose's heat kept the carcasses warm. Raif scratched his horse's neck. Moose had worked hard tonight, trotting down slopes thick with new snow and over ponds hard with ice, never once whickering when game was in sight, always holding steady for those long vital seconds when a bow was drawn above him.

"Orwin named you well," Raif said as he walked the horse over the graze toward the roundhouse. "I swear one morning I'll come to the stables and find two antlers sprouting behind your ears."

Moose turned his head toward Raif and let out a long disgusted grunt.

Raif grinned. He liked his borrowed horse a lot. Riding him, hunting from his back and at his side had helped the night pass quickly. And that was all Raif had wanted. It was difficult to sleep these days. More and more he needed to wear himself out before he dropped onto his bench or bedroll for the night. Sometimes it was better not to sleep at all. His dreams were never good. Tem was often in them, thrashing in his hide tent, beating against some invisible enemy, calling out to Raif to help him. Tem's skin was burned black, and his fingers had been chewed on by wolves. Raif shivered. Glancing up through the bank of frost smoke, he set his gaze on the predawn sky. This was one of those nights when it was better to hunt than sleep.

Few lights could be seen within the roundhouse. Most windows were either barred by stone or wood or both. Many clansfolk believed that Vaylo Bludd would arrive any day now and attempt to take the Hailhold in the same manner he had taken Dhoone. Raif wasn't sure about that. From what he'd seen and heard at Gnash, it looked as if the Dog Lord would have his work cut out for him just holding on to Dhoone. Dhoone was a huge clanhold, with more than a dozen war-sworn clans upon its borders. A good half of the Dhoonesmen had escaped to Clan Gnash and Clan Castlemilk, and they were madder than stags in rut. Raif couldn't see how even the Dog Lord could lay siege to one roundhouse while trying to secure another.

Frowning, Raif patted Moose's neck. Frozen mud cracked beneath his boots as he walked. No more snow had fallen during the night, but the temperature had dropped to the point where Raif had been forced to slather his cheeks and nose with grease. Every few minutes he had to brush ice crystals from his fox hood, where his breath had glaciated in the fur.

As he stepped onto the clay court, he spied movement to the side of the roundhouse. Pulling on Moose's reins, he altered his path and made toward the figures spilling from the door that faced the stables. Noises cut through the mist: the crunch of boiled elkskins on snow, the rattle of arrows in a bowcase, and the squeak of new leather, straining as it took its first weight. Someone yawned. Raif caught a glimpse of Corbie Meese's misshapen head, then Ballic the Red's great barrel-shaped chest. Clansmen, about three dozen in all, heading from the roundhouse to the stables.

Tugging Moose forward, Raif broke into a run. Even before he reached the half-light of the open door, Ballic the Red had his bow drawn and sighted. Dropping the reins, Raif raised both arms into the air. "Ballic. It's me. Raif Sevrance. Don't shoot."

"Stone balls, lad!" roared Ballic, lowering his bow. "What were you thinking? Running up like that! I came within a rat's tail of shooting the teeth right out of your jaw." The bowman wasn't smiling, and his words had a hard bite. "Where've you been?"

Raif patted Moose's flank. Dried, partially frozen blood had stained the gelding's back crimson. The carcasses strung across its rump hung limp like bags of feed. "Been out to the southern taiga. Hunting."

As he spoke, more men continued to pour from the roundhouse. All were dressed for hard riding, wearing oilskins and thick furs over steel. Weapons and supplies formed jagged lumps on backs and shoulders and around waists. Pouches containing neat's-foot oil, powdered guidestone, spare bowstrings, and dried meat hung on dog hooks from their belts. Raif saw Drey bringing up the rear. He was wearing Tem's wax-stewed greatcoat.

"Did you see anything while you were out there, lad?" Corbie said, his light brown eyes flickering toward the land far south of the roundhouse.

Raif shook his head. He didn't like the look on Corbie's face. "What's happening? Where are you going?"

Corbie Meese and Ballic the Red exchanged glances. Corbie made a rolling motion with his arm, indicating that the other clansmen move on ahead of him. "We're riding east past Dhoone, to the Bluddroad. Mace has had word that a party of forty hammermen and spearmen will be making the journey from Bludd to Dhoone three days' hence, and we're planning to set an ambush and take them."

Raif looked along the lines of men. He could see no sign of Mace Blackhail. "How does Mace know this?"

Corbie Meese ran a gloved hand over the hammer dent on

his bare head. "He came by the information at Gloon's Stovehouse. Two nights back, just before we returned to the clanhold, he split from the rest of us. Said he wanted to check what travelers and other such folk had heard about the Dhoone raid."

"Just as well that he did," Ballic the Red said, cutting in, "else we'd have nothing but fresh air to go on."

"Aye," Corbie agreed. "Turns out that more than a few patrons at Gloon's were loose-spoken, and Mace heard tell that the Dog Lord means to make the Dhoonehouse his chief hold. Everything—arms, furnishings, animals, even women and bairns—has to be moved from the Bluddhouse to Dhoone. The Dog Lord means to leave his eldest son, Quarro, to watch over the Bluddhold in his stead."

Raif nodded. It made sense. The Dhoone roundhouse was the strongest keep in all the clanholds, with walls sixteen feet thick and a roof made of ironstone. *So how had he managed to take it?* Against his will the memory of the badlands raid came back to him . . . the stench of hot smelted metal in the air.

"Are you coming wi' us, lad?" Ballic said, his great broom of a beard catching his breath and then turning it to ice. "Tem was always telling me how good you are wi' that bent stick of yours. We could do wi' an extra bowman. Eh, Corbie?"

Corbie Meese hesitated before answering, tugging on his dogskin gloves to make them sit right on his hands. "I'm not sure he should come, Bal. Mace said only yearmen and full clansmen. With the dangers involved, 'tis only right and fitting."

"Aye. You speak the truth." Ballic the Red set his fierce gray eyes upon Raif for a moment before turning his gaze to the animal carcasses riding Moose's back. Raif could see him counting. When he spoke it was to Corbie, not Raif. "Twelve skins in half a night, eh? Heart kills, too. And one of them's a snagcat. Quite a cache, and that's no mistaking."

"Lad's trouble, Bal," Corbie said. Then to Raif: "Nothing personal, lad. You've just reached that age when you're as much harm as help to have around. And Mace Blackhail has no love of you, that's for sure."

Ballic chuckled. "Aye, but try as he might he can't keep the lad from his meetings!" The bowman slapped Raif on the back with a hand that was gloved *then* mitted. No one took as much care of his bowfinger than Ballic the Red. "So, lad. Tell me the truth. Are you as fine a shot as Shor Gormalin and your da would have me believe?"

Raif looked down. How could he answer? "I'm better at some things than others. I'm no good at hitting targets, but game . . ." He shrugged. "I do well with game." As he spoke, clansmen began to emerge from the stables with their mounts. Drey was one of the first to trot his horse onto the court. Orwin Shank had given him a fine black stallion with strong legs and a wide back. Dawn light had started to shine across the snow, and Raif could clearly see the expression on his brother's face. It made something in his chest tighten. Drey did not want him along.

"How old are you, lad?" Ballic the Red's question seemed to come from a very great distance.

"Sixteen."

"So you're due for your yearing this spring?"

Raif nodded.

"Well, I say we call Inigar Stoop out here and now, and let him take your oath where you stand. Couple o' months will make no difference either way."

Corbie Meese sucked in a good deal of air. The cold had turned his lips gray. His wedge-shaped chest and ham arms strained against his elkskin coat as he stamped his booted feet upon the snow. "Stone Gods, Bal! Mace'll have a frothing fit if he learns you're planning on taking the lad's oath. Why, just last night—"

"Where *is* Mace?" Raif interrupted. "Is he riding with the ambush party?"

"He'll be holding back a day to stand vigil afore Inigar anoints him as chief."

Raif kept his features still, but he felt his pupils shrinking as they cut out a portion of the light. So Mace Blackhail would stand Chief Watch in the guidehouse, lashed to the north-facing plain of the guidestone through twelve hours of darkness, alone, unspeaking, eyes open to see the faces of nine gods. His spine would touch granite in three places, and

the chief's mantle that he wore would soak up graphite oil
and fluids from the guidestone. Afterward, when Inigar cut
him free with the Clansword, chiefblood would be let and
nine drops of Mace's blood would be allowed to fall into the
Gods Bowl hewn within the stone. Later Mace would speak
terrible oaths and pledges before the clan, renouncing his
birthclan and giving himself wholly to Blackhail for life.
Later still, he would draw a guide circle with his own hand
and step within it and ask the Stone Gods to smite him down
if they judged him unfit to be chief.

Aware of Corbie Meese's eyes upon him, Raif did not let
his anger show. But it was there, hot and twisted like a piece
of black iron in his chest. He hoped the Stone Gods sent
Mace Blackhail to hell.

"Mace will ride to catch up with us when he can," Corbie
said. "He sat up all night overseeing clan defenses." The
hammerman looked impatient to be on his way. He kept
glancing at the increasingly wide circle of clansmen who
had trotted their horses from the stables and were busy buckling bedrolls and feed sacks in place. "He's heard tell that
the Dog Lord has sent cowlmen to our borders. So none of
us can trust our own shadows from now on. Mace'll catch up
wi' us within a day."

*Cowlmen.* All thoughts of Mace Blackhail slid from
Raif's mind. He now understood what had made Corbie and
Ballic so nervous when he had first approached the court.
Cowlmen were the nearest thing in the clanholds to assassins. Named after the long, hooded cloaks they wore, which
were said to switch colors along with the seasons, they traveled into enemy territory, took up positions near game tracks
and trapping runs, and lay low for days on end, biding their
time until someone came along whom they could kill. The
casualties they caused were few in relation to raiding and
ambush parties—lone hunters usually or, if they were lucky,
small hunt parties—but that wasn't the point. They created
fear. When cowlmen were thought to be loose within a clanhold, no one could leave the roundhouse and be sure of returning home. A cowlman could shoot a woman out tending
her traps without once showing his face. They could be anywhere: high in the canopy of a purple blue hemlock, hiding

in the fecal-like sludge of a moss bog, or crouching behind the red spine of a sandstone ridge. In winter, it was said some cowlmen even buried themselves in snow, lying for hours with their weapons crossed over their chests, ready to bring cold death.

"Well, Mace Blackhail's gonna have to find my blunts and roast 'em, for the lad's coming wi' me." Ballic the Red's gaze was almost wistful as he studied the kills on Moose's back. "You know how valuable a good marksman is to an ambush party, Corbie. Heart kills like these will drop the Bluddsmen where they stand." Then to Raif: "Set here, lad, while I fetch Inigar Stoop." Without waiting for any response, Ballic made his way back to the roundhouse.

Raif watched him go. He didn't know if he wanted to ride with the ambush party or not. Moose would have to be left behind; the gelding had been hard ridden these past three days and needed sleep. Drey clearly didn't want him to go. Raif could see his brother now, astride the black, edging closer so he could keep track on what was happening between the two senior clansmen and his younger brother. Then there were the things that niggled away in the back of Raif's mind, things about Mace Blackhail. It wasn't usual for the head of an armed party to split from his men on the final leg of the journey. And from one short visit to a stove-house, Mace Blackhail had learned an *awful* lot, enough to spread fear throughout the clanhold and send an ambush party east to beset Bludd.

It didn't fit.

Raif glanced at Corbie Meese, wondering if he should speak such things out loud. The hammerman had been quick to pledge his arms to Mace Blackhail, yet what had happened last night in the Great Hearth had not sat well with anyone, and both Corbie and Ballic seemed less inclined to keep Mace Blackhail's good opinion than they were yesterday. Still, it would all be forgotten once Mace and Raina were wed. Raif pushed back his hood, suddenly feeling hot and trapped beneath it. He didn't like to think of Rain Blackhail with Mace. It was another thing that didn't fit.

"Here! Gather round now!" Ballic the Red's fierce booming voice broke the silence of the court as the bowman stepped from the roundhouse, dragging the little white-haired guide behind him. "Raif Sevrance is about to take First Oath."

A murmur passed through the ambush party. Bald-headed Toady Walker muttered, "He's gone and done it now." Behind his back, Raif heard Drey swear softly, not quite to himself.

Inigar Stoop did not look pleased. He was dressed in a pigskin coat, dyed black as was clan way. Disks of slate, sliced so thin they looked like scales, were attached to the collar and hem. The cuffs had been singed at the Great Hearth to mark the onset of war. Judging from the flatness of the clan guide's hair and the number of untied lacings on his coat, Ballic the Red had just pulled him from his bed. Pieces of slate snapped as he moved.

"Let's get this over and done," he said, frowning at the dawn sky. "Though I warn you now, 'tis not a fitting time and place."

Almost without thinking, Raif reached up to touch his raven lore. The black horn felt as cold and smooth as a pebble plucked from ice. He wasn't sure if he wanted to do this now, before three dozen clansmen, yet even as he let the lore drop against his chest, Inigar Stoop was taking a swearstone from the cloth pouch he wore at his waist. Warming the stone in his fist, Inigar named the Stone Gods. His voice was thin and wavering, and the gods' names had a sharpness to them that Raif had never noticed before. Ground mist receded. Light from the rising sun reflected off the downsides of clouds, washing the courtyard with a pale silver light. The wind had long since died, and the sound of Inigar's voice carried well beyond the court.

When all nine gods had been named, Inigar uncurled his fist and held out his hand. His black eyes never once left Raif as he waited for the stone to be claimed. Even though his raven lore was outside his coat, resting against oiled hide and waxed wool, Raif felt it was *inside* his skin. A strong desire to flee came upon him, to knock the swearstone from Inigar's hand, drive it deep into the snow with the heel of his boot, and run off across the frozen headlands, never to return. Things were moving too fast.

"Take the stone, Raif Sevrance." Inigar Stoop's eyes were as dark as volcanic glass. "Take it and put it in your mouth." Raif did not move, *could* not move. The guide raised his arm a fraction, made a jabbing motion with his hand. *"Take it."*

Over the guide's shoulder, Ballic the Red nodded vigorously at Raif. He had pulled an arrow from his case and held it in his fist, point facing down. Corbie Meese had freed his hammer from his strap and had it weighed across his chest. A glance to the side showed that the entire ambush party had drawn weapons, sliding them from horn couchings and leather cradles and scabbards lined with wool. All here had taken First Oath. Drawing weapons was a sign of respect.

Raif's mouth ran dry. Inigar Stoop's old brown face, with its beaklike nose and hollow cheeks, hardened. A thin breeze gusting across the court set his slate medallions tinkling.

*"Take it."*

Raif raised his hand toward the swearstone. As his shadow fell upon Inigar's open palm, a raven cawed. A bird, dark and oily as a piece of meat blackened on the fire, swooped down into the court. Descending on a cold current, it rolled its body, diving and shrieking, until a column of warm air gave it lift. Flapping its knife wings just once, it came to rest on the weathercock high atop the stable roof.

The raven watched with yellow eyes as Raif's hand closed around the swearstone. Small flecks of white metal dotting the stone's surface caught and reflected light as Raif brought it to his lips. Under his tongue it went, tasting of chalk and earth and sweat. Tiny bits of grit broke from it, filtering to the bottom of his mouth.

Inigar Stoop glanced once at the raven, then spoke. "Do you pledge yourself to the clan, Raif Sevrance, son of Tem? Your skills, your weapons, your blood and bones? Do you pledge to stay with us, amongst us, for one year and a day? Will you fight to defend us and stop at nothing to save us and give your last breath to the Heart of the Clan? Will you follow our chief and watch over our children and give yourself wholly for four seasons?"

Raif nodded.

*Kaaw!*

"And do you do this freely, of your own will? And are you free of all other oaths, ties, and bonds?"

*Kaaw!*

The swearstone was like lead in Raif's mouth. Minerals bled from it, tainting his saliva with a foul metal taste. *It isn't right,* he wanted to cry. *Can't you feel it?* Yet to do such a thing seemed like madness of the worst kind. He'd already gained a name for making trouble—even his own brother had said so. Stop First Oath now and he might as well run south to the taiga and never come back; he would never be able to show his face at the roundhouse again. No. He had to take this oath. For as long as he could remember he had lived his life *expecting* to take it. Now Inigar Stoop stood before him, the cuffs of his pig coat burned black for war, his breath rising in a blue line from his lips, waiting on the sign that would seal it.

Raif steeled himself. He nodded for a second time.

*Kaaaaa! Kaaaaa!*

Inigar Stoop jerked back as the raven screamed, bending at the waist as if he'd taken a blow to the gut. His eyes closed briefly, and when he opened them again Raif saw immediately that knowledge lay within them, like the core of blue ice that slept through summer deep beneath the badlands' crust. Quickly Raif looked away. Inigar knew. He *knew*.

"You have taken First Oath, Raif Sevrance," the guide said, the words falling like stones from his mouth. "Break it and you make yourself a traitor to this clan."

Raif could not meet his eyes. No one moved or spoke. The wind picked up, and the raven flung itself from the weather-cock and onto its mercy, wings unfurling like pirate's sails, black so they could sail through enemy waters by night.

*Kaaw! Kaaw! Kaaw!*

*Traitor!* Raif heard. *Traitor! Traitor!*

He shuddered. His lore lay like a dead weight against his chest, pressing so heavily he could barely breathe. Unbid-den, a vision of the little blond-haired luntman Wennil Drook came to him: Dagro Blackhail and liver-spotted Gat Murdock pushing the bloodwood staves through the pink hairless skin on Wennil's back. Later, when it was all over and done and Wennil's corpse lay blue and frozen on the barren earth of the fellfields, Inigar Stoop had taken a chisel to the guidestone and cut his heart from the clan.

"Who will stand second to this yearman?" Inigar said, turning to face the ambush party. "Who will vouch for him and guide him and stand at his side for a year and a day? Who amongst you will come before me and take a beggar's share in his oath?"

*Shor Gormalin.* Raif fought for a breath and held it. On the return journey from Gnash, the fair-haired swordsman had hinted that he would be willing to stand second to Raif's oath. Shor was not here, though. Raif didn't know where he was, couldn't even be sure if he had returned from his outing last night. And even if he *had* returned and was sitting in the kitchen drinking hearth-warmed beer and crunching on bacon, he would hardly be in a mood to bother with the yearing of some untested youth. The business with Raina Blackhail had gone hard on him.

Inigar Stoop waited for someone to speak. His beaklike nose cast a long shadow across his cheek. Raif thought he would be well pleased if no one stepped forward to back the oath. The raven circled over the court, silent except for the faint whistle of air through its pinion feathers. Corbie Meese and Ballic the Red exchanged glances. Raif saw Ballic the Red thinking hard, mitted hands smoothing the fletchings of the arrow he held in his fist. Raif could almost guess what he was thinking: *The lad is a bowman, like me. . . .*

"I will stand second to his oath." Drey. Drey kicking Orwin Shank's black stallion forward and trotting through the snow to stand at Raif's side. Drey saying, "I know I am only a yearman myself, but I have sworn two such oaths of my own and will soon swear a third, and I count myself a steady man who takes no responsibility lightly. If the full clansmen will permit it, I would back my brother's word."

A ripple of relief passed through the ambush party. For a moment it had looked as if no one were willing to step forward. Inigar Stoop did not look pleased, but it was out of his hands now. It was up to the clansmen with greatest due respect to say whether or not Drey, a mere yearman himself, could stand second to his brother's oath. Raif glanced at Drey. His brother made a small shrugging motion. Tem's elkskin coat fitted him well, made him look older than his eighteen years.

Corbie Meese cleared his throat. Slapping his iron hammerhead into his palm, he said, "You're a good clansman, Drey Sevrance. There's none here who would say otherwise. The past few weeks have been hard on all of us, yet you have kept your head and done your duty and proven yourself to be an asset to this clan. I for one can see no reason why you can't back your brother's oath. You have the heart for it and the steadiness of purpose, and if you are willing to stand before this party and swear that you will watch your charge well and closely, then that's good enough for me."

Ballic the Red and others nodded. The raven circled, slow and lazy as a dragonfly in summer.

Inigar Stoop's face showed no emotion. "Will you do as Corbie asks, Drey Sevrance?"

Drey slid down from his horse. His brown eyes sought Raif. "I swear."

Raif felt a tightness come to his throat. Drey had not wanted him along on this trip, had warned him only last night about the damage he was doing to himself and their family, yet here he was, standing before three dozen clansmen, speaking on his brother's behalf. Shame burned Raif's cheeks. He wished he could take back what had been said between them last night in the hall. Words couldn't be unsaid, though. Raif knew that.

"So be it." Inigar Stoop sounded as if he were proclaiming a sick man dead. He turned to face Raif. "Your oath has been spoken, Raif Sevrance. You are a yearman now in the eyes of clan and gods. Let neither party down." The wind switched as Inigar spoke, blowing hard against his face. He should have said more—Raif had been present at enough yearings to know that the guide was supposed to pass blessing and offer words of guidance to the sworn man—but Inigar just pressed his lips together and turned to face the wind full on.

In the uncomfortable silence left, Raif spat out the swearstone. Rubbing it dry against the fox fur of his hood, he waited for Drey to take it from him. Normally Inigar Stoop would transfer the stone from one clansman to another, yet Raif could tell from the set of the guide's profile that he wanted no more to do with this ceremony. To him it was already done.

All gathered were silent as Drey took the small dark swearstone and slipped it into one of the many pouches hanging from his waist. The ambush party was eager to be gone. Drey reached out and cuffed Raif's shoulder. "You'd better hurry and get your roll together for the ride . . ." He grinned. "Clansman."

Raif nodded. He couldn't speak. As he turned to enter the roundhouse, the raven began shrieking loudly. *Corpse! Corpse! Corpse!* Raif heard.

"Rider approaching!" Velvet-cheeked Rory Cleet made the call.

Even as Raif swiveled around, Ballic the Red brought his bow to his chest. The massive bowman bellowed for all to get out of his way so he could be sure of a clear shot if needed. Raif looked over the graze in the direction Rory Cleet indicated. A white gelding walked across the snow, picking its steps with enormous care, its back held artificially straight. Its rider was slumped forward in the saddle. The man's chest and head were resting against the horse's neck, and an arm trailed down over the gelding's shoulder, gloved fingers still tangled in the reins.

A muscle in Raif's neck began to pump. The gelding belonged to Shor Gormalin.

Slowly, over seconds that stretched like minutes, Ballic slid his arrow from the string. Corbie Meese's hammer thudded onto the ground, making a sound like a broken bell. Inigar Stoop's lips started moving, and even though the wind was still high and Raif couldn't hear what he said, he knew the Stone Gods were being named for the second time that day.

The gelding, long necked and finely cheeked, with large liquid eyes, slowly picked a path to the court. Everything within him was focused upon just one thing: bringing his rider home. One small misstep, one slight shake of his neck, and his rider would slide from the saddle into the snow. Shor Gormalin was dead. As the clansmen moved forward slowly, quietly, so as not to startle the fine white horse, Shor's fair hair could clearly be seen. Half the side of his head was blasted away by two fist-size quarrels shot at close range. One of the arrow shafts had broken off, the other jutted out from a mat of blood, tissue, and raised bone like something growing from Shor's head.

Without a word passing between them, the ambush party halted in a half circle and allowed the gelding to finish his journey home. Respect was due to such a horse, and twenty-nine men knew it. Shor had fallen slightly to the left, and every muscle in the horse's neck and shoulders was taut with the strain of holding his rider in place. Dried and partly frozen blood streaked the gelding's mane pink and black. As horse and rider drew close, Raif saw that Shor's small unpretentious halfsword still sat firmly in its scabbard. The finest swordsman in the clan had not been allowed chance to draw his weapon.

"*Cowlman*," whispered someone, perhaps Corbie Meese.

The gelding came to a halt before the clansmen, turned side-on, and then held his position, offering his rider to the clan. Cloud. The horse's name came to Raif like a gift. Shor had ridden him for eight years.

A soft tearing sound cut the air as the raven chose that moment to fly away. Watcher of the Dead, thought Raif with a dull stab of self-hatred. The raven had known all along.

# TWELVE

## *A Fistful of Ice*

STOMACH CRAMPS PUMPED IN Ash's stomach as she and Katia descended the stairs, heading toward the quad. She was sick of feeling ill all the time, tired of being cooped up in her chamber and tended day and night. She hated her dreams, too. They came every night now. *Every night*. She couldn't remember the last time she had closed her eyes and simply slept. Couldn't recall when she'd last awakened in the morning feeling rested. Instead she woke in the dead of night, in those dark standstill hours where no one but thieves and nightwatchmen were about, feeling as if she'd been running through the streets. Always she awoke drained of strength and shaking. Sweat poured down her neck, her heart beat like a mad thing in her chest, and the sheets were twisted so tightly around her throat, they raised weals that stayed for *hours*. Lately there had been bruises. . . .

Ash shook her head. Put *that* thought aside.

"What's the matter, miss. Cold already?"

"No. I mean yes. That's it. Cold, just cold." Ash cursed herself. She sounded like such a fool. "Hand me my gloves. Quick now."

Katia harrumphed. She might have said something, only they were approaching the lower rotunda and armed men dressed in the black leather cloaks of the Rive Watch, carrying blood steel at their hips and across their backs, were walking through the hallway on their way to the Red Forge. No one, not even a sulky maid like Katia, liked to draw the Rive Watch's attention her way. The sight of their blades alone could set maidens and goodwives fainting. The red pigment fired into the steel of their longknives and greatswords was said to come from a mix of mercury and human blood.

Suddenly nervous, Ash snatched her calfskin gloves from Katia and tugged them on with a great deal more force than was necessary. Knuckles cracked. "It's not snowing, is it?" she asked, stepping into the hallway. Perhaps a dozen or so steps above her Marafice Eye, Protector General of Spire Vanis and Lord of the Rive Watch, followed in her shadow like a terrible and silent hound. It really was quite ridiculous. Didn't he have something better to do? Ride down smugglers, burn thieves' hands black, hack the fingers from prostitutes who were slow in paying Protector's Trove?

"I *said*, it's cold and dry outside."

Ash jumped at the sound of Katia's raised voice. "I heard you the first time," she lied. Why did she feel so weak? Why did every sharp sound and creaking floorboard make her flinch?

Reaching the tall iron-gated door that led from the Cask to the quadrangle, Ash tied the last few ribbons on her cloak for good measure. Penthero Iss hadn't allowed her outside in weeks, and the last time she had ridden in the enclosed space of the quad was late autumn. Things had got a lot colder since then. Bracing herself, she stepped over the threshold. An awful lot colder.

The stone-flagged quadrangle formed the protected heart of Mask Fortress. Each of its points was occupied by one of the four great towers, and its walls were formed by fortress ramparts and great halls. The quad was long enough to race horses and wide enough to raise lists and stage tourneys each spring. In summer the grangelords held court here, and in the dark months leading to winter Penthero Iss oversaw the trials of high traitors from the obsidian ledge in front of the Bight.

A thin layer of snow covered the entire quad. Bitter frosts over the past week had glaciated the topsnow, making it crackle underfoot. Every time Ash took a step she felt as if she were breaking something. Most of the quad was paved, but the horse run along the outer wall had long since grown over with the tough yellow grasses that lived on Mount Slain. Shaggy weeds peeked through cracks in stonework, and oily green mosses coated flagstones around the bases of three of the four towers. Nothing grew close to the Splinter, not one spike of grass or cushion of moss. Nothing. The ice-bound tower had foundations like the roots of a black walnut, sending its poisons deep into the soil to kill anything that grew and threatened to rob its light.

Ash shivered. However did such nonsense get into her head? The ground soil was saturated, that was all. Too much water running down the walls. Aware that her thoughts were skirting dangerously close to the night she had stepped through the iron-plated door and walked along the abandoned east wing, Ash said the first thing that came into her head. "You don't have to walk beside me as I ride, Katia. You can stay in the stables and keep warm."

Katia grumbled something. Her dark glossy hair was currently waging war with a woolen cap, and from the looks of things the hair was winning. Great springy curls had succeeded in tilting the cap at an angle guaranteed to catch a passing updraft—one strong gust and it would be off. Ash watched the maid out of the corner of her eye. Even in a temperature cold enough to freeze the brine in the curing vats, Katia looked beautiful. Her skin glowed like buttered toast, and her lips were fat with blood. Ash knew her own cheeks and lips would be as pale and bloodless as day-old bread, and the harsh light of reflected snow would do the bags under her eyes no favors. The sight of her own face had begun to frighten her. She looked half wasted.

Not realizing Ash was watching her, Katia glanced over her shoulder toward the Knife. Something passed between them—Ash couldn't tell what—but a moment later the expression on the little maid's face changed. She shivered elaborately. "Ooh. But it's cold, miss. I swear I'll catch my death out here. I'm not like you: iceborn. Mistress Wence says that judging from the color of my skin and the sum of hair I have to pluck off my legs afore they're decent, my family must have come from the Far South. So perhaps I'd better stay in the stables like you said. I *am* feeling a bit middling."

*Iceborn.* Ash didn't like the sound of that one bit. Stepping over a pile of steaming horse dung, she forced her mind back to the subject at hand. Katia wanted to be with Marafice Eye, she was sure of it. The stables were a common enough place for romantic assignations. For as little as a meat pie or a wedge of good cheese, Master Haysticks would turn a blind eye to what went on in any number of his vacant stalls. Some held that the eye he turned wasn't nearly as blind as it might be, and he had actually carved peepholes in the doors, which he rented out for tidy sums. Ash thought about the peepholes sometimes before she fell asleep at night. It *would* be interesting to see what people got up to.

"Rest in the stables, Katia. I'll be fine on my own out here. I won't gallop off, I promise." Ash glanced at the limestone battlements that were topped with iron railings, archers roosts, and murder holes. She wouldn't be going anywhere.

Katia pouted prettily. "I'll stay in the stables if you say so."

Ash glanced over the maid's shoulder to where Marafice Eye stood watching from the shadows along the Cask's west wall. He had found something buried in the snow—a boulder, or a frozen hare carcass, or a bit of firewood—and was grinding it beneath the heel of his boot until it broke. When he noticed Ash watching him, he smiled. It was a terrible sight to see, such a small mouth stretching. The skin looked as though it might tear and bleed. Ash turned away.

"What are you waiting for?" she snapped at the maid. "Go on, off to the stables. Tell Master Haysticks to saddle and bring out Cob."

Something close to anger crossed Katia's face as she turned on her heel and made for the stables. Ash regretted her sharpness immediately yet didn't call the maid back. Rubbing a mitted hand across her face, she took a few deep breaths to calm herself. Coming outside hadn't been a good idea. Oddly enough, it had been her foster father who had suggested it, last night when he'd visited her chamber after dark. *You are so pale, almost-daughter, like a lily trapped beneath the ice. You must go outside tomorrow. Take a ride around the quad, stretch your legs, breathe in some fresh mountain air. Your room is filled with lamp smoke and old dust. I worry so about you.*

Ash kicked at the frozen snow. Iss was always *worried* about her.

Master Haysticks emerged from the stable block, trotting his old blue cob behind him. The stablemaster wore a coat pieced together from old horse blankets and bits of harness leather. His large head was covered by a halfcap woven from horsehair, and his stirrups had once been horse's bits. Nothing was wasted in Master Haysticks' stables. Once a day he sent out grooms to shovel dung in the quad.

"'Day, miss," he said, inclining his head. "Old Cob's ready for yer. Go easy on the bit; her mouth's scratched up bad. Been chewing on the stall door again." He shook his head. "Terrible splinters."

Ash took the reins from him. Although she didn't like Master Haysticks much, she *did* like the plain way in which he treated her. He had been stablemaster at Mask Fortress since before she was born, when Borhis Horgo was surlord and Penthero Iss held the same position as Marafice Eye did now. Master Haysticks remembered who she was. He knew she was nothing more than a foundling.

"Pass me yer foot, miss." Master Haysticks cupped his

hands and squatted low to the ground. Ash gave him her foot, and he heaved her up over the cob.

When she was settled in the saddle, she glanced back toward the Cask. Marafice Eye had gone; footprints driven deep into the snow led straight for the stables. Ash let out a guarded sigh of relief. It was good to be free of the Knife. "Come on, Cob," she said, kicking the old work mare's flank. "Let's take a turn or two around the quad."

Master Haysticks watched Ash with a critical eye, satisfying himself that her reinwork wasn't putting undue stress on the mare's mouth, before spitting in the snow and heading back.

Ash felt free to relax only when he was gone. Cob was just about the gentlest horse she had ever known, and in all the years she had been riding her, Ash had never managed to coax the old mare into anything faster than a trot. She didn't have a name. Master Haysticks called her Cob because that's what she was. This past year he had taken to calling her Old Cob, which meant she didn't have many horse days left.

Turning onto the horse run, Ash put aside all bad thoughts. Now she was higher from the ground, she could see a little of the city over the northern wall. Spires, sharply sloped roofs, and cast-iron turrets rose above the wall like weapons in an arms case. If she listened very carefully she could hear the clatter of carts in the street and the roar and bustle of Hoargate market.

Ash had always wanted to see Hoargate. Of all the gates in the city, Hoargate was considered the most beautiful. Its great arch was carved from a thousand-year-old bloodwood, cut and carted all the way from the Storm Margin on the western coast. Hoargate faced west; that was the thing. Each of the four gates was built from materials that came from the direction it faced. Vaingate was raised from the plain cream limestone of Mount Slain; Wrathgate, which faced east, was cut from a huge slab of granite quarried from the stonefields of Trance Vor; and north-facing Almsgate was cast from the blue iron that was mined beneath the clanholds.

Hoargate was the only gate made of wood. Yet according to Katia, who had seen it several times, it hardly looked like wood at all, more like shiny black stone. The masons had forced hardeners and preserves into the wood, turning its insides to steel. Even so, its elaborate facing still managed to attract a thick layer of hoarfrost in midwinter, and it was after this it was named: Hoargate.

Then there was Vaingate, the dead gate, built from plain limestone, carved with a mated pair of killhounds and their one silver blue egg. The gate where she was found.

Abruptly Ash looked away from the city. It wasn't worth thinking about. Her foster father had never once allowed her to step outside Mask Fortress. The most she had ever seen of Spire Vanis was when she was small enough to clamber over the battlements in the Cask and wriggle her way though to the archers gallery at the top. The entire city could be seen from up there: steaming and smoking, its snow black with cart oil, its streets clogged with barrow boys, dog carts, and horses, and its street corners afire with the red eyes of a thousand charcoal braziers.

Beneath it all, beneath the dark, diseased mass of Almstown, the fine mansions and lodgements of the grangelords, and the ever-expanding marketplaces with their hide-covered awnings and elk-bone struts, the hands of the original masons could clearly be seen. Walls were as wide and straight as ox backs. Original stonework was cut as precisely as clock parts, and roads were flat enough to skate on in midwinter, weighted down with enough hard stone to prevent even the dead from rising.

People said Robb Claw had broken the back of a mountain to build Spire Vanis. Ash wondered if the mountain would ever strike back.

Shifting her gaze forward, she saw that Cob was picking a path toward the Splinter. Even from this distance, wisps of ice smoke steaming from its walls were clearly visible. Ash shivered. Like a belt of blackstone pines along a timberline, the tallest tower in Mask Fortress created a climate all its own. It was *so* cold. Icy air slipped inside Ash's chest, wrapping long blue fingers around her heart.

It's just a tower, she told herself. Stone and mortar and wood.

Cold or not, Cob seemed happy enough to go there. Ash reasserted her grip on the reins, ready to pull the mare away, then remembered the splinters in the horse's mouth and let the reins fall slack. What was the harm in drawing close? She glanced at the sky. It was daylight, she was in full view of the Red Forge and the Cask, and it was impossible to enter the tower from outside. The external door had been sealed shut for years.

As rational as all that sounded, Ash still found herself stiffening in the saddle as she approached. Her thighs gripped the mare's belly tightly.

She was hardly surprised when Cob took it upon herself to step from the horse run and trot over to the path that led behind the tower. The old mare was bent on going her own way. Craning her neck, Ash risked a glance at the stables. Still no sign of Katia or the Knife. Katia had once told Ash that when a man and a woman took a tumble together, it took longer for them to unlace and unhook their clothes than to do the actual act. Ash frowned. She could have her own dress stripped off within a minute.

As she puzzled on that, Cob rounded the curve and entered the short run between the curtain wall and the tower. Puzzlement slid from her face when she spotted tracks in the snow. Footsteps, two pairs of them, and two thick drag lines leading straight to the spire's unused door. Fresh tracks, by the looks of them, leading in but *not* out.

"Easy now," Ash said, as much to herself as the mare. Looking ahead, she saw that the footsteps had come from the direction of the south gate. Ash knew from experience that if she were to head that way, she'd be stopped before she reached the endwall. The gate was patrolled by a dozen brothers-in-the-watch.

"Whoa," she murmured, pulling briefly on the reins. The old mare seemed happy enough to stop and quickly found something to sniff at alongside the curtain wall. Ash slid down, booted feet thudding onto hard ground. Glancing left, then right, she approached the tower door.

Wooden boards had been pried away from the frame, leaving an outline of bent nails around the door. Candle ice hung from the lintel in fat chunks, and Ash felt water drip on her hood. The keyhole was set in a brass plate as large as Cob's head, and someone had spent many minutes scraping rime ice from the lock. Ash hesitated, took a step back, then surprised herself by reaching out and pressing against the door. It held firm.

She should have been relieved, yet the nerves in her hand continued to register the contact seconds after she withdrew. Against her will the memory of the night she had walked along the east gallery came back to her. She hardly knew what she'd felt, had tried to convince herself many times that the whole thing had been a figment of her imagination, brought on by extreme cold and fear and darkness, yet the feeling of *want* returned so sharply it brought the taste of metal to her mouth.

Something in the Splinter wanted what she had.

A deep part of her mind had known it all along, from the very first instant she had felt the thing's presence in the tower, yet she had thrust it to the back of her mind with such force that everything had become jumbled and unclear. It was clear now, though. Perfectly.

Slowly, taking a child's careful steps, Ash backed away from the Splinter. She nursed her hand as she retreated; the fingers that had touched the door felt like ice.

"Come on, Cob," she said, hating how weak her voice sounded. "Let's get back to the stables." Cob paid her no heed, forcing Ash to spin around and fetch the mare herself. She didn't like turning her back on the door, and the desire to run was so strong that she had to bite down on her lip to fight it. Yet she couldn't very well leave a horse in the quad. Master Haysticks would have a few choice words to say to her if she did.

Cob was still sniffing at the wall, and as Ash dipped down to grab the bridle, she spied the object of the mare's attention. All the heat drained from her face. A blue ribbon lay embedded within the snow like a vein beneath a hand. She recognized it at once. It was a tie from a nightgown she had given to Katia to mend. The fabric was wearing thin, and several of the ribbons were loose. One or two had fallen off. Ash plucked the ribbon from the snow. Katia had asked if she had any clothes that needed mending before winter, and Ash had handed her an armful of cloaks, dresses, and night-gowns. They hadn't been returned, but that was nothing strange. Seamstressing was not one of Katia's strong points. It took her a whole morning just to pick the hem from a skirt.

The ribbon was cold and limp, a tongue of blue ice. Turning back to face the tower door, Ash studied the two drag lines that ran alongside the footprints. Something large and heavy had been hauled inside. *Like a bed.* Ash frowned. Where had such a thought come from? Any number of objects could have left similar tracks in the snow. In fact, things were beginning to make more sense now. The interior door was only half the size of this one, cut narrow to match the scale of the east gallery. Nothing wider than a man could be brought through. So if Iss needed something large brought into the Splinter, this was the only way he could do it.

Ash rolled the ribbon between her fingers. What had her old clothes got to do with anything?

*. . . and of course there'll be a new chamber . . .*

No. Ash shook her head, sending Katia's words away. It was madness. Her foster father couldn't be planning to move her here. Not to the Splinter. He loved her and worried about her, and just last night he'd told her how pale she looked and encouraged her to take a ride in the snow. Ash crushed the ribbon in her fist. She needed to get back to her chamber. Suddenly nothing felt right.

Walking alongside Cob, she made good time. Marafice Eye and Katia still hadn't emerged from the stables, and even Master Haysticks hadn't sent out a groom to watch for the horse. Ash was out of breath by the time she reached the stable door. Her stomach was cramping rhythmically. She hardly knew what to do, didn't know what to think, couldn't believe the ideas that kept shooting through her head.

"Whoa, lady. Watcha doing in 'ere?"

Ash wheeled around. She had walked straight into the stables without thinking.

A young groom with bad skin and a flat head stepped out from behind a stack of hay. "Best step outside, lady. Haysticks don't like no high collars strutting about when he's not around." The groom moved forward. "'Ere. I'll take Old Cob."

Feeling like a fool, Ash held out the reins. What had she

been thinking? Leading her own horse into the stables like a journeyman. Just as the groom took the reins, a great rumbling noise shook the building. Already on edge, Ash flinched. Suddenly the far end of the stable block was flooded with light as a whole section of the endwall was wheeled back. *Of course,* she thought, relaxing instantly, *the stable has a second entrance to service the trade gate.*

Marafice Eye picked that moment to emerge from the nearest horse stall. His big dog hands were busy with the buckle on his belt. As soon as he saw Ash he sneered and turned the simple business of belt buckling into something she couldn't bear to look at. Feeling her face growing hot, she turned and ran from the stables. Laughter followed her.

The moment she was free of the building, Ash threw the ribbon onto the ground and kicked it into the snow. She was sick of being out here. She hated Marafice Eye and the pimply groom and Master Haysticks. She hated all the things going on behind her back. *Where was Katia?*

"Aaw, miss. Are we going back so soon?"

Ash spun around. Katia, her wool cap gone and thick curls disheveled, leaned against the stable door and smiled lazily at her mistress. "I've come over all flushed. I swear I'll need to take a roll in the snow to cool my blood."

Three steps and Ash was on her. Grabbing Katia's arm, she marched the girl from the stables.

Katia fought back. "You're hurting me!"

Ash wrenched Katia's arm and twisted it behind her back. She was filled with fury, angry at everyone and everything, sick to her stomach of being afraid. "I don't care. Now walk on."

Katia did as she was told, yet it wasn't in her nature to go quietly. "You *told* me to go to the stables! Said you didn't want me around. 'Taint my fault if you're jealous of me and the Knife. 'Taint my fault you're flatter than sheet ice and no man would give you a second glance. What you need—"

"Be quiet!" Ash twisted Katia's arm another degree. Her own anger surprised her. She was shaking, yet for the first time in months it wasn't with fear. It felt good to have control over someone—even if it was just a servant girl. "Open the door. And be quick about it."

In the fourteen months that she had known Katia, Ash had never seen the girl move so quickly. She snapped down the door latch faster than she pocketed rose cakes. Two brothers-in-the-watch were walking along the great circular corridor of the Cask, their leather cloaks fastened to their tunics by lead broaches the size of sparrows. Both men wore quarter helms that cast shadows across their eyes. It was telling that neither man smiled or reacted in any way to what they saw: by now the whole fortress knew that wherever the Foundling was, the Knife was only paces behind. Ash slammed the door shut with her boot heel, then pushed Katia directly into the path of both brothers, forcing them to step aside to let mistress and servant pass.

Climbing the stairs to her chamber, Ash was aware of her heart racing in her chest. Just one touch! One touch and the thing, the presence in the Splinter, had known she was there. In all her life she had never felt such need. It pulled at something, some part of her she had no name for.

*Reach, mistressss. We smell you. Smell of blood and skin and light.*

"Aargh! Miss! You're breaking my arm."

Ash started. Looking down, she saw where she was holding Katia so tightly that blood had stopped flowing to her hand. Abruptly she let her go. Katia stumbled forward and immediately began rubbing her arm. She said things—a whole stream of them—yet Ash cut them away from her mind. Calmly, as if Katia were perfectly silent, not in the process of sobbing and issuing threats, she said, "Follow me."

Ash took the final steps to her room, secure in the knowledge the maid would follow. The door was ajar, and when she pushed it she came face-to-face with Penthero Iss' manservant, Caydis Zerbina. The tall dark-skinned servant stopped dead on the spot. His long, elegant arms cradled an odd assortment of her belongings: the green wool rug, a thick winter cloak, one of the amber lamps, a silver hairbrush.

Ash supposed she should be surprised at seeing him here, but she wasn't. The calmness was still upon her. She made a small bobbing motion with her chin, indicating the items he held. "It's all right, Caydis. Please continue. I realize you didn't expect me back from my ride so soon. The fault is entirely my own. My apologies. Please finish your business."

Caydis Zerbina bore Far South blood, as Katia did, yet unlike Katia, he was soft-spoken and gentle in manner. He worshiped with the priests in the Bone Temple and never wore any fabric heavier than linen, even on the coldest day. Common was not his language of birth. "So sorry, mistress. I stop now. Cause no more offense." He bowed deeply, the bone bracelets on his wrist chinking like falling rain. Slowly he began to back away.

Ash raised her hand. "No. I insist you carry on. Your actions cause me no offense." And the strange thing was, they didn't. Caydis Zerbina was just carrying out orders, like Katia and Marafice Eye. One person ruled Mask Fortress, one person had access to the Splinter, one person had suggested she leave her chamber this morning to go for a ride in the quad: Penthero Iss. Her foster father had wanted her out of the way so he could collect more things for her move. Chances were she wouldn't have missed anything except the rug and the lamp, and both those items were in need of cleaning or repair, and their absence could be smoothly explained.

Caydis Zerbina was clearly unhappy at being compelled to finish his business. His dark eyes, with their almond-colored whites and thick lids, flicked nervously as he moved about the chamber. Ash suspected that he collected things solely to satisfy her wish that he carry on, rather than from any real need to remove anything further. She held open the door for him as he left, inclining her head in a gracious farewell. "Caydis," she said after he had taken a handful of steps along the corridor, "I won't tell my foster father about our unplanned meeting. I trust you will do the same. There's little benefit in either of us admitting our mistakes."

Caydis bowed his long gazelle neck. "Mistress."

Even before he reached the steps, Ash had turned her attention to Katia. The servant girl was standing against the corridor wall, her face all red and puffy, rubbing her arm as if she couldn't quite believe it was hurt. One step forward was all it took to cower her. Ash supposed she should feel ashamed about having someone frightened of her, yet a teeny bit of her rather liked it. "Inside. Now."

Katia's eyes were huge with a mixture of indignation and suspicion. She moved, though. Quick enough to dislodge the last remaining hairpins from her curls. The pins struck the stone with musical notes as Ash shut the door behind her.

"Sit," she said, wagging her head toward the bed.

Katia sat.

Ash turned her back on her. "Now. I'm going to ask some questions, and you have two choices. One, you can answer them honestly and be away from here within the quarter. Or two, you can lie and deceive me and get hurt." She spun back. "Now which is it going to be?"

"You won't dare hurt me. I'll scream. I surely will."

Bending forward so that her face was only a breath away from Katia's, Ash said, "Go ahead. Scream. The Knife is out there. He'll hear if you make enough noise. But before you do, think for just one moment. You may know and bed him, but it's me he's charged to protect. Me. Not some scrap of a kitchen girl who doesn't know what's good for her. *Me*." Ash saw hurt in Katia's eyes but forced herself to continue harder than ever. "Ask yourself this. If *you* cry out and *I* cry out, which one of us is he likely to aid first?"

Katia made no answer. Her teeth pulled at the skin on her lips.

Ash straightened her spine. "Right. Why has my foster father sent Marafice Eye to watch me?"

"Don't know." Katia sounded sulky. "The Knife hisself thinks it's madness. Says he's sick of the sight of you, and that he's got better things to do than watch over a thin strip of bacon wi' no fat."

Ignoring the gibe, Ash said, "So he doesn't know why?"

"No. Says it'll be over soon, though. Vealskin promised any day now."

Ash frowned. Marafice Eye was Protector General; he would hardly agree to act as personal guard to a foundling without good reason. He knew something, Ash felt sure of that. And despite what he said to Katia, he took a cat's pleasure in watching and taunting her—though he wouldn't likely admit that to any girl he chose to bed. Suddenly uncomfortable with the turn of her thoughts and knowing that if she dwelled on them further, she would lose her nerve and weaken, Ash changed the subject. "What happened to the clothes I gave you to repair last week?"

"Iss took them."

"Where?"

Katia shrugged. "Don't know. Said he wanted to start collecting a few things here and there to make the move easier when it came. Said he wanted to surprise you, and to tell you I wanted them for repair."

"What other special instructions did my foster father give you?"

No reply.

"I *said*, what else?"

Katia shuffled her feet. "Nothing."

She was lying. Ash took a breath, thinking. After a moment she began to shake her head. "You know, Katia, my foster father isn't the only one who has power over you. I don't have to take you with me when I move to my new lady's chamber. I could tell my foster father that I no longer care for your services, that you bed any man who crosses your path, and that you stole one of my—"

"'Taint never stole nothing!" Katia stood, fists clenched. "You'd be lying if you say so. *Lying!*"

"Hush, girl," Ash said in a voice she hoped sounded bored. "I can claim anything I want and get away with it. Do you really think my foster father will take your word over mine? Do you?"

That made Katia stop and think. All the strength and light in her face faded, leaving her looking as young and vulnerable as the girl she really was. Fifteen, that was all. Ash felt her determination waver; all she wanted to do was go to Katia and put her arms round her and assure her that she'd never say anything bad about her—even if she really *had* stolen something. Katia was younger than her by almost a full year, yet up until today, until right this minute, Ash had always felt like the younger one. Strange, but the very thing that was frightening her was also making her strong. She had to know. And she would do anything, *anything*, to find out.

Steeling herself, Ash said, "I think we both know the answer to that question, Katia. You'd be back in the kitchens within a day on my say-so, no matter how diligently you carried out my foster father's orders. I am Penthero Iss' ward, his almost-daughter. Now tell me what I need to know, and I swear he'll hear nothing but good about you from me."

Although she was still standing, Katia seemed smaller than usual; her shoulders were slumped, and her back was bent. Even her curls seemed flatter. "Promise to take me with you when you go."

Ash closed her eyes. A pain, like a sore muscle, flared softly in her chest. "If I go to a grand chamber with isinglass windows and a fireplace all my own, then I promise to take you with me." She felt the lie as she spoke. It was the truth, but it was also a lie.

Katia, who was such a terrible liar herself, heard only the truth. She brightened immediately. "Well, that's settled, then. Isn't it?"

Ash nodded. She didn't know how she managed to stop her cheeks from burning.

"Well, miss, it's the strangest thing. Can hardly understand it myself—'less of course it's to do with your 'tility." Seeing Ash's blank look, Katia expanded, her love of sharing secrets now fully engaged. "Your *fertility*. You know, when you finally come into your blood and can be married and tumble with men. Well, ever since His Lordship engaged me, but most particular these past three months, he's asked that I check your chamber pot and sheets each morning for blood. You know, *women's* blood. Says he must be told the minute you come to your menses. Right fierce on the matter, he is. Gives me the dox just thinking about it."

"Sheets? Chamber pot?"

"Aye, and your nightdress and underthings, too."

Ash exhaled softly, her strength vanishing as quickly as it came. *You can't stay a child forever, Asarhia. The old blood will show soon enough.* Her foster father's words came back to her, each one a drop of ice against her face. Iss was waiting for her menses to come. All his pinching and prodding and watching was for just one thing. *Why?* What did he want with her? What would he do when her blood finally broke? The thought made cramps jab at Ash's stomach. Putting a hand on the wall to steady herself, she said, "Leave me, Katia. I want to be alone."

The little maid brought her lips together, took a step forward, hesitated, then took one back. "You won't tell Iss I told you, will you? He'd be madder than a snagcat in a trap if he knew. If mad's the right word for someone who never raises his voice, just fixes you with a cold stare and—"

"I promise I won't say a word." Ash cut her short; the last thing she wanted right now was a reminder of how cold-blooded her foster father could be. As Katia swung open the door, she said one last thing. "I'm sorry about hurting you before. Truly I am. It won't happen again."

Katia turned and smiled. "Weren't nothing really, miss. I used to get worse from Mistress Wence. A lot worse."

Ash tried a smile but failed. By the time she thought of a reply, Katia was gone. Ash stared at the closed door. Why had she never mentioned being beaten before?

It seemed like a very long time before she made her way to the bed. The cramps became stronger, rolling across her abdomen in sickening waves, and all she wanted to do was sleep. Later. She would decide what to do later. Her eyes closed, bringing darkness and peace, and before she could form another thought she fell into a deep numbing sleep.

*So cold, mistressss. So dark. Reach.*

Ash twisted in her bed, turning her back on her dreams. They pursued her, liquid shadows with hands that cracked and bled. Their shapes massed and shifted, darkness leaking from them like water weeping from ice.

*Reach, mistressss, pretty mistressss. Reach.*

Ash twisted again, saw the cavern of black ice ahead. *No.* Not there. She twisted back, felt shadows slide across her face, cold as water from the deepest darkest well. Things moved in the periphery, wet and twitching like skinned beasts. Ground shifted beneath her feet, and suddenly the cavern was below her, its entrance a vast hole blasted into sea ice, an ocean of black tar rolling beneath. Ash backed away. She wouldn't go there, wouldn't take that last step.

*Reach, mistressss. Reach.*

Wet fingers clawed at her arms, drawing them up and up and up. Ash fought to keep them from rising, but it was like trying to bend her knees backward: the joints would only work one way.

*Reach! Reach!*

No. She shook her head, tried to twist away. Nothing moved except her arms, which continued to rise until they drew level with her shoulders. Shadows pushed from all sides, eyes flickering like serpent's tongues.

*REACH!*

Ash didn't reach, she *pushed*. Palms falling flat against something that shone pale like ice, she thrust herself away from that place. A white-hot needle of pain raced along her arms to her heart. She felt something deep within her tear, heard a great weight of ice shatter as it hit hard ground, then staggered back and back and back . . .

She opened her eyes to a world dulled by pain. Belly down upon the bed, sheets bunched around her waist, she lay for a long moment without moving. Her hands were stretched high above her head, reaching for the nearest wall. Even as she worked muscles to pull them in, she knew something was wrong. The hot, angry pain that came with skin burns flared in her palms, making her wince. One palm was open, the finger and thumb pads red. Burned. Ash dragged her other hand into view. It was closed, the fingers stiff and set in place. She opened it slowly, aware of something hard pulling at her skin. When the fingers had curled halfway, a drop of clear liquid slid along her wrist. Shivering, she forced the fingers back all the way.

Ice. A chunk of ice slid from her palm onto the bed.

*Iceborn.* Katia's word was the first thought she had, before shock or fear or the need for explanations set in. The burns had been caused by ice, not fire.

The ice was wedge shaped, blue as frost, and stippled with the kind of pressure lines that Ash had seen on rocks dug from the base of Mount Slain. As she watched, the patch of damp beneath it spread.

Abruptly she looked away. What time was it? How long had she slept? Late afternoon light made everything in the chamber seem gray. No lamps had been lit, but the little charcoal brazier was still burning, giving off a puttering last-breath sort of light. Ash brought her burning hands to her face and blew on them. After a moment she braced herself and began to rise from the bed.

That was when she felt it. Halting on the spot, halfway up from the bed, her weight borne by one elbow and one knee, she reached down with her right hand, pushing through skirt fabric and linen. Seconds passed before her fingers found the right place. Ash tensed. Wetness, warm this time, between her legs. Slowly, as if she were moving through water, not air, she brought her hand back. She didn't want to look, didn't want to *see*, but matters were too far gone now, and of all the changes that lay ahead, surely this one would be the easiest to bear?

Dark blood rolled across her fingers like treacle. Menses. Ash breathed deeply, trying to recall the calmness she had felt earlier when confronting Katia and Caydis Zerbina. She needed it more than ever now. Time passed and still her hand shook, and she realized that this was as calm as she was likely to get.

Moving slowly, she brought her thighs together to prevent any more blood from staining her clothes, held her wet hand clear of the bed, and shuffled to her feet. Once she was satisfied there were no bloodstains on the sheets, she stripped bare, isolating her underskirt and underdrawers, which were the only items stained, then picked up the small fruit knife from the dresser and began to hack away at the linen. This took time. The knife was almost blunt and her hands persisted in shaking, and the linen was winter weave, so doubly thick. All the while, she pressed her thighs together and held something deep inside her clenched.

Well before she was satisfied with the smallness of the linen pieces, she began to feed them into the brazier. The charcoal took a lot of stirring and blowing before it produced a decent flame, but eventually the fire got under way. The linen pieces burned quickly, crisping to nothing within seconds. There was a great deal of smoke, and Ash supposed she should open the shutters and fan it out, but she had a lot of other things to do and even more things to think about, and she would get around to it soon enough.

Tying a linen strip between her thighs, she crossed back to

the bed. The ice was gone, melted to a dark puddle shaped like an eye. Within an hour even that would be gone, and soon there would be nothing left to prove that it had ever existed. Ash contemplated the drying stain. That's what she needed to do: melt away without a trace.

# THIRTEEN

## *The Bluddroad*

RED FOG SURROUNDED THEM like the haze rising from a vat of boiling blood. The air was bitterly cold and so still that the sound of lake ice cracking under tension could be heard five leagues away. It was dawn, and Raif supposed the sun was somewhere, rising over the tops of the Copper Hills, casting its strange and bloody light upon the road. Raif grimaced. He couldn't see anything beyond the two riders directly ahead of him.

Frost had warped his boiled leather cuirass, making it chaff against his neck. He had not slept well. *No one* had slept well. A cold camp raised along the northeastern edge of the Dhoonehold was no place for a Hailsman to rest.

*"All halt!"* Corbie Meese's hiss blew through the mist like a draft of cold air. His voice, which had been formed by the Stone Gods to do the one thing necessary to all hammermen as they fought—bellow at the tops of their lungs—did not sound right forming whispers. It was like listening to a dog meow.

Still, everyone was quick to obey him, reining horses within a space of twenty paces. Metal on all bridles had been bandaged to prevent frostbite to the horses, so there was little noise. Even the hammermen had rubbed oat flour into their chains to prevent them from rattling and betraying a position. Sharp winds two nights earlier had dumped the snow into drifts, and Raif's borrowed filly was up to her hocks in dry white powder.

The raid party formed a loose circle on the sparsely wooded slope, their mounts tightly reined, breath venting in white bursts, eyes dark as coals beneath their fox hoods. Ballic the Red had freed his bow from its case and was busy warming the waxed string between his fingers. Drey and several other hammermen adjusted the straps on their hammer slings for ease of draw.

Corbie Meese pulled back his hood so all could see his face. Jabbing his chin southeast, he said, "Road's below us, just beyond those stone pines. Should be plenty of cover, but with this piss-thick mist about us it's hard to tell a molehill from a moose. We'll know better when Rory gets back. Last time I rode here there were trees to either side of the road, but that was ten years back, and times have changed since then. The Dog Lord's no fool—you'd do well to remember that." A brief glance included Raif and some of the other younger yearmen. "And he knows a likely ambush site when he sees one. According to Mace, he's ordered the felling of all trees along the Bluddroad. 'Course, unless he's got an army of woodsmen hidden up his dogskin draws, he won't be reaching here anytime soon. But that isn't the point: The Dog Lord *knows* the dangers. You can bet your bowfingers that any man of his traveling this road will be armed to the teeth, nervous as a wench squatting in a bush, and ready to attack at the first sound of an arrow knocking wood.

"Now the mist's in our favor, but don't let it make you lazy. There'll be foreriders in the Bludd party, and when they can't see their own horses' heads afore 'em, they'll stop looking and *listen* instead. So keep your horses on tight rein and no moving or drawing steel once you're in position. Right?"

Raif nodded along with the rest. His mouth was so dry he could feel the ridges on his teeth. At some point while Corbie Meese was speaking, the fact of what they were planning to do had sunk in. He had never shot a man before, never set his sights on anything larger than a snagcat. But he knew, in that deep part of himself where the shots came from and the arrows passed through on their way to their targets, that he would be good at shooting men.

"'Course you'll need to keep an eye to the mist. If the

wind picks up, it'll be gone afore you've had chance to shift your arses in the saddle." Corbie Meese looked grim. The hammer dent in his head was filled in with a wedge of red fog. "More than likely we're in for a wait. The Bludd party could pass here any time between noon and nightfall, and we need to be ready when they come. So I'll have no man leaving his mount."

"Aye," chipped in Ballic the Red. "So piss now or hold it in."

When no one in the party moved, Toady Walker raised an eyebrow and said, "No pissing over the horses' backs, gentlemen. Riles 'em something rotten."

Everyone laughed in the quick, reflexive way that owed more to tension than to humor. While most in the party were busy making last minute adjustments to their weapons' casings, Drey trotted his black stallion over to Raif. Keeping his hood up so only those who were directly in front of him could see his face, Drey leaned close to his brother and murmured, "Whatever the split, you come with me." Before Raif could answer, he turned away.

Raif stared at the back of his brother's head. A split? This was the first he'd heard that the ambush party would be divided. Uneasy, he reached inside his oilskin and felt for his lore. It was the first time he had touched it in nearly a week—ever since the day Shor Gormalin's horse had brought its master home. Raif took a breath and held it in. The hurt of Shor's death had not passed. He could still remember the dark look in Shor's eyes as he left the Great Hearth, still see him flinch the moment Raina Blackhail admitted joining with Mace. Abruptly Raif dropped the lore. *Watcher of the Dead.* How many deaths would he watch today?

Snow crunched ahead, somewhere deep within the fog curtain. Ballic aimed his bow. Corbie Meese called softly, "Rory?"

"Aye! 'Tis me. Don't shoot, Ballic," came the reply.

Raif couldn't help but smile. From his position well below them, Rory Cleet couldn't possibly see Ballic the Red, yet he knew enough about the red-haired bowman to guess that he'd already drawn his bow.

Seconds passed, and then blue-eyed Rory Cleet rode into view, his hood pushed back, his sheepskin mitts caked in sap and pine needles, and his boiled-leather halfcoat weighted with clods of frozen snow. He wasted neither breath nor time. "Road's clear. No sign of horse or cartage since last snow. Five dozen or more stone pines have been newly felled on the road's south verge, but whoever was set to the task got bored or cold or sent to another section before he could finish the job. As it is, the area around first choice has been poorly balded, but three hundred paces beyond that there's an area of newgrowth above the road. The pine crowns are at a height to conceal mounted men, and directly across from them there's a copse of dogwood and ash. Between the two, there's enough cover to conceal thirty men."

Corbie Meese nodded. "Aye. Well done, lad."

Rory Cleet tried but couldn't quite stop his face from coloring with pleasure. Not for the first time, Raif found himself regretting the incident at the Great Hearth door when he'd forced Rory from his post.

"Right," Corbie said. "Ballic. You head the southern party. I'll take the north. We'll count a dozen men apiece, and the remaining five will form a rear guard, quarter league east of the ambush site, to block Bludd's retreat and pick off runaways." Corbie scanned the ambush party, his light brown eyes hard as flint, a muscle in his right cheek pumping. After a while his gaze settled on Drey. "Do you think you can handle the lead in the rear?"

Drey pushed back his hood. His hair was plastered against his head, sweat and six days of grease making it appear darker than the chestnut brown it normally was. His face was pale, and Raif was struck by how much older he looked than the day they had shot ice hares by the lick. It was never Drey's way to speak without thinking, and when he stripped off his glove and turned down his elkskin collar, Raif guessed he was reaching for his bear lore. Raif had always envied him the bear. Tem had been a bear, like his father before him and his uncle before that. Every generation of Sevrances produced a bear.

Watching as he weighed the bear claw in his fist, Raif realized why Corbie Meese had chosen him. Drey was solid, dependable, and he possessed none of the rash cockiness that took most yearmen five or more years to overcome. Raif felt his chest ache with envy and pride. *One day*, he thought. *One day Drey will make a fine chief*.

"I can handle the rear guard." Drey's voice was level. He slipped the bear lore beneath his softskins.

Corbie Meese and Ballic the Red exchanged a glance, and Raif knew that Drey had done right in their eyes by taking time to weigh his lore. Corbie beckoned him closer. "Right, lad. Here's the cut. If all goes to plan, there shouldn't be much for you to do. The Bludd party will pass you a good three minutes afore they reach us, so your job is to stay back from the road, high up beyond the tree line, and keep your men silent as corpses. There'll be no signaling done. I don't want to hear one clever owl hoot or loon call. Nothing. The only time you move from your positions is *after* you hear us attack. Then your job is to get onto the road as fast as you can, and take down any Bluddsmen who attempt to retreat. Understood?"

Hearing Corbie speak, Raif began to understand why the hammerman had given the command to Drey when there were full clansmen available to take it. The real danger and the real fighting would fall upon the two attack parties: It would be they who risked their lives, they who fought at close range. Corbie Meese wanted all the seasoned clansmen with him. Raif could not fault him for that. The retreat party would be there as a fail-safe to pick off any runners or stragglers.

Drey nodded slowly. "What makeup?"

"Yourself, another hammerman, two bowmen, and a swordsman. Remember that everyone in the Bludd party'll be a trained warrior. More than likely they'll be spearmen or hammermen. They fight fierce and their weapons are weighted, so unless you fancy a hammer notch to match mine, give them a wide berth." Corbie Meese poked his dent with a gloved finger. "Keep your bowmen above the road, and have them shoot from cover."

Party members were picked by Corbie and Ballic. When Ballic suggested that Raif go with Corbie in the north party, Drey spoke up. "I want him with me. Take Banron Lye instead."

Corbie Meese looked at Drey a moment, perhaps waiting for the yearman to explain himself, but when Drey said nothing further, he nodded once. "It's your party. The say is yours. The lad goes with you."

Minutes later they set off. Winding their way through paper birches as pale as wax candles, they headed east along the slope, high above the road. The horses' mouths had been soft bound with sheepskin to prevent them from blowing and whickering as they moved. Raif had braced his bow, and it was now balanced across his cantle. He rode with an arrow in his fist.

Overhead, the sky was the color of rotting plums. The fog had begun to thin, and much to Raif's disgust it had turned from red to pink. Slowly, gradually, one tree and sandstone crag at a time, the taiga northeast of Clan Dhoone was beginning to emerge from the mist. The land was a mineshaft of drops, cut banks, and jutting rocks. Pine roots burrowed deep into the soft blue sandstone, pulverizing bedrock as they grew, making for treacherous ground. Small ponds, deep and dark as wells, beaded the creases between slopes. All of them should have been frozen, but they weren't, and Raif could only guess mineral salts or mineral oil as the reason.

No one spoke. Raif doubted if there was saliva enough in his mouth to roll his tongue, let alone utter a word. All five of them were yearmen: Bullhammer, Bitty Shank, Craw Bannering, Drey, and himself. Craw was the second bowman. Raif hardly knew him; he was older than Drey, dark skinned, with a clever face and long, tattooed fingers. He might have been betrothed to Lansa Tanner, Raif wasn't sure. Bullhammer was Bullhammer, a great big bear of a man with bristles for eyebrows and the most frightening smile the clanholds had ever beheld. Everyone loved him; it was impossible *not* to love a man who could uproot a five-year-old foxtail pine with a single mighty hug.

Bitty Shank was the swordsman. Like all the Shanks, he had a face that looked cooked. Although he was the same age as Drey, his fair hair had already started to thin. Bitty swung between tarring down his hair to prevent further loss and vigorously tugging at what little remained to show how little he cared. He was in the devil-may-care frame of mind at the moment, but come spring and wenching season, there'd be tar in his waxing pouch again.

When the mist cleared enough to allow snatched glimpses of the Bluddroad, Drey raised an arm, gesturing all behind to slow. The path he chose became more elaborate, involving great doglegs and double-backs as he worked to bring them down the slope out of view of the road. Oldgrowth paper birches, with their long branchless trunks and high crowns, didn't provide the best cover, and bushes and ground birch were scant.

As Drey guided them toward a cluster of newgrowth two hundred feet above the road, Raif's stomach muscles began to clench. The two main parties would be in place now, waiting just off the road to ambush Clan Bludd. Raif had grown up listening to tales of Clan Bludd—their fierceness in battle, their swords cut with a central groove for channeling their enemies' blood, their terrible deafening war cries, and their weapons so heavily leaded that no non-Bluddsman could raise them—yet he had never seen a Bluddsman up close. To him they were the stuff of legend, like the people who were said to live in whalebone huts in the frozen North, or the Maimed Men who ranged across in the Want and were scarred by terrible beasts and crippling frosts.

Drey called halt so softly it was like listening to a thought. Raif reined his horse along with the others. Beckoning everyone close, Drey positioned the entire party behind a dense growth of yearling pines. The Bluddroad lay below them, dark and straight like a fault in the earth. Raif looked west but could see no sign of the other parties. Ballic and his team must have doubled back before crossing, to prevent hoofprints and scent on the road.

As Raif looked up, he caught a glimpse of his brother's face. Drey's eyes were two frozen points on his face. Seeing them, recognizing the one emotion that lay behind them, Raif felt his bones turn to ice. Drey wasn't waiting to fight Bluddsmen; he was waiting to slay the men who killed his da.

There was nothing to do but wait. Minutes passed, then an hour, then another, then they had to cut the sheepskin muffles from the horses to prevent them from becoming agitated. Then, just as Bullhammer reached back in the saddle to fetch a feed bag for his restless stallion, a low rumbling sounded in the east.

Everyone tensed. Bullhammer straightened his back, took his reins in both hands. Bitty Shank stripped the mitts from his swordhand, revealing fingerless gloves beneath. Craw Bannering pressed thin lips together and turned his cool archer's eyes to the road. Drey made no bid for his hammer. Glancing back at his men, he sent one word with his eyes. *Easy*.

The sound grew louder and began to separate into recognizable parts. Horses' hooves, too many to number, thumped down upon the hard surface of the road. Bushes and tree limbs cracked like whips, dumping their loads of snow. Dogs yipped and barked, carts creaked, harness metal jingled, and above it all something lurched, clattered, and shuddered like a great and terrible engine of war. Raif and Drey exchanged a glance. The mist was as stringy as rotten cobwebs. It was hard to get a clear view of the road, almost impossible to see the bend the Bludd party would round any moment.

A pair of snow geese took flight from the near side of the bend, their calls harsh as saws drawn over metal. Raif's whole being was focused on controlling his horse. Her ears were flicking, and she had begun to pull on the reins. The scent of strange dogs made her nervous. Raif found himself wishing he were on Moose, not some flighty filly borrowed from Longhead at the last moment.

All thoughts evaporated from his mind as a gust of wind shifted the mist, allowing a clear view of the Bludd party as they rounded the bend below. Tiny hooks of fear pierced Raif's chest. Dark and full of purpose, the Bludd party took the road as if it were territory to be claimed like a foreign shore or an enemy camp. Riding stallions as thick necked and muscular as wolves, the foreriders held spears of black steel couched in horn casings that hung from the saddles along with their stirrups. Bull-headed dogs raced ahead of them, black and orange like hellhounds. A supply cart came into view, then a second one loaded with iron-banded kegs. Raif strained to see more, but mist poured down the slope, resettling in the lowest points. Briefly he snatched a glimpse of a team of horses flanked by a quad of heavily armed hammermen.

The grinding, shuddering noise became deafening. White smoke gouted in the air above the road. With one single fluid movement, Drey pulled his hammer from its sling. Raif noticed the metal had been abraded with steel wire. As he looked up, he met eyes with his brother. Drey looked so much like Tem for a moment that Raif felt his hand leave his bow and reach out.

*Easy*, Drey said without speaking. *Easy now*.

Feeling foolish and confused, Raif worked to conceal his emotions. He returned his hand to his bow and nocked his arrow against the plate. *We are Clan Blackhail, the first of all clans. We do not cower and we do not hide, and we will have our revenge*. The oldest version of the Blackhail boast ran through Raif's mind as he sighted his arrow. Angry words. And not for the first time, he wondered what had prompted them.

The Bludd party was directly below them now. The team of horses pulled some sort of lurching contraption that was partially obscured by mist. Raif counted seconds. The screech of wheel axles turning in their housings set his nerves on edge. The cold weighed on his bladder, making him painfully aware of its fullness. Looking ahead, he thought he saw a sliver of steel in the young growth to the far side of the road. Ballic's crew.

The Bludd dogs yelped and brayed, running rings around the trotting horses in their eagerness to be on their way. As the lead dog found something to sniff at on the road's north verge, the surrounding mist switched like a horse's tail, allowing Raif a clear view of the team and its load.

Breath hissed softly in his throat. The *size* of the thing. A team of horses pulled a war wagon as big as a house, with iron-spined wheels as tall as men and whole elm trunks for sides. The wheels plowed into the road, churning up mounds of dirt and snow. Great gasps of smoke vented from a copper chimney fitted high into the timbered roof, and the entire structure huffed and shuddered with every rut in the road. Raif had never seen anything like it in his life. It was like watching an entire roundhouse on the move.

"Raif. Pull out your flint." Key's voice was as low and ragged as the mist. "Bull. Hand him the hard liquor from your pack. Easy now. All of you."

Raif understood at once. No one had been expecting this thing, this cart as big as a building. No one knew what horrors were housed within it. The only thing to do was set it alight. Ballic the Red and Corbie Meese were probably thinking the same thing, but just in case they weren't, or just in case they missed, Drey was making plans. Raif tore the thumb from his left mitt and used it as a hood for his arrow. Bullhammer handed him a silver flask, his meaty hands warming the metal where he touched.

As Raif doused the thumbpiece in the clear amber-colored liquor, the lead dog caught whiff of the ambush party's scent. Its joyous yelping turned to a low, dangerous growl. Raif felt the sound echo in the soft inner tissue of his bones, then all hell broke loose on the road.

A salvo of arrows cut low through the mist, aimed for the foreriders' mounts. Animals squealed in terror as metal broadheads, barbed for lightness and snagging flesh, punctured horseflesh. Rearing up, they kicked and bucked, thrashing their heads from side to side and screaming. Their fear spread through the remaining Bludd animals like wildfire, yet even as other horses began to whiffle and stamp, their riders and draymen worked to calm them. A word spoken softly but firmly, a steadying hand on a neck or a shoulder, a squeeze with the thighs, and the Bluddsmen saved their mounts from panic.

The foreriders were quick to abandon their wounded horses, dismounting with heavy grace. Thudding onto the snow, they drew their ten-foot spears from their couching. All escaped injury, though with four massive horses kicking and screaming in the confined space of the road, it hardly seemed possible. Raif had no time to think on that before Corbie Meese, Toady Walker, and eight other hammermen blasted onto the road. Screaming at the top of their lungs, they rode wide of the standing spearmen, driving for the hammermen behind. As soon as they were clear of the spearmen, a second salvo of arrows shot north across the road. Most hit the panicking horses, spraying horse blood in red arcs, but one spearman took an arrow to his shoulder, and another lost a piece of his face. The injuries caused neither man to break formation, and as a single unit the four spearmen turned to pursue Corbie and his crew as they met steel with the Bludd hammermen. It was, Raif realized, the only possible thing they could do. Standing free like that, they were a bowman's prayer, but no bowman in the territories would shoot an arrow into a fray where his own men were fighting.

Raif worked at the alcohol-soaked thumbpiece, pulling it down so the metal point of the arrowhead peeked through at the tip. The screams of the horses were terrible to hear, and Raif tried to cut them from his mind. He had known all along that Ballic and his crew would target horses first.

"Raif. Shoot." Drey. No mention of what he was to shoot or why, no caution concerning taking such a shot at such a distance. Just an order. *No*—Raif positioned the flint and striker in his hand—it was more than that. By saying the little that he did, Drey assumed not only that his younger brother knew his mind, but also that he was capable of making such a shot without injuring Corbie or one of his men.

It was a sobering thought. Raif tipped the hooded arrow on an angle to catch sparks and struck the flintstone. The alcohol on the thumbpiece ignited with a soft ripping sound that distressed the filly. Raif didn't have to worry about stilling her, as Drey was already at her head, leaning over to calm her with soft words and gentle scratches.

Raising the flaming arrow to his bow, Raif switched his mind to the battle below. The remaining hammermen and swordsmen from both Corbie's and Ballic's parties were now fighting on level ground. Corbie Meese screamed at the top of his lungs as he whirled his hammer in a liquid circle above his head, his face purple with rage, his stewed leather gauntlets butcher red with blood. He was, Raif realized with a stab of quiet pride, a truly terrifying sight. It was the hammer dent on his head that did it. The Bluddsmen danced around him, reluctant to go hammer to hammer against a man who had taken such a blow and lived.

With a ghost of a smile on his face, Raif aimed his bow. The war wagon was a large and barely moving target. If it hadn't been for the mist and the men fighting about it, it would have been an easy shot. Raif took a breath, relaxed his grip on the bow, decided upon the upper quarter of the wagon wall as his target, then felt for the still line that would lead the arrow home. He did not reach inside the thing. The wagon was dead wood, and there was no question of calling it to him—after the day at the lick, he knew and accepted that now. To try to find its heart was a mistake that would cost him both accuracy and time.

Everything slipped away. The string creaked with strain, a good sound that brought saliva to Raif's mouth. The flames from the thumbpiece licked at his cheek. A second stretched to breaking. Then, suddenly, the mist cleared, the riders parted, and the line between the target and the bow became as broad and inviting as an open road. Raif lifted his fingers from the string, and the arrow shot toward its mark.

Hearing the soft *thuc* of the bowstring, feeling the rough hand of the recoil snap at his fingers, Raif knew he had been wrong. There *was* life in the wagon, inside it, and for a brief moment as the bowstring whipped air and his eye held the target, he felt hearts beating from within Dozens of them. Racing and skipping with fear.

*You can't call on arrow back.* That was the first thing Tem had ever taught him about shooting, and Raif finally knew what he meant. A bowman delivered his blow the moment his fingers left the string, not seconds later when the arrow sank its barbs into enemy flesh. The small distinction had never meant anything to him. Until now.

The sound of the impact didn't carry, but the flames blanket-rolled across the wagon wall, changing color from blue to yellow as they spread. The shot was perfectly placed, the alcohol fire hot enough to kindle hardwood, and the arrowhead sat snug between two elm logs, driving the flames deep. Even the wind helped, gusting along the wagon like air from a bellows. Within a minute the entire upper portion of the wagon was alight. Sheets of yellow flame rippled over the wood, spilling between cracks like molten metal and belching black, greasy smoke.

The flaming of the war wagon had a profound effect on the Bluddsmen. The drayman riding the team worked frantically to turn the horses, whipping and hollering, standing on his plate and smacking the horses' rumps. Bludd hammermen and spearmen moved into position around the wagon, defending its team and driver with hard focused force. Toady Walker fell from his horse as a lead-weighted hammer smacked into his spine. Within seconds a Bludd spearman had moved in to spike his guts.

"Raif. Craw. Cover us as we go down. Once we're there, move closer and shoot as you judge safe." Drey's voice was rough. His gloved hands pressed against the leather mount of his hammer. "Do not show yourselves. Bull, Bitty. You're with me."

Raif barely had time to nod before his brother turned his horse and cantered down the slope. Bullhammer and Bitty Shank flanked him. Bullhammer tore the oilskin, from his back as he descended, revealing his iron-banded breastplate and freeing his arms for the powerful hammer moves that had earned him his name.

Raif pulled a second arrow from his case. Below, the war wagon lurched backward As one of its rear wheels rolled off the road. Saplings snapped like chair backs as the wagon tumbled into the newgrowth, sending a wedge of flames and sparks shooting into the branches. The drayman worked the team, lashing horseflesh with his whip, but the wagon was trapped in the ditch. Raif could see the outline of the wagon door and the great metal stave that held it shut. As he watched, the saw the door shake, as if someone inside were pushing against it.

A bowstring hummed to Raif's left as Craw Bannering let an arrow fly, shooting at a swordsman who had moved forward to intercept Drey and his crew. The shot was sound, catching the swordsman high in the neck, dropping him where he stood. Bludd hammermen fought around him, their sable cloaks fluid as running oil, their hammers breaking up the last of the mist. Raif drew his bow, waited for a clear shot at one of them. His concentration was not good. Red and black, the angry blaze, of the war wagon kept catching his eye. The door continued to shake, yet still no one broke out.

Almost without thinking, Raif dipped his bow, aiming his

arrowhead at the wagon door. Imagining it was game to be shot, he *called* the wagon to him. A seam of hot pain shot between his eyes as he forced his sights to focus *beyond* the door. It was like staring into the mist all over again. His eyes ached. Seconds of blankness passed, then just as he was about to drop his bow, he felt the wild thumping of many hearts. Terror filled his mouth like blood.

Trapped. They were trapped inside the war wagon. Heat had sealed the iron bolt in place.

Shaking with the force of their terror, Raif let his bow fall slack. A sour metallic taste ringed his mouth. Glancing at Craw, he saw the black-haired bowman braced to take a second shot. With a furtive, close-body movement, Raif switched arrows, choosing a thick-bladed hunter shaped to take down a horse in a single strike. The weight was wrong for a bow the size and shape of Raif's—he kept it only to shoot from Drey's longbow—yet he raised it to the plate all the same. If he was careful and he drew enough power into the bow, it just might go where he planned.

It took him less than a moment to sight the bow. The last ropes of mist felt like a noose around his neck as he searched for the line between the tip of his arrow and the iron bolt of the war wagon. The belly of the bow shook along with his hands. He didn't dare think, didn't dare question what he was doing and why. The memory of the hell inside the wagon was too great. The line calmed him. Once it was set in his mind, his hands stilled. Gentle as a breath taken in sleep, he released the string.

The arrow split curls of fire and smoke as it raced toward its mark. Even from where he stood, Raif heard the harsh clang of metal striking metal. The arrow hit, then dropped. A moment was lost to smoke, and when Raif caught sight of the door once more, someone inside was beating hard against it. After three blows, the iron bolt gave and the door blasted open. Smoke poured out.

Raif tugged a hand across his face. He had no way of knowing if his arrow had done the job, yet strangely it did not matter. The door was open, and even as he looked on, people began clambering out. Hands held to their faces, backs bent, they coughed and screamed and ran.

It took Raif a moment to realize they were women and children.

He didn't believe it at first. This was supposed to be a war party—Mace Blackhail had said so. What business did children have with war? Yet even as he groped for a reasonable explanation, he began to realize there had been a mistake. This was no war party. The quad of heavily armed hammermen, the foreriders with their case-hardened spears, and the swordsmen with their blades of blue steel were here solely to guard the wagon. The Dog Lord wasn't moving troops to the Dhoonehouse, he was moving women and children.

*And Mace Blackhail knew it.*

The thought seized his mind so swiftly, it was almost as if someone had spoken it out loud. No one had questioned how Mace Blackhail had come upon the information for this ambush. Corbie Meese said he'd picked it up from stovehouse talk, yet how could anyone other than a Bluddsman know about the Dog Lord's plans? Most especially when those plans concerned the moving of kin? Raif shook his head. All possible answers left him cold.

"Raif! *Children*." Craw Bannering nudged his bow arm.

Raif nodded, feeling a bite of disloyalty as he feigned seeing the open wagon door for the first time. "We'd better get down there."

The snow on the road was red and pink with blood. Four horses had fallen, two others fled. Toady Walker's body had been trampled facedown into the snow. Banron Lye lay in a ditch just off the road. He wasn't moving. Dogs sank their teeth into his collar and sleeves, tearing away great strips of elkskin to get at flesh. All the remaining Hailsmen, including Ballic and his bowmen, were now fighting hand-to-hand on the open road. Black blood and spittle frothed from Corbie Meese's mouth, yet judging from the volume of his screams and the swift circles he cut with his hammer, he wasn't badly hurt.

Drey and Bullhammer had wasted no time driving themselves into the middle of the melee. They worked well together, their hammers as dull and ashen as charred logs, as they moved to outflank a Bludd swordsman who had just lost his mount. The spearmen were the worst danger. Fighting in tight formation back-to-back, they made it impossible for anyone to get near them for a blow.

Reining his horse thirty feet above the road, Raif pulled an arrow from his case. The dogs worrying Banron Lye were the first things to go. They were easy targets; once he had their hearts in his sights he didn't worry about hitting Banron or any other clansman by mistake. Down the dogs went, one after another, legs crumpling beneath them in the manner of all heart-killed beasts. The Bludd spearmen were a more difficult problem. Guarding the drayman and his team, they formed a knot of grizzled steel at the center of the road. Raif couldn't get a clear shot at any of them. Corbie Meese and Rory Cleet were too close.

Sweat slid down Raif's neck. The war wagon roared with flames, melting the surrounding snow with snake hisses, dripping yellow fire onto the undergrowth, and setting whole runs of stone pines alight. Fire poured along the team's harness, and the drayman began hacking at the leather traces with his sword to free the horses. Raif could no longer see what was happening at the back of the wagon. Out of the corner of his eye, he was aware of people running to high ground through the trees.

It was hard to focus on the spearmen, harder still to call them to him in the split seconds when the way was clear. He loosed one arrow and it went wide, glancing off a Bluddsman's hammerguard. Cursing, he tried to control the fast beating of his heart. Rory Cleet howled as a spear ripped along his thigh. For a moment Raif saw white lines of bared sinew and bone, then blood welled over Rory's flesh and everything turned red. Face pale and shiny with sweat, hand pressed to the wound, Rory wheeled his horse.

Raif drew his bow, ready to let an arrow loose the moment Rory broke free and cleared the way. The spearman who had inflicted the wound moved forward for a second blow. He was armed for heavy marching, not for war, and wore a breastpiece of elkhide boiled in wax. His leather-bound topnotch swung like a sling as Raif caught his heart in his sights. A strong heartbeat slammed against his mind, shocking like a physical blow, knocking all thoughts clean away. Raif didn't need them: His eye knew to hold the target and his fingers knew when to release the string, and it was over in less than an instant.

Nausea bent him double as the spearman fell. His vision blurred, and sour acids from his stomach burned his throat. He lost his grip on the bow and let it drop to the snow beneath him, not trusting himself to rock sideways and catch it as it fell.

He shook his head, concentrated hard on keeping his seat. Killing men wasn't the same as game. He could do it, but it wasn't the same.

"Sevrance! Pick up your bow and ride down the survivors! *Now!*"

Raif flinched at the harshness of the voice. It sounded as if it were coming from behind him, but he knew now wasn't a good time to turn in the saddle and look. It took all he had to sit his horse.

A horse and rider bore down through the pines. Raif saw a hail of kicked-up snow, then felt something jab against the base of his spine.

"I *said*, go and run down the survivors."

Mace Blackhail. The new-made Hail chief. *Here?* Raif's thoughts came in clumsy lumps. How had he managed to catch up?

"Craw. Go and pull Drey and Bitty from the road. I need all three of you to ride east through the woods and pick off survivors. I'll have no Bludd breeders and bitches walking free from this ambush. Now go."

Raif spat to clean the metal from his mouth as Craw Bannering headed down the slope. Pulling himself to his full saddle height, he turned to look at the Wolf. Mace Blackhail's eyes were the color of frozen urine, his lips a hook of pale flesh. Wearing a cloak of slate gray fisher fur over a mail coat inset with wolf teeth, he sat high atop the blue roan, contemplating Raif. After a moment his jaws sprang apart. "I am your chief. You have taken First Oath. Do my bidding."

Raif flinched. He wished his thoughts were clearer. As he reached down to collect his bow, Mace Blackhail kicked the roan forward, ramming the filly's belly and trampling Raif's bow underfoot. The filly caught the sharp end of a spur along her shoulder and reared up, squealing in pain. Raif fought to keep his seat, pulling hard on the horse's mouth. By the time he had calmed her, the blue roan had stamped the bow into splinters.

"I've changed my mind," Mace said, starting down the slope. "Use your halfsword on the runaways instead."

Raif watched him go. The edges of his vision were blurred, and he could still feel the spearman's heartbeat rattling away inside his skull.

As soon as Mace Blackhail reached the road, he began working to take control of the battle. He moved quickly, and although he wasn't a powerful fighter like Corbie Meese, Bullhammer, or Drey, he was clever with his sword. Within a minute he had taken down one of the three remaining spearmen.

Drey and Bitty were slow to pull off the road, both clearly unhappy at the order to hunt down runaways. Seeing them move into the trees, Raif kicked the filly after them. He didn't spare a glance for his ruined bow. It was a relief to have it gone.

The war wagon collapsed inward as Raif rode past it, sucking air from his lungs. The heat was fierce. Bits of flaming matter floated through the stone pines like wasps. One of the Bludd dogs ran across the filly's path, howling and frothing at the mouth, its black-and-orange coat alight. Raif found its pain surprisingly easy to ignore. He hardly knew what he was doing. Thoughts came and then slipped from his head, and no matter how many times he swallowed and spat, the copper taint of blood stayed in his mouth.

He nearly rode past the first woman. Pressed against the trunk of an old growth pine, she held still until almost the last moment, then lost her nerve and broke into a run. If she hadn't moved, he would not have seen her. A long braid of golden hair thumped against her back as she sprinted away from the road. Her cloak was dark red with gold stitching around the hem, and her leather softboots had been sewn and dyed to match. She ran fast but straight, failing to take advantage of the trees, and the filly soon outpaced her. Raif drew Tem's halfsword. "You have it," Drey had said that first evening when they'd returned to the roundhouse. "I have his coat and his lore. It's only fitting you have his sword."

Raif rode the woman down. The thrill of the chase woke something in him, and he cut the air with his sword, growing accustomed to its balance and reach. A drift of new snow collapsed beneath the woman's weight as she stepped across a shallow draw, causing her to sink and lose her footing. Hearing the filly closing distance, she turned to face man and horse. Long strands of golden hair had worked free of her braid, framing a face hot with fright and exertion.

Seeing her, Raif realized she wasn't a woman at all, just a girl, a year or so younger than he himself. Her pale eyes widened as he raised his sword. Shivering in small bursts, she brought a hand to her throat as he approached. A deer lore was fastened about her neck on a strip of birch bark. Her knuckles were black with soot and smoke.

Tem's sword grew heavy in Raif's hand. Girls at home used birch bark for their lores. It was said to bring luck in finding a husband.

The girl shrank back, closing her fist around her lore. She had a small dimpled scar above her lip, the sort of mark that was left by a dog bite. When she noticed Raif's gaze upon it, her hand moved to cover it up.

Raif knew then that he would not kill her. She was too much like the girls at home, thinking that whenever someone looked at her it was always to find fault. Ridiculously, the scar made him want to kiss her.

Unable to look the girl in the eye any longer, he turned the filly and rode away. Bludd breeders and bitches, Mace had called them. What words would he use for the children?

A series of high-pitched screams led Raif to a clearing where Drey, Bitty Shank, and Craw Bannering had rounded up two dozen women and children. All were dressed finely, in thick wool cloaks, sable hoods, and softskin boots. Some women carried babes at their breasts, others hid small children behind their skirts. One woman, a tall matron with a braid that reached her hips and eyes as blue as ice, stood proud and stared her attackers down.

Realizing that Drey intended to cause no harm to the

women, simply capture them, Raif exhaled. He felt light-headed with relief. The madness of the day was finally coming to an end. All he wanted to do was roll in his blanket and sleep. He didn't want to think about the Bludd spearman, or the girl with the dog scar, or Toady Walker's horse-trampled body.

Chest shaking with exhaustion, head throbbing to a dead man's heartbeat, Raif trotted over to join his brother. The Bludd women watched him, their faces crusted with soot and snow, their hands forming knots against their skirts.

Drey's face was grim. "Pull up your swordarm."

Before Raif could obey the order, Mace Blackhail broke through the trees on the roan. His broadsword rested against his dogskin pants, a thin line of liver blood bleeding along the blade. He looked first at Raif, then Drey. "What are you waiting for? I said slay them."

No muscle on Drey's face moved. From the near side of the glade, Bitty looked his way, waiting to see what Drey would do.

"They killed our chief in cold blood," Mace Blackhail said, walking the roan forward, his yellow-and-black eyes fixed solely on Drey. "They slaughtered your father in his tent. Bitty's brothers were taken where they stood. And just five days ago, they sent cowlmen into our woods to slay our women and children on home ground. Yes, they shot Shor Gormalin, but don't be mistaken: If Raina or Effie had been riding that trail, it would have been they who rode home dead.

"Bludd broke faith first, Drey. Not us. If we let these bitches and their litters go, then both our fathers' deaths go unavenged." Mace Blackhail wiped his blade clean against his pants as he spoke. "We are Blackhail, the first amongst clans, and our chief's life is worth a hundred of their women's."

Mace Blackhail stared at Drey with such force, it was as if he were physically pushing against him. Drey didn't blink or move, but something in his face changed. Raif couldn't tell what his brother was thinking, didn't know what the sudden lack of light in his eyes meant, but words Drey had spoken on the journey home from the badlands slipped into Raif's mind like cold poison.

*We'll make Clan Bludd pay for what they did, Raif. I swear it.*

Raif had no way of knowing whether Mace Blackhail saw the answer he wanted in Drey's face or not, but *something* made Mace move. Kicking bronze spurs into the roan's belly, he began the charge. Light ran down his newly cleaned sword like water, gleaming with all the cold colors from white to blue. He howled as he rode, baring his teeth and drawing low in the saddle like something not quite human. The Bludd women and children began to run, scrambling awkwardly through knee-deep snow.

Afterward, when he thought back on it, Raif realized that by forcing them to run, Mace Blackhail changed them from wives and children and turned them into game instead. Drey Sevrance, Bitty Shank, and Craw Bannering could not have slain the women and children where they stood—Raif believed that completely. He had to. But Mace Blackhail had all the inborn cunning of his lore. A wolf hunts nothing that does not move, and when words failed him, Mace Blackhail fell back on instinct, changing slaughter to a chase.

Raif felt its pull. Tired and headsick as he was, part of him *wanted* to go after them, run them down, hack them at the knees with his sword, and bring them to ground. He wanted it so badly, the saliva in his mouth ran clean. The children shrieked and cried, herding close to their mothers as if somehow they could save them. Clumsy things, they were, foolishly heading into thicker drifts, bereft of even an animal's sense to pull out from the snow and head for the shelter of the trees. The women were worse, stopping to pull one another up when they stumbled or fell behind, lifting children too heavy to carry. They acted like a flock of mindless sheep. Covered in snow as they were, they even *looked* like sheep.

When Bitty Shank rode alongside a thin mewling child whose cheeks were showing the first yellow blush of frostbite and plowed his blade into the child's shoulder, forcing him under his horse, Raif felt a hot surge of excitement take his chest. The thumping in his head changed to a drumbeat, and the weariness in his bones shifted into something else. He wanted to join Bitty and take his share of the game.

The sight of Drey stopped him dead: Drey with his hammer whirling above his head, his eyes sunk deep into their sockets, and his lips pulled back to his gums. *Drey.* He was chasing a young mother and her two small children, and every muscle on his face and neck pressed against his skin like bone. Raif felt shocked to his core. His raven lore cooled against his skin, quick as red-hot metal plunged into snow.

Sobered as surely as if someone had slapped him in the face, Raif took an arrow from his case and reached to his saddlebag for his bow. He was going to bring down Drey's horse, heart-kill the beast, make it drop from under him.

Gone. The bow wasn't there. Raif swore as he remembered what Mace Blackhail had done to it. He couldn't understand why he'd just sat by and let him do it. What was wrong with him? Why hadn't he got angry? Raif shook his head. It didn't matter. He was angry now.

Kicking the filly into a gallop, he cut across the glade. A killing field of sounds filled his ears: terrible wails and screams and panting, the crack of severed bones, and the thick liquid gurgle of blades yanked free of flesh. Children rushed before him, bare hands clutching at their hair and faces, hoods and mittens lost in the chase. Mace Blackhail rode through them like the shadow of a Stone God, forcing them to move, flee, *run*. Any who didn't were cut down and then trampled, their bodies driven deep into the snow.

"*Drey!*" Raif screamed at the top of his voice as he drew close to the cut bank where his brother had cornered the young mother and her children. "*Stop!*"

Drey looked round. Momentarily his hammer slowed in his hand. He looked at Raif a long moment, a trickle of saliva rolling down his chin, then he turned and drove his hammer into the side of the woman's face. A sickening crack split the air as the woman's neck broke and her head twisted to a place where no amount of sideways glances would ever take it.

The two small children screamed. Tearing and clutching

at each other, heads and shoulders knocking together, they tried to squeeze themselves into one. A shudder worked through Raif's body, rattling his bones like pebbles in a jar. Wrapping the reins around his fingers, he bore down on his brother, setting his filly on a path to smack into Drey's horse. The filly turned at the last moment to save herself, and Raif's shoulders slammed into Drey's side. Drey was knocked forward in the saddle, his hammer losing momentum and crashing into his thigh. Furious, Drey shoved Raif with all his might.

"Get away from me! You heard Mace Blackhail. We weren't first to break faith."

Raif smashed the heel of his hand into Drey's hammer arm. "Run!" he called to the children. "*Run!*"

The oldest child simply stared at him, and the younger one sat down in the snow and began shaking his mother's arm as if she were asleep and needed waking. Raif wheeled the filly around, preparing to scare the children into running. As he dug his heels into horseflesh, a fist of pain exploded in his lower back. Breath rushed from his lungs in a harsh gust, leaving a sucking emptiness in his chest. His vision shrank to two dots, and he grasped at air and bridle leather as he fell into a tunnel of spiraling darkness where the snow was as hard as glass.

HE CAME TO. A spasm of pain ripped along his backbone, sharp as if someone had gouged a rusted nail down his spine. Rolling over, he coughed blood into the snow. Something warm pushed against his ear, forcing him to twist back and confront whatever it was: the filly, her great wet nostrils pulling in his breath, testing if he were still alive. Raif raised a hand and pushed her nose away. The effort cost him. He lost seconds as he dealt with the pain. Slowly his eyes grew accustomed to the glare of snow. Three dark forms, impacted in the snowdrift like rocks, broke the line of perfect whiteness. A pitifully small amount of blood stained the surrounding snow.

Raif closed his eyes. His heart grew unbearably light in his chest. Both children had been younger than Effie.

Sounds far behind him told of a hunt still running. Those

still alive had little breath to scream, and hoarse cries and sobs were almost drowned out by the noise of hooves churning snow. Pushing himself up on his elbows, Raif caught sight of Corbie Meese and Ballic the Red entering the clearing from the west. Blood had turned their horses and armor black. When they saw what was happening they exchanged a small, worried glance. Hope surged in Raif's chest. Corbie and Ballic were good men; they would do what was right.

"Stop her! She's getting away!" The call came from Mace Blackhail, who rode across the glade toward the two men, chasing a heavyset Bluddswoman before him. Mace Blackhail could have taken the woman himself—she was struggling in the snow less than thirty paces ahead of him—but that wasn't what he wanted. Raif knew that at once. The Wolf needed to share the responsibility for the killing. He needed the two senior clansmen to run with his pack.

Raif watched for a while, long enough to see Corbie and Ballic succumb to the lure of the chase and move swiftly to head off the enemy that Mace Blackhail was intent on driving toward them, then turned away. Softly he called for the filly. Leaning heavily against her, he rose and brushed himself clean of snow. His back burned. When he probed it with his fingers, tears filled his eyes. At the very least he would have a hammer-size bruise there tomorrow.

Not trusting himself to mount, he took the filly by the reins and led her northwest from the glade. He had to get away. Suddenly he didn't know his brother or his clan.

# FOURTEEN

## Escape

*I MAY STOP BY and visit the Knife tonight. What's it to you?* Katia's words echoed in Ash's mind. The tiny dark-haired maid had said them four hours earlier, and Ash stood in the shadows behind her chamber door and waited to see if they were true. Her back ached from standing still for so long, but she didn't dare risk moving away. Barring opening the door and checking for herself, listening was the only way she had of knowing for sure if Marafice Eye had left his post. She didn't want the Knife catching her peeking around the door. It would only make him suspicious. No. Better by far to keep her position and wait.

*Katia has been telling me how your charcoal brazier was choked with ashes the other night, almost-daughter. You haven't been burning anything upon it, have you? I'm sure I don't need to tell you how very dangerous such a thing would be.*

Ash shivered. Penthero Iss had visited her room late last night, and although he'd said many different things on many different subjects, she was sure all he had really come to say was that he knew about the extra cinders in the brazier. He was sly like that. What the whole thing really meant was that from now on he would be watching her more closely, as he was now well aware that she was up to something improper. Ash cursed Katia under her breath. Cinders in the brazier? Was there no secret, no matter how inane, that the girl wouldn't tell?

Frowning, she turned her attention to the door. Little mouse steps pattered on the stone beyond. Something creaked. Silence . . . then a bright laugh quickly muffled. Katia. Katia was on the other side of the door, talking with the Knife.

*Please take him to your room, Katia. Please.* Ash hated herself for wishing it, hated the thought of Marafice Eye's massive hands pressing against Katia's spine, yet she needed the little maid to distract the Knife. She had to leave Mask Fortress. Tonight. And the only way she could slip from her chamber undetected was if Katia lured the Knife away for a bedding.

*Bedding.* Ash rubbed a hand over her eyes, trying to dispel the image the word showed her. Bedding wasn't the right word for it at all.

Feeling her cheeks grow hot, she risked taking one more step toward the door. Marafice Eye could speak quietly when he chose to, and she couldn't hear his voice, though a conversation *was* taking place. Katia spoke, her voice low for moments, then high with excitement as she continually forgot the need for secrecy. Ash caught the words *kiss* and *gift*. A long silence passed, and when it broke rough breaths could clearly be heard.

"Witch." Marafice Eye's voice cut through the wood. The word had a nasty edge to it, and Ash felt the flesh on her arms pucker. Sounds followed, a whole lot of them, then two sets of footsteps padded along the hall. Ash rested her head against the door. They were gone, but she didn't like it one bit. Was it her imagination, or did the lighter set of footsteps appear to drag? Knowing such thoughts would only slow her down, she pushed them aside. This wasn't the first time Katia had been with the Knife. The little maid could look after herself.

Ash moved around her chamber, checking the body-shaped lump of cushions beneath the sheets, pulling on her thickest, plainest cloak, and opening the shutters so that those who eventually discovered she was gone would think she had somehow managed to escape by lowering herself down the Cask's outer wall and so misdirect the search. Stopping at the brazier, she raised the brass lid and thrust a mitted hand into the black, powdery soot. The soot was hot as she worked it into her hair, hot and itchy as sin. It caught in her throat and made her eyes tear, so she scrunched up her face until she was done. When she opened her eyes a minute later by the mirror, she saw a strange girl staring back. Matt black hair did not suit her at all, making her face look like something preserved in wax. Abruptly she turned away. It would have to do.

What to take with her? What would she need? She had thought everything through beforehand, thinking of little else for the past six days, but for some reason she had avoided thinking about what she would have to take. Everything in her room belonged to Iss. Oh, he said it was hers and made a point of giving her many pretty and inexpensive gifts, but when it came down to it he took them back at will. She'd seen the truth of that herself these past few weeks, as Katia and Caydis Zerbina plucked objects from her room on his say. She wasn't Iss' real daughter at all; he never let her forget that. *Almost-daughter* was what he called her. Almost daughter was what she was.

Foundling, Ash told herself. Left outside Vaingate to die.

Angry now, she felt less inclined to leave empty-handed. That silver brush on the dresser would fetch a price at Alms Market, and the pewter cloak pin was set with some kind of red jewel that might be worth something to someone. She snatched them up and bundled them into her cloak lining before her resolve had chance to turn. What else? Spinning, she examined her chamber. Horn books bound with pigskin, their library chains still attached, would be worth a good few coins apiece, but Ash quickly rejected them. Too heavy. Too noisy. If she tried to sell them, the chains would surely give her away.

Abruptly she turned toward the door. She didn't have time to conduct an inventory of her chamber. It was leave now or lose her chance.

*If only I could be sure.*

No. Ash shook her head so hard a cloud of black soot wafted from her hair. She had to go. Stay and she would be a fool, and anything that happened to her would be no one's fault but her own. She was a foundling; no one would care for her but herself. Penthero Iss did not have her best interests at heart. Worse than that, he planned on taking her to the Splinter and . . . Ash hesitated, took a breath. Truth was, she didn't know what her foster father intended to do. She only knew that her belongings had been taken to the Splinter, the second most powerful man in Spire Vanis had been set to watch her door like a common foot soldier, and every morning while she washed her face and dressed her hair, her maid rifled through her underclothes, looking for blood.

Ash took a final look around the room. None of those were the real reason she had to go, though. Whatever was trapped inside the Splinter, aching with hate and need so great that all she had to do was put her hand against the door to feel it, was what finally forced her into action. Just the memory of the thing's desperate, unspeakable misery was enough to turn her stomach to lead.

It wanted what she had. And Ash March, Foundling and almost-daughter, wasn't prepared to give it one whit.

Steeling herself, she pushed against the door. Cold bit her like a snake, and she had to fight the urge to step back. Weeks of poor sleep had worn her down, and little things like the constant cold in Mask Fortress now affected her more than they used to. Almost as if she were about to plunge into water, not darkness, Ash took a breath, held it in, and stepped into the corridor. It was deathly quiet. One greenwood torch smoked above the stairs. No light at all reached beneath Katia's door.

Ash moved quickly. She had already lost minutes to indecision, and she knew from observation how little time it took Marafice Eye to do his business. He might step from Katia's room any moment, hands tugging at the leather straps on his pants, small mouth still wet with Katia's saliva.

*Promise to take me with you when you go.*

Katia's words made the heat come back to Ash's face. It was the only serious promise she had ever made in her life, and although she had chosen words to deliberately mislead the little maid, she felt no better for it. After tonight Katia would find herself back in the kitchens, and that was the one place in the fortress she didn't want to be.

*Better the kitchens than where I go.* Hardening herself against emotion, Ash rushed down the stairs. Tonight was Slaining Night, and the Rive Watch would be out in force, patrolling the city and keeping order. Brothers-in-the-watch would be thin on the ground within the fortress.

Slaining Night was the oldest of the Gods Days, and people celebrated it only after dark. Ash was not really sure what the festival marked. Her foster father said it was a celebration of the founding of Spire Vanis, marking the erection of the first strongwall at the base of Mount Slain by the Bastard Lord Theron Pengaron. It sounded reasonable enough, and people *did* warm rocks from Mount Slain in their hearths or charcoal burners, yet Ash had heard other things said. Old servants in Mask Fortress talked about death and sealing darkness and keeping old evils in their place. Ash had even heard that the name Slaining Night had nothing to do with Mount Slain at all and that in some cities to the east it was called by its true name instead: Slaying Night.

Ash frowned into the darkness. What in the Maker's name

was she doing? Tonight was quite frightening enough without digging up a lot of old nonsense to frighten herself even more. Sometimes she could be as dim as a lamp trimmer. Tonight was her best chance of escaping from Mask Fortress. She had spent all day hoping Katia would lure the Knife from her door, and now that she had gotten her wish and was well under way, she had to keep her mind to the task in hand.

Setting her jaw in place, she approached the last run of stairs. A graymeet bench and its accompanying alcove created a trap for shadows on the landing. Torches were sparse, as any flame without a Slain Stone at its base was considered ill luck tonight. Ash shivered. Penthero Iss probably hated that. He hated the old ways and the old traditions—anything that spoke of Spire Vanis's barbaric beginnings and past.

Hearing footsteps below, she slipped into the graymeet alcove to wait until whoever caused them passed. The limestone wall was as cold as iron against her back. The stone bench, with its hard seat and sculpted backpiece, couldn't look less inviting to sit on. Funny to think that grangelords and their ladies had once sat here and flirted, their golden wine cooling as they stole kisses and slid their hands beneath silk. All gone now. Penthero Iss had seen to that. He claimed to be a man who liked culture and art and high things, yet although he tore down or put an end to many things that had been common in the fortress in Borhis Horgo's day—dances held in the barbaric light of a burning pyre, death duels fought with broadblades in the quad, and the yearly slaying of a thousand beasts to mark winter's end—he seldom introduced anything new in their place. Penthero Iss seemed more concerned with destruction than creation.

Chilled, Ash slipped from the graymeet and took the last steps down to ground level. The footsteps faded into the distance, and she guessed that a single brother-in-the-watch was making his rounds of the Cask. That meant she had only a few minutes before he appeared again.

The black oak door and its gate were open and raised. Even though Ash knew brothers-in-the-watch used the gate constantly throughout the night to move between the Red

Forge and the Cask, it didn't stop her from feeling relieved when her booted feet sank into snow. Wind ripped the cloak from her chest, driving the metal fastening against her throat. Tears stung her eyes as she forced the door closed and stepped into the shadows close to the wall. The snow was old and slippery, polished to ice by the winds of Mount Slain.

It was not dark. The Red Forge was kept burning through the night, and the red light from the forge fire combined with lamplight from the three occupied towers to make the snow glow like human skin. The Horn was especially bright. The most intricately worked of the four towers, with its iron outwork and lead cladding, was positioned due west of the Cask. Katia said that the Lord of the Seven Granges was holding a gathering there tonight. *Wicked it is, miss. Right wicked! There'll be prostitutes and shaven women and worse!*

Ash edged along the west gallery wall, heading in the direction of the Horn. The faint, tinny sound of muffled music grazed her ears. Singing followed, then high tinkling laughter, then the wind blasted it all away.

Ash fought with her cloak. "Thirteen," she whispered softly to herself for no reason. Thirteen doors and gateways led out onto the quad. As a child she had sat on the practice court and counted them. She could recall a time when twelve of the thirteen had been in use, but then Penthero Iss had shut down the entire east gallery and sealed off the Splinter, and now only eight doors were left. Eight. And the Rive Watch had keys to them all.

Directly opposite, set deep within the carved limestone facade of the east gallery, lay the boarded and defaced Shrine Door. The door, which led down to a small crypt once used by the Forsworn, was made of wood that had been ported all the way from the Far South and was gray and hard as nails. It had defied defacing by Spire-made chisels and blades and had been painted with a grotesque likeness of the Killhound instead. The bird leered at Ash from across the quad, its sexual organs red and swollen, not like a bird's at all. Ash could not remember a time when the door was unmarked. In Borhis Horgo's day the knights who named themselves the Forsworn because they renounced all prior oaths upon entering the order had moved freely about Spire Vanis. They had helped Horgo defeat Rannock Hews at Hound's Mire; and forty years later Iss had expelled them for it. Like everyone else, Ash had heard the tales about the twelve old and infirm knights who had fled to the crypt during the expulsions, sending messages to Penthero Iss, begging for asylum. Iss had supposedly granted their request, commanding carpenters to seal the Shrine Door and the crypt's three small windows, interring the men alive.

Abruptly Ash took her gaze from the door. Suddenly everything she looked at seemed to be warning her to turn back, to return to her chamber by the fastest route and put all thoughts of leaving behind her. It was unnervingly easy to imagine herself in a room built of stone with no way out.

No. No. *No.* Ash fought the fear before it came. Tonight or never, she told herself, deliberately increasing her pace.

Ahead a pale slash of light marked the stable door, drawn together but not yet closed for the night. Lying halfway between the Cask and the Horn, the stables were her intended destination.

As she headed for the light source, she heard the Cask door creak open behind her. Not daring to look around, she stopped dead. Her heart thumped like a cracked bell in her chest. *Remember the hares*, she told herself. *Only things that move get hunted.*

Sounds were difficult to catch in the wind. Ash heard nothing she could put a name to at first. It could be a routine patrol, a brother-in-the-watch changing guard, servants bringing spitted meat and kegs of black beer to the Horn. Surely the fact that no one was shouting and running was good? Ash thought it highly likely that news of her escape would be greeted by something harsher than a softly creaking door.

Having waited for over a minute, she risked glancing back. The Cask door was closed. No one was in sight. The chains holding the gate raised were still. Satisfied, she carried on toward the stables.

Sounds of music and laughter from the Horn grew louder. A side door opened as she watched, and a fat man dressed in shiny silk stumbled out. Bending double, he promptly vomited against the wall. Ash didn't stop. The man was too drunk to notice anything moving in the shadows behind his back.

A half-moon rode low over Mount Slain, casting a well-defined shadow for the Splinter. Ash tried not to look at the ice-bound tower, preferring to watch steam rise from the fat man's stomach contents, ice crystals form on her boots—*anything* rather than the Splinter itself. It was foolishness of the worst kind, yet she couldn't help herself. To look meant to think, and Ash didn't want to turn any portion of her mind that way. Not now, while she was this close.

Paces away from the massive crossbeamed door of the stables, she stepped as quietly as she could. The dry, saw-dusty odor of hay and oats mingled with the stench of horse sweat and urine. Ash was glad of smells that had names, rather than the strange, slightly chemical odor that blew with the wind from Mount Slain. Rubbing her eyes to clear away the last traces of wind tears, she padded to the door's edge. All was quiet, and after a moment she braced herself and peeked inside.

Master Haysticks and two grooms sat on wooden crates with their backs to the door, drinking something hot from pewter tankards and playing blocks with the hard focused attention of men serious about their game. The stone floor was brushed clean and all the horses were boxed. A pair of safe-lamps hung from brass pegs on the wall above Master Haysticks' head, their horn guards yellow as an old nag's teeth.

Ash didn't pause to take a breath before entering. She had to risk this. The stables were her best chance—she had known that from the moment she had decided to go. The gate beyond the stables was the most used and the least checked. The brothers-in-the-watch who manned it were more interested in who was going in than coming out. Those who entered through the stable gate were usually tradesmen or deliverymen or fellow brothers-in-the-watch. Grange-lords, petty gentry, rich merchants, and anyone else who thought enough of themselves to worry about appearances always used one of the other gates, preferring to call grooms to lead their horses away.

Master Haysticks and the two grooms did not hear Ash

enter. A groom with a neck as red and shiny as a loin of beef had just thrown the blocks, and Master Haysticks and the second groom were studying the lay of the wood. They did not look pleased. Loin Neck had thrown a good hand, and Ash could tell from the shell-like clink of coinage that money was riding on the wood.

She took a moment to recover from the ravages of the wind and cold. The stables were dim despite the two safe-lamps, and sounds of horses blowing, feeding, flicking their tails, and snoring were comforting to her ears. She liked horses. After a moment she began edging toward the long line of horse stalls that lay directly across from where the men sat gaming.

She had to get to the far door. The stables were the reason the brothers-in-the-watch manning the gate were lax; they knew that whoever presented themselves for leavetaking had already passed through the stables and therefore the inspection of the stablemaster and his grooms. Ash had thought this through. She wouldn't stand a chance at any other gate. Brothers-in-the-watch were on guard day and night. They asked questions and would call a commanding officer rather than risk letting anyone of uncertain credentials pass. Why, the west gate alone was manned by a full sept and lit by so many torches that Katia said that all the snow for thirty paces melted.

Ash sucked in her cheeks. If there was any way to leave Mask Fortress other than through one of its four gates, she wished she knew it. Climbing over battlements and roofs was out: She had broken her arm falling against an iron siege guard when she was six. She knew just how treacherous the walls of Mask Fortress, with their iced-up stonework, murder holes, and spiked embrasures, could be.

"Hey! That throw doesn't count. Bloody rat over there turned the tally." Master Haysticks' voice rose in anger. "Throw again or I'll have you on dung duty for a week."

"'S not my fault the rat—"

"Throw again!"

Sounds of crates creaking and grown men huffing muffled the click of Ash's bones as she crouched close to the floor. Shadows deepened as she crawled toward the line of stalls that ran the length of the stables. Every stall in the stables had dividing walls that came to an end a full foot above the floor. Once a week the stables were sluiced clean, and the gap between the walls and the floor was needed to allow all the horse muck, shed hair, and moldering grain to be carried away.

Tucking her head close to her body, Ash ducked under the wooden divide and into the first stall. It *had* to be safer than iced-up stone.

A black gelding stood asleep close to the door, its legs locked in position, its eyes closed and tail slack. The sound of hay snapping beneath Ash's chest woke it instantly. Ash held herself perfectly still as the large, liquid brown eye of the horse regarded her. The gelding dipped its head and smelled her breath. Dust itched in Ash's nostrils and hay stalks scratched against her cheek as she worked to control the impulse to shy away. The gelding's forehooves were big as war hammers, shiny with neat's-foot oil, and shod with iron.

The gelding whickered and shook his head. Prodding Ash with his nose, it waited to see what she would do. Ash glanced ahead. The stone manger for the feed and the leather water bucket were pushed hard against the back wall. To keep as far away from the gelding's hooves as possible, she would have to scramble over them to reach the next stall. Gathering the ends of her cloak to her chest so they wouldn't snag on splinters, she began crawling forward . . . slowly.

*Only a short stretch*, she told herself, gaze darting between the next divide and the gelding. It was a good horse, she was sure of that. But it was used to seeing rats, not humans, crawling in its stall after dark.

Scrambling over the stone manger proved difficult and painful. Ash struck her shin on a sharp edge, and although she didn't dare spend a minute inspecting the damage, she knew there was blood. The gelding watched her. Any time she moved too fast, it changed positions, stamping its hooves onto the dung-packed stone. Ash's heart beat unsteady in her chest. The skin on her face felt too tight. Every second she expected to hear a cry rip through the fortress and the night come alive with armed men and light. Where was Marafice Eye? Was he back outside her chamber? Had Katia slipped inside to check on her one last time before she slept?

"*Damn!*" Ash cursed under her breath as her elbow caught the water bucket, causing it to tip over onto the stone. The floor slanted forward slightly, and the water ran straight under the stall door.

"Damn black's knocked its bucket again!" came Master Haysticks' voice. "Skimmer, spread some new hay before the damp gets in his hooves."

Free of the stone manger and the bucket, Ash pushed herself through to the next stall. Her cloak caught on a bit of wood, and just as she tugged it free the black gelding's door swung open. Ash froze. The groom called Skimmer whistled as he spread fresh hay. The gelding, angry by now at all the disturbances, snorted and kicked. Skimmer swore. Master Haysticks and the other groom laughed. Ash thought she heard the faint click of wooden blocks, then Skimmer closed the door.

"Bloody black's a devil," he said. "That's the last time I go in there after dark." He crossed back to the crates. "Hey! Thems blocks been handled! They weren't laying like that afore I fetched the hay!"

A lively argument broke out between the men, where Master Haysticks and the second groom swore by every blind dog that had ever frozen to death on a street corner that they hadn't even *looked* at the blocks, let alone handled them.

Ash turned her attention to the stall she was in. Apart from a harness of fine dark leather hung from a dog hook next to the door, it was empty. The red-and-black insignia of the Killhound on the Iron Spire was stamped across the noseband, indicating that a member of the Watch normally stabled his horse here. Ash didn't permit herself a sigh of relief, though she *was* relieved. Most of the Watch were out in the city, patrolling the Slaining Night crowds, and that meant many of the stalls would be empty.

She moved quickly after that. The argument over blocks raged nicely—Master Haysticks' voice rising from mild indignation to thundering outrage as Skimmer continued to accuse him of cheating—and the sharp voices helped mask all the little noises Ash made as she crawled from stall to stall. A fair number of stalls were empty, as she had predicted. The more crusted in hay, horse muck, and horsehair she became, the more the horses seemed to accept her. Apart from a nasty clip from a pregnant mare who was sleeping lying down and struggled to stand as her stall was invaded, Ash avoided further injury. The secret, she found, was to turn on her back, then stay perfectly still for a moment, offering up the soft flesh of her throat, until the horse had smelled and inspected her. They usually let her pass after that.

Finally she found herself in the stall nearest the far door, sharing space with a one-year-old filly who was bright, alert, and not the slightest bit sleepy. The filly was wary at first, but after a few minutes of continuous sniffing, she began nudging Ash's cloak for treats.

"Sorry, girl," mouthed Ash, strangely affected by the gentleness and beauty of the young mare. "No treats tonight."

After a quick peep under the stall door had assured her that Master Haysticks and his grooms were too caught up in their argument to notice someone slipping through the outer door, she mouthed her farewell to the filly and slid under the wall.

Slipping into the deepest shadows, following the line of the stable wall, she worked her way toward the exterior door. The men's gazes were turned inward, heads wagging, booted feet cuffing stone. The argument had turned nasty. Money was under dispute now, not wood. One of the safe-lamps was now burning dregs, and the flame was orange and weak. Ash chose her steps carefully, pressing her chest against the damp stone and walking on the balls of her feet. She wanted to run as fast as she could for the door, but the noise and sudden movement would give her away.

Like the quad door, the far door was open slightly to let in latecomers and brothers-in-the-watch. Ash felt a stream of cold air blow against her cheek. As she took the final step toward the opening, the quad door rattled into motion. Quick as she could, she shrank back into the shadows. Someone was entering the stables from the other side.

The quad door rumbled open, and the massive, bull-necked form of Marafice Eye stepped into view. Cloaked in the skin-soft leather of his office, he carried a horn lamp burning with a hot blue flame in one hand and a crab-hilted dagger in the other. Master Haysticks and the grooms fell silent. The wooden blocks tumbled from Skimmer's hands onto the floor.

"You!" said the Knife to Master Haysticks, stabbing the air with his dagger. "Has the Surlord's ward come this way tonight?"

Master Haysticks shook his head with feeling. "No, sir. All's quiet. No one but the Watch and their parties have passed through."

The Knife grunted. His small mouth gathered to itself like something pulled shut with a wire. Watching him, Ash felt the bones in her legs turn to water. How much of the stables could he see from where he stood? Were the safe-lamps throwing light to the far door or shining in his face? "Get this place lit up! Lock all doors and let no one pass until you hear from me again. Is that clear?"

"But, sir, what about the other brothers-in-the-watch. . . ."

Marafice Eye didn't have to say anything to make Master Haysticks fall silent. His eyes glittered, that was enough. With a shrug of his shoulders that in any other man would have been a gesture of uncertainty, but in the Knife was a violent switch of muscle and bone, Marafice Eye turned and walked away. A line of blue light trailed behind him like smoke.

Master Haysticks followed after, a lot happier to talk to the Knife's back than his face. "As you say, sir. As you say. Skimmer, get the lamps. Cribbon, help me with this door."

Ash didn't wait another moment. While all three men were intent on watching Marafice Eye leave, she slipped from the far door out into the night.

Cold and darkness enveloped her so completely it was like diving into a pool of black water. The wind hissed. Hard snow squeaked beneath her boots as she moved. Walls, their mortar fresh and in good repair, towered to either side like stone giants. Thirty paces ahead lay the gate.

Stable gate, trade gate, whatever one chose to call it, was an iron jawbone of spikes. Two guardhouses, cut from pale limestone and scoured smooth by centuries of hard wind, flanked the gate itself. The gate was up, its great metal teeth suspended above the crossbeam, dripping clods of snow and horse dung onto the ground below. Chain rigging held it in place. Stretching from the crossbeam to the guardhouse, wrapping around gears and levers, forming knots of black iron, the gate chains shuddered like metal foliage in the wind.

Ash stood and looked, her breath shallow and halting. Her only chance now was if the brothers-in-the-watch guarding the gate hadn't heard of her escape. She knew they shouldn't have—someone would have had to travel through the stables to tell them, and Ash knew for a fact that had not happened—but the presence of Marafice Eye made her unsure of herself. He would crush her skull between his bare hands if he could. . . .

*Stop it.* Ash jabbed her knuckles against her forehead, trying to knock out the fear.

The snow at her feet began to glow as many lamps were lit in the stables behind her back. Hearing the door rattle closed, she stepped aside and waited until it was locked and bolted. The fortress was coming to life. The stables weren't the only new source of light, and quick glances to either side showed torches being lit around the curtain wall. Sounds broke through the driving roar of the wind: shouted orders, the whir and clank of sealed gates, and the harsh percussion of metal arms.

Ash stepped toward the gate. Tidying herself as she moved, she brushed scraps of hay and muck from her cloak and tucked her hair beneath her hood. She smelled bad and couldn't decide if that was a good thing or not. A square of pale light escaped from the grille-covered window on the left gatehouse, and several lines of freshly trodden snow led to and from the door, so Ash headed that way. A man appeared at the grille as she approached. Knowing she was being watched made it difficult to appear natural, and her movements became jerky and stilted.

The gatehouse door swung open, and a brother-in-the-watch stepped out. The man was young and black haired, with a well-shaped mouth and eyes set too far back in his skull. A cruciform insignia stamped high upon his steel gorget marked him as a grangelord's third or fourth son. He drew his sword. "Who goes there?"

The second man behind the grille raised a bright-burning lamp to the window, throwing light onto Ash and the surrounding ground.

Ash blinked. She thought a moment, then curtsied. With her gaze carefully lowered, she said, "Please, sir. May I pass?"

The guard took a step forward. Like all members of the Watch, he was clean shaven and clad in soft beaten leathers worn over plate. The red steel of his blade shimmered and rippled as the patterns forged into the metal drew the light. Out of the corner of her eye, Ash saw his gaze flick behind her to the growing ring of torches spewing light and black smoke over the wall. When a cry broke through from the other side, he stilled himself to listen.

Ash held her jaw so tight it ached. Grinding the heel of her boot into the snow, she forced herself to stay calm. She was a servant, a messenger girl, a seamstress. She couldn't afford to act afraid.

"One of Till Bailey's girls?"

Ash had been concentrating so hard on grinding her heel into the snow that the question startled her. Lifting her head, she risked glancing at the watch brother.

He did not look pleased. Sharp noises continued to sound within the fortress. "I said, are you one of Till Bailey's?" He made a cutting motion with his sword in the direction of the Horn. "One of those brought in for Slaining?"

Ash took a breath. He thought she was a prostitute.

"Answer, girl." The guard's well-shaped lips slid across his gums, revealing small, yellow teeth.

"Yes." Ash nodded, her eyes fixed on the man's sword. "One of Till's."

The watch brother spat. Ash thought for a moment he would let her go. He altered his grip on his sword, preparing to resheathe it, but as he did so a great bell began to toll within the fortress. Ash's heart dropped in her chest. It was the Quarter Bell, hung in the topmost chamber of the Cask. Sounded in times of war, riots, or sieges, it was the signal to secure all gates.

Lunging forward, the warden caught hold of Ash's arm and yanked her toward the gatehouse window. Sharp fingernails, the same yellow as his teeth, hooked into her flesh. Inside the gatehouse, the second man moved away from the window, and a moment later metal chains began to shudder and hum as gears and pulleys creaked to life. Stable gate was being lowered.

"Please. Could you let me out before it drops? Till's expecting me back." Ash tried to match the sly charm Katia used when rooting after favors or rose cakes. It was a mistake. She ended up sounding desperate instead.

The watch brother pulled her up to the window and forced her face against the grille. "Grod. What should we do about this? She's one of Till's."

The one called Grod was working the crankshaft. He slowed but did not stop as he took a look at Ash. Graying and nearly bald, he had the look of a man who had soldiered for many years. His eyes were sharp as a pig's, and he wore no fancy insignia at his breast, shoulder, or throat. Ash's first reaction was to back away, but the first brother had his hand on her scalp and was holding her fast against the grille. The crisscross iron cut her face into squares, and she could feel the cold metal stealing warmth from her cheeks. Slowly, carefully, using the arm that was pressed against the gatehouse wall, she reached inside her cloak for the jeweled pin she had taken for selling.

The bell continued to toll, sending out deep, wailing notes that hurt Ash's ears. Overhead, the gate clattered and screeched, descending in small, lurching stages as its weight fought against the chains.

As Ash's fingers found and then closed around the smooth brass of the cloak pin, Grod shook his head. "She's not one of Till's. Thin scrap of nothing like that. With that hair and that mucked-up cloak. Till likes 'em plump and pretty, not dark and scraggy as a strip of trail meat." Grod's eyes narrowed. His gaze focused on a lock of Ash's hair that had poked through the grille. Releasing his hold on the crankshaft, he straightened his back and snatched the lock. Ash's eyes teared as he ran his fingers along its length.

Soot rubbed off in his hand. A cold smile hardened his

face as he rolled the newly cleaned lock between his finger-tips. Abruptly he tightened his grip. "This one stays with us. Bring her round, Storrin. And we'll bind her fit for hauling."

On the word *hauling*, Ash yanked her head free of the grille. Pain stung her scalp as she lost a lock of her hair to Grod. Swiftly she swung her arm forward and drove the brass spike of the cloak pin into Storrin's well-formed mouth, driving hard through lip tissue and gum to the smooth bone beneath.

The man swore viciously. Blood welled from his upper lip as he lashed out in anger with his fist. Ash took a hard blow on her shoulder but managed to keep her footing. She had to get through the gate. Inside the gatehouse, she was aware of Grod working on the crankshaft, meaning to lower the gate before he came to the aid of his partner. It was the move of someone practical and cold-hearted. Ash despised him for it.

She ran for the gate. Storrin was faster, seizing her cloak tails and yanking her down into the snow. Falling to her knees, Ash struggled with the ties at her throat. She couldn't breathe. Snow crystals ground into her shins like powdered glass. Storrin held her cloak like a leash as he jabbed his blade into her back and yelled at her to stop fighting. Ash felt little pain. She was concentrating on loosing the ties and freeing Storrin's stranglehold on her throat.

The gate juddered to life almost directly above her, fresh gobs of snows dislodging from its spikes as it dropped. Ash's hands felt big and clumsy as she clawed at her neck. *Why won't the damn thing come undone?*

Storrin yanked hard on her cloak, making Ash slide backward in the snow. A moment was lost to blackness as she fought to regain her footing and stand. *Jab! Jab!* Storrin poked his blade into her ribs.

"Stop fighting me, bitch!"

Ash's mouth flooded with something that had to be blood. Her head felt heavy and swollen, and suddenly there was no room for her thoughts.

*Reach! Reach!*

Voices hissed through her mind like scalding steam. The pressure was unbearable, forcing blood and heat to her face.

Another yank on the cloak. "Get back here."

*REACH!*

Ash reached. With numb, frozen fingers, she reached into the taut hollow of her throat and tore at the cloak. The fastening broke. Hot blood rained down her neck, steaming in the freezing air. Gasping and shaking, she took a diving man's breath. Stumbling forward, she dug the toe of her boot into the snow. Storrin was at her back, still pulling on her cloak tails. It took him a moment to realize she was no longer attached.

The second was all Ash needed. Forcing strength into legs that felt cold and oddly numb, she hauled herself to her feet. And ran.

The gate was two-thirds of the way down. As Ash fell under its shadow, she heard a high-pitched wail crack the air. All the chains rattled, and gears and pulleys began to spin out of control. The gate dropped. Ash screamed. Storrin reached.

Two tons of black iron smashed to the earth. A soft gurgle sounded, like water forced from a pipe. Ash felt air and snow and something else spatter against her back. She was on the outside. *Outside!*

Behind her, she heard the gatehouse door blast open and Grod cry out to the Maker. Strange. He didn't sound angry. He sounded scared.

Ash glanced back. Storrin was under the gate. An iron spike had entered his spine. His legs were jerking, the muscles contracting and relaxing so it looked as if he were performing an obscene dance in the snow. Blood from the impact had sprayed all the way to her feet.

Ash swayed and nearly fell. Turning, she ran into the night.

# FIFTEEN

## *Within Mask Fortress*

SHE ESCAPED THROUGH THE stable gate. Grod watched her run east. By the time he'd raised the gate and called for aid she was gone. Lost in the Slaining Night crowds.

"And the other man . . . What was his name again?"

"Storrin." Marafice Eye spat the word, clearly displeased that Iss had already forgotten the man's name. "He's dead. It wasn't the falling of the gate that killed him, but the raising."

Iss nodded, interested despite all he had on his mind. "Yes. I've seen things like that before. As long as a man isn't moved and the spikes stay in place, he lives. The moment one tries to free him, the internal organs tear apart and the lungs flood with blood. Unfortunate. Most unfortunate. You have saved the body?"

"You're not having it." The skin over Marafice Eye's lips stretched white as he spoke. Seeing him standing there, his back to the great Roundroom fire, his boots dripping snowmelt onto the gold-and-turquoise rug, his entire body shaking with fury, Iss decided to say no more. Marafice Eye was protective of his men, fiercely so. The Red Forge would burn long and bright this night in memory of a brother lost.

Turning his back on the Knife, Iss stared into the yellow flames blazing in the hearth. How could Asarhia have gone? Didn't she know he would never hurt her? Hadn't he told her a hundred times that he loved her more than any real father could? Damn her! She had to be found. There was no telling whose hands she might fall into out there. The Phage might find her . . . or even the Sull. Iss took the black iron poker from its stand near the hearth and turned over piece after piece of burning coal. After a few moments he had collected himself enough to finish the matter at hand. "Have Storrin's body brought before the White Robes for blessing and annunciation—wake them if you must. If they complain, tell them that the Surlord himself commands it. And see to it that the man's widow, his mother, or whoever else he leaves behind is adequately compensated for the loss."

Marafice Eye grunted. Even in a chamber the size and height of the Roundroom, which occupied a full quarter of the ground floor in the Cask, the Protector General of Spire Vanis dominated the space. He was a dangerous animal, not to be toyed with—Iss knew that.

"You never mentioned what business was so pressing it pulled you away from Asarhia's door."

"No. I didn't." Marafice Eye stood his ground, his eyes hardening along with his tight little mouth.

Iss held his gaze. Information was cheap to come by in Mask Fortress: He'd have answers soon enough. Caydis Zerbina, with his soft linen slippers that never made a sound and his long agile fingers shaped for foiling locks, would see to that. There was little Caydis and his dark-skinned brethren did not know about Marafice Eye. *The Knife prefers to court his women in the dark, Sarab*, Caydis had once breathed in his soft musical voice. *His night mushroom is sadly misshapen.* Iss found such information both useful and distasteful. And he always sent Caydis in search of more.

Returning the charred black poker to its stand, he said, "No matter. Asarhia must be found. The servant girl must be questioned. It seems highly unlikely to me that Asarhia could have orchestrated such a clever escape on her own. My ward is a bright girl, but far too naive and timid to have carried off something so cold-blooded without help. Soot in her hair, crawling under horse stalls, strutting to the stable gate, and declaring herself a prostitute!" Iss paused, his pale hand knotted around the poker shaft. "The servant girl *must* be involved in some way."

He looked at the Knife without seeming to. The man's face gave nothing away as he murmured, "I'll take the truth from her."

"Call her now."

Iss released his grip on the poker as Marafice Eye left the room. The Roundroom was bright and warm, decorated with silk hangings and silk rugs and thirteen black pewter lanterns that burned the fragrant flume of sperm whales, giving off a sweet childlike scent. Iss had taught Asarhia to read and write here, beneath the light of the pewter lanterns. Once when she was nine years old her feet had frozen to blocks in the quad, and he had stripped her down in front of the fire and warmed her pale little toes in his fists.

"The girl will be here soon." The Knife strode back into the chamber, shaking tapestries and wall-mounted weaponry as he moved. "Ganron has reported back. Watch has been tripled on Almsgate, Hoargate, and Wrathgate. The east—"

Iss flicked a wrist, silencing the Knife. "Vaingate must also be watched. I want a triple guard posted there as well."

"Vaingate leads nowhere. No one in their right mind

would leave the city by way of Mount Slain. I'll not waste my men setting them to guard a dead gate."

"Indulge me," Iss said. "Waste them."

Marafice Eye glowered. His big hands crunched the Killhound broach at his throat, forcing the soft, lead-based alloy into a shape that looked more like a dog than a bird.

The Surlord explained himself only once his Knife had nodded and said, "Aye."

"You know Asarhia's history as well as I do, Knife. She was abandoned outside of Vaingate. *Vaingate*. Now, for the first time in her life she's free to go where she chooses. If you were in her position, wouldn't you be curious about the place where you were found? Wouldn't you like to stand upon that frozen ground and spend a moment wondering why your mother left you for dead? Asarhia is a sensitive girl. She hides things even from me, yet I know she feels her abandonment keenly. Some nights she even calls out in her sleep."

Marafice Eye took this information and chewed on it, his hands dropping to his waist where his red sword was sheathed and hung. After a minute of silence he spoke. "If you're so sure she'll visit Vaingate, then I say we don't increase the guard at all. Visibly. The girl's not stupid—we've seen the truth of that ourselves tonight—and she won't show herself by the gate if she judges it unsafe. Let her come. Let her see only beggars and vendors and street filth. Let her come in good faith, unawares. And let me be there to stop her when she does."

"She is not to be harmed, Knife."

"She killed one of my men."

Iss felt the anger come to him but did not show it. His voice was quiet as he said, "You will not hurt her."

"But—"

"Enough!" Iss kept his eyes upon Marafice Eye until he was satisfied that Asarhia would be returned to him whole. Turning his back on the Knife, he contemplated the stone reliefwork above the hearth. Impaled beasts, two-headed wolves, goats with women's heads and breasts, and serpents with the angled, segmented eyes of insects looked down at him from their limestone poles. Iss shivered. *Asarhia! The stupid girl.* He would not have hurt her if she had stayed.

Caydis would have seen to it that she had every comfort. Her life would have barely changed.

Knuckles rapped against wood. "Girl's here, sir."

Marafice Eye opened the door, and a brother-in-the-watch pushed the little dark-haired maid into the room. With one quick movement the Knife caught the girl's arm and twisted it hard behind her back. The girl let out a small cry but was sensible enough not to fight him.

"Leave us," Iss said to the watch brother. When the door was closed, he turned to the servant girl and shook his head. "Katia. Little Katia. I trusted you and you let me down. Now look at the terrible mess you are in."

Katia's lips trembled. Her fine dark eyes glanced sideways toward the Knife. He looked away.

Iss took pity on the girl. She was so very frightened, and she had already been beaten once this night. "Let her go."

The Knife released her immediately. The girl let out a sob and stumbled forward, hardly knowing what to do. She looked around the room for a moment, then flung herself at the Surlord's feet. "Please, sir. *Please*. I didn't know what she was planning. I swear it. She told me nothing. Nothing. If I'd known I would have come to you . . . like I always do. I would have told you, sir. I swear." Finished, she broke down into soft, shuddering tears, her head shaking, her little hands grasping at the watered silk of Iss' robe.

Iss patted her shiny curls. "Hush, child. Hush. I know you would have come to me." His fingers slid under her chin, forcing her to look up. "You're a good girl, aren't you?" Katia nodded, tears pooling in her eyes, mucus running from her nose to her mouth. "There. Wipe your face . . . That's better, isn't it? No need to cry. You know me and you know the Knife, and neither of us has ever hurt you, have we? So there's nothing to be afraid of. All we need from you is the truth."

Katia was quiet now but still shaking. "Sir, I told you all I know. Ash—I mean Miss Asarhia—said nothing to me about wanting to leave the fortress. She kept to herself this past week. Ever since the day she went riding in the quad and came back and found Caydis in her chamber, she—"

"She saw him there?"

Katia nodded. "Yes, sir. Made him feel bad. Promised that she wouldn't tell on him being slack about his business if he didn't tell on her."

"I see. And did she say anything to you?" Katia hesitated. "Tell me the truth, child."

"Well . . . she hurt my arm, and said she'd hurt me more if I didn't tell her what you asked about whenever you summoned me to your chamber." Katia twisted silk in her hands. "So I told her how you're most particular in wanting to know when her menses start . . . but that's all I said. I swear it. She was right queer that day. All cold and angry. Told me to leave straight after."

Iss patted the girl's head. "Good girl. You're doing very well. Now. This past week, have you seen any sign of her menses? Think hard, girl."

"No, sir. All her underthings were as clean as if she'd never even worn 'em."

A soft breath puffed from Iss' lips. "As if she'd never worn them." He exchanged a glance with Marafice Eye. It took him a moment to settle his mind. "Now, Katia. One last thing and you may go. Have you taken inventory of all the items in Asarhia's chamber?" Katia nodded. "So, discounting the jeweled cloak pin we found in the snow and the silver brush we found in her cloak, do you know of any other items she may have taken?"

"No, sir. The brush and the pin are the only things that have gone."

Iss continued to stroke Katia's hair. "So she has nothing to sell for coinage, and no cloak to keep her warm. What a poor affair her first excursion into the city is likely to be."

"She'll end up in Almstown, most like." Marafice Eye had sat himself on one of the dainty satin-upholstered chairs near the door, and judging from the way he was pressing his forearm against the armrest, he seemed intent on breaking it. "I'll double the Watch numbers there as well."

Iss nodded, well content to abide by the Knife's judgment. He'd never had occasion to doubt its worth before. Turning his attention to Katia, he said, "Look at me, girl." Katia raised her chin. Such a pretty, plump little thing. A perfect mix of servant girl cunning and little girl fear. Asarhia had cared for her very much.

"Please, sir. I won't have to go back to the kitchens, will I? *Please*." Large brown eyes pleaded as small, slightly grubby hands clawed at the silk of his robes.

Iss was not unmoved. His hand slid across her hot cheek. "No. You won't have to return to the kitchens. I promise."

The girl was so relieved and delighted, her face was a genuine pleasure to watch. As she kissed his silk robe, teared, and murmured a hundred little words of thanks, Iss nodded to Marafice Eye across the room.

Katia was so caught up in relief, she didn't hear the Knife approach. For an instant, as his hands clamped around her head, she thought it was a caress. One of her hands even fluttered up to touch him. Then the Knife's grip tightened and she knew to be afraid, and the look she sent Iss tore at his heart.

One quick wrench was all it took to break her neck.

\* \* \*

*PEOPLE WILL DIE FOR THIS.*

Fire and ice burned his flesh and his soul. The pain was as deep and many layered as rock formed and then compressed over millions of years beneath the sea. The Nameless One knew pain. He knew its weights and measures, its aftertaste and its cost. His joints ached with the soft calciferous pain of old age, and even to rest them curled and at ease brought no relief. His broken and mismended bones burned within his flesh like heated rods, and his organs shrank and hardened, losing function bit by bit. He no longer knew what it was to straighten his back or urinate without pain. He could not recall when last he had taken a breath that satisfied him wholly or chewed a piece of meat until it was flat.

Pain he knew.

The past he did not.

He strained for it every day, strained until blood vessels broke in his belly and spine, until his jaw locked, his wounds wept, and the shaking of his body opened sores upon his skin. His fear of harming himself—once so strong that it was the only thought he could retain in his mind from one year to the next—had now faded to a mild concern. The Light Bearer always fixed him. The Light Bearer with his salves and bandages and gauze bags and tongs. The Light Bearer would not let him die. It had taken many years for the Nameless One to learn this, and more after to accept it, but now it was set firmly in his mind.

Knowing this had freed him, not from pain—nothing and no one could free him from that—but from fear of death. The Nameless One no longer had complete control over his face muscles, but bitterness still leaked across his face. Even pain so terrible it tore whole years from his life could not make him welcome death.

He did not want to die; that was another thing he knew. In time he would know more.

Waiting. That was his life. Waiting, pain, and hate. He waited for the Light Bearer to come, waited for the scraps of light and warmth he brought, ate them up like a dog after bones. A hand on his shoulder, a warm hand, could burn him now. He yearned for the warmth and the touch and the contact, but when he received it, it was too much. When the touch was withdrawn he felt nothing but relief, yet even before the memory faded and the imprint of the Light Bearer's hand left his skin, he yearned for it all over again.

Loneliness wasn't like pain. It had no degrees and niceties; it did not shift and deepen and lighten, or change from day to day. It fed consistently moment after moment, hour after hour, year after year, gnawing away at the back of his throat, consuming him piece by piece. What it left behind scared him. The confinement he could stand, the torture and usage he could stand, even the red-and-blue flames of fire and ice that burned in place of his past. But the loneliness, the utter loneliness, ached with a pain he could not bear.

It turned him into something he hated.

The Nameless One shifted in the iron chamber that was his home, his chamber pot, and his bed. Chains, their metal mottled and corroded by years of sweat, urine, and feces, did not rattle so much as crack like the knuckles of a young and soft-boned child.

Hate was not new to him; that was the last thing he knew. It came too easily and fit too well to have been something newborn during his confinement. Even as he craved each visit from the Light Bearer, craved the world of light, warmth, and people, he hated all he craved with utter coldness. Loneliness fed off him, and he fed off hate. Hate was how he lived through years of darkness, how he survived the aching stillness and the separate weights of physical pain. It was how he faced a world with neither day or night, seasons, sunlight, nor cool rain. It was how he clung to the last shred of self.

*People will die for this.*

Counting was beyond him—he knew nothing of numbers and their kind—but the words he whispered into the darkness had the feel of things many times said. They were a comfort to him. They made tolerable the wriggling and pinching of the creatures inserted beneath the skin on his forearm, back, and upper thigh. They turned the sawing of their chitinous mouthparts into a soft bearable hum.

Skin on the Nameless One's face cracked and bled as he forced muscles to work upon a smile.

*People will die for this.*

All he had to do was remember the past, that was the thing. Remember who he was.

Already he was stronger than he had been. The Light Bearer did not know this; he thought his charge the same. But he was wrong. The Nameless One added to himself in cornea-thin slivers, cumulating in the darkness like rotting meat growing mold. He could retain thoughts from one day to another now. It cost him in other ways, forced his body to fight the pain alone as his mind wet-nursed a thought, and his joints ached to bleeding as he held himself still while he slept. Still, he *knew* things now, and he judged it worth it. For uncountable years he had known as little as the creatures that grew to maturation beneath his flesh, aware of nothing except hunger and pain and thirst.

He had himself now. And he spent his days waiting for the chance to reclaim more.

When the Light Bearer took, when he descended into the chamber with his light and his warm packages oozing honey and bean juice and stole that thing he needed from the Nameless One's flesh, he uncovered a river of dark currents as he worked. These glimpses of darkness, swells, and eddies of liquid glass whetted the Nameless One's tongue. The current ran for him alone. And every time the Light Bearer slit open skin with his thin engraver's knife and extracted what he needed with his little silver tongs, the river's bank meandered closer. One day it would come close enough for the Nameless One to enter. One day he would use its waters to douse the flames that burned in place of his past.

Settling himself in the position that brought most comfort, with his legs tucked beneath him and the chains pulled high across his chest, he began straining for the name he'd lost. Time came and went. Darkness endured. Somehow, despite all his efforts and his deepest wishes, his mind slipped from his task, and loneliness came to feed upon him once more. Eventually he slept. His dreams when they came were all of warm arms, touching him, holding him, carrying him up toward the light.

# SIXTEEN

## A Visitor

HEAVY SNOWS HAD FALLEN on the clanhold during the ten days he was away. The filly didn't like the soft, often chest-high drifts and left to her own devices chose paths that were indirect, to say the least. Raif let her have her say. The roundhouse was in sight now, and he could find nothing inside himself that welcomed the thought of coming home.

Overhead the sky was striped gray and white by high winds. A storm far to the north, born in the frozen waste of the Great Want, was working itself out beyond the horizon. At ground level the wind it generated was biting. The filly got the worst of it, and her nose and eyes were crusted and weeping, and ice crystals formed continually around her

mouth. Every hour or so Raif would stop and clean her face
and bridle and check the flesh around her mouth for
chilblains. He could muster no such enthusiasm for himself.
His fox hood was stiff with ice; five days' worth of breath
had accumulated in the guard hairs, turning each strand of
fur into a brittle quill of ice. The parts of Raif's cheeks that
touched the hood were numb.

His eyes stung, part snow abrasion and part snow blindness. Everything he'd looked at for the past two days had
been blurred. The others probably had the sense to sit out the
worst days of the storm, raise camp hard against a leeward
slope, and cover their tents in snow. Raif forced his wind-
cracked lips to stretch to a hard line. He wouldn't think
about the others. They would come back, perhaps two or
three days later than he, but they *would* return, and when
they did his life in the clan would be over. Mace Blackhail
would see to that.

*Raif Sevrance ran from battle*, he would say. *The yearman
broke his oath.*

Raif closed his fist around his lore and squeezed. He had
done Mace Blackhail's work for him. And, if time could be
turned and he could go back to the Bluddroad and the ambush, he couldn't say if he would do it again. The horror of
killing women and children had seemed so clear then. Riding alone for the past five days had dulled it.

Pulling the filly from her path to one of his own choosing,
Raif steeled himself against doubts. The past was the past,
and wishing it different never brought anyone relief.

As he cut across the graze, a line of blue smoke rising
from the near side of the roundhouse caught his attention.
He rubbed his sore eyes, making them worse. When the
stinging subsided, he concentrated upon the smoke, tracking
its source to the blue stone roof of the guidehouse. Uneasy,
he kicked a better pace from the filly. The guidehouse had no
hearth or chimney, only a smoke hole for letting out lamp
fumes, yet from the volume of smoke escaping from the
roof, it looked as if someone had built and lit a fire.

Everything else about the roundhouse seemed normal.
Longhead and his crew had cleared the snow from the court,
and a handful of young boys were out taking advantage of

the cart-size snow piles that had been shoveled aside. The boys stopped playing and turned to watch as Raif approached. Berry Lye, a great turnip-headed youth with red ears who was younger brother to Banron, brushed the snow from his buckskins and ran forward to greet Raif. He wanted to know what had happened at the ambush. How many Bluddsmen had Banron unseated with his hammer? How had his new armor stood up to the fight? Raif silenced him with a single look. He was in no mood to talk to children. Berry's face reddened to match his ears, and for a moment he looked just like his brother. Raif turned away, suddenly ashamed. He didn't even know if Banron was alive or dead.

Berry ran for the roundhouse, eager to be first with the news that at least one of the ambush party had made it back alive.

Raif slid from his horse and led it to the stables. He felt sick to his stomach. What was he going to say? How could he tell the clansmen and women with due respect what he had done?

Pretty, copper-haired Hailly Tanner emerged from the stables to take his horse. She actually blushed as their hands touched over the reins. Raif, like many young men in the clan, had wasted hours dreaming about Hailly's pale, lightly freckled skin and perfect strawberry mouth. Until today she had never deigned to notice him, let alone gone out of her way to tend his horse. Now she stood before him, asking quite coyly if the filly needed hay or oats. Raif showed a grim smile. He was a yearman now; that was the difference. Before he had been nothing, a lad with a borrowed bow and no oath, unworthy in every way of her attentions. He gave her his instructions and left.

Ignoring the small crowd of women and children who had begun to gather at the main entrance, Raif headed for the side door instead. Before he did or said anything, he needed to visit the guidehouse. Alone.

Anwyn Bird stood in the entryway, arms folded, watching him. Raif thought he might be in for a grilling, but something must have been showing on his face, for the gray-haired matron let him pass unchallenged. As he headed along the stone passage to the guidehouse, he heard her calling for a keg of warm beer and a platter of fried bread. Despite everything, Raif felt his mouth watering. He had trail meat in his pack, but if he had eaten any on the way home, he had no memory of it.

The door to the guidehouse was open. Tattered scraps of smoke and burned matter sailed from the doorway as he passed inside. He thought for a moment, then shut the door behind him, taking time to ensure it was firmly closed.

The interior was as dark and suffocating as a smokehouse. Raif's eyes stung fiercely. He couldn't see anything at first except the massive blocky outline of the guidestone. Gradually he became accustomed to the darkness and began to pick out details in the room. He was standing at the foot of the guidestone. The granite was slick with graphite oil. Pockmarks in the age-old stone were crusted with hard, milky mineral deposits that glinted like exposed sections of bone. The stone itself seemed darker than he remembered. Perhaps it was the smoke.

A small fire was burning in the west corner, its densely packed timbers wetted with hog's blood to stop the wood from burning with a hot, fast flame. Directly above, the smoke hole had been newly enlarged, and fresh tar had been painted around its edges. No tallow or oil lamps were lit. The guidehouse floor was littered with debris, and bits of rock crunched beneath Raif's boots as he stepped toward the stone. Despite the fire, it was deathly cold, and a harsh acrid stench rose above the gamy aroma of cooked blood.

Uneasy, Raif stripped off his soft inner gloves and dropped to his knees by the guidestone. He wasn't good at prayers. Tem had taught both his sons that it wasn't right to ask the Stone Gods for anything for oneself. They were hard gods, not easily moved by suffering. A man's life and his problems were nothing to them. They watched over the clanholds and the clans, demanding their proper place in each roundhouse and around each clansman's and clanswoman's waist. Yet they gave little back . . . and they answered no small prayers.

Raif's fingers hooked around the time that hung from his belt. Weighing the antler tip in his fist, he suddenly realized there was no need to pray: The Stone Gods had been at his side through the ambush and long journey home. They were here in the powdered guidestone at his waist. They knew all he had come to say.

Not knowing if that thought gave him comfort or made him afraid, Raif reached forward and laid his palms on the guidestone.

The stone was as hard and cold as a frozen carcass. Raif had to fight the desire to withdraw his touch, knowing that to do so would be a kind of defeat. Forcing his jaw together, he pressed his flesh harder against the stone. Numbness took his fingertips, then knuckles, as blood vessels carried the stone coldness toward his heart. A dull pain sounded in his upper left arm. The light entering his pupils wavered, and his vision flickered and dimmed.

The numbness crept across his palms, tingling like alcohol evaporating from his skin as it spread. After a few minutes he could feel nothing of the guidestone's surface. The pain in his arm throbbed like a pump drawing up water. For the briefest of instances, Raif was taken with the idea that he was siphoning something from the guidestone, pulling it inward toward himself. He felt a moment of utter stillness, heavy as the deepest sleep, where he understood that if he could just reach *beyond* the stone's surface, everything would become known to him.

"What makes you think you can heal the stone?"

The voice snapped the thread. The pain and the pulling stopped. The stillness collapsed inward, creating a rush of light and darkness that formed images as it slid back into the stone. Raif saw a forest of high trees, their foliage rippling from blue to silver like the sea; a lake of frozen blood, its surface hard as hammered metal, its depths dark with distorted shapes trapped within the ice. Other things came and went, moving too quickly for him to capture or understand: a city with no name or people, a pair of gray eyes, frightened, and a raven flying north in winter when all other birds flew south.

Before he could commit it all to memory, someone tugged at his wrists, pulling his hands from the stone. Raif's hands peeled away slowly, making sucking noises as his skin fought to keep hold. He felt no pain, only a vague sensation of loss. Turning, he found himself looking into the black eyes of Inigar Stoop.

"You should not have touched the stone, Raif Sevrance," he said quietly. "Did you not see that it is broken?"

Raif's heart was still racing from all the guidestone had showed him, and it took him a few seconds to decipher what Inigar had said. He shook his head. "Broken? I . . . I don't understand what you mean."

The guide held out a hand dark and twisted with age. "Then I shall show you."

When Raif gave Inigar his hand he did not expect to need the guide's help standing, but his legs buckled as they took his weight and he stumbled against the stone. Surprisingly, Inigar pulled him up, steadied and held him until he had regained enough of his strength to stand alone. Looking at the small, sunken-chested guide with his white old man's hair and his dark, membrane-thin skin, Raif wondered how he could manage such a feat.

Inigar smiled, not kindly. "Follow me." Disappearing into the smoky darkness, he gave Raif little choice but to do as he said.

Coming to a halt at the opposite side of the guidestone, Inigar wagged his head and said, "This is why I burn the smoke fire. This"

Raif followed Inigar's gaze. A deep fissure ran from the top edge of the stone halfway to the floor, exposing the wet and glistening interior of the rock and gathering shadows like a fault line in the earth. Graphite oil oozed from the cleft like blood.

"It happened five days ago." Inigar looked at Raif sharply. "At dawn."

Knowing there was a question in the guide's words, yet unwilling to answer it, Raif said, "The ambush went well. The others will be back within a day or two."

Inigar ignored his words completely. Running a hand along the crack, he said, "The Stone Gods watch over all clans. Despite the claims of each and every clan chief since the Great Settling, they have no favorites. Blackhail, Dhoone, Scarpe, Ganmiddich: They are all one and the same to those who live within the stone. If Scarpe wins a victory over Gnash, they are not displeased. If Ganmiddich takes the Croser roundhouse and makes it their own, they find no reason to be enraged. The Stone Gods created the clans, they put the craving for land and battle within us, so they do not grieve when clans make war and lives are shed. It is their nature as well as our own.

"However, when something happens that goes against all they have taught and bred within us, threatening the very existence of the clanholds themselves, then the gods get angry." Inigar punched the cracked guidestone with the heel of his fist. "And this is how they show it!"

Raif stepped back.

"Yes, Raif Sevrance. Perhaps you had better step back, for all our sakes."

Feeling his face grow hot, Raif began to shake his head. He couldn't bear to look at the crack in the stone. "I . . . I . . ."

"Silence! I don't want to be told what happened from your lips. Some news can come too soon, when a man is not ready or able to chew it." Inigar Stoop looked straight into Raif's eyes. "Like oaths."

Raif winced. The pain returned to his arm, soft and sickening like a pulled muscle.

"We three knew, didn't we? Eleven days ago on the court. Me, you, and the raven." The guide grabbed Raif's elkskin, tore the ties apart to reveal the raven lore beneath. He plucked the piece of horn from Raif's neck, snapping the twine. Closing his fist around the lore, he said, "I was not the one who gave you this—that shame is not mine—and perhaps it is as much the old guide's fault as it is yours. Either way, you are not good for this clan, Raif Sevrance. You are raven born, chosen to watch the dead. And I fear that if you stay amongst us, you will watch us all die before your eyes have had their fill.

"Already you have watched the deaths of your father, ten of our best warriors, and our chief. Yet that still wasn't enough, was it? You had to watch the death of Shor Gormalin, too. Shor. The finest man in this clan. An eagle, he was. Tell me, what right has a raven to watch over an eagle's death?"

Raif looked down. He had no answer.

Still Inigar Stoop wasn't finished. "And what of your brother, Raif Sevrance? Who seconded your oath and took possession of your swearstone. What new shame have you brought him? If I had such a brother, who loved me with all the fierceness of his bear lore, who spoke up for me when no one else would, and linked his fate to mine without a moment's hesitation, I would count myself blessed. I would revere and obey him and spend all my days repaying his trust. I would not shame him with my words or my deeds."

Raif covered his face with his hands. He had spent the last five days pushing all thoughts of Drey from his mind. Now the guide was pushing them back. And Raif knew he spoke the truth.

Inigar opened his fist and let the raven lore drop to the floor. "You came here to seek the Stone Gods' guidance. So look hard upon the guidestone and see if it does not offer the answer you need." He glanced once at the fissure in the stone, just long enough to ensure that Raif understood his meaning, then turned and walked into the smoke. "When you are done, go and join those gathered to greet you on the court. A visitor awaits you there."

Raif closed his eyes. He stood and did not move, fearing to touch the stone again. It was a long time before he scooped up his lore and left.

"LEAVE HIM ALONE! ALL of you!" Anwyn Bird broke through the crowd of people on the court, laden tray held out before her like a battering ram. "Can't you see the yearman needs food and drink before you go bothering him with questions?" The clan matron favored Raif with a smile so gentle and proud, it made him ashamed. "Here, lad. It's the best dark beer I have. Drink it."

Raif took the horn from her, grateful to have something to focus his attention upon. The sunlight reflecting off the snow was dazzling after the darkness of the guidehouse, and the river of faces before him, all chattering and asking questions at once, made him want to run away. He stood his ground. These people were his clan, and they had a right to know of their kin. He held the horn to his lips, inhaled the rich, woodsy aroma of beer aged in oak barrels and then warmed slowly over the hearth for three days. Anwyn was right: It *was* the best she had. And that was why he chose not to drink it.

Resting the horn against his chest, he tried to pick out the faces of Raina and Effie in the crowd. He couldn't spot them. A small group of people stood in darkness behind the greatdoor; perhaps they were among them.

"We must know what happened, lad." It was Orwin Shank, his big red face grave and worried. "Take your time, tell us as you see fit."

Raif nodded slowly. Why was everyone treating him so kindly? It only made things worse. Forcing himself to meet Orwin Shank's eyes, he said, "Bitty is alive and well. He fought bravely, and his blade took at least two Bluddsmen that I counted."

Orwin Shank reached out and clamped a hand over Raif's shoulder. Tears sparkled in his light blue eyes. "You always bring news to ease a father's heart, Raif Sevrance. You're a good lad, and I thank you for it."

Orwin Shank's words were in such contrast with those he had heard earlier from Inigar Stoop that Raif felt his eyes stinging. He didn't deserve them. Glancing around, he addressed the crowd, fearing that if he didn't get it over and done with soon, he would lose his nerve. "The ambush was a success. All went as planned. Corbie Meese led a crew from the north of the road, Ballic the Red from the south. My brother was chosen to lead the rear. The battle was fierce, and the Bluddsmen fought hard, but we wore them down and forced them into the snow, and then took victory for ourselves." Raif's gaze sought out Sarolyn Meese, Corbie's plump, sweet-natured wife.

"Corbie fought like a Stone God. He was beautiful to watch."

"Is he hurt?" Sarolyn touched Raif's arm as she waited for his reply.

"No. A few nicks, perhaps. Nothing more."

"And what of Ballic?"

Raif couldn't tell whom the question came from, but he answered it as well as he could. Other questions followed, everyone wanting to know of their loved ones and kin. Raif found himself relaxing as he spoke. It was surprisingly easy to avoid speaking of what came later in the clearing. All that mattered to the clansfolk was if their sons, husbands, and brothers were alive and well and had fought bravely. Raif was relieved to find himself telling truths that hurt neither himself nor any member of the ambush party.

When Jenna Walker stepped forward and asked about her son, Raif's relief left him as quickly as if it had never been there at all.

"Toady was badly injured. He may be dead."

Jenna Walker shook off the people who moved swiftly to support and comfort her. Green eyes, sharp with anger, pinned Raif to the spot. "Why do you not know for sure? Why are you here before the rest? What happened after the raid?"

Raif took a breath. He had feared this moment for five days.

"What happened to Banron?" It was big, turnip-headed Berry Lye, pushing his way to the front of the crowd. "How many Bluddsmen's skulls did he crack open with his hammer?"

"Tell us why you're here, Raif Sevrance." Jenna Walker's body shook as she spoke. "Tell us."

Raif looked from Berry to Jenna Walker. He opened his mouth to speak.

"Enough!" Raina Blackhail stepped from the shadows behind the greatdoor. Dressed in soft beaten leathers and fine black wool, she looked every bit a clan chief's wife. Sable fur at her throat and cuffs rippled with every breath she took, and a silver knife slung at her hip caught the light. The crowd parted for her as she made her way forward. "The yearman has had a hard journey through new snow. Let him name those he believes wounded or dead, then allow him time to rest and eat."

Despite all her finery, Raina's eyes were dull, and her face had lost all its fat. Raif was shocked to see her widow's weals still bleeding. "Tell Berry of his elder brother."

It was a command, and he obeyed it, seeing in his mind Banron Lye's body lying in a ditch being worried by dogs as he spoke. He gave Berry and his kin little hope, telling them that Banron had not moved even after the dogs had been shot. The belief that his clansman was dead grew in Raif's mind as he spoke. He remembered standing across the Bluddroad from Banron. *Watching. . . .*

*You are raven born, chosen to watch the dead.*

"Any others?" Raina's voice cut through his thoughts.

He shook his head. "I saw no others fall."

The relief of the crowd showed itself in relaxed fists and downward glances. Some of the older clansmen touched their measures of powdered guidestone, giving thanks. Raif saw Jenna Walker's questions held, unspoken, on many faces. Raina ensured that no one spoke them out aloud, guiding everyone back to the roundhouse by the simple act of heading there herself. Anwyn helped, promising hot ale and fried bread to all who came inside out of the cold. Raif stood his ground, watching the clansfolk disappear one by one into the roundhouse. More than anything else he wanted to go inside and find Effie, seize her in his arms, and press her child's weight against his. Yet he no longer knew if that was the right thing to do. Raina had kept her away from the meeting on purpose, wanting to shield her from harm.

That was what *he* had to do now: shield Effie, Drey, and his clan from harm. Inigar Stoop had made him see that clearly.

"Raif."

Raif looked up as his name was spoken by a voice he had not heard in five years. A broad bear of a man, with stubbly reddish blond hair and light coppery eyes, stepped from the roundhouse onto the court. Squinting into the snow clouds, he said, "I was hoping for a more favorable light. With a good set of shadows upon me I swear I look a full stone lighter."

"Uncle."

It took Angus Lok only three strides to reach Raif's side. Catching him in a massive bear hug, Angus crushed him so tightly, Raif felt his rib cage bend. Just as quickly, Angus let him go and stood exactly an arm's length from him and examined him as thoroughly as if Raif were a horse he meant to buy.

Dressed in undyed suede pants and saddle coat, with high black boots and enough leather belts crossing his chest to harness a team of horses, Angus Lok looked every bit the seasoned ranger that he was. His cheeks were red with snow-burn, his lips were smothered with beeswax, and his ear-lobes were bound with soft leather strips to prevent chilblains and the 'bite.

"Stone Gods, lad! But ye've grown!" He knuckled the twelve-day beard on Raif's chin. "What d'you call this? When I was your age I barely had that much hair on my head, let alone my jaw!"

There was no answer to that. Raif smiled. Angus was here, and he didn't know if that was a good or a bad thing, but he knew that Angus could be trusted and was owed due respect. Tem had said so many times, even after the person who had brought the two men together had died: Meg Sevrance, wife of Tem, mother of Drey, Raif, and Effie, and sister to Angus Lok.

Abruptly Angus' face changed. Hazel eyes watched Raif closely. "I arrived early this morning. Raina told me about Tem. . . . He was a good man, your father. A fine husband to Meg. Adored her, he did." Angus smiled softly, almost to himself. "Though I must admit I hated him at first sight. There was nothing that man couldn't do better than me: hunt, shoot, drink, dance—"

"Dance? My father danced?"

"Like a devil in the water! Tem only had to hear a tune once to start snapping his heels and making steps. Quite a sight, he was, with his bear-claw cap and bearskin weskit. I do believe it was the reason my sister first fell in love with him, as he was hardly the handsomest of men. 'Least I didn't think so at the time."

Stupidly, Raif felt close to tears. He had never known Tem could dance.

Angus touched Raif's shoulder. "Walk a while wi' me, lad. I've been in the saddle for two long weeks, and I've a hankering to stretch these old legs."

Raif glanced back at the roundhouse. "I need to see Effie."

"I've just been with her. She's in good hands with Raina. She can wait a little while longer for her brother."

Raif wasn't convinced, yet it was obvious that Angus wanted to talk to him, so he let himself be led away.

Sunlight had turned the graze into a perfect slope, white and smooth as a hen's egg. Hemlock and blackstone saplings were no longer recognizable as trees, just strange, man-size mounds of snow that most clansmen called pine ghosts. The snow underfoot was loose and grainy, the motion of the wind preventing it from freezing hard. A few hare tracks broke the surface, soft and discreet as snagged wool.

Raif found little comfort in walking through familiar surroundings. Inigar Stoop's words prayed on his mind. *I fear that if you stay amongst us, you will watch us all die before your eyes have had their fill.* Raif shivered. Everything looked different now the guide had spoken. Trying to save the Bludd women and children from burning in the war wagon had been a mistake. No lives were saved. And in the end he had only created something worse.

"Here. Drink this."

Angus Lok's voice seemed to come from a very long way away. It took Raif a moment to pull his thoughts from the field north of the Bluddroad. Angus pressed a flask into his hand. Raif weighed it for a moment and then drank. The clear liquid was so cold it stung his gums, completely tasteless, and strong enough to render his breath invisible in the freezing air. Angus slowed his pace. After a few minutes he stopped by a pine ghost and rested his back upon it. Clods of snow dropped from the branches onto his boots. He made a small motion toward the rabbit fur-covered flask, encouraging Raif to drink more. Raif took only enough to heat his mouth.

"You had a hard time on the Bluddroad." It was not a question. Angus unbound his wrist ties and stripped off his fine sealskin gloves. His undyed clothes, the plain journeyman's blade strapped to his thigh, and his short-cropped hair marked him as an outsider. He was not clan. Tem had said that Angus and his sister grew up in the cityhold of Ille Glaive, close to the Ganmiddich border. Tem had met Meg during the year he was fostered at Ganmiddich, when that rich border clan held a summer dance for its yearmen and clan maids. Angus had been invited—Raif could not recall why—but he did remember that Crab Ganmiddich, the Ganmiddich chief, had forbidden him to come unless he brought a woman of his own to dance with. Angus had brought Meg. Tem saw her, and according to Gat Murdock, who was also present, he never gave her chance to dance with another man all night. They were married two months later, on the very day that Tem was released from his yearman's oath.

Meg Lok never returned home. On the day she married Tem Sevrance she became clan.

"Raina told me that you can shoot targets in the dark." Angus busied himself as he spoke, turning his gloves inside out and scraping the lining clean with a handknife. "She also said that when you and Drey returned from the badlands, you mentioned something about sensing the raid as it happened."

Raif felt his face grow hot. What right did Raina have to say such things to an outsider?

"Others tell me you're having problems with Mace Blackhail, arguing with him in front of clansmen, disobeying his orders—"

"Say what you mean, Angus. I know well enough how things stand in this clan."

Angus was unaffected by Raif's outburst. Finished with his gloves, he reversed them and pulled them back on. Only when he had cleaned and resheathed his knife did he see fit to reply. "I have business that takes me south to Spire Vanis. I think you should come along."

Raif met Angus Lok's eyes. Irises shot with flecks of bronze returned a steady gaze. *How much does he know? Has he been talking to Inigar Stoop?* "Why make such an offer now?"

Angus Lok gave Raif a look that made him wish he hadn't spoken. Angus wasn't clan, but he *was* kin. Respect was his due.

"When a man arrives back ahead of his party, it's usually a sign that there's trouble between him and the other members of that party. And when a clansman walks away from battle, he makes himself a traitor to his clan." Angus' face hardened along with his voice. "I'm not a fool, Raif. I heard what you said on the court. You knew enough about the fighting, but you said as good as nothing about the wounded. You don't even know for sure who's alive and who's dead. It's obvious you didn't see out the fight. Something happened, didn't it? Something happened to make you ride away."

Angus held up a hand to stop Raif from speaking. "I don't want to know what it was. Clan business is not my business. My sister's kin *is*, and from what I've heard this morning, Mace Blackhail has a mind to be rid of one of them. Now, by walking out on an ambush, that kinsman has as good as sharpened the staves for his own hanging."

Raif looked down. One afternoon, two people. Two people telling him it was best if he left the clan. His hand rose to weigh his lore.

Clan was everything.

All he loved and knew was here. Only eleven days ago he had sworn an oath binding himself to Blackhail for a year and a day. If Inigar Stoop had refused to hear his oath, refused to warm the stone for his yearing, then everything would be different. He would have been just another lad in the clan, not sworn to anyone or anything. If he had left the battle as Raif Sevrance, he would have been forgiven. Raif could almost hear Orwin Shank or Ballic the Red speaking up for him: *The lad is young, unsworn, and untested. Who can blame him for acting like a pelt-shorn fool?* Instead he had left as a yearman. And no one would wear their jaw finding excuses for a yearman who had left the field before battle's end. Disobeying an order, quarreling with the clan chief, even wasting arrows on a war wagon that was already alight, were offenses that could be dismissed as heat-of-the-moment anger or overzealousness. Clansmen could and *would* forgive such misdeeds. But for someone to leave the field while the battle was still raging, ride away without word or warning . . .

Raif closed his fist around his lore. Angus was right: Mace Blackhail would see him staved and skin-hung. The truth of what happened, the hunt and slaughter of the Bludd women and children, would be forgotten. It had to be. Raif knew he would never mention it in his own defense. To do so would dishonor Drey, Corbie Meese, Ballic the Red, and all the rest.

He would not bring such shame upon his clan.

Better to let Mace Blackhail smooth over the incident; let him spin some wolf tale where the Bludd women were armed and trying to escape, let everyone who took part in the slaughter return home believing it, and let the truth lie dead on the Bluddroad.

Raif felt a finger of ice tap his cheek. *Watcher of the Dead.* For the first time in his life, he understood what it meant to be raven born. The raven circled overhead, watched and waited, and then picked at the lifeless remains. Inigar Stoop had the truth of it in the guidehouse: He was not good for the clan.

The fifth Blackhail guidestone, which had been quarried from the stonefields south of Trance Vor and had stood within the roundhouse for three hundred years, had split because of his actions. The very stone itself had told him to go. Raif could not recall all the images the guidestone had shown him, but one thing was certain: None of the places was home. The Blackhail clanhold harbored no bloodred lakes or forests of silver blue trees. The guidestone had told him to go and shown him the way.

Raif shivered, suddenly colder than the day itself. He looked up and met eyes with Angus Lok. Angus' large hearty face and bright coppery eyes showed no signs of the temper he had displayed minutes earlier. He looked worried now and kept glancing east, perhaps searching for signs of the ambush party or to track the progress of the storm.

It had been five years since he had come here last. Effie had been little more than a baby at the time. Raif tried to recall all he knew about his uncle. He had a wife and children, yet Raif found he had no memory of where they lived or what they were called. He didn't even know how Angus made his living. Raif knew Meg had loved him dearly, and when she had been alive Angus had visited the roundhouse twice a year. He always brought gifts, good ones, such as practice swords made from petrified wood, chunks of green seaglass, thumb rings carved from walrus ivory, bowstrings woven from human hair, and little fur pouches made from whole collared lemmings, just the right size for holding flints.

Raif smiled as he remembered how he and Drey had fought over the gifts. One of them would always end up bleeding, Tem would clout both of them, and then Angus would miraculously produce a second identical object from his pack. After that Meg would scold everyone—Angus and Tem included—and shoo them all away until they had found some good sense.

Slowly Raif's smile faded. He glanced back at the round-house. Clan was everything: home, memories, kin. To leave would mean never coming back. A man could not break an oath and desert his clan and ever expect to return home. A muscle pulled high in Raif's chest. He loved his clan.

"So. What do you say, lad? Will you come with me to Spire Vanis? I'm not as young as I once was and could do with a young buck to watch my back."

*Yes, Raif Sevrance. Perhaps you had better step back, for all our sakes.*

Raif closed his eyes and saw the guidestone's leaking wound. Opened his eyes and saw Drey as he last glimpsed him: a hammer in his hand, saliva rolling down his chin, mouth filled with words Mace Blackhail had given him. No. Raif stopped the memory before it burned itself more deeply into his soul. Instead he forced himself to remember Drey on the court the morning they had left for the ambush. Out of twenty-nine men, he had been the only one willing to come forward and second his oath. *If I had such a brother . . . I would not shame him with my words or my deeds.*

Raif pulled himself up to his full height, hand coming to rest on the hilt of his halfsword. Inigar Stoop was right. Stay, and no matter what happened he would only bring shame to Drey.

The day grew darker and the badlands storm rolled south as Raif spoke his reply to Angus Lok.

# SEVENTEEN

## And Now We Must Bring Them War

VAYLO BLUDD KEPT HIS stallion on a tight rein in the snow. The old horse's eyesight was failing, and despite its advancing years it was still as mean as a pike. Any man or horse who drew too close could still find themselves the recipient of a swift kick to the shins or balls courtesy of the stallion who answered to the name of Dog Horse. Vaylo Bludd had a soft spot in his heart for the old nag. Although it had long since willfully disregarded all its obedience training, it still remembered two basic things: Dogs and small children were *not* to be kicked.

Smiling, Vaylo revealed his black and aching teeth. He'd had a terrible time training the stallion. It was a bad horse, everyone who saw it said so, yet here they were eleven years later, the Dog Lord and his bad horse, trotting through territory gained, as comfortable with each other as a man and mount could be.

"Light the torches, man! Light them!"

Riding at the head of the party of twelve, Vaylo heard his sixth son shout for light. Hanro had done little but shout orders all day. Vaylo wasn't quite sure whom he was trying to impress but swore to himself that next time his sixth son called for torches, scout reports, or wet halts he would make a point of riding Dog Horse close enough to land a swift kick to his vitals. Just because a man shouted orders, it didn't mean he was leader of the party. Hanro needed to learn that. All his sons did.

Not liking to dwell on the weaknesses of his seven sons, Vaylo turned his attention to his surroundings. Late afternoon light was fading rapidly, turning the snow underfoot blue and translucent like ice. Ahead lay the Copper Hills, once key to the Dhoone's greatness and military might. Copper mined there had made Clan Dhoone rich, allowing them to build the largest roundhouse in the clanholds, dam rivers, divert streams, and cart a mountain's worth of topsoil to the northern fellfields, converting barren land left by the retreating Hell's Tongue glacier into prime livestock graze.

This was the first time Vaylo Bludd had been out riding in the Dhoonehold since he had taken it, yet he had little mind for the fine grasses, the well-stocked trout lakes now sealed for the winter beneath a crust of freshwater ice, or the herds of elk traveling southeast through the blackstone forests, fat and glossy from two seasons of good grazing on the badlands to the north. All he had eyes for was the Bluddroad.

His grandchildren were four days late. The party had been

set to leave the Bluddhouse thirteen days back. They should have arrived at Dhoone by now. Drybone thought it likely that the party had met with bad weather in the hills and had set the great war cart down on its trusses and made camp until the worst of the storm had passed. It sounded likely, and Drybone was a cautious man—for a Trenchlander—yet Vaylo couldn't shake off a feeling of unease. His dogs were fussy and quick to bite, and the scent of Sarga Veys hung around the Dhooneseat like peat smoke.

In a way it had been a relief to leave the roundhouse. Clan Dhoone was not home. Perhaps in time that would change, when his sons' wives and their children arrived and claimed the hold as their own, but for now it was a place of strange echoes and foreign shadows and large empty rooms that no amount of birch fires could warm or light. The place made his teeth ache. To add to his troubles, four of his seven sons were living there with him, fighting like foxes down a hole, scheming, bickering over land and borders, and getting drunk as fools each night. And each and every one of them thought he could take the Dog Lord's place!

Vaylo Bludd spat out a wad of black curd. The dogs trotting at the stallion's hocks growled and snapped, shaking their heads and worrying against their leather collars and harness. They hated being spat at.

"Use your noses, then," he barked at them. "You weren't brought here to plow snow. Search. Find." Just to spite them, he made the stallion rear and kick out its hooves. Damn dogs! They'd been traveling since before dawn, and the only scents they'd caught were a lone broadback ewe, which they'd sent cowering up a slate crag, and a raven-killed eider whose flesh was one-day froze. Still, even though Vaylo was inclined to be churlish with his dogs, he was secretly quite relieved. No scents meant no people, and no people meant no foreigners on the road.

Indeed, the snow underfoot was as white and level as the head on a good stout. They had seen no sign of riders all day, and now that the light was failing they wouldn't be able to spot either tracks or camp smoke. Which was why the dogs needed to earn their keep.

The dogs, instantly recognizing the change in their master's temperament, ran ahead of the party, bounding or pushing through the snow, depending on the length of their legs. Vaylo sat back in the saddle, his ancient leathers creaking along with his bones. Stone Gods! But it was cold! Made him want to piss by the minute. He remembered once when he was young, riding from the Trenchland border to the Bluddhouse in a single day, not stopping once to empty his bladder or ease the chaff around his thighs. Damn fool thing to do! Probably damaged something internal along the way.

"Vaylo. We can't ride for much longer. Even with the torches lit." Cluff Drybannock, better known as Drybone, fell in at Vaylo's side. Even as he adjusted his horse's pace to match his chief's, Vaylo could hear the slap and patter of a second horse hurrying to catch up. Vaylo didn't have to turn his head to know who the second rider would be. Hanro wouldn't want to miss out on anything Drybone was likely to say.

"We'll ride a while longer," Vaylo said, deliberately speaking loudly to relieve the burning in his sixth son's ears. "Give the dogs chance to spot a league or two." As he spoke, he glanced over at the man he trusted most in the clan. Drybone was a great wall of a man, with barricades for shoulders and skin the color of red clay. He was not clan, not quite. His mother had been a Trenchlander whore, and his father . . . well, whore's bastards seldom knew just *who* their fathers were. When Drybone turned seven, his mother had sent him from the Trenchlands to the Bluddhold and told him never to come back. He was not one of their kind, and he was not wanted anymore.

Vaylo sucked on his old teeth. He hated Trenchlanders. What sort of woman would do that to her child? He still remembered Cluff being brought to the Bluddhouse by massive, bulb-nosed Yagro Wike, who had caught the lad tickling for trout in the Flow. Thin as a fence post, he was, and nearly wild with hunger and sunstroke. When asked what he was doing on Bludd territory, he had replied just the way his mother had taught him: "I'm a Trenchborn bastard. My father was a Bluddsman, and I'm searching until I find him and make him pay his due in my rearing."

The lad had such a fierce look in his bright blue eyes and

such a hard sense of purpose within his small clenched fists that Vaylo had taken to him on the spot. "A bastard, eh?" he'd said, ruffling the lad's night black hair. "Well, you should fit in just fine here. If no man speaks up to claim you, then I'll take you as my own."

That was twenty-five years ago. Drybone was a fullsworn clansman now and the best swordsman in the clan, yet the bastard was still in him. It never went away. Vaylo knew that. They understood each other, the whore's bastard and the clan chief's bastard. They knew what it was to give up their places at table, to fight a real or imagined insult until their mouths filled with blood, and to watch the laughter and scolding of legitimate children with envy so potent that it took something from you as surely as a long day's hunt in the woods. Vaylo had seen to it that Drybone had fared better than he, but you could not shield a child against the cruelty of other children. And to try to was a mistake of a different, greater kind.

Drybone had grown up well enough. He was a good solid fighter, a hard worker, and as vigilant of people's moods and motives as any bastard ever was. Vaylo knew his sons resented him, yet he didn't care one jot. Let them fret over who would take over his chiefdom when he was dead and gone. Worry might make men of them yet.

"Balhagro would have pulled well off from the road to make camp," Drybone said, squinting into the darkness beyond the pale sheets of torchlight. "And would have thought to cover the wagon's tracks."

The Dog Lord nodded. Drybone had a better opinion of Balhagro's initiative than he had, but that didn't mean he wasn't right. Age had brought Vaylo the slow realization that he would never know everything about men and that even those he knew best were capable of surprising him. Balhagro was a steady man; that was why Vaylo had chosen him to lead the moving party. That and the fact that Balhagro's eldest daughter had just produced his first grandchild, so the man knew just how fiercely grandchildren must be guarded.

"Aye," Vaylo said, suddenly hopeful that Drybone was right and Balhagro *was* the sort of man to take extreme caution. "We should have brought the hawks. They'd be better than the dogs in the snow."

"Your best pair were out last time I looked." Drybone glanced at Vaylo, a question in his sharp blue eyes.

Vaylo Bludd seldom lied. He either spoke the truth or said nothing. Looking at Cluff Drybannock, he saw a man who took care that his appearance was neither lesser nor greater than those around him. His braids were closely tied, but not excessively so; his furs and leathers were of good quality, but he wore no sable, lynx, or stillborn calfskin. The greatsword at his waist was shorter than most swords given that name, but it was polished to a high sheen and couched in the best lamb's wool. Vaylo didn't have to look around to know how his sixth son was dressed in comparison. Hanro was the dandy of the bunch. Spent more time oiling his braids than most women did plucking their leg hair. His crown was always shaved so smoothly that sometimes Vaylo wondered if he wasn't just plain bald.

Kicking his stallion forward, Vaylo made a minute gesture to Drybone to keep up, and the two rode ahead along the darkened road, leaving the rest of the party to the light of the torches. Hanro followed his father for a while, trotting awkwardly in the middle of the two groups. Then, obviously deciding he looked ridiculous attempting to listen in on his father's conversation, he slipped back into the main party. When Vaylo heard his sixth son's voice cracking orders in the peeved tone of a slighted dance partner, he knew he was free to speak.

Leaning in toward Drybone, he said, "The pair should have homed by now, Dry. I sent them to Duff's Stovehouse to see if the stovemaster had given ale or warmth to Sarga Veys."

Drybone took this information and thought on it, the muscles on his lean beardless face giving nothing away. "Storms?"

Vaylo shook his head. "Storms have been to the north. Duff's is to the south."

"You think the birds were shot?"

"No. I think they were stopped."

"By Veys?"

"He's a magic user, Dry. They can spell birds out of the sky."

The word *magic* was enough to make Drybone sign to the

Stone Gods, touching both his eyelids and then the copper vial at his waist containing his measure of powdered guidestone. "If he is a threat to the clan, say it, and I will take the south road and tend his throat myself."

Hearing Drybone speak, Vaylo felt the muscles in his old heart tighten. Drybone was not a man to make such statements lightly, and Vaylo knew he meant what he said. "I don't know if he's a threat or not, Dry. I don't even know what he and his master want. I just know I don't trust either of them. And when my two best hawks fail to home from a journey I've sent them on a dozen times before, then it sets my mind to worrying."

It would have been easy then for Drybone to point out that Vaylo should never have accepted Sarga Veys' offer of help in the first place, yet if the thought was on his mind, he didn't speak it. Vaylo was grateful for that. He needed no reminder of his mistakes. Living with them was penalty enough.

"You think Sarga Veys met with someone at Duff's?"

"I think it's possible. The morning he visited the Dhoonehouse he was poking around, asking questions of the stablehands and pot boys. He's a sly one, that Veys. I don't trust any man whose jaw is as smooth as his arse."

"Did he ask for anything in return for his master's help with the Dhoone raid?"

Vaylo looked at Drybone. It was a bold question he asked. Many Bluddsmen knew that something had happened the night of the Dhoone raid to give them an unnatural advantage; fewer knew that their clan chief had arranged it; and fewer still knew whom he had arranged it with. None knew the terms of the deal. Now Drybone was asking for that confidence.

Perhaps it was the darkness and quiet along the Bluddroad, or the thought that his grandchildren could be out somewhere in these hills, freezing and hungry, their wagon mired in thick snow, their fuel running low, but for some reason Vaylo *wanted* to speak. He had been the Dog Lord for over thirty years, and at no time during his tenure could he remember feeling so uncertain about the future. All his life he had taken what he wanted. Now he feared the Stone Gods wanted it back.

Keeping his voice low and his left hand resting on his guidestone pouch, he said, "Veys and his master are up to some kind of doggery, Dry. When they first came to me six months back, they said they wanted nothing in return for their help. Said the clanholds needed to be united under one firm leader, and that I, as chief of the mightiest of the clans, was just the one to do it. Veys swore his master would never ask for anything in return. And to this day he hasn't. Yet I know in my gut it isn't right. I have a suspicion I'm being used, but can't for the life of me work out how."

Drybone's expression never faltered as his chief spoke. If he was shocked, angered, or disappointed, he did not show it. After taking a moment to correct his gelding's path, he said, "Then we must be watchful, you and I. All our actions from now on must be well thought, and our priority must be to secure the Dhoonehold and prepare for an unknown threat from outside."

Reaching over, Vaylo clasped Drybone's arm. They were bastards together, and they knew what it was to defend their possessions against those seeking to take them away. Just knowing he had Drybone's support was enough to set his mind at ease.

As Vaylo's eyes met Drybone's and recognized and acknowledged the loyalty there, a wolf howl broke through the glassy stillness of the night. Keen and hard, it drove through. Vaylo's mind like a stave through his heart. The hairs on the back of his neck bristled, and deep within his stomach the remains of his last meal turned to lead. The wolf dog. Even as he took his next breath, he heard the other dogs yipping and barking as they rushed toward the call.

Swinging his great weight around in the saddle, Vaylo followed the wolf dog's cry with his eyes. It came from the north, on the wooded slope that lay above the road. Without pausing to give orders or finish his business with Drybone, Vaylo kicked his old stallion into a canter.

He followed the road for as long as he could, his eyes aching with the strain of holding a path in the darkness. The snow reached the stallion's fetlocks, and great clouds of blue crystals shot into Vaylo's face as he rode. Dimly he was aware of the rest of the party following, but he had no mind for them. The boiled-leather body armor that stretched across his chest felt as tight and constricting as a corset, and Vaylo swore curses to the man who had buckled it. The wolf dog's howls made him mad with fear. Three years he had owned that beast, yet he had never once heard such a sound from its throat.

As he took the slope, a pair of dogs sprang forward, frothing and howling and throwing their heads from side to side, eager to lead the way. Vaylo spoke words to the stallion, and the old beast allowed the dogs to guide him.

Limber pines, their spines bent by the weight of newly fallen snow, shivered like caged animals as he passed. Saplings spilled their loads as the stallion brushed against them, snow hitting the earth like fallen fruit. The exposed pine needles glistened with protective resin, scenting the air with the smell of winter and ice. The cold made Vaylo's eyes water, and he wiped tears away with fingers encased in dog's-hide gloves. The fur around his collar was stiff with breath ice, and his woolen cloak pulled at his throat, its fibers heavy with massed snow.

The dogs led the stallion along a cut bank where runoff flowed in spring and through dense clusters of black fir and stone pines. Vaylo thought he detected an unevenness in the snow underfoot, but he couldn't be sure if it was due to tracks lying beneath the surface or uneven ground. His heart felt too big in his chest, as if some unknown disease had enlarged and distended it, causing chamber walls to thicken and muscle to bloat. He could hardly breathe.

Abruptly the dogs separated, allowing the stallion to step ahead of them into a gently sloped clearing high above the road. The wolf dog, with its thick-muscled neck and metal-colored snout, stood in the center and howled one last time as its master approached. Vaylo slid from his horse, letting the reins fall slack over the stallion's neck. Behind him the other dogs waited, their yelps growing increasingly softer until there was no sound at all. The wolf dog's eyes were two coals burning in the darkness. Vaylo stepped toward them, knowing as he did so that he would find nothing good. He was the Dog Lord, and it had been many years since he had last fooled himself with false hope.

*We are Clan Bludd, chosen by the Stone Gods to guard their borders. Death is our companion. A hard life long lived is our reward.*

The Bludd boast echoed in the back of Vaylo's throat. Words that had been said so many times over so many centuries that their truth had been deadened by layers of callused skin. Vaylo did not want to think on their meaning. Not tonight.

Bones cracking, furs shedding ice, he stepped toward the wolf dog. The dog shrank as he approached, crouching on all fours and lowering its belly to the ground. A soft whine vibrated deep within its throat, and it began to lick and snuffle at something that stuck out from the snow.

Vaylo fell to his knees. Lashing out violently, he sent the wolf dog away. Speaking words harsher than he had ever spoken before, he made sure it would not return for the rest of the night. Oblivious of the creature's slow, reluctant withdrawal and the thin, almost human cries it made as it left, Vaylo stripped off his gloves and thrust his bare hands into the snow.

He dug until his fingers turned blue and his skin cracked and blood rolled over flesh he could no longer feel. He dug until his leather cuffs froze solid and his knuckles were bared to the bone and snow driven deep beneath his fingernails was ground into lenses of ice. He dug until his hands and wrists swelled with frostbite, blood ceased flowing to his fingers, and flesh died. Others came and offered help, but he would let no one near him. Light was brought, words were spoken, but all he had mind for was digging his granddaughter's body from the snow.

Nine, she was. The fiercest little thing that had ever worn a braid on the Bluddhold. She beat all the boys her age at swordplay, and she fought hard and dirty, and Vaylo still had the sore spots to prove it. Just before he'd left, she'd jumped him in the storeroom and stuck him in the knee with her older brother's training sword. Vaylo smiled as he remembered her wild, triumphant giggling. *That girl*, he thought. *That girl is a Bluddsman through and through.*

Her eyes were closed, but her mouth was open and full of snow. The hammer blow that killed her had not drawn blood. As Vaylo dug and scraped and freed her body from the snow, he spoke words, scolding her for playing in the snow. What had Granda always told her? Never play in the snow in unknown woods.

When finally she was free, he tugged the cloak from his back, wrapped her tightly, and carried her to where Dog Horse could watch over her. He never kicked children; she would be safe with him.

That done, he went back to the snow and dug again.

It took him all night to free his grandchildren. Others worked on the women, and more still worked on the road, digging out the men who had fought to save the party. Vaylo paid them little heed. His grandchildren were cold, and they needed their Granda to warm them, and he couldn't stop until he had lifted each tiny body from the snow.

Dawn came, bringing light that was not welcome and a new day that was wanted even less. Clouds smothered the sky. The snow turned pearly and gray, the color of uncooked seal flesh. The pines around the clearing were perfectly still.

"The Sull did not do this."

Vaylo looked up from where he was crouched by the body of his newest grandchild, a baby boy no more than ten months old. Drybone stood above him, his face dark with grief.

"The Sull would never kill children."

Vaylo nodded. He knew why it was important for Drybone to speak: He was half Trenchlander, and the Trenchlanders were part Sull. Turning back to the frozen body of his grandson, Vaylo began to brush the ice from the child's fine black hair. "Clan Blackhail did this," he murmured. "And now we must bring them war."

Somewhere many leagues to the west, the wolf dog began to howl.

# EIGHTEEN

## *Leaving Home*

EFFIE AND RAINA CAME to see them off. As Raif held his sister, pushed his cheeks against her soft, beautiful hair, he was aware of something moving in the darkened hallway beyond the roundhouse door. Wooden boards creaked, and a slight form slipped into the cave of shadows that existed beneath the stairs.

"That's just Nellie Moss," Effie said without looking around. "She's always following Raina about. One day she'll end up dead in the snow."

Raif pulled back from Effie so he could look at her face. Huge blue eyes, the color of the sky at midnight, regarded him with a level gaze. "What do you mean, Effie? Why will Nellie Moss end up dead?"

Effie shrugged. The russet-colored dress she wore was woven from heavy goat's wool and made her look like a doll dressed in grown-up clothes. "I don't know. She'll just be dead, that's all."

*Oh, gods.* Raif rocked his sister against his chest. She was such a small thing—too small for her age. When had she learned to speak of death so calmly?

Gently he set her down on her feet. A few strands of hair had fallen over her eyes, and he took a moment to push them back. He had to believe she would be better off without him. He had to.

"Effie will be safe with me and Anwyn," Raina said, taking hold of Effie's arm and leading her away. "And Drey will be back today or tomorrow, and you know how much he loves her."

Raif did not speak.

Angus touched his arm. "Come on. Dawn's cracking. We'd best be on our way." With that, he led Moose and his own horse, a muscular bay with clever eyes, across the court.

A light snow was falling, and Angus' hood was up. The fur around the hood was dark and glossy, and Raif could not tell what animal it came from.

Raif turned to face Effie and Raina Blackhail one last time. Raina had worked through the night to get supplies together for the journey south. She hadn't once asked why he was leaving, but she knew about the guidestone and had guessed that something other than a battle well fought had taken place on the Bluddroad. Like Inigar Stoop, she had refused to hear the details. Raif didn't know why she was going out of her way to help him. It might be that Inigar had told her he was bad for the clan. Yet somehow Raif doubted that. Raina Blackhail wasn't the kind of woman to act on someone else's words.

Yet she had married Mace Blackhail that same day he had been made chief, with Dagro less than forty days dead. According to Anwyn, the ceremony had been short and joyless, and not one sworn clansman had come forth to dance above the swords. Raina herself had retired to the guidehouse straight after, and no one, not even Inigar, had been able to persuade her to come out and eat at her own bride's feast. Anwyn said that Mace had been in a fury and would have broken down the door if the thought of missing the ambush hadn't pulled him away.

Raif reached for the usual anger, but it wasn't there. Mace Blackhail had won. He had everything: the clan, the clan chief's wife, a successful ambush to boast of when he returned. All those who had questioned his leadership were either dead, muzzled, or gone.

"I will speak to Drey on your behalf," Raina said, breaking into his thoughts. "My husband's voice won't be the only one he heeds." She met Raif's gaze, and in that instant he knew the real reason she had married Mace Blackhail.

Strangely, it made it easier for him to go. If she could marry a man she hated just to guard over the clan, then surely he could do this for Drey? Quietly he spoke his last words to Effie and then walked the short distance to where Angus Lok was waiting with his horse.

When he was mounted and ready in the saddle, the reins couched in the split in his thick dog's-hide gloves, he spun his horse to face south. He did not look at Effie or the round-house again.

*You are not good for this clan, Raif Sevrance.*

Without another word, Raif kicked Moose hard and rode away.

Angus Lok caught up with him an hour later as Moose worked his way through the old snow on the outskirts of the graze. Raif guessed Angus had held back to talk privately with Raina, but he wasted no thoughts on what matters had passed between the two. He concentrated only on the way ahead.

Dawn was a slow process. Light came, but it had no direction or visible source. The ground snow stripped shadows of their depth, and the distance to the sandstone ridge and taiga beyond was hard to judge. Raif had hunted in the great pine forest more times that he could count. When he was a child he had imagined it went on forever; in all the rangings he had been on, he had never once made it to the other side.

Angus rode in silence. After an hour or so he spoke a word to the bay and took the lead. Guiding them down to the base of the ridge, he followed a hunting track Raif had little knowledge of or feel for. Clansmen seldom took the ridge to the east, preferring to walk their horses up the more gentle inclines to the west. The snow was thinner here, and Moose stepped on hard ground for the first time all day. Young hemlocks and stone pines glistened with rime ice like bodies emerging from water. Even with their outer bark and needles hard froze, their sharp, resinous smell still spored the air.

Raif kept an iron grip on his thoughts, blocking out everything but the little needed to get by.

Hours passed. The temperature rose along with the light. Ptarmigan shrieked from the cover of snow-laden ground birch, and far in the distance a black-tailed deer brayed like a mule.

"That's a good horse you have there."

Raif's mind was so tightly locked on the many small adjustments necessary for riding up a rocky slope, it took him a long moment to realize that Angus had spoken. Glancing up, he saw Angus had pulled back so the bay was almost alongside Moose. Obviously Angus was well used to travel:

Every part of his body was oiled, bound, waxed, hooded, and insulated against the cold. His face alone boasted separate areas of beeswax, elk fat, and neat's-foot oil.

Seeing where Raif's gaze lingered, Angus grinned. "My wife would have me heated in a dry pan and then trodden to death by donkeys if I let anything happen to this handsome face."

Raif made a smile. He didn't want to talk.

" 'Course, when she sees you, I'm counting on her turning a blind eye to the odd broken vein. She should let me live . . . as long as I don't lose half a nose to the 'bite."

Even as he realized it was Angus' intention to get him talking by any means he could, Raif couldn't help but be interested in what he said. He knew almost nothing about his uncle's family. Angus kept all the details close. "We're going to your home?"

If Angus Lok was pleased that Raif had spoken, he did not show it, merely concentrated on keeping the bay's coffin bones clear of the rocks. "Perhaps, when my business in the south is done. It's been a long time since my wife last saw you and Drey, and she's never once set eyes on Effie. She'd skewer my ears if she knew I had you with me and didn't bring you home. Right fierce, she is. Especially in the cold months."

*Drey.* How long would it take him to crush his brother's swearstone to dust? Raif heard his voice say, "I don't remember your wife ever coming to visit the roundhouse."

"Aye, lad, well you wouldn't. Wee bairn, you were. Drey was still in his pelts. Had the meatiest little calves I've ever seen on a boy his age. Knew how to kick with them, too—just like his da." Angus Lok looked up. Bits of reddish blond stubble had already grown through the lard smeared on his chin, giving his face the fierce look of a stinging fish. His eyes were a different matter, shifting color from copper to dark amber as quickly as if pigment had been poured into his irises. "It's for the best, you know. Effie and Drey will get by without you. Good people are watching out for them, don't forget that. Mace Blackhail is just one man. He might lead the clan, but he *isn't* the clan. Men and women like Corbie Meese, Anwyn Bird, and Orwin Shank are the clan. They will follow Mace only so far."

Raif wanted to believe what Angus said, but Angus hadn't been party to the ambush on the Bluddroad. He didn't know what good people were capable of when a man like Mace Blackhail stood behind them. In the short time Angus had spent with the clan, he had uncovered a great deal of its business from the private conversations he'd had with Raina, Orwin Shank, and others, but he didn't know Mace Blackhail. Raif set his lips in a hard line, tasting the frost that had formed there. No one but he knew the Wolf.

Angus said no more on the subject. Instead he concentrated on guiding the horses up the slope. The sandstone cliffs were slick with ice. Underground streams forced water through the soft, porous rock, creating a breaking ground of loose gravel and split stones. Ferns and bladdergrass lashed at the horses' cannons as they climbed, and great beds of frozen moss made it difficult for even the bay to keep his footing. Angus dismounted and led the bay, and after a few minutes Raif did likewise.

In the three hours they had been traveling, Raif had seen no sign of Angus' incoming path. Snow had been light for the past day, and up within the protected folds of the ridge wall there was little coverage, so Raif had expected to see some indication—flattened grass, broken ice, horse tracks—that his uncle had traveled this way less than two days earlier. He looked and looked, but there was nothing. As they crested the rise and Raif saw nothing but level snow stretching out toward the great black body of the taiga, he drew level with Angus and said, "Why aren't we taking the same route out of the clanhold as you took coming in?"

Angus Lok's eyes shifted color for the second time that day, and Raif saw tiny flecks of green in the irises he had not noticed before. Pulling back his hood, he said, "You've got a good eye on you, lad."

Raif took out a shammy and began cleaning ice and mucus from Moose's nostrils as he waited for his uncle to say more. Angus turned out his hood to air it, then took his rabbit flask from his pack. He drank a good portion. When he was done he did not offer the flask to Raif.

"Ranging is my business. I've traveled the Territories for twenty years, and it's my wont never to take the same route twice in a season." Angus smiled, showing good straight teeth. "'Course, me being me, I took the easy way in, so now we're stuck taking the bastard's way out. I'm always doing that, lad. You'll get used to it given time."

Raif felt the force of his uncle's charm and goodwill working to settle his mind. Before he'd had chance to frame a reply, Angus spoke to change the subject.

"What say I take out some of those calf livers Anwyn bled until they were dry as bone and then boiled until they were boot leather, and eat them in the saddle? I'd like to get to the pines before next snow." He squinted into the dead whiteness of the sky. "Looks as if we're in for some bad weather before dark. What do you think?"

Raif shrugged, letting the matter drop. His uncle's evasions were more telling than any straight answer. Just a couple of sentences and Angus Lok had put the old subject to a quiet death while blithely introducing at least another two to block the way back. It was a clever feat, and one Raif made a mental note not to forget.

As he put his boot in the stirrup to mount Moose, the gelding turned and Raif was forced to swing round to keep his footing. Abruptly he found himself staring back over the ridge toward the roundhouse. He wasn't prepared for it. All day and he had never once looked back. Muscles in his chest tightened.

The round, snow-covered roof of the roundhouse was clearly identifiable, floating within the moat of cleared ground that was the court. Smokestacks showed up as black rings against the white roof, and the steam and soot they belched looked like fumes venting from an underground fault. Dark dots moving through the graze told of a hunt party out to shoot wild boar, ptarmigan, and deer. Raif strained to hear the yelps of the setters. When his ears finally picked up the high, familiar braying, he suddenly wished he hadn't heard it and turned.

He made a lot of noise settling himself in the saddle and kicking Moose forward. When that wasn't enough, he spoke, saying the first thing that came into his mind. "How is your daughter? Is she wed yet?"

Angus had also mounted and was now sitting in the saddle, chewing on a liver. He seemed glad of an excuse to spit it out. "Cassy's not wed. No." He was silent a moment, his face thoughtful. After breaking the bay gently into the knee-high snow, he said, "'Course, you wouldn't know about the other two, would you? There's Beth now—my second girl— and my little one, Maribel. Though call her that and she won't know who you're talking to. Doesn't even know her own name. Little Moo she is, and Little Moo she'll stay." Angus smiled softly to himself. "Can't think what the young men will make of it when time comes for courting."

Fearing silence just then, Raif said, "Tem said you live near Ille Glaive."

"Aye, that we do. Couple of days away, nothing more." Angus swung around in the saddle and unhooked his bow-case from the bay's hipstrap. "Here," he said, holding it out for Raif to take. "You carry it for a while. I see you haven't one of your own, and it would be a shame to waste the only bow in the party on the man who's least able to use it."

Raif took the bow automatically, even though he knew his uncle was being modest. Tem was fond of telling the story of how Angus had once shot a wild boar through goosegrass at two hundred paces. "Twilight, it was," Tem had said. "And even the shadows had shadows."

Only when Raif had stripped off his outer gloves and was busy with dog hooks, fastening the bowcase to Moose's leatherwear, did he realize that Angus had changed the subject yet again.

"Orwin Shank said that on the morning the party formed for the ambush, you returned to the roundhouse with a dozen heart-killed beasts. Quite a haul for a night's work. Tem must have been a good teacher."

"He was."

Ignoring the hostile tone of Raif's voice, Angus carried on. "I knew a man once who could heart-kill any beast he set his sights on. He could even do it in the dark. We shared a season's hunting together, many years back now. Whenever we made camp, I'd sit around the cookfire facing in, and he'd sit facing out, bow on his lap, bowring on his finger, watching the darkness for game. Sooner or later some poor possum or shoat would always draw close to investigate the fire and the smell. That was when Mors would take them, clean as if it were day."

Angus put his hand on his chest. "Never saw as much as a cleft foot or a red eye myself, and I'd sit by that fire thinking the man I'd chosen to camp with was as mad as a dog with a stick in its eye. Yet off he'd go, trekking into the darkness, and sure enough five minutes later we'd have fresh kill to roast. Took me quite a while to get accustomed to it, I can tell. And just between you and me heart-killed possum tastes like shit."

Raif smiled.

Angus grinned, his eyes turning coppery again. "I used to say to him, *Mors, can't you hit them in the head or something?* and he'd say, *No. Only the heart.*"

The quick, appraising look Angus gave him as he spoke sobered Raif completely. "Who was this Mors?"

"Oh Mors is still alive. Though he's a bit different now than he was twenty years ago. Who knows, one day you may meet him." Angus was silent as he guided the bay through a drift of snow that reached to the gelding's chest. When they were free of the incline, he said, "I asked Mors once if he could kill men the same way as he killed beasts."

"And?"

"Said it wasn't the same. He'd tried, but couldn't do it."

Inside his fox hood, Raif's neck and cheeks flushed hot. He saw the Bludd spearman tearing flesh from Rory Cleet's thigh, remembered finding the man's heart in his sights . . . then shooting him dead. Heart-killed. Suddenly feeling as if he couldn't breathe, Raif pushed back the fox hood. All the sickness and weakness that had seized him after the killing came back with such clarity it was like feeling it over again, here, on the taiga's edge.

"Here. Drink this."

Raif looked up. Angus Lok was holding out his flask. Raif shook his head. How long had it been since he'd torn back his hood? Surely only a moment? Yet Angus had had enough time to find and uncork his flask.

Shrugging off Raif's refusal, Angus took a swig from the flask himself. Smiling fondly at the flask as he corked it, he said, "We'll rest a bit once we're under cover of the trees.

Feed the horses. The snow in the forest should be light enough for us to make a fair pace before dark."

This time Raif was grateful for the change in subject. His heart was racing, and the taste of metal leaked through his mouth like blood from a sliced gum. Although he didn't much feel like it, he forced himself to speak. "Will we travel south through the taiga until we reach Black Spill?"

Angus shook his head. "No. We'll head south a bit, then east. There's a few places I mean to visit along the way."

"Stovehouses?"

"Aye. I have a habit of running out of good liquor in the most inconvenient of places, so I never miss the chance to top my load. Besides, the stovemaster's wife at Duff's has a way with needle and thread. And Darra would have my eyeballs for chewing curd if I passed that close and didn't bring her back a length of cloth."

Raif nodded, but not lightly. Stovehouses were the backbone of the clanholds. Any mud-and-hide mound, felt-covered dugout, log cabin, or ancient barn could be named one. All a stovehouse needed was a stove. Some of the larger ones like Duff's were more like inns, with a stovemaster to keep the stove lit day and night, cots to sleep on, hot food, warm ale, and stalls to box the horses. Others were little more than deserted shacks, their walls plugged with wax against the wind, their stoves cold, a cord of logs stacked in the corner, and dried food packed high in the rafters, out of reach of bears. All clansmen traveling from one clanhold to another used them. They were a basic necessity in a land where storms could roll from the Great Want in less time than it took to skin an elk.

Stovehouses were no-man's-land. Any man or woman from any clan had right of refuge in every stovehouse in the clanholds. Wars, border disputes, clan feuds, and hunting rivalries were all set aside once a clansman stepped within shadow of a stove.

Stove laws were sacred in the clanholds, and although many legendary fights and battles had taken place in the woods and balds directly surrounding the great stovehouses, no one ever bared weapons inside. To do so would bring shame and condemnation upon oneself and one's clan.

As he rode through the thick, powdery snow, Raif worked out who he would be likely to meet at Duff's. His mood darkened. Any number of clansmen could be there, hunting by day in the winter game runs east of the taiga, warming themselves around the great copper stove shaped like a brewer's vat at night.

And then there would be Bluddsmen.

Raif felt for his raven lore for the first time that day, turning it in his hand like a game piece. He didn't want to think about what would happen between Bluddsmen and Hailsmen once news of the Bluddroad slaying leaked out. Stove laws would be tested to breaking then.

"Have you got that bow of mine braced and ready?" Angus called from ahead. "I'll be expecting a pair of ice hares in payment for the lending. Fat ones, mind. Not some skinny albino rats."

Raif looked over Angus' shoulder to the black wedge of forest they were about to enter. By turns scattered, dense, fire leveled, and wind stunted, the taiga stretched for hundreds of leagues south and west of the clanhold. A stand of old, perfectly straight black spruce formed the forest's north wall, and Raif was aware of light and wind levels dropping as he approached. It was like entering a building. The snow underfoot became firmer and more shallow with each step. Noises fell away. Overhead, the limbs of the spruces created a ceiling of nursed snow.

Raif swallowed as he took the bow from its case. He couldn't get the taste of metal out of his mouth.

Angus slowed the pace. After a few minutes he looked over his shoulder. "What say we stop and nosebag the horses?"

Raif shook his head. He didn't want to stop. Already he was searching for game. It was a reflex action of all clansmen upon entering the taiga, but none more so than those who chose the bow as their first weapon. Even as he hated himself for it, part of him welcomed the relief. Hunting meant not having to think.

Time passed. Angus was silent, his hood pulled close to his face. The taiga deepened, revealing narrow corridors leading to frozen ponds, standing stones ringed with crowberries, and clearings bedded with icegrass and touch-me-nots. The smell of pitch settled in Raif's clothing like dust as he watched the ground for game.

A ptarmigan, fat as a loaf of bread, flew up through the spruces, dislodging snow as its wings clipped pine needles. Raif drew his bow, sighted the bird, then *called* it to him. Blood warmth flooded his mouth. The rapid beat of the ptarmigan's heart pulsed like a vein in his cheek. The bird was young, strong, its belly full of crowberries and soft willow leaves. Raif breathed once on the bowstring to warm it and then let the arrow fly.

A soft *thuc* sounded, then the arrow hit the ptarmigan with such force, it knocked the bird from the sky. Raif didn't have to see the body to know that the arrowhead had found its heart.

"A pretty shot," Angus said.

Raif glanced down. His uncle was watching him intently, his eyes the color of old wood.

After a moment Angus turned his horse. "Wait here. I'll fetch the bird."

Spitting to clean his mouth, Raif watched his uncle slip through the trees. Absently he ran a hand over the bow. Made of a combination of wood and horn, and tilled so smoothly that it was like touching glass, the bow was unlike any other he had held before. Silver and midnight blue markings had been stamped deep into the riser, but Raif couldn't work out how.

By the time Angus returned with the ptarmigan, Raif had shot two hares. The first he saw clearly as it ran from the path of Angus' bay. The second was crouched in a head of sagebrush, and Raif told himself he had seen it *before* he released the string.

"We'll eat well tonight," Angus said, pulling the shafts from the hares and bagging them along with the bird. "I can see it's going to be useful having you along, Raif Sevrance."

Raif waited for his uncle to bring up the fact that all three creatures had been heart-killed, yet his uncle said nothing, merely busied himself with cleaning the arrow shafts before the blood froze.

They fastened feedbags on the horses and rode until dark.

Angus led them to a deserted stovehouse that Raif thought only clansmen knew of. Dug out of sandstone and clay, the stovehouse was little more than a hole in the ground. Hidden in the center of an island of stone pines, the entrance was covered by a slab of slate as big as a wagon wheel. Raif worked to clear the moss and rootwood from around the edges as Angus took his pickax to a nearby spawning pond and broke out some freshwater ice.

Raif worked himself hard, pushing aside the entrance slab by himself rather than waiting for Angus to lend a hand. When that was done, his muscles were aching and his inner woolens were soaked with sweat. It wasn't enough. Taking the hand ax from his pack, he went to cut wood.

Angus found him an hour later, his gloves and oilskin glued with sap, pine needles stuck to his sleeves, veins in his chopping hand open and bleeding, and the yellow bruises of imminent frostbite coloring his skin. A pile of logs, cut almost to splinters, was heaped at his back.

"You've done enough now, lad," Angus said, taking the ax from him and guiding him away. "Come wi' your old uncle. The stove's glowing like a warm heart, and there's good food upon it, and you may not have your clan this night, but you and I are kin."

Raif let himself be led to the stovehouse.

Angus had done a good job of turning the clay-walled hollow into a place filled with warmth and light. A damp cloth was steaming against the belly of the brass stove, and Angus took it and wrapped Raif's hands closely to stop chilblains from forming. Next he bit the cork from the rabbit flask that had been cooling in a pot of snow. "Drink," he said, and Raif did. The alcohol was so cold it *burned*.

The stovehouse was tiny and low ceilinged. Pine roots had broken through the walls in some places, jutting out like bones from a rain-worn grave. Raif sat on the ground in front of the stove and ate and drank what Angus gave him. The skin on the roast hares was black, and it crackled as it broke, releasing hot juices and scalding steam. The ptarmigan meat was rich and fatty. Angus had stuffed it with wild sage and roasted it in its feathers.

There was a lot of smoke. The smoke hole was open, but the stove was old and warped, and fumes and soot leaked from the stack.

Raif felt numb. He couldn't remember the last time he'd rested or slept.

"That bird was a beauty," Angus said, sucking on a wing bone. "Daresay it would have been better for a plucking, but for the life of me I hate pulling feathers." He watched Raif through the smoke, his large keen face now cleared of its protective oils. Setting aside his dish of bones, he said, "When you shot the bird, did you taste or smell anything?"

Raif shook his head.

"Nothing coppery, like blood or metal?"

"No," Raif lied. "Why do you ask?"

Angus shrugged. "Because that's what happens when a man draws upon the old skills."

"Old skills?"

"Sorcery, some would call it. I've never cared for the word myself. Frightens people." A quick glance at Raif. "Better to use the Sull name: *rhaer'san*, the old skills."

Hair on Raif's arms lifted at the mention of the Sull. The Sull were seldom named out loud. The Trenchlanders, who lived on Sull lands and were part Sull and who traded fur and lumber with the clanholds, were different. Clansmen often took their names in vain. But the Sull . . . no clansman ever dealt with the Sull. The great warriors of the Racklands, with their silver letting knives, pale steel, recurve bows, and proudlocks, wasted neither breath nor time on clan. Raif tried to keep his voice light. "What are the signs that a man is using the old skills?"

"Well, as I said, the one who draws it often tastes and smells metal. He'll weaken, too. His vision can blur, his stomach cramp, and often he'll get pains in his head. It all depends upon the level of power drawn. I saw a man fall from his horse once, just plain keeled over into the mud. It was a full week before he could stand on his own two feet. Drew too much, you see, tried to do something he had neither the power nor the skill for. Nearly killed him."

Raif felt his cheeks burn. He had come close to falling from his horse after he had heart-killed the Bludd spearman.

"There was a time when those who could draw upon the old skills were valued, when mortar binding the Mountain Cities was white as snow, and the clanholds had kings instead of chiefs. Indeed, you'll find some who'll tell you that the masons who built Spire Vanis owed as much to the old skills as they did to their chisels and lathes. A few will even swear that Founding Quarterlords had more than a few drops of old blood running in their veins."

"Old blood?"

Angus' eyes shifted color. "It's just a term. Old blood. Old skills. The two are one and the same."

It was an evasion, and Raif guessed Angus would work quickly to cover it. He was right.

"'Course in those days, it wasn't unheard of for clansmen to draw upon the old skills. Small things: healing and foretelling and the like. It wasn't until Hoggie Dhoone's time that the clanholds turned their backs on sorcery."

"No clansman worth his lore would take part in anything unnatural."

"Is that so?" Angus scratched his chin. "And how do you suppose a clansman *gets* his lore? Chance? Fate? Or does the guide pluck straws from a hat?"

"He dreams."

"Aah. That's it. He dreams. Nothing unnatural *there*, that's for sure." Angus tilted his head one way and the other, making a great show of thinking. "And then there's the guidestone itself. . . . I suppose each clansman carries its powder with him at all times so he's never caught short of a spot of mortar. Must come in mighty useful those times when you're out ranging and you see a poorly built wall. A few cups of water, some fire ash, and a handful of powdered guidestone, and you'll have it repointed in no time."

Raif glowered at his uncle. "We carry our guidestone with us because it's Heart of Clan. It's what we've always done."

Surprisingly, Angus nodded. "Aye, lad, you're right. It was wrong of me to bait you. Can't help myself sometimes—I'm wicked like that. If Darra were here, she'd have me out packing snow by now." Standing, he fed the ptarmigan bones to the stove.

Raif watched the flames shiver through the smoke hole. His cheek and fingers were throbbing where they had taken the frost, and a deep weariness stole over his body like rising water. He was annoyed at Angus but too tired to make anything of it. "Does anyone use the old skills today?"

Angus did not stop tending the stove, but something in his body changed as Raif spoke. Shrugging to the flames, he said, "Some. A few."

"In the cityholds?"

"Aye, perhaps. But it's frowned on there, just as it is in the clans. The cities have their One God, and he's a jealous one at that. Any powers not of his making have long been forced into the shadows, their time nearly past. Hoggie Dhoone recognized that a thousand years ago, when he drove all who used the old skills from the clanholds. The One God has long arms. He lives within the Mountain Cities, but make no mistake: His reach extends to the clans."

"But we worship the Stone Gods."

"Aye, and you've got the last of the great Clan Kings to thank for that."

Raif ran a hand through his hair. He didn't understand what Angus was getting at. "Why do you keep mentioning Hoggie Dhoone? He hated the cities and their one jealous God. His armies slew ten thousand city men at the Battle of Stone Cairns. He made the Bitter Hills his wall, swearing that no man who was not a clansman would ever raise a roof beyond them. He *saved* the clanholds. And he had no dealings with the One God."

Angus began packing the stove for the night, adding only the largest chunks of firewood to the stack. "Aye, you're right about Hoggie Dhoone: He *did* save the clanholds. He saw the cities for what they were. He knew that given half a chance they'd march their armies over the Bitter Hills and shatter clan guidestones to dust. He knew what they thought of the clanholds and its nine gods. Hoggie Dhoone was no fool. He fought the cities with one hand, and met them halfway with the other."

"Hoggie Dhoone never met anyone halfway."

"Did he not?" Angus shrugged. "So it's just coincidence that he began outlawing the old skills at the same time the Mountain Cities did? Not the act of a clever man who saw the way the world was turning and chose to turn *with*, not against it."

"I don't understand."

"It's simple. Hoggie Dhoone was not prepared to give up the Stone Gods. He knew the Mountain Cities thought them cruel and barbaric, and he also knew that the sort of fanatic wars that raged in the Soft Lands to the south could easily break out in the North. So rather than set himself and his gods apart and risk the self-righteous might of the cities falling upon him, he chose to run with the pack. Everyone who used the old skills was exiled or hounded. It was nothing to him. The Stone Gods have always been hard gods. They're not known for weeping over the dead.

"In one canny move, Hoggie Dhoone turned the Mountain Cities into his allies. Oh, there were battles aplenty—you know that better than me—but they were always over land, not religion. Shared beliefs may be a powerful thing. But nothing quite binds like shared hatred."

Raif stared at Angus; he didn't know what to think. Hoggie Dhoone was the last of the great Clan Kings, and no one in the clan had ever told his story quite like that. It lessened him. "If the Mountain Cities were as fanatical as you say, then why didn't they go after the Sull? Their gods are older than the clans'."

Angus closed the stove door, creating darkness. "Because it suited them to strip land, not gods, from the Sull."

Raif closed his eyes. He thought Angus might say more, but he didn't and began settling himself down by the opposite wall. Raif almost spoke to break the silence. Suddenly he didn't want to be alone with his thoughts. Time passed. Angus' breathing grew shallow and regular, and Raif imagined his uncle asleep. *How long before I sleep?* he wondered. How long before the nightmares come?

# NINETEEN

## *Swinging from a Gibbet*

ASH HELD HER BREATH, scrunched her face as tight as it would go, and began to hack away at her hair. She couldn't look. Couldn't bear to see it fall to the snow. Stupid, she told herself. Vain, weak-minded, and stupid. It was only hair. It would grow back. Still, she couldn't quite bring herself to cut it as short as she had intended. She tried, but her hands kept defying her, and the knife kept sliding downward, and she didn't have the heart to fight it.

She had originally planned to cut it as short as a boy's, but that decision was taken in the broad light of day, when decisions were easier to make and keep. Now, at midnight, sitting on an iron bench cleared of snow in the Street of the Five Traitors in Almstown, hemmed in by shadows, overhanging eaves, and mounds of black, shoveled slush, she didn't much feel like doing anything. And she *was* very much attached to her hair—even if it wasn't curly and bright like Katia's.

Vain, weak-minded, stupid, Ash scolded herself again as she sawed the blade through the last strands. There. Done it now. Running a hand through her ragged, shoulder-length hair, she tested its new feel and weight. Her head felt uncommonly light, as if she'd drunk too much red wine at supper. Pale silver strands, long as snakes, curled in the snow at her feet. Kicking them with the toe of her boot, she told herself they were nothing really, just a heap of old straw.

Hearing footsteps and thin jabs of laughter, Ash bent forward and scooped up the hair, then folded it into the cloth bag tied at her waist. She could get good money for it on Shorn Lamb Street, but she was no longer sure if selling it was a good idea. She had heard the talk in the city. Everyone who was anyone was looking for a tall, slim girl with long pale hair and no breasts. Ash glanced down at her chest.

Slowly, little by little, that particular aspect of her description was being rendered obsolete. It was quite amazing how fast a body could grow when it had a mind to. Even when the body in question was being fed nothing but goose grease and oats.

Ash concentrated on staying as still and silent as she could until the laughter and footsteps had passed. Her rough wool cloak itched, and things living within it crawled as slowly as things living in cloaks *did* crawl on cold nights in early winter. At least they weren't biters. Ash supposed she should be grateful for that.

She had sold her old clothes the very same night she had broken free of the fortress, before word of her escape had had chance to leak through the city and everyone knew to be on the watch for a girl matching the description of Penthero Iss' ward. Her dress had been plain but of excellent quality, and her calf-leather boots were the best to be bought in the city. The old bidwife who had purchased them had been happy to give Ash a whole outfit in exchange, complete with a lined and hooded cloak, thick wool leggings and mitts, a dress dyed a forgettable shade of brown, and a stout pair of "whore's boots." According to the bidwife, the boots were named for whores because they boasted soles so thick that a girl could walk the streets all day and not feel the pinch.

Ash wondered about that. Sometimes she caught men looking at her feet. The toes were capped with a particularly bright strain of copper that could be seen across a fair-size street. Just this afternoon she had worked charcoal and horse dung over the metal, hoping to ward off speculative glances from men and ill-humored appraisals from other girls.

The leather belt with a silver buckle that she had worn during the escape had also been sold, and the three silver pieces she had haggled from the bidwife had been enough to buy a loaf of oats and a sausage skin full of goose drippings every morning for the past five days. She had one silver left.

At night she slept alongside beggars and street whores. It was easy, really, watching people, seeing where they went and what they did. Early in the evening, even the poorest and sickest slid away to known dens to sleep. Wedge-shaped spaces under stairs, sewers blocked with ice, collapsed watch towers with makeshift roofs of elkhide, disused roast pits, abandoned outhouses and dry wells, burrows dug into the great mounds of snow that built up along the city's south wall, and cracks in the very city itself, leading downward to vaults of precision-cut stone and warrens of crawl spaces, underspaces, and sinkholes: Ash had seen people slip into them all.

The first night had been the worst, after she had left the bidwife's stall with money in her hand and nowhere to go. She didn't trust places that were dark and deserted and had chosen to stay on noisy, crowd-filled streets. Through the course of the night she had walked the length of the city, across the great stone court known as the Square of Sorrows, where Garath Lors had declared himself king before being cut down by his brother's darkcloaks; along the Spireway with its crumbling stonework and rotted spikes; and down into the dim and slushy streets of Almstown, where the soot from a thousand charcoal fires turned every wall, roof, and walkway black. Even the falling snow was black, catching minute flecks of burned matter as it sailed toward the earth.

Ash thought Almstown was a kind of hell. Katia had always spoken about it with a sort of wistful affection, telling how you could buy whole sides of bacon, steaming and ready to eat, warm your hands with mugs of beer so hot that you could set them on the ground and melt snow, and walk down any street and see dark-skinned women dressed in cloth-of-gold hoods and thin-lipped assassins glittering with knives. Ash tried, but she saw only the filth and the smoke and the open sores on people's faces. She had no money to buy bacon or beer, and the only people she saw were prostitutes fighting with their pimps, pot boys shoveling slush, charcoal burners tending their smoke fires, and tired old men getting drunk.

No one trusted anyone. Ash had learned quickly to keep her hands and eyes to herself. It didn't do to look too long at anyone or stand too close to a man selling hot food or cold beer.

Still, Ash thought, rising from the bench and stepping into the street, Almstown *was* a good place to get lost in. No one cared about finding the Surlord's ward. There was money in it—Iss had offered a crow's weight in gold for information leading to her capture—but the inhabitants of Almstown didn't think for one moment that any fine lady from Mask Fortress would ever find her way *here*.

Ash had heard people talking about it. Women joked that they'd dye their hair with lye, bandage their breasts, and go and claim the reward for themselves. Men spoke in hushed voices, murmuring about the Rive Watch, forced searches, torchings, and how Marafice Eye had blinded a carcass gutter for claiming, wrongly, that he had seen Asarhia March enter the Bone Temple and ask the tall and silent priests for asylum.

Ash shivered. Sometimes she wondered if Marafice Eye hadn't done such a thing just so news of it would reach her and make her afraid.

Determined *not* to be afraid, she headed south through the butcher's market and onto the paved streets beyond. When the pale, straight-as-arrow forms of the Horn and the Splinter drew her eyes, she did not look away. At this distance they were the only structures within Mask Fortress that were visible. Ash knew that all she had to do was head north for a few streets to lose sight of the Horn, but she had yet to find one street corner, alleyway, or ditch within the entire city of Spire Vanis from which the Splinter couldn't be seen. In a way it was a good thing. All she had to do was look up into the southern sky to see the reason why she had fled.

Before she pulled her gaze downward, she couldn't help but linger on the sloping roofs, flickering watch towers, and hammered iron domes of the southern skyline. At the farthest point south lay Vaingate.

Vaingate. The last built and least used of the four city gates. Ash didn't know how many hours she had spent imagining what it would feel like to walk through the limestone arch and onto the mountainside beyond. Vaingate was her one connection with her mother, the only thing they shared. Both of them had passed through that gate.

Ash took a breath and held it. All her childhood dreams had begun with her standing outside Vaingate. She imagined finding the place where she'd been abandoned, running her hands through the loose scree and dry brush, and finding something that no one else had found before. Some bit of parchment, a rusted locket, a scrap of fabric, anything that she could hold and say, *This once belonged to my mother*. In her more elaborate dreams, she'd find something that told her who her mother really was, and she'd search the city and find her, and her mother would turn out to be warm and glowing and utterly good . . . yet she never had a face. Ash smiled bitterly. She saw the dreams for what they were today.

There was no hidden marker waiting for her on Mount Slain. Her mother had set her down to *die*; she would have left nothing that could give her away. It was a sin against the Maker to abandon a healthy child. And even if she *had* dropped something—a hairpin or a ribbon or a bit of lace from her dress—sixteen years of snow and floods would have washed it clean away.

Ash continued to look south. Even if she went there and found something, there was no telling *whom* it had once belonged to. Besides, it wasn't safe. Vaingate was too close to Mask Fortress. No one but sheep drovers, hunt parties, holy men traveling to the Cloud Shrine, and healers in search of mountain plants passed through. She would be spotted the moment she drew near the gate.

Somehow, despite everything, Ash found herself moving south. Five days had passed since she'd escaped—enough time for the Rive Watch to grow bored and ease off the hunt. They had a whole city to search. How could they possibly watch over every street corner and marketplace? *I'll just get close enough to look*. It was midnight. She could cross the city and reach the gate before dawn. As long as she stayed clear of Mask Fortress and the watch towers, she'd be safe.

Gradually she increased her pace. Walking with her head down and her hand on her hood, she avoided all contact with strangers. When she drew close to the massive shantytown of animal hides, elk bones, and ice-rotted timbers that had grown up along the city's west wall, she altered her course to avoid it. The smell of deer fat, dung smoke, and thousands of unwashed bodies was enough to keep her away. Even from a safe distance, she could still see the massive circle of snowmelt caused by the heat and the filth.

The farther south she traveled, the cleaner the city became. Narrow streets gave way to wide causeways and smoothly paved squares. Brightly lit taverns and coarsehouses were replaced by limestone halls and tightly shuttered manses with bronze doors. Fewer prostitutes stood warming themselves by charcoal braziers, and fewer drunks urinated against walls. Even the snow underfoot grew lighter—not white exactly, but certainly *gray*.

It took Ash a full five minutes to walk past the unlit facade of the Quarter Court, where the grangelords stood in judgment of all crimes except treason. It had been built by the tenth Surlord Lewick Crieff, Lord of the High Granges, whom everyone called the Halfking, and his badge of a halfmoon shining above the knife-edge peak of Mount Slain was cut into every limestone cap, ledge, and corbel. After checking to see if anyone was watching, Ash stopped and rested her back against the black, soot-encrusted stone. She was growing tired, and tiny hobnails in her whore's boots were cutting into her feet. Ash cursed the bidwife who had sold them to her, thought for a moment, then cursed all whores as well. She was beginning to wonder if heading for Vaingate had been a good idea.

Ahead lay a vast cleared space surrounded by a circle of standing stones known as the Dreading Ring. Six gibbets stood in the center of the circle, massive T-shaped timbers forming a dark scaffold against the sky. Justice was swift in Spire Vanis, and once a man or woman had been convicted of a crime, he or she was marched straight from the Quarter Court and punished in the stone circle for all the city to see. No one was ever hanged—the grangelord's executioners were chosen for their skills with knives, not rope—but the bodies were hauled up later to feed the crows.

All but one gibbet was empty. The small body that was roped there hung like an empty sack. A sharp burst of wind made the rope creak and set the body swinging.

Ash edged back along the wall, suddenly unsure of herself. Running away had been a mistake. She had nowhere to go, no one to help her, no plans beyond the need to survive. Soon she'd run out of money . . . then what? She had no skills. Her description was posted around the city. Many of the brothers-in-the-watch knew her by sight. Pushing back her hood, she took a long hard look at the gibbets. Her scalp was hot, and sharp edges of newly cut hair prickled her skin. She longed for the safe enclosed space of her chamber, for Katia's endless chatter, warm baths, sweet food, and clothes without rough edges. She wanted her old life back.

Abruptly she pushed herself off from the wall. She had made her choice five days ago, and giving in because she was tired and her feet were aching and she didn't like the look of the way ahead was stupid. *Stupid.* She *would* carry on walking. She *would* go to Vaingate and see the place where she was abandoned and then found.

*Kaaw! Kaaw!*

Ash jumped as the shadow of a raven glided over her face. Looking up, she saw the great bird swoop down from the roof of the Quarter Court and soar toward the gibbets. As it entered the circle of ancient stones, it rolled its wings, catching an updraft that lifted it almost vertically alongside the occupied gibbet. Hovering for a long moment, it jabbed its bill into the face of the corpse and pecked out some bit of sinew that snapped like a snake as it came free. With the morsel held firmly in its bill, the raven beat its wings and rose to the top of the gibbet. Settled, it threw the strip of sinew into the air, caught it, and gobbled it up.

With its throat muscles still working to push down its meal, the raven swiveled its neck and looked at Ash. Bobbing its head up and down, it clucked and cooed like a mother hen.

*Come. Join me. Good flesh.*

Ash shivered. Although she didn't much want to, she took a step forward, then another. The snow was sticky under her feet, streaked with tar and spilled blood. Moonlight poured into the stone circle, running like liquid silver along the crossbeams of the gibbets. The wind dropped as she neared the center, and for the first time all night she felt the cold. The bird, black as the bricks at the back of a hearth, fussed and cooed until it came to rest by the occupied gibbet.

The body was strung up by cordage as thick as a man's wrist. Tarred ropes wound between its legs, around its neck, and under its arms. It took Ash a moment to realize the body was naked, as the flesh was stained dark by what might have been excrement or mud. Crows had been pecking for days, and the soft flesh of the belly had been opened and the guts spilled. The eyes were dark holes, picked clean. Teeth roots showed where lip and gum tissue had been torn away. The head was shorn.

Ash swallowed softly. It was a woman. It hardly looked it, as the breasts were gone and the genitals were obscured by a knot of rope and clotted blood, but what was left of the waist and hips formed a slack pouch of curves. Frightened, Ash gazed upon the face once more.

That was when she saw it. A lock of hair caught in the rope. Dark, curly hair.

*Promise to take me with you when you go.*

Ash took a step back. *No . . .*

Moonlight shifted, and shadows on the corpse's face fell into place. Ash saw the high curve of a cheek, the dimpled hollow of a chin.

*Why, you're wicked, miss. Plain wicked!*

Ash began shaking her head. Her stomach churned and churned until she thought she might be sick. The corpse, the *thing* that was and wasn't Katia, watched her with dead eyes as it swung upon its rope.

*Katia! Katia! Katia!* The raven took to the air, beating its knife wings, screaming and triumphant as it vanished into the night sky.

Ash did not know how long she stood in the stone circle, facing Katia's corpse. *Not long enough,* a small voice told her. *If you stayed here forever, it wouldn't be long enough.* When a gray sun began to rise in the east and the city started to creak to life, she turned and fled north . . . deserting the little maid one last time.

# TWENTY

## Duff's

THEY ROSE BEFORE DAWN and headed southeast. High winds
blew, creating a snowstorm from old frozen snow. Raif
pulled his fox hood over his eyes and mouth so only his nose
showed. The small specks of taiga he saw through the fur
were all he needed to guide his horse. The wind came from
the north and blew at his back, and it seemed to push him
away from the clanhold.

Angus took the lead, taking Raif along gullies and over
frozen ponds, finding trails long lost to the snow. Neither he
nor Raif spoke. They sat, hunched low on their horses, and
suffered the battery of the wind.

Raif's bowhand was swollen, and the skin on his fingertips had begun to shed. An ugly blister, dark and bloody as a
kidney, had formed on the heel of his hand. Every time he
grasped the reins to make an adjustment, pain made him
close his eyes. Beneath the fox fur, his mouth set in a grimace. Well, that would teach him to go axing wood on a
night as cold as hell.

After six hours spent in darkness, dreaming violent unspeakable dreams, the biting whiteness of the snowstorm
and the mindless monotony of riding through the taiga were
a relief. Raif had risen before Angus. He had heated fat and
stock from the ptarmigan in a small tin pot, and while he was
waiting for the steam to thin, he had made the only decision
he could. Clan was behind him now; remembering it, longing for it, believing that somehow in the future he would find
a way back, were things he could not allow himself.

He had fixed his own fate, and now he must live with it.
He was no longer part of the clan.

He had thought long and hard about discarding his lore, of
throwing it in the iron stove along with the remainders of the

last meal or taking it outside and burying it in the snow. But each time he grasped it in his hand and pulled on the twine, he heard the old guide speak.

*It's yours, Raif Sevrance. And one day you may be glad of it.*

So Raif kept it. He rode, his thoughts sealed as deeply as cached meat, his raven lore a cold bit of horn against his skin.

Half a day passed with no relief from the storm. The snow, rolled to hard pellets by the wind, rattled like hailstones against the trunks of stone pines. Great clumps of snow dropped from overhead branches, dislodged by the violent push and pull of the air. Raif did not hunt. His right hand wept pus and blood into his mitt, and the storm created a whiteout. Yet almost against his will he found himself searching for game.

Even on a day like this living things were out in the forest. A weasel, white and sleek as a dish of milk, watched Raif's passing from the cover of a paper birch. An ice hare popped its head out of its burrow, its cheeks puffing as it drew breath. In the overhang above a frozen stream, a snagcat broke shrew bones with a single snap of its jaw. Raif was aware of all these things, swore he *saw* them, yet when he peered through his fox hood, little more than the white haze of snow on the move met his eyes.

Darkness came early. The wind died with the light, leaving the forest feeling hollow and used up. All the trees had been stripped of snow, and many of the first-year saplings were snapped and broken. Overhead, the sky shifted from gray, to charcoal, to black.

Angus led them to the strip of taiga that bordered along the Southroad, and they followed the road's path from a discreet distance through several hours of darkness. Wagon tracks, horse dung, bones, and cast-off scraps littered the road, reminding Raif that soon he would come into contact with clansmen. In fine weather, taking a direct route, a man could ride from the Blackhail roundhouse to Duff's in a single day. Even the Dhoonehouse was only four days' hard ride from Duff's, and Gnash and Dregg were nearer.

When the glow of Duff's Stovehouse finally appeared over the rise, Raif was stiff with cold. His neck ached with a hard, nagging pain, and his hand burned. Angus made a signal, and they cut onto the road. Quarter of an hour later they reached the stovehouse.

Duff's was a stocky building with rounded walls and a rounded roof. Built from great, tree-size elmwood timbers and banded with iron staves, it looked like a giant beer barrel knocked on its side and sunk deep into the snow. Two doors led inside. The largest led to the stables, and Angus and Raif headed there first. Raif brushed down Moose and the bay while Angus exchanged quiet words with the groom. The groom was young, blind in one eye, and he spoke with a soft, hesitant stutter. Raif had seen him many times over the years, but until he watched Angus speak with him, he had never seen the young man laugh or smile. When the exchange was over, Angus grasped the groom's hand and bade him, "Stable the horses near the door."

Raif glanced around the dark, well-ordered stables. Over half of the two dozen boxes were occupied, and a handful of sturdy cobs and mountain-bred ponies stood in the lean-to outside.

It was a long walk to the stovehouse's second door. Piles of newly dumped snow mounded along the stovehouse walls. Hoarfrost sparkled on the timbers, and high upon the roof, where the brick chimney cut through the wood, snow could be heard hissing and sputtering as it melted.

Heat, smoke, smells, and sounds blasted against Raif's face as he pushed open the door and entered Duff's. Even as his eyes worked to grow accustomed to the light, his mouth watered at the smell of charred fat, elk meat, and onions. Normally at this hour someone would be singing and some crusty old clansman would be blowing the pipes. People would be laughing and arguing and gaming recklessly, yet although over thirty men and women sat or stood in the bright, wood-walled stoveroom, they kept themselves in small groups. Raif recognized a small party of spearmen from Clan Scarpe, their hair either black by birth or dyed that way, their weapons sheathed in intricately plaited cords that were designed to show the sharpness of their blades. A man and woman from Clan Gnash sat warming themselves by the great brick and metal stove. The woman wore her waist-length red hair unbound in the manner of all Gnash women. She was dressed in soft pigskin pants, and the belt around her waist was weighed with the Three Daggers: one horn, one steel, and one flint. A great circle of Dhoonesmen dominated the room. Massive men, they were, with blond hair, full beards, and blue ink tattooed into their faces. Strapped to their backs, waists, thighs, forearms, and calves were their weapons. Steel as perfect and brilliant as running water sent knifelight flashing through the room.

"Step away from the door, lad," murmured Angus close to Raif's ear. "Let's not give the patrons too long to think on who we are, or why we're here."

Raif, as if woken from a trance, obeyed his uncle's order and made his way to the back of the room. Talk, which had come to a dead halt the moment he and Angus had entered, resumed with the hushed frenzy of cockroaches escaping from light. As Raif picked a bench to sit at, as far away from the stove as it was possible to be, Angus exchanged nods with the stovemaster.

Duff had a bit of every clan in him, at least that was what he claimed. He was the hairiest man Raif had ever seen, and in his youth he had been famous for his teeth. Logs, barges, carts, carrion, and sleds: With a rope between his teeth, Duff had hauled them all. His teeth were still splendid to this day, and as he brought over a tray steaming with hot shammies, hot beer, and hot meat, he grinned broadly, revealing surprisingly small but perfectly even teeth. Raif remembered Tem asking Duff once how he had got his teeth so strong. "I used to crush pond ice with them," he had said.

"Angus! You old dog! How long's it been?" Duff's brow reflected a moment of strenuous thought as he loaded his goods on the table. "Aye, I canna be bothered thinking. Too long, that's for sure."

"Duff. You've grown fatter and uglier. By the Stones, man! That neck hair needs a shearing. If I was your wife, I'd bind your arse to that stove and shave you."

Duff's laugh was his second wonder. Rich and hearty, it rolled up from his chest like breaking waves. "If *you* were my wife, Angus, I'd bind myself to the stove and light it."

Raif grinned, suddenly feeling better than he had all day.

He had forgotten how much he liked Duff. The two men continued on, railing each other with such unabashed relish and affection, it was obvious they were old, old friends. A few heads turned at the laughter, but no one took longer than they should paying heed to the stovemaster and his guest.

As he took a draft of bitter foamy beer, Raif spent a moment studying those people who had not caught his attention when he had first walked through the door. A small party of trappers kept to themselves in the far corner, chewing on long strips of birch bark as they mended the wires for their traps. An old Orrlsman, his eyes milky with snow blindness, sat close to the stove with his dog. Across the way, a woman wearing the gray leathers and moose felt of Bannen was busy finishing her supper of fried onions and elk meat. Like all women from Bannen, she carried a longsword of black steel on her back. Two men sat in the shadows directly opposite Raif, nursing half-empty tankards between gloved hands. They were clansmen, but their hoods were up and they were dressed in dark oilskins and Raif could not place them. There were no Bluddsmen. Which, considering a circle of Dhoonesmen commanded the room, was lucky for patrons, staff, and stove laws alike.

Raif knew that everyone in the room saw him as a Hailsman. Blackhail was the most austere and least given to show of all the clans. It had been stripped of its badge five hundred years earlier when Ayan Blackhail took the life of the last Clan King, and no one had worn the Hail Wolf since. Even so, the silver cap on Raif's tine, the beaten silver strip that tied his hair, and the black leather of his belts, scabbards, and fronts placed him from Blackhail as surely as the blue tattoos on the Dhoonesmen's faces named them Dhoone. Blackhail was the only clanhold where silver was mined, and the metal was worked into the hilts of all handknives and swords. Tem's halfsword had a layer of silver wire wrapped around the grip, and the leather scabbard it was housed in was dyed black to match the graphite lesions in the Hailstone.

"You won't mind keeping your own company for a while, Raif," Angus said, slapping a hand on his shoulder. "Duff's going to take me in the back so I can pick a length of cloth for my wife."

"Aye," Duff said. "Me poor wife hates to show herself once she's plaited her hair for bed."

Raif nodded to both men. He thought they spoke a little too casually, but it was no concern of his. Angus shrugged off his coat and packs and followed Duff to a small door in the back of the room. Raif watched them go. Did Angus greet the trappers along the way?

"Raif Sevrance."

Turning, Raif came face-to-face with the two men who had been sitting in the shadows wearing oilskins. They were Hailsmen: Will Hawk and his son, Bron, who had been fostered to Dhoone for a season. Bron was the one who had brought news of Dhoone's defeat to the clan. Raif was immediately on his guard. He gave back greetings but did not ask what business brought father and son to Duff's.

Will, a somber man with the kind of pale skin that showed many veins, sat on the stool that had just been vacated by Angus. "I see you're here with your uncle. The ranger."

It was an invitation to speak, not a question. Raif nodded.

Will made a gesture toward Bron, bidding that he sit. Bron's mother was a Dhooneswoman, and he had the fair hair and light eyes of the Dhoones. He was known for his swordsmanship, Raif recalled, and, strangely enough, for his fine singing voice. Raif thought he didn't look much the sort to break into song.

When father and son were settled close, Will took a heavy breath and said, "How did the ambush go, lad?"

Raif worked to keep his face still. He had been expecting the question—as a senior clansman, Will Hawk would have taken part in planning the ambush—yet Raif found it difficult to speak. He had spent the past two days sealing off his memories of the clan, and he did not want to reopen them. Not here. Not now. He glanced into Will Hawk's eyes. Genuine concern nestled there, along with growing impatience. Raif did not know Will Hawk well, yet he was a full clansman and was therefore owed respect. "The ambush went well. All was as Mace Blackhail said."

"Who amongst us took hurt?"

"Banron Lye. Toady Walker."

Both Will and Bron touched their guidestone pouches. Silence followed. After several minutes Will said, "And so you're heading south to spread the word to Scarpe and Orrl?"

Raif shook his head. He would not lie to a clansman.

Will waited for him to explain himself. Raif breathed and did not speak. After a minute of silence, he could no longer look his clansman in the eye. Bron took a ewe's heart from a platter and began to chew on it.

In the corner of his vision, Raif saw Angus emerge from the back room of the stovehouse. He was carrying a dainty bundle with exaggerated care, and one of the trappers made jest of him. Angus laughed along with the rest, falling into an easy conversation that grew lower as the minutes passed.

"So you are just traveling with your uncle for a while," Will said at last.

*He knows*, Raif thought. *Will knows I have broken my oath.*

Will stood. His eyes carefully avoided Raif as he said to his son, "Come. There is no company worth keeping here tonight." Puzzlement shot over Bron's face, but he obeyed his father, swallowing the last of the heart and standing. Together they walked back to their place at the far side of the room.

Raif did not move. Shame burned him. There were no excuses he could give, nothing he could say to bring Will back to his table. He had broken his oath, and no words could change what that made him.

Blackhail was the oldest of the clans, and there were many who held it was the hardest, too. It had its traitors, Raif knew it *must* have traitors—three thousand years of wars, successions, and infighting had to produce some men who had broken their oaths—yet their names were never spoken. Their memories died before they did. Once when he was younger, Raif remembered asking Inigar Stoop why there was a deep black pit in the farthest corner of the guidestone, big as a wolf and filled with oil that had hardened over centuries to dark jewels. Inigar had run his stick fingers over the hollow and said, "This is the place where we cut traitors' hearts from the stone."

Raif felt the shame heat sear him. How long would it be before Inigar picked up a chisel in his name?

Hard footsteps crunched on snow and then the stovehouse door burst open. The temperature dropped immediately as a cold wind circled the room. Raif looked up to see four Bluddsmen enter the stovehouse. Faces hard, bodies weighted with steel, they stopped just beyond the doorway and surveyed the room. Air and space contracted. The Dhoonesmen stood as a single body, swordhands dropping to the hand-and-a-half hilts of their greatswords. In the far corner Will and Bron shifted themselves without seeming to move, making body and weapons ready.

Raif felt the full force of the Bluddsmen's attention. He watched as their gray and dark blue eyes seized upon the silver piece in his hair and on his tine. He saw them hate.

Hair shaved clean around their faces, braids descending down their backs like rope dipped in tar, they looked like no other clan. Their leathers were tanned in different ways, and their weapons were heavy forged. Seeing them here, at close quarters, Raif realized how little he had learned by fighting them on the Bluddroad. Clan Bludd was a force unto itself.

"Close the door, Chokko. Bring your men to warm their bellies at the stove." Duff moved into the strip of space separating the Dhoonesmen from the Bluddsmen.

The one named Chokko raised a gloved fist. "Nay, Stovemaster. This is not something to be smoothed over with beer and warming. Our clan bleeds this night."

"Take it outside, Chokko. No misdeed is greater than breaking the law of the stove."

Chokko shook his massive head. "I have respect for you, Stovemaster. Know that. And I come to pick no fight with the Dhoone." He and the head Dhoonesman shared a long, bitter glance. "But I *will* fight this night. I have to. My heart will not let me rest until I have taken Blackhail blood."

A murmur of cold fear passed through the room. The Dhoonesmen's faces darkened. The woman from Gnash slid her hand down toward the Three Daggers at her waist. The Scarpemen, war-sworn allies of Clan Blackhail, bristled like hackles on a dog. Will and Bron Hawk shed their oilskins and walked with hard dignity into the center of the room.

Beneath the table, Raif's fist closed around Tem's sword. His heart hammered, yet strangely he felt something close to relief. *So this is how it would end, fighting Bluddsmen.*

"The stove laws work two ways, Chokko," Duff said, holding his position directly in front of the Bluddsmen, barring them access to the rest of the room. "If men are at my stove, keeping my peace, I will not allow anyone to force them outside against their will."

"Bravely said, Stovemaster," said Will Hawk, entering the Bluddsmen's space. "But we are Clan Blackhail, and we will not cower and we will not hide, and if Bludd wants the chance to best us, then so be it." The last words were addressed to Chokko, and the stovelight seemed to dim as they were spoken, leaving the two men in a place of their own.

Chokko did not blink—hardly, in fact, seemed to breathe. He spoke, and although his words were said to Will Hawk, he meant the whole room to hear them. "Our chief sent a dog to us—we, who were camped along the Elk Trail— telling of what Blackhail had done. The bitch died even as I took the bale from her collar, so hard had she traveled in two days and one night. The message told of an ambush along the Bluddroad, and how three dozen of our wives and children were hunted like animals and then slain in the snow, in cold blood."

A hiss, like the sound of trees whipped by high wind, took the room. Duff closed his eyes and touched his lids. The couple from Gnash signed to the Stone Gods. The woman from Bannen touched the black iron pendant containing her measure of powdered guidestone and spoke a single word: *"Children."* Even the Dhoonesmen looked down.

Will Hawk shook his head. "You lie, Chokko of Clan Bludd. My clan would never slay wives and children in cold blood."

The Bluddsman at Chokko's side pushed forward. "We do not lie. Our chief does not lie. We are Clan Bludd, and even when the truth is hard we speak it." Chokko gripped his clansman's arm to stop him from drawing his sword.

"It is the truth, Hailsman," he cried. "And you will know it soon enough when you receive the swift judgment of our blades."

A muscle pumped high on Will Hawk's cheek. His eyes glittered in the stovelight. Raif tensed, his chest as tight as a bow at full draw. Will Hawk turned toward him. "Tell them they lie, Raif Sevrance. That I may carry the pride of my clan to this fight."

All eyes fell on Raif. The Bluddsmen, realizing straight-away the full implication of Will's appeal, sent looks filled with such loathing that Raif felt them as blows against his skin. All was quiet for one terrible, unbearable moment. The knowledge Raif held damned them all. Bluddsmen and Hailsmen would fight this night regardless of what he said—that much was clear—but how could he send Will and Bron Hawk into a fight with no honor? Four massive Bluddsmen in their prime, against three Hailsmen, two of them yearmen newly sworn?

They would die. He, Will, and Bron would die.

Raif swallowed hard, gathered himself in. Clan was everything. What he was didn't matter—his soul was already lost—but he couldn't send Will and Bron to their deaths on a lie.

He stood. "We did what we had to."

Gasps erupted. The Bluddsmen drew steel. The expression on Will Hawk's face was a kind of death for Raif. He knew he would never be forgiven for the words he had spoken.

Will struggled with the truth for only a moment, yet when he turned to face the Bluddsmen he was no longer the same man. "Hold your steel until we are outside," he said, his voice hard and weary in one. "I will not confound one wrong with another, Bron." He looked at his son. "Your yearman's oath to Dhoone still stands. This is not your fight."

Bron shook his head. "Tonight I am a Hailsman," he said.

A look of pure pain crossed Will's face. By the time he spoke it was gone. "Come, then, son. Let us fight for our clan."

Father and son moved toward the door.

Raif stepped forward, following them.

Hearing the scrape of his chair and the slap of his foot-steps on stone, Will Hawk turned and held up his hand.

"Nay, Raif Sevrance. Take your seat. I would rather a Bluddsman cut out my heart than a traitor fight at my side."

Will held his position for one moment and then walked outside. The Bluddsmen followed. Bron followed. Someone shut the door.

Like a ghost, Raif continued walking. Slowly. Unstoppable.

Angus came and fought him, big meaty arms clamping around his chest, knees jabbing at his shins. Duff slid a bar across the door, then came to Angus' aid. Raif fought back. Hands pushed, feet kicked, chests blocked his way. They slowed but could not stop him. He took great hurt and gave great hurt, yet it all seemed as unreal as any dream. All that mattered was the door. Not once did he doubt that he would reach it. Like game, he had set its oak and iron heart in his sights. It was his, and he would take it. If Angus and Duff had known that, if he could only have explained, they would have let him go. But they didn't, so he fought them, and all three took harm.

Sometimes he caught glimpses of himself in other men's eyes. A Dhoonesman held his hand to his tine, as if he were seeing something unspeakable like a Stone God come down for vengeance. The Scarpemen looked afraid.

Hot blood ran down Raif's nose to his mouth. Yellow fluid slid across his eye. His fists were like machines, up and down they went, smashing flesh, as his feet claimed ground beneath him. Filled with the same inevitable force as an arrow in flight, he had no choice but to move toward the door.

Then, suddenly, Angus spoke a word. He wiped blood from his face and shook his head, and then he and Duff fell away. Raif barely registered their withdrawal. It was nothing to him. He would have reached the door without it. His hands came up and dealt with the bar, and a moment later he stood facing the snow and the night. Cold breezes worked his skin as he took in the last seconds of the fight. One Bluddsman was down. Bron was down. The remaining Bluddsmen delivered long thrusts with their swords, impaling the flopping, powerless form of Will Hawk. Only their blades kept him standing.

Raif lost himself after that. Afterward he would remember things, or perhaps what little Angus Lok told him *became* memory, but when he stepped through the threshold and into the snow he became something else.

Swords don't ring when you draw them, yet to Raif it seemed as if his did. His mouth was dry, utterly dry. His raven lore burned like white-hot steel against his skin.

*Watcher of the Dead.*

That was his last thought before his mind spiraled downward to a place where all that mattered were the Bluddsmen's beating hearts.

# TWENTY-ONE

## *Sarga Veys*

PENTHERO ISS STOOD HIGH in the cool marble blackness of the Bight and watched as Sarga Veys entered Mask Fortress. Not for Veys the soldiers' sparseness of stable gate or the common squalor of north gate. No. Veys took the east gate, whose fine marble columns and wrought-iron gratings were usually reserved for lords, ladies, and those of high office, not second-rate envoys who had knowledge of the old skills. Iss exhaled softly into the shadows. Sarga Veys was an interesting piece of flesh.

As he crossed the quad, Veys kept turning his head toward the Splinter. After a moment he stopped, spun his heels, and spent a full minute contemplating the ice-bound tower. Iss didn't like that. He didn't like that at all. A small *drawing out* of himself, like a long sniff or a wet finger thrust into the air to test wind speed, served to assure him that Veys was studying the Splinter purely with his own two eyes, not probing it with sorcery as he feared.

Withdrawing back into himself, he became aware of the taste of metal in his mouth and a drop of urine sliding down his thigh. It was disgusting to feel the wetness there. He despised his weaknesses. Working the tainted saliva into a wad for spitting, he looked once more upon the white-robed form of Sarga Veys.

Sarga Veys was looking directly at him.

Unsettled, Iss took a step back. *I am in shadow*, he told himself, *and five stories above him. How then does he know I am here?* The drawing! Sarga Veys had sensed the drawing. Iss' face darkened. The power he had drawn to test for sorcery was so slight, a little moth on the wing, it should not have been detectable. Yet there was Sarga Veys, smiling now, raising his arm in greeting. Iss turned and exited the room. Veys would know now, with utter certainty, that something was housed within the Splinter that his Surlord wished him not to see.

Descending the ice-cold stairs of the Bight, Iss prepared himself to meet with Sarga Veys. Although the sun had newly risen above Mount Slain, the day was already little to the Surlord's liking. Only an hour earlier, beneath the darkly sloping ceiling of the Hall of Trials, the Lady of the Eastern Granges and her beswarded son the Whitehog had challenged his right to apportion land along the city's northern reach.

"My grandfather's brother owned hunting rights to the Northern Granges," Lisereth Hews, Lady of the Eastern Granges, had said, her voice rapidly becoming shrewish. "And I claim them here and now for my son." It was a ridiculously trumped-up claim, of course, but Lisereth Hews was a dangerous woman. The white and the gold of the Hews suited her just as well as it suited any man. She *would* cause trouble over this. Four of the past ten surlords had come from House Hews, and the good lady was scheming to place her son as the fifth. The matter of the Northern Granges, newly come into dispute owing to the death of its lord, Allock Mure, had provided her with a convenient excuse to show her teeth.

Iss bared his own teeth. Lisereth Hews was a fool if she thought she could take him on. He would not sit and grow old and wait for the assassins to come. The great old houses of Hews, Crieff, Stornoway, Gryphon, Pengaron, and Mar would find battles aplenty soon enough.

Once within his private chamber, Iss took time to change his clothes. The urine stain on his robe was a tiny thing, but Sarga Veys had quick eyes and a quick mind, and Iss would not allow him the satisfaction of putting two and two together and realizing that his Surlord was not as powerful as he seemed. Sarga Veys was a skilled and subtle magic user, and that meant he was dangerous as well as useful.

Iss dressed without haste, content to let Caydis Zerbina fasten the dozen pearl buttons on each cuff and lace the ties on his silk coat so that they formed an elaborate herringbone design across his chest. He was indifferent to clothes but knew well enough their many uses and always made a point of dressing in expensive silks, heavily weighted and exquisitely cut.

When he was satisfied that he had kept Sarga Veys waiting long enough, he indicated that the Halfman should be let in the room. Caydis moved to the door without making a sound.

"My lord." Sarga Veys entered the chamber and then bowed, awaiting his Surlord's pleasure.

Iss studied the curve of Veys' neck, the texture and pigment of the skin. Even though Veys had just returned from a journey lasting several weeks, no dirt from the road clung to him. He must have stopped in the city and bathed before presenting himself at the fortress. Not liking the cool detachment such an act betokened, Iss made a note to have Veys followed while he stayed in the city. He already knew much about the Halfman, but it never hurt to know more.

"Sarga Veys. I trust I find you in good health?" Veys opened his mouth to reply, but Iss blocked him. "I failed to notice the sept as you returned. I trust the brothers-in-the-watch came to no harm?"

"They asked if they could ride on ahead of me when we came within sight of the city. I saw no reason to refuse their wish."

He lied. No member of the Rive Watch would ever ask anything of Sarga Veys. More likely they had abandoned him as soon as they'd judged it safe. Iss nodded. "I see."

Suspecting his lie had been detected, Sarga Veys straightened his shoulders. "Next time I ride on your behalf, my lord, I would prefer to handpick the sept myself."

"As you wish." Iss didn't care either way. Let Veys try to handpick a sept. It would be interesting to see just how far he'd get before Marafice Eye stepped in to have his say. "Have you any further demands before we begin? Perhaps a new horse, or a new title, or a new set of robes with gold trim?"

Sarga Veys' violet eyes darkened. His throat muscles worked, and for a moment Iss didn't know if he meant to draw sorcery or to speak. Veys hardly seemed to know himself. After a moment he calmed himself, swallowing whatever sorcery or wordage had massed upon his tongue. "I apologize, my lord. I am tired and ill worn. I do not much care for the cold open lands of the North."

Iss was immediately conciliatory. "Of course, my friend. Of course." He touched Veys' arm. "Come. Sit. Wine. We must have wine. And food. Caydis. Bring us what you know is good. Make it hot. Yes, by all means see to the fire first. How right of you to think of our visitor's well-being as well as his belly." It was interesting to watch the effect the little show of pandering had on Sarga Veys. He liked being courted. That was one of his weaknesses, his belief that he was entitled to better than what he got.

When Caydis left the room, closing the door as softly as only he could, Iss turned to Veys and said, "So. All has gone to plan in the clanholds?"

Veys' smooth skin glistened like linen dipped in oil as he said, "They're fighting like dogs in a pit."

Iss nodded. He did not speak for a moment, wanting to settle the knowledge in his mind and claim it for his own. Absently he ran a hand over his mouth. "So Mace Blackhail acted upon the information you gave him?"

"Immediately. It was a massacre. Thirty women and children slain in cold blood—most of them kin to the great Dog Lord himself. Now Bludd is at Blackhail's throat, Dhoone *and* Blackhail are at Bludd's throat, and all the clans in between are scrambling to take sides." Veys smoothed the perfectly white sleeves of his robe. "The Dog Lord will find thorns growing on the Dhooneseat soon enough."

"Perhaps." Iss had a higher opinion of Vaylo Bludd than Sarga Veys did. Sarga Veys saw only the crudeness, the spitting and swearing and dogs. Iss saw the ruthless determination of a man who had lorded Clan Bludd for thirty-five years and was loved as a king by his sworn men. Besides, Sarga Veys was missing the point. The Dog Lord was just one chief among many. Clan Croser, Clan Bannen, Clan Otler, Clan Scarpe, Clan Ganmiddich, and all the rest had to be brought into the war. It wasn't enough that Blackhail, Bludd, and Dhoone fight; all their war-sworn clans must, too. When the time came to send a host north for battle, it would be the promise of easy land and easy wealth that stirred the grangelords and their armies. The fat border clans would be first taken. The cold giants of the Far North, with their massive stone roundhouses, steel forges, and ice-bred warriors, would come later . . . once they'd fought themselves bloody over years.

Iss ran a pale hand over his face. Could he do this? Did he have a choice? The world was changing, and the Sull would ride out from their Heart Fires soon enough. If ever there was a chance to seize greatness and power, this was it. If Spire Vanis didn't move to claim a continent, then Trance Vor, Morning Star, and Ille Glaive would. An empire *would* be created. And he, Penthero Iss, son of an onion farmer from Trance Vor and kinsman to Lord of the Sundered Granges, would not stand by and watch as others took what should be his.

"I picked up one or two other intelligences whilst I was in the North," Veys said, his voice slicing through Iss' thoughts like cheesewire. "I think you may find them interesting."

It was an effort to bring his mind back to the subject at hand. "Go on."

"Our old friend Angus Lok is on the move again. Heading north to the clanholds, last I heard."

This was news. Angus Lok had been to ground for six months. None of Iss' spies had been able to locate him. *He and his family live within a few days' ride of Ille Glaive*, was all they could ever tell him. "If Angus Lok is on the move, then so is the Phage."

Sarga Veys met eyes with his Surlord. "I wonder why."

*I bet you do*, thought Iss. Not for the first time he contemplated ridding himself of Veys. The Halfman was too clever, too sharp. He had already betrayed one taskmaster. How much easier would a second betrayal be? "Seems you were one of them once, you tell *me* what the Phage are up to."

Veys shrugged. "With the Phage . . . who can know for sure? They keep themselves as close as bats on a cave wall. In the whole of Spire Vanis there are probably only five people who have ever heard of them, and two of them are sitting in this room." Veys moved forward in his seat, and Iss knew to expect a second revelation. "Of course, there *was* that raven Stovemaster Gloon brought down."

"What raven?"

"Well, apparently the good stovemaster lives in fear of ravens flying over his chimney—you know how superstitious stovemasters can be about their god-cursed stoves." Veys waited for his Surlord to nod. "So, whenever Gloon climbs up on his roof to clean his stack he always carries a braced bow with him in case he spot a raven flying overhead. He likes to take potshots at them. Hangs them from the rafters like trophies. Anyway, seven days before I arrived, Gloon brought down the biggest raven he'd ever seen. He couldn't stop bragging about it. The man exaggerated, of course—little men like that always do—but when he cut the bird down to show me, I noticed a line of sinew wrapped around its leg."

"A messenger bird."

"Yes. And it was heading north toward the ice."

"There was no message."

"No."

Then the bird was homing, toward the Ice Trapper tribe. No others besides Ice Trappers and the Sull used ravens. Invisible hairs on Iss' arm rose. "What direction did it come from?"

"South. Just south." The look on the Halfman's face told Iss that he had already made the connection between the bird and Angus Lok. He was clever, so clever.

But the news *was* tantalizing. That was the problem: Veys

had a way of uncovering just the sort of information that Iss liked to know. And he was so very useful, so very adept with sorcery.

Iss attended the tray of food and wine that Caydis had discreetly slid upon the marble-topped table. All things fragrant were upon it: the wine warmed with cloves and then poured into cups rubbed with lemon, the egg yolks shuddering like oysters under the weight of turmeric and sesame seeds, the fried figs split and steaming, and lamb's tongues spread with rose jam, musk, and amber. No one prepared food like Caydis Zerbina. No one could find the things he did.

Offering a silver cup filled with wine to Sarga Veys, Iss contemplated all he had learned. So the Listener of the Ice Trapper tribe had sent a raven? That meant the North was prepared itself for the dance of shadows to come. Iss sat back in his chair, stilling himself with deep breaths held long in his lungs. *Let them dance*, he thought. *Let the Sull dance with shadows and the clanholds dance with swords, and let those bold enough to move while the music plays steal a world from under their feet.*

Sarga Veys popped a fat fig into his mouth. He was looking more than a little pleased with himself. "I hear your ward has gone missing. The sweet and lovely Asarhia. I could help you track her down if you like."

"No." Iss let the word stand alone. He would not explain himself to a second-rate envoy who had neither land nor family allegiances to call his own. The thought of Sarga Veys even *touching* Asarhia filled Iss' chest with cold unease. Asarhia was so young, so unknowing . . .

Iss put down his wine cup untouched. She had to be found. The city was no place for her to be. She could get hurt, raped. She could lose her fingers overnight to the cold, starve to death in some dingy little tent in Almstown, or curl up in the cairn-size snowdrifts that massed along the city's north wall and sleep her way to death. Iss had seen it happen. Every spring, during first thaw, a hundred or more bodies would be carried through the sluice gates along with the snowmelt. The poor fools all died with smiles on their faces, thinking that the blue tongues of frost that killed them were as warm and soothing as flames.

Iss breathed heavily. He needed to call the Knife. The search must be expanded, the reward doubled, Almstown and all its shanties razed to the ground. Asarhia must be brought home. He had not spent sixteen years in her rearing to let her fall into another's hands.

Catching Veys looking at him with eyes that knew and guessed too much, Iss rose and walked to the door. Caydis Zerbina waited on the other side, and one word was all it took to give him purpose.

"Will you need me to head north again, my lord?" Veys said.

Iss shook his head. "No. It's a delicate game we play, this making of wars. Push too often and we risk making our intentions known. Far better to watch and wait and see. Blackhail has lost its chief, Bludd has lost women and children, and Dhoone has lost its clanhold: Let clannish pride and clannish gods do the rest."

"But what of their war-sworn clans? What of Ganmiddich, Bannen, Orrl . . ."

"All in good time, Sarga Veys. If the game slows or the rules change, you'll be the first to know."

The Halfman bowed his head. "As you wish."

Iss waited for the next question, knowing full well what it would be.

"And my next duties?"

"I haven't given them much thought, my friend. There's nothing pressing. Obviously, I'd be grateful for any word you might bring of Angus Lok and his family. Apart from that I suggest you rest yourself after your long journey, take time to enjoy the refreshments of the city." Iss flipped the lid on a silver box crusted with emeralds that had once belonged to the Surlord Rannock Hews, whom Borhis Horgo had slain in the black mud of Hound's Mire forty years earlier while five Forsworn held him down with the heels of their boots. Taking something from the box, Iss smiled indulgently at Sarga Veys. "Here," he said pressing the object into the Halfman's hand. "Spend it wisely."

Sarga Veys' face was a thing to behold as he stared at the golden piece the Surlord had given him. The idea that he wasn't needed, that he could be dismissed as easily as a wetted prostitute, was something that had never occurred to him before. He was the young and brilliant Sarga Veys, the Phage's greatest find in over a decade. Who would not want or need him? Any other time Iss might have been tempted to smile at the specks of stricken pride shining like salmon roe in Sarga Veys' eyes, yet for some reason he did not. Veys was dangerous. And although it *had* been necessary to teach him a lesson, he was exactly the sort of person who collected and nursed his slights.

Iss was saved further thought on the subject by the arrival of Marafice Eye, swiftly brought by Caydis Zerbina. The Knife neither knocked nor waited. He entered the room, claimed space, then set his small blue eyes upon the game: Sarga Veys.

Instantly Iss regretted summoning him. His intent had been to intimidate the Halfman and put him in his place. Yet the business with the gold piece had already achieved part of that, and Iss knew he was in danger of going too far.

Sarga Veys, who still hadn't recovered from the blow of being judged unnecessary to his Surlord's immediate plans, colored slightly under the force of the Knife's gaze. Without realizing what he did, he shrank back in his chair.

The Knife did nothing except stand; he needed to do no more.

Iss looked from one man to the other. A change of plan was in order. Taking a shallow breath, he addressed himself to the Knife. "The sept you sent north with Sarga Veys needs disciplining. See to it."

Marafice Eye scowled. Iss turned his back, dismissing him.

Footsteps shook the room and then the door was slammed with enough force to split the frame.

Iss turned to Sarga Veys. "I will not keep you idle for long."

The Halfman's cheeks glowed prettily with spite; he had very much enjoyed the dressing-down of Marafice Eye. "I await your call, my lord." Standing, he slipped the gold piece into a fold in his robe. "I trust my lord was pleased with the duties I performed in the North?"

All this and praise, too? Iss' dislike for the Halfman deepened. Smiling, he crossed to the door and opened it. Splinters of wood fell in great chunks to the floor. "You have more than proved your worth."

Sarga Veys continued to glow as he walked through the door.

As soon as he was out of earshot, Iss called to Caydis to bring back the Knife.

# TWENTY-TWO

## *Matters of Clan*

PAIN RODE WITH HIM like a second skin. Boot-shaped bruises marked his flesh, organs and soft tissue leaking blood beneath. Wounds sewn closed with black thread punctured with soft hisses, spilling pus. Hurts riddled his body like pine beetles in wood. His sliced lip throbbed. His black eye turned every blink into an agonizing procedure of weeping flesh and pain. Crusted yellow stuff accumulated in his swollen ear, and the blister on his right hand was fire upon the reins.

Miserable, cold, and tucked deep into a place well warded against thoughts, Raif Sevrance rode at Angus Lok's side. Bleak, gray light shone upon a landscape glittering with frost. A predatory wind stayed close to the ground, content to let the terrible cold weaken its victims before moving in for the kill. Stands of hemlock, their trunks dulled by rime ice, rose like a ghost army to block the advancing night.

Angus rode in silence, his back bent and his head sunk deep within his hood. Although Raif could not see his uncle's face, he knew all about the bruises and lesions there. Raif shuddered to think of them. There was even a bite mark.

How many days had passed since the night at Duff's Stovehouse was difficult to tell. Perhaps a week. Maybe longer. All days and nights were the same in the taiga. Raif could remember little about the night of the fight. Dimly he recalled Angus leading him away from the hacked pieces of flesh that had once been the Bluddsmen's bodies. He remembered the looks of fear and horror on the faces of the Dhoonesmen, then the coming together of Scarpe, Dhoone, Ganmiddich, and Gnash to draw a guide circle around the six bodies in the snow.

They couldn't wait to be rid of him. Angus and Duff had taken him to the stables and seen to his injuries there. As soon as Duff finished the stitching, Angus had forced a flask full of malt liquor down his throat and hefted him over Moose's back. Raif's last thought was that one of Duff's famous teeth was now missing: He would never pull a sled that way again.

Only later, much later, did he realize that *he* had been the cause of Duff's missing tooth and the bite mark on Angus' cheek. It didn't bear thinking about.

Angus had told him what little he judged it necessary for him to know. Raif knew he was holding back and was glad of it. He didn't want to hear all the details of the fight. Angus himself had been strangely quiet these past days, holding his peace around the stove at night, speaking of little but the weather and journey by day. Glancing over at the hunched, frost-dusted form of his uncle, Raif felt a rough soreness press against his throat.

*You are not good for this clan, Raif Sevrance.*

Now Angus knew the truth of it, too.

"Angus," Raif said, surprising himself by breaking the silence.

Angus turned his head so Raif could see his face. All the cuts and bruises were heavily waxed; broken and damaged skin was an invitation to the 'bite. "What?"

Raif felt his nerve waver so rushed on before he had chance to think. "Why did you let me go? You and Duff fought me all the way to the door, but then you said something and both you and he pulled away."

A soft grunt came from Angus' lips. Turning his attention back to the way ahead, he said, "Aye. You would ask that. And you'll be wanting the truth of it, too."

He was silent for a while, guiding his bay around a thicket of frozen thorns. Just when Raif had given up hope of an answer, he spoke again, his voice lower than the wind. "There came a point when I knew you couldn't be stopped, just knew it in my old Lok bones. To carry on fighting would have only brought Duff and myself more harm. Yet it was more than that." Angus sighed heavily. Bits of ice on his saddle coat slid into his lap. "I have a trace of the old skill in me, Raif. Just a wee bit, enough to sense when others around me use sorcery, and a few small things like that. I'm not a magic user, don't hear me wrong. I couldna shift air and light if me own life depended on it—and if we're ever in a situation where that sort of thing is called for, then remember Angus Lok *isn't* your man. As I said, though, I can sense things when I have a mind to. And that night when you kept fighting and fighting, butting old Duff in the teeth and kneeing me in the knackers, I felt something—"

"Sorcery?"

"No. Fate." Angus held the word a long moment, then shrugged. "Call it an old ranger's fancy if you like. Call it bloody delirium brought on by having my balls disbanded. All I know is there came a moment when I thought to myself, *As terrible as this is, it's meant to be.*"

Raif took a breath. Pain from his stitches and blistered hand made him wince. Fate. He wanted none of it. Yet even as his thoughts pounced, ready to attack the idea, fragments of memory slipped through his mind. A red lake, frozen, a forest of silver blue trees, and a lightless city without people: The places the guidestone had showed him.

"Fate pushes," Angus said, breaking through Raif's thoughts. "Sometimes, if you lie under the stars at night, you can feel it. Children sense it—that's why they always get so excited at the thought of camping out. They *know*, yet can never put it into words. As for myself, I've felt fate only a few times in my life, and always it made me change my course. The stovehouse was one such push."

"Yet I might have died."

"Aye. And I canna say if I would have stepped in to save you." Angus turned and looked at Raif, his coppery eyes flecked with green. "You know that word of what you did will reach every corner of the clanholds. To slay three Bluddsmen single-handed is a feat not soon forgotten."

Raif shook his head. He hated what he had become when he'd walked through the stovehouse door. There was no pride in slaying men so; he had been little more than a wolf tearing out throats. It sickened him to think of it. He had a memory of the snow outside of Duff's saturated with blood. "Blackhail will sing no songs in remembrance of me."

"Maybe not. But thirty pairs of eyes saw what you did, and songs don't always need to be sung to be heard." Angus stared hard at Raif a moment, then kicked the bay forward onto ground that had once been marshy and wet and was now fast with ice.

Raif followed after. Soon they came upon a frozen stream and took the cleared and frozen path it offered them through the hills and ravines of the taiga's edge. By the time they left the ice to make camp for the night, the trees surrounding them had stopped being a forest and become a loose collection of woodland instead. A quarter moon rode low on the horizon, making the stream ice glow like blue fire.

"What will happen now between Blackhail and Bludd?" Raif asked, banking snow against the base of the tent to weigh it against the wind. His hands ached as he worked, yet the pain was a small thing. This was the first night there had been no stovehouse to stop at . . . the clanholds were coming to an end.

Angus had peeled off his gloves and was busy stripping wood. His knife never stopped dancing as he spoke. "You know what will happen, Raif. War. It's in the clanholds' nature to make battle. Look at your clan boast: *We do not hide and we do not cower. And we will have our revenge.* And Dhoone's: *We are Dhoone, Clan Kings and clan warriors alike. War is our mother. Steel is our father. And peace is but a thorn in our side.* Bludd claims that death is their companion, Castlemilk swears they'll be fighting the day the Stone Gods shatter the world, and even cursed Clan Gray holds that loss is something they know and do not fear." Angus sniffed. "Quite brings a tear to a man's eye."

Raif frowned at him, yet he seemed not to notice. Resting his blade, he said, "The point is, the clanholds have been at each other's throats for three thousand years—probably more if you count the time before Irgar drove them north across the Ranges. Clan Withy and Clan Haddo keep the histories, and believe me, those histories are grim. Grim. You've fought yourselves, the Sull, the city men, the Forsworn, Trenchlanders—anything you could see and shake a stick at and a few things you could not. The past forty years have been different, and you have the old Dhoone chief Airy Dhoone and Dagro Blackhail's father, Ewan, to thank for that. Both grew up during the River Wars, both lost kin on the banks of the Wolf and the Easterly Flow. Airy lost his sister Anne, whom he loved above all others, and Ewan lost two of his three sons. Such losses shape men. Airy rode the thirty leagues from the Flow to the Dhoonehouse with Anne's body laid over the back of his mare. Her death fell hard upon him. Some even say it turned him mad, and that he kept Anne's dried-up corpse on a chair made of willow wood next to his bed."

Angus smiled softly, reached for another log to strip. "With chiefs, who will ever know the truth? But both Airy Dhoone and Ewan Blackhail *did* withdraw to their roundhouses, ordered their clansmen to retreat, turned their backs on their gains, and left their war-sworn clans to battle amongst themselves. Gullit Bludd did well by them, as did Roy Ganmiddich and Adalyn Croser. All got the land and water they wanted.

"Five seasons went by where Ewan Blackhail and Airy Dhoone watched as their war-sworn clans pushed north against their borders. By this time Dagro had grown to manhood and taken his first yearman's oath, and Vaylo Bludd had put a dagger to his father's heart and taken over the lording of that clan. That was when Ewan and Airy began to see a future where the clanholds were ruled by Clan Bludd. They knew what sort of man Vaylo Bludd was, that early, even before he started calling himself the Dog Lord and braiding his hair in the manner of the Dhoone Kings.

"Vaylo Bludd shook Airy Dhoone and Ewan Blackhail from their mourning. Both chiefs took command of their war-sworn clans. They met at the House on the Flow, with the river brown as mud beneath them, and brought an end to the war by speaking a treaty there. They met only the once, yet both men spent the rest of their chiefships building bonds of fosterage between their clans that have stayed in place to this day."

Raif nodded. He knew this well enough. Only two winters earlier Drey had been set to leave for a year's fosterage at Dhoone. Mannie Dhoone, nephew to the Dhoone chief, Maggis Dhoone, had been set to come to Blackhail in Drey's stead. But Mannie was thrown by his horse while out hunting in the blue thorngrass south of the Dhoonehold, and both his legs were broken, and the fosterage had never gone through.

Standing and brushing ice from his oilskin, Raif said, "Dhoone *will* join with Blackhail to defeat Clan Bludd, won't they?"

Angus let the last of the logs fall to the snow, then reached inside his coat for his rabbit flask. In no hurry to drink, he simply turned the flask in his hand. "I canna say, Raif. Dhoone is scattered and broken. Maggis and his sons are dead, and no one knows when a new chief will be named. They lost three hundred clansmen and yearmen in that raid. They lost their forge, their stockpile of pig iron, their livestock." Angus shook his head. "Dhoone is as close to being lost as Clan Morrow was on the eve of Burnie Dhoone's wedding."

Raif touched his measure of powdered guidestone, as all clansmen did when the name of the Lost Clan was spoken. Clan Morrow had once stood east of the Dhoonehold, rivaling Bludd and Blackhail in size. The Dark King, Burnie Dhoone, spent thirty years destroying the clan when his young wife, Maida, left him for Shann Morrow, eldest son of the Morrow chief. Only outsiders such as Angus ever called Clan Morrow by its name. To clansmen it was always the Lost Clan. Raif remembered Tem telling him once how he and Dagro Blackhail had come upon the ground where the Morrowhouse had once stood. *Nothing remains, Raif, not even a cairnstone, and no plants but white heather will root there.*

Angus took a swig from his flask, swallowed, then took one more. "Blackhail will fight alone. Dhoone has battles and demons of its own. The war-sworn clans may help, yet I have a feeling that they'll be too busy saving their own necks to worry about Blackhail and Dhoone."

Raif looked hard at Angus. The wind had dropped, and the hard frost turned each of his uncle's breaths into a spell of ice and light. "What do you mean?"

"Naught except that in all wars it's every man for himself." Slipping the flask beneath his coat, Angus stooped to pick up the stripped logs. "I'd better get a fire started or we'll be eating cold kidneys tonight. And I don't know about you, but I've a fancy that once a kidney's been left to cool overnight, it makes a better weapon than it does a meal." He grinned. "Put one of them in a slingshot and I'm sure we could bring down a bird. A big one, mind. Maybe even a goose."

Raif watched as Angus built the fire close to the tent's entrance. It wasn't worth restating the question. Angus Lok said nothing he had no mind to. He knew more about the coming war, that was certain, but he would speak it only in his own good time. Bringing his hands to his face, Raif blew on his cold, aching fingers. It had been full dark for several hours, yet he was still careful not to turn his gaze north. Clan was behind him, and that was the way it had to be.

After a time, he made his way to the tent. As he crawled through the flap, he felt the stitches on his chest pull at his skin. It took him a moment to deal with the pain. He stripped off his oilskin and eased himself down amid the blankets and elkhides. He had no desire for food, neither hot nor cold, and settled his body into the position that caused the least hurt and waited for sleep to come.

*Blackhail will fight alone.*

He did not rest easy, but he slept.

The next morning when he woke and crawled from the tent to relieve himself, he caught a glimpse of a new landscape far below the southern rise. A massive, partially frozen lake stretched as far as he could see into the distance. Its shore was gray with grease ice, yet its center was black, oily, and steaming with frost smoke.

"The Black Spill," murmured Angus, coming to stand at Raif's side. "The deepest lake in the Territories. Ille Glaive claims its shore to the east. We'll be heading around its western shore, toward the Ranges."

Raif nodded, suddenly acutely aware of how far he was from home. He had never been this far south, never before stepped upon soil that did not belong to a clan.

*Effie, Drey . . .*

Abruptly he turned and went to feed and water Moose. They broke camp soon after, heading southwest and then south toward the towering peaks of Spire Vanis. The weather warmed and the winds quickened and storm clouds began to gather in the north.

# TWENTY-THREE

### *Vaingate*

ASH SCRATCHED HER SCALP. Mites, she thought as she watched the distant arch of Vaingate, got everywhere. And no amount of wind and frost could kill them. She supposed she should be horrified at the idea of things living on her body, but she hadn't eaten in over three days and she was seriously beginning to consider them as a meal.

That thought made her smile in a grim way, and *that* made the ice sore on her lip crack open. Seconds later she tasted her own blood, warm and briny like salt water. Eating snow wasn't a good idea. She wished someone had told her that before her mouth had gotten sore. Still, it did have its advantages. Ash couldn't imagine anyone recognizing her now, not even Penthero Iss. Her hair was dark and greasy, her clothes were stiff with mud, and her skin felt like something a carpenter might use to sand a chair. Heaven only knew what she looked like. She hadn't seen her reflection in days and had now reached the point where she was quite sure she didn't want to.

Her stomach rumbled noisily, pulling her thoughts back to Vaingate. It was early morning and the rising sun had turned the gate's three-story arch into a bridge of golden light. Just watching the sunlight flow across the bias-cut limestone filled Ash with such longing, it stopped her hunger dead.

*Reach, mistressss.*

*So cold here, so dark. Reach.*

The voices jumped her, beating against her mind like a flock of dark birds. Ash fought, as she always did, yet more and more these days she had less and less to fight with. A razor's edge of darkness cut her thoughts, splitting and resplitting until there was nothing but a thin line left.

SHE BLINKED AWAKE. SUNLIGHT streamed into her eyes, dazzling and making her feel sick. Pain squeezed along her forehead as she rolled sideways and vomited onto the snow. Wiping her mouth clean, she forgot about the ice sore and winced as the edge of her hand knocked the scab. When she was ready, she looked at the sky again. The sun was now high in the south. It was midday. She had lost four hours. *Four*.

Frightened, she sat upright. *It's all right*, she told herself. *No one could have spotted me up here.*

She was sitting on the flat roof of a broken-down and abandoned tannery. Ever since she had discovered the building a week ago, it had become her favorite place in all the city. The area around Vaingate was crowded with disused buildings, but all were carefully chained and boarded to prevent anyone in need of shelter from breaking in. The tannery's windows were nailed shut, and it had enough chains around its doors to contain a prison full of thieves, yet at some point the weight of snow on the roof had caused a portion of the upper floor to collapse. A season of floods, frosts, and thaws had gone on to break the walls, and it hadn't been difficult at all to find a way in.

Unlike most other buildings in the city that were built with sloping roofs to shunt snow, the tannery roof was mostly flat. Ash supposed the flat sections had been used for pegging out tanned skins to dry. She could still see some of the remaining pegs, poking up from the rooftop like stone weeds.

It wasn't a very high building, yet its position a quarter league north of the city wall afforded it a good view of Vaingate. It soothed Ash to come here and just look. Yet now, glancing at the boarded-up buildings across the way and the lifeless streets below, she knew she couldn't risk coming here again. This wasn't the first time the voices had made her black out, and it wouldn't be the last. They were getting stronger . . . and they had learned ways to reach her while she was awake.

Ash shivered. *Four hours.* What if she had not woken? What if she had lain here, unseen and undiscovered, all day? One night spent outside would kill her. Last night it had been so cold that she had felt the saliva freeze against her teeth.

A sound halfway between a grunt and a sob puffed from her lips. She desperately needed to drink, but the thought of eating more snow made her mouth curl. Slowly she struggled to her feet. She tried not to look at her body as she brushed the snow from her cloak, but bony edges kept catching her eye. Stupidly, ridiculously, it was her breasts that worried her the most. Just two weeks ago they had been heavy and round, growing so quickly they *ached.* Now they were small again, barely there. It was as if her body had reverted to childhood, leaving only her hands and face to age.

Straightening her back, she turned into the wind and pulled the odors of the city through her nostrils. Saliva pooled in her mouth as she tasted the scents of woodsmoke and charred fat. She was fiercely hungry. Money had run out five days ago, and unless she sold her cloak and boots she had no chance of getting more. Stealing scraps of food from the charcoal burners who stood on street corners day and night, grilling bacon and goose sausages over their dark-fires, was becoming increasingly tempting to Ash. Yet she knew from watching children quicker and cleverer than she that being caught was another horror, every bit as dreadful as starvation. Whenever a charcoal burner caught a child robbing, he would hold their hands over his grill and sear their skin like a piece of meat. At first when Ash had seen this happen, she'd wondered why the children took the risk. Now she knew. The smell of grilled fat and onions was enough to drive a starving child insane.

Walking a little bit to test the strength of her legs, she felt her gaze returning to Vaingate. The gate tower looked so quiet—only one brother-in-the-watch that she could see—and the portcullis itself was up. It would be so easy to walk over there and slip through. No one would recognize her; *that* much was certain. And she knew from watching the gate for the past few days that no special arrangements were in place: just one sworn brother, occasionally two at changing watches. Even the beggars and street vendors never changed. Surely it would be safe?

Ash's stomach growled as she reached the roof wall. Soft cramps had begun to sound in her lower abdomen, and she wondered if her second menses were due. She had to take the gate now. The voices might come back at any time, and she didn't know how much longer she could fight them, didn't know if she could survive blacking out another time. Two hours yesterday. Four today.

Ash shook her head. It was now or never.

Decision made, she felt herself filling up with a splintery, last-stand kind of strength. Once she had been through the gate and seen the place where she had been found, everything would change. She would be free to leave the city and go where she pleased. She could read and write; those skills had their uses. Perhaps she could find a position as a ladies' maid or traveling companion or even a maiden scribe. Maybe she could travel east to the Cloistress Tower at Owl's Reach and ask the green-robed sisters for asylum. If only it wasn't winter . . . and so cold that the wind blew your breath back as ice.

Ash drew her cloak close as she made her way down through the treacherous landscape of the tannery. She was Ash March, Foundling, left outside Vaingate to die.

\* \* \*

"Er . . . NAY, LAD. I think we'll be taking the back door in." Angus grinned at Raif in the way he always did when he was about to do something that made no sense. "A wee hike around the back of the city will do the horses a power of good. Work the colic from their bellies."

Raif knew better than to argue. He and Angus had been traveling together for two weeks now, and Raif could spot one of his uncle's diversions a league away. Angus Lok seldom took the most straightforward route anywhere. *As the blind crow flies, as the wounded crow crawls,* and *as the dead crow rots* were favorite sayings of his, used to excuse his eccentric methods of getting from one place to another. If there was a road, Angus would not take it. If there was a bridge, Angus would not cross it. If there was a city gate, Angus would examine it from a distance and then shake his head.

"Come on, young Sevrance. Stare up at Hoargate any longer and the guards'll have us pegged as a dimwit and his fool."

Raif continued to stare at the black and icy arch of Spire Vanis's western gate. It was massive, cut from a single bloodwood as big as a church. The bark had been stripped away, and the remaining heartwood had the smooth gleam of obsidian. The carvings that chased around the arch were thick with hoarfrost, yet all things the west represented—the setting sun, the bloodwood forests, the Storm Margin, the Wrecking Sea and the whales that swam within it—could clearly be seen etched beneath the ice. In all his life Raif had never seen such a thing. Nothing in the clanholds matched it.

Ever since they had caught sight of the city walls two days back, Raif had felt a cold chill of excitement quickening in his gut. The creamy white stone of Spire Vanis glowed in every kind of light that shone upon it. Sunrise, sunset, moonlight, and starlight: The city took something different from them all. Here, in the bright sunlight of late morning, the towering walls shone like forged steel. The entire city seemed to throb and breathe like a living thing. Smoke rose from the stone mass like exhaled breath, and beneath his feet Raif felt the earth shudder and rumble as if a dragon were sleeping in a chamber far below.

"That's Mount Slain," Angus said, grabbing Raif's arm, not gently, and guiding him away from the gate. "It moves year-round. You'll get used to it after a while."

Raif nodded absently. Spire Vanis. He could hardly believe he was here.

The journey around the Black Spill had taken a week. The Bitter Hills north of the lake marked the clanholds' southern border, and it seemed to Raif that as every new day passed the clanholds receded deeper into the mist. He had not seen a clansman or clanswoman in days. The stovehouses they had stayed at were large and gloomy, not really stovehouses at all, rather places that sold ale. If you had no coin to buy food and drink, the stovemaster threw you out—in the *cold*—and when fighting erupted, there was no talk of stove laws or due respect, only the cost of broken tables and chairs. Raif had sat in these new nonclan stovehouses and watched these things happen and let the truth of them settle against his skin. Stoves were not sacred here. Old laws did not bind. The One True God of blind faith and fresh air had no love for the men who worshiped stone.

Angus was as at home here as he was in the clanholds. He knew many people and had many different ways of associating with them. Some men he would laugh and talk with openly in full sight of all; others he would simply nod to or happen to meet outside near the jacks or the smokehouse and exchange a few words with as he pulled on his gloves and hood. Some men he pretended not to know at all, yet Raif had little to do but watch his uncle these past weeks and he had seen things a casual observer would not. Angus had a way of acknowledging men without even looking their way. He could communicate a thought with the smallest shrug of his shoulders or arrange a meeting with the slightest narrowing of eyes.

Four nights back, when they were settling down by the fire in a dingy stovehouse on the western shore of the Spill, Raif had discovered he'd left his handknife in his saddlebag. When he'd run over to the stables to retrieve it, he'd come upon a man slipping a square of folded parchment under the bay's blanket. Raif had pretended not to notice. If a stranger wanted to pass a note to Angus, it was nothing to him. The man, a toothless birch eater in a moose coat, was one of a group of five drovers who were driving their cattle upland in search of graze. Angus had not once looked his way all night.

Although Angus liked to *visit* stovehouses, he seldom chose to spend the night there, and more often than not he and Raif camped out under the stars. The warmer temperatures in the cityholds made it bearable, yet the open farm-lands and clear-cut hillsides made cover increasingly hard to find. Angus liked cover, Raif had noticed, and often traveled several hours past sunset in search of a dense stand of bass-woods, a bank cut low into the hillside, or a favorable cluster of rocks.

Angus set a hard pace, and Raif was glad of it. There was a lot to be said for falling into an exhausted sleep each night. Long days in the saddle, battling the wind, the ice storms, and the aches and pains of a mending body left Raif too tired for thought. He rode, ate, stripped logs for the morning cookfire, melted ice, skinned hares, plucked birds, and took care of Moose. He did not hunt. The blister on his right hand was purple and bloated with blood.

Pain was something he lived with. The stitches on his chest itched and burned as the skin knitted itself together. The urge to tear off his clothes and claw the healing flesh was overpowering, and he would have scratched his chest raw if it hadn't been for the sheer number of layers between his fingers and his skin. It drove him mad. He cursed his mitts, his oilskins, his softskins, his elk coat, and his wool shirt. To make matters worse, Angus had insisted that the wounds be covered in purified butter and he now stank like something kept a day too long in the sun. By comparison, the cuts and bruises on his face were bearable. A scab the size of a leech clung to the cheekbone directly below his left eye, and a hairline split on his lip made smiling more trouble than it was worth.

"This way. We'll make better time the farther we travel from the wall."

Raif followed Angus' direction, leading Moose through the bald and rutted ground that surrounded the west wall. A sharp wind blew down from the mountain, hissing in his ears and driving ice crystals into his face. Ahead, the north face of Mount Slain rose above the city like a frozen god, its cliffs and high plains blue with compacted snow, its skirt black with pines. The air smelled of something Raif couldn't put a name to, some faintly sulfurous mineral that belonged deep beneath the earth. Underfoot, the ground snow was hard and unforgiving, harboring no shadows to reveal its depth. The city itself tantalized Raif with brief glimpses of iron spires, blazing watch towers, and stone archways as smooth and pale as the bones of a long dead child.

Angus was quiet as they made their way south along the wall. He had not applied any protective waxes or oils this morning, yet his face looked as pale as if he had. Leading the bay at a brisk pace, he grew impatient whenever snowdrifts slowed them.

Raif glanced at the sky. Midday. "Do you come often to this city?"

Angus sent Raif a sharp glance. "I have no love for this place."

It was the end of the subject as far as Angus was concerned, for he turned his attention to trotting the bay through the tangle of weeds and mud ice that lay in the storm channel ahead. Raif knew his uncle expected him to say no more, but his chest was itching and the devil was in him, and he was getting tired of Angus and his evasions. "Why come here, then?"

Angus' shoulders stiffened at the question. He pulled hard on the bay's reins, causing the gelding to whiffle and shake his head. Raif thought his uncle wasn't going to answer, yet when they reached the first in a series of giant buttresses that supported the main wall, Angus turned to face him.

"I come here because I have people I must see and others I must take heed of. Don't think, Raif Sevrance, that you are the only one in this world who is troubled and hard done by. The clanholds are just the start. There are people who would see more than Clan Bludd and Clan Blackhail at each other's throats. Some of them are in this city, some of them scheme in bed each night and call themselves clansmen when they wake in the morning, and others are hidden in vaults so deep that even the sun can't find them. There is danger here for me, and that means there is danger for you also. Soon enough you will attract enemies in your own right. For now be content that the burdens of danger and protection fall on me."

Angus took Raif by the shoulders and held him at arm's length. His face was grim. "I am your kin, and you must trust me. Save your questions for a place far away from these walls. There's nothing but ill memories here for me."

Raif looked at his uncle carefully. He could see him shaking, feel the heat of his body through his sealskin gloves as he waited for Raif to speak. Raif wanted to know more. How was it that Angus knew so much about the Clan Wars? Was Mace Blackhail one of the clansmen he mentioned? Who were the men whom no sun could reach? Raif frowned. Although he didn't much want to, he said, "I'll hold my questions for now."

Angus nodded back at him. "That's favor enough for me."

The sky darkened as they led the horses around the buttress walls and on toward the mountain. Snow clouds were rolling south and the sun was soon hidden from view. Two tall structures rose against the city's west wall, one dark and ringed with metal outerwork, the other as pale as ice and so tall that Raif could not see its peak.

"The Horn and the Splinter," Angus said, slapping his coat in search of his flask. "That's Mask Fortress on the other side of the wall. Home of the surlords of Spire Vanis."

Raif could not take his eyes from the tower called the Splinter. It wasn't merely the color of ice, it *was* ice. A rime of it covered the stonework like fat around a skinned carcass, gleaming yellow then blue in the light. Raif shivered. He was cold and empty, and he needed a drink.

Angus handed him the rabbit flask. The alcohol had been spiked with birch bark, and it tasted sweet and earthy like newly turned soil. One mouthful was enough. Thumping the cork in place, Raif said, "Does anyone *live* in that thing?"

"The Splinter? Nay, lad. It was flawed from the day it was built. Too high, you see. Milks the storm clouds. By all accounts it's little more than a broken shell inside. None except Robb Claw ever lived there, if *living*'s the right word for it. Holed himself up one winter, he did, and never came out. They found his corpse ten years later. Took five men to carry it to the light of day, as it had turned as hard as stone." Angus sniffed. "That's the story, anyhow."

Raif looked away. He knew little of the Mountain Cities and their history. Some of the border clans had dealings with

Ille Glaive, but few clansmen had words, good or otherwise, to spare for the cities and their closely guarded holds. "Who was Robb Claw?"

Angus slowed his pace as they reached the southwest cornerstone of the city and the bay was forced to pick its way through the rocks, dead rootwood, and loose shale that had rolled down from the mountain. The path steepened and narrowed, and then there was no path at all. Raif felt sweat trickle along his stitch lines.

"Robb Claw was the great-grandson of Glamis Claw, one of the Founding Quarterlords of Spire Vanis."

"Was he a king?"

"Nay, lad. No king's ever ruled in Spire Vanis, though it's not from want of trying. The Founding Quarterlords were the bastard *sons* of kings; their fathers ruled lands far to the south, and each king had enough true sons to ensure that neither lands nor titles would ever cede to their bastards. This pleased the Quarterlords not at all, and there were many battles fought and many knives slipped into princeflesh. Two of the four were the brothers Theron and Rangor Pengaron, and they joined with Glamis Claw and Torny Fyfe to raise a warhost and march it north across the Ranges. Theron was their leader, might have even crowned himself a king if it hadn't been for the other three lords at his back. As it was, he led the host against the Sull, founded the city, and built the first strongwall of stone and timber where Mask Fortress lies today." Angus wagged his head toward the Splinter. "Though it was Robb Claw who built the four towers."

As Raif followed his uncle's gaze, the mountain shivered beneath his feet, sending chips of shale rolling down the slope. The ice on the tower made a soft, knuckle-snapping sound as a hairline crack ran down along the rime. "Why don't they just knock it down?" he heard his voice say.

"Pride, lad. The Killhound of Spire Vanis is said to roost upon the Iron Spire that caps it. Five hundred years ago they'd haul traitors up there by a great contraption of metal and rope and impale them on the spire. The winged beasties were said to gobble them up for breakfast." Angus squinted into the clouds that wrapped themselves around the tower. "Or was it supper? I forget now."

They led their horses away. Raif grew hotter and more uncomfortable as they hiked across a shoulder of pitted limestone and then down into a ravine. Massive stone conduits built to divert the runoff around the city had to be crossed with care, as the ice was unstable and wet. Moose tore his left hock on a jagged edge, but Angus refused to stop and bind it, and they left a trail of horse blood in their wake.

An hour later, when the gate finally came into view, Raif felt nothing but relief. His stitches itched like all the hells, and so much fluid had leaked from his blister to his glove that the hide had hardened to armor and set itself in a permanent curve around the reins. Raif wanted to go to some dark stovehouse and sleep. He was tired enough that he would not dream or, if he did, not remember it later.

Angus gave the gate a name and struck a path down from the mountainside toward the wall. It was smaller than Hoargate, made of plain stone that arched as gracefully as a drawn bow. No road of any kind led from it. No one stood waiting for admission—indeed, there was *nowhere* for anyone to stand as the gate opened directly onto a grassy slope. As they drew level with the first gate tower, a hoarse cry split the air.

*"Get her!"*

A child stepped through the gate. A girl. Hearing the cry, she hesitated, glanced back, then started to run. Two men, dressed like beggars but carrying swords of bloodred steel, emerged through the gate and ran straight for her. The girl was weak and very thin, and they caught her in less than ten seconds. She fought them in a quiet, almost animal way, not making a sound, but kicking and jerking furiously, making it difficult for the men to hold her. Her hood was torn off and then her gloves. Her shoulder-length hair was caked in dirt. An ice sore cast a shadow across her lips.

More men came. One man was massive, with hands that swung at his side like lead weights. His small eyes glinted like iron filings. Raif watched in growing anger as the big man approached the girl and smacked her full in the face. The girl's neck snapped back, and she stopped struggling. Blood trickled from her nose to her lip. The big man said something to the others, making them laugh in an excited, nervous way that seemed more to do with fear than amusement. He struck the girl again, casually this time, with a half-closed fist.

Raif felt his blood heat. He stepped forward.

Angus put a hand on Raif's arm, barring him from taking another step. "There's trouble here we want no part of. That's Marafice Eye, Protector General of the Rive Watch. If he chooses to torment a beggar girl outside one of his own gates, there's nothing you or I can do about it."

Raif continued to press forward. The man named Marafice Eye tore off the girl's cloak. Fabric ripped. A breath of fear puffed from the girl's lips.

"Easy, lad," warned Angus, fingers digging deep. "We canna afford to draw attention in this place. More than your life and mine depend on it."

Raif glanced at his uncle. Angus' face was grave, the lines around his mouth as deep as scars.

"If it were just you and me alone in this, I would save her. Believe that. I would not lie about another's life."

Raif did believe him. He saw what was in his uncle's eyes. Angus Lok feared someone or something greatly in this city ... and he was not a man who feared lightly. Raif stopped pushing. Angus released his grip.

A group of six armed men now surrounded the girl. All but two were dressed in muddy cloaks and ragged pants, yet Raif began to realize that none of them were beggars. Their steel gleamed with linseed oil, their hair and beards were trimmed and clean, and their arms and necks were corded with the sort of hard muscle that was built during long practice sessions on a weapons court. The one named Marafice Eye was dressed in a rough brown robe, like a cleric or a monk. Despite his size he carried only a handknife. All the men deferred to him.

The girl had lost the sleeves and collar from her dress. She was being held by three men, only one of whom was dressed in the same oiled and supple leathers worn by the guards at Hoargate. The girl's body was twisted so that her skirt rode up around her thighs and her head hung down, unsupported.

"Let her drop."

Raif heard Marafice Eye's words clearly. Immediately the

three men released their hold, and the girl slumped to the ground. She remained silent as Marafice Eye poked her with the toe of his boot.

"Thought you'd run away, eh? Thought you'd made a fool of the Knife?" He jabbed her twice in the ribs. "Thought you'd get away with leaving one of my men to die." Bringing the heel of his boot down on her hand, he drove her fingers into the snow. Something snapped with the soft click of rotted wood. Still, the girl did not cry out.

Raif felt the anger come to him. He imagined killing the six men in slow and hideous ways. Clansmen would never do such a thing to a woman. A small voice whispered, *What about the Bluddroad*? but he cut it from his mind.

"Go on. Run. Let's see just how far you'll get." Marafice Eye shoved his foot under the girl's back, raising her torso off the ground. "*Run*, I said. Grod here has a fancy for the hunt. You remember Grod, don't you? You left him a lock of your hair."

The girl tried to struggle to her feet. She was so thin; Raif wondered where her strength came from. Making the mistake of putting her weight on her damaged hand, she inhaled sharply and collapsed back into the snow.

That was when she spotted them.

The six armed men had spread out, allowing her room to stand, and the space between her and Angus and Raif was now clear. Raif got his first real look at the girl free from shadows and darting bodies. Something in his throat tightened. She wasn't as young as he had first thought.

Storm clouds parted and sunlight streamed down onto the girl's face, illuminating her skin with silver light. Raif felt his body cool. One by one the hairs along his spine rose, and the skin beneath them pulled as tight as if ghost fingers were laid upon it. Even as he shook the chill from him, something hardly important and yet at the same time vital fell into place inside his head.

She was not looking at him.

She was looking at Angus Lok.

Gray eyes drew Angus' coppery ones to her as surely as if they were connected by a thread. A second hung like dust in warm air as they locked gazes. Everything stopped. Wind and cold and sunlight died. Raif felt like a shadow, like nothing. Angus and the girl were all that counted.

Then he heard his uncle draw breath. A word was spoken—Raif heard it clearly but did not understand its meaning. *Hera*, Angus said.

Angus Lok drew his sword. Plain it was, steel as gray as sleet. He stepped forward, and as he did so, something shed from him like old skin. He grew larger and taller and more terrible. His eyes stopped being copper and became golden instead.

"Hold the horses," he murmured without once looking Raif's way. "Hold them and wait."

Raif took the bay's reins instinctively. Fear filled the hollow spaces in his chest. He didn't understand. Did Angus think he could fight six armed men? What was happening here?

Angus walked forward, his fist curled around the leather grip of his sword. He was shaking intensely, almost vibrating. The girl was still on the ground. Marafice Eye was shoving her with his boot, in the manner of a hunter who wasn't quite sure whether or not the game he had just brought down was dead. The guard dressed in black leathers noticed Angus first. Raising his red blade, he nudged the Knife.

Marafice Eye looked up. Angus was about thirty paces away from him. Slowly Marafice Eye wiped the spittle from his lips. His eyes brightened. "Drop the gate," he shouted to some unseen guard in the gate tower. "I think I'll take this fight inside." Without once taking his eyes from Angus, he gestured to his men to gather up the girl and carry her into the city. Three men dealt with the girl, while the other two moved to flank their leader. Marafice Eye held his position, watching Angus approach. Above his head, metal gears whined, then the gate shuddered into life.

Raif pulled the horses toward a dead birch and tethered them. His eyes were on the gate, watching as spiked gratings black with mud began to descend with a stop-and-start motion. The moment his hands were free of the reins, he broke into a run.

Angus stepped onto the gate platform. Marafice Eye smiled tightly, then backed away, allowing the two men flanking him to cut first steel. Swords, red as if blood were already upon them, angled upward toward the light. Pulleys screeched overhead, spinning out of control, and the gate began to plummet. Angus leaped forward, dodging the iron spikes by a hair-thin slice of a moment. Raif ran and ran and *ran*. He had to get to Angus.

Too late. The gate crashed to the ground as he stepped onto the platform. Clumps of greasy snow fell onto his head and shoulders as he grabbed the grille and rattled it with all his might. *"Angus!"*

Paces away on the other side, five armed men formed a baiting circle around his uncle. Angus' face was dark and still. His blade edge was already tipped with one man's blood, and as he cut a defensive circle around his position, he wounded two more.

Three men in black leathers rushed from the gate tower and attended the girl, dragging her back from the fighting. Raif counted nine red blades in all. Marafice Eye stood off to the side, watching. His small lips twitched as Angus took a cut to the ear.

Raif's heart hammered in his chest. He had to do something. Wildly he looked around. He saw Moose and the bay nosing snow to get at the tufts of fat thistlegrass buried beneath. A wing-shaped piece of leather riding high on the bay's back caught his eye: Angus' bowcase.

Raif raced for it. A soft cry sounded at his back: Angus had taken a second hit. Raif took a short breath. He couldn't risk thinking about that now; it would only slow him. As he fumbled with the brass buckle on the bowcase, his hands had never felt so big or so clumsy. Grease from the gate made everything slippery, and his fingers wouldn't *bend*.

Bracing the bow seemed to take hours. The waxed string was cold and stiff; it kept breaking free of the knot. He had to use his teeth in the end, pulling the thread through with a violent snap of his jaw. Running his shaking fingers along the belly of the bow, he tried to calm himself. The bow was exquisitely carved, deeply inset with silver and midnight blue horn. Touching it helped. He had drawn it before; he knew its measure and its hand.

Turning, he slid Angus' quiver around his waist and

sprinted back to the gate. The iron grating was densely woven. Bars as thick as a man's wrist crossed at right angles, leaving two-inch squares in between. Raif drew an arrow from the quiver. Its leaded head was heavier than he was used to, and in a deep, instinctual part of his brain he knew it would take more pull and height to aim it.

On the other side of the gate, one man was down, floored by a gash to his shoulder, and another two men were bleeding from snipe cuts to the arms and legs. Only one guard looked after the girl now, twisting her arm behind her back to keep her close. The seven remaining red blades were all focused on containing Angus Lok. Angus was clearly frustrated by their baiting tactics. If one or two swordsmen had come forward to engage him, he would have bettered them; Raif saw how swiftly his uncle moved, how certain he was with his plain journeyman's sword. But the red blades preferred to play a waiting, tiring game. They knew Angus was dangerous. It was easier and safer to wait for a mistake.

Marafice Eye watched from his position on the periphery, jabbing only occasionally with his crab-hilted knife. Unlike the men under him, he chose his moments with care, and his blade always came away wet. A ribbon of blood, dark and slow as molasses, ran down Angus' right cheek and across his jaw. He kept pushing forward toward the girl, but the red blades kept him back.

Raif swallowed a mouthful of saliva. What had driven Angus to attack? It was madness. Standing back from the gate, he nocked the lead-packed arrowhead and raised the bow to his chest. The stitches across his rib cage burned like new wounds as he drew the string. Fighting the pain and the hot salty tears it brought, he concentrated on picking out a target. He had counted five arrows in Angus' quiver. Five. None could go astray.

Focusing his gaze beyond the steel-rimmed eyelet, Raif chose the man who presented the most immediate threat to Angus: a thin, dark-haired weasel dressed in sackcloth and stewed leather who had grown impatient with baiting and was gradually working his way under Angus' arm. He was fast and vicious, and he reminded Raif of a Scarpeman.

Raif aimed for his upper chest, sighting him purely

through the notch on the riser. He wanted no heart kills, nothing to sicken or stain him. That was one madness he would not bring to this fight. As he searched for the still line that would lead his arrow home, the blister on his hand cracked open and a line of yellow fluid oozed along his wrist.

He released the string. The arrow shot ahead. The bow recoiled, slamming in his hand like a bird. *Thwang.* Metal slammed against metal. Orange sparks sprayed through the grille. Raif cried out in frustration as he watched his arrow nosedive into the snow beyond the gate. The arrowhead had hit the iron grating. One of its flight feathers was lodged in the grille like elk hair on a fence.

*"Aargh!"*

Raif focused his gaze on the fighting beyond the gate. The weasel man jerked his blade free of Angus' shoulder. Blood pumped from a dark hole in Angus' buckskin coat. His face was gray and twisted with pain. The red blades needled him, drawing pinpricks of blood. Angus roared. Swinging in a mighty turning circle, he severed one man's hand and sliced deeply into another's hip.

Raif glanced down at his quiver. Four arrows left. Seven men. *Gods help me, I can't miss another shot.* Cursing his shaking hands, his weeping blister, and the fierce burning in his chest, he drew the second arrow from the quiver. Angus was slowing; his left arm was dragging and he was taking hard, frothing breaths. Watching him, watching muscles in his cheeks pulse with anger and some other unknowable emotion that lay between sorrow and dread, Raif knew what he had to do. It wasn't a matter of choice anymore. It was a matter of shared blood.

The arrow was nocked and primed in less than an instant. Raif held it fast against the plate as he drew the bow. The weasel man grew large in his sights, big as a giant. Raif *called* him nearer. The space between them contracted, and then suddenly there was no space at all. Raif smelled sweat and the secret scent of blood and waste that lay trapped beneath the skin. Then nothing mattered but the heart.

Engorged with blood, heavy with life force, driven by the one thing that the gods had no power over, the heart filled

Raif's sights like a glance into the sun. Things became known to him, small things about the body that surrounded the vital, pumping core. The weasel man's blood ran too fast, rushing through his body like hot steam in search of release. His liver was hard and dimpled, dark with disease, and only one testicle hung from his groin.

This and more Raif knew in less time than it took for a used breath to ascend from his lungs. It meant nothing. Nothing. The heart was his.

He kissed the string and released the arrow, and by the time his shoulders had dealt with the recoil, the weasel man was dead. Heart-killed. His legs dropped beneath him, his bladder failed, and he was gone.

Metal flooded Raif's mouth. A pain, like the sickening wrench of a bone pulled from its socket, worked its way through his chest. *Is this what I am? Cold killer of men?*

It was a question he had no time for. Another arrow was already in his hand, though he had no memory of drawing it, and he brought it to the plate and pulled once more upon the string. His powers of discrimination had gone—blasted away by pain and madness—and he set his sights on the first red blade who crossed his plate.

The heart came to him, faster than an eye focusing on a distant object. Young and strong, this heart, with a body only lately visited by disease. Something dark grew in the deepest underlevel of the lungs, a lobe of quiet flesh. He spared it no thought as he released the string. The *thrum* of the arrow merged with the soft gurgle of a stopped breath, and then another faceless body hit the snow.

Raif drew the third arrow. Pain blurred his vision, saliva corroded his gums. On the far side of the gate, Angus was taking advantage of the fear spreading through the remaining men. As Raif pulled his bow, Angus slid his steel into kidney flesh, and a red blade fell to the ground, screaming and clutching at his gut. Behind the circle of armed men, the black-cloaked guard in charge of the girl was beginning to panic. He threw her onto the ground and put the point of his sword against her neck. The girl's chest rose and fell, rose and fell. Her fingers scratched the snow.

Even before he was aware of what he was doing, Raif *called* the guard's heart to his sights. It happened so quickly he barely got an impression of the man before he released the string. The arrowhead shot through a break in the fighting and entered the guard's heart from behind, pinning his cloak to his spine.

Raif swayed. His head rang with pain. Dimly he was aware of objects hitting the metal grating, as knives and missiles were flung his way. None got through. He could see little now, only sharp edges and glimmers of light. He saw a moving blur that he knew to be his uncle, and three or perhaps four figures surrounding him. His thoughts came slowly, clumsily, floating in his mind like pieces of driftwood. One arrow, that was all he knew. One arrow. One shot. *Must take it.*

He couldn't see, but he could *feel.* As he drew the bow, something within him fastened on to the nearest heart. It happened with the speed and certainty of a stone dropping in a well . . . and it made Raif sick to his gut. His arms adjusted their positions and his bowhand ceased shaking and he knew with utter confidence the exact instant to release the string. *Dead,* he thought dully, *gone the moment I found his heart.*

After that, someone else went down: one of the red blades dressed in shabby stripes. Angus landed a blow that made another man squeal like a pig. Raif swayed. Stumbling forward, he grabbed hold of the grille for support. His eyes cleared for a moment, and he saw Marafice Eye looking straight at him. Raif took a breath. The Knife stood apart from his remaining men in the shadow of the east gate tower, his eyes as pale as gristle in a piece of meat. As Raif watched, he turned his gaze first to the girl, then to Angus Lok, deciding what he would do. The girl was thirty paces away from him, and even as Marafice Eye stepped toward her, Angus moved to block his path.

Raif felt himself failing. With his last scrap of strength, he focused his eyes hard on Marafice Eye, holding the man in his sights, *willing* him to turn and look. When the Knife shifted his gaze and their eyes met, Raif released his hand from the grille and reached down toward the quiver at his waist. In that moment Marafice Eye *knew* he was going to be shot, heart-killed like four of his men. Raif saw the realization in the man's eyes, saw the understanding that he could not reach the girl before the arrow reached him and that it was better to withdraw than die. As Raif's hand closed around fresh air, Marafice Eye barked an order and fled.

Raif's legs collapsed beneath him, and he slid down to a place where the walls were formed from darkness and the edges creased with pain.

# TWENTY-FOUR

## The Gods Lights

THERE WERE TWELVE SECRET uses for whale blubber, and this night Eloko, widow to Kulahuk and mother to Nolo and Avranna, had promised to show Sadaluk one of them. Eloko was a fine woman, with teeth as tiny as a baby's and the belly of a fat snow bear. She was not young, but Sadaluk was not fussy about that. When a tribeswoman offered comfort to an old man, it was something to be celebrated, not picked apart like a whale carcass after a kill. Eloko had been widowed for ten months, and it was fitting that she had chosen to break mourning with an elder of the tribe. It showed respect. The Ice God could not fault her for that.

The Listener permitted himself to think about Eloko and her plentiful supply of whale blubber for only a short while longer. Eloko had waited ten months. Sadaluk himself had waited that and more. It would do neither of them much harm to stand at opposite sides of the village, one in a house made of driftwood and clay and the other in a ground dug from hard earth and braced with whalebone, and watch the Gods Lights for a few hours more.

The sky was clear tonight, dark and brilliant as the hole in the center of a man's eye. The Gods Lights raged to the north like flames from a wildfire burning beyond the horizon. Pink and green, the lights flashed, the colors of all living things. Every winter the Gods Lights unfurled like banners in the clear night sky. Their slow, languid movements reminded Sadaluk of seaweed floating in deep water, limbs unfurling with the grace of weightless things. If you listened very hard, you could hear them. The noise sounded like the cracking and ripping of wind in the sails of a ship. Some said it was the same noise you heard before you died, but Sadaluk did not know about that.

He did know that the lights were a message from the gods. *Look at us*, they proclaimed. *See how beautiful and terrible we are. See how we come to you in full winter, when your sons and daughters need us the most.*

It was impossible to look upon the northern lights and deny the presence of the gods. Lootavek, the one who had listened before him, said that the Ice Trappers would know when the end of the world was coming, as the lights would burn red. "The gods will give us warning," he said one night as they camped on the sea ice, butchering seals. "They will send us a sky filled with blood."

Sadaluk remembered looking down at his own wet and bloody hands and asking, "How do you know this?"

Lootavek had given him one of his looks. "You ask the wrong question, Sadaluk. How is not important, it is the *why* that counts."

"Why, then?"

"So that we will be the first to know."

Sadaluk had finished the butchering in silence, not really understanding what the Listener meant but unwilling to ask any more questions. He had been young then, in awe of the Listener, as was right and proper for a young hunter in the tribe. Now, tonight, watching the Gods Lights dance in the northern skies, he wished he had asked more. The lights seemed darker than he remembered them, the pinks deeper, the greens flickering and strangely distorted. Sometimes he thought he saw flashes of red in the farthest reaches of the corona. *It's nothing*, he told himself. *There have always been streaks of red in the lights.*

But surely tonight there were more?

Frowning at the wildness of his own thoughts, he turned his back on the sky and entered his ground. Eloko would be getting impatient and might yet close the door in his face. A woman's pride was a fierce thing, and making her wait was one thing, but making her wait *too long* was quite another. And it would be good to feel warm arms around his back and the touch of another's hands on his face.

Why, then, could he not get Lootavek's voice out of his head? *So that we will be the first to know.* There had been pride in that statement, Sadaluk realized that now. Ice Trappers were always the first to know. "We live on the edge of the world," Lootavek had said another time, during summer, when swarms of blackflies formed clouds in the sky and even the dogs stayed indoors. "We pay a great price in hunger and death, and for this we bear the messages of the gods. We are closest to them, Sadaluk. Never forget that. After I am gone, you must listen to your dreams and wait for the messages to come."

Sadaluk *tsk*ed. If he were a sane man, he would be reaching for his bear coat and gloves; he would march across the village and take himself quickly to Eloko's door. An offer had been made, and a short walk would secure it, and he would be an ice-rotted fool if he let the opportunity pass. But he wasn't sane, and the Gods Lights worried him, and thirty days and thirty nights had passed and still Black Claws had failed to home. The Listener did not think the raven would be coming back. The thought pained him, for he had loved Black Claws the most, and the idea of the raven lying dead on some glaciated cirque or frozen lake was upsetting in strange new ways. Had he been attacked by other birds or the hand of man? Had he delivered his message before he went down, or had the small strip of spruce bark fallen into unwelcome hands? The Listener shook his unease away. *It's only a raven*, he told himself. *One less bird to find scraps for through the long winter's night.*

Stretching his hard old hands upon the door frame, he prepared to go inside. It was high time that another message was sent. The Old Blood had to be told that the dance of shadows had begun. They must send Far Riders to him and make bid upon the future and stand upon the sea ice and see the Gods Lights for themselves.

Pulling a strip of birch bark from a peg near his door,

Sadaluk took one last look at the sky. Red, he saw, a world flickering red.

\* \* \*

IRON CHAINS RATTLED. METAL groaned. Feet thudded over compacted snow. "Drink. Drink."

Raif instinctively shied away from the cold, stinging fumes that rose from a nozzle thrust toward his face. He did not want to drink.

Fingers, neither clean nor fragrant, thrust themselves into his mouth, forcing his jaw apart. Liquid was poured. A moment passed while the open cavity of his mouth was filled, and then the liquid streamed down his throat. Raif gasped and spluttered and raised his head. Spitting, he cleared his mouth of the foulness.

Angus frowned at him. "You must drink your fill, lad. I know it tastes like lamp fuel, but I swear it will do you good."

Raif glanced around. The sun had sunk behind the mountain, and the sky was dark and silvery, transforming itself into night. He was lying in soft snow by the gate. The grating had been raised, and six bodies lay in the plowed field of blood, mud, and slush on the other side. His hand rose to feel for his raven lore. The horn was as smooth as a pulled tooth, hotter than his skin. He drank more of the liquid. Already he felt his body working, tingling, as if it had been whipped with dry birches. His mind sharpened. Suddenly he realized that Angus was wounded; blood was gouting from a hole in his buckskins. Raif began to rise.

Angus put a hand on his shoulder and forced him back down. "Easy, lad. Give the ghostmeal chance to work."

"Ghostmeal?"

"Medicine to you." Angus looked over his shoulder, wincing as muscles in his chest were stretched. "Come. Please. We will not hurt you."

It took Raif a moment to realize his uncle was speaking to someone else. The girl. Edging around, he saw she was standing by the far gatepost, watching them. Ragged bits of her dress blew in the wind, and her pale hair sparkled with ice. Dried blood formed a black line around her jaw. She did not speak.

Angus stood heavily and at great cost, pressing a hand to his chest. "You must come with us, with Raif. They will be back soon. You are not safe here anymore."

"Who are you? Why did you help me?"

Raif was surprised by the calmness of the girl's voice. Her gray eyes were cool, and there was an air of confidence about her that he had not expected from a beggar girl.

Angus' gaze flickered to the city behind her back. "I am Angus Lok of Ille Glaive, and this is my kinsman Raif Sevrance. We helped you because you were in need. We would help you again if you will allow us. You need food and clothing and protection. Come with us and we will take you to a safe place."

"Where?"

Raif almost smiled. The girl wasn't about to be fobbed off with one of Angus Lok's typically vague replies.

Strangely, Angus smiled too. His entire body strained toward the girl as he said, "We head for Ille Glaive."

The girl nodded slowly. She looked at Raif. Shouts and horse thunder sounded within the city. Her face stiffened as she listened.

"Please," Angus murmured. "I swear on all that is precious to me I will not harm you."

Raif had never heard his uncle speak so quietly before. It disturbed him. Why had Angus risked his life to save this thin scrap of a girl?

"Will we leave through Vaingate?" The girl's calm demeanor was wearing thin as the thud and clatter of armed men grew louder. Her shoulders twitched as a voice bellowed, *"To the gate!"*

"You and Raif will. I'll drop the gate behind you so it looks as if you're still within the city with me. Then I'll lead the Rive Watch on a fair chase and meet you on the east road past midnight."

"No. You can't stay in the city alone." Raif struggled to his feet, battling pain and nausea with clenched fists. "I'm coming with you."

"No. You must stay with the girl. A party outside the city

gates is too easily found. Someone needs to draw the Rive Watch away." All the hearty redness drained from Angus' face as he spoke, and suddenly he looked like a stranger to Raif. "You must go now. As your uncle I command it." Without waiting for a reply, he turned and walked toward the gate. Raif thought he would touch the girl as he passed, for his hand jerked awkwardly toward her, yet he didn't. Turning, he headed for the gate tower instead.

Pulleys creaked a moment later as the break was kicked free of the crankshaft, and then the gate descended with a crash. Spikes rattled in their sockets like bones in a jar, and plates of ice that had quickened over the limestone arch above the gate fractured and fell, revealing a carving of a great winged beast. The girl began to walk toward Raif. Her eyes were bright and hard, and they stirred a memory within him. . . . He tried but could not place it. Shrugging, he slipped the flask containing the last of the ghostmeal into his coat. He felt light-headed and full of false strength. *What in all the gods' names is that stuff?*

Angus emerged from the gatehouse seconds later. The bloodstain on his buckskin coat had spread, and the great mass of his body pitched unevenly from step to step. "Ride, do not walk," he said to Raif. "The ghostmeal only gives so much; you'll feel worse for having drunk it come dark. Head southeast. In about an hour you'll cross a game trail above a stand of hemlock. Follow it. It should keep you out of sight of the wall. When you come to Wrathgate head east. I'll find you along the road."

*Let me go in your place*, Raif wanted to say. Yet he guessed his uncle's argument even before he spoke it: Angus *knew* Spire Vanis; he did not. A clansman with no knowledge of the city couldn't hope to evade the red blades. Looking into his uncle's copper eyes, Raif knew he could do nothing but nod and say, "Until midnight." Anything more would have cost Angus time.

The clatter of hoof irons grew louder. A series of orders was shouted, and the scrape of steel against leather told of weapons being drawn.

"Take care of the girl," Angus warned. Before Raif had chance to answer, he was gone.

Raif turned away from the gate. Four dead men had his arrows in their hearts: It was not a sight he wanted to dwell on.

The girl was no longer at his side. She had stepped clear of the platform and was now walking through the grainy snow and loose rocks on the slope. Raif ran to fetch the horses. He caught up with the girl on the far side of the gate and forced her to step back against the wall. Night was rising in the east, sending shadows spilling over the snow like black oil. The limestone was cold against Raif's back, smoother than any stone ought to be. As he pulled the horses to him, the ground shook as an armed force descended upon the gate. Breath ached in his throat as he listened to the red blades rein in their mounts. It would be so easy for someone to raise the gate.

For the longest moment all was quiet and still. Raif imagined the red blades standing in silence over the bodies, their gazes moving from heart to heart. Moose snuffled. Raif sent Orwin Shank's horse a look to silence the dead. Booted feet crunched snow. The gate grille chimed softly, moved by either hands or wind. *Make them turn*, Raif thought. *Gods, make them turn.*

A call sounded from within the city, high like the howl of a wolf. *Angus*, Raif knew in an instant. A cry went up. Horse leather cracked like whips, and then the ground shook once more as the red blades charged from the gate. *Hunting.*

Raif took a breath. Anger toward the girl welled up inside him. She was the reason Angus was running through the city alone. He turned to face her . . . and saw that she was kneeling in the snow. Her chin was resting on her chest and her face was curiously still, the muscles relaxed as if she were sleeping. Raif pulled the horses forward. What was wrong with her? Was she half-witted?

The girl didn't raise her head as he approached. For the first time he noticed how pale she was, like a statue carved from ice. As he opened his mouth to speak, her arms began to rise, gliding up through the air like weightless, boneless things, reaching for something he could not see. Raif felt a pulse of fear beat close to his heart. Her eyes were closed.

He didn't know what made him act. He just knew that

something was wrong and he had to stop it, and he reached out with his blistered hand and grabbed the girl's arm.

*Reach for us, pretty mistressss. Break our chains of blood. So close now . . . so close. Reach.*

Voices crowded Raif's mind. Terrible, inhuman voices, insane with need, panting with the cold hiss of gases escaping from decaying flesh. A landscape of black ice opened before him, a wasteland of jagged peaks and gleaming edges and dark, dark trenches. Raif's lore flared hot against his chest. His first instinct was to pull away, sever whatever connection held him here: This was no place for him to be. Yet the girl's presence held him. Her heart beat in a way he recognized immediately, and she stopped being a stranger and became known to him instead.

Suddenly his raven lore was white-hot steel. It burned through his skin, to the muscle that lay beneath. Raif gasped for breath. It felt as if the girl were entering him, boring through his chest along with his lore. She opened her eyes. Gray eyes. And he knew then that he had seen her before: The guidestone had shown her to him.

The memory was like cold water on his skin. Using all the false strength the ghostmeal had given him, he wrenched his hand from the girl's arm. Air snapped as they parted. Droplets of Raif's blood formed a red arc between them. The girl swayed, reached back in the snow to steady herself. Raif stumbled forward, bringing his blistered hand home to his chest; it felt as if it had been dipped into the substance of another world.

The girl moaned. Raif paid her no heed. Turning from her, he tugged his oilskin apart. His undamaged left hand fumbled with clothing, desperate to get at skin. The raven lore was unchanged, dark and cool: a bloodless piece of horn from a bird long dead. Even his skin seemed unaffected. There was redness and a shallow pressure mark, but no great open wound, no tortured purple flesh. Raif frowned. But he had *felt* it! He could feel it now, whatever it was, a burn, a presence, a taint. It was as if a red hot poker had been inserted beneath his skin.

Fear brought back his anger. He wheeled around to face the girl. "Get up. We must be gone."

She looked at him with eyes that were impossible to read. With her right hand she cupped the portion of her arm he had touched. "How long?"

Raif did not understand the question. He made no answer.

"I said *how long*? How long was I kneeling here before you came"—she struggled for words—"and woke me?"

*Woke*? Raif thought it an odd word to use. He said, "Only minutes."

The girl nodded.

After a moment, when she made no move to speak further or rise, Raif said, "We must leave now. The red blades will be back."

She made a small gesture with her head toward the gate. "Will he be all right?"

He wanted to say no, tell her that Angus was in grave danger and it was all her fault, yet he found himself saying something else instead. "Angus is no fool. He can take care of himself. If there's a safe way out of the city, he'll find it." The words were little enough, but he felt better for saying them. He almost believed they were true.

The girl's face relaxed just a little. Brushing snow from her ruined skirt, she struggled to her feet. Raif moved forward to help her, then stopped himself at the last instant. He didn't know if he wanted to touch her again.

"Please, could you leave me alone for a moment? I'll come and join you by the horses as soon as I . . . I'm finished."

Raif made a point of glancing to the gate. "Be quick." Purposely he kept his back toward her as he walked the horses away. He was curious about her request—and he didn't think she meant to relieve herself in the snow—but he wouldn't question her or spy on what she did. He made himself busy fetching things from Angus' saddlebag: blankets, a spare pair of gloves, a day-old roasted plover packed in a greased cloth, a cake of sheep's blood and whey, a skin of snowmelt kept liquid by its nearness to Moose's rump, a little jar of Angus' beeswax. Things for the girl.

By the time everything was pulled out and ready, the burn in his chest had subsided to a mild ache. His hand throbbed, but that might have been the blister. Shuddering slightly, he set his mind away from what he had seen and heard. That was the girl's business, not his.

"I'm ready to go now." She stepped alongside him.

He had not heard her coming. He covered his surprise by asking her if she could ride. When she nodded, he cupped both hands to take her foot and hefted her onto the bay's back. Her boots were thick, and when the leather soles pressed against his palms he didn't feel as if he were touching her at all. That seemed like something to be thankful for.

He passed her the blankets and the beeswax first. She accepted the jar of wax in a way that made Raif think that she was accustomed to having things handed to her. Her calmness broke when she took possession of the roasted plover, and she tore at the bird with gusto, eating skin, gnawing on bones, licking her fingers for grease.

Raif smiled as he mounted Moose. He liked her better now. "What's your name?"

"Ash."

"I'm Raif."

"I know, the other man . . . Angus . . . said."

Raif felt put in his place. He searched for something else to say, yet the only subjects that sprang to mind seemed too dangerous to speak of there and then.

"Raif. You must promise to wake me again if . . . if I fall asleep." Gray eyes met his. Knowledge passed between them, and somehow she knew all that he had seen and heard. She touched her arm. "They call me," she said. "The voices."

Raif nodded. That much he understood. Knowing it wasn't his right to question her, he passed her the whey cake and the waterskin. Their fingers touched over the creamy surface of the cake, but he felt nothing, only the thinness of her skin. "I'll watch out for you," he said.

MOUNT SLAIN'S PEAKS VANISHED into darkness as they rode, claimed by a moonless, starless sky. Flames from the city's watch towers cast a halo of red light upon their backs and set their shadows flickering. No snow fell, yet the wind was white, shifting drifts from the high slopes to the low slopes in quick, brutal bursts.

The deer path was easy to find and follow. Raif had the feeling that Angus' bay had traveled this way before, for the gelding anticipated every twist and hook in the trail. Raif was glad to let the horses lead the way. The fast, brittle strength that had filled him earlier was gone, drained away as completely as if it had never been there at all. Ghostmeal: It seemed important to remember that what it gave wasn't real. Raif felt as if his body had been trampled by a cart. The only thing that kept him awake was the familiar torment of his stitches. That and his promise to the girl.

He glanced over at her. She sat hunched on the bay, her shape obscured by blankets, her head upright, her chin nodding with the movement of the horse. They had not spoken since earlier. The shadow of Spire Vanis was too great a presence between them. It was unthinkable to Raif to speak of small things to pass the time while Angus was trapped inside the city. The girl had her miseries and he had his, and there was companionship to be found in shared silence.

Raif watched her as they wound through the pines. It was impossible not to. She had bewitched Angus with a single look, and with just one touch she had . . . *What*? Raif turned his hand so that his blister showed, fat and purple like a tick gorging on his blood. What had happened between them as she'd knelt in the snow?

He would never forget the voices. They were inside his mind for life.

*Drey.* Longing for his brother suddenly overwhelmed him, making him feel weary beyond knowing. If Drey were here now, he would know what to do and say. He wouldn't have let Angus go off alone. Raif's lips formed a faint smile. And even if he had, Drey would have stood outside the gate and *waited* until Angus returned. Drey always waited. Of all the traits a brother could have, that suddenly seemed the best one of all.

"Wrathgate."

The girl's voice drew Raif back. He looked at her, and she nodded toward the shimmering mass of darkness that was Spire Vanis at night. A ring of blue fire framed a portal three hundred feet below the deer path.

"They keep the oil lamps burning day and night. It's the most heavily used gate."

"Does the east road lead directly from it?"

"I'm not sure."

Raif looked at the girl's face, Ash's face, he reminded himself. She lived in this city yet didn't know its roads? Who was she? What sort of trouble was she in? Shrugging, he told himself it meant nothing to him. "We'll head east a while, then start making our way down."

The girl, as if embarrassed by her lack of knowledge, made no reply.

Raif turned his attention to breaking a path through the shifting snow and loose scree of Mount Slain's northeastern skirt. In his anxiousness to find the east road and meet with Angus, he pushed on ahead of Ash.

The farther they traveled from the city walls, the darker the night became. Spire Vanis felt like an enemy at his back. He had not once stepped inside it, yet he had killed men there. Another four to add to his tally.

Lights appeared in the landscape below, scattered over the rolling darkness like grain waiting to take seed. Some moved. Carts, Raif realized with a small thrill. The lights were torches burning on the guardrails of carts. East road. After glancing over his shoulder to check that Ash was still keeping pace, he began weaving his way down to the moving lights.

Everything that grew on Mount Slain was crippled and hard formed. Moose picked his path with care, hesitating whenever the mountain shivered or twisted bits of dead wood poked rotten limbs through the snow. Raif was so tired his eyes ached. *Angus has to be here. He has to be all right.*

By the time they reached the road, the lighted carts were long gone, and the crowds of towns and villages had thinned, giving way to plowed fields, fenced grazes, farmhouses, and unlit strongwalls built from rough-hewn stone. A lone man rode a horse in the distance, but Raif knew it wasn't Angus: too thin, too dark, too *upright* to be a wounded man. The road itself was wide and gently graded, the snow upon its surface packed to the hardness of ice. To

the north lay the Vale of Spires, prime farmland and graze-
land that sloped gently for thirty leagues. Angus said that in
its center lay a strange formation of granite spires that most
people believed had been formed by nature, carved by a
hundred thousand years of wind and hail. A few claimed the
spires were the work of man, erected in the Time of Shadows by sorcerer-masons who spent their lives working with
stone. Fewer still whispered about dark horselords and dark
beasts and things impaled upon granite spikes. Raif didn't
know what to think of *that*. Sometimes he swore Angus told
him such things just to see how he'd react.

According to Angus, it was the granite spires that gave the
city and the vale their name: Spire Vanis. Vale of Spires.

Raif waited for Ash to join him before turning onto the
road and heading west. The relief of riding on cleared
ground almost canceled out the fear of being out in the open.
It was bitterly cold, and he could feel the freezing air hardening the threads that held his stitches. Ignoring the pain, he
began pulling food and drink from the nearest saddlebag. He
wasn't especially hungry, but eating gave him something to
do. The wind-dried mutton Angus had purchased ten days
ago had the taste and texture of old string. It was easier to
*suck* than chew it. Unwilling to trust his body to alcohol, he
washed down the meat with clear water.

As he wiped his mouth with the back of his hand, he was
aware of a sense of loss, almost as if he were drifting away
to sleep. The muscle lying directly beneath his raven lore
*wrenched* softly, as if something had pulled on it.

Without thought he turned to Ash.

Her eyes were closed, and her head was slumped forward
onto her chest.

Raif pulled on his reins, leaping down before Moose had
chance to halt. He stilled the bay with a word and then
reached up and pulled Ash from the saddle. She weighed almost nothing. As his left arm slid beneath her to support her
legs, he felt something wet roll over his hand. *Let it not be
blood*, he thought as he hefted her fast against his chest.

Picking a spot fifty paces from the road's edge, shielded
from casual eyes by a grove of sticklike birches, Raif laid
her down on the blankets she had been using as a cloak.

Quickly he ran back for the horses. As he led Moose and the bay through the brush, he reached inside his skins for his lore. The horn felt cold, and heavier than it had a right to be.

Ash lay where he had left her, perfectly still, breathing fast, shallow breaths. A dark stain on her skirt grew as he looked on, pluming outward like dye poured in water. The horses smelled blood. Raif pushed up his sleeves and knelt in the snow. He hesitated before touching her again. He had felt nothing when he'd pulled her from the bay, but what if the voices had returned? Swallowing hard, he reached out and brushed the hair from her face.

*Reach for us, reach. We cannot wait much longer, we are cold, so cold, our chains cut us, how they cut us, we want, we need. Reach.*

Raif's first instinct was to pull away. *Run,* said something within him. *Run and never look back.* He didn't run, though he could not say why. Instead he took Ash by the shoulders and shook her. "Wake!" he cried. *"Wake!"*

No muscle in her face or body moved. She was limp beneath his grip, a doll made of rags. Still he shook her; he didn't know what else to do.

Gradually, over the course of many seconds, her shoulders stiffened beneath him. Imagining she was coming round, he took his hands from her and sat back in the snow. He wondered why he felt no relief. A long moment passed, where the wind died and the snow settled, and then Ash's arms began to rise, slowly, mechanically, like machines worked by ghosts.

Gooseflesh rose on Raif's arms. Hardly aware of what he was doing, he slammed his fists into her shoulders, forcing the muscles flat. She would not reach out to them. He would not let her. It was madness and he didn't understand it, but he had heard the voices call to her and knew they loved her not.

Ash's body fought him, but not in a forceful way, more a slow relentless push. New blood flared over her skirt, soaking through to the snow beneath. Raif didn't want to risk letting her go to deal with it. There was too much to be woman's blood, that he knew.

Then, suddenly, Ash stopped fighting him. Her body stilled. Raif felt a bead of cold sweat trickle along his stitches. All was quiet for a moment as the night entered a new phase of darkness, then Ash's mouth fell open.

The stench of blood metal came out. The same odor Raif had smelled the day his father died.

Sorcery, and she was drawing it.

Raif howled Angus' name into the night.

# TWENTY-FIVE

## *Tunnels of the Sull*

PENTHERO ISS WAS STANDING in the Rive Hall, in the heart of the Red Forge, watching Marafice Eye snap a sword over his knee, when the night came alive with sorcery. The Knife's leathers were stiff with mud and blood, his face smeared with soot, his fingernails jutting from his fingertips with the pressure of wedged dirt. Fury was upon him, though he did not shake and he did not fume; he took things in his hands and broke them.

"Six of mine dead. Another three wounded in the chase. And they got away—all three of them." Marafice Eye raised the two separate pieces he had made of the sword. "And this is all I got from Angus Lok. *This!*"

That was when Iss felt it: strong, metallic, reverberating with the pure tone of a struck bell. Sorcery, and it shot through the room like siege fire. Iss' tongue wetted, and the glaze on his corneas dried in an instant, leaving a scum of salt and dust that stung his eyes. Fear relaxed muscles in his lower abdomen, and he had to work quickly to stop urine from dribbling down his thigh. Yet even as terror took him and his skin soaked up the aftermath like a rag dipped in oil, he probed the nature of the drawing with small mental jabs.

Iss breathed through his mouth, letting minute particles of airborne metal settle upon his tongue. Straightaway he learned things. The drawing was unfocused, the work of a beginner. It came from somewhere close and to the east. If he had been a stronger sorcerer himself, he might have forsaken his body and tracked it back to the source. Almost he didn't need to. He knew who had drawn it and where she was likely to be.

Asarhia. The air *tasted* of her. A small thrill fingered Iss' throat and groin. His almost-daughter was close by, probably on the east road or traveling just above it, doing what she had been born for: reaching from this world to the one that lay beyond.

Abruptly the flow of sorcery stopped, halted so quickly that Iss was left snapping tongue flesh. He felt disoriented for a moment, as if he had been passing through a doorway that was suddenly and unexpectedly shut. Aware of Marafice Eye's hard blue eyes upon him, he worked to bring his body and mind under control. Only those who could use sorcery could sense it.

"Trapped wind?" Marafice Eye said, throwing the broken pieces of sword onto the exquisitely woven rug that covered the length of the Rive Hall. "Too many quails eggs at supper. You should try eating real meat instead."

Iss made no reply. Marafice Eye's crudeness was nothing to him; he'd had more than fifteen years to grow accustomed to it.

Taking a moment to still himself, Iss regarded the vast stone-ceilinged chamber of the Rive Hall. Row upon row of red swords armed the walls, hung from their crossguard and pointing down toward the earth. Blood steel, forged in the great black furnace in the adjoining chamber, cooled in oil drawn from the tar pits of the Join. Only two people in the Watch knew the secret of its making: the Iron Master and the Rive scribe. The scribe kept a written record of the brazing. The text was rumored to fill three leaves of parchment and be written backward in the manner of sorcerer's spells.

Iss turned to face the Knife. "Asarhia is no longer in the city. She's east of here, either on the road or just above it."

Marafice Eye's mouth twisted unpleasantly. "I'll leave within the quarter." He turned to go.

"No." Iss found himself strangely unsettled by Asarhia's drawing. Its aftermath still lived within him, running like fever through his blood. He forced his mind to focus above the roar of the forge. "Not yet. I must know more about who we are dealing with. This stranger . . . the one with the arrows—"

"That bastard shot four of my men, dropped them where they stood."

There was that hint of possessiveness again: *my men, mine*. Iss wasn't sure that he liked this new protective Knife. "What did he look like?"

"Dark haired. Rough clad, like one of those demon clansmen. Had a silver piece in his hair."

"A Hailsman, then." Iss felt better for knowing that one small fact. "And he shot the brothers *through* the grating?"

Marafice Eye stamped a booted foot on a section of the broken sword and ground it into the rug. "Space no bigger than a piss hole."

Iss ran a hand over the cleverly weighted silk of his robe. He had felt four jolts of power earlier: rough, hard, and stinking of the Old Blood. He had assumed it was Angus Lok, an old dog who had learned new tricks. Now it seemed it was someone else. "When you chased Lok through the city, did you catch sight of Asarhia or the clansman again?"

"No."

So it was likely the two were together. Now. The thought of Asarhia in the company of some rough-skinned clansman who could draw upon the Old Blood turned him cold. And then there was Angus Lok. . . . Iss' fingers tightened around the silk. Asarhia was his. He had found her. He had raised her. She called no one else Father but him. Armed men were no longer enough. "You must take Sarga Veys with you when you leave. Asarhia must be brought back."

"The Halfman." Marafice Eye spat the word.

"Yes. The Halfman. He will be able to track Asarhia in ways you cannot."

"I will not have him in any sept of my choosing."

"Don't be a fool. If this clansman is a demon, as you say, then who better to deal with him than a demon of our own?"

Marafice Eye grunted.

"And you *do* want them back, don't you? All three of them. Asarhia must be brought to me alive and unharmed, but the men . . ."

"They slaughtered my own."

"Precisely. Kill the clansman where you find him. Angus Lok must be brought to the Cask and tortured. He's so full of secrets his skin will likely burst the moment we strap him to the wheel." Iss glanced quickly at the Knife, then added, "You can have him when Caydis is done."

"Don't make light with me, Surlord. I'm not one of your grangelings."

"No. But you want Lok and the clansman, and it seems to me that Sarga Veys is your best chance of getting them." Iss' temper rose as he spoke. The thought of Sarga Veys tracking down Asarhia chilled him, yet time was running out and new dangers had come into play, and Asarhia must be found. A dry sept might easily lose her, especially now that she had the protection of a man who could heart-kill seven brothers with seven arrows if he chose. A fully formed sept was the answer: six armed men and one magic user. Such small, fast-moving forces had once been the scourge of the North.

Marafice Eye glowered. "Very well. I'll take him with me, though I can't vouch for his good health on my return."

Iss forced himself to smile. "As you wish." Perhaps things wouldn't be so bad after all. The Knife would keep an eye on Sarga Veys . . . that and one of his dog-size fists. "Send him to me before you leave."

"Here?" The Knife snapped his head in a circle, indicating the walls of red steel, the embossed shields and iron bird helms arrayed on racks, the life-size statue of the Killhound standing at the foot of the great fireplace, carved from marble so black that to look at it hurt one's eyes, and the tapestries nailed to the ceiling for want of a better place to hang them, tapestries depicting Thomas Mar, Theron and Rangor Pengaron, the Whitehog, and a dozen other men armed to the teeth and bathed in blood.

Iss saw the Knife's point. "No . . . tell him I'll meet him in the guardroom instead."

*That* made Marafice Eye smile. "There are a lot of angry brothers there tonight."

Iss shrugged innocently. "Then he won't be lonely if I'm a little late."

* * *

"KEEP THE RAG IN her mouth until she wakes." Angus stood, grimacing as his muscles stretched and twisted. He thrust a fist against the wet sparrow-size hole in his chest, counted twelve seconds under his breath, then spoke again. "You'd better take another draw of the ghostmeal. We have a long night ahead."

Raif was kneeling over Ash's lifeless body. Angus had found them an hour ago, drawn by Raif's cry. Shaking with fatigue, his fingers yellow with the first sign of frostbite, and his face black with blood, he had barely spared a glance for Raif before starting work on Ash. After wadding a horse shammy into a ball, he had thrust it into her mouth, then held her jaws together, until nothing, not even breath, could leak out. Raif felt the sorcery stop as quickly as a candle snuffed by hand. Even before the stench of metal had dissipated, Angus began working on something else. He lit a small alcohol-fueled fire, heated snowmelt in a tin cup, then added dried herbs and roots to the liquid once it had boiled. The concoction soon turned yellowy green and gave off an odor that reminded Raif of the Oldwood in spring. "Bethroot to slow bleeding, valerian to calm her mind," Angus said.

As he turned back to tend Ash, Raif noticed that his uncle's sword was gone. The sheepskin scabbard was limp and misshapen, striped with sword cuts and dark with blood. After a moment Raif looked away. It was hard to think about what Angus must have gone through to reach here.

When the green concoction was ready, Angus came and knelt at Raif's side. Gently he eased the wadded shammy from Ash's mouth and dribbled steaming liquid down her throat. He said things, whispers too low for Raif to understand, all the while rocking her back and forth against his chest. When he was satisfied that she had swallowed enough of the liquid, Angus glanced at Raif. "Turn your back." It was fiercely said, and Raif obeyed immediately. Sounds of fabric being lifted and torn followed. Water was poured. Rags were wrung dry. "Hand me the clean shirt from my pack." Raif did so without once glancing at Ash. He wondered how Angus could continue working with his chest wound still open and leaking. The hole needed to be cleaned and stitched, yet Raif knew his uncle would welcome no reminders.

The sound of fabric being knotted was soon followed by a series of commands. "I need grease. Warmed wax. The silver vial from my pack. Whatever spare clothes you have must be cut to a size to fit her. Beat the ice from my buckskin mitts, then take the chill from them over the fire. Quick now. There is little time."

Raif didn't know how long it took to fetch all the things Angus needed, yet the steady drop in temperature made him aware of time passing. The night had turned as dark and still as the inside of a sealed cairn. The fierce blue flames from the alcohol fire gave off more heat than light, and Raif wondered how his uncle could see to work. When Angus was done with tending to Ash, he returned the shammy to her mouth and bade Raif watch her while he saw to his own hurts.

He was a good deal harder on himself than the girl. Tippling frequently from the rabbit flask, he cleaned and stitched his own flesh. There was a lot of blood, and Angus was by turns anguished then impatient. He swore like a hammerman. When he was finished he had an ugly mass of black stitches on his chest. Raif thought they looked like a heap of dead spiders, yet didn't say anything. Angus stamped out the fire. "Get the horses ready. I'll wake the girl. Have you taken that ghostmeal yet?"

Raif shook his head. Ghostmeal was as false as the twin landscapes that hovered above the earth on cold, bright days in the badlands. It fooled the senses, nothing more. Raif preferred to be exhausted and *know* he was exhausted.

Brushing snow from his dogskin pants, he rose and made his way to the horses. Moose welcomed his approach by snuffling gently and nudging Raif's chest with his head. The gray was a good horse, well suited to long treks through deep snow. Raif brushed him down, cleaning ice from his eyelashes and nostrils. "It's been a long day for you, too," he said, thinking of Orwin Shank and all the fine horses he had bred. "Not much farther to go tonight."

A faint groan sounded, and Raif looked over Moose's shoulder to where Angus was crouched over Ash. "Wake now, little lass. You're safe. Safe and amongst friends."

Ash opened her eyes. A wary, animal expression crossed her face, and she shied away from Angus' touch. Angus let her go, yet Raif sensed he did not want to.

"It's all right," he said softly. "I'm Angus, and that's Raif, and we're taking you somewhere safe."

"How long was I . . . asleep?" Ash frowned as she spoke, her mouth twisting as if she'd tasted something unpleasant.

"A wee nonce, nothing more." Standing, Angus held out his hand for her to take. Once she was upright she glanced around, at Raif, the horses, their surroundings. Last, she looked down at her clothes.

"Your dress was as stiff as a board when I got here, so I had little choice but to strip it away." Angus met Ash's eyes, and after a moment she looked down, suddenly finding a leather strap that needed retying beneath her chin. Angus did not share her embarrassment. Clapping his hands together, he said, "Well then. We'd better make a start. Raif. Roll the blankets. I'll take Ash on the bay wi' me."

Despite Angus' casual tone of voice, they broke camp quickly, burying the remains of the fire and filling the empty waterskins with snow. As Raif turned Moose, ready to head back onto the road, Angus stopped him with an almost imperceptible nod in the direction of Spire Vanis. "I think we'll take the high road," he said.

Which meant they took no road at all. Angus made his own trail through the gorse and malformed pines above the road, Ash pale and silent at his back. Raif took up the rear. From the pace his uncle was setting and the small gesture he had made toward the city, Raif knew there was a good chance they were being pursued.

The thought did not make for an easy ride. Raif found himself wishing he had reclaimed the arrows from the dead men at Vaingate. Angus' sword was gone, the bow was useless without sticks to fire, and between them they now had nothing more deadly than a pair of belt knives and a half sword. Neither of them was in any fit state to fight if it came to it, and fleeing in haste was no longer practical, as Angus' bay was loaded with weight.

Frowning, Raif turned his attention to Ash. She was now dressed in a blue wool shirt donated by Angus and a tanned hide coat and pants that had once belonged to Drey. Raif had to admit that they suited her well enough. Strands of hair peeking through her fox hood flashed silver in the snowlight. Why had Angus risked everything to protect her? And what would have happened if he hadn't come along in time to halt her sorcery? Deciding the answers didn't bear thinking about, Raif turned his mind to following the path instead.

The slope above the east road was heavily canted, mined with bog holes and draws. Snow made the uneven ground difficult to read. Bitter cold made breathing, moving, even *looking*, an ordeal to be endured. No one spoke. Angus appeared to have a destination in mind, as he picked each step with a deliberateness that Raif found vaguely reassuring. Angus always knew a back way, a hidden path, a break between the rocks.

As they rode through a stand of limber pines, Raif became aware of noises sounding in the road below. The drum of hooves, the tinny clink of tack, and the rough bark of someone coughing wafted up the slope along with a growing tide of mist. Angus said nothing, merely increased his pace. Most of the metal on Moose and the bay was covered with sheepskin to prevent frostbite in the colder temperatures to the north, so the horses made little sound as they trotted.

Eventually the ground began to level off and a path of sorts opened up before them, narrow and soiled with deer droppings. The going became easier, and it took Raif some time to realize that they were actually back on some distant eastern slope of Mount Slain. The steady pace of the horses rocked Ash to sleep, and her head came to rest against Angus' shoulder. Strangely, Raif wasn't worried about her; she wasn't absent, as she had been earlier. She was simply exhausted and sleeping.

After a while Raif risked speaking to Angus. "Where are we headed?"

"Aye. You *would* be wanting to know that." Angus' voice was softer than the mist at his heels. "If your old uncle's memory serves him well enough, there's a bit of a tunnel somewhere along this path that leads down from the mountain and under the east road."

Raif wasn't sure how he felt about tunnels. "Won't those following us simply take the tunnel, too?"

"Nay, lad. The sept'll likely stay on the road and wait for us to come down. They know we can't stay up here forever. It leads nowhere."

"They know we're up here?"

"If they're using a fully formed sept, they will."

"Fully formed sept?"

"Six blades and one magic user. It's the way sorcerers have been hunted for centuries. Irgar the Unchained, the Red Priest Syracies, Maormor of Trance Vor, and Asanna the Mountain Queen all used them. It takes a magic user to find one. Force isn't enough. Some with the old skill can stir air and water and earth. They can crack ice that a squad treads on, fuel storms that they ride through, and shake earth they sleep upon in the dark hours of night. They can turn hunting dogs mad and make them attack their own pack brothers, and ignite tiny sparks of sorcery inside a stallion's heart." Angus glanced over at Raif.

Raif felt his cheeks heat. He pulled hard on the reins, treating Moose roughly.

"A trained sorcerer is capable of great subtlety. They can do more with less. They are taught how to deflect and contain powers greater than their own, how to shield those around them by setting bloodwards, and hook their claws into others like themselves, and leech the power from them bit by bit. They can confuse and disorient an enemy, weaving a fine mesh of sorcery called a fret." Angus frowned into the mist. "And they hunt magic users like dogs."

Raif shivered. The mist was heavy and wet, like a shifting sea around them. Suddenly it was impossible to see more than ten paces ahead. "How do they hunt people?"

"They hunt sorcery, not people, Raif." Angus glanced over his shoulder, pinning Raif with his coppery eyes. "All sorcery leaves an aftermath that can be tracked. Users can *taste* the blood of a person who draws the old skill, smell the metal they feed into the air. Even weeks later residue can still cling to a user's hair and clothes, leaving a trail as surely as a deer musking pines in a forest."

"So what Ash did . . ."

"Aye, lad. A sept is likely tracking her aftermath as we speak."

"Then how can we hope to escape? Even if we find a way down from the mountain, they will know it."

Angus was silent a moment as he walked the bay through a crop of oily rocks. Ash, disturbed by the change in motion, made a soft, snuffling sound and resettled herself against Angus' back. When Angus spoke again, Raif had to strain to hear him.

"Tracking someone with sorcery is a risk unto itself. Sometimes a sorcerer must take drugs and forsake his body while he searches. Such skills never come cheap. They use a man up completely, leaving him as weak as a horse ridden clean through the night. Sometimes those who forsake their bodies never come back. The firmament glitters for them, tempting them out toward its cold, hard edge. Secrets lie there, they say. All things become known at the moment of death. Men who cannot resist simply leave their bodies behind. Their minds die the instant their spirit touches the roof of the world, but their bodies waste slowly over weeks."

Cold. Raif felt so cold his lungs ached. He found himself looking up at the black arc of the sky. *Yes, I can see how a man might be tempted.*

Angus saw where his gaze had rested. "I can't say as we'll be tracked that way tonight, not with us being so close to the city. The cost is too high for it to be lightly done. Any time a man or woman draws upon the old skills it takes something from them. The body pays a price. Different people weaken in different ways. I've seen some men bleed from the mouth, and others shiver as if a fever is upon them. A few lose part of their memories or their minds. I knew a man once, one of the Storm Dogs who live on the high slopes of the Join, whose body wasted in small portions every time he broke a storm. The first time I met him I thought he'd been burned. His arms and legs were black and withered. Dead."

Raif turned away. He hated sorcery. Clansmen would have no part of it. Strength of mind, will, and body was what counted in the clanholds. Sorcery was the weapon of the weak and the damned. Raif remembered watching as Dagro Blackhail and Gat Murdock clubbed a dark-haired girl senseless one cold winter's morning on the court. Raif couldn't recall who the girl was, perhaps a sister to Craw

Bannering or a daughter to Meth Ganlow, but he knew the girl had been discovered calling animals to her without speaking words. She had died a week later. No one, not even her family, mourned her. And then there was Mad Binny, living in her ancient crannog over Cold Lake, exiled from the roundhouse for thirty years. She could make ewes drop their lambs, people said, tell which winters would drive the hardest and cull the most deaths.

"Most magic users need rest after a drawing," Angus said, pulling Raif back. "Many need to sleep. Some take drugs to lend them strength."

"Like the ghostmeal?"

"Yes, like the ghostmeal."

Raif looked round to find Angus watching him, and he suddenly realized the purpose of everything his uncle had said. *Accept what you are*, he seemed to say. *You possess the old skills, I have shown you that. I have spoken of their dangers and forewarned you of their limits. Now you must learn to accept it and stomach your distaste.*

Mist washed in and out of Angus' mouth as he breathed. "Not all people condemn the old skills. There are places that would fail to exist without them, where they are woven so tightly into the threads of history that you cannot separate the people from their sorcery. Perhaps you and I will travel to those lands one day."

Raif made no reply. He didn't want to hear any more. He longed for clan, imagined riding across the thick white snow on the graze, shooting targets with Drey on the court, and sitting so close to the Great Hearth that its hot yellow flames burned his cheeks.

"The girl is waking," he said after a time.

Angus' eyes narrowed. A fraction of a second later Ash moved against his back. Before he turned his attention to her, Angus searched Raif's face, and Raif guessed he had given something away. He had known Ash was waking before his uncle had felt a thing. Abruptly he pulled on Moose's reins, dropping back.

Angus and Ash spoke softly for some time, Ash turning once to retrieve a parcel of trail meat and a waterskin from Angus' pack. Raif thought she looked little better for sleep.

Following her lead, he drank some water himself. The liquid was thick and icy, and it numbed something within him for a while.

The landscape changed as they threaded through the upper reaches of the tree line, becoming rougher and more inhospitable to plants. Bare rocks rose to either side of the path, swept clean of snow by persistent winds. Pines twisted close to the ground, their trunks smooth as bones, their needles shriveled and gray. The air smelled of resin, and the mist was sticky, as if it had slipped into the heartwood and stolen the sap from the pines.

Angus trotted the bay through a series of sharp turns and then surprised Raif by calling a halt and dismounting. "Wait here," he said, handing Raif the reins. By the time Raif had dismounted himself, Angus had disappeared into the mist. Ash stared after him.

Silence followed. Raif had no desire to speak. He felt a dull resentment toward the girl; it was almost as if she'd stolen upon him while he slept, slit the skin on his wrist, and made a blood kin of him. He'd been given no choice in the matter, yet somehow he felt bound. And she was so young and thin, her face red with snowburn, her hair matted with many kinds of dirt. Only her eyes held his interest: huge gray eyes that shone like polished metal, silver one moment, iron the next.

"Good. You've both dismounted. We're on foot from now on." Angus' voice emerged from the mist ahead of his body. "Raif. Cut a torch from that hemlock. Strip it until the juices run."

Raif was glad of something to do. He cut three sticks, hacking at the branches until his dogskin mitts were soaked with sap. Shaving the sticks with his belt knife, he created a series of thin wood curls to catch the sparks from his flint and hold them against the sapwood until it kindled. The business of making fires in snow and ice was something he knew well, and it felt good to do something plain and honest with his hands.

The first torch was lit by the time Angus had brushed down the horses. Ash had taken charge of Moose and was saying horsey things to him and scratching behind his ears.

Moose seemed stupidly pleased, snuffling and clucking like a hen. Raif glared at him. Traitor horse.

Angus led them into a deep draw between the rocks. The pale, ice-riven banks grew higher as they descended, and the path began to narrow and steepen. Soon the walls curved overhead, and Raif got the sense that they were traveling *into* the mountain. The same kind of oily stone they had passed earlier caught and reflected light. When flames from Raif's torch licked against the wetness, it hissed. Mist rolled around the horses' fetlocks like seafoam, turning from gray to green with each flick of the light. The air became noticeably colder.

Then, suddenly, there *was* no draw. The rocks fused overhead, and what might have been a water channel during spring melt became a tunnel instead.

Raif felt his stitches itch. The raven lore was as cold as a fossil against his chest.

"Easy now," Angus said. "Stay close. There are ways here that are not ours to take. Raif. Step forward with the torch. Ash. Keep an eye to Moose. Don't forget to tear a bit of rue leaf now and then and chew on it."

As he positioned himself at the head of the party, Raif was aware of the ground changing beneath his feet. What minutes earlier had been rough, uncut rock now had the smooth shine of stone once tended by a chisel. The walls were more lightly touched, hewn only to prevent sharp edges. Something—mineral oil or water—tapped away in the distance like a leaking roof. All surfaces collected shadows as easily as ditches filling with rainwater.

Raif's first thought was that Effie would have loved this. No one knew the caves in the clanhold like Effie. The only time she ever came out of the roundhouse in summer was to explore the sandstone caverns around the Wedge. Raif smiled. He remembered taking her out one summer morning and having to wait for *hours* while she explored some odd bit of a pothole not much wider than her own head. He wasn't about to go in after her, and Tem would have given him a beating if he'd left her to return home alone.

"What *is* this place?" asked Ash.

It was hard for Raif to pull back from his memories. For no reason other than she *wasn't* Effie, he felt a tide of ill feelings toward the girl. She wasn't who she showed herself to be. Her voice was clear and insistent, and she sounded like no beggar girl in any story Turby Flapp or Gat Murdock had ever told.

"It's just a wee tunnel, nothing more." Angus took a slug from his rabbit flask. "It was cut many thousands of years ago, before Spire Vanis was even built."

Ash reached out a hand and touched the wall. "Who built it?"

"The Sull."

Raif sucked in air and held it in his lungs. This was the third time Angus had mentioned the Sull, yet the word sounded no better for repetition. The Sull were enemies to all. They hated the Mountain Cities *and* the clans. And even though they protected the Trenchlanders with their lives, they hated them, too. Hiding in their vast forests, amid their cities of blue and silver stone, they refused to trade and treaty. Rumor had it they emerged from the Racklands only to defend their borders and reclaim their dead. "What use is a tunnel here, in the west, to the Sull?"

"Do you think, Raif Sevrance, that this land has always been held by the Mountain Cities?" Angus' tone made Raif wish he hadn't asked the question. "Before there were cities, before even there were clans, there were the Sull. Clan Blackhail might call itself the first of the clans, yet it's a poor claim when compared to the Sull's. They call themselves the First Born, and they do not mean solely in the Northern Territories."

Ash spoke after a moment of silence. "The Sull were the first men in the Known Lands?"

"So legend says. The same legends that tell how they were driven first from the Far South, and then the Soft Lands of the middle, finally making a home of the North. All of it, not just the Boreal Sway and the Great Snake Coast and the Red Glaciers they claim today. All of it, from the Breaking Grounds in the farthest north, to Old Goat's Pass in these Ranges." Angus' voice was hard, his eyes dark. "So this small tunnel, cut so the Sull could cross the mountains and descend Mount Slain without being sniffed out by the Mountain Queen's septs, or scented by Wetcloaks and their hounds, may not be much use to them now. But it once was, and there are a score of others like it in the Ranges."

"Who is this Mountain Queen?" Ash said. "And the Wetcloaks? I've never heard of them."

Angus shook his head. "People and forces from another age, before the Red Priest and the Founding Quarterlords were born, before religion took its hold on the Soft Lands to the south, when the world was ruled by emperors and kings, and sorcery was their weapon of control."

Raif held the torch away from his body. The damp air was making it crackle and spit. "You said the Sull could use sorcery. So why didn't they build an empire of their own?"

"Once they did," Angus said quietly. "Once they did. Now . . ." He shook his head. "Now they seek only to survive."

Frowning, Raif walked deeper into the tunnel. What Angus said didn't fit with clan beliefs about the Sull. "But the Sull are the fiercest—"

"Aye," Angus said, cutting him short. "The Sull *are* the fiercest warriors ever to raise their banns over the North. They have to be. They are a people unto themselves, deeply private and self-sustaining, and every king, emperor, and warlord in the Known Lands for the past thirteen thousand years has feared them. The Sull have been driven north and east through three continents, and now all that's left to them is the Racklands." Angus' voice quieted and turned oddly cold. "And I pity anyone who tries to take it from them . . . for they have nowhere else to go."

Raif and Ash exchanged a glance, both affected by Angus' words. Ash's eyes looked almost blue in the cave light.

"We must leave something for the journey," Angus said, working to regain his good humor. "'Tis an old custom and doubtless seems foolish to do so when none but dark-winged bats will likely collect it. But Darra would have my earlobes for salt dishes if I failed to pay my due."

"Darra?" asked Ash.

"My lady wife."

Ash made no reply, and silence grew around them.

Reaching back behind his neck, Raif felt for the band of silver that bound his hair. With one swift movement he tugged it free. "Here," he said, offering it to Angus. "Take this for the journey."

Angus closed his large red hand around Raif's. "Nay, lad. That's a clan token. Keep it. I'll pay this passage."

"Take it."

There must have been something in his voice, for Angus looked at him hard a moment, then nodded. "As you wish."

No one spoke for a while after that. Angus took the silver band in his fist and began kneading the metal as he walked. The tunnel grew narrower and the rock ceiling dipped, so both Angus and Ash had to be careful where they led the horses. Moisture wept from cracks in the stone, forming oily pools that everyone avoided.

Raif lit the second torch, and the fresher, brighter light illuminated markings on the stone. No, not *on* the stone, he corrected himself, *in* it. Drawings of the moon and stars, inked in dark blues and liquid silvers, shone through a layer of rock as thin as the membrane on a fish's eye. Somehow the artist had inserted the pigment below the surface, like a tattoo. Raif thought back to Angus' bow; that had an inlay beneath the wood too. *Angus has a Sull bow?* Raif held on to the question as they entered a section of tunnel partially collapsed by flood damage, trying to decide what it meant.

Every so often, turnoffs would present themselves: black holes in the rock face that always led down. Angus insisted that everyone stay close to him as they passed them. The largest was as dark and steep as a mineshaft, cut with a thousand narrow steps that seemed to lead straight down to hell. Raif felt cold air kiss his cheeks as they passed it. Ash looked as if she felt something else. When Angus reached out to hold her arm, she made no effort to pull away.

"Take a bit of the rue leaf and chew on it," he said. "Remember what I said?"

"You said scribes use it when they work through the night. You said it would clear my head."

"That's right. Yes, chew, don't swallow now. What does it taste like? I've quite forgotten."

Raif listened as Ash spoke her reply, quite aware that Angus' main aim was to keep her talking. After a while Raif joined in, and together they nursed Ash through the deepest sections of the tunnel. At some point during the process, when the conversation had shifted to long winters—one of the few subjects they could share without prying into anyone's past—Raif began to feel something himself. At first it was just a knot of tension in his shoulder blades, a strain he put down to lack of sleep, but the sensation spread to his chest, where it pressed against his heart and lungs like a secret, inner rib cage growing quietly beneath his own.

It happened so slowly, over hours, that Raif didn't immediately recognize it as fear.

Even when the tunnel's end came in sight and Angus halted the party while he performed a small ritual around the silver band from Raif's hair, Raif still hadn't worked out *what* he was afraid of. Then, over Angus' bent back, he locked gazes with Ash.

She knew. She knew what it was. "Mount Slain runs deep," was all she said, yet it was enough for Raif to begin to understand. Something was within the mountain with them. Something knew they were here.

*"Ehl halis Mithbann rass ga'rhal."* Angus' words seemed to come from a long way away. Raif did not recognize the language. After placing the silver band on a spur of rock, Angus sprinkled it with the last drops of alcohol in his rabbit flask, then lit it. Blue flames leaped for the briefest moment, then died, leaving the silver with a dusky tarnish, patterned like tree mold. "There," he said softly. "That should please the Sull gods. The offerings they like best are blood and fire."

Straightening, Angus reached for the bay's bridle and began walking toward the tunnel's end.

After a moment Ash followed, and Raif was left alone by the rock. The desire to reach out and touch the silver band one last time was great, but he fought it. Instead he ran his hands through his loose, shoulder-length hair. From now on when people saw him they would not immediately recognize his clan. It's for the best, he told himself, unhooking his belt knife and cutting a leather tie from the neck of his oil-skin. He didn't believe it, but perhaps belief would come later.

Tying back his hair with the leather strap, he followed the others from the tunnel. A pair of ravens drawn to guard the entrance barely caught his eye.


# TWENTY-SIX


## *Secrets in the Kaleyard*


EFFIE SEVRANCE SAT CROSS-LEGGED in her special place beneath the stairs, and watched the raiding party return. Great big clansmen, their axes dripping chunks of frozen blood and muck onto the stone floor, their faces grave and hard, crossed beneath the greatdoor and into the entrance chamber, bringing with them the quality of silence that Effie knew meant death.

She tried not to be scared. Her hand squeezed her rock lore as she looked into the face of every man who crossed the threshold, searching for Drey.

So many men, some dragging bloody legs behind them, others with fierce bruises on their necks and faces, and many with their wounds hidden beneath their oilskins, the slowness of their walk and the blue tint of their lips giving their injuries away. A few were brought in on dragsleds, and Effie's eyes scanned their clothing, searching for the zigzagging pattern of Da's elk coat. She knew Drey had worn it the day he went away.

Raina, Anwyn Bird, and the other women with due respect moved among the injured, tending wounds, bringing black beer and warm clothing and good plain meat. As always when Anwyn was in charge, there was no fuss or wailing from the other women: Anwyn wouldn't allow it, saying that it only upset the men. Raina didn't speak, though she did *count*, taking careful note of each man who entered, keeping a tally of their numbers in her head. Her widow's weals were healed now, the skin pale and raised like cornrows around her wrists. She hardly ever spoke to Effie these days. She *cared*, making sure that Effie was fed and clothed and never too long alone, but she seldom brought the food or the blankets or the company herself. Effie knew they shared a bad secret. The badness made it difficult to sleep some nights, and Effie ran off more and more to the little dog cote. The shankshounds loved her almost as much as Raina . . . and they didn't look at her with dead eyes.

All thoughts vanished from Effie's head as she caught sight of a big silhouette in the doorway. *Drey*. He moved slowly, a little bent at the waist to relieve pressure on a wound. His face was a mask of dirt and blood, and there was a deep gash in his breastpiece. His eyes began searching even before his foot hit the stone floor of the roundhouse.

Effie rose, her heart beating rapidly in her chest. *Drey*.

He saw her the moment she was free of the stair space. Something deep and massed inside him relaxed, and for a moment he looked young, like the old Drey, like he had been before all the badness had started and Raif went away. Without a word he opened his arms. If her whole life had depended on it, Effie could not have resisted him. She wanted to hold him so badly, her insides ached.

She didn't run; Anwyn didn't approve of that. Instead she walked forward with slow, deliberate steps. Drey waited. He didn't smile—neither of them smiled—just took her in his arms and held her for a long time.

They pulled apart without speaking, Drey catching her hand in his. He turned his head for a moment and gave an order to a new-sworn yearman concerning the state and treatment of some men. The yearman, a small youth with a sword that was nearly as tall as he was strapped to his back, was quick to do Drey's bidding. Dent-headed Corbie Meese stopped and asked Drey something. Drey thought before answering, as he always did. Corbie nodded his agreement, then left.

Anwyn Bird caught his eye, a question on her large horsey face. In answer, Drey held up both his and Effie's hand. Effie didn't quite understand, but Anwyn obviously did, for she nodded in a knowing way, then changed her path, bearing the tray of beer and bannock she was carrying toward a group of hammermen sitting on the floor.

Drey tugged on Effie's hand. "Come," was all he said as he led her across the river of clansmen and clanswomen toward the guidehouse.

"Clan Croser has been threatened by Bludd."

". . . a hundred Dhoonesmen dead."

"We had to speak treaty before Gnash would let us pass."

"Corbie dragged him away from the body. He hasn't spoke a word since. His heart is with his twin."

"Nay, Anwyn. See to Rory first. This wound is naught but a ticking."

Effie listened to the soft voices of her clan as she walked at Drey's side. War was full upon them now, and raiding parties like the one led by Corbie Meese left every day from the roundhouse. Two nights back, a squad of Bluddsmen had broken bounds near the lowlands strongwall and slaughtered a dozen crofters. Effie had seen the bodies. Orwin Shank and his sons had ridden out to bring them back. One of the shankshounds had found a baby alive in the snow. Orwin said the bairn's mother had swaddled the tiny thing in sheepskins and hidden him in a drift at the side of her croft as the Bluddsmen approached on their warhorses. Jenna Walker was looking after the baby now. Orwin had brought the bairn straight to her, saying he had such a strong little heart and such hard little fists that there must be something of Toady in him. Every nursing mother in the clan had come forward to offer milk.

Effie thought about the baby a lot, thought of him trapped beneath the snow. She wanted to ask Orwin which of his hounds had found him, but Orwin was fierce and important, and she didn't have the nerve.

Drey pulled Effie into the smoky darkness of the guidehouse and bade her sit at one of the stone benches while he approached the stone. One or two other men from the raiding party already knelt by the guidestone, foreheads brushing against the hard, wet surface. All were quiet. Drey found a place and joined them. He was silent for a very long time: walking with the gods, as Inigar always said.

Effie knew the guidestone well, better than anyone else except Inigar Stoop. She had spent much of her life in its presence, curled up beneath Inigar's chipping bench, staring at the face of the stone. It *had* a face, that she knew. Not a human face, for it had too many eyes for that, but it could see and hear and feel. Today the guidestone was sad and grave. The deep, salt-encrusted pits that were its eyes glistened with wept oil. The dark gashes that were its mouths were filled with gray shadows, and even the new flaw that ran the length of the stone and everyone said was a bad omen and a sign of the coming war looked like a deep worry line on the cheek of an old, old man.

Quickly Effie took her gaze away. She couldn't look at the flaw without thinking of Raif.

Her lore had told her he would go, pushed the knowledge into her through the skin on her palms. He *had* to go, the lore had said. Even before he'd returned from the Bluddroad she had known it was so. Sometimes she wished she could tell Drey, to ease his mind, but she didn't have the words. Drey was angry at more than Raif. He was angry at Angus, too, for taking Raif away. He didn't even call Angus *uncle* anymore, just *that man Angus Lok*. Effie frowned. A week ago she'd caught Drey standing outside the greatdoor, staring south. At first she thought he was checking to see if the latest storm had passed. Then she saw the look on his face. He was watching for Raif . . . even though Raina had told him Raif wasn't coming back.

That thought made Effie's insides pull tight, and her hand crept up her dress toward her lore. The stone was asleep now, cool and lifeless as a hibernating mouse. It was better that way. It never told good things. She dreaded it telling her that Drey would go away.

"Come, little one." Drey stood heavily and awkwardly, not once touching the guidestone for support. Walking with the gods had taken something from him, and he looked tired and old and more troubled than before.

Effie went straight to him, her hand finding his through the smoke.

"Drey."

Both Effie and Drey looked around in time to see Inigar

Stoop emerge from the darkness at the far end of the guide-house. The guide's face was gray with wood ash, the cuffs and hem of his robes scorched black for war. His dark eyes glanced only briefly at Effie, yet she knew he saw her completely for what she was. The guide knew all about the Sevrances.

"Inigar." Drey closed his eyes and touched both lids.

"Corbie says you fought hard and well, and took the lead when Cull Byce went down."

Drey made no motion to reply. Effie knew he was awkward around praise, but it did not account for the hardness in his face as he looked at the guide. She wondered how Inigar had managed to speak to Corbie Meese so quickly; last she'd seen of the hammerman he was battling with Anwyn for more beer.

"You must put the past behind you," Inigar said. "All of it. Clan needs good men like you. Do not let bitterness steal your strength. Things are as they are. Dwell on what they might have been, and the ghosts of the past will eat you. They have sharp teeth, those ghosts; you will not feel them bite until they start tearing at the marrow in your bones. You must put them behind you. Bears do not look back."

"You don't know of what you speak."

Effie took a quick breath; no one spoke to the guide that way. No one.

Inigar wagged his head, shaking the words away as surely as if they were raindrops on oilskin. "My lore is the hawk, Drey Sevrance. I see much that a bear cannot. Do not suppose that I know nothing of what happened on the Bluddroad. Do not suppose that I pronounce you free of blame. But know this: What is done is done, it is what comes *after* that concerns me now."

Drey rubbed his hand over his face. When he spoke he sounded tired. "I must go, Inigar. You must not worry about me. I know my place is with the clan."

Inigar nodded. "Have you thrown the swearstone away?"

Drey turned his back on the guide before answering. "Yes."

Effie felt Inigar's gaze on her and Drey as they walked the length of the guidehouse. Drey was silent as they made their way to the kitchens and then picked bread and meat for them both. Effie saw him wince as he stretched a muscle that shouldn't have been stretched, felt his body tremble for a moment as he dealt with the pain.

"Let's find somewhere quiet to eat," he said.

"We could go to the kaleyard. It's quiet there, and the walls are high so there's hardly any wind." Effie was pleased and a little bit anxious when Drey nodded. She dearly wanted him to like her choice.

The kaleyard was a small square of ground at the rear of the roundhouse that had been set aside for growing herbs. Tall walls kept freezing winds at bay year-round, and someone long ago had thought to build a pair of brick benches so that two or three people could sit and take advantage of the walled haven. The kaleyard was Anwyn's territory now, and every flake of snow that dared to land there was hauled away before it had chance to settle. Anwyn only had to *look* at Longhead to make him start hauling snow. She had that effect on a lot of men, Effie noticed.

Kale, which Effie classified in her mind as tough cabbage, was no longer grown in the kaleyard. Dagro Blackhail had forbidden it, calling kale "that foul leaf." Effie rather liked it, though she did allow that it took quite a chewing. Now Anwyn grew herbs in its place, lots of them, like leeks, black sage, and white mustard, all pulled up for winter so that nothing but mulched-over soil remained.

Effie felt her heart race as she walked around the exterior of the roundhouse. She tried to keep her eyes on her feet and not look up at the wide-open spaces, but sometimes she forgot and found herself staring north toward the badlands and the Want . . . places that had no *end*. Only when the gate on the kaleyard was closed and bolted and her world was reduced to a size she could walk across in less than a minute did she begin to feel safe.

Drey sat on the nearest bench. Effie, still a little breathless from the walk, chose to sit on the second bench, across from him. She watched as her brother took in the details of the kaleyard, trying to decipher the look on his face. A willow planted in the farthest corner of the yard creaked like a loose shutter in the wind.

"Last time I was here I got a beating from Anwyn Bird," Drey said after a while. "I was out throwing spears behind the stables, and the wind caught one of them, sent it clear over that wall. Took the heads off at least a dozen cabbages. Of course, Raif tried to fix them. Stuck the heads right back, he did, smearing them with mud to make them stick. . . ." Drey's voice trailed away to nothing. The hard look came back to his face. "Anyway, it's been a good many years since I was here."

Effie nodded. She could think of nothing to say.

Abruptly Drey leaned forward. "Effie, there is just me and you now, and we must look out for each other. We must stay close. While I was riding back with the raiding party, I had time to think. Arlec lost his twin. Bullhammer lost his foster brother. . . ." He shook his head. "I'm not much for saying things—I don't think anyone in our family ever was—but I see things, and I've stood and watched as you've grown more and more into yourself. I've known something was wrong, but I kept saying to myself, Effie will be all right. Effie's a good girl, she won't come to any harm. Now I think you must tell me what's wrong. Every time I see you there's less than the time before. Raina tells me you take food, but she doesn't know if you eat it. Anwyn tells me that since the night Raina became betrothed to Mace, you only leave your cell to visit the dogs. What are you afraid of? Has anyone said anything to you? Frightened you? Please, Effie, I need to know."

Effie, who had been looking into her brother's brown eyes from the moment he began speaking, looked down as he spoke the last few words. It was the longest speech she had ever heard Drey make. It made her feel sad. She made no reply.

"You went to the woods that day with Raina, didn't you? That day when she and Mace—" Drey stopped himself. "The day when they became betrothed."

A small shaking motion was all Effie could manage. She didn't want to think of that day. Wouldn't.

Drey rose from the bench with great difficulty, his hand bracing his lower abdomen as he moved, and came and sat next to her. "You're frightened of something, Effie. I can tell. I saw you hiding under the stairs in the entrance chamber. You didn't want to be seen. I know these past months have been hard, and I know you miss Da . . . and Raif. But I think there's something different here. A secret."

Effie looked up at the word *secret*.

"Please, Effie. If something is wrong, I must know."

"Secrets have to be kept."

"Not bad ones. Never bad ones."

Effie's hand found her lore.

"Bad secrets lose their power when they're told. The badness is shared."

"Shared?"

"Yes. Between you and me."

"You and me?"

Drey nodded. He looked so old, like a proper clansman in his boiled-leather breastpiece with its ribs of steel. And he was hurting so much—she could tell by the border of sweat around his hairline and the uneven rhythm of his breaths. She didn't want to disappoint him or lie to him. She didn't want to lose him, too, the way she had lost Da and Raif.

A quick squeeze of her lore steadied her, and then she spoke. She told her brother everything about the day in the Oldwood: how Raina had woken her and bade her come to check on the traps, how Mace Blackhail had come upon them, his horse lathered and muddy, and told Effie to leave as he wished to speak to Raina alone; how she had scrambled onto the cliff above them and what she had seen and heard. She told about the threat Mace had made to her, and the dead look in Raina's eyes. Effie wasn't good with words, and sometimes there *were* no words to describe what had happened between Mace and Raina, but she told everything as best she could, encouraged by Drey's silence and patience and the unchanging expression on his face.

When she had finished, he nodded once. He did not question her in any way or ask her if she was *sure*. He took her hand in his and sat and thought. Effie had started shaking sometime during the telling and continued to shake now as she waited to see what her brother would do. She noticed that the sky was almost dark. It was very cold, but only her outsides felt it. Inside she was hot and rigid.

After some time Drey rose. "Come, little one. Let's go inside."

Effie rose with him. She hated how tired he sounded. She hated how she couldn't tell what he felt.

The walk back to the roundhouse took forever. Effie looked down at her feet, crunching frozen weeds from step to step. They found the entrance chamber much changed from when they had left it. Torches burned, clansmen were gathered in small groups, speaking in hushed voices and drinking beer. Four young boys were sitting around a pile of mud- and hair-matted weaponry, cleaning hammer and ax heads in silent awe. Massive red-haired Paille Trotter was singing a song about the Clan Queen Moira Dhoone and the Maimed Man she had loved and lost. All the wounded had been carried away.

Effie thought that Drey would lead her through to the kitchens or the Great Hearth or even her own cell, but he cut left across the hall, toward the little crooked stair that led down to the chief's chamber. Realizing straightaway what he meant to do, Effie pulled back, but Drey held her firm and would not let her go. They met man-chested Nellie Moss on the stairs. She was carrying a fiercely flaming lunt, which she made no effort to shield as they passed. Effie felt the heat of the flames singe hairs around her face.

Clan Blackhail had no seat like Clan Dhoone. No Hail chief had ever called himself a king, though over time many had gathered items of kingly power to them. The Clansword was one such thing, known throughout the clanholds as the symbol of Blackhail power. Clan Bludd had the Red Axe, which wasn't really red at all and was said to be older than the clanholds themselves. Ganmiddich had a great plate of green marble known as the Crab Lode, as it had a giant fossilized crab in its center and had been quarried a thousand leagues from the nearest sea. Effie could recite all the clan treasures and emblems. Her favorite was Clan Orrl's; they weren't known by some grand weapon or polished stone, rather a simple oakwood walking stick known as the Crook.

Effie liked the thought of these treasures. They seemed beautiful to her. Precious. Once, when she had been reciting the emblems of each clan to Raina at the ladies' hearth, Dagro Blackhail had walked in. She had stopped straightaway, but Dagro had bade her continue, and she'd gone through the clans from Bannen to Withy, pausing only once to show respect for the Lost Clan. When she had finished, Dagro Blackhail had laughed heartily—but not in a mean way— ruffled her hair, and told her that no one in the clan, not even Gat Murdock, could remember all those things. Dagro Blackhail had then thrust out his hand toward her and said, "You'd better come with me, young clanswoman, and I'll show you our treasures firsthand. That way if anyone ever makes off wi' them in the dead of the night, we can send you straight to the smithy. Between your memory and Brog's hands, we'll have new ones forged within a day."

Effie had loved being called *clanswoman*. She had loved going to the chief's chamber with Dagro Blackhail even more. Dagro had talked for hours about the clan treasures, holding them up to the torchlight and polishing them with the cuff of his sleeve before he'd let her look. It was the last time Effie had been in the chief's chamber, a year before Dagro's death.

These thoughts and others passed through Effie's mind as she and Drey descended the stairs. It seemed a very long time since Dagro Blackhail had been chief.

Reaching the glistening, tar-blackened door of the chief's chamber, Drey paused to push a hand through his hair. He took a breath, then shouldered open the door and forced his way into the room. Mace Blackhail, who had been sitting on a hide stool behind the square stone table that everyone called the Chief's Cairn, stood. He was alone. His eyes flickered yellow and black in the torchlight. As he looked from Drey to Effie, his hand slid down to rest upon his swordbelt.

"What is the meaning of this?"

Drey tightened his hold on Effie's hand. He took a breath, then said, "Effie told me what happened in the Oldwood. You are not worthy of my respect, Mace Blackhail. I call you out onto the court, here and now, to settle this matter with swords."

Effie let out a choked cry. *No*. Drey couldn't fight with Mace Blackhail. Not now, while he was injured. Not ever.

The sword was Mace Blackhail's chosen weapon, Drey's was the hammer. Why had she told? Why? Why? *Why?*

Mace Blackhail looked at Effie, his thin lips curling to something between a sneer and a smile. A finger came down upon the Chief's Cairn, casually, as if he were testing the surface for dust. "So you would cross steel with me, Drey Sevrance? Raina's honor means that much to you?"

Drey made no reply. His body shook him with every breath.

"Now I come to think of it, it was you who thought to bring my foster father's last token back from the badlands. You who tanned the hide, making it soft for Raina's back."

Drey wrenched his head savagely. Effie didn't understand what Mace Blackhail was getting at. Of course Drey cared about Raina . . . everyone did. The chief's chamber, which was small and coved like a bear cave, suddenly felt as hot and dangerous as a firepit primed with fat.

Mace Blackhail made a negligent gesture with his hand. He was dressed in wolf hides dyed black. "No matter, Sevrance. You're not the only yearman who feels . . . *protective* of my wife. I know how highly she is regarded. And while your concern for her honor is touching, your rashness is a grave mistake. I—"

"This isn't about Raina's honor, Mace. It's about yours— your lack of it."

Effie swallowed air. Part of her wanted to cheer at Drey's words. The other part of her was deeply afraid for her brother. Mace Blackhail was dangerous in different ways from other clansmen. He wasn't hot-blooded like Ballic the Red, or fierce like Corbie Meese. He was as cold and sharp as the spikes of needle ice that formed on the bottom of melt ponds in spring, impaling bears and dogs by the act of simply existing.

"I wouldn't be so foolish as to challenge my chief's honor on the word of a half-grown girl."

"My sister is no liar. I would lay my life on that."

"I didn't say she was a liar, Drey. She saw some things and heard some things, but only through the eyes of a *child*. She doesn't understand what goes on between a man and a woman when they're alone and in private. Tem lived like a hermit. She never happened upon *him* lovemaking, that's for sure. She doesn't even know what lovemaking is. Think, Drey. When Effie spied upon me and Raina in the Oldwood, what did she see? She saw Raina playing coy and slapping me away—what woman would not do that? You know how they are. We tussled in the snow, I will not lie about that, and I daresay I pinned her down and she cuffed me for my trouble. A woman like Raina needs her loveplay rough—"

*"Stop it!"* Drey lashed out at the space separating him from Mace Blackhail, his face contorted with rage. "I will not hear such filth about Raina."

"No. And I wouldn't have had to speak it if it hadn't been for your little sister here. It's not her fault. Of course what she saw distressed her—all lovemaking looks like violence to a child."

"You threatened her."

"Yes, I did, and with good reason. I didn't want the truth of what had happened coming from anyone's mouth but mine or Raina's. The child had no right to tell. It was not her business."

"You're lying. You have no honor."

"Don't I? Perhaps we should call Raina in and ask *her* the truth of it. She was the one who agreed to be my wife."

Effie saw something within Drey waver. He didn't step back exactly, but he let out a breath, and part of him seemed to withdraw as he did so. Effie felt sick with relief. She didn't care about Mace Blackhail's lies—and she knew they *were* lies. Mace Blackhail would kill Drey in a fight.

"Drey, heed me in this. I am your chief. I will not stand by and watch as you take the same path as your brother. You are too valuable to me and this clan. I see how the yearmen respect you. Corbie and Orwin are full of your praises. Just this past quarter, Corbie was here telling me how you saved Arlec's life at battle's end. I need men like you by my side. Good men, whose honesty and loyalty I can rely on.

"What has happened here in this chamber need go no further. You heard something and acted from your heart; I cannot fault you for that. I respect your challenge to fight me on the court, and hope that if the time ever comes when I'm in want of a clansman's justice, you will stand where you are right now and make that same challenge again."

Drey continued looking at Mace long after he had finished speaking. Mace's expression did not change, but he brought himself up to his full height and sent a hand out to trail along the wall where the Clansword was mounted on wooden pegs. His eyes were all darkness now; there was nothing of wolf yellow in them.

After what seemed like hours, Drey turned to face Effie. Kneeling on one knee, he took both her hands in his. His face was pale, and she could see the uncertainty in his eyes. "Do you think you may have been confused by what you saw, little one? Did you actually see Mace strike Raina in a proper way, like I would strike a man in a fight?"

Effie's chest was heavy with love and sadness. She had brought this mess upon him, and he had done what was right and proper and absolutely *good*. Even now he would fight. Even now, on just her say. The thought was almost too much to bear. Either way she harmed him. Lie, and she became a conspirator with Mace Blackhail, leading Drey away from what was right and true. Hold to the truth, and he would end up dead or gone . . . like Da and Raif.

That could not happen. Effie knew it in the deepest bit of her insides, yet it didn't stop her from hating herself as she opened her mouth to lie. "I'm not sure anymore, Drey. Not sure. I thought . . . but then what Mace said—"

"Hush, little one. Hush." Drey hugged her to him, wrapping his big arms about her like a cloak. She shook with relief and a dreadful kind of shame. It was as if she had betrayed him.

"I am glad in my heart this matter is settled," Mace Blackhail said, moving out from behind the Chief's Cairn and offering his hand to Drey. "It is behind us now, and we shall not speak of it again."

Drey released his hold on Effie and stood. He stepped toward Mace, and the two clasped forearms without exchanging another word. Their gazes held, and Effie could almost feel Mace Blackhail's will working upon Drey, like when Brog Widdie took white-hot metal from his oven and pulled it into the shape he needed. Mace slapped Drey on the shoulder as they moved apart. "Get yourself to Laida Moon. Have her take a look at whatever injury you're nursing beneath that breastpiece. I need you well. I heard a rumor that the Dog Lord is set to march on Bannen, and we ride south tomorrow to steal his thunder."

Mace Blackhail ushered Drey to the door. Effie followed after. As Drey turned his attention to the first of the stairs, Effie felt Mace Blackhail's finger slide across her throat. "What did I say would happen if you went telling tales?" His voice was softer than the sound of Drey's boots against the stone.

# TWENTY-SEVEN

## *Dancing on Ice*

SKINNED HANDS CLAWED HER. Faces burned by something darker and more terrible than flames pushed against her, openmouthed and pleading. Seared tissue cracked, revealing pale pink flesh beneath. Proud flesh: raised and stippled and full of lifeblood. The first sign of healing.

*Reach, reach. We must have it . . . we need it . . . give us what we need . . . you must . . . we will make you . . . we know ways to harm you . . . we have waited too long. Reach!*

Red eyes glowed with malice. Lips spread, revealing night smiles. She turned, but there were more at her back. She crumbled their substance in her fists, breaking them down into ash and fire scraps, but for every limb she broke, another dozen rose to haunt her. Glancing into the distance, through the charred and greasy timbers of their arms and legs, she saw the wall of black ice. The ice cave. Suddenly it no longer seemed like a—

"Wake up! Ash! Wake!"

Hands of flesh and blood pulled at her, tugging her back through so many layers of sleep that she felt like a diver emerging from water.

"Wake! Please wake."

She opened her eyes. Daylight flooded in like salt water, harsh, stinging, and unwelcome. It had been pitch dark in her dream, she remembered. She always dreamed of night.

"Angus. She's awake."

Hands touched her forehead and cheek, warm hands, rough and gentle, not like her foster father's hands at all. A face appeared before her. Raif, she thought, pleased at her ability to find names.

"It's me. Raif. You're safe. Angus is here. We're three days north of Spire Vanis, in the spruce woods east of the Spill."

It took Ash much time to decipher what he said. She looked into his eyes: What color were they? An inky blue? A shade between midnight and black? After a moment she asked the only question that mattered. "How long?"

"All of last night and most of the morning."

Feeling she might be sick, Ash tugged herself free of his hold and twisted her head toward the ground. *Half a day! How long will it be before no one can wake me*? Aware of Raif's eyes upon her, she straightened her spine. She decided she would not be sick in front of him. After a moment she felt well enough to sit. The action made her hurt in new ways. The third finger on her left hand felt big and sore, tucked away in its splint. Her shoulder *ached*, and her mouth tasted of saddle leather and horses.

"Here. Drink this."

Ash took the offered waterskin and let some of the icy water run over her face. Raif watched her as she opened her mouth to drink. He knew about the voices. She didn't know how it was possible, but he knew.

"I felt you . . . go last night, just before we made camp. We tried to wake you, but you were far away. Angus thought it better to let you sleep."

"He bound my mouth?"

Raif nodded. "And your hands." They both looked away.

Ash scanned the surrounding territory. Camp had been made on a hillside above a wooded valley. Great columns of black spruce, weighed down by ton upon ton of new snow, rose up like a city around them. To the south the blue giants that were the Southern Ranges floated above the horizon, shimmering with ice. Overhead the sky was thick with snow clouds, and it was impossible to tell where the sun lay. Ash shivered. She had no memory of coming here.

As she turned back to face Raif, she heard hounds howling and barking in the distance. Following the sound with her eyes, she looked down across the valley and into the deepest depths of the spruces, whose needles shone black as night.

"I think we'd better be on our way." Angus strode into her line of vision, his big red-stubbled face as calm as if he had heard sparrows singing, not hounds. "Ash." He held out a gloved hand for her to take. Ash grasped it, and he pulled her off the ground as effortlessly as if she were made of twigs. "Raif. Saddle the horses. I'll see to the remains of the camp."

"What should I do?" Ash forced a calmness into her voice that she did not feel. She didn't like appearing weak before Angus.

"Fill the skins with snow." Angus fished inside his buckskin coat and took out a package wrapped in linen. "Take this and eat every scrap of it, even the fat around the eggs. I know you don't feel much like it, but you must force yourself. You haven't eaten in over a day."

Unable to think of a reply, Ash nodded. In a strange way Angus' vigilance reminded her of Penthero Iss; they both wanted to feed and watch over her.

The past three days had been a new kind of nightmare for Ash. Her life had changed absolutely and forever the moment she had stepped into the shadow of Vaingate. Marafice Eye had conjured himself up from a pile of beggar's rags. Two charcoal burners attending a brazier had peeled red blades from their sides like strips of skin. An old drunk lying in the snow had shaken off his years and infirmities like a leper touched by the gods, and one guard standing alone in the gate tower had suddenly turned into three. Ash had seen it as a kind of magic, the sort used by street corner magicians, all misdirection, mirrors, and smoke. She had continued running for the gate anyway. To be that near and not cross to the other side was unthinkable, a failure of the worst kind.

After that, madness took her. She remembered only fear and death. When it was over and the man who called himself Angus had asked her to travel with him and his kinsman to Ille Glaive, all that had mattered to Ash was getting through the gate. That was why, in the end, she had agreed to go with them: They were heading her way.

She had not counted on what had happened next. Somehow, as she'd sunk to her knees in the hard snow outside of Vaingate, she had lost herself to the voices. There had been a moment, just before they claimed her, when she thought she saw her mother's face. It was there and then it was gone. Robbed. She could remember nothing . . . except a feeling . . . a feeling that the woman who had abandoned her had cared. Probably nothing but a fancy, and she could never, ever be sure. The voices had seen to that. Perhaps they'd even conjured the image up to fool her. They were desperate and they would do anything to seize her. Forcing their way into her mind, they had dragged her into their world. Raif had pulled her back. He had touched her arm, and as he'd done so knowledge had passed between them. Ash shook her head. It was more than that, almost as if something inside her had reached out toward him—an invisible tentacle probing and binding—yet the idea of that was so distressing, she shied away from it. They were connected now, that she knew. And it was *her* doing, not his.

Ash frowned as she scooped snow into the horn nozzle of the waterskin. The cry of the hounds was louder now, more insistent. Almost against her will, her gloved hand rose up to the part of her arm Raif had touched.

"Ash. To the bay."

Hauling the waterskins over her back, she obeyed Angus and crossed to where Raif held the horses. Raif did not speak as he took the skins from her. He was not like Angus; he never made conversation for the sake of passing time.

Mounting the horse wasn't easy for Ash. The quick movement made her head spin, bringing back flashes of the dream. Surely there had been something . . . some revelation, something she had to remember? As quickly as she thought of it, the idea flitted away.

As soon as she was settled behind the saddle, Angus came striding over—not running, exactly, but moving more quickly than was his wont. His copper eyes kept flicking to the valley below. Following his gaze, Ash saw a blur of movement gliding across the packed snow. Unconsciously she squeezed the bay with her thighs. The sept had caught up with them at last.

The Sull tunnel had given them a quarter day's start. Angus had kept them traveling through the night and on into the next day. His knowledge of the roads and ways helped, and the nearer they drew to Ille Glaive, the greater his knowledge became. He could read snow and ice like other men read books. He knew when snow lay over ice, not solid ground, where drifts were deepest, and where pond ice was thinnest and liable to crack. He could spot an animal trail lying beneath two days of snowfall and could tell when a hard frost was coming just by sniffing the wind.

He always seemed to know when it was time to move on. Ash had sat behind on the bay and felt as his shoulders stiffened for no reason that she could hear or see. Always at such times he'd kick the bay into a canter or send Raif to high ground to check the trail.

Angus knew lots of things for a man who claimed to be a humble ranger. Ash was sure he knew who she was. He never asked what she had done to warrant being chased and tormented by Marafice Eye. Nor did he show any curiosity about her second name, her position in the city, or her life before she had met him. It wasn't politeness that halted his tongue, rather a desire that nothing be said until they reached Ille Glaive. Ash went along with this because it suited her. The longer she could put off telling either of these two men anything about herself, the better.

Angus Lok was no fool. It might suit him to play one now and then, but that wasn't who he was.

"Northwest through the trees, Raif. Then hard along the stream." Angus gave the bay its head, and they took off after Raif at full gallop.

Ash held on tightly as the bay charged through the spruces. Behind her she could hear the high, excited braying of the hounds. A horn blared, brash and triumphant, growing louder and louder as seconds passed. The hair on Ash's neck prickled. Was Marafice Eye one of the seven?

"Hounds are a quarter league ahead of the sept," Angus said, perhaps speaking to calm her. "And likely they've been traveling through the night."

Ash struggled for his meaning. "So their horses will be tired?"

"Aye. Unless they've been given false strength."

"Like the ghostmeal?"

"As close as damnation would have it." Angus kicked the bay up a bank. White breath pumped from the gelding's nostrils in thick bursts. Raif had already gained the stream and was now waiting for them to catch up. "Damn the lad," hissed Angus under his breath. "He gets that from his brother—infernal waiting."

Ash watched as Raif turned the gray, a strange tightness pulling at her chest. She hadn't known Raif had a brother, hadn't thought of him as having any family other than Angus. For some reason she had thought he was an orphan . . . like her.

Raif reached over Moose's dock and slid his bow from its soft leather case. With practiced movements he strung and braced the bow, rolling the twine between his fingers as he tied a series of knots. His face was gray with shadows, his eyes focused on the road below. *Can he see the sept from where he's sitting?* Ash wondered. The thought turned her cold.

She had seen what he could do with a bow. That day at Vaingate, while Marafice Eye and the others had watched his arrows, Ash had watched his face. Even through the grating she had seen the hunter's glint in his eyes, recognized death as a presence behind them. Even now, days later, the memory chilled her like cold breath upon her spine.

"*No!*" Angus screamed. "No arrows. Not at the men."

Raif, who had taken an arrow from his case and was in the process of raising it to his bow, halted in midnocking. Ash frowned. She had thought he had no arrows left. Where had they come from? As the bay drew nearer she saw the arrow was crudely shaped, whittled from pine, not hardwood, fletched with horsehair and tipped with flint. He had made it himself. But when? Ash answered her own question: while she had slept through the night.

"Do not target the men. Any of them. Understand?" Angus' voice was harsh as he flanked Moose. "One of them is a magic user—we have no way of knowing which. Sight his heart and you give him a weapon to kill you."

"But—"

"No, Raif. Do not question me on this. There's no time to explain. When the dogs get close, shoot at them if you must. For now, though, put the arrow away. Distance is our best protection." With that Angus kicked on ahead, leaving Raif to the ridge top and the stream. Moments later Ash heard Moose gaining speed behind them. She breathed a sigh of relief.

Below the ridge, the spruces rippled like things made out of water, not wood. Ash tried to spot the sept, but every tree and bush moving in the wind looked like a horseman. Ahead, the ground began to level off. The stream slowed, and cords of ice smoke rose from its partially frozen surface. The impact of the bay's hooves along the bank was enough to crack shore ice as they passed. Ash's heart beat fast in her chest. There was a fierceness in her, and she wanted to ride and ride and never stop.

She still couldn't believe she was free. Sixteen years she had lived in Spire Vanis. Sixteen years of being watched, cosseted, and confined. All she knew was within the city; all her dreams had ended five paces south of Vaingate. When she was younger, Penthero Iss had taken pains to teach her about the world in which they lived. He had brought her books, beautiful fantastic books, painstakingly written in High Hand, illustrated by master engravers, and colored by oathbound scribes. Ash had seen the tall spiraling form of the Cloistress Tower at Owl's Reach, surrounded by its ring of petrified trees; she'd studied the ruins at Morning Star, the giant steps that led nowhere, and the runners of silver ivy that climbed them year by year; she'd gazed upon the vast stonefields of Trance Vor, the iron cairns sunk deep into the soil of Hanging Valley, the Towerlode at Linn, the sheer cliffs that rose around Raven Head, and the golden walls of Ille Glaive with their windows shaped like tears. She had seen the world from those books, yet she had never once dreamed she'd be part of it.

Spire Vanis was her home. Mask Fortress was her home. Now she was riding around a lake she had only read of in books, on her way to a city she knew only through lines of ink. She supposed it felt like freedom, if freedom was a fall into the unknown.

"Cross the stream!" Angus called. Raif was ahead of them again, leading Moose along the bank with a tight rein. On Angus' word, he descended the shallow slope to the water's edge.

The stream was frozen along its banks, yet green water still ran at its center, frothing over unseen rocks. Ash feared for Moose. She saw his hooves break rotten ice, watched his momentary hesitation as he fought his natural instinct to back away. Raif stroked his neck, spoke soft words that Ash couldn't hear. Slowly Moose moved forward through the shore ice into the center of the stream.

The bay, who as far as Ash could tell had a name that Angus preferred no one to know, knew no such fear. It was almost as if he had been ice trained, for he seemed to *test* the ice before he broke it. When they came to a small runoff pool where the water was mostly undisturbed by the stream's current, the bay made no attempt to break the ice at all: He simply knew it was thick enough to take the combined weight of himself and his riders. Angus said nothing during the process, but Ash could tell he was proud of his horse as he scratched the bay's neck and shoulders continually.

As they scrambled out of the ice on the far side of the stream, the lead hound broke from the trees. Snapping and snarling, it made for the bank, its orange-and-black body humped with ribs, its docked tail quivering like a second snout. A second emerged a moment later, then another. Suddenly the sound of their calls was unbearable. The pitch changed, growing higher and more frenzied. They had the quarry in their sights.

Angus turned the bay in the last of the ice. Freezing water

splashed as high as Ash's face. The bay's tail whipped against her thighs.

"Carry on along the bank!" called Angus to Raif. "They'll cross long that way. If we're lucky, we'll lose some to the water."

Ash didn't understand what he meant, but Raif did and he turned Moose quickly, staying as close to the stream as he could. With Moose's hooves barely a pace above the shore ice, horse and rider broke into a gallop. Angus followed suit, the bay keeping perfect pace.

Ash risked glancing back, then wished she hadn't. Half a dozen dogs swarmed like wasps on the far bank. Yellow teeth glinted in ice-reflected light. Pink-and-black gums wet with saliva reminded her of scorched flesh.

As Moose and the bay picked up speed, the dogs began to shadow them along the bank. Soon Ash didn't need to turn her head to see the dogs, as they pulled level with Moose within a matter of seconds. Only the stream separated them now. Then, as Ash looked, the first of the dogs scrambled onto the shore ice. Ash dug her fingernails into Angus' buckskin coat to stop herself from crying out. The dog skidded over the ice effortlessly, its weight not great enough to break the surface. Others followed, howling and shaking their heads like things possessed.

Only when they entered the water did Ash begin to understand what Angus had meant by "crossing long." The dogs, seeing how their quarry was racing ahead of them while they splashed in the water, actually began swimming *upstream*, rather than take the shortest route across. If Angus had simply ridden away from the stream and out of the dogs' sights, the dogs would have crossed in a straight line. This way he tormented them into trying to keep pace.

Not all the dogs were fooled, and some began to swim through the froth toward the far bank. Seeing their sleek wet heads bobbing toward the shore ice, Raif reined in Moose. "Keep going!" he shouted to Angus as he kicked Moose onto the rise above the bank. Already he had one of the pine arrows in his hand.

Ash felt Angus' body stiffen. He drew breath to speak yet stopped himself at the last moment, perhaps deciding it was better not to repeat his earlier warning. Despite Raif's cry, he pulled on the bay's reins, slowing the gelding to a trot. "How many dogs?"

It took Ash a moment to realize Angus was speaking to her. She glanced over her shoulder at the stream. One dog had already reached the far shore and was shaking its body viciously, spraying a fine mist of water droplets into the air. Another two dogs were skating over the shore ice toward the bank. A fourth was trying to scramble onto the ice from the water but was obviously tired, as the current kept tugging it back. A fifth dog was still in the free-flowing water at the center of the stream, paddling furiously. The sixth had fallen back. Ash watched as its small head went under, saw panic in its amber eyes as it emerged once more from the froth.

*Thuc.*

Glancing in the direction of the soft, knuckle-snapping sound, Ash saw Raif sitting high in his saddle, his left arm absorbing the shock of the recoiling bow, his eyes focused on the bank below. The first dog was dead. Ash pressed her hand against her mouth, holding her breath. It was a terrible thing . . . *terrible* . . . to be able to kill another being so surely.

"Five dogs," she heard her voice say. Even as she spoke, Raif's second arrow found another heart.

As the third dog tore toward Raif, the spruces on the far bank came alive with noise and movement. Branches thrashed air, snow spewed upward in a glittering arc. Seven silhouettes came into view. Swift moving, dark as beasts that hunted by night, they rode in a close V formation with only the space of a child's hand between them. The Rive Watch. Ash had seen them ride that way before, watching them from the high windows of the Cask as they drove a wedge into an armed and angry mob. A man had been hung, a popular rogue and ladies' man, and the people of Spire Vanis had taken offense at his death. Not the fact of his death, rather the manner of it, for Penthero Iss had ordered his handsome face cut off and then stitched on backward. Ash swallowed hard. Sometimes her foster father did things like that just to see what such horrors would look like.

The riot had been quelled within an hour. Marafice Eye had spearheaded the first sept. Just the *rumor* of his presence had been enough to take the fight from the crowd. No one in the city, not even Penthero Iss, was stupid enough not to fear the Knife.

"No, Raif!" Angus screamed at the top of his voice. "No more shooting!" He spun the bay, depriving Ash of her view of the sept.

Ash lost sense of what was happening as she was forced to hang on to Angus as they crashed through shore ice and frozen reeds toward Raif. Suddenly a dog exploded from nowhere. Ash felt air pump against her thigh, then the dog's muzzle sprang open, ripping hair and skin from the bay's rump. The horse screamed and bucked. Angus bunched the reins in his fist. "Take the knife from my belt."

Ash did as she was told. The dog danced around the bay's rear hooves, then launched itself once more at its rump. Ash's only thought was for the bay. Already she could see two holes full of blood where the dog's canines had bit deepest. Anger made her lash out violently, uselessly, at the dog's snout. Angus whipped the bay's head back, making the horse wheel so quickly, the dog was left snapping at air. Ash cursed her own uselessness.

"Wait until its snout touches horseflesh." Angus' voice was low, almost threatening. His teeth were clenched.

Ash readjusted her grip on the knife. The hilt was carved from rootwood, but some unseen metal at the center made it heavy in the hand. As she waited for the dog to attack, she risked glancing back across the stream. The sept was clear of the trees now. The lead rider shouted an order, and the V bore down upon the stream. The leader was huge, dressed in the black and the red of the Watch, with the Killhound sewn above his heart and a black iron bird helm forming a cage around his face. Ash looked into the shadows behind the helm, and slowly, so slowly, her belly shrank to the size of a fist. Marafice Eye rode at the head of the sept.

Something dark streaked below her. A muzzle packed with teeth came straight for her thigh. Ash shifted back in horror. Small orange eyes closed in self-protection as the dog sank its fangs into her thigh. Shock and pain tore through her like a jolt from a lance. Hot tears filled her eyes. Rage drove the knife. She hardly knew what she was doing, hardly bothered to place the blow, yet she drove the blade in with all the force she possessed. Bone split with a wet crack. The dog's eyes opened, and its jaws sprang apart. As the creature fell away from her body, Ash yanked the knife back. She wasn't about to lose her blade to a dead dog.

"I said horseflesh. Not girlflesh." Angus seemed angry. He drove the bay up the slope in silence, making his way toward Raif. Ash held her hand to her thigh and pressed. She was angry herself. She had expected Angus to praise her.

Raif waited for them at the top of the hill. He had stowed his bow and now had a short double-edged sword in his hand. Two dogs lay butchered by Moose's hocks. Both Moose and Raif were scratched and bloody. Raif was breathing heavily, and his face was all angles and grayness. *It takes something from him*, she thought with cold certainty. *Killing the things he does, the way he does, hurts him in some way.*

Catching a glimpse of something dark and sparkling over his shoulder, Ash strained to see more. The Black Spill stretched out in the valley below them like a beast under glass. Ledges of ice crusted the shoreline, supporting great frozen piers that extended toward the heart of the lake and the black steaming water that ran there. A haze of mist floating above the surface mirrored each curve and break of the shore, forming a ghost lake above the Spill.

Ash breathed softly, letting her hand relax against her thigh. The eastern shore of the Black Spill, where the Maker of Souls had shown himself to the Condemned Man, Rob Ruce, who went on to take Ille Glaive; where the Red Priest had washed his hands of the blood of the Five Sisters, who saw visions and spoke in Old Tongue; where Samrel of Spire Vanis had met to exchange hostages with the Clan King Hoggie Dhoone; and where Sorissina of the Elms had drowned beneath the ice as she followed her lover's calls into the mist. Ash sat, transfixed for the briefest moment, and watched the play of light and shadow on the surface of the lake. She had always felt a kinship for Sorissina of the Elms: She had been a foundling, too.

"Cut the saddlebags."

Ash was brought back to the present by the sound of An-

gus' voice. Before she could decide whether or not he was
speaking to her, he jumped down from the horse. His boots
crunched snow as he moved to inspect the wounds on the
bay's rump. "I *said* cut the saddlebags."

Ash exchanged a glance with Raif.

"Both of you. Hurry. Ash. Move forward into the saddle."
Angus opened the saddlebag on his near side and took out a
handful of small hide-bound packages, then slipped them
beneath his tunic. He moved quickly, continually looking
over his shoulder to check the progress of the sept.

Marafice Eye was clearly visible now, his gloved hands
like twin ravens at a kill as he reined in his stallion for the
descent to the stream. As Ash sawed at the pannier harness
to release the bags, she noticed that one man in the sept had
broken formation and was now straggling behind. Although
he wore a black cloak like the others, he held no weapon and
obviously needed both hands for his horse. As his cloak tails
caught the wind and ripped behind him, the white colors of a
cleric or anchorite were revealed at his chest. Ash felt a
small thrill of remembrance. She had seen the man before.
She recognized his pale skin and the sharp set of his shoulders. He was one of Penthero Iss' creatures, one of those
special people whom Caydis Zerbina brought to his chambers after dark.

"Sarga Veys." Angus plucked the name from Ash's
tongue, making it sound like one of Marafice Eye's curses.
For a moment his copper eyes turned red, as if the metal
there had been heated by a burst of flame. "Raif. Hand me
the bow. *Now.*"

Raif, who had cut his saddlebags moments earlier, un-
buckled the bowcase and quiver and handed them to his uncle. Angus did not take his eyes from the sept as he hooked
the quiver to his belt. "We must part now," he said. "All of
us. There are seven of them and three of us, and our only
hope is to split them. Raif. You will follow the shoreline
north. Fight only if you must. Better to flee and be safe. If
you are pursued by many, cross onto the ice. Moose is less
laden than the sept's horses and will be more readily borne.
Do not venture farther from shore than the length of four
horses." Angus waited for Raif to nod. "Good." The sound of

the small word was nearly drowned out by the noise of Marafice Eye's horse fracturing ice as it entered the stream. Others followed, and the slim body of water became alive with dark, pitching forms driving toward the bank.

Angus ran a finger over the bowstring, warming. "Ash. You must go directly onto the lake ice. You're the lightest among us—"

"*No*," hissed Raif. "She'll be killed. There's no telling how thick that ice is past the shore—"

"Do you not think I know the dangers, Raif Sevrance?" Angus asked quietly, a muscle pumping in his cheek. "I know the Spill better than you know the graze around the roundhouse, and the bay knows ice better still. He will lead her safely across." Angus turned to Ash. "You cannot fight, lass. You have only my belt knife as a weapon. The best way I can protect you is to lead you to a safe place. No man can follow you deep onto the ice—the Maker help them if they do. The frost smoke will shield you from arrows. You must trust the bay. Old Blood runs in his heart. He will deliver you from harm. I would not let him take you if I did not believe this wholly."

Ash looked into Angus' eyes. He was shaking slightly; the force of his words still upon him. She believed what he said absolutely. She had seen for herself the bay's knowledge of ice as they crossed the stream, and if Angus had wanted to kill her, he could have done so a dozen times before now. No. He wanted her alive and safe . . . the truth of that was in his eyes. *But why*? What made him shake? What emotion was he controlling within himself when he spoke? Did he fear her? Thrusting that thought aside, she glanced across the lake. The Black Spill. It never froze completely, not even in deepest winter. Sorissina of the Elms had taken that truth with her to her death.

*Left outside Vaingate to die*. The words came to Ash, as they always did, as a kind of prayer. They were her life, those words. They made her who she was.

She took the reins.

Angus breathed heavily, showing no sign of relief. His eyes flicked to the stream. Marafice Eye's spurs claimed horseflesh as he forced the beast through the last of the ice.

His small mouth was clearly visible now, pale and twisted like butcher's string around a roast.

"*Go!* Both of you." Angus smacked Moose's rump as he spoke. "Raif. Watch Ash as far as you can, but do not follow where the bay leads. Moose is a good horse, but he's no skater. Don't test him. Ten leagues north of here, where the lake bends inward like a quarter moon, you'll find a grove of white oaks above the shore. If I don't find you before then, I'll meet you there after dark."

Raif nodded. He did not look pleased. Ash could tell he wasn't happy about leaving her to ride on the ice. Their gazes met, and Ash watched as he raised his hand to his throat and touched the piece of horn that hung there. Unsettled, but not sure why, she looked away.

Angus had hold of the bay's bridle. "*Tharra dan mis,*" he murmured. Then quickly to Ash: "Trust him. He'll lead you a fine dance. When all is quiet I'll call you back."

Ash jerked her head in something she hoped was close to a nod. She could not speak. She wanted to ask him what he would do on foot, but there were only seconds left between them, and she feared to detain him with thoughtless speech. Sliding her feet into the stirrups, she took control of the horse.

"Go," he said. "Hold your mind in the now."

Ash turned the bay and let the gelding find his own way down the slope. Already she could hear the whip of leather and horse tails as the sept sloughed off water from the stream and re-formed themselves into a V. When she glanced over her shoulder, she caught a glimpse of Angus running down the slope away from her, making for the cover of a dense island of spruces.

"Maker save him," she whispered, suddenly wishing she had spoken up after all. She should have told him to keep himself safe, asked him the true name of the bay, found out why he'd taken the bow from Raif the moment he'd spied Sarga Veys.

"*There she is! On the bay! Shoot the horse from under her!*"

All thoughts were expelled from Ash's mind at the sound of Marafice Eye's voice. She felt as if she had been punched in the stomach. Her child's terror of him bubbled up from the past. Clutching at the reins, she kicked the bay hard—harder than she knew she should. A salvo of orders followed her down the slope. Marafice Eye was screaming at the top of his voice. *"Thray, Stagro, with me. Malharic, Hood, after the clansman. Crosshead, to the trees. Stagro, flank Veys."* He wanted her to hear him. He knew the quality of her fear.

The bay cantered down the slope toward the hard-froze mud that formed the lakeshore. An arrow shot past his hocks, a second sailed wide of his head. Ash ground her teeth together. The world around her was a blur of trees and harsh, ice-reflected light. Which way had Raif gone? North? She looked that way but could not spot him. *The clansman*, she had heard Marafice Eye call him. Some small part of her had known that all along, recognizing the rough, almost barbaric manner of his dress from descriptions she'd read in books. Yet he'd never once mentioned his clan.

The bay slowed his pace as he hit the lake ice. Tugging his head forward, he demanded more rein. It was against all Ash's instincts as a rider to allow him the freedom to choose his own path in such a place. *Trust him*, Angus had said. Ash frowned, slid her hands a small way down the reins. She was just beginning to realize how hard such a thing would be.

The bay's iron-shod hooves made the shore-fast ice ring like a bell. The water was frozen solid, offering no give, and Ash was jolted around in the saddle as they entered the wall of mist. The temperature dropped immediately, making her cheeks smart as if burned. The light changed texture, and suddenly there were no shadows or highlights—no structure for judging distance or depth. Frightened, Ash looked down. The surface of the lake shone beneath her: wind scratched, snow encrusted, the color of diamonds and salt.

*"Follow me! Don't lose her!"* Marafice Eye's voice carried perfectly through the mist. Seconds later the lake ice began to vibrate as other horses gained the shore. Ash heard Marafice Eye spit a curse at the mist. Softly he said, "Do your business, Halfman. She must not be lost."

Ash shivered. The mist surrounding her was as ragged as rotten linen. Could Marafice Eye see her? She didn't want to risk looking back.

The bay's huge liquid eyes were fixed upon the ice, his entire being bent upon the path ahead. Ash could feel the blood humming along his spine, see the rigid set of the muscles in his withers and neck. Abruptly he changed his course. Straightaway his hooves began to make a flatter tone when they hit the ice, and Ash caught his ears twitching accordingly. *He's listening*, she thought. The revelation filled her with wonder. Where had such a creature come from?

Behind her she was aware of other horses slowing. They were close now. Even the sound of their breaths carried.

Ash gave the bay more rein, squeezed his ribs with her thighs. She thought she smelled something familiar, like copper or the stench of lightning during a storm. The sensation passed as the bay altered his course once more, turning into the wind. They were very far out on the ice now. Ash looked ahead into the peaks and plains of frost smoke. Was this what Sorissina of the Elms had seen before she died? This world of white, captured light?

Something prickled the back of Ash's neck, like an insect's touch or a fingernail scored down her spine. Fear came alive in her chest. Everything was quiet. *When did I last hear the sept's horses*? She found she could not remember. She didn't want to turn and look behind her. Didn't want to see what was there.

"Stop where you are, Asarhia March," came a voice from close behind. "Or we'll shoot the horse."

Ash looked back. Four men rode on the ice thirty paces behind her. Marafice Eye, Sarga Veys, a watch brother with a thin face and a nose made ugly by scar tissue, and a fourth man farther behind. Thin Face had a cranked and loaded crossbow resting in the crook of his arm. Marafice Eye was hunched low on his horse, his arms drawn close to his body, his gloved hands knotted at the reins. Beneath the wire of his bird helm, his eyes glinted like lenses of ice. Sarga Veys rode in the middle, his pale and unprotected head rising from the leather plumage of the Rive Watch cloak like something already dead. He was breathing hard, and a film of gray sweat shone on his nose and brow.

Then it struck her. There was no mist between them. She shouldn't be able to see them at all; the mist was too thick for that. Ahead she could barely see five paces, yet behind her a tunnel of clear air had been created.

She swallowed hard. It was an aberration, wrong in every way, like water running upstream or the sun coming out at midnight. The mist had been held back, molded, forced to do the bidding of one man. It made Ash's flesh crawl. *So this is what sorcery is? Not gaudy tricks and flashing lights; control over nature.*

*Tht.* An arrow shot over the heads of the three men. Even as Ash recognized the crude shape of the shaft and the horse-hair fletchings at its tail, she kicked the bay into a gallop. Angus must have fired high because he couldn't be sure where she was and didn't want to risk hurting her. It wasn't much, but it was a distraction. As she lowered her body over the bay's neck, she heard the crisp *thuc* of the crossbow discharging. The bay was in the process of switching its path, and the crossbolt scraped along his rump, taking hair and skin with it.

Ash pressed her lips together to stop herself from crying out. Horse blood spilled over her boots. Beneath the gelding's hooves, the ice began to creak. Horses charged after them, tracing the bay's path. Marafice Eye shouted an obscenity at Sarga Veys. Ash heard metal rattle as Thin Face cranked the bow for a second shot.

The bay galloped faster and faster. Looking down, Ash saw where the ice had grown darker as the deep, lightless water began to shine through. Her foster father had once told her that a man could stand on freshwater ice as thin as a hen's egg. But what about a girl on a horse? She could recall no wisdom to cover that.

Ash felt the ice *move* beneath her. The bay veered keenly to the left. One of his hooves broke the surface with a sharp, wet snap. Crack lines began to appear in the ice, running through the bay's legs like fast little ants. Lather foamed along the gelding's neck as he danced across the fracturing plates. Ash felt freezing water spit against her face. Behind her, ice snapped with the force of a felled tree. Someone screamed. A horse squealed, high and terrible like something being slaughtered. Ice pitched and rolled, causing the lake water to swell. The shelf of ice the bay ran across bobbed like a raft in a storm.

Ash risked a glance over her shoulder. Frost smoke spewed from the surface in a shower of blue sparks. Horses and men plunged through the erupting ice field, arms flung outward, eyes wide with terror, fingers clutching air. Marafice Eye's horse plummeted into the lake, its forelegs kicking wildly, its rider clawing at its neck. The last thing she saw before turning her back was a pair of gloved hands struggling for a handhold in the cold black water.

Ash rode across the ice, dancing with the bay.

# TWENTY-EIGHT

## *Strike upon Bannen*

THE DOG LORD STOOD in silence as his fifth son, Thrago, fastened his armor to him. The plate was thirty years old, bashed in places, its many punctures packed with solder, and its pot-black finish scratched to hell. Vaylo almost smiled to see it. Two stone of case-hardened iron . . . and it had been with him longer than any friend.

"Not so tight, Thrago. I'm not a chicken to be trussed for the spit."

Thrago Bludd looked at his father with eyes that were the exact same shape and color as those of old Gullit Bludd. It gave Vaylo a chill to see them. Gullit Bludd was dead thirty-five years now, yet his likeness was borne by all seven of his grandsons. Sometimes Vaylo thought the Stone Gods had arranged such a thing just to spite him.

He scowled as Thrago tightened the cinches around his waist. Five winters ago this armor had fitted him perfectly; now it rode over his belly like a loose collection of bowls. Damn the thing to hell! Who'd have thought iron plate could shrink?

"You should have Croda forge you some new plate," Thrago said, putting his back into the task of making the runnels meet. "Else use the Bludd armor Gullit had made for his—"

"No." Vaylo's voice was hard. He would not wear that man's armor.

*Put the knife here, boy, so that it will enter the upmost chamber of my heart.* Vaylo breathed hard at the memory. He could still see his father lying on his bench of old black wood, his face shrunk with disease, his eyes bulging with swollen veins. *Do it! For gods' sakes, do it! We both know you've dreamt of little else for the past seventeen years. Now, when I finally hand you the knife, you stand there with your balls shriveled to hailstones and a bastard's fear upon you. What's the matter with you, boy? I thought you had more jaw.*

That was when the knife went in. To this day Vaylo truly didn't know if he thrust the blade or his father moved forward to take it. It hardly mattered. *His* hands had been on the hilt. *His* fingers were covered with the red wetness that gushed from the hole. So much blood . . . pouring over the bench and onto the floor, running between the cracks in the stone. And his father's eyes . . . *triumphant*. He had thought himself rid of his bastard son.

Vaylo rubbed a hand over his face. It had all gone as smoothly as any epic sung by a hearthsinger. Right on cue Arno and Gormalic had burst into the room. He was still standing there, knife in hand, his father choking on his last breath below him. Vaylo hoped very much that he hadn't seen his father smile then, that the stretching of Gullit Bludd's lips was nothing more than a death rictus or a trick of that bloody light. Of all the things that happened that day in the chief's chamber at Bludd, that was the one thing that haunted him the most. That smile.

Arno and Gormalic had come at him with steel bared. Two longswords against a knife made for slicing fruit. Yet Vaylo could honestly say that there was not one instant when he'd thought he might die. He knew his half-brothers well. Arno and Gormalic practiced for two hours every day on the court. Vaylo practiced for four. Arno and Gormalic were filled with the rage of legitimate sons who had just seen their father murdered by a bastard. Vaylo was filled with a bastard's rage. *His father had tricked him!* Gullit Bludd had been dying for months, his teeth rotting from the bone, his gut shrinking to a loose flap of skin, and his fingers shriveling to bird claws. When he called his bastard son to his chamber, he was as good as dead. He would not have lived out the month. Yet this was Gullit Bludd, son of Thrago HalfBludd, and his pride would not allow him to die alone. He had sought to take his bastard with him.

*Put me out of my pain, boy. I cannot bear it. It eats me, how it eats me. Would you see it turn me into a shitting, drooling babe?*

Gullit had readied the knife himself, Vaylo remembered. He had it waiting beside him on the bench. Blue steel with a hilt of sacred ash. With fingers so pale and wasted they seemed already dead, Gullit Bludd had raised the point to his heart.

Vaylo closed his eyes for a moment. It might have happened yesterday, so clear were the memories. By the time that day was over three Bluddsmen lay dead in the chief's chamber, and Vaylo could recount every blow it had taken to send his brothers to the floor.

They called him the Death Lord later. Legends grew, as legends always did, and suddenly he was no longer a bastard yearman celebrated for stealing the Dhoonestone from Dhoone, he was a killer of men. A usurper. A kinslayer. A chief.

He had offered no explanations or denials. Even then, thirty-five years ago, he knew it was better to say nothing and let men think what they would think. Who would have believed him, anyway? It was well known he hated his father and his half-brothers. Who would have believed he had killed his father as a mercy, that Gullit Bludd had directed the knife himself and begged his bastard son to thrust it deep to cut the great blue vein?

Touching his fifth son on the shoulder, Vaylo said, "Enough. I'll see to the helm and gorget myself."

Thrago nodded. "I'll ready the horse."

Vaylo watched as his fifth son climbed the narrow stair that led up from the chief's chamber at Withy. It was a strange place, this Clan Withy roundhouse, built to confound outsiders. It made no sense, what with its maze of tunnels, mine holes, dead ends, secret chambers, and traps. A man could lose himself, turn a wrong corner, and find himself falling through a trapdoor and into a pit floored with spikes. Molo Bean had broken his ankle when a stone flag had given way beneath him, and Pengo had taken a fall and ended up with a spike through his cheek for his trouble. Vaylo thought his second son looked no worse for the spike hole, yet it had certainly darkened his humor.

They had taken over Clan Withy ten days ago for no other reason than its roundhouse was southwest of Dhoone. Pengo had led the assault, backed by three of his seven brothers and nine hundred hammermen and spearmen. Vaylo almost pitied the Withymen. The anger was upon Clan Bludd, and the proud Withymen, who had lived in Dhoone's shadow for two thousand years, must have thought the Stone Gods had deserted them. Perhaps they had; the Dog Lord claimed no knowledge of such things. He *did* know that Withy had received the fury meant for another clan.

*Blackhail.* Vaylo's entire body stiffened at the word. It was Clan Blackhail his four sons had attacked that day, not Withy. It was Mace Blackhail's face they saw in their minds as they smashed every bone in the Withy chief's corpse. It was Raif Sevrance, he who stood at Duff's and proudly admitted slaughtering Bludd women and children, whom they imagined gutting with their three-bladed spears.

Pengo, Hanro, Gangaric, and Thrago had killed two hundred Withymen between them that day, and another eleven hundred had died by other hands. Proud Withymen, who wore ringmail over coats stuffed with blue fox fur, and boasted, *We are the clan who makes kings.*

The boast was true enough. It was a Withyman who had proclaimed the first Dhoone King and a Withyman who crowned him.

Vaylo buckled his gorget to his plate. If Withymen made kings, then it was Blackhail who slew them. Oh, people forgot that now. Five hundred years had passed since Dhoone last had a king, and in that time Blackhail and Dhoone had cozied up like two blind men with sticks. Bludd was the en-

emy. Godless, ruthless Bludd. Yet it wasn't a Bluddsman
who put an arrow in Roddie Dhoone's throat, it was the
Hailsman Ayan Blackhail. Vaylo's blue eyes shrank. Roddie
Dhoone may have been a mother-spoiled weakling with a
cruel streak as deep as the Black Spill, yet an arrow was no
way to kill a king. A Bluddsman would not have killed Roddie Dhoone at distance; he would have walked straight up to
him and thrust cold steel through his Dhoonish heart.

*No matter, no matter. What does anything matter?* Vaylo
grabbed his gray braids in his fist and held them down while
he fixed his horned helm in place. Other men wound their
braids beneath their helmets to help buffer blows, but not the
Dog Lord. *His* braids streamed free in battle. It was a small
thing, but such small things made men who they were. And
when the battle was joined this night, two thousand Bludd-
sworn eyes would be looking toward his braids.

Vaylo touched the red leather pouch containing his measure of guidestone before he tucked it beneath his plate.
*Stone Gods, see my clan through this night.*

The Clan Withy roundhouse was only a tenth the size of
Dhoone's, yet its builders were artful and had shown a pen-
chant for building *down*, not up or outward. The chief's
chamber was sunk far below the earth, perhaps even to a
depth of a hundred feet. Vaylo could only wonder where the
Withy chief had dressed for war, for it hardly seemed likely
that he'd willingly climb the hundred and twenty steps to the
surface while loaded with two stone of plate.

Vaylo climbed and puffed and was careful where he put
his feet. Already all thoughts were falling from him. He was
the Dog Lord, and he must lead his clan to battle as he had
led them a hundred times before. If the Stone Gods showed
him grace, then dawn would find him one step closer to taking the Hailhold. If they turned their cold cheeks toward
him, then he would strike somewhere else another day.

For he would have Blackhail. He was the Bludd chief, and
a hard life long lived was his reward. Gullit Bludd had died
in his sixties, yet Thrago HalfBludd had lived until he was
eighty-two and Wolver Bludd before him had seen out
ninety-four years in the Bluddhouse. Vaylo expected he
would live for another thirty years himself . . . and by his

reckoning that was more than enough time to send Mace Blackhail to hell.

"Vaylo. The Bludd host waits upon your word."

It was Cluff Drybannock, crossing over from the boatsize piece of white oak that formed the Withy door. Drybone was dressed in armor only marginally less battered and worn than his chief's. A hand-down from Ockish Bull, who had been dead these past five years and who had stood second to every oath Drybone had ever spoken. Oil lamps flickering in the perfect circle of the entrance hall showed the hard bones in Drybone's cheeks and the brilliant blueness of his eyes.

A young scrap of a boy came running over with Vaylo's war hammer, the metal all shiny and near dripping with oil. Vaylo didn't have the heart to tell him that he had not wanted it cleaned, that he liked it good and worn to match his armor, his sword, and his horse. "Strap it on me," he commanded the boy, who might have been Strom Carvo's son.

It was an honor, and the boy's hands shook as he laid the great spiked and lead-weighted hammer in its cradle of soft suede and fastened the steel chains about it. As always when the hammer was laid against his back, Vaylo felt the first stirrings of battle fear. So many battles, so many melees, yet in all this time he still hadn't found a way to calm the turmoil in his stomach and the hammering of his heart.

Thrago had the Dog Horse standing ready as promised, and as Vaylo and Cluff Drybannock passed under the oak door and emerged into the late afternoon light, he trotted the old black stallion forward. Vaylo stood on the steps a moment and looked out upon the sea of red that was his men. Pengo was there, on his great gray warhorse, his hammer as big as his head. Gangaric, Vaylo's third son, stood at the fore, dressed in new-forged plate, a troop of Clan HalfBludd axmen surrounding him. Vaylo recognized men from Clan Otler, with their maroon-colored battle cloaks and clean-shaven faces, and men from Clan Frees with copper wire braided into their hair, and the bones of their ancestors forming bosses on their shields. Even little Clan Broddic had sent sixty men, who sat high upon their snowy horses, resplendent in oxblood leathers and hound-skull helms. All the Bludd-sworn clans had sent men, even cursed Clan Gray

who could ill afford them, and that meant something to the
Dog Lord. No matter that of the two thousand horsed upon
the Withy greatcourt, fifteen hundred were Bluddsmen. No
matter at all.

Ties of blood and battles bound Bludd to HalfBludd,
Frees, Otler, Broddic, and Gray. Dhoone had more clans
sworn to it than Bludd, but ties didn't run as deep in the middle of the clanholds as they did in its farthest reaches. All
clans here today knew what it was to defend themselves
against the Mountain Cities, against Trance Vor and Morning Star . . . and against the cold quick arrows of the Sull.

Vaylo took a hard breath as he descended the steps. He
would not think about the Sull . . . not here, not now.

Using the bottom step as a platform, Vaylo mounted his
horse. The beast was lively today and fought the reins the
moment he pulled them. Vaylo fought back, and the Dog
Horse screamed and reared and other horses shied away to
give it space. Vaylo was not displeased. Drawing his
greatsword from the hound's-tail scabbard at his side, he
looked upon the faces of his men and roared, *"South to
Bannen!"*

The howls of two thousand warriors followed him as he
rode to the head of the line.

The Dog Lord set a hard pace. The day was cold and
clear, and the wind was changing, and there'd be a halfmoon
rising soon enough. The territory north of Withy was
wooded with elms and white oaks, with many groves cleared
to provide forage for wild boars. The grazing land and wheat
fields lay to the north. To the northeast, the dull brownish
waters of the Easterly Flow could be seen, as they bow-
curved north toward Dhoone. Southwest, toward Bannen, lay
a landscape of gentle rolling lowlands seeded with white
heather, thistlegrass, and oats.

Vaylo pulled great quantities of air through his lungs as he
rode, savoring the coldness of the day and the ice upon the
wind. The snow underfoot had a crust to it that snapped with
a pleasing sound as the Dog Horse claimed ground beneath
him. At his back, Vaylo heard the thunder of his men, and
the noise made the bloodlust rise within him.

Bannen. They had once sworn oaths to Blackhail, had fought beside the Hail chief at the battle of Mare's Rock, yet that almost wasn't important. It was where they *lay* that counted. The Banhold pushed far into Blackhail's southern reach. Take it, and Bludd would have a base for attacking the Hail Wolf himself. Vaylo had thought long on this and knew that an attack upon Blackhail would be better coming from the south, not the east. Gnash could not be bested; the Gnashhold was crammed with Dhoonesmen and its roundhouse was as good as a fort. Bannen, though . . . Bannen was something else. Bannen could be taken. Blackhail and Dhoone would be expecting the Dog Lord to strike west, take Gnash or Dregg. They would not think he would move south instead. Bannen herself would not be expecting an attack; her doors would not be barred, her livestock would be afield, and the foot-thick layer of sod that lay over her roundhouse could be doused and set alight.

Vaylo arched low in the saddle, letting the wind stream his braids behind him. Once he had Bannen, he could begin taking Blackhail's sworn clans. Scarpe first. The Hail Wolf's birthclan. No one would weep to see them taken. Dregg next, though the Dreggsmen were hard-bred warriors and Vaylo knew they would give him a fight. Orrl last. Vaylo had respect for Orrl; like Bludd, they knew what it was like to live on the far edge.

"Do you mean to outrun your army, Bludd chief?"

Vaylo looked around to see Drybone pulling alongside him on his gray. In the fading light he looked little like a clansman, and Vaylo found himself wondering why his Trenchland mother had sent him away. Surely he would have fit in well enough in Hell's Town?

The Dog Lord managed a grim smile. "What's the matter, Dry, frightened I'll get to Bannen ahead of you?"

Drybone shook his head. "Just worried about an ambush, that's all."

"Cautious as ever."

"Tell me you haven't thought of it yourself."

Vaylo could not. There was *always* chance of an ambush.

"Open ground between here and Bannen. We'll be there before the moon peaks."

"We're close to Gnash, Scarpe, Dregg . . . even Ganmiddich. The middle clans are all pressed close."

With a small pull on the reins, Vaylo slowed his horse. He knew better than to trade words with Cluff Drybannock. It was close to dark now, the sun sinking in a red sky. The dying wind smelled of cold things from the north, of frozen lakes and ice fields and glaciers. Vaylo tasted old memories in his mouth, and the old desires rose with them. Looking into the blackness beyond the setting sun, he said, "Sometimes I wish I could just ride away, Dry. Head north and never come back."

"Join the Maimed Men?"

Vaylo laughed. "It wouldn't be the worst thing. I swear I thought of it a thousand times when I was a boy. To have the badlands and the entire Want as my ranging ground, to ride with storms against my back and the Gods Lights in my face and a hard frost beneath me."

"And to lose two ears, three fingers, and a nose to the 'bite?"

It was true enough. The Maimed Men were an unhoused, unnamed clan who wandered the farthest reaches of the badlands. It was said that no man or woman among them was whole, that all had lost limbs or appendages to the frost. It was also said that the Maimed Men had come into being the year Morrow was wiped out by Dhoone and that many who rode their ranks could trace their ancestry back to the Lost Clan. Vaylo didn't know the truth of it. As a child he had started north to join them a dozen times. He was a bastard, and his father wished he had never been born, and everyone knew the Maimed Men accepted traitors, exiles, and bastards.

Suddenly sober, Vaylo said, "We'll ride at trot to Bannen."

Two thousand men slowed to Drybone's shouted order. Drybone himself moved back into the ranks; he was seldom comfortable riding at the head of a line.

Vaylo rode south and then west as the terrain demanded. The moon rose, half of it, and silver light ran upon the snow. Vaylo kept his mind in the now as he rode, determined not to think of another night similar to this one, of another ride upon the white.

The northeastern border of the Banhold was formed by a giant stand of black spruce, each tree as tall as thirty men. There were streams to be forded and ancient glacier tracks to circumvent and pale stone ruins where the horses feared to tread. As they neared the trap rock cliffs that protected the Banhouse, Vaylo sent six men forward as scouts.

Only one came back.

The man, a little red-haired bowman from Broddic, had taken a quarrel to the meat of his upper arm—clean through the stewed-leather munnion he was wearing. Vaylo called a halt, and all his sons and warlords and the warlords of his sworn clans gathered in a great circle around the bowman.

"They know we're coming," said the bowman, still atop his horse. "And there's more than just Bannen."

"Cawdo!" shouted the Dog Lord to the Bludd healer who was far back in the ranks. "Come forward and see to this man." Then to the bowman. "Who else is present, and in what numbers?"

The bowman swallowed. His face was ghastly pale. "I saw Dhoonesmen . . . I'm not sure of their numbers. They were waiting below the cliff, quiet as the dead. What I saw had spears." He grimaced as the healer bade him slide from the horse. "A Blackhail bowman—"

"*Blackhail?*" The words fell like ice from the Dog Lord's mouth. A ripple of quiet, made up of held breaths and un-moving limbs, spread through the company of two thousand men. Suddenly it did not matter how the ambush had come into being, who among the Bludd-sworn clans had given word to Bannen. It mattered only that Hailsmen stood in the valley below.

Cawdo Salt pressed hard fingers into the bowman's arm as he snapped the arrow shaft near the base. Wood broke with a sickening crack. The bowman swooned, but Cawdo held him firm. Vaylo could not take his eyes off the man's blood, black and shiny in the moonlight.

"How many Hailsmen did you see?" he heard himself ask.

"Not many. Less than two hundred. Mostly it's Bannen and Dhoone."

Cawdo held a flask to the man's lips and bade him drink.

Pushing away the flask, the bowman said, "They've taken the best positions at the neck of the valley, along the rise, behind the Banhouse. All high ground except the cliff is theirs. We'd have to ride through the bottleneck of the valley to reach them."

The Dog Lord nodded. "Drink, man," he murmured. Cawdo Salt had a silver-bladed knife in his hand, and Vaylo knew the healer was readying himself to cut out the arrowhead.

"We must turn back," Drybone said in a strange voice. "We don't know their numbers. They're well entrenched in their positions, they know the ground, and they haven't just come off a five-hour ride."

"We strike now, bastard," Pengo Bludd hissed. "There's Hailsmen in that valley, and I for one don't care whether they hold all the ground between here and the Night Sea. I'd ride through wildfires and ice storms just to place my hammer into a single Hailish skull."

Not one muscle in Cluff Drybannock's face changed as Pengo spoke, yet Vaylo saw the anger in his eyes. He was probably the only one among two thousand who did.

"We can split up," Thrago said, his hammerman's chains rustling as he kicked his mount forward. "Take the cliff from two sides. Have the Broddic archers cover us as we go down."

Pengo was quick to nod, one of his black braids falling loose from his helmet as he did so. "And we can send a troop of spearmen wide to attack the rear."

"Aye," agreed the HalfBludd warlord, "and post another west to flank them."

"And hold two hundred pikesmen in reserve—"

"*Enough!*" roared the Dog Lord. "We will not split ourselves a dozen times over, like a leg of pork carved at table. We are Bludd and Bludd-sworn, and we are the Stone Gods' chosen, and we will not ride like cravens to this or any other fight. Pengo. You will take a hundred men only and ride wide. Take up position a league south of the Banhouse, ready to cover a retreat if needed."

Pengo glowered. "You said we would not ride like cravens. Yet you talk of retreat in the same breath."

"It's one thing to act bravely, another thing entirely to act like a fool. There is danger here. As Cluff Drybannock said, there is much unknown to us. I will not lead men into this battle without being sure I have a way out." As he spoke, Vaylo was aware of Drybone, sitting his horse at the far edge of the circle, watching him with Sull-blue eyes. *I know you are right, Dry,* he wanted to say. *This is not a wise thing to do, but sometimes we must do things out of rage, not wisdom. If you were wholly clan, you would know that. But you are not, and I would have you no other way.* Instead he said, "Dry, I want you and your swordsmen with me."

Drybone nodded.

It would have to do. There was no time for anything more. While Cawdo Salt cut a cross into the Broddic bowman's arm, turning the circular wound into something larger that could be more easily stitched, the Dog Lord and his warlords planned their strike. They settled on riding for an extra ten leagues and approaching the valley from the west, not the northeast as expected: Strike hard and fast and work their way south toward Pengo's position.

A second silent strategy lay beneath the spoken one, and fifteen hundred Bluddsmen knew it: Kill every Hailsman in sight.

Vaylo led the main body west. The ground shook beneath the Bludd host, and the night wakened to their calls. Screams and terrible low bellows, Stone Gods named and named again, wolf howls, and desperate low keening thickened the air like smoke. Vaylo pulled his hammer from its sling and whirled it high above his head. Three stone of lead, limewood, and steel, yet it moved like a goddess in his hand. The bloodlust was upon him, and for the first time in eleven days and eleven nights, he allowed his mind to settle in the place where he kept his losses.

Seventeen grandchildren dead.

When he descended to the valley floor and the Dhoone host rose to meet him, he saw fear in their gray blue eyes. His hammer smashed into a iron-helmed skull, unhorsing

the first foe that he met. Sword blades licked him like cold
fire. All around, black spruces bent and rippled in the quickening wind. Torches circling the Banhouse burned red, but
the half-moon stole their glory, turning the fields of snow
blue. Vaylo smelled resin and sword metal and the stench of
his own fear. Ahead he saw the Dhoone foreguard and the
wing of spearmen that flanked them. The Bloody Blue Thistle had been raised above the black dome of the Banhouse,
and the standard blew straight and true and to the south.

Blackhail arrows rained from the sky, their shafts black as
night, their arrowheads bound to their nocks by cords of silver wire. Vaylo swatted them from the air with his hammer,
furious that the men who sent them were out of sight. The
Dhoone foreguard felt his wrath as he rode upon them, howling like the Dog Lord that he was. Ranks of mounted
Dhoone swordsmen closed around him, yet any man who
drew within hammer range received a kiss of lead and steel
for his trouble.

Dhoone steel screeching against his armor, braids lashing
against his back, Vaylo screamed for Blackhail to take the
field.

At his back Cluff Drybannock killed men with a cool effi-
ciency that Vaylo found mildly disturbing. Dry's longsword
was sharp and heavy, and its double-edged blade could
pierce all but the thickest plate. He was deadly silent as he
fought, his face unmoved by fear or anger, his eyes always
looking two moves ahead.

With Drybone at his back, Vaylo felt safe to push farther
into the Dhoone line. To the east, he saw the first of the Bannen swordsmen moving to cut off the Bludd rearguard. The
Bansmen were dressed in cloaks of gray leather trimmed
with moose felt, and their swords were things of clannish
beauty, the steel burned with acid until it shone black. The
Bansmen sang a slow metered deathsong as they marched
down the slope, wailing about some ancient battle where the
Wolf River ran with blood.

The deathsong drove the Dog Lord to distraction, and he
prayed that some hawk-eyed bowman would put an arrow
through the head singer's tongue. Vaylo was choked by

Dhoonesmen, tantalized by brief glimpses of Hailsmen on the far edges of his reach. His hammerman's chains rattled in fury as he swung his hammer in ever widening circles. His throat was hoarse from screaming. Dead men rode past him, slumped over their horses' necks, blood oozing from cracks in their plate. A piece of a man's face was glued to his hammerhead, yet he could spare no moment to pick it away.

This battle was madness, *madness*, yet he had no choice but to keep moving forward. A lance shattered against his breastplate, sending splinters flying into his eyes and knocking him sideways in the saddle. When a hand reached over to steady him, he didn't need to glance over his shoulder to know who it was.

Mist began rolling north from the Wolf River, and soon the snowfields were a sinking ground of scattered forces and unhorsed men. Vaylo's shoulder ached with a deep and terrible pain, yet he kept his hammer swinging in spite of it. There were Bludd swordsmen ahead of him now, hacking at Dhoone spears. Vaylo saw one man with a spear rammed so far down his throat that he had been impaled upon his fallen horse. *An axman from Clan Gray*, the Dog Lord thought with a small shudder. *Truly, they are the cursed clan.*

Finally they broke the Dhoone line . . . and Vaylo did not fool himself for one instant that it was his doing. Yes, he had rage and a hammer that never stopped. But it was Drybone and his crew, going one-on-one against the Dhoonesmen, that saved the day. Cluff Drybannock came alive in moonlight. His movements had a grace that all other clansmen lacked, and once he found his rhythm he could strike or unhorse a Dhoonesman with every blow. When the mist came and Vaylo was hard-pressed to see ten feet ahead of the Dog Horse's neck, it was Drybone who forced a path in the whiteness, Drybone who stood upon his stirrups and murmured, "There's a break in the Dhoone line to the west." Vaylo looked and squinted but could see nothing but the arses of Bluddsmen's horses.

He let Drybone lead the flight to the south, where Pengo and his hundred men were waiting to escort them off the field. They would not stay and fight. The Dog Lord knew a rout when he saw one. Bannen would not be taken this night . . . and far too little Blackhail blood had been spilled.

Unsated, the Dog Lord turned for home.

# TWENTY-NINE

## *By the Lake*

RAIF SAT WITHIN THE circle of light created by the white oak fire and cut arrows. They would not be good ones, for the wood was unseasoned and widely grained and would likely split upon impact, but it was something to do. He had a stone warming at the base of the fire, ready to heat and straighten the shafts when he was done. Later, much later, he would think of sleep.

It was dark, sometime past midnight, and moonlight came and went as the wind shifted clouds overhead. Angus was kneeling by the bay's forelegs, rubbing them softly with a shammy. His gloves were clotted with pine sap and blood, but he was too caught up in tending his horse to clean or care for himself. Ash sat on the opposite side of the fire, her face made golden by the flames. Moose's horse blanket was wrapped around her shoulders, and Angus' buckskin coat lay across her lap, yet neither stopped her from shaking.

Raif had watched as she rode off the ice, her hair sparkling with frost, her eyes fierce and full of light. It was as if he were seeing her for the first time. Suddenly she wasn't a skinny girl in borrowed clothes, she was a young woman with fine shoulders and a sure way of sitting a horse. The brightness within her had faded as they'd made their way north to the campsite. The reality of wet clothes and aching muscles had set in, and by the time Angus found them an hour later, Ash was crouched in the snow, shivering. Angus had called her his "wee lassie of the ice" and built up the fire to warm her. What destruction she had left behind could not be known. All was hidden by the mist over the lake.

At least two of the sept were dead. Raif had killed one of them himself. It had been a nasty fight . . . one he'd found he had little stomach for. After he'd taken two fingers from the second red blade's swordhand, he had shown the man grace and let him live.

Shor Gormalin had taught him about grace. "You must learn to recognize when a fight is won," the small fair-haired swordsman had said one spring morning as he'd put Raif through his paces on the practice court. "Some wounds will take the fight from a man as surely as a dragon breathing fire. Others will just make him angry and want to hurt you more. The secret is knowing the difference."

Raif remembered waiting for Shor to continue, certain that the swordsman would tell him to be on the lookout for spilled guts, bits of bone poking through skin, or wounds that bled and bled and wouldn't stop. Instead Shor had said, "The truth of it's always in your opponent's eyes. I've known hammermen who could fight from noon to sunset with wounds the size of rats in their chests, and I've seen swordsmen turn tail and flee with nothing but a fine set of scratches on their necks." Shor had raised his hand to his own neck, perhaps reassuring himself that there were no scratches *there*. "When you've wounded a man and looked into his eyes and seen for yourself that you've taken the fight from him, then you must decide whether to take his life or spare it.

"Grace is a matter between a clansman and the Stone Gods. They give you a choice—and make no mistake, they'll judge you for it—yet none but they know the rights and the wrongs of it. Never assume that leaving an opponent alive on the battlefield will gain you entrance to the Stone Halls that lie beyond. With our gods nothing is ever certain. They damned Bannog Tay of the Lost Clan for choosing *not* to kill his brother at the Battle of the Verge."

Shor's words had run through Raif's mind as he'd looked into the red blade's eyes. The man's sword was lying in the snow alongside two fat fingers and a pool of blood. *The fight's left him*, Raif had thought, a strange tightness pulling at his chest, and he'd turned his horse and fled.

Raif felt that same tightness now. Abruptly he thrust the last of his arrows into the fire and watched as the yellow flames warped the wood then turned it black. Truth was, he didn't really know if he'd shown grace at all, not in the way Shor Gormalin meant, where one clansman spared another out of respect. It had sounded good in the telling, and even Angus had nodded and said, "That's your right, Raif, and I will not question it." Yet Raif wondered if he hadn't spared the red blade simply to prove to himself that he *could*; that not every fight he fought and every arrow he loosed was destined to end in death.

*Watcher of the Dead.*

Raif shivered, fed another arrow to the fire.

"Do you think Sarga Veys is dead?" Ash's voice broke the silence of the camp like a tree snapping under the weight of winter snow. Raif couldn't recall the last time she had spoken, and he and Angus exchanged a small, worried glance.

Angus left the bay untethered and came and crouched by the fire. Peeling his stained gloves from his fingers, he said, "I will not lie to you, Ash. I have an inkling he's still alive."

"But the ice. . . . I saw—"

"Aye, but did you *smell*? I heard the ice break, heard the horses scream, but I also smelled sorcery moments later. Sarga Veys is a clever sorcerer. Powerful, too. You may have left him to the frozen waters of the Spill, but such a man is seldom easily killed. There are things he could have done, bodies he could have robbed heat from, drawings he could have made to still and stiffen the ice."

Ash looked down. After a moment she said, "What about the Knife?"

"Marafice Eye is Penthero Iss' right hand. Veys would be a fool to leave him to damnation. Veys wants power in his own right, yet he knows he won't get it by returning to Spire Vanis alone. If there was any way he *could* pull the Knife from the water, then we must assume that's exactly what he did. I doubt very much if there's any love lost between those two, but Sarga Veys has a high opinion of himself, one that doesn't allow for failure."

"You know Sarga Veys?" Raif asked.

Angus fixed Raif with his copper eyes. "Aye, you could

say that. We've crossed paths before in our time . . . and I'd sooner not think on it now." It was the end of the subject. Angus made that clear by standing and stretching and turning his back on Ash and Raif.

Raif traced a line in the snow with the tip of an arrow. His uncle had as many secrets as Anwyn Bird had recipes for mutton. Always there were evasions, lines that couldn't be crossed. After today there were more mysteries than ever. A sept led by the Protector General of Spire Vanis had hunted them down like game. Sorcery had been used out on the lake. Raif signed to the Stone Gods, touching his closed eyelids and the tine at his waist. Angus might speak casually about sorcery, but as a clansman Raif could not. Some things were too deeply engrained. Clan was earth and stone and mud, things that could be held in the hand and weighed. Sorcery was air and light and tricks.

Raif sighed heavily. Sorcery had been used in broad daylight, under an open sky. And for what? At first he had thought Angus was the main quarry of the sept, yet the magic user and the Knife had followed *Ash* onto the lake, not Angus. Glancing through the yellow needlework of flames, Raif looked at Ash. Who was she? The Surlord of Spire Vanis wouldn't send his Protector General to track down a girl off the streets. Raif took a breath, drawing in the warm air and gray smoke from the fire. The newly knitted skin on his chest pulled tight as he filled his lungs. The stitches were gone now, winkled out by Angus and his knife. The scars left behind reminded Raif of widow's weals.

"Why did Marafice Eye come after you?" Suddenly it seemed easier to ask than think.

The question was meant for Ash, yet Raif saw Angus' shoulders stiffen as it was asked. For half a moment he thought Angus would speak up and end the subject on her behalf, but he didn't. Instead he busied himself with his gloves, scraping away ice and pine needles with the edge of his knife.

"You think he came after me?" Ash raised her head from her knees. A sheen of sweat glistened on her brow, and even the smallest movements she made seemed powerless and disjointed.

Raif was already beginning to regret the question. Mist trapped in Ash's clothes would turn to ice through the night. She needed fresh linens, hot food, and extra blankets—none of which they had now that the saddlebags were gone. Angus had taken a few things—some trail meat and medicine, as far as Raif could tell—yet he had no clean cloth to bandage Ash's thigh and the bay's rump, and only a splash of alcohol to clean them. Raif shook his head. "No. It doesn't matter."

Ash looked at him with large gray eyes. After a moment she made a small warding gesture with her hand. "It does matter, Raif. It matters because you don't know what you're putting yourself in danger for. Even if Marafice Eye and Sarga Veys both died out on the lake, Penthero Iss will send more to replace them. He wants me back . . . I'm his foster daughter, Asarhia March."

It took Raif a moment to understand the words. "The Surlord's daughter?" he repeated stupidly.

"His almost-daughter." Ash glanced quickly at Angus.

Raif caught the look, understanding it immediately. "You knew," he said to Angus.

Angus put down his knife. "Yes."

"And that's why you moved to save her by the gate?"

"What do you think?"

"I think you won't tell me the whole truth."

"Why ask, then?"

Raif pushed himself to his feet. "I asked because I'm sick of lies, because every time I get close to the truth, you push me away. We are blood kin, yet you do not trust me. I have followed you blindly, trusted you blindly, yet it's Ash who finally speaks the truth to me, not you."

"I have told you no lies, Raif Sevrance. Be sure of that. If I have held things back, it is to protect you. If I have kept knowledge to myself, it is because some things are better not known. I have learned many things and gathered many burdens. Such truths as I hold come only at a cost. What sort of kin would I be if I passed all the horrors I have seen and all the fears that I live with onto you? Once something is spoken it cannot be unsaid."

Angus' voice was low and dangerous, yet Raif hardly

cared. He took a step forward. "Don't treat me like a fool, Angus. You're content to let me share the danger when it suits you. In the past three days I've been hunted, ridden down, and attacked. What more has to happen before you'll speak?"

"The less you know, the safer you are."

"Why? Who are you protecting me from? Penthero Iss' sept seemed more than happy to slit my throat regardless of what I knew or didn't know. No one slowed down between blows to ask questions."

Angus shook his head. "Don't make the mistake of supposing that you are the only person I must protect. Some secrets are not mine to tell."

"Tell me what *is* yours to tell, then. Why was it so important to visit Spire Vanis? What happens when we get to Ille Glaive? How do you know Sarga Veys? And why did you take the bow from me the moment you knew it was him? I had a full flight of arrows. I could have shot the other six."

"And the bay," said Ash, softly. "Who taught him how to dance upon the ice?"

Both Angus and Raif turned to look at her. In the heat of the exchange she had been forgotten. The Surlord's almost-daughter, cold and shivering like a child.

Angus' face softened. "The bay was given to me as a gift. I saved a man's life once, a Sull warrior named Mors Stormyielder. He promised me then that he would breed and train a horse in payment. The Sull do not take such things lightly, and the horse was many years in the breeding. Mors' pride demanded that he send me only the best of his stock, and it took eleven years and two generations of foals before he was satisfied that a horse fitting his debt had been born. He spent another three years training the horse in the Sull manner, teaching it how to hold itself steady beneath an archer taking aim, how to survive in white weather and keep moving through thick drifts, how to endure the sudden pains of rocks and arrows without throwing its rider, how to war in formation with other horses, scent trails, read snow, and dance ice. When Mors was finished he sent the horse to me."

"Fourteen years seems a long time to repay a debt," Ash said.

"Mors was bound by his word, not by time. The years that passed between my deed and his repayment were nothing to him. He is Sull, he sees things differently from you and I."

"What's the bay's name?"

The bay, as if knowing it was being spoken of, whickered softly and stamped snow. The makeshift bandage covering its hindquarters had already been thoroughly sniffed at, then chewed on for good measure.

"He has a Sull name, one that can't properly be translated into Common." Angus smiled as he saw Ash's next question, already formed, in her eyes. "*Ehl Rhayas Erra'da Motho*. It means 'One Who Is Born for a Debt but in the Rearing Becomes More.'"

Ash smiled sleepily.

"It's easier to call him the bay."

"I see that now." She yawned. Closing her eyes, she pulled the blanket over her chest and lay down in the snow. "*Ehl Rhayas Erra'da Motho*," she whispered. Then, a few minutes later, "I'm so cold."

Raif and Angus exchanged a glance. Raif began to tug apart the ties on his elk coat. He wasn't angry at Angus anymore. They would speak later when Ash slept—the look Angus had given him had promised that. For now he had to look after Ash. Walking around the fire, he braced himself for the shock of cold air and then stripped off his coat. Frozen leaves and forest matter crunched like glass beneath his feet. As he knelt to tuck the coat around her shoulders, his hand brushed the side of her cheek. Her skin was as cool as ice.

Slipping beside her, he took her in his arms and pulled the elk coat over them both. He held her, shivering and silent, until she fell asleep.

Raif's mind drifted with the icy stillness of the night. Angus kept watch, occasionally walking between the horses and the steep bank that led down to the lake. Strings of mist from the Spill slithered across the snow like snakes. Overhead, the half-moon shone through a mesh of clouds. Raif thought of Drey, of the time Drey had fallen through the ice in Cold Lake and Raif had held him as he held Ash now. Tem had been mad with anger, furious at Drey for running

opened his eyes and looked at Raif. "That's one of the reasons I wouldn't let you target the sept."

"But I've targeted men before now without being harmed."

"That's part of your gift. What you do happens in less than an instant. Your mind enters another's body, joins with the heart, then leaves within an eyeblink. You don't damage or interfere with the heart in any way, you *mark* it. It all happens so fast that the victim doesn't have chance to respond. And even if they did, your arrow hits them a second later and then they're dead.

"You use sorcery as your *accomplice*, not your weapon. It's a subtle difference at best, but that, and the sheer speed of what you do, saves you from any backlash."

Raif tilted his head back and looked up through the clouds to the stars. His heart was beating rapidly in his chest. What Angus had said disturbed him deeply; he'd described exactly what happened when Raif drew his bow, right down to marking the heart. "How do you know so much?" he asked.

"I know a man with nearly the same gift as yours—"

"Mors Stormyielder. The Sull."

If Angus was surprised at Raif's guess, he did not show it, merely ran a hand over the rough stubble on his jaw. "Aye. He's the one. Can kill any animal he sets his sights on."

"And it's the same for him as well?"

Angus nodded. "Close enough. Animals have wills to survive just as you and I do. They cannot be interfered with lightly. Mors knows that. I never knew him to spend a moment longer than necessary in any beast."

"Yet he couldn't target people?"

"No." Angus looked at Raif only an instant before looking away.

Raif waited, but the silence between them only deepened, and Raif guessed he had touched upon yet another subject that Angus had no liking for. Having little liking for it himself, Raif let it go. Perhaps his uncle was right: Some things were no better for the knowing.

Shifting himself against Ash's body, he said, "I still don't understand what this has to do with Sarga Veys. If I can target people as quickly as you say, where's the danger?"

Angus seemed relieved at the question. During the silence he had taken to looking longingly at the empty flask. "It's simple. You should never set your sights on *any* sorcerer. Ever. They'll know the moment you enter them, and if they're quick enough and clever enough, they'll send your sorcery back home with a vengeance. It doesn't matter that what you do is little more than a sighting, a bowman taking aim on his target. The act of *severing* is where the power comes from. By severing the thread between you, a sorcerer can take a small insignificant drawing and whiplash it into a force."

Angus still wasn't finished. Now that he had decided to speak, he seemed determined to say the worst and have done with it. "From the night we left Spire Vanis I knew we were being tracked by a magic user, yet until I saw Sarga Veys on the ridge I couldn't be sure who it was. If it had been another man, I might not have taken the bow from you. As long as you'd targeted the other sept members, chances are you would have been safe. But Sarga Veys isn't like most sorcerers. Sorcery lives within him like the future lives within prophets and hell lives within the insane. He can do things that no one else can, clever things, subtle things, things that people say canna be done. As soon as he realized you had a man's heart in your sights, he could have slid his power in beside yours and sent your drawing snapping back like hellfire."

Angus showed his teeth. "And such a small thing like that, a little snapping motion, wouldn't even weary him to the point where he needed a ghostmeal."

Raif held his body still, determined to show Angus nothing of the fear that lived within him. Suddenly he longed for Drey and Effie and clan. "If Veys has so much power, why didn't he strike sooner, from afar?"

"Sarga Veys knows his limits. More than likely he was saving his strength for when he caught up with us, in case you used your trick with the bow, or Ash did something that sent everyone running. No matter what happened, he would have left the killing and capture to the sept. Sorcery is useful in many ways—you heard what happened on the lake, how he pushed the mist aside so the Knife could follow Ash—but if you've a mind to kill someone, you're safer using an arrow or a sword."

Several things struck Raif about what Angus had just said, and he was silent for a while as he thought. *Or Ash did something that sent everyone running.* The words had been spoken lightly enough, but the idea behind them was hard to comprehend. What could Ash do that would make a full sept, half a dozen dogs, and a sorcerer run away? Raif pressed Ash's body against his. She was breathing steadily, no longer shivering, relaxed in a deep dreamless sleep. Penthero Iss' almost-daughter. As soon as she had told him that, he had assumed they were being hunted because the Surlord of Spire Vanis wanted his daughter back. Now it seemed there was more.

Raif glanced at his uncle. With Angus there was always more.

Then there was the other thing that struck Raif. Twice now Angus had said that sorcery was no good for killing. Yet he, Raif Sevrance, could kill with it. Oh, Angus would say that the arrow killed, not the drawing. But Angus was wrong. Vaingate had proven that. At some point while he'd stood shooting men through the grating, Raif had realized that as soon as a heart was within his sights the man whom it beat for was as good as dead. The arrow was just the medium, like wine carrying poison; the *act* of killing had already been made.

So what did that make him? Raif shook his head slowly, forbidding the answer to come to him. Inigar Stoop knew; perhaps even Angus knew: It was better left at that.

Angus touched Raif's shoulder. "You should get some rest. I'll be waking you at dawn."

Raif nodded. Suddenly he wanted very much to sleep.

"I canna tell you what business brought me to Spire Vanis," Angus said, adjusting the elk coat around Raif and Ash so it let in no drafts. "That city is alive with secrets, it was built on them, and you shouldna blame your old uncle for holding a few of them back."

"And Ille Glaive?" Raif asked, barely able to keep his eyes open.

"Aye. The City of Tears. A man lives there whom I must

visit. He's a tower-trained scholar and as stingy as a goat, but he does have a talent for finding truths. I remember once when I was coursing for gray foxes along the Chaddiway . . ."

Raif drifted into sleep. Perfect darkness folded around him, creating a secure place where no dreams or thoughts could enter. Time passed. Sounds began to niggle at the back of his mind, and he turned restlessly from them. Still they pursued him, louder now, dream voices, egging for something he did not have and could not give. Irritated, he turned from them once more. Couldn't they see that he slept? At last they went, leaving him to a deep stupor that lasted through the night.

When he awoke at first light it was pain, not voices, that stirred him. He was lying on his stomach, and something cold and sharp pressed against his chest. Thinking it was a stone, he reached beneath himself to push it away. As soon as his fingers touched the surface of the object, he knew it was his lore. *Ash* . . .

His eyes shot open and his hand reached upward, but already he knew it was too late. She was cold, motionless, lost to the world of voices.

He called Angus, and together they tried to wake her, but her eyes would not open and her body lay heavy and unresponsive, and finally Angus lifted her onto the bay, strapped her against his back, and set a grim pace for Ille Glaive.

# THIRTY

## *Frostbite*

SARGA VEYS OPENED HIS EYES. Unlike other men who needed time to come around, put the dreamworld behind them and recall the day ahead, Sarga Veys knew all instantly the moment he awoke. He never dreamed. That was one human weakness he was free from.

The timbers above him were black and furry with mold, and the entire ceiling bowed under the weight of accumulated snow. The trout guddler's cabin had not been lived in for at least two seasons, yet the stench of fish and old men remained. Ancient oilcloths, now brittle and dusty, hung from the walls along with snowshoes, rotten nets, and racks for drying fish. The oak floor was crusted with salt. In the far corner, hiding behind cords of rotten firewood and split crates, lay a small basswood shrine to the Maker. Sarga Veys' lip curled to see it. Fishermen, whether they manned trawlers on the Wrecking Sea or sat upon a lakeshore fishing with their hands, were always superstitious about God.

Gathering his strength to him, Sarga Veys raised his shoulders from the floor. Naked beneath the buckskins he had found folded in a pile near the saltpit, his entire body shuddered and worked against him as he moved. Sour liquid rose in his gullet, and he fought it by forcing his lips against his teeth. He would not vomit. Such foulness would not pass from his stomach to his mouth.

After a few seconds the sickness lifted, leaving him feeling little better for it. His head throbbed, and his legs felt swollen and full of water. The smell of his own body disgusted him, the drowned-man's stench of fish oil and algae and fear.

Veys exhaled softly. He very nearly *had* drowned out there, in that greasy body of water so rightly named the Black Spill. The first shock of the cold had been breathtaking. He remembered freezing water seizing his throat and his groin, and utter darkness robbing his thoughts. It had been a kind of hell. Cold hell. The screams, the cracking ice, the horses . . . Veys shuddered. It had made animals of four grown men.

But, he thought. *But.* It had been a trial of ice and darkness that he had passed. Surely now he must be stronger? He, Sarga Veys, son of no man willing to claim him and a mother who had taken her own life by slashing her stomach a dozen times with a jeweler's knife, had swum in the Black Spill in midwinter and *survived*.

He should not have been able to do it. Only minutes before the ice cracked he had spent everything within him opening a corridor in the mist. Such drawings never came cheap. Sarga Veys could do a hundred things more showy and more impressive: little tricks with fire and smoke guaranteed to make children and goodwives fear him. Yet parting mist, which impressed no one, most especially not the Knife, had a cost far above such japery. For five long and excruciating minutes, Sarga Veys had set his will against nature.

It had left him barely enough strength to breathe and think. When the ice cracked and day turned into night and black water rose to take him, he had been as limp and powerless as a man made of straw. Yet fear of death had woken something in him. A tiny spark of hidden strength had ignited close to his heart. It wasn't much, but he was Sarga Veys, the most brilliant sorcerer born in half a century, and he could turn *not much* into quite a lot.

The horse was close to death when he had taken it. Bereft of strength of will, it could do little to fight the drawing. As its insides had kindled and horseflesh had cauterized then cooked, the carcass had floated upward toward the light. Sarga Veys had ridden it to the surface like a wraith riding his ghost horse from hell. The heat from its flesh had warmed him, and the buoyancy of its gas-filled body had been more than sufficient to float his own. Clinging to the black, stinking flesh, he had paddled with his legs and feet toward the nearest ledge.

Raped of power and strength, he had hauled himself onto firm ice. How he had crawled across the lake and up the bank to shelter was an ordeal he would sooner forget. The skin on his elbows and knees would grow back. Chilblains and frost sores would fade. The burns on his hands were another matter, but he had read the secret histories of all the brilliant sorcerers, and such scars and deformities were common among them. All who were born to greatness were marked in some way.

Only when he had found the trout guddler's cabin and stripped the stiff, icy clothing from his back had he given himself over to exhaustion. Judging from the light slicing under the door, he had slept for close to a day.

Overcome with thirst and the sudden need to relieve himself, Veys tested his strength by extending his leg across the salt-encrusted floor. Weakness made him cringe like a child. Hate for Penthero Iss filled him. How dare that man send him north again! His talents were wasted here on the east shore of Black Spill, chasing the Surlord's errant daughter and the Phage's trusty sheepdog Angus Lok.

Anger succeeded in rousing Veys sufficiently to the point where he could stand, and he gathered the coarse hide around himself and stumbled toward the door. Of course, the very fact that Iss had sent him north in a sept with Marafice Eye told of just how important the task of returning Asarhia March was. She was dangerous, that girl. Veys had felt the truth of it the night Iss had summoned him to the Red Forge and bade him travel from the city to find her. Power had been drawn that night. Dark and unfamiliar, it had switched against his skin like a draft of air from a mineshaft or the deepest, driest well. It had come from Iss' almost-daughter, and it excited him in ways he hardly understood.

He had been following its aftermath ever since. It wetted his tongue even now. She was moving north again. He knew it without even probing outside himself, so strong was the trail she left behind.

Reaching the door, Veys steadied himself against the jamb, taking a moment to regain his strength. He cursed the loss of his saddlebags. Drugs, waxed bandages, oil of cloves, blood of the poppy, eyebright, handknives, coiled wire, combs, wax candles, flints, honey, sweetened milk, spare clothes, and clean linen had all been lost. All things except food he could do without, yet he had little liking for making do. A childhood spent living in the filth and glossy mud of Dirtlake had seen to that.

Glancing back at the frozen, greasy heap that was his clothes, he shuddered. The action pulled muscles in his chest and groin. He needed a ghostmeal badly. He craved warm milk thickened with honey and the soothing sap of eyebright dropped from a hollow needle into his eyes. His eyes were not troubling him now, but they would soon enough. Weak eyes prone to redness and infection were his curse. "It is their color," a man in Ille Glaive had once said. "So unusual . . . startling, even. In a woman they would be celebrated, painted. In a man they are considered ill luck. Either way you will have much trouble with them. Purple is the color of the gods."

Not displeased by the memory, Veys unhooked the latch and stepped outside.

Cold air blasted his face, and the sharp tang of snow filled his nose and his mouth. A white landscape presented itself to his watering eyes. He saw the lake down below him, cloaked in mist, saw tall spruces and white oaks glittering with hoar-frost, and his own bloody trail stamped into the snow. He had not come as far as he'd thought. The trout guddler's cabin was a mere forty paces from the water, set in a crown of man-high birches above the bank. Veys shrugged tightly. He told himself the distance hardly mattered; it did not de-tract from his feat.

Out of the corner of his eye he caught a movement. In-stinctively he stepped back, into the shadows provided by the door. Shifting his gaze to the left, he saw the movement again. There, down by the shore, something gray moved. Sarga Veys licked dry lips. It was a man . . . no, *two* men. One lying down on the shore ice, another kneeling, tending him. Veys' stomach twisted into a knot. The kneeling man's outer cloak wasn't gray . . . it was black leather crusted with snow. The Rive Watch. He had thought he was rid of them.

A long moment passed where Veys contemplated the shore-fast ice, speculated how thick it was and whether there would be sufficient water underneath to drown two men. Yet ice was a mystery he knew little of, and he set aside the idea of murder before it was fully formed.

"Halfman! Over here!"

Startled, Veys focused his gaze upon the kneeling man. He had his hand raised over his head, and Veys saw immedi-ately that something wasn't right with it. Two bloody stumps waggled where fingers should have been. Perceiving the weakness made Veys' heart beat more calmly, and he stepped from the shadows into the light.

The man's name came to him as he treaded through the snow toward the bank. Hood. A filthy guardsman with dirt under his nails and shredded food between his teeth, who claimed kinship to Lord of the Straw Granges and as proof wore a grangelord insignia—arms set in a cruciform—at his chest. Veys detested him. He was Marafice Eye's creature—all the sept were—but he more so than the rest. He could not open his mouth without speaking filth.

"Help me get him to the cabin. His foot is hard froze."

Veys paid little heed to Hood's words as he picked his way across the rutted and frozen mud along the shore. He now had a better view of the second man, and his heart had started beating wildly once more. The huge head, the fine light brown hair, and the shoulders the size of sheep: It was Marafice Eye. Sarga Veys' skin paled. He had thought the Knife dead, lost to the black waters of the Spill.

"Aye, Halfman. You left me to the devil, and the devil spat me back." A small eye, perfectly blue, regarded Sarga Veys with something akin to satisfaction. The Knife was lying on his side, half on the bank, half on the ice. The skin on his face was yellow and waxy, his cheeks and nose split by tissue expanding as it froze. Strips of flesh hung from his small mouth, flapping as he breathed and spoke. One eye was frozen shut. One hand was curled like a bird's claw, yellow and scaly and twitching. The frozen foot was still booted, resting on the ice like a shovel.

Marafice Eye smiled, a terrible sight to see on a frozen face. "You may well look frightened, Halfman. I saw you with Stagro's horse. I clawed after you in the water, watched as you pulled yourself onto the ice."

"I looked for you, but the ice was churning. It was impossible to see—"

"Save your lies for those who need them, Halfman."

Marafice Eye winced as Hood began to cut the boot free of the frozen foot. "The only thing that matters to me is whether you acted from cowardice or spite. Did you wish me dead, eh? Or were you so involved with saving your own skin that you didn't give me or my men a second thought?"

Veys shifted ground. He saw Hood slow down with the sheath knife, awaiting his reply. Marafice Eye breathed steadily, good hand clenched to control the pain. Two men, both injured but still dangerous. Veys swallowed bile then spoke. "I do not wish you dead, Knife. You cannot doubt that. The ice was not under my control. It was the girl's fault it broke . . . she led us too far. Her horse was more lightly burdened, and it knew how to dance. When I fell into the water I had no mind but to get to safety. I was hardly thinking. . . . Stagro's horse was close . . . I did what I had to. By the time I crawled from the water I had no strength for anything else."

"Yet you made it to the cabin," said the Knife.

"And stripped the frozen clothes from your back," added Hood.

"I did these things without thinking. I—"

"Hush, man. You bother me like jiggers at my crotch. You claim to be a coward, not a murderer. Then you must prove that by using your foul magics upon me. I will not lose my foot and my hand. I will not. You will save them for me."

"But—"

The Knife slammed his good hand onto the ice. "I saw how you were with the horse. You took its flesh and warmed it. Now you must do the same for me, only gently, without scorching. Hood will stand by. He will see you do no harm."

Hood smiled pleasantly, displaying filaments of trail meat packed between his teeth. "Devil help you if you hurt him, Halfman."

Veys actually took a step back. To perform a healing—on the *Knife*. The idea was horrifying to him. He was not a physician, he had not been trained in the ways of blood and organs as some sorcerers were. Sickness and disease were abhorrent to him. Marafice Eye's yellow swollen flesh repulsed him as surely as the sight of maggots at a corpse. And then there was the loss of strength. How could he be expected to draw power after all that had happened yesterday? He needed to rest, sleep.

"Come. You must help Hood carry me to the cabin."

"I cannot heal you. It's impossible. Impossible."

Marafice Eye shook his head. The strain cost him dearly, pulling tissue and ligaments that should not have been pulled. "Nay, Halfman, I'm not giving you a choice. Four of my best men have died. One with an arrow in his liver, another with a blade-sized hole in his heart. The other two died here"—he punched the lake ice with his fist—"in the Spill. And if you'd had the balls, you could have saved them. Mind me well, Sarga Veys, for I know the blackness in your heart.

You meant to walk free from this place, travel back to Spire Vanis and your master Penthero Iss, spin a tale with you as the hero and me and my men as victims of the lake. That will never happen. Hood may have lost two fingers, but he's still a better man with eight than you are with ten. He'd kill you now on my say, and do not think I'm not tempted. Your only use to me now is as a healer. So heal me, and perhaps Hood will forget the loss of his sworn brothers and let you live."

Veys looked into the Knife's open eye. Even lying prostrate on the ice, he was a dangerous beast. Veys believed him capable of any sort of violence, and he was just the sort of man to survive if abandoned in this frozen waste. *He pulled himself free of the lake!* That act alone told of the strength of his will.

"Ready to weep, Halfman?"

Veys glared at Hood and had the satisfaction of forcing the thick-necked badger of a man to look away. This was not the first time one of the sept had passed comment on his red and stinging eyes. Savagely he wiped away the tears. "Let's get him to the cabin."

The Knife said nothing as they carried him up the bank. Hood took most of the weight, and Veys was left to haul the legs and feet. It was a difficult journey and Marafice Eye must have suffered much in the handling, yet he did not cry out or curse or show any but the briefest signs of pain. Veys supposed some men would call such stoicism bravery, but he had little care for it. Dread of the task that lay ahead weighed like lead upon his chest.

When finally they arrived at the trout guddler's cabin, Veys became aware of a new pressure pushing against his mind with the steady throb of a sore tooth. "Take him inside," he said to Hood, "and strip him. Pry up the floorboards for firewood. We will need a quick fire."

"Don't settle yourself by the door, Halfman. You're coming with us." Hood dragged Marafice Eye across the threshold. The Knife himself did not speak. Perhaps delirium had set in. Veys hardly cared.

"My master calls me. I must speak with him."

The words had a profound effect on Hood, who like all the barbarians in the Rive Watch feared sorcery like the Skinned

One himself. His hand rose to touch the grangelord insignia at his breast, and he muttered the Maker's given name under his breath.

"Go," hissed Veys, pleased by the man's superstitious dread and well aware that it would do him no harm to play to it. "You would not want to risk standing here when his fetch appears before me."

Hood worked the latch quickly for a man with eight fingers. In his haste he trapped his cloak tails in the door, and Veys heard a tearing sound come from the other side as the man decided it was better to lose a fistful of leather than re-open the door and risk seeing a fetch.

Veys smiled with spite. Fetches, wraiths, scantlings: They were always good for scaring children and witless men.

The smile faded as quickly as it came as Veys steadied himself against the cabin's exterior wall and laid himself open to the one who called him.

Shock and pain took his breath. Penthero Iss was there, suddenly inside him like a new heart. Every hair on Veys' body bristled, every pore opened and exuded sweat. How could he do such a thing? The power it took to perform such a drawing from such a distance was unthinkable. This wasn't simply far-speaking, this was the breaching of another's flesh. And then there was the threat of the backlash. True, he had invited Iss in, but the mind and the body did not always work together in matters of sorcery, and the instinct to protect oneself was greater than any given thought. What if the drawing snapped?

*Calm yourself, Sarga Veys. Did I not tell you that I would speak with you along the way?*

Veys shuddered so deeply bones cracked in his spine. Fear burned with a pure and fierce flame, like alcohol igniting on his skin. *What do you ask of me?*

*Is Asarhia with you?*

*No. She travels north to Ille Glaive. The Knife tried to take her yesterday on the lake, but the ice broke beneath us and she escaped.*

*And the sept?*

*The sept is gone. The Knife suffers from frostbite; Hood has lost fingers on his swordhand. The rest are dead.* It did not occur to Veys to lie. Iss was inside him; what else could he do?

*I will send another sept to you. Make your way to Ille Glaive and await them there.*

*But we must return to Spire Vanis. The Knife needs—*

*See to him, Sarga Veys. That is why you are there. Asarhia must be followed north. She must be brought back. Angus Lok's family lives near Ille Glaive; he will not pass that close without seeing them. Find them for me also.*

Veys knew he could not argue. Penthero Iss seemed so much *more* than he was. His power was potent, foreign. It tasted of another world.

*Do not fail me.* The words stretched southward across a continent as Iss withdrew to Spire Vanis and the craven warmth of his flesh.

Veys slumped against the cabin wall, his shoulders scraping the skin of rime ice from the timbers. The vestiges of Iss' drawing had left a gritty film in his mouth, but he did not like to spit, so he swallowed it instead. How did Iss get the power? He was a weakling; Veys had known that from the day they'd first met, when a discreet and gentle probing had told him all he needed to know. Now this.

Running a hand across his jaw, Veys worked to calm himself. A day's growth of beard made his mouth shrink in distaste.

"Get in here, Halfman!"

Hood's call made Veys flinch. Taking a series of fast, shallow breaths, he pushed himself off from the wall and made his way inside the cabin. Marafice Eye waited there, his foot made yellow by frozen bile, the chilblained skin on his face shedding in strips as wet and slippery as vegetable scrapings. Veys gathered power to himself, fear leaving him as quickly as fear *did* leave a man who was angry and eager to prove himself to those who considered themselves his betters. So Hood would kill him if he failed, eh? Well, who was to say that one day Hood wouldn't wake to find his remaining eight fingers gone the way of the other two? And who was to say that one day Penthero Iss wouldn't wake to find his *own* body invaded and the secret source of power he tapped into taken over by a better man than himself?

Such thoughts stayed in Veys' mind only long enough to calm him. He had a job to do, and although he hated Marafice Eye with bright malice, his pride demanded that he perform no drawing that wasn't equal to his best.

Suppressing a shudder of revulsion, Veys entered the frozen canals of the Knife's frostbitten flesh.

## THIRTY-ONE

### *Ille Glaive*

RAIF RECOGNIZED THE DHOONESMEN at five hundred paces. War dressed in the blue and copper of Dhoone, mounted on fully laden shire horses, spears so highly polished they shone like glass, they rode south along the Glaive Road, forcing farmers and cart boys from their path. Two men only, there were, yet they had a power to them that drew the eyes as surely as a mountain made of steel. They sat high in their saddles, backs straight, eyes forward, left hands on the shafts of their couched spears, blue tattoos pulsing like veins beneath their Dhoonehelms.

Angus said something, perhaps a warning to keep eyes down as the Dhoonesmen approached, but Raif had no mind for it.

*Clansmen, here in the Glaivehold.* Without thinking, Raif reached behind his neck to the leather strip that held his hair. The Blackhail silver was long gone. Even the black thread on his elkskin coat now lay concealed beneath a layer of muck. All he had left to tell of his clan was the silver cap that sealed his measure of guidestone in his tine, and the bit of silver wire around the grip of Tem's sword. Soon even his hair would outgrow his clan. Hailsmen kept their hair shortest of all clans, scorning the intricate plaitings, braidings, oilings, and part shavings that were as much a part of the clanholds as the white heather that bloomed on the fellfields each spring.

"Raif. Ease to the side of the road and let them pass."

Out of the corner of his eye, Raif was aware of Angus pulling the bay's reins and setting the Sull horse on a path to lead its riders from the road. *So even Angus makes way for Dhoonesmen.* The thought made something ache in Raif's chest.

The heavy-shod hooves of the shire horses set the packed-earth road ringing. The late afternoon sun shone directly onto the Dhoonesmen's faces as they rode toward Raif at a trot. Raif saw their eyes flick to him, then just as quickly flick away. Even though Raif held the center of the road, they made no motion to alter their path and continued to head straight for him as if he were nothing more than a speck of dust.

Abruptly Raif kicked Moose into a turn and headed off the road. Even before horse and rider gained the ditch, the Dhoonesmen claimed the space they'd left behind. Heads held high, never once looking back, the Dhoonesmen continued south.

Minutes passed. Flecks of gray snow kicked up by the Dhoonesmen floated back down to earth. Raif could feel Angus' gaze upon him, yet he did not turn to look at him, even when his uncle spoke. "Let's head back onto the road. I want to reach the Glaive before dark."

Raif breathed and breathed, and after a while he nodded. After turning Moose out of the ditch, he took the road ahead of Angus, deliberately setting a pace that would keep him well ahead of the twice laden bay.

He had been less than nothing to the Dhoonesmen.

Raif bound Moose's reins around his fist as he rode the winding curves and humpbacks of the Glaive Road. The Spill lay below him, its oily surface turned the color of bird blood by the first real sun to shine in days. Farms, mills, smokehouses, stoveshouses, broken watch towers and fortifications, and crannogs extending out over the lake on stilts, all lay within a short distance of the road. Other people traveled the road, mostly carters, drovers, and market traders, but occasionally a fine lady dressed in scarlet velvet and sables, accompanied by her men-at-arms, or a pair of Forsworn knights, wearing iron scale gleaming with bone oil, cloth-of-skin cloaks, and the thorned collars known as the Penance, would pass by or overtake them.

Raif paid them little heed. Angus shouted ahead, informing him that the city itself would likely come into view any moment, yet Raif made no effort to search for it. The blank, disinterested gazes of the Dhoonesmen filled his sights. He wasn't one of them now. Somehow, though his clothes hadn't changed and his hair had barely grown, the weeks spent with Angus had changed him. A month ago the Dhoonesmen would have hailed him, asked what news he had of Dhoone yearmen fostered at Blackhail, what lakes had frozen on the Hailhold, what he was doing so far from home, did he need help or food or company. They would have seen him as one of their own. Instead they had seen nothing but a man on a horse who had no status or due respect in their world.

Raif breathed heavily. With an effort he loosened his grip on Moose's reins and set his mind elsewhere. Lowering himself in the saddle, he concentrated on guiding the gelding up the steep slope to the headlands that lay high above the lake.

The surface of the road was especially bad on the incline, and mud broke away in frozen clumps as Moose searched for hoof holds in the ice. Five hours' worth of sunlight had melted parts of the surface, and Raif's gaze had settled upon a particularly treacherous-looking ditch filled with loose stones and wet ice, when Angus whistled softly at his back. Straightaway Raif looked up.

Ille Glaive rose before him like a cliff of golden light. He saw stone walls and slate rooftops and needle-thin towers, all transformed in the sunset to gleaming metal things. A thousand tear-shaped windows collected shadows the color of dark amber, and a network of bridges, ledges, and battlements glinted like human spines dipped into gold. At the foot of the southern wall, the lake reflected a smaller, smoky version of the city, a mirror image seen through old glass.

As Moose topped the slope, Raif studied the lakeshore, wondering how many men it took to break and clear the ice. Then he noticed the steam and bubbling water forming a stewpot along the bank.

"Natural springs," Angus said, pulling alongside him. "Ille Glaive was built on them. They feed the lake year-round."

Raif nodded. Following his trip to Spire Vanis he had no love of cities, yet he couldn't help but admire Ille Glaive's golden sandstone walls. Savagely he scratched the scars on his chest. The skin was fully healed now, but the ghosts of the Bluddsmen's swords would not leave him. Two mornings ago he'd awoken to find dried blood driven deep beneath his fingernails and the scars scratched raw and peeling.

"I think we'll take the beggar's entrance," Angus said, squinting ahead. "We should be safe going through the market at this hour." Making a small movement to indicate Ash, who was riding at his back, he added, "The sooner we get our wee lassie here to Heritas Cant, the better."

Raif made no reply. Cities were Angus' affair. It was up to him to say how they entered and where they stayed. As long as Ash was seen to quickly, little else mattered to him.

Glancing over, he saw she was still the same. She sat, slumped against Angus' back, her eyes closed, her eyelids pale and unmoving, her hair pressed flat where it rested against Angus' shoulders, and her small pink mouth open just enough to let in air. She had not spoken since the night by the white oaks. Both Raif and Angus had tried to wake her many times in the past four days, yet although her body seemed to respond, sometimes cringing or pulling away from a harsh or unpleasant touch, her eyes seldom opened. Angus had taken great pains to force her to drink, holding her jaw apart and pouring clear broth or water down her throat. Yet he could not make her eat.

Sometimes, as this morning before they'd broken camp, she became agitated and her arms would slowly rise from her sides. Whenever that happened, Angus would force her wrists behind her back and bind them together with sheepskin, hobbling her as if she were a dangerous horse. Sometimes he wadded shammies in his fist and thrust them so deeply into her mouth that they rested against the back of her throat. Raif hated to see it. What within her was so terrible that she had to be bound and gagged?

Running a hand over his week-old beard, Raif frowned. Even now, when he wasn't looking at her and they were separated by twelve paces of air, he was aware of her presence pushing against him. Always he felt her in his lore. Somehow she pushed herself into his mind, claiming space that belonged to Drey and Effie and Tem.

With a violent shake of his head, Raif stopped his thoughts from moving farther past that point. Last night, when he had taken a damp cloth from the fire and cleaned the road grime from Ash's face, Angus had said, "You treat her as gently as if she were Effie." Raif had had to stop what he was doing and walk into the shadows beyond the fire. Asarhia March was no Effie, and he hated Angus for putting them in the same sentence and linking them. He looked after Ash because that was what he and Angus had done since the moment they had saved her at Vaingate. It was a necessary thing, like brushing down the horses and lighting a drying fire for their clothes each night. Ash was not kin. She would never replace Effie or Drey in his heart.

Yet she *had* told him the truth. While Angus had danced around the truth like a clan guide around the Gods Night fires, she had told him who she was. *That* he valued. That was an action worthy of a clanswoman.

"Hold the reins a nonce, Raif, while I see to our drunken lassie here." Copper eyes twinkling, Angus handed the bay's reins to Raif and then busied himself with other things. Yesterday morning he had made Raif wait with Ash in the cover of a grove of sister aspens while he'd visited a farmhouse set a quarter league off the road. An hour later he had returned bearing fresh food, new waterskins, an ancient and crusty leather saddlebag, a pail of fresh milk, and a newly fattened rabbit flask, filled to the cork with the sort of stinging birch alcohol that Angus had a taste for. He took the rabbit flask from his buckskins now, bit the cork free, and began anointing Ash's head and shoulders with droplets of clear alcohol.

"If anyone asks, she had a skinful at nooning."

Raif nodded. Ash's breaths were very shallow now, and her lack of response to the icy drops of liquid worried him. Glancing ahead, he judged the time it would take them to reach the city. "Will this man we're going to see be able to help her?"

Angus thumped the cork on the flask, then motioned for Raif to hand back the reins. "Heritas Cant knows many things: storm lore, the true names of all the gods, how to read the secret language of prophecies and speak the Old Tongue of the Trappers and the Sull. He can bind hawks to fly on his bidding, recite lists of battles from the Time of Shadows, heal sicknesses of blood and mind, and find patterns in the stars. If anyone can help her, he can."

"Is he a magic user?"

Angus sucked in breath with a small hiss. "He will do whatever he must."

Unable to decide what sort of answer that was and in no mood to dance lies and truth with Angus, Raif let the matter drop. Fixing his gaze firmly ahead, he set his mind to contemplating Ille Glaive. The city was set at the head of a narrow plain. Furrow lines in the snow, tarred-log farmhouses, and trails of blue woodsmoke told that the surrounding land was used mostly for crops. A sparse forest, heavily logged, reached westward around the farmland, and the low craggy peaks of the Bitter Hills stretched northeast into the Bannen, Ganmiddich, and Croser clanholds.

Now that the brilliant light of sunset had faded, Ille Glaive looked older, smaller, and less glorious than it had when Raif had first seen it. Where Spire Vanis had the hard lines, white mortar, and precision-cut stones of a young city built by a single generation of masons, Ille Glaive had the layered, worn, disorderly look of something built over centuries by many different hands. Unlike Spire Vanis, Ille Glaive did not live solely within its walls, and pothouses, stables, barracks, covered markets, pieces of freestanding stonework, broken arches, and lightning-cracked towers spilled from the split skin of its east wall.

Angus guided the bay from the road and headed toward the clutter of buildings and markets. Raif smelled woodsmoke and scorched fat, and then the faintly sulfurous odor of hot springs. The wind carried broken bits of sound: a baby crying, meat sizzling on a grill, a pair of dogs scrapping, and the hiss and clang of water forced through pipes. As they approached the first line of buildings, Angus motioned for Raif to dismount. Angus had scraped the oil and wax from his face with the blunt edge of his knife and now began to unravel the leather jesses around his ears.

Snow was light on the ground, and Raif found walking a relief. He understood why Angus wanted him on foot: Two armed men on horseback drew looks. Discreetly he slid the scabbard containing Tem's sword along his belt, tucking it into the shadows of his coat. He didn't need Angus to tell him to avoid everyone's eyes, and he saw little save the boot leather of the first few people he passed.

Angus led them through the market, tracing a fox's path of quick turns and sudden stops. Timber stalls, roofed with hide or woven spruce branches, reminded Raif of the clan markets held on the Dhoonehold each spring. Many of the same items were for sale: handknives with carved boxwood handles, dried fishskins for bow backing, grouse feathers already bound and cut for fletchings, archers' thumb rings, horn bracelets set with Blackhail silver, pots of beeswax, neat's-foot oil and bright yellow tung oil imported in birds' craniums all the way from the Far South, lynx pelts and sea otter pelts, brilliantly colored leathers from a city called Leiss, amber beads threaded on caribou sinew, shimmering purple silks from Hanatta, blue mussels, dried mushrooms, green seal meat, pickled sweetbreads, whole eider ducks, wheels of marbled yellow cheese, warm beer thickened with eggs, hot sausages stuffed with unknowable meats, and fat white onions roasted until they were black.

Raif's mouth watered. Food had been sparse and cold for the last three days. Angus showed only passing interest in the food and continued weaving through the aisles in the manner of a man strolling idly through a market. "Here they come," Angus said under his breath. "Don't look up. I'll do the talking."

Raif, who had been looking longingly at a roasted leg of lamb crusted with white pepper and thyme, had no idea who *they* were. Slowing down to match Angus' pace, he found something of interest to stare at on the toe of his boot.

Footsteps, two pairs of them, pounded against the hard-froze mud. Raif heard the dull ring of metal, thinly couched, then watched as the tip of a knotted willow stick was jabbed at the bay's coffin bone.

"What 'ave we here, Fat Bollick?" came a low, rasping voice.

"Newcomers, Nouse. Poor if ye look to their clothes, rich if ye ken their horses."

Raif glanced up. Two men wearing the white of Ille Glaive with the black, red, and steel tears at their breast stood at the bay's head. Nouse, the man with the stick, had the small eyes and shiny black head of a magpie. Fat Bollick had the plumped-up wrinkly look of fingertips soaked too long in water.

Angus addressed himself to Nouse. "Good eve to you, gentlemen. If the Master cares for tribute, then he'll gladly let us pass." Somehow, despite both his hands resting on the reins in plain view, Angus managed to generate the sound of coins clicking together as he spoke.

"The Master don't need no tribute," Fat Bollick said. "He takes it simply because he can."

Inclining his head, Angus once again addressed his words to Nouse. "Naturally I didn't mean to imply that the Master has need of funds. I just want it to be known that my purse is overheavy, and I would count a favor in its lightening."

Nouse's eyes narrowed as he stroked the oily plumage of his beard. "What d'you ken, Fat Bollick?"

Fat Bollick shrugged. "The man speaks with respect, and I'd be inclined to lighten his purse and let him pass. Though I must say the girl at his back worries me. We wouldn't want no foreign fevers brought into the Glaive."

Angus glanced over his shoulder at Ash. "Her? Fevered? I wish it were so. She's as soaked as a brewer's rag . . . and Maker help me if my lady wife ever hears about it, for she's handy with her skinning knife and well inclined to use it."

Nouse prodded Ash sharply with his stick. "Potted, you say?"

"Aye." Angus' voice was level, but Raif saw how his knuckles whitened around the reins.

"She smells like it," Fat Bollick said. "I say we take the Master's tribute and let 'em pass."

Nouse's sharp little eyes narrowed as he looked at Angus. "I've seen you here afore."

"Aye, and you'll likely see me again. And each time you do, you and the Master will end up a wee bit richer for it." Angus peeled his hand from the reins and reached inside his coat for his purse. It was the size of a sheep's bladder and bunched full with coins. He threw it, not gently, at Nouse, who caught it like a punch to his chest. "Now, if you gentlemen will excuse me, I have a daughter in need of sobering, an apprentice in need of a wenching, and my own handsome face in need of a good shave and some wifely fussing." With that Angus kicked the bay's flanks and started forward. "Kindly give my regards to the Master."

The willow stick twitched in Nouse's left hand as he weighed the purse with his right. Fat Bollick made eye signals to him. Nouse's gaze dropped to the purse. Finally he cracked his stick on the bay's flank. "Aye, go on then. Pass. Me and Fat Bollick will be watching ye. Piss too high against a wall and we'll know it."

Raif led Moose past the two men-at-arms, his gaze carefully avoiding Nouse. He didn't know what to make of the exchange among the three men. The Master of Ille Glaive ruled the cityhold from the Lake Keep, and Angus said he was more a king than the Surlord of Spire Vanis, as the title of Master was passed from father to son. *Threavish Cutler likes to call himself the King on the Lake*, Angus had said just that morning as the trail they traveled joined the Glaive Road. *And his sons and sworn men call themselves thanelords. Mark my words, one of these days old Threavish is going to take all the gold he's collected in tributes, melt it in a pot, and forge himself a crown. A big one, mind, one large enough to cover his swollen head.*

"That was easy enough," Angus said once they were out of earshot of Nouse and Fat Bollick. "Cost me my purse *and* saddle last time."

Annoyed at Angus' humor, Raif said, "I wouldn't have given them anything."

Angus sighed, not heavily. "Lad, you have a lot to learn. Those two practitioners were playing a well-turned tune. They knew we wanted to slip into the city unnoticed; we'd have gone the way of Shallow Gate otherwise. They simply made us pay for the privilege."

Raif made no reply. He was pretty sure the tune would have changed in an instant if Nouse had prodded Ash a fraction harder with his stick. "Let's get Ash somewhere safe."

Angus gave him a hard look. "You're going to have to get used to the way things are done in cities, Raif, like it or not. Stove laws, rights of passage, due respect: They all vanish quicker than snow on a grate the minute you leave the clanholds. Don't think those two Dhoonesmen who forced us from the road did any different. Their tribute alone will have been enough to keep Fat Bollick in beer and sausage for a week."

Heat came to Raif's face. "They would have taken the gate."

"Would they now? Two clansmen armed to the jaws?" Angus shook his head for a long time. "No gatekeeper worth his rations would let a pair of war-dressed Dhoonesmen in the city, not the way the clanholds are at the moment. Nay, laddie. Nouse and Fat Bollick would have taken them for a grand sum."

Raif pulled far ahead of Angus, not wanting to hear any more. All the earlier shame he had felt from being overlooked by the Dhoonesmen came back, causing hard knots in his chest. He was so close to the clanholds . . . a day's hard ride would take him into Ganmiddich territory. It was said that Crab Ganmiddich, the Ganmiddich chief, could row out to his island in the Wolf River that was known as the Inch, climb the watch tower there, and see the lights of Ille Glaive at night. Raif raised his chin and looked north. The sky above the Bitter Hills was already black and full of stars.

"Through the arch, Raif."

Acknowledging Angus' direction with a curt nod, Raif led Moose through a timber-supported cleft in the wall and entered the city of Ille Glaive. The light level dropped immediately, turning late sunset into darkest night. Raif paid scant attention to his surroundings, heeding only the directions Angus gave at irregular intervals regarding turns and crossings and places to be avoided. Ille Glaive was old, *old*. It smelled of passing centuries, mildew, butchered carcasses, and slowly rotting things. Roads were cobbled and seldom straight. Sandstone buildings were worn, crumbling, propped up by massive bloodwood stangs, and leaking smoke and lamplight from a thousand cracks and chinks. Mazes of hog-backed bridges connected battlements to ring towers and stone barracks, and far to the west the leadcapped domes of the Lake Keep caught the last of the sun's red light.

Raif had little mind for any of it. The only thing that drew his attention was the figure hunched at Angus' back. Ash's breathing grew heavier as they made their way along streets no wider than two pigs. When Raif drew close he heard air scraping through her throat. After a time Angus halted and hobbled her arms with rope. He said nothing to Raif, but his face was grave and his movements were hard on himself and the bay. When they started up again, Ash's wrists strained against the sheepskin tethers, sawing back and forth until the skin began to redden and break. Raif quickened his pace.

"Here. Through the iron gate."

The sound of Angus' voice pulled Raif's mind only so far away from Ash. He barely noticed the stone wall and the gated archway they had arrived at, and he dealt clumsily with the heavy bolt and chain on the gate, making much noise. A dimly lit courtyard lay beyond. A narrow three-storied manse, its stonework hidden by the hard clay of five hundred years of bird droppings and a rack of dead vines, commanded the fourth wall. The manse's windows were tightly shuttered, and its door was banded with cords of iron that were, Raif noticed, the only thing in sight that looked to be well tended. Angus bade Raif go forward and knock on the door while he dismounted and saw to Ash.

Raif held his raven lore in his fist as he thumped the wood. He didn't like the enclosed space of the courtyard.

The door opened silently, gliding on well-oiled hinges. Momentarily dazzled by the sour light of a goose-fat lantern, Raif took a step back, his hand dropping automatically to Tem's sword. A moment later he made out the slight, bow-shouldered form of a very old woman. Robed in dark blue wool with a cap of coarse netting pinned against her scalp, she reminded Raif of the clan dowagers who always dressed plainly when washing the dead. Her cataract-stained gaze traveled from Raif's face to the hilt of his sword. Immediately feeling foolish, Raif snapped his hand away.

"Cloistress Gannet." Angus pushed past Raif and nodded curtly to the old woman. Ash was pressed close against his chest.

"It's been forty years since I last rendered souls in a cloister, Angus Lok. I have no claim to any title you give me." The old woman's voice was dry and hard. The hand that held the lamp did not shake. "Come, enter. I see you have brought a sick birdie for the master."

The cloistress led them along a dark corridor toward the back of the house, then showed them into a room where a fire burned with tired red flames. Angus laid Ash on a rug near the fire. Raif knelt by the hearth and warmed his hands before he touched her. He did not hear the cloistress leave.

"What is this? What is this?" A twisted creature with misshapen legs and too many bones in his chest walked into the room with the aid of two sticks. *Click, click, click.* Sharp green eyes assessed Raif in less then an instant, then moved swiftly to Angus and Ash. A bone grown high in the man's shoulder twitched. "I am not in the business of receiving visitors after dark. Warm yourselves, then begone. You shall get no more fire out of me."

"Heritas, this is my nephew Raif Sevrance." Angus spoke in a voice Raif had never heard before, stilted and full of emphasis.

Levering his body around, Heritas Cant adjusted the curve of his neck and fixed Raif with a hard stare. Uncomfortable, Raif looked away. His gaze rested on Heritas Cant's pale, bone-filled hand. The knuckles were out of alignment. Two had twisted around completely and now faced downward along with his palm.

As he straightened up, Raif caught the end of a look passed between Angus and Heritas Cant, a message-filled look, where the crippled man looked grim and Angus appealed to him like a puppy who had dug up some piece of nastiness from the garden and brought it into the house.

"I suppose you'll be wanting supper?" Cant said, each word a little stab with a knife. "And this late, too. You won't get anything hot, mind. I won't have the oven fired for a ranger, a clansman, and a sick bit of a girl. You'll have to make do with cold mutton, thinly sliced, and such crusts as I could not eat myself. *Woman!*"

The cloistress appeared in the doorway.

"Supper for these people. Light no extra tallow and serve them only with the third best bowls."

The cloistress said nothing, merely inclined her head.

"And watch your own trips as you go, woman. Come here but once to bring the food, then not again. I will not have the carpet worn by undue steppings." Heritas Cant turned to Raif. "Nor will I have the heat from the fire hogged by just one man."

Raif pressed his lips to a line and moved a few paces from the fire. He didn't like this petty little man.

Cant clicked his sticks on the plank floor as soon as the cloistress was gone. "So you've brought me something sick to look at, Angus Lok. I trust she is not fevered, for I'll have no catching sickness in my house." As he spoke, he labored across the room, making his way toward Ash. His movements reminded Raif of an aging black bear that Drey had shot at distance one summer in the Oldwood. Drey's arrow had found the bear's lower spine, and the creature had lurched into the undergrowth before either he or Drey had chance to kill it.

To cover up the awkwardness of Heritas bending to tend to Ash, Angus spoke. "Heritas is treasurer of all monies levered from the Old Sull Gate."

Heritas blasted air through his nostrils. "And they give me nothing but a copper on the crow-weight for my troubles. More gold rubs off in the gatekeepers' pockets in a single afternoon than I see in a whole month of counting coin." Heritas Cant's good hand traveled along Ash's body as he spoke, pressing the base of her throat, the hollows beneath her eyes, her stomach, and the muscles in her shoulders and sides.

Raif feigned interest in the topic of conversation, though in truth all he was concerned with was watching Heritas Cant's hands on Ash. "Why is it called the Old Sull Gate?"

"Because that's what it's always been known as." Heritas Cant slipped something between Ash's lips, something dark and brittle like a dried leaf. "Master Threavish Cutler would have it otherwise; he's tried calling it King's Gate, Lake Gate, and even Heron Gate, after his damn fool of a brother who died in waist-deep snow battling a dozen Crosermen on disputed ground. Cutler's aim, besides appeasing his own undeniable grief, was to make everyone forget that this city once belonged to the Sull."

"But I thought—"

"You thought what?" Heritas Cant sent Raif a withering look and then answered his own question. "That Ille Glaive has always counted itself one of the Mountain Cities? That the Sull have always lived in their forests in the east and never built anything more ambitious than a stone redoubt and a ring of cairns? No. The Sull were the first to cross the Ranges and settle the Northern Territories. Before the clans and the driven ranks marched north, the Sull came here, to the shores of the Black Spill, and built a fine city around the springs. That city still stands today if one cares to look. It exists at the base of old buildings, beneath thickly worked plaster and hastily laid tiles. Aboveground there is nothing—the towers, statues, and earthwork have all gone, systematically wrecked by a long line of Threavish Cutler's ilk—but belowground, at the heart of Ille Glaive, lie Sull foundations, Sull tunnels, and Sull stone."

Raif didn't care for Heritas Cant's tone of voice. If the man hadn't been a cripple, he would have dearly liked to hit him. For Ash's sake, he made an effort. "So the lords of Ille Glaive forced the Sull from the city?"

Heritas Cant took his left hand from Ash's stomach and massaged the misshapen hump of bones that was his right wrist. "Yes and no. A siege took place, many battles were fought, but in the end the thanelords of Ille Glaive earned their tears' worth of Sull blood cheaply. The Sull have demons that are not of man's making. They fought for this city and would have held it if they hadn't had older, more pressing battles to win. They as good as gave this city to the thanelords and their leader, Dunness Fey . . . and it wasn't the first time such a gain has been made at the Sull's expense. Yet we should all pray that it be the last."

Raif felt his face burn as Heritas spoke. He was angry, but

there was something more here. Almost against his will, Raif's hand moved to touch his raven lore. Heritas Cant's sharp green eyes caught the action even as Raif stopped himself short.

"What is your lore?"

It was a rude question, and Heritas Cant knew it. When a clansman met someone from another clan, he would never ask him outright about his lore. That sort of knowledge always came secondhand. Raif considered not answering. Heritas Cant was something unknown; just because Angus trusted him didn't mean that *he* should. Yet something else struck him about the small, broken man: He had known Raif was a clansman. Angus had not introduced him as such, and Raif knew his clothes and ornaments no longer proclaimed him as clan—the Dhoonesmen's indifference on the Glaive Road had told him that. So, did Heritas Cant know him as clan because he'd seized upon something subtle like his accent or his manner, or had Angus discussed his sister's family in this house once before? Either way Raif found little reassurance. He glanced at Cant. The man's shrewd, pain-sculpted face glowed like polished wood in the firelight.

"I am raven born," Raif said.

"Watcher of the Dead." Cant clicked his sticks. " 'Tis a hard lore. It will drive you fierce and use your flesh and leave you little but loss in payment."

Raif did not move; he neither blinked nor breathed nor trembled. The words felt like a sentence, and it seemed all he could do was stand and accept them. The same nameless fear he'd felt moments earlier when Cant spoke about the Sull filled his chest.

Angus shifted his weight, causing a board to creak beneath him. "Come now, Heritas. You need not be so bleak. Ravens are clever beasties. They're the only birds who can live out a full winter in the Want. Strong, they are, with wings like knives and voices to match. True, they're not the prettiest creatures, but if the clan guide gave out lores on looks alone, we'd all be kittens and doe-eyed . . . *does*."

Heritas Cant had stretched his dead hand upon Ash's forehead as Angus spoke. Now he arranged the twisted fingers with his good hand, spreading them wide, into her hair, over the bridge of her nose, and across her eyebrows. "True enough," he said as he worked. "The raven is a clever bird. It favors shadows and waits upon death."

With those words Cant changed, becoming for a moment something else, as if a heavy substance, like molten rock, had been poured into his body and then flash-hardened in an instant. The dead hand that could only be moved with another's help *gripped* Ash's flesh. Cant's mouth opened, and he uttered something that was not speech.

Ash's entire body moved toward him. Her head rose from the floor. Her mouth gasped open, revealing the dead leaf on her tongue. Raif saw the tendons on her neck and wrists working, *straining*. The stench of smelted metal was suddenly there in the room, so strong it could be tasted as well as smelled. Pinpoints of spittle frothed from Heritas Cant's lips. His sticks clattered to the floor. All was still for the briefest moment, then Cant swayed and nearly fell and Ash slumped back onto the rug.

Angus rushed to Cant's side, supporting him, helping him rise, leading him to a chair.

Raif paid them no heed. He crossed to where Ash lay and knelt in the warm space Cant had just vacated. Even as he reached out to touch her, her eyes opened.

Relief flooded over him, leaving him feeling drunk and breathless and so stupidly pleased, he could have laid down Tem's sword and danced above the blade. All talk of ravens and death was forgotten. Swiftly he gave thanks to the Stone Gods; they were jealous and demanding and might take something back if not appeased. Ash was *awake*. Her large gray eyes, first shown to him weeks ago by the guidestone, looked and saw and recognized.

"You're safe," Raif said. "We're in a friend's house." He hesitated, knowing their peculiar relationship demanded that he always tell her how long she had been asleep. He didn't want to upset her with the truth, yet he would not lie to her, either. "You've been asleep for four days."

Ash's eyes looked into his. Her lips trembled.

What had she been through? He found he did not like the thought of her suffering. Slowly, deliberately, he bent down and gathered her up, pulling her fast against his chest. She was so cold it frightened him.

"Easy, Raif." Angus put a hand on his shoulder. "Let her be."

Raif shook his head. "I will not let them take her again."

Crouching, Angus brought his face close to Raif's. He studied whatever was showing there for a long moment and then said in a weary voice, "And so it begins."

A quarter passed before Raif could finally be persuaded to let her go.

# THIRTY-TWO

## *Named Beasts*

I HAVE PUT WHAT WARDINGS I can between Ash and that which calls her. Later, I shall do more. Yet know this: The Bound Men and Beasts of the Blind will not be held off indefinitely. They know what Ash is, and they will not let her rest until she gives them what they crave."

Heritas Cant's wheel-broken body rested in a chair of hard black wood. An hour had passed since Ash had awakened. A light supper of watered beer, bread, and roasted mutton had been eaten by all, during which Cant had complained heatedly about the number of guests, the amount of food eaten, the crumbs wasted, the gristle spat, the strain on the dying fire, and the wear on his rugs, chairs, wooden bowls, and spoons. After supper he had called the cloistress to him and informed her that he was taking his guests "to the warren" to show them his collection of foreign coins. The cloistress had bobbed her head sharply, like a sparrow plucking insects from air, yet even as her face and chin pointed downward her milky gaze had followed them from the room.

The warren was located at the far edge of the plot of land that lay at the rear of Heritas Cant's house. Constructed entirely underground, it reminded Raif of the rendering pits in the badlands, dug so that thirty head of elk could be sweated at one time. Its mud walls were braced with crossing timbers as big as a full-grown man, and its ceiling was formed from whole basswood logs mounted on brackets. Things grew in the spaces between the logs: silvery weeds that moved with every breath Raif took. The floor was good firm stone, blue slate, and much worn. The air above it smelled of wet soil and old age.

Heritas said it had been built half a century earlier by the last owner of the house, an eccentric man who had been convinced that one day headless demons would walk the earth and only those living beneath it would be saved. Raif had laughed. Angus had suggested that the man's real motive may well have been to get some peace from his wife. Heritas Cant had greeted both reactions with ill humor.

He was ill humored now, sitting awkwardly in his chair at the head of a broad oak table laid with chained books, rolled hides, and copper tablets as thin as blades. Mud glistened on the walls behind his back, oozing softly as the goose-fat lantern warmed the chamber.

"I don't understand," Ash said. "What is the Blind?"

Heritas Cant and Angus exchanged a glance. Raif watched his uncle's face carefully, trying to see beyond Angus' guard of good humor. Angus and Ash were sitting close, sharing a bench across the table from Cant. Raif sat with his back against the far wall, glad of his place in the background in the dim low-ceilinged space.

"The Blind is a place of darkness," Heritas said. "Some would call it the underworld, others would say it is the boundary where hell and earth meet. More learned men will tell you that it is a place of holding, a prison if you like, where beings that should never have been brought into existence are walled in by the bricks and mortar of ancient spells." A pause followed, where Heritas settled his crippled legs into a more comfortable position against the chair. When he resumed speaking his voice was sharp with pain, but as he continued, everything—the chamber, the mud walls, the light from the lantern, and even his own pain—fell away.

"The Blind is home to those who should be dead. Things live there who crave the light and the warmth of the world we inhabit. Hunger is all they know. Need is all they feel. For a thousand years none amongst them have reached the light, but still they do not forget or stop craving. Desire only deepens with time. The Blind is as cold and empty as eternity; it is fed by the dark rivers of hell, held in place by spells so terrible and lasting that closeness to its boundaries can kill.

"The creatures who wait there are chained in blood. They hate living men with all the substance of their souls. Once they were human. Once they walked our world as men, yet dark times came and some would say the world cracked open and through the breach rode the Endlords. They have many names, these lords: Lords of Shadow and Lords of Night, the Unleashed, the Condemned, the Shadow Warriors, and the Takers of Men. One touch is all it takes for an Endlord to claim a man's body and soul. Their flesh bleeds darkness. Cut them open and the black substance of evil leaks out. In the Time of Shadows they massed great warhosts that stretched from sea to sea. They were terrible to behold, human yet not human, wearing the faces of men and women they had claimed, stinking of death, their eyes burning black and red, their bodies shifting shadows beneath them. The Endlords rode at the head of their armies, great beastmen on black horses, with weapons forged from voided steel that reflected no light.

"It is said that they were birthed at the same time as the gods, and if it is the gods' purpose to make life, then it is the Endlords' purpose to destroy it. Make no mistake, the world *will* end, perhaps not for a thousand thousand years, but when it does it will be the Endlords who will dance upon the wreckage.

"They ride the earth every thousand years to claim more men for their armies. When a man or woman is touched by them, they become Unmade. Not dead, *never* dead, but something different, cold and craving. The shadows enter them, snuffing the light from their eyes and the warmth from their hearts. Everything is lost. Their memories leave them first, seeping from them like blood from skinned flesh. The ability to think and understand comes next and with it all emotion except need. Blood and skin and bone is lost, changed into something the Sull call *maer dan:* shadow-flesh.

"These men and women are known as Shadow Wearers, the Bound Men, Wralls, and the Taken. The Endlords have taken others, too, beasts from forgotten ages, things that are half man and half monster, giants, bloodwraiths . . . things that no longer walk this earth.

"All have but one memory left: the knowledge they were once counted amongst the living. This is the core of their existence. It is what drives them to battle . . . and to hate.

"There was a time when the Shadow Wearers and their masters rode unchecked in our world. Their numbers massed and their power cumulated and the long night of darkness began. Terrible wars were fought. Wars so ancient and devastating that only scraps of their history remain. Wars of Blood and Shadow, the Ruinwars, Wars of the Blind. Hundreds of thousands of lives were lost. Generations of sorcerer-warriors were massacred. Losses became so great that those fighting could see no end, only the complete and utter silence of destruction. That's when the Hearth of Ten came together to bring an end to the wars and banish the Shadow Wearers and the lords who had made them, exile them to a place where their powers were rendered futile and they could no longer walk the earth.

"I do not know if the Hearth of Ten created the Blind or found it. Some say the Blind is where the Endlords first came from, that they originated in a place beyond the boundaries of our world and that the Hearth of Ten did nothing but drive them back. Others will tell you that the Blind is wholly the creation of man, that it is as artificial as a glass eye and as monstrous as a cage riven with inward-pointing spikes.

"One thing is certain, though: The Hearth of Ten *sealed* the Blind. The ten greatest bloodlines of sorcerer-warriors came together and worked upon the sealing for ten generations. Spells and dark sorceries, heavy with kin-blood, thick with time's passage, shared sacrifices and loss, were woven over the course of three hundred years. The Hearth of Ten created new sorceries as they worked, inventing new methods of seeing, new ways of combining their powers, and massing them over time.

"By such methods they built a wall around the Blind, such a wall as had never been seen or imagined, one that could never again be duplicated, whose secrets died with the generations of sorcerer-warriors who had created it, their blood, bones, ashes, and souls ground into the substance of the wall.

"And so the Blind was sealed and remains sealed, and those beings that feed on men abide there, remembering, waiting, living quarter-lives in an absence of light. The Blind is their prison and may one day be their tomb, and no man, woman, or sorcerer may go there. No one except a Reach."

At some point while he spoke, Heritas Cant had stopped being a crippled man with stunted, misshapen legs and a listing spine and become a powerful sorcerer instead. Now, finished, he set his green eyes upon Ash and watched to see what she would do. He shrank as he waited. The distance between his shoulder blades contracted, his chest sagged, and the skin on his hands settled, revealing white ridges of bone.

*He is two people,* Raif thought, *one broken and twisted like his body, and one powerful and in pain and not often shown.*

No one spoke. Ash sat and suffered Heritas Cant's gaze as if it were a necessary torture. Since she had been wakened an hour earlier she had said little and seemed glad to sit and listen. Now all eyes were upon her as she readied herself to speak.

Raif kept his face still, as he had done all through Cant's speech. He would not show his fear to this man . . . or Ash. Especially not Ash.

Finally she moved, rocking forward on the bench so that her face caught the light. Angus' hand came up to touch her wrist, but she shook it away as if it were a moth or a bit of dust. Gray eyes met and held Cant's gaze, and then she spoke a command. "Tell me what I am."

Heritas' good hand came up to support his drooping jaw. A thin line of drool slid along his chin. "To know what a Reach is you must understand where the Blind lies in relation to our world. The two exist alongside each other and *within* each other, yet remain wholly separate places. They are divided by a gray plain, a no-man's-land known as the borderlands or the Gray Marches."

"The Gray Marches," Ash repeated, showing her teeth.

"Yes. March is an old word meaning the boundary between lands." Heritas Cant's smile was knowing. Angus had not told him who Ash was, yet it was obvious he had already worked it out. With a little click of his sticks, he carried on. "These borderlands hold the Blind apart from our world. Powerful sorcerers can enter them, some may even catch a glimpse of the Blindwall, but no one but a Reach can know them truly. And no one but a Reach can lay her hands upon the wall and *breach it.*"

Ash flinched at the word *breach.* Angus muttered something to whatever gods he believed in. Raif concentrated on the mud walls behind Heritas Cant's back, watching them ooze and drip and deteriorate as he imagined putting his fist into Cant's face. The cripple was taking pleasure in this. His green eyes glinted as he took another breath and spoke.

"A Reach is born every thousand years, a man or woman who can enter the dead space of the borderlands, approach the Blindwall, and free the creatures who lie beyond it."

When he was sure the anger had left his eyes, Raif turned to look at Ash. Almost she didn't shake. Her hands were clenched on the table before her, the tendons on her wrists pulsing. Slowly her gaze rose to meet his. A question filled her large gray eyes, and even before he fully understood what it was she asked, Raif answered with a swift jab of his jaw.

Acknowledging his reply with a smile not quite cool enough to hide her relief, she turned back to Heritas Cant and said, "So you think me a Reach?"

"Yes."

"And you think I was born to free the creatures in the Blind?"

"Yes."

"And if I tell you that for the past six months I have dreamed of creatures calling me, begging me to reach out and help them, then you will tell me I have been listening to the creatures of the Blind?"

"Yes."

A muscle at the corner of Ash's lips began to quiver. She

worked quickly to stop it, white teeth jabbing at lipflesh. "Answer me this, then, Heritas Cant. If I am not the first Reach to be born, why is the Blindwall still intact?"

Angus and Heritas Cant exchanged a glance. Heritas shifted in his chair, his good hand dealing awkwardly with his legs. When he spoke his voice was peevish. "The wall is still in place for several reasons. First of all, breaks can be sealed if swift action is taken and certain conditions are met. Second, not all Reaches have lived to an age where they could cause a breach. And third, a place exists where a Reach can discharge the power that builds within her without threatening the integrity of the wall."

Raif frowned. Compared with Cant's other answers, this one was short and evasive. Raif thought of asking why it was that some Reaches didn't live long enough to cause a breach, then decided against it. All possible answers worried him.

Ash did not reply straightaway. Her fingers traced along the table's edge, fingernails collecting wax. Finally she said, "Do I have no choice but to discharge this . . . power that is building inside of me?"

Heritas Cant nodded. "You are the Reach and you have newly come into womanhood and by all rights you should have caused the breach by now. Great power masses within you; I felt it when I laid my hands upon your skin. It pushes with cold force, displacing organs, feeding upon your blood, forcing the air from your lungs. It must be released or it will destroy you."

"But she has fought it so far," Angus cried.

"Yes, and look what it has done to her. She is being eaten from inside. Her body is skin and bone, her skin is yellowing with jaundice, her breathing is shallow. And you cannot see what I have felt: the punctured kidney, the compressed chest organs, the poisons cumulating in her liver, the rapid beat of her heart. Soon her mouth will run dry, her gums will turn gray and crack, her eyes will sink into their sockets, her hair and fingernails will—"

"*Enough!*" Raif stood. In his anger, he sent his chair cracking against the wall. Angus and Ash turned to look at him. Heritas Cant regarded him with interest, as if he were seeing some new species of insect for the very first time.

Raif sent a look to wipe all fascination from his face. "Tell us what we must do."

Again, a certain unspoken communication passed between Angus and Cant. Raif hardly cared. *Will you help me in this?* Ash had asked him across the room moments earlier. *Yes,* he had replied in an instant.

Crossing the room, Raif was aware of the size and health of his own body compared with the wheel-broken shell that was Heritas Cant. He saw envy and even the cold sparkle of fear in the man's green eyes, and he could not say he was sorry for it. Drawing himself up to his full height, he sent a hand down for his sword.

Heritas Cant shrank back.

*"Raif,"* Angus warned.

"Stay out of this, Angus," Raif said without looking around. "If I were to harm anyone over this matter, it would be you. You knew it all from the start, from that very first moment outside Vaingate. That's why you saved her: to bring her here to Cant."

"No." Angus rose. Raif heard the soft scrape of chair legs, saw Angus' growing shadow on the wall. "I moved to save Ash for other reasons. I—"

"I know what you *mean* to say, Angus. You have your reasons yet cannot speak them." Raif turned to face his uncle. "Don't think that just because you switch a subject or avoid it completely you can stop me from thinking on it. You are my uncle and my respect is your due, but I will not stand by and let you deliver Ash into this man's hands." Only as he spoke did he realize the truth of what he said: Heritas Cant *did* want Ash. With all his broken bones and misjointed limbs he suddenly looked like a spider to Raif.

Angus shook his head softly, though his eyes were hard gold. "No one wants Ash harmed here. No one. Heritas has told us of the dangers, and he does not lie. Now we must find a way to save her. You heard what he said—she will die if we do not act."

Raif waved his uncle's words away. He believed Heritas Cant had spoken the truth—some of it—but he also believed that Cant was more concerned about a possible breach to the Blindwall than he was about Ash. Turning to Cant, he said,

"What is the name of this place where she must go to release her power safely? I will take her there."

"There is not much time," Heritas Cant said, anger at being forced to cower in his chair making his voice shrill. "You have seen her blackouts for yourself. These will only get worse. Her health will only get worse. As I said earlier, I can set wardings to keep the voices at bay, give drugs to steel her mind, but these measures will prove effective for only so long. This place lies several weeks to the north. It is not an easy journey at any time of year, but now, in winter . . ." Cant clicked his sticks. "Gods spare us all."

"Just tell us where it is." Ash sounded tired. Raif saw where she had scratched the varnish from the table with her nails.

"I'm not sure of the exact location of the Cavern of Black Ice. . . ."

"Black ice?" Ash said, paling visibly.

"Yes. The cavern lies beyond the Storm Margin in the west. I've heard tell that it sits beneath Mount Flood, in the crease where the mountain and the Hollow River meet, ten days south of Ice Trapper territory."

"What is it?" Angus asked Ash, ignoring what Cant was saying completely.

Ash lowered her head. "I've had nightmares about a cavern for as long as I can remember. Terrible dreams, where I'm trapped or crushed or lost."

"And were the walls of this cavern formed from black ice?" Cant's green eyes glowed with interest. Ash nodded, and he made a little satisfied sound. "Then your dreams have been showing you how to survive. This cavern is as old as the Blind, and may indeed be made from the same substance. I cannot be sure. What I *do* know is that it had been used by Reaches before you. It is said to absorb a Reach's power, hold it within its walls, and stop it from causing a crack in the Blindwall."

Ash didn't look convinced. She glanced at Raif, but he could offer her no help. "But the nightmares . . ."

Cant made a calming gesture with his hand. When he spoke his voice was surprisingly soft. "The creatures in the Blind can infiltrate your dreams; that is how they call to you.

Every time you fall asleep you are vulnerable to them. Now that they sense you are close to releasing your power, they have grown bolder and have laid siege to your waking mind as well. Their weapon is fear. You have fought them so far, bravely, with such strength as I can hardly imagine." With a small shrug of his shoulders, Cant highlighted his own physical weakness. "Do not let them stop you from doing what you must."

Raif leaned against the table. Suddenly he didn't know what to make of Heritas Cant. Nothing was straightforward here. Secrets and traps lay behind every word. There was truth, but it was not the *whole* truth, and he wondered how much Cant was keeping to himself.

Smoke from the lantern rose and shivered like a fifth presence in the room. Raif watched as Ash breathed it in as she spoke. "If I go to this cavern, will it be the end of this . . . this thing that I'm part of?"

Cant sighed heavily, the nostrils on his still fine nose flaring to two dark holes. "Yes and no. The power that is building inside you has only one purpose, and once it is safely discharged you will never know its like again. Yet you will still be a Reach; that will not change. You will be able to walk the borderlands at will, hear and sense the creatures that live there, and your flesh will become *rahkar dan,* Reach-flesh, which is held sacred by the Sull. Why, I do not know. Why Reaches exist, I cannot tell you. Perhaps the sorcery that originally sealed the Blind was flawed. Perhaps it is impossible to build a prison without a key." Cant smiled briefly. "Perhaps one day when you ask me that same question I may have an answer that suits us both. One thing I am sure of, though, is that if the Endlords and their Taken are freed from the Blind they will destroy us all. They walk in death, they are sustained by hate, and their memories last as long as the sun.

"Yes, Asarhia March. You do well to look afraid. I, who have spent a lifetime learning about these matters, am more afraid than you can see. I know the names of the beasts. I know what is in there, some of it, and even that small portion of knowledge burns like the fires of hell in my mind. So travel north along the Storm Margin with this young man who has broken one of my chairs and does not trust me, go and wade through waist-high snow, crawl over black ice, and release your power safely. And when you're done, come back to me, and then perhaps I'll tell you about the creatures of the Blind, recite a list of their names and their deeds. For if I told you now, I would only be unburdening myself at your expense. And although I am a sick man, with little but knowledge and counting to live for, I seldom act out of spite."

Green eyes made brilliant by speech and strong emotions glanced briefly, accusingly, at Raif. " 'Tis better that *I* know much and you know little. Let me worry and you act."

Raif felt blood pumping up through his neck to his face. He didn't know if Cant's words were meant for him or Ash. Either way he felt frightened and stirred. He wanted to be gone, now, away from Cant and the spinning silk of his knowledge, away from Angus and his hidden motives, back to the wide-open spaces of the clanholds. He was boxed in by secrets. Getting at the truth seemed an impossible task; Cant was too clever, and Angus was too well practiced. Together they were bent on controlling Ash and probably him as well.

The door to the chamber looked inviting; one push and it would open, one short walk through the adjoining tunnel and he would be outside in the night. Punish Moose, and he'd be in the clanholds in less than a day. Blackhail would never have him back, but Dhoone might take him, or one of the lesser clans like Bannen or Orrl. Outcasts could find homes in other clans; Gat Murdock had been taken in by Ewan Blackhail after he'd fought with Wort Croser over a woman and her dowry of two poorly drained fields. Raif tried to think of others but failed. He looked from the door to Ash, and as soon as their eyes met he knew he would go nowhere, not tonight. She had asked him to stand by her, and he had agreed. And as a clansman he was bound by his word.

A small sound, like half a breath, escaped his lips. Who was he to take refuge in a promise? He, who had broken faith with his brother and his clan? Raif closed his eyes for a moment, willed the pain not to come.

"I know the Storm Margin as well as any man," Angus

said, breaking the silence that had possessed the chamber since Cant had finished speaking. Uncharacteristically, he seemed ill at ease and could find nothing to occupy his large hands. "Let me take you and Raif as far as Mount Flood. You'll need someone to show you the ways of the ice. The Margin is beset by white winds in winter. It's easy to become lost or fall victim to cold sickness or the 'bite. I can teach you how to wait out storms, show you how to find food beneath the rime, and make shelter by burrowing into old snow. Packs of ice wolves range the Margin, and in dark seasons they become desperate enough to attack men. I know their signs and their trails and how best to avoid them. I'll see that you get to Mount Flood alive and unharmed and in good time."

Finished, Angus looked from Ash to Raif. It was the closest thing to a plea Raif had ever seen his uncle make. Raif knew Angus possessed skills that he did not, yet every clansman worth his lore learned early about hard living in the white weather. Wolves and ice storms were part of clan life. Raif sucked in breath. Why, then, was it so important to Angus to come with them?

Ash looked first to Raif, then to Angus. "How soon do we leave?"

It was all planning after that.

Heritas Cant left them as they spoke of supplies and routes and clothing and horses. Rising gracelessly from his black wood chair, he muttered something about things that needed to be prepared. Watching him support his broken body with the aid of two sticks, Raif found himself admiring the strength of will that lay like an iron plate beneath Cant's skin. He did not trust him, yet he respected him, and it occurred to Raif that perhaps in the cityholds that was the most he could expect from another man.

With Cant gone, Angus took control of matters and began to plan a route that would involve only minimal time spent in the clanholds. Raif recognized his uncle's consideration and was grateful for it, and as the night wore on and he learned more about the Storm Margin and the bleak windcarved wastes that surrounded Mount Flood, he gave thanks to the Stone Gods that Angus would be with them.

Later, much later, when the goose-fat lantern had all but dried and the flames chewed away at the last bit of rope, Cant returned to the chamber bearing two copper bowls and a knife of gray steel. Angus, who had been in the process of warning Ash about cold sickness, stopped speaking in mid-sentence and rose to help Cant. Angus' great red face was showing signs of strain, and his ready smile was missing as he greeted the broken man.

It had been a long day for all of them. Ash and Raif watched each other across the table as Angus and Cant arranged things at the other end of the room. Raif suddenly wished they were alone. There were things he wanted to say to her, small things that no one else had asked or said. He wanted to know if she felt strong enough for the journey north, if she was afraid, how much she believed of what Heritas Cant had said.

Ash smiled gently, rubbing eyes that were nearly red. "You wouldn't let anyone near me earlier."

Raif felt heat come to his cheeks. "I didn't want you to fall asleep again," he said. Even to his own ears, his voice sounded gruff.

"I'm glad you're coming with me."

With those words the night changed one last time. Cant came forward, bearing the first of the copper bowls. His eyes glittered like two pieces of seaglass as he said to Ash, "Lie down on the bench. I must place what wardings as I can upon you."

Ash's eyes flicked to Raif. Her mouth made a small grimace of fear.

"I will not harm you," Cant said. "The cost is only to myself."

"But . . ."

"But what? Would you rather I did nothing and allow the creatures of the Blind free rein to take you? Your mind was last held by them for four days; would you wish to let them seize it again?"

Ash shook her head.

"Lie down then, and let me do what I must."

After a moment's hesitation, Ash brought her feet off the

floor and lowered her back onto the bench. She was shaking, Raif noticed. So was Cant.

"Angus. If this young man is to stay and watch, you must take him in hand. I will not have him throwing his fine clansman's body around, raging about things he does not understand."

"Aye, Heritas." Angus beckoned Raif to his side. "The lad will stay by me, I'll see to that."

Raif did not like being spoken of as if he were a child, and he suspected Heritas Cant had done so to punish him one last time for breaking the chair. Still, he crossed to where Angus stood at the head of the table and settled himself in place against the edge.

Cant's spine had too many vertebrae. As he bent to loosen the ties at Ash's throat, they poked through the thin fabric of his robe like fishbones. *Who broke him?* Raif wondered. *What crime bears the sentence of the wheel?*

"Place this upon your tongue." Cant held out a dried leaf for Ash to take. "Bite through it when I say so." Ash did as she was told. Raif was watching her so intently, he didn't see Cant draw the knife.

"Easy, lad," Angus said under his breath, reacting to the tension that shot through Raif's body like lightning.

Easing back to reassure Angus, Raif watched as Cant drew the knife to his wrist. The blade rested there, above a vein as thin and insubstantial as a curl of smoke, while Cant's lips spoke words that Raif could not hear.

The room dimmed. Air became thicker, colder, harder to expel from the lungs. The stench of copper and blood rose in the room like mist rising from a field at battle's end. Raif's mouth watered. Sickened, he swallowed hard.

Ash's face shone with sweat. Her eyes were closed and her mouth was open, and the skin Cant had bared at her throat flushed pink. Cant stood above her, joined to her by the substance pouring from his mouth. Raif saw it as thick shadow, a mixture of words and air and something else he had no name for. Light ran along the knifeblade as Cant sliced into his skin.

Blood welled in a perfectly straight line, so bright and

hearty it was shocking to see it pump from such pale, misshapen flesh. Following the line of the blade, it dripped into the hammered copper bowl, pattering like a child's footsteps on tile.

"Bite the leaf," Cant said.

Ash's mouth closed. Her jaw worked once and then was still. Cant dropped the knife and placed his good hand on the tissue of Ash's throat. The air in the room shifted, as if moved by an opening door. Raif felt the raven lore grow hot against his skin. Cant's presence became somehow *less* than it was, wavering as if seen through the heat from a fire. Pulse racing, Raif became acutely aware of the danger. Ash was a *Reach*; it meant old skills and old knowledge and power beyond anything he knew. If she fought against Cant, she could kill him.

Raif glanced at Angus and saw the same knowledge reflected in his uncle's eyes.

Ash and Cant were as one now, joined as surely as two stags with antlers racked. Raif shivered as the image came to him. Three summers ago he and Drey had come across a pair of elk carcasses at the foot of the balds: bodies head to head, torsos picked clean, antlers locked together so surely that neither animal had been able to free itself from the other's hold. They had died that way, struggling to pull apart over countless days and nights. Rut deaths, Tem had called them. He said it only happened when two beasts of equal strength were matched.

Blood smoke rose between Ash and Cant as the contents of the copper bowl began steaming. Cant's face was gray with strain. His mouth worked furiously, speaking a clotted mix of words and sorcery.

Unable to watch any longer, Raif turned away. His eyes settled on the shadows cast on the wall, and after a while he couldn't even look at them. Sorcery had never seemed so wrong and unnatural, and for the second time that night he found himself staring longingly at the door.

The clanholds lay one day's ride to the north, yet they might as well have stood in the frozen heart of the Want. Raif had never felt farther from all that he knew as he did waiting for Heritas Cant to be done.

# THIRTY-THREE

## *Shankshounds*

EFFIE'S LORE *PUSHED* HER AWAKE. She'd been having such a strange dream about Raif, about how he was trapped underground with no way out, when her rock lore pressed so hard against her chest, it hurt. Effie opened her eyes immediately. The quality of darkness in her cell told her it was still properly and completely night. Frowning, she reached beneath the neckline of her wool nightdress and took her lore in hand.

*Push.*

Quick as if she'd picked up a hot coal from the fire, Effie let the stone drop.

She had to go, leave her cell right now.

The idea didn't come to her in words; it wasn't really an idea at all. It was just something she knew, like the time of day or whether the air she breathed was cold or warm or damp.

Sitting up, she swung her feet onto the floor. Boots or slippers? *Boots are warmer,* said a little voice. *Slippers are quieter,* said another. Effie poked her feet into the darkness until her toes brushed against the shaggy softness of her squirrel fur slippers. That done, she pulled the rug from her bed and wrapped it around her shoulders. She didn't have time for a shawl.

Her legs didn't help much as she stood. They felt like rain-soaked twigs that had nothing to do with the rest of her body and no intention of carrying her weight. Effie felt her bottom lip start to tremble as she shuffled to the nearest wall.

*Push.*

"Stop," she whispered, glad of the chance to give her treacherous bottom lip something to do. "I *know*."

Thinking about what Inigar Stoop would likely say to her if he knew that she spoke to her lore made Effie feel better.

Rufus Pole had been the laughingstock of the roundhouse last summer just for speaking to his sheep. Effie had seen Rufus' sheep—they were clean and healthy and fat as rain clouds—and she'd very nearly giggled out loud when he'd said he'd rather speak to them than a good quarter of the people in the clan.

Sheep thoughts helped, and Effie felt her legs harden beneath her, ready for flight. Clutching the bed rug around her throat, she moved toward the door.

It was closed, of course—open doors were the next worst thing to open spaces—but both Raina and Drey had warned her about bolting herself in. Fingers sliding over the bolt, Effie considered drawing it and simply hiding from whatever danger was on its way. She knew straightaway that was foolish, though. Doors could be easily broken. Taking a shallow breath, she pushed against the wood and stepped into the new darkness waiting on the other side.

The roundhouse at night was icy cold, peopled by strange drafts and grinding noises. Effie knew it well. The noises came from stone blocks in the walls moving against each other as the timbers separating them cooled and the drafts blew from secret rotting holes in the peat-and-graystone roof. Longhead said swallows nested there in spring, and Effie thought about that for a bit as she walked along the tunnel leading from her cell. She was just wondering what swallows found to eat up there when she heard footsteps pounding on the stone steps directly ahead. A halo of light descended from above. Someone, a man, coughed with a hard hacking sound that produced something worthy of spitting. Effie, still standing in the darkness close to the wall, felt for the nearest door.

Her hand found the splintery roughness of wood as the man's booted feet came into view. Thanking all the Stone Gods—even Bethathmus, who always gave her a chill and few except hammermen ever named—she pushed open the door and stepped into someone else's cell. Doors were never locked in the roundhouse, and Effie found herself glad of that fact for the first time in her eight-year life.

More darkness occupied the cell—so much, in fact, that she couldn't even see the hand she used to close the door. A series of soft snoring sounds rose from somewhere close by. People sleeping. At one time Effie would have known the names and faces of everyone who occupied the cells close to her own, but now she couldn't be sure who slept where. The roundhouse was swollen with tied clansmen and their families, all come to seek protection from the Dog Lord. Most slept wherever they could. Some had caused fights. Just last week Anwyn Bird had beaten a tied clanwife with a wooden spoon for daring to spend the night in her kitchen. By all accounts the woman had gotten off lightly, and the bruises were said to be nothing that a few weeks of bed rest couldn't cure.

Sniffing slightly, Effie peered through the shadows in the room. After a few moments her eyes began to pick out shapes: a box pallet with several hunched forms lying upon it, a bloodwood stang propping up the ceiling, and a line of fat grain sacks hanging from the rafters to keep their contents dry. Effie listened to the sound of breathing and snoring rising from the pallet, assuring herself that those who lay there were fast asleep. Then, just as she felt safe enough to think about what to do next, a sliver of light shone under the door. The man on the stairs was walking this way!

Effie stilled herself. Footsteps tapped close . . . the light brightened . . . and then receded as the man on the stairs walked past the door. Suddenly realizing she had been holding her breath, Effie exhaled in a great gasp of relief. As she did so, she heard the familiar whine of hinges so badly rusted by damp that no amount of calf oil could silence them. Her cell door. Effie breathed in, snatching back her relief. Her lore beat against her chest like a second, smaller, heart.

Pressing her forehead against the door, she listened for more sounds from the man on the stairs. Nothing. What was he *doing* in there? Effie imagined his boots; the leather was greenish, moldy, the toes ringed with watermarks, and the soles caked with muddy bits of hay. Not a full clansman's boots. Effie shook her head. Not even a yearman.

The whining noise came again, pushing all boot thoughts from her mind. Effie tensed. Suddenly she couldn't breathe. Her throat felt as if someone had their hands around it.

Footsteps again. *Slap, slap, slap.* They were so close,

Effie could feel their vibration on the part of her head that was touching the door. They slowed. Stopped. Effie imagined monsters. She knew what the man's boots looked like, but what about his face, his *teeth*? Tiny, hard contractions punched at her belly. Should she wake the other people in the cell? Might they be monsters, too?

Then, abruptly, the footsteps started up once more, receding with a slowness that was another torture in itself. Effie waited. Even after the footsteps had long faded and night sounds took over again, she waited, forehead pushed against the bloodwood door, body held so still that dust settled upon her back.

The soft crunch of a body rolling over dried grass broke the waiting spell. Effie lifted her head from the door and glanced over her shoulder. A tiny crack high in the roof let in a trickle of dawn light. The box pallet was clearly visible now. Three bodies vied for space upon its grass-filled mattress: a thin crofter with a silvery beard, a woman with dark hair and a pale back, and a young dark-haired child. It took Effie a moment to realize that the child was awake. His eyes were wide open, and he was looking at her in the interested way children looked at things that might, or might not, be dangerous.

Pressing a finger to her lips, Effie warned him not to cry out. He was small and skinny and a good deal younger than she, and even though Effie wouldn't normally deign to notice such a boy, she knew they were made of the same child substance. The boy knew it, too, and acknowledged her sign with a similar one of his own. Effie was careful not to let her relief show. They might both be children, but she *was* the elder, and even after favors were granted she had a certain superiority to maintain.

They held their places for a good long time, watching each other in the growing light, neither friendly nor unfriendly, waiting. When the child's mother stirred, sending out a hand to feel for her son, Effie knew it was time to go. Part of her didn't much like the idea of venturing outside, but the sensible, thinking part knew that dawn was properly here now and no one would dare harm her in the good light of day.

Raising her hand, she thanked the boy with a seriousness befitting his deed, then let herself out the door.

The corridor was no longer dark. Sounds of clattering metal pots, thudding footsteps, and sharply spoken orders filtered down from the floors above. Anwyn was in her kitchen, stoking the fires and warming last night's broth and bannock. Effie glanced toward her cell.

*Push.*

No, better not go back there yet.

Massaging the part of her forehead that she had ground into the wood of the cell door, Effie thought about what to do. Drey would be in the Great Hearth, sleeping close around the fire like all the other yearmen. He was becoming important these days. Rory Cleet, the Shank brothers, Bullhammer, Craw Bannering: All the yearmen looked to him to lead raids, settle disputes, and talk with Mace Blackhail on their behalf. He was often away from the roundhouse: riding the borders, scouting as far as Gnash, carrying messages between Blackhail and exiled Dhoone. Last week he had ridden with Mace Blackhail and a host of two hundred full clansmen to defend Bannen against the Dog Lord's forces.

Drey said the Dog Lord was working to take over all the Dhoone-sworn clans and fortify his position in the Dhoonehold. Already he'd taken over Clan Withy, whose funny little roundhouse with its mineshafts and mole holes lay two days south of Dhoone. Even with the combined forces of Dhoone, Blackhail, and Bannen working to defend the Banhold, the battle had not gone easy. Drey said the Bluddsmen had fought like men possessed, and the Dog Lord himself had ridden at the head of their line.

"You should have seen him, Effie," Drey had confided upon his return. "He rode an ugly black horse and carried the plainest of weapons, yet no clansman who matched hammers with him lived to tell of it." After that Drey had shivered in a funny way, and Effie had asked him what was wrong. "He was screaming at us, Effie. Screaming for Blackhail blood."

That had made Effie shiver, too. According to Drey, the battle lasted well into the night, and even though Bludd was outmanned they managed to break through the Dhoone lines and take more lives than they gave.

Drey had been injured in the Bludd retreat. Mace Black-hail had sent him and two dozen other hammermen after the Dog Lord and his sons. Ten of the hammermen had died. Drey had been unseated by a blow from a spiked and lead-weighted Bluddhammer. The spikes had pierced his plate in two places, and he'd taken a bad landing upon stony ground.

Effie sucked in her cheeks. Raina said that once the swelling and bruising had gone down it wouldn't be that bad. He'd only broken two ribs.

With a small shake of her head, Effie made the decision not to go and seek out Drey. She knew he would see her no matter how busy he was—hers was the first face he looked for whenever he returned home from a raid and the last name he spoke in his words to the Stone Gods each night—yet she didn't want to be a burden to him. He had too many worries already.

Raif's leaving still hurt him. He never spoke of it, and Effie had seen him stiffen in anger when anyone in his presence dared to mention Raif's name. Yet these days it was hard *not* to hear talk of Raif Sevrance around the Great Hearth at night. All the clanholds were in uproar about what happened at Duff's Stovehouse. Three Bluddsmen had died by Raif's hand. Three. Effie shivered. It was unthinkable. Watcher of the Dead, they called him now.

Effie climbed the steps to the entrance chamber. She wished Raif were here now. She couldn't tell Drey about the man on the stairs; he'd go straight to Mace Blackhail, and this time they might actually fight. Effie shook her head. That couldn't happen. Mace was a bad man. Drey was stronger and a better fighter, but somehow Effie knew that wasn't enough. Mace hurt people in different ways. He had hurt Raina, changed her. He might send Drey from the clan, or worse.

By the time she had walked through the entrance chamber and past the kitchen, her mind was set. She told herself that she didn't really know whether or not Mace Blackhail had any connection with the man on the stairs, couldn't even be sure if the man had meant her harm. Fearing a push from her rock lore, Effie knocked it impatiently with her fist. Suddenly she very much wanted to go to a place where she knew she'd be safe.

Reaching up on her tiptoes, she worked the latch on the side door that led out onto the court. Cold air blasted her face as the door opened. Snow was swirling in heavy gray flakes, and the wind was hard and from the north. *Another storm,* Effie thought as she stepped outside. The third one in as many days.

The big stable door had been shut and barred against the wind, and she concentrated on its shape and *thereness* as she made her way across the court. The open space of the graze, the distant rise of the Wedge, and the far line of the horizon were blurred by the storm, yet Effie knew better than to look at them even now. Just the fact of their presence made her heart race. *Not far to the little dog cote,* she told herself. *Not far now.*

Jebb Onnacre, one of the Shanks by marriage and caretaker of all their horses and dogs, passed within a few paces of Effie on his way back from the stables. Seeing her, he smiled and raised his hand in greeting. Effie liked Jebb; he was quiet and good with animals and never said anything to anyone whenever he found her in the dog cote. Normally she always waved back, yet today she put her head down and ignored him. His boots were caked in mud, she noticed. He might have sat and taken breakfast with the man on the stairs.

Disturbed by that thought, she broke into a run, heading north along the stable wall and into roughs beyond. By the time she arrived at the dog cotes her squirrel slippers were stiff with ice. Clutching the bed rug close about her chest, she picked her way around the largest of the two cotes and made for the small stone structure that lay behind them, its round walls sunk deep into the snow like a miniature version of the roundhouse. The little dog cote. Effie's chest tightened to see it.

Dog smells and dog noises defied the bluster of the storm. Already one of the shankshounds had gotten wind of her scent and was howling like a mad thing through the roof. Effie grinned. That was Darknose, by the sound of it; he was always howling about something. Crouching down by the little dog-size door, she worked the latch and then jiggled the hinges as necessary. By the time she had forced the door open, a wall of dogs was waiting for her on the other side.

Effie's heart filled with joy. "Stop that! Easy now. No chewing on my slippers. Give me that rug back! Bad dogs. Bad dogs." The dogs accompanied her into their warm, dark lair, tails wagging, tongues licking, amber eyes bright with interest and affection.

Most people in the clan held that the shankshounds were the nastiest, evilest, most foul-tempered beasts that had ever fetched a stick on the Hailhold. *Hell-bred,* Anwyn called them. *Bears with tails,* said someone else. Of course, since one of them had found the crofter's baby buried alive in the snow, a sort of legend had grown up around them. Due respect was given . . . but always from a safe distance. Anwyn had taken to sending Mog Wiley out to the cotes with kitchen scraps, and Jenna Walker, who now acted as foster mother to the rescued child, would not hear a bad word said against them. Orwin Shank, who everyone held was the wealthiest man in the clan, had even sent one of his best breeding ewes in payment to Paille Trotter for making up a song about them. Effie had heard the song. It wasn't very good, containing in her opinion far too many words that rhymed with *dog,* but even she had to admit it was a jaunty tune.

With Effie the shankshounds were as soft and playful as kittens. Sometimes they didn't realize their own strength, and once or twice she had returned to the roundhouse with nips and bruises from where they had scrambled and jumped all over her in their eagerness to greet her. That never bothered Effie much. The bruises hardly ever hurt at all.

Perhaps sensing some vestige of her earlier fear, the dogs were especially gentle with her as she settled herself back against the closed door. Darknose probed her face with his handsome wet nose, sniffing and concerned. Lady Bee came and sat close, pushing her warm body against Effie's, giving her heat to the scrawny little thing that had come in from the cold. Effie stroked her fine black-and-orange neck. She had long ago worked out that Lady Bee thought she was one of her pups. Old Scratch simply laid his great old head on her lap and promptly fell asleep. Cally and Teeth worried at her slippers, making small breathy noises as they nipped around her toes. Cat came and sat at a dignified distance from everyone, waiting for a sign from Effie before she deigned to come close.

Sitting on the hard-packed earth of the cote with all the shankshounds around her, Effie finally felt safe. Her lore was quiet now, sleeping. The thought of the man on the stairs no longer frightened her, and she began to wonder if she'd made too much of a fuss over nothing. Already she felt bad about ignoring Jebb Onnacre on the court.

Darknose watched her with his clever dog's eyes as the other shankshounds settled down in readiness to sleep, each one determined to use some part of her body as a pillow. Effie loved the feeling of their heavy heads and paws on her skin. Even aloof and dignified Cat came to her in the end, tempted by a hand stretched her way and the soft click of Effie's tongue.

Effie loved the shankshounds. They were good dogs. They smelled a bit, but Jebb Onnacre had once told her that she probably smelled just as bad to them as they did to her.

Snuggling down beneath her blanket of dogs, Effie began to drift off to sleep. She was ever so glad she hadn't gone running to Drey. The shankshounds would protect her.

Dreams of dogs followed her to sleep.

*Grrrrrr.*

Effie's sleeping brain first responded to the sound of a dog growling by making it part of her dream. Yet the growling went on and on, and soon other dogs joined in and the noise became too loud to ignore.

Effie blinked awake. Strips of light from the dirt hole at the back of the cote took a moment to get used to. Even before she could fully see, she became aware of six dogs standing in a half-circle around her, hackles raised, heads lowered, tails flat against their docks. There was a moment where all she could really see was yellow fangs and burning eyes, when she suddenly understood all the bad things people had ever said about the shankshounds. They could kill a man and not regret it.

Then, even as she raised a hand to calm them, she heard voices from outside. Two of them. A man and woman, shouting to be heard above the storm.

"She's witched, that girl. Witched. Cutty swore she disappeared right afore his eyes. Reckons she knew he was after her the moment he darkened the roundhouse door. It's that lore of hers. If you ask me . . ."

Effie strained to hear more above the howling of the wind and the snarling of the dogs. Pushing her palms through the air, she worked to silence the dogs without speaking. She had recognized the speaker instantly. That deep mannish voice belonged to the luntwoman Nellie Moss. Cutty Moss was her son. He was about Drey's age yet had never made yearman. Last summer he had been caught stealing chickens from Merritt Ganlow's coop, and the winter before that there had been some incident involving the Tanner girls that Effie had only vague ideas about. She hardly knew Cutty Moss at all and was quite sure he didn't live in the roundhouse most of the year. The only thing Effie could remember vividly about him was that one of his eyes was hazel and the other one was blue.

*"Hush, woman!"* cried a hard male voice, cutting the last of Nellie Moss' words clean away. "I'll listen to no more of your superstitious chaffing. The Sevrance girl is no more witched than you or I. If she did slip away, then it was likely because she heard that worthless son of yours coming."

All the dog-given heat left Effie's face. The second speaker was Mace Blackhail, she was sure of it. His voice penetrated the stone walls of the dog cote like icy drops of rain.

"Cutty's no fool," snapped Nellie Moss. "He did as he was told."

"Then he'll have to do it again, for I won't have that little bitch sneaking around the roundhouse, telling tales and watching me with her father's dead eyes."

Hounds from the larger cotes yipped and howled as Mace spoke, yet all he had to do to silence them was whip a piece of leather through the air. The soft jingle of metal followed, and Effie guessed that Mace had brought leashes to the cotes meaning to save his best dogs from the storm.

"Making ye feel guilty, is she?" Nellie Moss sounded pleased.

"Just do as we arranged."

" 'Twould be easier for everyone if she could be caught outside by a cowlman's arrow . . . like Shor Gormalin."

A quick series of sounds followed. Boots thudded snow, fabric rustled, and then Nellie Moss issued a low throaty wail.

"You'll not speak of Shor Gormalin again, woman. Is that clear?" A moment passed where all Effie could hear was the wind and the soft persistent growling of Darknose, then, "I *said*, is that clear?"

A breath was taken sharply. "Aye. 'Tis clear. No one will hear the truth of it from me."

"Good." A sound, like many knuckles snapping, accompanied the word.

Effie sank back amid the shankshounds, deeply shaken. Lady Bee began licking Effie's ears as she would with a sick pup. Old Scratch, Cally, and Teeth were still intent upon the people outside, spines lowered, snouts bunched and quivering. Darknose and Cat, whom Effie always thought of as the leaders of the pack, were alert, trotting to and fro in front of the door, listening, *ready*. All of the dogs except Lady Bee continued to growl.

Shankshounds. That had been Shor Gormalin's name for them. Effie remembered smiling when he'd first called them by it. Now she knew it was their real name. The only one that suited.

A space opened in Effie's chest. Shor Gormalin had known about dogs. He had known about her, too. He was the only person who understood why she had to run and hide sometimes. He'd even said he did it himself. That meant something to Effie. It helped cancel out some of the bad things Letty Shank and the others always said. She couldn't be *that* different. Not when the best swordsman in the clan told her she reminded him of himself when he was growing up.

Now something terrible had happened. Nellie Moss had spoken as if Shor Gormalin wasn't really killed by a cowlman at all, that somehow Mace Blackhail had arranged it.

Effie began to rock back and forth on her haunches. She

felt violently sick, as if she'd eaten a meal of dirt and grease. When Lady Bee licked her ear again, she pushed the dog away. *Shor Gormalin.* Mace Blackhail had killed Shor Gormalin. He had hurt Raina and . . . Effie stopped rocking as a thought smashed through the others like a rock breaking ice.

Mace had killed Shor because of Raina. Shor loved Raina. He would have protected her, stopped her from marrying Mace. Effie had seen how Shor was around Raina, how gently he'd tended her when she'd first heard about Dagro's death. Anything he *could* do for her he had. He'd taken over her duties with the tied clansmen, seen to the stores of grain and oil . . . he'd even ridden out to the Oldwood to check on Raina's traps.

Effie's stomach turned to liquid. Shor had been working on Raina's behalf the day he had found her here, in the little dog cote. Sickness flooded Effie's head and chest, and she turned away from the dogs to vomit. Even as she ran her fist over her mouth to clean it, Lady Bee began lapping away at what had been produced.

"What was that?" Mace Blackhail's voice suddenly sounded close.

"Shanks dogs. With any luck a fever'll take 'em."

Mace Blackhail grunted. "Be off with you, woman. And don't follow me here again. People will mark our meeting." The leashes he held jingled. "Do your business."

"Cutty'll bide his time. He'll wait till things settle and the girl has long forgotten him, and then he'll take her in such a place as she canna get away."

A disgusted breath was almost lost to the wind. "I want her gone, and quickly."

"My Cutty won't be rushed. Not now he knows she's witched."

Mace Blackhail said something, but the wind drove the words away.

"Me and Cutty need no lessons in trespass from you."

"And I need no lessons in man-craft from a woman who lights torches for her supper. *Go.*" The word was spoken in a whisper, but it carried better than anything else Mace Blackhail had said. So strong was its compulsion that Effie found herself obeying it, edging farther away from the door. Even the shankshounds quieted.

Footsteps receded toward the roundhouse. All was silent for a long moment, then Mace called to his dogs. A door creaked open, dogs shrieked and howled and dashed through the snow. A wet nose probed the door to the little dog cote. And then a command was spoken and Mace Blackhail led his killers away.

Deep inside the cote, Effie hugged her knees. The shankshounds formed a barrier of dogs around her, yet for the first time in all the months she had been coming here she no longer felt safe.

# THIRTY-FOUR

### *Men Buying Clothes for a Girl*

How DO YOU FEEL?" Raif's face was grave as he asked the question. A scarred hand smoothed the edge of the blanket that covered her.

"Well . . . I think." Ash rubbed her eyes. "I feel a bit knotted inside, as if Heritas Cant had bound all my organs with string." Raif didn't like Heritas Cant; Ash could tell that from the brief twitch of muscles around his mouth as she mentioned his name.

"Are you well enough to ride?"

"Do I have a choice?"

Raif made no answer. He looked at her with dark eyes then turned away.

They were sitting in the room Heritas Cant had first greeted them in last night. Judging from the bands of gray light that shone beneath the shutters, it was sometime after midday. Ash had slept on a padded bench close to the fire. She had no memory of being brought here, didn't even know if she had walked on her own two feet or been carried inside.

The last thing she remembered before waking and finding herself snug and well wrapped by the fire was the sound of Heritas Cant's blood dripping into a bowl. Ash shivered. She could still taste the fear in her mouth.

"I'll leave you for now," Raif said. "Eat your breakfast." He frowned. "Angus and I went to the market this morning. We bought you some new clothes. They're in the basket by the table." He opened the door. "And there's a pony outside, too."

Ash raised herself up from the bench. "A pony?"

"Yes. She's mountain bred. Gray as a storm cloud."

"You picked her?"

Raif nodded. Their eyes met.

A moment passed. Then Ash said, "I won't hold you to any promise you made last night. It was all so . . ." She shook her head. "I had no right to ask for your help."

An expression that Ash didn't understand glowed with cold light in Raif's eyes. For a moment he looked older, harder, like someone she might cross the street to avoid. "I'll take back no promise, spoken or unspoken. I owe loyalty to my uncle and will say no word against him that is not to his face. Nor will I speak ill of Heritas Cant, for I respect his strength of mind and am grateful for all he has done. Yet know this. My reasons for helping you are not the same as theirs. I have no interest in the Reach."

"I know. That's why I turned to you last night. That's why I told you the truth by the Spill."

Raif looked at her and did not speak. After a moment he turned to leave.

"I'm sorry," she said, halting him.

"For what?"

Ash found herself struggling for words. He was giving her so much . . . quietly and with no fuss. "For letting you touch me that day by Vaingate."

Raif's hand rose to his throat, where it probed until it found the black bit of horn he called his lore. Surprisingly he smiled, and it was such a beautiful thing to see that Ash caught her breath. "You are worthy of respect, Asarhia March."

Before Ash could decide what sort of answer he had given

her, the door clicked closed and he was gone. Stupidly she stared at the space he had left behind.

She took her time getting ready after that, pausing to eat slices of cold fried bread and sour winter apples. Someone, probably Cloistress Gannet, had seen to it that she had everything she needed to take a bath. It seemed a long time since she'd last had the luxury of soap and water, and she stripped off her clothes and stood naked in the copper tub and let the hot steam soak her skin. After a time she scrubbed the grime from her body and worked her hair into a frothy lather that smelled of oats and winter mint. The water beneath her soon turned gray, and for the briefest moment she considered calling to Katia to bring more.

Ash stepped out of the tub. The water seemed suddenly cold, and she could not dry herself quickly enough. Katia was dead. Gone. Hung on the gallows for crows to pick at and all the world to see.

And Penthero Iss had put her there. Ash dropped the wool towel into the tub and watched as it soaked up the dirty water. She understood more about her foster father now. Last night while Heritas Cant spoke of Reaches and the Blind and the creatures who lived there, Ash had thought of Iss. Everything he had ever done and said to her—every kindness he had shown, every kiss he had given, every little attention he had paid her—was a lie. She was a Reach, and he had known it. It was why he had come to her late at night, asking slyly worded questions about her dreams. It was why he had set Katia to watch her chamber, the Knife to guard her door, and Caydis Zerbina to steal away her things.

Penthero Iss had wanted his own Reach.

Ash stood in the center of the room and let that fact sink in. Gooseflesh pricked along her arms and chest, and after a while she began to shake uncontrollably. Her foster father had planned to lock her away in the Splinter and keep her for himself. Already he had something, someone, imprisoned there, and she was the next piece he meant to add to his collection.

How long had he known what she was? Always? Had it been the only reason he had saved her?

Ash didn't know how long she stood there, shaking, didn't

even know if she shook from anger, shock, or cold. Heritas Cant's words had remade her life. Her memories were now as dirty as the water in the tub.

The hard clack of wood hitting wood jolted her from her thoughts. "Yes?" she called, falling back into her old ways of command as easily as if she had never left Mask Fortress.

"It is Heritas Cant. I must speak with you before you leave."

"Wait a moment while I dress." Ash's voice was as cold as her body. She crossed to the table where the basket of new clothes lay and began sorting through them. Two men buying clothes for a girl! Ash smiled a crazy tear-filled smile as she looked on what they had bought. They meant to spoil her. They had thought of everything and nothing, buying red silk skirts and pretty embroidered blouses and the finest, softest woolen cloak she had ever felt or seen. Everything was dyed in bright and lovely colors: a waistcoat of peacock blue, ribbons as green as emeralds, and suede boots the color of rust.

Ash found herself laughing and crying as she held up a needlepoint bodice as fine as anything she had ever seen on a grangelord's wife in Mask Fortress. There were slippers and wraps and fine woolly mittens, lace collars, bone buttons, and shoes: everything two men thought a girl needed. Everything they thought she'd love.

She did love them. She loved them so fiercely, she hugged them to her chest like living things. The thought of Angus and Raif walking around a market, choosing colors, feeling textures, guessing sizes, and talking trim made her giggle like a child. On the other side of the door, she heard Heritas Cant wheezing. One of his sticks tapped impatiently against the floor.

Time she was dressed. Only she could find neither wool stockings nor small linens in the basket. Ash shrugged. Men couldn't be relied on to think of *those*. She'd have to make do with the ones she had.

Having picked out the plainest wool skirt, a white blouse embroidered with tiny forget-me-nots, and the peacock blue waistcoat, Ash began folding the other clothes away. As she picked up the red silk skirt, a small muslin bag fell from its folds. She scooped it up and untied the string. Underthings. The bag contained pretty ladies' underthings, all scented and fastened with bows. *Angus,* she thought immediately. *Angus remembered to buy these.*

Five minutes later, dressed and ready, she opened the door to Heritas Cant.

He did not look well. The twin sticks he used to walk with shook with the force of his weight. Immediately feeling guilty about making him wait, Ash came forward to help him. He shook her away, and they both spent an awkward few minutes as he made his way toward the fire and then settled himself on a high-seated, high-backed chair that Ash guessed had been specially built for his use.

His first words to her were, "Money wasted." And it took her a moment to realize he was talking about her new clothes.

She said nothing.

"Are you well?" Cant's green eyes seemed to extract the answer from her before she spoke, and the nod she gave had the quality of an afterthought. "Good. Good. The bloodwards I have set are in place, then. Can you feel them?"

"I think so. My insides feel tight, almost as if they've been battened down."

"In some ways they are." Cant struggled to adjust his right leg, which rested in an odd way beneath him. "Wardings do two things. First, they conceal you, making it difficult for magic users and the creatures of the Blind to track you down. Now this doesn't mean they won't or can't find you, for if you draw upon your Reach power, you might as well light a beacon on the highest hill, put a horn to your lips, and blow. No. The wardings are just a trick to fool those who don't look too close."

Ash made herself nod.

"Second, wardings protect you. The restraint you feel is part of the barrier I have erected. Your body is bound by cords of sorcery. They wrap around your heart, your liver, your brain, and your womb, shielding them from harm or interference. They are strong now, yet time will wear them. I pray they will last until you make it to the Cavern of Black Ice, but in truth I cannot be certain. You can help by making yourself strong. Eat well and often, sleep for as long as you can, do not drive yourself hard, and never put yourself in a position where fear might lead you to draw sorcery."

"I'm not sure I understand."

"As a Reach you were born for one thing: to make a rift in the Blindwall. The power is here"—he poked a finger at his chest—"inside you. And nothing of flesh and blood can stand against it when you draw it forth and reach." Cant's eyes were suddenly hard, green jewels in a face so pale it could have belonged to a corpse. "You think I mean to scare you, Asarhia March. Well, perhaps I do. Perhaps I myself am scared. This is an old land we live in, and old myths and old powers sustain it. Before the clans and the city men came here, before even the Sull settled in their cities of icewood and stone, there were others, not men, not as we would name them, yet they had eyes and mouths like men, and built great halls of earth and timber in the heart of the Want. I cannot tell you how many centuries they lived for, but I do know they died out within a hundred years, slaughtered or taken by the creatures in the Blind. The Sull call it *Ben Horo,* the Time Before. They hold the knowledge of these others close, pass it down from generation to generation, even though they share neither blood nor kinship with them. This they do to honor the memories of the Old Ones as they named them, and to keep fear of the Endlords alive."

"Why tell me this now?"

"Because you must know what is at stake. Any magic user who is untrained is dangerous. Anger, terror, fear: Any strong emotion can concentrate power. You must guard yourself against such things. Lash out in anger, and sorcery may be released with the blow. You cannot afford to lose control of your emotions. More than your own life depends on it."

Ash decided she would say nothing . . . and not be afraid.

"If there were more time, I could show you what the Sull call *Saer Rahl,* the Way of the Flame, which teaches men and women how to master their emotions and never act out of anger or fear." Cant smiled thinly. "I never took to it myself, but then I was born on the slopes of the Shattered Mountains, and no flames I knew burned cold."

Cant clicked his sticks against the floor. "So I must send

you north with nothing but bloodwards to protect you. And perhaps we should both pray that next time we meet your Reach power will be gone and you'll have no need of lessons in self-control from an old man such as me. Just know this: Any kind of sorcery you draw before you reach the cavern will blast through my constraints." Spittle shot from Cant's lips. "Is that clear?"

"Yes."

"The wardings will not withstand Reach power." A pause followed, and then he murmured, "Little can."

Ash held herself tall. She would show no reaction to this man.

Cant watched her for a moment, then shrugged. "Well, that's all I mean to say." He began the long process of rising to his feet, and Ash turned away to give him privacy to position his legs and sticks. His breaths sounded like discharged arrows at her back.

When finally he had moved himself close to the door, she turned and said, "How did my foster father know I was a Reach?"

"Do you really mean *how* or *when*?"

Surprised by his cleverness, Ash confessed the truth. "Yes, when?"

An expression looking much like sympathy charged the slack muscles of Cant's face. "Prophecies that foretell the coming of the next Reach have been passed from mouth to mouth ever since the last Reach died ten centuries ago. I have read or heard many of them myself. Some are obvious fakes, written by the sort of men and women who take pleasure in hoaxes and tricks. Others are food for scholars, filled with so many archaic references and metaphors that no two people can agree on their meaning. Others still are written in dead languages that once translated lose their subtlety and sense. A few, just a few, have the ring of truth about them. One such prophecy is a child's verse. It has been known and spoken in the North for many years." Cant hesitated.

"Say it."

Cant nodded. He adjusted his sticks to better bear his weight and then spoke in the soft voice of secrets and confessions.

*First to breathe upon a mountain*

*First to gaze upon a barren gate*

*First to Reach in the hands of her captors*

*Last to learn her fate.*

Silence filled the room like cold water. Ash breathed and thought and did not move. Cant waited. The air surrounding them was thick and dark, filled with the scent of old things. Ash met Cant's gaze and held it until he looked away. She had no desire to discuss the verse with him. Its meaning was clear. She had been left on the north face of Mount Slain, five paces away from Vaingate, the *barren* gate, and Penthero Iss, Angus Lok, and this man standing before her had all known who she was before she had known herself.

Yes, Cant had answered her question, the real one she had not asked. Her foster father had known all along. Scores of children were abandoned each year in Spire Vanis, left in doorways of grand manses, on the steps of the Bone Temple, or at the foot of Theron Pengaron's statue in the Square of Four Prayers. Hundreds of children must have passed through Iss' hands, yet he'd chosen to keep just one. A baby girl left outside Vaingate to die.

Ash closed her eyes, told herself she must be strong. "Go now," she said to Cant. "Tell Angus I am ready."

Cant's mouth worked upon a word but did not speak it. Like a servant obeying orders, he bowed his head and left.

Only when the door had closed behind him and she heard the click of the latch did she reach over and grab the table for support. She had thought her father loved her.

Minutes later when Angus entered the room, she was composed, her face cleared of all emotion. She was surprised at the wave of relief she felt upon seeing his big red face. He looked well and had taken the trouble to shave his beard and trim his hair.

"You look beautiful," he said, his gaze missing no detail of her hair, clothes, or feet. "Blue suits you. I thought it might."

She had forgotten about her new clothes, forgotten even

that she was wearing them. She went to reply, but for some reason it was hard to speak. Smiling instead, she made a litle twirl to show off her dress. As the wool skirt whipped against her ankles, it occurred to her that she had performed this little ceremony countless times for Penthero Iss.

Angus looked at her without smiling. Suddenly he didn't seem much in the mood for talking, either.

"I want to thank you," Ash began, "for all the lovely things—"

"Hush," Angus said, not gently. "It was nothing. Nothing." His voice had a roughness to it that she didn't understand. "Well, we'd better be on our way. Raif's waiting outside with the horses." With that he scooped up the basket containing the remainder of her clothes and made his way from the room.

Ash put on her new cloak and gloves, then followed him. In the darkness of the hall she met gazes with Cloistress Gannet. The tiny black-clad woman gave no greeting, save to pinch her dry little mouth into an even drier line.

Angus held open the door against the wind. A storm was picking up, and snowflakes sailed through the doorway, coming to land on the red-and-cream rug that covered the floor. *Cant won't like that one bit,* Ash thought, fastening her cloak ties in haste.

Her new boots sank deep into the snow as she walked across the courtyard toward Raif. He was standing by a black iron gate, holding Moose, the bay, and a full-grown pony with thick legs and a strong neck. The creature was gray, like Moose, but darker and more blotchy, not so elegantly turned, as Master Haysticks would say. She had a large head and three white socks and wasn't a bit like a grand horse at all.

Raif grinned as she approached. The storm suited him. He didn't shiver or stamp his feet as most people did in foul weather. Tilting his head toward the pony, he said, "She's a beauty, isn't she?"

"Yes." Ash stopped short of the creature so as not to alarm her on their first meeting. "What's her name?"

"Snowshoe." Raif continued to grin.

Ash grinned madly back. "It's a perfect name. Perfect." Stripping off her new gloves, she moved wide of the pony so she could approach her from the side. "Snowshoe," she said softly, to get her attention. Arms down at her side, Ash stepped closer, presenting herself for sniffing. Master Haysticks had always been particular about that. *Let a new horse sniff you before you touch it,* he'd said. *Else it's like a total stranger coming up to you and poking you in the neck.* Ash very much wanted Snowshoe to like her. It was suddenly the most important thing.

Snowshoe sniffed and looked, then made a rolling motion with her head. Ash glanced at Raif, who nodded. Leaning in toward the pony, Ash raised her hand and stroked the bottom of the creature's neck. Snowshoe's huge brown eye watched her closely. By the time Ash had worked her hand down to the withers, Snowshoe was moving her chest forward to meet each stroke. Ash's heart tightened with joy. When Raif held out his hand, presenting her with a small green apple to give to the pony, she thought she might cry.

"Take it," he said. "The last owner said they were her favorites."

The apple was offered and taken. Snowshoe allowed her mane and back to be stroked while she crunched it.

"Aye, you've made a friend there," Angus said, approaching with the last of the packs. Ash smiled at him as he loaded the horses. The hound bites on the bay's flanks were no longer bandaged, and she was relieved to see they were closed and dry. When she raised her gaze from the gelding's flank, she noticed Heritas Cant standing in the doorway, watching her.

"Here, give me your wee footie." Angus bent at the waist, ready to help her mount.

A little unnerved by Cant's presence, Ash placed her left foot in Angus' cupped hands and levered herself onto Snowshoe's back. The saddle fit perfectly, and Raif moved quickly to adjust the stirrups to her leg. Snowshoe held herself steady all the while, as calm as if she met new riders every day in a storm.

When everyone was mounted and ready, Cant called out from the doorway. "The north road should be clear. Follow it until dark and then turn west when you pass the twin stormbarns of Clan's Reach."

Angus nodded. "Aye, Heritas. We'll do just that. I thank you for the warmth of your hearth and the knowledge you have given. Gods willing, we'll meet again afore winter's end."

Cant made no reply, save to click his sticks against the stone step.

"I owe you a debt, Heritas Cant," Raif said, his voice rising to compete with the storm. "When we meet again I'll repay it."

Cant shook his head. "I will not add to your burdens, Clansman, by claiming a debt against you."

Ash watched Raif's face as he listened to the reply. A muscle high on his cheek pulsed, and then he bowed his head and looked away. Ash stroked Snowshoe's neck, searching for warmth. Turning the pony into the street, she nodded her farewell to Heritas Cant.

Ille Glaive was differently made from Spire Vanis. As Ash trotted the pony down the street, past crumbling stonework, slate-roofed mansions, sealed-up sewers, and lead pipes venting steam, she began to see layers in the stone. The lower cellar levels that were only partially visible from the street were built from finely hewn stone that was black with soot and age. Ash saw moons and stars carved into the risers of cellar steps and the undersides of arches. Aboveground the stone was newer, lighter, the walls constructed from softer, more workable sandstone. Everything seemed to be heaped upon everything else, and buildings creaked and listed under the weight of added stories, ring towers, and timber bridges. In the distance the five lead-capped domes of the Lake Keep could clearly be seen rising high above the great curtain wall of ironstone that surrounded them. The Three Tears of Ille Glaive—the Black Tear of the Spill, the Red Tear of Sull blood, and the Steel Tear of Dunness Fey's sword—flew on stiff white banners from their hoardings. Ash remembered her foster father telling her that the Lake Keep was built around a pool of black water known as the Eye of the Spill. The pool was said to be deeper than the lake itself, and strange blind fishes were said to swim there.

The nearer they drew to Ille Glaive's north wall, the more squalid the city became. Many buildings were little more than occupied ruins. Ash studied the caved roofs, boarded windows, and iced-up drains with eyes that had seen such things before. She knew what it felt like to be out on the streets, cold and hungry and alone. A journey north along the Storm Margin was nothing compared with that.

Quickly, before her mind turned to the subject of Heritas Cant and all that he had said, Ash began patting Snowshoe's neck and saying horsey things out loud. She couldn't think about being a Reach. Not now. Not yet.

The storm darkened as they approached the Old Sull Gate. Mounds of brown snow had been piled to either side of the gateposts, and rows of icicles hung from the gate and its rigging, wet and dripping like monster's teeth. Angus dismounted but indicated that Ash should keep her seat. He appeared calm, yet Ash saw the way his gaze flickered from the gate tower to the guards in white mail shirts to the bowmen walking the wall.

The north gate of Ille Glaive was old and beautifully carved from honey-colored stone. It matched neither the color nor the style of the wall in which it was set. Unlike the gates in Spire Vanis, it had not been designed to impress anyone with its size and grandeur and existed simply as a thing of beauty, like an entrance to a holy place. A landscape of gently sloping hills, valleys, thick forests, and gorges alive with crashing water was carved across its posts and arch.

"The clanholds," murmured Raif.

Ash turned to look at him. Snow swirled around his face, switching this way and that with every change of the wind. He held Moose's reins at tension, and Ash was reminded of what he looked like when he was drawing a bow.

"Aye," Angus said. "There's parts of Dhoone and Blackhail and Bludd up there. The stone was cut and carved by Sull masons. All their gates tell stories of the lands that lie beyond."

Raif did not acknowledge what he said. Ash watched him as they joined the thin line of people waiting to take leave of the city. His gaze never returned to the gate.

A woman farmer with a dog and cart and an old trapper dressed in rabbit furs that stank like all the hells stood ahead of them in line. Two guards wearing the Three Tears at their breasts gave them little trouble as they passed. Ash expected Angus to be relieved when they took the gate unchallenged, yet no part of his body relaxed. *What is he afraid of?* she wondered as she caught him looking over his shoulder one last time.

Beyond the city walls the storm raged. Ash's eyes and mouth filled with snow the moment the pony cleared the gate, and she was forced to pull her fox hood so close that she looked at the world through a filter of gray fur. The north road stretched out ahead of her, straight as an arrow and wide as four carts. The cityhold of Ille Glaive, with its sprawling farms, stout outwalls, and tight little villages where every building shared walls with another, spread across the horizon like a land made of snow. Everything was white, even the sky. The only dark patches were chimney stacks and smoke holes on the roofs of a thousand farms.

Angus mounted and set a brisk pace north.

Snow drove into the horses' faces all the way. Darkness came early, moving south through the cityhold like a second storm. The wind died along with the light, and the sudden drop in temperature bred frost. Ash huddled in her oilskins, aware of every gapehole, eyelet, and poorly stitched seam. Cold settled in her chest like a disease. Every breath she exhaled caught in her hood and turned to blue ice. Lights from roadside taverns began to look tempting, yet Angus showed little interest in stopping. Smoke smelling of roast meat and onions burned black blew across the road, making Ash's mouth fill with saliva and her stomach growl. Hours passed, yet Angus still refused to call a halt.

Ash sank into the misery of aching thighs, numb fingers, cracked lips, and a full bladder. She took to looking at the starless sky and wondering how long it would be before dawn. She had already decided that Angus meant to ride through the night.

Finally Raif spoke up, saying something to Angus that Ash couldn't hear. Whispers passed between the two. Angus shook his head. Raif's voice dropped dangerously low . . . Ash heard him speak her name. Angus' shoulders stiffened for an instant, yet on his very next breath he relented. Glancing over at Ash, he said, "Aye. A short stop will do no harm."

Ash tried not to let the relief show on her face.

They rode a while longer, until they were free from the light of nearby villages and Angus was satisfied with the density of trees along the road. Ash smelled the sharp vinegary scent of resin as they headed for a stand of blackstone pines. Snowshoe was delighted to be off the road and found much to sniff at beneath the snow. Ash looked over the tops of the pines as she waited for the pony to raise her head. The northern horizon was dominated by a row of jagged peaks, dark shadows against a nearly black sky.

"The Bitter Hills," Angus said as his boots thudded into the snow. "The clanholds stand beyond them. Ganmiddich, Bannen, and Croser lie that way."

Hearing Angus speak, Ash knew she had been watched. Did he always mind her so closely that he could tell where her eyes focused? She dismounted Snowshoe in silence, unwilling to draw Angus out on the subject of clans. Something inside her knew that Raif would not welcome it.

"On certain days if you look northeast, you can see a light above the hills. Ganmiddich has a tower, though I can't say as they built it, and they light fires in the topmost chamber so the blaze can be seen throughout the North."

Ash glanced at Raif. He was down from Moose, busy tending to the gelding's nose and mouth. He gave no indication of having heard what Angus said, yet sound traveled well in the makeshift hall of pines.

Angus began filling snufflebags with oats. "Last time I saw the tower lit was when the old chief Ork Ganmiddich died. They doused the timbers with milk of magna to make the flames burn white."

Out of the corner of her eye, Ash saw Raif's hand come down to touch the silver-capped horn he wore at his belt. *He's showing his respect,* she thought.

Perhaps Angus noticed the gesture too, for he didn't speak anymore about the tower or the clans, simply walked among the horses, bringing snowmelt and grain.

Ash worked the cramps from her legs by stamping her feet in the snow. After a while Raif came over bearing food.

There was square-cut oatbread that Raif called bannock, crumbly white cheese, cold black bacon, hard apples, and flat beer. They ate it sitting on a storm-felled pine, and it tasted like a feast. Angus joined them halfway, consuming everything with gusto except the beer. "I canna do it," he cried, slapping a hand upon his heart. "I'll drink warm beer, cold beer, beer thickened with oats, iron filings, and eggs, but I canna drink a flat brew. A man must draw the line somewhere."

It was good to laugh. Angus passed around his rabbit flask, insisting that both Ash and Raif take a mouthful of some "real warmth" instead. Ash drank, though the contents tasted like lamp fuel and smelled of dead trees. "That's the birch," Angus explained as Ash's eyes watered. "There's a curl of bark in the bottom of the flask. It'll make you grow as tall as a tree . . . or is it as thick as one? I canna remember which."

Ash grinned. It was impossible not to like Angus Lok. Handing back the flask, she stood and brushed the snow from her skirt. "Just going to stretch my legs a bit."

"I'll come with you," Raif said, making to stand.

Angus put a hand on his arm. "I think our wee lassie of the ice needs a spot of privacy."

Raif look puzzled for a moment, then understanding dawned on his face. Quickly he settled himself back on the log.

Angus' copper eyes twinkled as he turned to Ash and said, "Go ahead. We'll be here if you need us."

Unable to decide if she was embarrassed or amused, Ash walked away. Angus Lok knew a lot about girls.

Finding a sprawling tangle of dogwoods, she relieved herself in the cover they created. The fastenings on her new clothes caused her much irritation, and her fingers were half-frozen and nearly useless. By the time she arrived back in the clearing, both Raif and Angus were mounted and ready to move on. Snufflebags and pigskin water buckets had been packed away, and all that was left of the meal they had eaten was a handful of brown apple cores in the snow.

Snowshoe showed no signs of weariness and held herself still while Ash mounted. Determined not to let her own exhaustion show, Ash made a point of sitting high in the saddle as Angus took them north through the pines. Eventually they came upon a game trail that led west, and Angus seemed content to follow where it led. They rode for some time through the dark hours of night, passing abandoned farm buildings, frozen streams, and forests steaming with mist, then Angus surprised everyone by signaling a halt.

Turning due east, he stood high in his stirrups and looked back along the path they'd just traveled. Shaking his head, he said, "It's not the finest ghost trail I've ever set, but it'll just have to do." He kicked the bay forward. "As it's high time we turned for home."

# THIRTY-FIVE

## *Finding Lost Things*

MEEDA LONGWALKER'S DOGS found the raven's frozen corpse beneath two feet of glaciated snow. She was minking in the mew-fallen snow nineteen leagues east of the Heart, when her team of terriers began excavation on a new set. Meeda had been minking on the high plateau known as Old Man's Rib for fifty years, and she knew the moment her dogs started digging that there was nothing but hard rock beneath the snow.

She nearly called them off. Across the empty streambed, on the thickly wooded bank where ten thousand years of willow and spruce growth had broken down the bedrock into fine powdery soil, had been her intended destination: soft land where she knew a mother and her three cubs lived. Yet the dogs were excited about something, and there was always a chance of a carcass. Meeda had known bitches to tear limbs and genitals from male minks in a frenzy of protective mothering, then leave the males for dead. A frozen and bloody mink pelt was no good for a cloak or a coat, but it could be washed and used as lining for gloves, game bags, and hoods. It was worth the time and effort of pursuit. Barely.

Slipping a strip of inner birch bark between loose lips long drained of pigment by age, Meeda stood back and waited for her dogs to finish digging. Her terriers, much maligned by male hunters for their small size, small brains, and small muzzles, shredded the snow with claws so sharp and strong that even now after fifty years of living with their breed, Meeda feared to let them close to her face. The male hunters were right: They *did* have small brains. But Meeda Longwalker had long realized that a small brain acutely focused was often more effective than a large one split by many thoughts.

When she caught her first glimpse of the dark form beneath the snow, Meeda spat out the birch bark and issued a few choice curses to the Lord of Creatures Hunted. Dark was not what she wanted. Dark was not what Slygo Toothripper had promised to trade her for a pair of good new boots and a metal spearhead. Slygo wanted white. Dark mink pelts were worth double their weight in arrowheads. White pelts were worth ten times that and more.

*"Mashi!"* Meeda cried to the terriers, halting them instantly. She would waste no more time digging a dark and bloody carcass from the snow.

The terriers feared Meeda even more than they loved to dig flesh, and to a dog all stepped aside from the excavation, allowing their mistress space to inspect their work. Meeda prided herself on being the greatest living minker in the Racklands. Fifty years of experience, eleven generations of dogs, five thousand leagues walked and another ten thousand ridden, and only twenty-eight days lost to childbirth, grief, and sickness. What man could boast such a record? As always before she had bagged her first catch of the day, Meeda was impatient with herself and her dogs, but she knew that certain rituals had to be maintained.

Terriers were like children: When they went to the trouble of excavating a den, a freshly killed carcass, or even a set of old bones, they needed to be praised for their efforts. Meeda looked down at four sets of dark eager eyes, and although she didn't much feel like it she drew her icewood stick from her belt.

"What have we here?" she said, prodding at the topsnow covering the dark, mink-size carcass. Two sons she had birthed, yet their names had been spoken less than those four words.

Muscles in the terriers' necks strained. One, a young pup barely eight months old, sprayed the snow with urine in his excitement. Meeda frowned. She would have to beat that out of him: What if a perfect white mink had lain dead instead of—

A raven.

Meeda Longwalker's face cooled beneath her lynx hood as she upturned a clod of snow to reveal the blue gleam of a raven's bill. *Ill tidings.* The thought came so swiftly, it was as if a stranger had leaned over her bent back and whispered the words in her ear. Meeda had half a mind to walk away, call her dogs to heel, and walk as fast as her knee joints would permit toward the empty streambed and the wooded bank. She was a minker, nothing more. It was not her place to deal in messages and omens. Yet even as she puffed herself up with excuses, she knew that it was her fate to find the raven and her duty to bring it home.

There would be no mink trapped today.

Speaking more harshly than was her wont to the terriers, she kept them at a distance while she finished the excavation with her own gloved hands. The raven had been killed by a pair of hawks. Its eyes had been plucked out, and the soft black down on its throat was stiff with the shiny substance of dried blood. The hawks had attacked it in midflight, and the impact of the fall had severed its left wing and sent its rib cage smashing into its heart. Meeda clucked softly as she scraped away the snow. Hawks had little love for any predatory birds entering their territory, but seldom had she witnessed the result of such a violent attack. Never had she known them to take down a raven.

As she freed its lower body from the snow, Meeda noticed something silver and scaled, like fishskin, flash as it caught the winter light. Meeda Longwalker knew then that an ill omen was not the only thing the raven had brought to the Racklands. It had brought a message as well.

Stripping off her thick horseskin work gloves to reveal

hands crossed with the scars of dozens of sharp mink teeth, Meeda dropped to her knees in the snow. Her knife was in her hand before she knew it. A package the size of a child's little finger was bound to the raven's left leg. The silver material was pikeskin—her hunter's eyes could not help but pick out that one detail even as her mind was intent on something else. Should she open the package, read it?

The raven had come from a long way away, Meeda knew that. No one in the Racklands used pikeskin to bind messages to birds, and only two men in the Northern Territories used ravens to send them. The first man she knew little about; he was one of the Far Family and lived upon a distant western shore, where he feasted on the fat of the great whales in summer and sat deep within the ground, chewing sealskin, through the long winter nights. The second man was her son.

This message was for him, could *only* be for him. And judging from the desiccation of the raven's corpse, it was already eleven days late.

Meeda Longwalker cut the message free. The dry, freezing winds had long robbed the bird of all its fluids, yet even now she did not forsake her minker's caution: Never break the skin. It was foolishness, she knew, but there it was. She was too old to change her ways now.

Too old also to wait upon her son's hands and eyes to open and read the message. It was for him—she could not and would not pretend otherwise—but *her* dogs had dug it from the snow. The find was hers. And in Meeda Longwalker's adopted world of hunters, coursers, minkers, ferreters, badgerers, and trappers, that meant she could do with it what she wished.

With hands that were deceptively agile despite their age and scarring, Meeda slit the pikeskin package down the center where it had been fixed with fish glue. A piece of white bark, not dissimilar to the strip she had spat into the snow earlier, fell into her palm. It was soft, excellently worked with both saliva and some kind of animal fat she did not recognize. The message was burned into the wood.

Meeda read it slowly over minutes, though in truth it was barely two sentences long. Her father had been a learned man who believed in tutoring both his sons and his daughters in letters, lore, and history, but for as long as she could remember Meeda had valued freedom of her body more highly than freedom of her mind. As a child she had run from her lessons, even in full winter when her father and his High Speaker swore that the temperature outside was cold enough to kill a soft-skinned girl within minutes. Meeda had proven them all wrong, though now, in her old age, she felt a portion of shame for having mocked and disobeyed her father so completely and with such terrible joy. The High Speaker, unlike her father, still lived. He was the oldest man in the Racklands, second in power only to her son. He had no eyes, yet that did not stop Meeda from avoiding his blind gaze even now.

Shivering, she folded the message and slipped it into her game belt. The terriers, thinking she was reaching for her treat bag, began to snap and jostle for position. Meeda shook her head. No treats. Not today.

*"Mis!"* she told them. Home.

It was nineteen leagues back to the Heart of the Sull. Meeda Longwalker walked them no more quickly or slowly than normal, yet they cost her more and wore her more than any other leagues in her life. As the path rose from the valley floor and the white chalk cliffs of High Ground became visible above the Heart Fires, she spotted two mounted figures in the distance.

Ark Veinsplitter and Mal Naysayer.

Far Riders, returning from whatever journey her son had sent them on at Spring's End. Meeda dropped her hand to the belt, felt the message carried there. The two men did not know it, but they would barely have time to bleed their horses and blacken their hands in the ashes of the Heart Fires. They would need to travel north now. Meeda Longwalker, Daughter of the Sull, had listened to her father's teaching long enough to know that Far Riders responded to the silent summons of the gods.

\* \* \*

THEY RODE EAST THROUGH the night and much of the next day. A new dawn brought more snow and the kind of low, gusting winds that came from all directions and were impossible to guard against. The farther they traveled from Ille Glaive, the emptier the landscape became. Villages were rare occurrences, and the land became peopled with backbreaking rocks, frozen mudholes, and forests of tall, silent trees. Raif called it taiga. He said that much of the clanholds was like this.

They rested during the evening of the second day, making a cold camp some distance from a tiny village that boasted an alehouse, a dry forge, and an ancient retaining wall built to prevent snow and mud from sliding down the Bitter Hills and overrunning livestock and farms. A pair of ewes and their yearlings penned on a nearby slope were their only company as they slept through the night.

Ash was woken by Angus. It was still dark, but a blush of light on the southeast horizon told of imminent dawn. Ash had slept on a mattress of piled snow, wrapped in two layers of oilskins and wearing a mask of greased linen over her face. Frostbite was a real and constant danger, and at various points in the night she had been aware of hands touching her nose and cheeks through the cloth. Angus insisted on checking her now, his rough fingers feeling for any stiff or frozen skin. Raif saw to the horses, then laid out a breakfast of cold store. The bannock, which one night earlier had been soft and toasty, now had ice crystals at its heart.

While Ash and Raif filled the waterskins with snow, Angus hiked onto high ground and surveyed the surrounding land. Now, finally, Ash knew the reason behind his constant watchfulness: He didn't want any uninvited guests following him home.

He hadn't trusted Heritas Cant, not fully. Ash clearly remembered him telling Cant that they would travel north and then west. Only he'd never had any intention of doing such a thing. As soon as he'd judged it safe he had turned east instead. "Just a wee visit," he had said last night. "It'll only slow us down by three days—a day there, a day back, and one in the middle for some decent rest under a safe roof and a spot of scolding from my wife."

Ash had accepted his decision without question. She could not stop Angus and Raif from visiting their family.

How could she argue against the wish of two men to see their kin—she, who knew nothing of fathers and daughters and cousins and aunts? Cant's wardings would stretch the extra days. They had to.

The tail end of the storm had passed in the night, and the snow underfoot was still finding its level. The going was hard, but sunlight broke through the clouds at midmorning, creating a world of sparkling blue frost. Everyone's spirits lifted. Angus hummed a selection of tunes as he rode; Ash recognized one of them as "Badger in the Hole." Raif remained silent, but his hands were lighter on the reins and he often leaned forward to scratch Moose's neck and say some bit of nonsense to the horse. Watching the men's obvious excitement about the homecoming, Ash felt herself growing nervous. The thought of Angus' daughters knotted her stomach.

"Raif," Angus said as the snowbound roofs of a small village appeared on the horizon, "what say you take out that borrowed bow of yours and bring down something fitting for Darra's pot. She'd have my hamstrings for slingshots if I brought her two extra guests and no extra food."

Cords rose in Raif's neck as his uncle spoke, and Ash thought he might refuse. Yet after a moment he reached back over Moose's quarters and unfastened the bow from its case. The bow was one of the few things that had not been lost by the lake. It was a thing of beauty, horn and wood fitted together and then worked to a high sheen. Raif stripped down to bare hands to brace it. He worked quickly, tying knots, warming the wax-coated string, kneading the belly of the bow as he curved it. The bowcase now boasted a dozen straight, well-tilled arrows, and Raif drew one at random and put its head to the bow.

Something in his face changed as he scanned the surrounding territory for game. Ash saw nothing, only blackstone pines, hemlocks, bladdergrass, and snow, yet Raif's gaze focused on the spaces *between* things, and his eyes flickered as if they were tracking invisible beasts. Minutes passed. Angus busied himself by scraping the dirt from his fingernails with the tip of his belt knife. Ash could not take her eyes from Raif. He became something else when he had a bow in his hands, something she tried but could find no name for.

*Thuc!* The bow *thwacked* back, rattling as Raif's hand absorbed the recoil. Ash followed Raif's gaze but could see nothing. No creature cried out in pain or shock. A smell, like sulfur or copper, filled her nose and mouth. By the time she swallowed it was gone.

Angus, who Ash guessed hadn't really been interested in cleaning his nails at all, turned the bay toward the shot. Even as the bay's hooves sent snow flying, Raif released a second arrow.

"A pair of ptarmigan should be enough," he said softly, after a moment.

Ash did not know how to reply. She nodded quickly.

He turned to look at her. His drawhand was free of the bow, and she could see the pink, herringbone flesh of a recently healed injury on his palm. "You look frightened."

She tried a smile but failed. "I've seen you shoot things before."

"That's no answer."

It wasn't, and she knew it. Looking into his eyes, she saw how dark they were, even with the sun full upon them. She tried a second smile and said, "Are you afraid of *me*?"

Raif's own smile was slow in coming, but when it did it warmed her heart. "Not yet."

The moment between them lasted only as long as it took Angus to return with the ptarmigan, yet it was enough. They pulled their horses apart as Angus held the two fat white birds above his head and cried, "I'll be sleeping in the big bed tonight!"

Both Ash and Raif laughed.

The journey went quickly after that. They talked and rode and swapped stories. Ash was surprised to learn that Raif had never visited Angus' farm before or met any of Angus' daughters. She thought it strange that Angus had never brought his daughters north to Blackhail to meet their cousins, but Angus made a joke of it, saying he'd already lost one sister to a clansman and had no intention of losing his three girls as well. Ash laughed along with Raif, yet she was beginning to wonder what Angus feared. Why was it so important to hide his family from the rest of the world?

As midday approached they neared the village that had first appeared on the horizon. The ground was hard here, good for nothing save stone walls and sheep. The Bitter Hills rose to the north, sending winds whistling through tough gray grasses that somehow kept their heads above the snow. Sheep farms dotted the slopes. The air smelled of woodsmoke and manure and damp wool. A necklace of frozen ponds strung across the hills told of glaciers long gone.

The village itself consisted of two streets of stone-built houses sealed with tar. Ash saw signs of pride in ownership in the cleared ground surrounding each building and the well-maintained shutters and doors. Like the bay, the village *had* a name, yet Angus preferred not to give it.

Angus also preferred not to approach the village too closely, and he took them along a series of low roads, sheep runs, and dry creekbeds, changing course at least three times. By the time they arrived at the bank of a green-water river Ash had lost all sense of direction and couldn't have pointed the way back to the village if her entire life had depended on it. They followed the river downstream for an hour or so until it ran through a forest of ancient hardwoods. Towering elms, basswoods, and black oaks rose like an army around them. The wind was quiet here, and the only sound came from the horses' hooves snapping forest litter with every step.

Ash was the last to see the farmhouse. The forest did not thin: It stopped. One moment they were walking through deep green shade cast by hundred-year oaks, then suddenly there were no more trees. Sunlight dazzled Ash's eyes. Raif took a hard breath. Angus said a single word: *"Mis."*

The rear of the Lok farm lay a quarter league ahead, set into a stretch of softly worked farmland and framed by a white elm as tall and stately as a tower. The roof of the house was blue gray slate, and the walls were pale yellow stone. A low door, carved from honey-colored oak and gleaming with newly applied resin, formed the center of the main building, and all paths, partition walls, lean-to's, and outbuildings were built in an arc around it.

As Ash looked on the door opened. A woman . . . no, a girl . . . stepped onto the path. She was wearing a blue wool dress with a white collar and sturdy work boots. Her auburn hair reached past her waist. "Mother! Beth!" she called, her voice high and excited.

Angus made a sound deep in his throat and jumped down from his horse. Ash glanced at Raif, thinking that he would do likewise, but something must have been showing in her face, for he sent her a look that said, *I'll stay here with you.* Ash was surprised by her own relief.

Two other figures appeared in the doorway, a woman with dark gold hair and a girl of six or seven, dressed in the same plain wool as her older sister. The woman held something in her arms, and it took Ash a moment to realize it was a young child. The two girls raced down the path, shouting, "Father! Father!" The woman waited in the doorway, watching. Ash noticed her eyes flick to Raif and then to her. A small chill took Ash as she sat upon her pony and received the woman's attention.

Angus ran onto the path to meet his daughters. Catching them in a bear hug, he lifted them clean off the ground and swung them in a great circle, all the while calling them "his best girls."

Ash had to look away.

Raif, who had taken control of the bay's reins, clicked his tongue, encouraging all three horses to step forward. Snowshoe moved without Ash's consent. Ash wanted to stop her, *considered* stopping her, yet in the end she didn't. *It's just Angus' family,* she told herself. *I'm making a fuss over nothing.*

She just wished he had sons. Not daughters.

Angus put his daughters down, and both girls stepped away from him, allowing him a clear view of their mother at the door. Angus stripped off his gloves, pulled down his hood, and stood and looked at his wife. His eyes were dark as he waited for her to beckon him. With half a smile she called him forward, and the space separating them contracted to nothing at all as Angus moved toward the door.

Ash knew then that Angus had lied about his wife. All the threats she supposedly issued, all the rules she supposedly made, were nothing more than thin air.

Turning away from them, Ash met eyes with the eldest of the two girls. She was beautiful, Ash realized that straightaway, with hazel eyes and skin that glowed with good health. As the girl looked at Ash, her hand moved up from her side and was taken immediately by her younger sister. Such a little thing, yet neither girl even glanced at the other as they touched.

"Darra, I have brought visitors." Angus' voice broke the moment. Holding his wife's hand, he pulled her down from the step and onto the path. "Raif's come all this way to see you. He's brought a fine pair of ptarmigan."

Hearing Raif dismount at her side, Ash did likewise. Her eyes never left Angus' wife.

Darra Lok was dressed in a plain wool dress without jewelry or trim of any sort. Her fair hair was piled on her head in a style that Ash knew took only minutes each morning to fix. As her dark blue eyes met Raif's, she let the child she had been carrying at her hip slide to the ground. The little blond-haired girl headed straight for Angus, crawling fiercely through the snow and calling, "Papa!" loudly. Angus snatched her up and threw her into the air like a sack of grain. The child loved it. Giggling madly, she demanded, "More! More!"

With both arms empty, Darra looked to Raif.

"Da's gone," he said quietly.

"I know," she murmured. "I know." Ash could see that she wanted to take hold of Raif and hug him, yet he stood apart from her and all she could do was touch his sleeve. "Tem was a good, good man. I never met anyone more honest and more fair."

Raif nodded.

Darra smiled. "And he could dance . . . my, how he could dance. . . ."

No longer nodding, Raif turned away.

Darra's hand moved in the air after him.

"Cassy, Beth!" Angus said. "Run and open the barn." He held out his youngest daughter. "And take Little Moo with you. Hurry now."

The middle daughter pouted. "But Father, we want to meet the lady with silver hair—"

"Later."

The girls heard something in their father's voice that made their backs straighten. The eldest came and took Little Moo from her father's arms, and the three sisters headed for the side of the house. Ash watched them disappear, envy stabbing softly at her chest. When she glanced up, she saw Darra Lok watching her.

Angus gripped his wife by the wrist as he led her toward Ash. "Darra, this is Ash. She's from Spire Vanis. We're taking her north with us."

Darra's face was as pale and smooth as wax. She was shaking in a strange way, as if she were either very cold or very afraid.

Ash didn't understand what was happening. Darra's large eyes were filled with so much emotion, they frightened her. Glancing over her shoulder, she looked for Raif, but he was some distance behind her now, tending to the horses.

"Ash." Darra seemed to test the word as she spoke it. "Welcome to our house."

Ash didn't know what to do. This was no time for smiles. Darra Lok looked distraught. Her welcome seemed almost to hurt her as she spoke it. "Thank you," Ash said. "I'm glad to be here."

Darra Lok made a nervous gesture with her hands, brushing imaginary dirt from her apron.

Angus moved himself into a position between his wife and Ash, touching both of them on the shoulder. "Well, ladies," he said. "I think we should all go inside and have a little brose by the fire."

Ash didn't know what brose was. Suddenly nothing made any sense. Did Darra Lok know she was the Reach? Was it fear she saw in the older woman's eyes or something else?

Angus held on to both of them as they walked toward the house. Raif followed after, leading the horses. When the eldest daughter returned from the barn, carrying horse blankets and feedbags, he called her by name: Cassy. What the two said to each other, whether they touched, or hugged, or kissed, was something Ash never knew, as she stepped into the warm, firelit interior of the house, leaving Raif and Cassy to the snow.

In the short time it took to walk to the door, Darra Lok had composed herself, and when she turned to Ash and bade her strip off her cloak and take the seat closest to the fire, she looked and acted like a different woman. Smiling gently, she helped Ash with cloak ties, her fingers making quick work of the hooks and laces. Angus stood in the doorway, watching them, an unreadable look on his snowburned face.

"Well, don't just stand there, Angus Lok," said his wife. "Stoke the fire and fetch me the heavy iron pot—the one for heating bathwater. Oh, and you might as well fill it while you're on your way."

Angus smiled at Ash. "I told you what she was like." With that he went about his appointed task with all the grumbling and puffing of a man perfectly happy yet pretending not to be.

Ash looked around the large farmhouse kitchen. Undressed stone walls glowed like old parchment in the firelight. The blue slate floor was covered in worn rugs of all shapes and sizes and thicknesses; the oldest one looked to be a balding fox pelt that lay like a faithful dog beside the hearth. The fireplace was as big as a shed, and cast-iron shelves, roasting racks, and gridirons were suspended at various heights above the flames. An armory of knives, graters, skewers, roasting forks, and nut-and-bone crackers hung above the hearth on meat hooks, and a great black warming stone sat in the middle of the flames.

It was a hard-used, well-cared-for place. The large birch table that sat in the center of the room had been scrubbed down to the raw wood, and every chair in sight boasted a slat, spindle, or leg that had been repaired with newer stock.

"Sit," Darra said, hanging Ash's cloak over the back of a chair to dry. "I'll warm us some brose."

Ash did as she was told, finding a stout little stool to her liking. She watched as Darra poured frothy amber beer into a pot, then thickened it with a hand of oatmeal. "I'm sorry if my coming here has upset you."

Darra did not stop what she was doing as she replied, "No, Ash. It's me who should apologize to you. I offered a poor welcome. I . . . you . . ." She struggled for words. "It's not often Angus brings visitors to the house."

She had meant to say something else, Ash was sure of it, but before she had chance to question Darra further the door opened and Raif and all three of Angus' daughters burst into the room.

"Look, Mother!" cried the middle daughter. "Raif brought down two ptarmigan on the dog flats. He said they were flying as fast as eagles when he took them. And he's promised to teach me how to shoot."

Raif's smile was tactful. He had probably said no such thing.

"Hush, child," said Darra. "Raif, come and warm yourself by the hearth. We haven't got any black beer, I'm afraid, only brose."

"Brose will be good."

"I don't doubt it," Angus said, emerging from another door with a huge iron pot filled to the rim with water. "Tem's black beer has doubtless ruined your palate for life."

"It was useful for keeping flies away in summer," Raif said.

"Aye, and women and maidens, too!"

Everyone laughed. Ash guessed that Tem's beer was famous for being bad. She smiled, then joined in the laughter. It was good to learn something small and homely about Raif's life back in the clan.

"*Father.*" The middle daughter turned the word into a reprimand. Her large gray blue eyes rolled in the direction of Ash. "We haven't met the lady yet."

Ash felt her cheeks color. Cassy sent her a sympathetic *Sorry my sister's acting like a fool* look.

Angus frowned. He fitted the iron pot onto the warming stone, where its height and breadth halved the light in the room. That done, he turned and surveyed his three girls, who were lined up from smallest to tallest by the door. After a moment he growled at them, sounding just like an aging and much-put-upon wolf. Little Moo growled right back, mimicking him perfectly. The two elder girls tried but did not succeed in keeping straight faces.

"Daughters!" Angus complained to no one in particular. "Who would have them?"

"Grrrrrr." Little Moo growled again. She was really very good at it.

"All right! All right! You've worn me down!" Shaking his head, Angus turned to Ash. "Ash, these are my daughters: Casilyn, the eldest, and close to you and Raif in age. Beth"—Angus glowered theatrically at his middle daughter—"the talker of the family. And Maribel the—"

"Growler," said Beth, quick as only a child could.

Angus very nearly gave himself away by laughing. "The baby."

"Moo! Moo!" said Little Moo.

"Aye," Angus said. "My youngest child, for reasons known only to herself, refuses to answer to any name other than Little Moo."

"Moo! Moo!" repeated Little Moo, eminently satisfied that her name situation had been explained.

Ash smiled shyly at the three girls. Cassy smiled back; Beth curtsied in an elaborate manner, losing her footing on the knee bend and knocking into the door; and Little Moo giggled, growled, and said, "Moo! Moo!" a few more times for good measure.

"Girls," Angus said, "this is Ash. She's traveling with me and Raif for a while. And tonight she's our special guest and must be treated so by all of you. Understand?" All three girls nodded. "Good."

"Father, can Ash sleep with me and Beth tonight?" Cassy raised her bright hazel eyes to meet Ash's. "If you'd like to?"

Ash nodded. Cassy was almost as tall as she, but better filled out, with proper breasts and hips. Her hair was glorious, sometimes red, sometimes golden, thick and wavy and full of light. Ash thought for a brief moment of Katia, of her dark beautiful hair that no amount of pins could tame, then shut the memory away.

"Cassy, why don't you take Ash to your room?" Darra poured hot cloudy liquid into a set of wooden cups as she spoke. "Help her bathe and change if she'd like to. She's had a hard journey and may want to rest before supper."

Ash sent a look of thanks to Darra. Meeting Angus' family had left her shaken and exhausted.

"Can I come, too?" Eagerness lit up Beth's small pink face. "I'll help with her clothes and hair."

"No," Darra said. "Just Cassy."

"But—"

"I said *no*. You can go up later, once she's rested."

Beth closed her mouth. Her bottom lip trembled.

A moment passed. The kitchen was so quiet Ash could hear the impurities in the firewood sizzle as they burned.

Then Raif stood and extended his arm toward Beth. "What say you and I go outside and shred some wood? I'll have you hitting bull's eyes by sundown."

Ash loved him for that. It was the act of someone who knew what it was to have sisters and brothers of his own.

Issuing a high, excited scream, Beth ran to Raif's side and hugged him fiercely. Together they left the house, Beth hitting Raif with a barrage of questions about bows, arrows, ptarmigan, the lady with the silvery hair.

Angus and Darra exchanged a glance, then Angus slipped on two thick sheepskin mitts and picked the now hot iron basin from the hearth. "Follow me," he said to Cassy and Ash.

He led them up a flight of stairs and into a tiny, odd-shaped room. Once he'd placed the iron tub on the floor, he lit an oil lamp and left. Ash noticed how his hand came up to touch his daughter's cheek as he crossed toward the door.

"Would you like to wash now, or rest?" Cassy gestured toward one of the two boxed pallets that lay against opposing walls. The room was sparsely furnished, with plain walls and a rug of woven rushes. The only item of furniture beside the pallets was a small table that had originally been built for carpentry work, as the many hammered nailheads, saw marks, and chisel gouges attested to.

"I'm sorry the room's a bit bare. Beth and I hardly spend any time here."

Ash shook her head, thinking of her own silk-lined, thick-rugged, amber-warmed chamber in Mask Fortress. "No. I like it very much. The bathwater looks tempting. I think I might wash first."

Cassy came forward to help her with the hooks and eyes of her skirt. Her hands were rough and calloused, split in part by old scars, and Ash reminded herself that Cassy lived on a working farm.

"Father's away a lot some years," Cassy said, obviously noticing wherever Ash's gaze rested. "Last spring Mother and I had to shear the lambs ourselves. They kicked a lot."

Ash made no effort to hide her own street-worn hands.

"Usually Father tries to go away in the winter, when there isn't much to do except feed the chickens and milk the ewes. But sometimes the birds come in summer and spring and there's nothing he can do about it."

"Birds?"

"Messages . . . from people."

"Oh." Ash waited, but Cassy said no more. "Can no one in the village help with the sheep?"

Cassy shook her head, sending her auburn hair dancing.

"No. We never talk to anyone in the Three Villages. We keep to ourselves."

Ash thought that strange yet didn't say so. Stepping out of her skirt and underskirt, she watched as Cassy tested the bath. What was Angus afraid of? What made him hide his family away?

"The water's not very hot, I'm afraid. Father still imagines that girls are like men: One quick dunk and we're done."

Ash grinned. She liked Cassy very much.

"Your father's a kind man."

"Tell him that and he'd spend more time denying it than he would if you swore he was a rogue."

Bracing herself against the coolness of the water, Ash stepped into the iron basin. Cassy began making lather with a hard wedge of charcoal soap and a linen cloth. Ash guessed the cloth was Cassy's best, as it had little birds embroidered around the border.

Cassy began washing Ash's hair with the firm, capable

movements of a girl who probably performed the same duty each week on her sisters. "How long will you be gone?" she asked as she poured rinse water over Ash's scalp. "If it's all right to say."

"I don't know. Not long, I hope. A month, perhaps." As she spoke, Ash imagined a map of the Northern Territories in her head. The Storm Margin lay far to the west, caught between the Coastal Ranges and the Wrecking Sea. She knew only bits of things about the Margin; about the chain of Floating Isles just off its coast that were surrounded by mist year-round and where the Sull King Lyan Summerled was said to have died; and about the Ice Trappers in the Far North, who camped upon the sea ice in midwinter and chewed upon squares of frozen seal blood like clansmen chewed upon curd. Far to the south lay the Seahold, where the Trader Kings lived.

"I envy you."

Ash looked up to see Cassy Lok watching her closely. It was in her mind to say something lighthearted and dismissive, something about trekking across thick snow in winter not being the sort of thing any sane person would envy, yet when she saw the expression on Cassy's face, Ash knew instantly that Angus' daughter meant what she said. Cassy Lok wasn't the sort of person to say anything lightly.

"I envy you," Ash replied, and meant it.

## THIRTY-SIX

### A Moon Made of Blood

BREAKFAST WAS EATEN IN SILENCE. Crusty bread, smoked bacon, and mushrooms drenched in butter were washed down with ewe's milk flavored with pine nuts. All the plates and cups were made of white oak, so even the business of cutting and spearing did little to break the hush.

Angus ate as slowly as a condemned man, cutting his bacon into ever smaller bits until a substance resembling sawdust filled his plate. Raif sat by the kitchen's only window, a tub of wax floating in a bath of hot water by his side. Every now and then he'd scoop some of the wax with a cloth and work it into his bow. "Weatherproofing," he had said earlier to Beth, who never stopped asking him questions. More often than not his gaze was on the dark gray sky outside the window.

Cassy sat beside Ash on the bench by the fire. They did not speak, but the silence between them was comfortable. Cassy had Little Moo on her lap, and the little blond-haired child was sucking on a rasher of bacon as stiff as a twig. Darra Lok sat at the table with her husband and her middle child. Every now and then Ash was aware of Darra's gaze upon her. She pretended not to notice, but it worried her. What had Angus said to his wife?

Angus chose that moment to push his plate into the center of the table and stand. "We'd best be on our way."

Everyone, including Raif, stood up on hearing his words, and within seconds the Lok farmhouse became alive with activity. Cassy ran upstairs to fetch Ash's things, Beth ran to the stables to saddle the horses with Raif, Angus topped his rabbit flask from a keg by the door, and Darra began winding the remains of last night's ptarmigan in strips of waxed linen.

Ash started the long process of wrapping, buckling, and caulking herself against the cold. She didn't know if she was sorry to leave or not. Angus' family were close to what she had always imagined a family should be, yet she had no place in it, and that knowledge left her strangely cold.

She was Ash March, Foundling, left outside Vaingate to die.

The words—*her* words—made her stronger, and she said her good-byes to Angus' family and went to join Raif outside.

Saddlebags and bedrolls were buckled onto the horses, last words were spoken, and then the three travelers mounted and rode south through the forest of old trees.

Angus did not look back. Ash did, and she saw Cassy Lok's hazel eyes filled with longing and Darra Lok's blue ones filled with fear.

They followed the green river west for many leagues,

shoulders hunched against the wind, heads down, silent. Storm clouds formed troughs and swells in the sky, and it wasn't long before Ash felt rain spit against her face. Warm air driven south before the storm had caused a minor thaw, and the snow underfoot was wet, and not all pond ice could be trusted. Snowshoe was no dancer like the bay, but she was a wily pony and soon learned to follow Angus' gelding step for step. Gradually the old hardwoods gave way to open fells and stunted pines.

After a noonday meal of cold salted ptarmigan, Angus turned northwest toward the Bitter Hills. Ash sat and suffered the wind and rain. She would have been grateful for any sort of conversation, but neither Angus nor Raif had a mind to do anything but ride.

The Bitter Hills changed color the nearer you drew to them. Ash had first thought they were gray, then blue. Now, as she and her two companions headed straight for the walls and cirques of the hills' southern approach, she saw veins of green copper, white shale, and red iron threaded through the rock. Ash remembered her foster father telling her that the Bitter Hills had once been named mountains by the people of Ille Glaive, but visiting clansmen had laughed at them, saying, "These wee things? Why, they're naught but hills." With storm clouds massed at their throats like furs around a king, the Bitter Hills looked like mountains to Ash.

As darkness came and the rain cooled to sleet, Angus turned his party once more. Locating a path at the base of the hills that ran above an ice-sealed stream, he led them west along the border between Ille Glaive and the clanholds.

They traveled through much of the night. The hills acted as a barrier between the horses and the worst of the storm. As the hours wore on, Ash became increasingly aware of Cant's wardings. They dug into her chest like wire, painful sometimes when she moved too quickly or breathed too hard. She still didn't know what to make of Cant's claim that she was a Reach. Before Cant had spoken she had never heard that such a thing existed. And if a Reach had been born a thousand years ago, why did no one in Spire Vanis know it? Ash knew her history. Haldor Hews was the surlord

then, and he had reigned for sixty years. During that time he
had extended the reach of the cityhold to the southern tip of
the Black Spill and brought so much wealth into the city that
he became known as Haldor the Provider. Ash frowned. Yet
a Reach had been born then; Cant had said so. And a thousand years earlier . . . Ash thought a moment as she checked
her dates . . . Theron and Rangor Pengaron had ridden their
warhost north and founded the city itself.

Puzzled, Ash shook her head. It really didn't seem as if a
Reach could bring all the horrors that Cant said.

Not quite feeling relieved, Ash kicked her heels into
ponyflesh and turned her mind to other things.

Not much later Angus called a halt, and camp was made
hard against the stream. Raif lit a fire, but no one had the in-
clination or energy for chopping and stripping wood, and it
fizzled quickly after the ptarmigan fat had been rendered to
make stock. Ash fell asleep with grease on her lips, bundled
deep within a goosedown quilt that had been a gift from
Darra Lok.

A second, greater storm front moved south across the hills
overnight, and Ash was woken by a pebble spray of hailstones on her back. Locks of her hair that had escaped her
fox hood were stuck to the ground with frost. The temperature had dropped again, and when she crouched in the
bushes to make water, she half expected her urine to freeze.
It didn't. At least not in the time it took to straighten her
stockings and skirt.

No one spoke as they broke camp. The wind howled
through ridges and canyons, shifting pitch like a human voice.
Raif and Angus rode to either side of Ash, buffering her
against the storm. There was no true daylight to mark the
day's passage. The farther west they traveled, the flatter and
more rounded the hills became. Clouds boiled above them,
sending sprays of ice and snow to sand already smooth slopes.

"Ganmiddich Tower should be in that bank ahead," Angus
shouted as the stormlight began to fail, flinging his arm toward the clouds. "If we turned north here, we'd be at the
pass within an hour."

Ash looked but could see nothing except hailstones and
clouds.

Darkness descended even as Angus returned his hand to the reins. Ash kept glancing north, hoping for a glimpse of the tower.

After a while she became aware of a pale glow above the hilltops. Thick curtains of cloud hid its color and center, and at first she thought it was the rising moon or the north star. Then the wind gusted west, clearing a small portion of sky, and a ball of red fire was revealed.

Ash felt something drop in her stomach. Reaching over, she touched Raif's arm. His gaze followed hers, and she watched as his eyes and face turned red with reflected light.

"Light in the tower," he said quietly. "The red fire of Clan Bludd."

Those were the last words she heard him speak that night.

A flight of arrows skimmed the air, whirring as softly as a fisherman dropping a line. Something *thwacked* against Snowshoe's rump, making the pony rear and break with the other horses. Ash sawed at Snowshoe's mouth, but the pony was scared and determined to flee.

Similar impacts hit Moose and the bay. Raif fought his horse, pulling hard on the reins and wheeling the gelding through a half turn. As Ash looked on, he bit off one of his gloves and spat it into the snow. The bay stood his ground. Sull trained, Ash remembered, glimpsing twin flashes of steel as Angus drew both knife and sword.

A second arrow hit the pony in the chest. This time Ash got a quick look at the head before it fell: a thumb of rounded wood capped with lead. A blunt. As she tried to make sense of what that meant, a troop of mounted clansmen descended the southern slope. Ash saw long oiled braids, sable cloaks, dull plate, and boiled leather dyed the color of blood.

*Crack!* Ash's world flashed red and white as a blunt clipped her chin. Her teeth roots rang with pain. Working to steady herself in the seat, she pulled so hard on the reins that Snowshoe reared and screamed. Cool air whiffled past Ash's cheek as another blunt sailed wide. The arrows were coming from the east. To the north, the mounted clansmen spread wide as they reached level ground.

Out of the corner of her eye, she saw the rising arc of

Raif's bow. It *was* Raif's bow now; it had been Angus' once, but seeing it bend like a dancer's spine in Raif's hand, she knew Angus could never ask for it back.

Fear filled Ash's mouth the instant he released the string. She didn't need to look over her shoulder to know that the point would find a clansman's heart.

Coldness took her. *It's so easy for him,* she thought. *If he had enough arrows, he could kill them all.*

Suddenly Angus was beside her, wheeling the bay so tightly that clods of snow and frozen dirt spattered against her leg. "Behind me," he said.

The bay's steady presence calmed Snowshoe, and she stopped fighting against the bit and allowed Ash to maneuver her against Angus' flank. A blunt skipped off the bay's neck, yet the great Sull horse held his ground. Ash looked into the gelding's brown liquid eye and felt a moment of pure reverence. *We've danced together, you and I.*

A dozen clansmen bore down on them across the runoff plain at the base of the hill. There were more somewhere, hidden in the darkness to the east, shooting blunts. Ash watched as the warriors uncouched their steel points and lowered them as they rode. Spearheads set with back hooks to snag flesh reached ten paces beyond the horses' heads.

Raif took one down, then another.

"Who are they?" screamed Ash.

Angus' weapons wept oil as he raised them. "Bluddsmen. They've taken Ganmiddich and want the world to know it . . . that's why they lit a fire in the tower."

"Why bother with us?" Ash was close to hysterical. The sight of Raif drawing his bow was terrible to her. She wanted Angus to stop him.

Pointing his knife at Raif, Ash, and then himself, Angus said, "Take your pick. All three of us are prizes worth taking."

Ash didn't know what he meant. What would clansmen want with her? And then: What had Raif done to warrant taking? Even as that thought burrowed deep in her thoughts, a storm of blunts hit Raif and his horse. Moose kicked and howled as his forelegs, ears, and snout were smacked. Raif was struck in the throat and the bowhand, causing him to lose his grip on the bow. Hands scrambling for the reins, he worked to control the thrashing horse.

Ash let out a small cry. Raif's skin was gray, and something close to madness shone from behind his eyes. Without a thought, she kicked Snowshoe's flanks. She had to go to him.

Angus' hand shot out, gripping her wrist so tightly that knuckles cracked. *"No!"*

Furious, Ash fought him, lashing out with her free hand and driving Snowshoe into the bay. Her fingernails hooked Angus' cheek, and she scraped four strips of skin from his face. Still he would not release her.

The line of clansmen were closing on Raif. Their steel points shone as red as Rive Watch blades where they caught the tower's light. Calls passed between the clansmen, terse words roughly spoken. Their black armor had been tarnished so that it reflected no light, and their cloaks-of-fur rippled like living shadows at their backs.

To the east, the company of bowmen finally showed themselves, trotting wide on horses bred for the darkness of their coats.

"Calm yourself," Angus said, twisting Ash's arm to stop her fighting. "They will not harm him."

It was then Ash realized they were going to be taken. She shot Angus an accusation of a glance.

"I will not endanger you by fighting against such odds." Blood rolled down Angus' cheek where she had scratched him, yet he heeded it not. His eyes were on Raif. Sobered, Ash let her arm go limp in Angus' grip.

Raif now had Moose under control, and his halfsword was drawn and ready. He was facing the line of Bluddsmen, yet he glanced over his shoulder and met eyes with his uncle. An unspoken communication passed between the two, and Raif nodded imperceptibly. Turning to meet the Bluddsmen, he raised his sword over his head, skimming the cutting edge against his free hand to draw the blood that was needed as a sign of submission.

*For her.* Ash knew that in every cell of her being. If she had not been here, riding with these two men, the fight would still be waging. Perhaps Angus would have come up with some clever way to retreat, perhaps not. But Raif would have fought to the end. Ash had seen that madness in him . . . he was never far from death.

The Bluddsmen slowed but held their points. A leader emerged from the line, indistinguishable in every way from his companions except for the fact he pulled ahead. He wore no helm, and the shaved portions of his head had been painted with red clay. When he judged the distance sufficient, he raised a fist and stopped both warriors and bowmen dead.

Ash had never seen a Bluddsman before, but like everyone else in the North, she believed them to be the most savage of the clans. It took all her will not to call to Raif, to have him turn and look at her one last time before he was taken.

*"Do not speak his name,"* Angus warned, renewing his grip on her wrist.

All was quiet except for the wind. The red fire in the uppermost chamber of the Ganmiddich Tower shone like a moon made of blood. Two men stood twelve paces apart: one with his sword lifted high above his head and a line of dark blood snaking down his wrist, the other with his spear pointed straight at the first man's heart.

With his free hand, the Bluddsman lifted his lore from his chest and weighed it. *Just like Raif,* Ash thought, hairs on her arms rising.

After a time the Bluddsman let the small token drop to his chest. Taking his spear in both hands, he broke the shaft in two. The crack sounded like nothing else Ash had ever heard, like a great stone split open or a tree falling to the earth. Bluddsmen signed to their gods. Some touched the hide pouches and horn vials that hung from their equipment belts along with blade grease, sheath knives, and dog hooks. A night heron took to the air, its wings curling upward as it crossed the light of the red moon. Somewhere far to the north a wolf howled to its pack members, telling of carrion found and waiting.

Angus whispered two words under his breath. "They know."

Hearing them, Ash was filled with dread. She wanted to

ask what it was they knew, yet her throat had lost its power to form words.

Raif's shoulders held firm. He had neither wavered nor flinched at the spear breaking, and Ash was filled with the certainty that he had been expecting such an action from the moment he had raised his sword.

"I am Cluff Drybannock of Clan Bludd," the leader said, speaking in a low voice, "and I claim your heart for the Dog Lord, Raif Sevrance of Clan Blackhail, for wrongs done to our clan."

A cold light shone in the Bluddsman's eyes for one long moment, then Cluff Drybannock turned his back on Raif. Addressing himself to no one particular in the line, he said, "Strip him of his guidestone. One such as he deserves no protection from our gods."

Ash glanced at Angus. For the first time since she had met him, Angus Lok looked afraid.

\* \* \*

MARAFICE EYE'S FOOT STANK. Blisters the size of eyeballs wept fluid onto the inn floor. Black and purple skin floated over a mass of swollen tissue. Beneath the shell of dead and shedding skin, the plump pinkness of proud flesh could just be seen. The proud flesh was a good sign: It meant the foot would survive intact.

Well, nearly. The tip of the Knife's big toe had already come away, cast off in a jelly of red translucent flesh like something birthed in the deepest troughs of the sea. Sarga Veys shuddered at the memory. He hated sickness in any form.

"How much longer before I can put this damned foot in a stirrup, Halfman?" Marafice Eye spoke from the largest chair, set closest to the fire, in the third finest inn in Ille Glaive.

Hood, sworn brother-in-the-watch and distant kinsman to the Lord of the Straw Granges, sat across from his general on a birchwood bench, working his way through a keg of black beer thickened with egg and a haunch of roasted elk as big as a child. Hood and Sarga Veys had ridden to the city while the Knife was carted in a one-horse wagon like a bale of hay. Hood's excellent horsemanship had not been affected in the slightest by the loss of two fingers on his right hand. Indeed, the man seemed determined to make the best of it. Veys thought him mad. Just last night Hood had stopped him in the corridor and waggled the stumps in his face. *Make you sick, do they?* he had said, his wet lips coming close to Veys' ear. *You should see how they pleasure the wenches.*

Veys' face darkened at the memory. He hated being holed up with Marafice Eye and his thick-necked crony. Where was the sept Penthero Iss had promised? Veys wouldn't have put it past the Surlord to slow their sending just to torture him further. Everyone was intent on causing him harm. Letting his anger seep into his voice, Veys said to the Knife, "The top layer of skin must shed before you can strap on a boot."

"And how long might that be?"

"A week," Veys replied, deliberately adding a few extra days to the tally.

The Knife cursed. Swiping a hand across the table, he sent dishes and flagons crashing to the floor. Beer hissed where it landed on the hearthstone. "A week! A week! You said it was cured. Now look at it." He thrust the blistered and weeping foot toward Veys. "Your foul magics have made a leper of me."

"I *said* that I had warmed the flesh as best I could. You will not lose your foot. You will be able to walk and ride as normal. What is happening now is just the natural course of events. I cannot make your skin heal any faster."

"Aye, but you'd make it heal slower if you could." Hood turned over a cracked dish with the toe of his boot. "If the limb festers, you die, Halfman. My own eight fingers will see to that."

Veys pinched his lips tight. He didn't understand Hood's loyalty to the Knife, yet he knew it was something real. Hood *would* kill him, and it *would* be out of some strange and twisted brother love for Marafice Eye.

Pale eyes glinting in anger, Veys watched as the innkeeper—a fat man with womanish breasts—shoved one of his girls toward their table to clear up the mess. The girl was blond, fleshy, and brazen, exactly the kind of woman Veys despised and Hood and the Knife well liked. Deciding it was time to leave, Veys stood. He had no wish to witness Hood and the Knife exchanging the kinds of obscenities they took for flirting with some cheap, overfed whore.

Looking to the Knife's foot, he said, "As long as it's cleaned and packed with dog mercury each night, the skin will not fester."

Marafice Eye grunted.

Hood smiled slowly, revealing a good portion of unswallowed elk between his teeth. Grabbing the blond girl by the waist, he forced her into his lap. "Running off to your bed, Halfman? The thought of our little Moll here scares you that much!"

The sound of Hood's laughter accompanied Veys from the taproom.

Holding his white robe above the stair level so it didn't catch dust from the floor, Veys mounted the inn's main staircase and headed for his private chamber. The third best inn in Ille Glaive was named the Dropped Calf, and calf hides, calf pelt rugs, and paintings of calves formed the main decorations. Even the wax candles that lit the stairwell shone from scrubbed calf craniums, giving Sarga Veys the feeling he was being watched by the spirits of long-dead grasseaters as he made his escape.

The quiet grandeur of his room soothed him. No dirty rushes, no cheap boxed pallet, no tallow, unwashed linen, or pests. Instead there was a proper pitch pine floor, a bed carved from fruitwood, a dozen beeswax candles whiter than his own teeth, bed linens as crisp as autumn leaves, and nothing but stray filaments of dust buzzing around the light. Gratifyingly enough, upon their arrival at the Dropped Calf the innkeeper had mistaken *him* for the head of the party and had housed Marafice Eye and Hood on the far side of the inn, in a chamber that looked out across the vinegar brewery next door. Veys had at first been surprised when Marafice Eye discovered the error and chose to do nothing about it, then contemptuous. The Knife could think no further than the Rive Watch and his men.

Of course, the passing days had shown the innkeeper who the real leader was, yet it pleased Sarga Veys' vanity to remind himself that on first look *he* had seemed the superior man.

The greasy smoke in the taproom had agitated Veys' eyes, and he crossed to the nearest of the two north-facing windows and flung back the shutters to let in the night. Icy darkness soothed him like a dip into a still pool.

The Dropped Calf was situated close to the north wall of the city, and its height and elevation allowed Veys a view across the battlements to the cityhold beyond.

The glacier-ground peaks of the Bitter Hills were a distant break on the horizon, topped by a crown of silver storm clouds. Each winter a hundred storms traveled south from the clanholds and the Want, some so close behind each other that three had been known to hit in the course of a single day. The Bitter Hills took punishment from them all. Perhaps once they *had* been mountains, yet between the grinding of ancient glaciers and the lashing of a million storms, they had been reduced to that awkward height that man had no right name for. Clansmen called them hills, yet that was just clannish bravado. And Veys knew all about that.

Making a small grimace of distaste that exposed his fine, inward-slanting teeth to the light, Veys sat at the oak desk that was positioned in front of the window. An excellent, large-scale map of the Ille Glaive cityhold lay unraveled and pinned to the wood. The map had cost Veys a small fortune, purchased earlier that day from a young ambitious chartmaker named Siddius Horn, and it merited every coin paid and more.

"All villages within thirty leagues of the city are marked and plotted," boasted Siddius Horn from behind the shabby, acid-burned counter of his shop. "All hamlets, all *proper* farms, all roads, shared cattle trails, and elevations."

It was a *very* good map.

Veys trailed a finger over the bleached silk-rag paper, tracing the course of Ille Glaive's northern road. The road, painstakingly traced in iron ink with a hair-fine sable brush, led directly from the Old Sull Gate to the Ganmiddich Pass. Angus Lok and his two companions had taken that road from the city. Veys knew that. He also knew that instead of continuing north to the pass or turning west toward Clan Blackhail, they had turned *east* instead.

The first piece of information had come cheaply enough. Gatekeepers were as willingly bribed as small children. It had taken Hood but quarter of a day to find the right gate and the right gatekeeper and purchase what intelligence was needed. The second piece of information was all Veys.

Yesterday morning, after Hood had returned to the Dropped Calf, Veys had paid a visit to the Old Sull Gate himself. More coins had changed hands. All bore the fine undetectable film of grease that formed on objects much handled and much used, yet one bore a little something extra as well: a compulsion. Compulsions were high sorcery, and Veys was good at them. More often than not a compulsion was spoken, not passed from hand to hand, but Veys didn't have the voice for it. A warm, rich, *compelling* voice was best. The sort of voice that encouraged a man to take part in one's schemes, that flattered his ego, and played tricks with his reason, and made the most irregular requests sound sane. A good voice and a commanding presence were half the work of a compulsion. Without them, such sorcery was hard work.

It had taken Veys most of the night to fix the compulsion on the coin. It was a simple one, of course. Compulsions only worked when the request was modest and of a nature that did not antagonize the victim in any way. Mostly they were good for information. With a compulsion upon him, a jailer might let slip the time of day when his prisoner was fed and the cell door was open, a pretty chambermaid might disclose her mistress's bedtime indiscretions, and a respectable innkeeper might point the way to the room of a guest who had just paid him good money for silence. The trick was in making the person *want* to fulfill one's request.

With the five silver coins that Veys had passed to the lean-bodied, smoke-eyed guardsman, he had also passed along the suggestion that the man ask all who passed into the city that morning a simple question. Had they seen two men and a woman riding together, the men mounted on good horses and the woman atop a gray hill-bred pony?

The guardsman's eyes had turned from smoky to blank as Veys spoke his request. No power was present in Veys voice, yet the coin pressing against the red flesh of the guard's palm had burned cold with sorcery. The guard had nodded his assent even before Veys had reached the words *gray hillbred pony.*

Half a day had been enough. After a small but excellent noonday meal of pheasant prepared in a crust of its own blood, Veys had returned to the guard and the gate. The guard related his intelligence in a voice that was fast and furtive— somewhere deep inside he knew that what he did was wrong. Several people had sighted the three companions heading north toward the pass, and Veys was about to conclude that Angus Lok and his party had indeed crossed into the clanholds when the guard offered his last piece of information.

"A drover and his son said they saw such a party heading east three nights back. Said they were about ten leagues off the north road, traveling along a cattle path known only to locals and drovers."

Veys made no reply—one did not thank an ensorcelled man—simply turned his back and walked away. A few discreet inquiries produced the name of the best chartmaker in the city, and not many hours later Veys was back in the comfort of his well-appointed chamber, plotting Angus Lok's journey with a pot of lampblack ink and a twig.

The guard's information was sound. It was just like Angus Lok to know the back ways: the low roads, cattle paths, game tracks, and dogtrots. If a drover had claimed to see him in such a place, then the drover was likely right.

Satisfied in that regard, at least, Veys sat back and contemplated Siddius Horn's map. Until an hour ago he had assumed that Lok's final destination lay east. Now he wasn't so sure.

Asarhia March's trail was dead. Either the sorcery that had clung to her had worn off or she had been warded by someone very clever indeed. Warding was a difficult business. One could not set wardings in place without giving something of oneself to the person who was being protected. Only few magic users could manage them, and almost all were likely members of the Phage.

Veys' lip twisted with the force of unwanted memories. Yes, there were one or two people in this city capable of warding Asarhia March . . . but that was not what concerned him now. Other sorceries did.

An hour earlier, while he had sat with Marafice Eye and Hood in the taproom, wetting his lips with beer he found too coarse to swallow and cutting slivers of meat from the *inner* loin of elk, he had felt a different source of power in the North. Three fast jabs, one after another. Barely sorcery at all, so instinctively was it used by he who drew it.

The Clansman.

Veys had perceived him twice before. Once, in Spire Vanis as he heart-killed four sworn brothers in the shadow of Vaingate, and again on the shore of the Black Spill when he took down a pair of hounds. His aftermath reeked of Old Blood. It made Veys' skin crawl. As soon as he perceived it, it was gone.

North was all Veys knew. North, not east. *North.*

A clean and perfectly filed fingernail scratched a furrow in Siddius Horn's map. After a three-day detour east, Angus Lok and his party were back at the Ganmiddich Pass.

To Sarga Veys that meant only one thing: Angus Lok had taken his new friends home. Smiling softly to himself as he worked, Veys began to work out how far three people mounted on good horses could travel east in a day in thick snow.

# THIRTY-SEVEN

### In the Tower

THEY SEPARATED HIM FROM Angus and Ash—that he was grateful for. That was one thing to hold on to in the darkness that was to come: Ash would not see or *know.*

The skiff traveled smoothly over water as slick and black as volcanic glass. The storm had long passed, and the Wolf

River was sleeping after a night spent howling at the moon. Raif could smell the thick animal odor of the water, water that in spring moved so swiftly and with such force that it killed more elk, horned sheep, snagcats, bear cubs, and small game than the largest pack of wolves in the North. It smelled of those kills now, of carrion suspended, half-frozen, in water so thick and cold that nothing would rot until spring.

The Ganmiddich Inch lay ahead. The Inch was a shoulder of granite that broke water in the river's middle, rising above the surface like the dome of an ancient temple, long sunk. The Ganmiddich Tower was built upon its bedrock. The red fire burning in the tower's uppermost chamber provided the only light for the skiff's skipper to steer by.

It was close to dawn. Raif could tell that much from the lay of the stars and the restless switching of air currents as night made way for day. He lay bound in the belly of the skiff, the booted feet of six Bludd oarsmen keeping him in place. A rope lashed across the bridge of his nose made it difficult to breathe, and another binding the soft tissue of his throat made any but the slightest movements impossible. He had not been beaten, but rough handling had broken open the hard, inflexible scar tissue on his chest. Bluddsmen's spit was still wet on his face and neck, and scratches on his temples and forehead leaked blood into the hull of the boat.

Cluff Drybannock stood at the prow, one foot up upon gunwales, his entire body leaning forward toward the Inch. Earlier, as they'd ridden north toward Ganmiddich, he had let down his braids, and now his waist-long black hair streamed behind him in the predawn chill.

Raif knew Cluff Drybannock by reputation—all clansfolk did. He was the Dog Lord's right hand, his fostered son, a fatherless Trenchland bastard who was named after the first meal he had eaten at Clan Bludd: dry bread. Now he was known to all as Drybone. He was the only man the Dog Lord trusted, people said, the only one who could speak and fight in his likeness. And he was the best longswordsman in the North.

A rasping noise broke the quiet of slow-moving water as the boat's keel scraped against granite pebbles on the Inch's

shore. The oarsmen raised their oars and waded into the
river to haul the body of the skiff ashore. Cluff Drybannock
worked with the men as one of the team, the tail ends of his
hair floating in the animal-scented water as he shouldered
his portion of the weight.

Raif looked up at the vast five-sided tower that had been
standing since before the clanholds were settled. Algae,
mud, and mineral stains ringed the tower's lower chambers,
each ring marking high water levels of ancient floods. The
stench of the river clung to the stone, hiding in pockmarks
and clefts in the granite. Ice, colored green and orange by
rust, hung in storm-broken fingers from the tower's ledges,
overhangs, and mooring rings.

The skipper tied the skiff to the nearest ring and then fell
in line with the oarsmen, awaiting Cluff Drybannock's
word.

Time passed. Cluff Drybannock stood, half-in, half-out
the water, watching the red fire burn thirty stories above him.
Weariness was a hard presence on his face, and Raif wondered what it had taken for him and his men to capture Ganmiddich's roundhouse and hold.

Finally the Bluddsman spoke, his vivid blue eyes not once
leaving the light of the fire. "Take him inside and beat him."

The words were heavily said, and the six oarsmen and the
skipper reacted to the tone of their leader's voice by moving
slowly and silently about their task.

Raif felt large cool hands grasp his shoulders, ankles, and
wrists. Somewhere ahead, an iron door creaked open, and
for the first time that night Raif felt his stomach betray him
by clenching in fear. Chains rattled as he was lifted from the
stench and dampness of the skiff. Fresh air skimmed across
his face, but the ropes at his nose and throat stopped him
from inhaling deeply. The Bluddsmen's breaths came short
and ragged as they hauled him inside the tower.

Inside all was as still and dark as a mineshaft. Wet mud
sucked at the Bluddsmen's boots. Leaking moisture dropped
like slow rain on their backs. The smell of the river was concentrated to a thick stock of meat, minerals, and mud.
Smoke filtering down from the Bludd Fire provided the only
relief from the stench. Raif watched stone ceilings pass

above him as he was carried into the tower's heart. He thought perhaps they would take him upward, but they bore him down instead.

Mud turned to wet slime and then thick, blood-colored water as they descended. No one spoke. No tallow was lit to guide the way. Thin shavings of dawn light came from sources Raif could neither identify nor see. River sounds filled his senses. Even in winter, when the water was thick · with suspended ice and sluggish with cold undertows, its current throbbed against the watch tower like a stallion's heart. All around water trickled and dripped, poured and rushed, making the tower echo like a sea cave.

A second door opened. Water sloshed around the Bluddsmen's ankles, then Raif was thrown to the ground. His shoulder and temple struck hard stone. Water filled his mouth and nose. The rope at his throat was suddenly tight enough to choke him. Someone said, "Cut him free," and cool blades licked his skin.

Raif saw pale edges: a curved endwall, the lip of a stone bench, a square grille overhead that let in a keyhole's worth of light. River water, foul smelling and turgid with algae and gelatinous strings of animal matter, formed a shin-high pool above the floor. Raif had no time to take in more details before the first blow was struck.

Pain exploded in his head, streaking the world white and gray and filling his mouth with hot blood. Other blows followed, swift, well placed, each one a hard wedge in the soft belly of his flesh. Bluddsmen grunted. Water rode high against the walls, spraying the cell like a ship's prow in a storm. Raif rose and fell with the waves, grasping water, then air, fingers scrambling for handholds in the stone.

His jaws clenched and unclenched as he accepted the Bluddsmen's blows. Boot tips hammered at his spine. Knuckles found the same places in his ribs . . . again and again, like a machine. Boot heels were thrust below the water level, seeking out the hidden tissue of thighs and groin. Raif thrashed like a hooked fish, knowing the same terror and confusion. Pain tore at his senses, causing him to breathe water and swallow air. Still the blows came, so many kicks and punches that soon they could not be separated or counted. Hard dots of white light burned in place of his vision. Vomit blocked his nasal cavity and flooded in and out of his mouth like driftwood carried on the tide.

Soon he lost all sense of where he was and what was happening. Blows and dealing with the pain of them were all he knew. Water buoyed but did not cool him. His back was afire, stripped of skin and bleeding acid in place of blood. His stomach contracted in hard waves, yet each time he tried to raise his knees to his chest to soothe the cramping, he was beaten below the water . . . held under by booted feet.

He lost time. Slaps revived him. A half-closed fist thudded against his chest, forcing water from his lungs. Fingers found his raven lore, twisted it round and round until the twine that held it was like a garrote against his throat. Breathing was impossible. . . .

More time lost. Through closed eyes he judged an increase in light. His eyelids were gummed together—whether by blood, mucus, or swollen tissue, he did not know. His throat burned. Breathing caused excruciating pain. A voice grunted words he could no longer understand, then something that could only have been a human hand pressed against his skull, forcing his head under the water once more.

When he came to again he was no longer in the water. Hard stone dug into his spine and ribs. His clothes were sodden. Daylight was gone. People were gone. He was alone in the darkness with his pain.

Hours passed before he could work up the strength to move his right hand. He wasted nothing of himself by trying to open the bruised flaps of flesh that were eyelids or lick lips that were so dry that a single breath exhaled through the mouth could cause them to crack and bleed. Everything within him he put toward raising his hand to his throat.

Pain made him pass out more than once. Sour matter in his mouth stung his gums. The desire for water, just a few clear drops, was strong. But the desire to reach his raven lore was stronger.

Fingers swollen with bruises grasped at the horn that had been embedded in his throat. Blood made the ivory slippery. Gobs of flesh came away as he pulled on the twine and closed his fist around the lore.

*Ash.* He felt her presence immediately, like a warm breeze or a sliver of sunlight shining upon his back. She was close and unharmed.

*Close and unharmed.*

Those words made the next beating bearable.

They came for him at some unknowable point in the night, or perhaps it was the next night and he had slept or been unconscious through a full day. This time they brought a hood for his head. He wanted to tell them not to bother, as he could not open his eyes, but instinctively he knew that any words spoken would condemn him to torture of a worse kind. They beat him in silence, always silence, grunting softly when striking a blow, breathing hard when tired by their exertions. Someone brought a knife and slit open skin on his thighs and buttocks. Someone else urinated on the wounds.

Days passed. For hours at a time he was strung up on dog hooks hammered into the cell wall. His arms were dead. The hood over his face made every breath taste of his own trapped sweat. He was not fed, and what water he drank came from the cell floor. Sometimes the river rose then fell, washing his own filth away.

*Close and unharmed.*

Whenever he woke, he spoke those words to himself. Time came when he no longer knew their meaning, yet even then they calmed him, like a prayer in a foreign tongue.

Often he dreamed of Drey: Drey racing through the long summer grass in the graze; Drey teaching him how to tie and trim trout lures in the dead of winter when all the trout lakes were frozen; Drey waiting for him on the camp boundary the day they set Tem's corpse ablaze. The ambush on the Bluddroad always played itself out one beat slower than real time. Time and time again Raif saw the two hard points of his brother's eyes as he swung his war-scratched hammer into the Bluddswoman's face.

*No.* Raif's dream-self fought the memory. That was not his brother swinging the hammer that day on the Bluddroad. That was not the Drey he knew.

Hunger gnawed at Raif's body, then his mind, robbing flesh and sanity and the simple ability to rest in peace. Waiting became worse than the beatings. Waiting, he was alone, utterly alone. Thoughts and dreams tormented him. Inigar Stoop pointed a finger, calling him *Watcher of the Dead.* Tem walked from the badlands fire, his body alive with flames, his mouth opening and closing as he spoke the names of the men who had killed him. Raif strained and strained but could not hear them. Later Effie was there in the cell with him, standing knee deep in water, calmly reciting a list of the lives he had taken . . . and somehow Shor Gormalin and Banron Lye were on the list, and he wanted to tell her that she was wrong, that he had killed no Hailsmen, but she disappeared before he could form the words. Later still Mace Blackhail was there, beneath the water, his wolf teeth flashing yellow as he laughed and said, *I knew you'd push me too far, Sevrance.*

Pain was something Raif passed out from and woke to every day. Bruises blackened his body, yet he could not see them. Split skin knitted and festered, healed and reopened, raising scars and welts that only his fingers knew. Unseen Bluddsmen choked and suffocated him into submission every night, his head held underwater until his lungs burned like furnaces, the cord that held his lore twisted until it robbed his breath. Soon the sickening blackness of unconsciousness was all he knew of sleep.

Then one day the beatings stopped. The high whine of the cell door woke him from unknowable hours of senselessness. Through the fog of wakening senses, Raif waited for the first blow to land. His body was stiff with pain, his stomach sick with it. Above his head his arms ached with the strain of bearing his weight. Every breath cost him. A muscle spasm in his knee made his entire body jerk.

*Close and unharmed.* Who? Effie? Was she here?

All thoughts left him as air switched against his throat. He hated his body for flinching, hated the fear that came to him as instantly as if he were a child listening for monsters in the dark.

The expected blow did not come. Instead hands worked on the rope that bound his wrists to the dog hook. The sour taste of helplessness stung his mouth. The routine was to beat him while he was strung, then later, when he was incapable of taking action to protect himself from a fall, let him drop to the stone bench or the floor. The change in tactics made him nervous. When firm hands took him by the shoulders, he heard himself make an animal sound, like a hiss.

Fingers grabbed the base of his hood, snapping his head back. "Now is no time to fight, Hailsman." The voice was rough, heavily accented. Its owner took Raif's weight when the last of the ropes was cut and then laid him down upon the bench.

Relief soaked through Raif like water through a rag, leaving his body cold and limp. Another pair of hands clutched his throat, but he hardly cared. At least he would be beaten lying down.

A knife point pricked his jaw as the rope that held the burlap hood in place was sawed. Blood rolled into the crease between Raif's lips. The Bluddsman working the knife smelled of the last meal he had eaten. The stench of scorched animal fat and roasted leeks drove Raif to open his mouth and make a bloodmeal of the fluids accumulated there. When the rope was severed, the Bluddsman's fingers hooked the hem of the hood and pulled it free.

Raif squeezed his eyes more tightly closed. It had been days since he had last seen the faces of those who beat him, and he had no wish to see them now. Fresh air buffeted his face—also unwelcome. Suddenly he wished very much the beating would begin.

Water sloshed as the man who had handled him left the cell. Raif heard the door close, yet he did not trust his senses and kept himself still. They had never left him awake before. Minutes passed. The Wolf River rolled like liquid thunder against the tower's exterior wall. Somewhere high above him, water dripped in perfect time like a pulse. Nothing moved in the cell. Raif concentrated on breathing . . . that, at least, was something he could do.

"Open your eyes and look at me."

The voice came from close to the door. It was not the same man who had spoken earlier, though both shared the Bluddsman's accent. This voice was harder, older, wearier.

Water lashed against the cell's walls. "I said *LOOK AT ME!*"

Raif obeyed. Skin on his eyelids tore and bled as he

forced the gummed tissue apart. Through a film of blood he saw a man of medium height, heavily built and turning to stoutness, with hair of such brilliant grayness that the braids that hung down his back seemed like something woven from silver, not human hair.

The Dog Lord.

Raif knew it instantly. The man's presence filled the cell like a guidestone. It was impossible not to look at his deep blue eyes, impossible not to edge back in his presence. How had he stood there for so long, watching in utter silence, without making himself known?

The Dog Lord said nothing. He looked *at* Raif and *through* him, his eyes pulling answers, his entire being pressing against Raif with a force so great it made breathing impossible.

Raif held his gaze steady. He thought of the four Bluddsmen at Duff's Stovehouse, the Bludd women and children running through the snow the day of the ambush. Shame burned him.

The Dog Lord continued looking, seeing, *knowing*. His heavy breaths made the shin-deep water ripple as if with dropped stones. Suddenly he moved. Raif braced himself for a blow, but instead the Dog Lord turned his back.

A cold dagger entered Raif's heart. The contempt of the gesture cut him to the core. *You are not worthy of my fist,* it said. *You are not worthy of my breath.*

As the Dog Lord opened the cell door and entered the world waiting on the other side, Raif felt himself shrink and wither like a dead leaf cast from a tree. He was nothing. The Bludd chief's scorn had stripped away what the beatings could not. He was an oath breaker, an outcast, a killer of men. As Angus had promised, the story of the killings at Duff's Stovehouse had spread. Raif Sevrance's name and his deeds were known to all. His presence at the Bluddroad ambush was known, and the betrayal of his clan.

Raif brought his knees to his chest and prayed for the senselessness of sleep. He did not want to feel or think. The pain was not enough, though. The leaking eye, the cracked ribs, the slit ear and lip, and the torn muscles in his arms and thighs were suddenly hurts that could be borne. He lay there in the quarter light and suffered the voices from his past.

*You are no good for this clan, Raif Sevrance,* murmured Inigar Stoop. *You are chosen to watch the dead.*

*You knew I would leave!* Raif fired back at him. *So why did you not stop me from taking First Oath?*

Inigar Stoop shook his head from his place behind the shadows, the silver medallions sewn to his pig coat making a sound like breaking glass. *Ask that of the Stone Gods, Raif Sevrance. It is they who form your fate, not I.*

Raif turned away, shifting limbs that felt hot to the touch. Still the voices hounded him. Raina warned him about Effie: *Just you be careful with her, Raif Sevrance. You and Drey are all she has.*

And Drey spoke up for him that day on the court: *I will stand second to his oath.*

Raif howled into the darkness.

Hours later, fever finally took him to sleep.

When next he woke the world was soft around the edges. Someone, a Bluddsman, placed a bowl containing thick gray liquid beside him on the bench. Raif watched the bowl intently. He did not move. Fever lines spreading along in his chest made his body tremble. Thirst tore at his throat, yet he could take no action to relieve it. Watching the bowl was all he could manage, and he did it diligently until he knew no more.

# THIRTY-EIGHT

## *Lords and Maidens*

VAYLO BLUDD SLIPPED A square of black curd into his mouth and chewed on it. The wolf dog and the other dogs sat in a circle around their master, their great jaws firmly closed, their ears pinned close to their heads in sign of submission.

Occasionally one would moan softly, making a sound as if in physical pain.

Vaylo sat in silence, chewing. Ahead in the distance lay the shimmering black line of the Wolf River and the dark hump in its center that formed the Ganmiddich Inch. It was bitterly cold, yet the Dog Lord felt little of it. The night air was still, and the sky above the clanhold was cloudless, revealing a clawed moon and a thousand ice blue stars. Sitting where he was, on a block of trap rock used for blunting hammer edges and filleting trout pulled from the river, Vaylo could see both the Ganmiddich Tower and the roundhouse. All his now. All the land south to the Bitter Hills was his.

Footsteps crunched in the snow behind his back. The Dog Lord did not need to look around to know the identity of the one who approached. The reaction of his dogs told him all he needed to know.

"Does he still live?"

Cluff Drybannock made no answer, yet Vaylo knew well enough the question had been heard and understood. Coming to crouch by the dogs, Drybone gazed out across the river as he warmed his hands against the wolf dog's throat. After a while he said, "He's still fevered. Cawdo doesn't know how he's made it through the past five days. Says any other Hailsman would be dead by now."

Vaylo spat the curd into his glove. Suddenly he didn't want to be out in the cold any longer. He wanted to be close to the hearth, his arms full of the two grandchildren he had left. Without a word, he stood.

The dogs were as much a part of him as the gray braids that fell down his back, and they rose as a single body the moment they heard their master's boot leather creak. Drybone also rose. He need not have done—Cluff Drybannock had led the raiding party that took the Ganmiddich clanhold, and his due respect was now great enough that he need stand for no man, even his chief—yet he did so as quickly as always. Others might have dismissed the gesture as mere force of habit, but Vaylo knew better than that. Cluff Drybannock stood because he was a bastard and that's what bastards did.

Vaylo placed his hand on Drybone's shoulder, and together man and chief took the short walk back to the roundhouse.

The Ganmiddich roundhouse was small compared with those of Dhoone and Bludd. Built of trap rock and green riverstone, it commanded a high bank above the river and the forest of oldgrowth oaks known as the Nest. The main structure rose a full six stories aboveground, in fitting with the Ganmiddich boast: *Over mountains and our enemies we tower alike.* Like most northern clansmen, Vaylo felt nothing but distrust for a roundhouse that rose to meet the clouds. A roundhouse's strength should come from the earth and the Stone Gods that lived there. Yet many of the southern clans built high roundhouses, betraying the influence of the Mountain Cities and the god of sky, air, and nothingness that the city men prayed to.

The Dog Lord shook his head as he and Drybone entered the storm-smoothed edifice of the roundhouse's southern wall. He found little joy in possession. Crab Ganmiddich, the Ganmiddich chief, was a man who had come to power only five years after he had. Crab swore like a trapper, would start a fight with any man who looked at him the wrong way, and had fathered as many bastards as most men had eaten meals, yet Vaylo had liked him well enough. He never lied, never failed to acknowledge his bastards, and once ten years ago when wetpox killed off all of neighboring Clan Withy's spring lambs, he had sent sixty head of blacknecks as a gift.

Vaylo sucked on his aching teeth. He had no grievances with Crab Ganmiddich, none save the man's newly struck friendship with the Hail Wolf. The attack on Bannen had made the Crab chief nervous, and rather than rely solely upon Dhoone for protection, he had been making overtures to Blackhail. Dhoone was weak, broken, and dispossessed. Blackhail was strong and getting stronger. Who could blame the Crab chief for dancing to two fiddles? As for Mace Blackhail . . . well, he had fought beside Dhoonesmen to save Bannen, and once the battle was done and he had returned home to that dark stinking Hailhold of his, he must have turned his gaze south and asked himself, "What did I get for my trouble?"

The Dog Lord shook out his braids. Next time Clan

Blackhail came to the defense of a Dhoone-sworn clan, he doubted very much that the Hail Wolf would return home empty-handed. He had ambitions, that one. Vaylo recognized the taint.

"The Crab's fled east to Croser," Drybone said, as always his thoughts closely following his chief's. "He's gathered forty score men about him and taken possession of the old fortalice."

Vaylo grunted. Slowly his enemies were mounting on his borders. Dhoone was split among Gnash, Bannen, and Castlemilk, and now Ganmiddich was housed at Croser. Any other time these facts would have consumed him, yet here and now his mind would not settle. The Hailsman was too close. Half the rooms in the Ganmiddich roundhouse looked out upon the tower and the Inch. All Vaylo had to do was raise his head and look.

He looked now, one last time before Drybone drew the great clan door closed, shutting out the frost and the night. Thirty stories of green granite rose above the river's surface like a Stone God's finger pointing at the sky: Ganmiddich Tower. Raif Sevrance was held there at water level. Watcher of the Dead.

A shiver passed along the Dog Lord's body, making his seventeen teeth rattle in their casings of bone.

"Nan. Bring the bairns to me. I'll be in the chief's chamber." He spoke to a middle-aged Bluddswoman with braids the color and texture of sea rope, who approached with beer and sotted oats as he and Drybone crossed the vaulted expanse of the great hall. The woman met eyes with Vaylo for half an instant, nodded, then withdrew.

Nan Culldayis had traveled down from Dhoone with him. She looked after his grandchildren now that their mother and elder sister were gone. Vaylo trusted Nan with his life. She had nursed his wife through the last year of her illness and cared for his grandchildren and sons' wives since. For many years now she had provided him with what private comforts he needed. She was of an age where conception and childbirth were well behind her, and that suited Vaylo well enough. Thirty-five years ago on his wedding day he had sworn to himself he would father no bastards.

Vaylo's thoughts were broken by the soft burr of Cluff Drybannock's voice. "Say the word and I will assemble a troop of hammermen and escort the bairns back to Dhoone."

Halting by the chief's door, the Dog Lord turned and looked into the man's Sull-blue eyes. "You don't think I should have brought them here."

It was not a question, yet Drybone answered it anyway. "No. This roundhouse is no place for them. It's only a matter of time before the Crab tries to reclaim it."

"And what if I had left them at Dhoone, with their father? How safe would they be there?"

"Safer than here, on the cityhold border, in a roundhouse only a day's ride from Bannen and Croser, and not much farther from Gnash."

Vaylo slammed a fist against the door. The dogs at his heels skittered and shrank to their haunches. "Don't you think I know the dangers? Don't you think I lie awake each night, thinking and rethinking them?"

Drybone did not respond in any way to his chief's anger. Instead he held his fine head level and spoke in a quiet voice. "Every journey you take them on is a danger. They are best kept at the Heart of Clan, at Dhoone."

He was right, and Vaylo knew it. Entering the green-walled interior of the chief's chamber, he turned to Drybone and said, "I fear to let them out of my sight, Dry. Two now, only two."

Cluff Drybannock nodded, once. He offered no comfort, made no attempt to remind him that his sons were still young and would father dozens more, and Vaylo was grateful for that. For the second time that night he touched Drybone on the shoulder. "I'll let you take them in a few days."

As Drybone assented with the briefest of his always brief smiles, the two children in question came bounding through the door. Ignoring their grandfather completely, they made straight for the dogs.

After watching them wrestle, tumble, and shriek in delight at the black-and-orange beasts known throughout the North as the Dog Lord's knuckles, Vaylo turned to Drybone and grinned. "I can't say they'll miss me much."

Cluff Drybannock turned to go.

Halting him with a small turn of the wrist, Vaylo said, "How is the girl?"

"Well. Nan visited her room today. Says she's not the sort to starve herself or throw tantrums. I think she's quite taken with her myself."

Vaylo rubbed his jaw, soothing his aching teeth as he thought. "How old is she?"

Drybone shrugged. "Just a girl. Tall, thin."

"Have her brought to me, Dry. I would look upon the Surlord's daughter myself."

"Here?" Drybone's gaze flicked to the children, who were giggling wildly as they groomed the wolf dog's belly with their feet.

"Aye. If Nan thinks well enough of her, then I'll trust her at my hearth."

Drybone left, closing the door behind him as quietly as if he were a servant, not the man who only seven days ago had claimed Ganmiddich for Bludd. *Give me two hundred swordsmen,* Dry had said the day before he'd left, *and your silence until the deed is done.* Even now Vaylo did not know how he'd managed it. Two hundred men to take a roundhouse the size of Ganmiddich? And it hadn't been a bloodbath, either . . . not like Withy.

Easing himself onto the maid's stool close to the fire, Vaylo slapped his thighs for dogs and children alike. Many feet, both hairy and hairless, scampered over the stone to reach him by the shortest, quickest route. The two children came and sat at his feet while he unhooked the leather cinches from his belt and began lashing the dogs into a team. The dogs hated being bound, but the children's presence tempered their normal reaction, and Vaylo managed to collar them with only a minor loss of skin and blood. When he was done, he looped the main lead over a spit hook in the hearthwall.

"Granda, why do they have to be tied?" Pasha, now his eldest grandchild, sent a long, sympathetic look the wolf dog's way.

Vaylo brushed the girl's jet black hair. Her mother had Far South blood in her, and the child was dark skinned and dark eyed and beautiful to behold. "Because I'm expecting a visitor, and the dogs seldom take kindly to those."

One of the dogs, a lean bitch who was all teeth and snout, growled. Vaylo hissed at her, though in truth he was not displeased. As he returned his gaze to his granddaughter, a red light shining through the slitted window in the opposite wall caught his eye: the Bludd Fire burning in the upper chamber of the tower. Seven days and nights it had blazed, long enough for all in the cityholds to know that the Dog Lord now stood at their door.

Vaylo tried to tear his eyes away but couldn't. There had been a time when taking Ganmiddich would have meant something, when the thought of war and raids was what roused him from his bed every morning and kept him awake past midnight with his warlords every night. He fought because he had the jaw for it, because he loved to win more than he loved life itself. Now, though, he fought from hate.

And fear.

Vaylo rose and closed the iron shutters, engaging each of the seven clasps and drawing the bar.

Blackhail was the reason Cluff Drybannock had moved against Ganmiddich. He had been there the night the women and children were found off the Bluddroad. He had helped excavate the bodies. Any clan who might form an alliance with the Hail Wolf and his clansmen had to be sent a message of death. Drybone knew it. The Dog Lord knew it. And although no word had passed between them, they both knew the war would not end until Blackhail had been destroyed.

Vaylo put a hand on the iron shutters, resting the heavy bulk of his standing weight. The Ganmiddich Tower and its red fire still burned upon his irises. The Hailsman who lay imprisoned within it still burned upon his soul.

He was just a *lad.* When Vaylo had entered the tower yesterday at noon he had not known what to expect. Watcher of the Dead, people had started calling him after the night he'd slain three Bluddsmen at Duff's. He'd fought like a Stone God, they said, and freely admitted to being present at the Bluddroad ambush before he'd forced his way through the door.

Vaylo's hand cooled to the temperature of iron. Now he had this Hailsman here, imprisoned upon the Inch. He had seen him with his own two eyes, minded his wounds, and sniffed his stench. Cluff Drybannock and the others had expected him to finish the Hailsman off. He saw that on their faces, later, when he had emerged from the tower and they stood waiting in a half circle about the skiff. Drybone had even given orders that no beating was to be so great as to threaten the Hailsman's life or limb: that privilege belonged to the Dog Lord.

Yet Vaylo had not used it. He hardly knew why himself. Seeing the Hailsman lying there on the bench, beaten, his clothes dark with blood and river grime, Vaylo had tortured himself: How had it happened, that massacre on the Bluddroad? Did the Hailsmen go in expecting to kill women and children? Did one man panic and kill one child out of anger or surprise and the others followed suit? Had any of the women fought back? How long had it taken for his grandchildren to die?

Vaylo closed his eyes, let the iron shutter take more of his weight.

No. He had not killed the Hailsman. He would, because he was the Dog Lord and no one could slay his kin and survive, yet there were things he needed to know. Things only someone present that day could tell him.

The dogs stood and growled. Immediately Vaylo looked to the door. A few seconds passed, and then knuckles rapped against the wood. A moment later Drybone entered the room, leading a girl before him. Depositing her in the center of the room, he turned to leave without a moment's hesitation. Vaylo knew he would wait outside, at a distance where he could be sure not to overhear a word.

Penthero Iss' foster daughter matched gazes with the Dog Lord. As Drybone had promised, she was tall and thin, yet Vaylo knew enough about young women to realize that the thinness would leave her soon enough. A few weeks of lard and oats would see to that.

"What have you done to Raif Sevrance and Angus Lok?" The girl's voice was cold, and for the briefest moment Vaylo was reminded of her foster father, Penthero Iss. He had reared this child from birth.

Vaylo gave no answer. Instead he walked from the window to the hearth and came to sit in the company of his dogs. His two grandchildren scrambled quickly to his feet, the youngest tugging at his dogskin pants, demanding to be picked up and held in his granda's lap. Vaylo was aware of his grandchildren's unease: They had sensed the fear of the dogs.

Normally when a stranger entered their master's territory, the dogs were quick to show their teeth. Growling, they would test their leashes, lower their tails, and watch the intruder with eyes that held memories of pack kills on the frozen tundra of the Want. Yet from the moment Iss' foster daughter had entered the room all the dogs had been silent. Not one of them growled, not even the wolf dog. They lay on their bellies, rumps pushed up against the hearthwall, ears flat against their skulls. As Vaylo picked up his grandson, one of the bitches whined softly and withdrew farther into the pack.

Vaylo watched the girl as she waited for his reply. Her silver gold hair brushed against her shoulders, falling as straight as if each individual strand had been weighted with lead beads. Her eyes were the same gray as the sky before a storm, large and clear, with silver filaments in the irises that reflected light. Everything about her looked conjured up from silver, water, and hard stone. Yet she was little more than a child, and she was afraid; Vaylo wasn't fooled about that for an instant. He saw how she clutched at the fabric of her skirt to prevent her hands from trembling, how a muscle in her throat bobbed when she swallowed . . . and she swallowed a lot.

It was interesting that the first question she had asked had concerned her companions, not herself.

Vaylo said, "You have been well treated by my clan?"

"Answer my question."

"Answer mine."

The girl flinched at the hardness of his voice.

Vaylo pressed his hands against each of his grandchildren's shoulders in turn, calming. Their granda's anger frightened them.

"I have been treated well enough. Fed. Clothed. Confined." The silver in the girl's eyes turned to something darker, like steel. "Now tell me what has become of my friends."

Vaylo made her wait upon an answer. He was impressed by her courage—he couldn't recall the last time anyone had demanded *anything* from him—yet he had been the Dog Lord for too long now to let a surlord's daughter force him into speaking before his time.

When he was good and ready he said, "Angus Lok is being held in the pit cell directly below my feet. His only harms have been the dampness of the four walls that surround him and the poorness of his diet. By all accounts he has little taste for raw leeks and sotted oats."

"And what will you do with him?"

It was on Vaylo's mind to reply, "Whatever I wish," yet the girl chose that moment to push back her hair. The curt, guileless flick of her wrist was the action of a child, not a woman. To Asarhia March her hair was still a hindrance, something to be flicked away like a mosquito or a bit of dust, not a veil to be toyed with for the benefit of men. Vaylo almost smiled but didn't. The ghosts of granddaughters lost began to gather in the room.

"I shall hold Lok here in Ganmiddich until such a time as I see fit to move him. When I am ready I will either ransom or exchange him. There are some in the North who would pay good money for his head."

If this was news to the girl, she didn't show it. She merely blinked and said, "And Raif?"

"He will die by my hand."

The girl took a breath. The light in her eyes dimmed, actually dimmed, as if something within her had blocked the fuel they needed to burn. A noise such as Vaylo had never heard before sounded deep in the throats of his dogs. The skin along his arms puckered with gooseflesh as he listened to the fearful keening.

Letting his grandson slide to the floor, he stood. "Raif Sevrance and his clan slew our women and children upon the Bluddroad. In cold blood they drew steel, and with cold hearts they rode down my grandchildren as if they were nothing more than sheep." Vaylo didn't take his eyes from the Surlord's daughter as he spoke. Every sense he had told him there was danger here, from this slip of a girl, and he never questioned his instincts. He was the Dog Lord: He lived by them.

The girl stood perfectly still. Light from the fire seemed *pulled* toward her, as if she were sucking it from the hearth. The air in the room moved, puffing through the dogs' coats and the children's fine black hair.

Unnerved, Vaylo continued speaking, his voice becoming louder as he approached the center of the room. "Raif Sevrance is a slayer of children. A murderer. An enemy to this clan. I will kill him because I have no choice. Nine gods demand it." Barely an arm's length from the girl now, he reached out and touched her cheek. It was like touching stone.

Muscles in the girl's throat began to move.

*Sorcery.*

Recognizing it for what it was, Vaylo snatched back his hand and sent it plunging downward to the gray iron clansword at his waist. As he drew metal from the hound's-tail scabbard, the girl's lips fell open. Something dark and liquid, like molten glass, purled on the tip of her tongue. Shadows lived within it, floating slowly through its liquid eye like specks of dust in oil.

Vaylo's skin cooled. Deep within him, in the blood vessels that connected his mind to his heart, he felt the nearness of something he could only name as evil. His dogs felt it, too. Behind his back he was aware of them, whimpering and scratching at the floor. He was aware also of the wolf dog moving into place by his grandchildren.

*"I shall not kill him yet."* Vaylo spoke because he knew exactly how fast he was with the blade, exactly how long it would take him to cut through the girl's neck . . . and he knew it wasn't enough.

The words were softly spoken, whispered darts, each one making the girl blink. The light in her eyes brightened. The dark mass on her tongue hung, half in the Dog Lord's world, half in the moist cavern of her mouth. Its surface rolled like hot tar. Vaylo saw his own death reflected there before the girl inhaled, sucking the substance she had created back into her lungs.

The chief's chamber trembled. Ceiling timbers ticked and shuddered, and a thin stream of masonry dust showered the hearth.

The dogs began to howl.

"Granda! The lady looks sick!" Vaylo's granddaughter spoke in a child's idea of a whisper that was actually louder than her normal speaking voice. "Shall I bring her the stool?"

Vaylo considered the Surlord's daughter. The blankness of moments earlier had gone from her face, leaving her looking like a young girl who had played too hard and stayed up too late. She swayed, and Vaylo automatically put out his swordhand to steady her. Glancing over his shoulder, he said to his granddaughter, "Yes, fetch the stool. Quickly, now." Then, to the dogs, *"Silence!"*

Vaylo couched his sword. His hands were trembling, but the blade slid into the scabbard on first attempt. What had just happened here? Part of him almost knew, almost recognized what the girl had brought forth, yet when he probed for a memory that might explain it, he drew blank. All sense of evil had left him. The girl was just that: a girl. As his granddaughter dragged the maid's stool across the floor, Vaylo shouldered more of Ash's weight.

Blood trickled from her nostrils to her mouth as he lowered her onto the stool. She was trembling, and Vaylo sent his granddaughter and grandson to fetch a good malt from Nan Culldayis. He was glad to have them gone from the room.

"Here." Vaylo handed the girl the soft red kerchief from around his neck. "Clean yourself."

He watched her do so, taking deep breaths to calm the worn muscle that was his heart. He needed a drink. Badly. The faint odor of urine in the room testified to the fear of one of the bitches. Vaylo could not find it in himself to discipline her.

"I should slay you now, Surlord's Daughter. Do the whole of the Northern Territories a favor."

She looked up at him, her gray eyes as clear as a child's. "But you won't."

She had the truth of it; he needed her alive and well. Yet he would not let her know that. "What are you?"

"You do not want to know."

She was right. He was the Dog Lord, and he existed in a world of earth and clay, where roundhouses were seldom built more than three stories above the ground and all gods worshiped lived in stone. What he had seen upon her tongue was something else, something that belonged to another people and another place. And as that thought turned over in his mind, he finally realized what part of him already knew.

This girl did not belong with Penthero Iss in Spire Vanis. This girl belonged to the Sull.

Seventeen teeth ached with raw, needling pain as Vaylo thought upon his old enemies. Bludd shared borders with the Sull, with the Trenchlanders who were part Sull, part clansmen, part anyone else who stayed long enough in their slash-and-burn settlements to give birth or spread their seed. Trenchlanders were one thing. The real Sull, the *pure* Sull, were something Vaylo feared above all else.

He clearly remembered the day, thirty-four years ago now, when he had led a raid on the Trenchlander settlement of Cedarlode. He had been chief less than a year, and a dry spring had forced the Cedarlode Trenchlanders out of their forests and onto his borders to search for game. Trenchlanders hunted by setting fires. They torched whole corridors of forest to force the creatures living there to flee ahead of the flames. If a fire went well and the winds blew true, they could kill enough game in a single day to feed an entire settlement for a season. While Trenchland hunters stood at the fire's mouth, waiting to spear fleeing game, cindermen moved across the scorched and smoking charnel, bagging freshly charred carcasses.

Vaylo shuddered. He hated Trenchlanders. He had seen them destroy a thousand-year-old timber line in half a day.

When they started lighting fires on his borders, he had been quick to act. Eight score of his best hammermen and spearmen rode east with him to Cedarlode. A skirmish of sorts had taken place. Trenchlanders were no match for

Bluddsmen, and even before the battle was met the Trench-landers began to withdraw. Vaylo's lips stretched in something close to a smile. Stone Gods! He had been arrogant that day. Suddenly, in the heat of easy victory, it wasn't enough to force them back to their own bounds. Why not drive them farther? Claim land along the Choke River that Bludd had always coveted? It was so *easy*. Vaylo clearly remembered laughing with Jon Grubber and Masgro Faa as they'd bludgeoned a dozen Trenchlander cindermen along the red mud banks of the Choke.

Four hours it took them. Four hours to claim the river and the high bluffs beyond. Afterward they danced in the shallows. Masgro Faa found women, as Masgro always did, and although Vaylo himself didn't take part in the rapings, he watched as others did. When they had done with the women, they drank themselves stupid on elk milk turned green and beer as watery as piss. In the morning, still drunk with victory and the lingering effects of green milk ale, they headed back to the Bluddhold.

Less than an hour later the Sull halted them in their tracks.

Five hundred of their warriors surrounded them. Pure Sull, dressed in lynx furs so rich and supple, it seemed as if they rode with living predators at their backs. Their horses were like no others: breathtaking, silent, oiled like machines. Long recurve bows gleaming with rendered wolf fat rose above the horses' haunches like masts.

Until the Sull had shown themselves, Vaylo had not seen or heard a thing, so softly did their horses' hooves break ground.

Vaylo clearly remembered that not one Sull—not even the foreguard—drew a single arrow from his case. They didn't need to; Vaylo knew that straightaway. Superior numbers, superior ground, superior weapons, formation, and foreplanning were all theirs. He also knew that if he'd had twice or even three times their number, the Sull would still have bettered him.

It was the first real lesson he had learned as the Dog Lord: The Sull were not to be crossed.

The Sull held their positions for as long as they chose to. To this day, Vaylo could not decide how much time passed as the two mounted camps faced each other. Sometimes he thought perhaps it was minutes. Other times he knew it was hours. Then, suddenly, without an order being called or any signal that Vaylo could see being made, the Sull turned as a single body and headed back into the woods. Vaylo could still remember the breeze of air and clay dust they created, still recall the equal mix of fear and wonder he had felt.

No words had been exchanged, no weapons drawn, yet the message was unmistakable: Trenchland is Sull land. Stay clear.

Vaylo had never set foot on Trenchland since. He protected his borders—vigorously—yet never once had he or any Bluddsman under him claimed as much as a hair-thin strip of Sull land for his own. Sull borders were sacred. He had known that even as he had ridden to Cedarlode with his men that first day, yet he was chief, and he was shiny with new power and brash with jaw, and he'd thought he could take them on.

Thinking back on it now, Vaylo knew he had gotten off lightly. The Sull could have slaughtered them all that day. Yet they had chosen to teach a lesson in might instead.

And the Dog Lord never forgot those.

Frowning, Vaylo studied the Surlord's daughter from the safe haven of the hearth as she sat on the maid's stool and held the bloody kerchief to her nose. If she had any Sull blood in her, nothing in her coloring or face betrayed it. Still, he could not discard what his instinct told him. The Sull were not people of earth and clay like clansmen; they lived in a land of cool nights and silver moons, surrounded by oceans of rippling icewoods as tall as mountains and pale as frost. Sorcery lived in their blood. All their cities were built to let in the light of the moon. The Sull were night and twilight, shadow and shade, and Vaylo knew in his bones that the substance he had seen rolling upon Asarhia March's tongue was something they would recognize and claim as their own.

"Vaylo," came a soft voice through the wood of the door. "I have brought food and malt."

"Enter, Nan," he called.

At nearly fifty years of age, Nan Culldayis moved more

gracefully than any other woman in the clan. Vaylo watched her as she walked across the room, her fine head held perfectly level as she bore, then deposited, the tray. He noticed how little lines above her brow deepened as she looked at the girl. The habit of care ran deep within her. Like Cluff Drybannock an hour earlier, she left the room without a word.

Vaylo took the malt and drank from the jar. Food, all his favorites—charred blood sausage and pork leg roasted so slowly that it fainted from the bone—had been laid out on a platter with sotted oaks and the kind of fancy honey cakes that all women loved yet Nan knew he hated. Vaylo took a second mouthful of malt, letting its sweet, hellish flames burn his tongue. Nan thought to slip a treat to the girl.

Shrugging, he tipped a full measure of malt into the hollow jug stopper and handed it to the girl. She drank it in one, then looked up for more.

Vaylo brought the jug. "There's fancies if you want them," he said, topping up the stopper. "Honey and spices and like."

The girl looked at him. "I'd rather have the meat."

It was then, under the scrutiny of those clear gray eyes, that Vaylo Bludd began to regret what he had done. Asarhia March didn't belong with Penthero Iss in Spire Vanis, in his world of silk-lined walls, rose-scented candles, and chamber pots with lids that fit so tightly that not even light could escape. Yet he was going to send her back there all the same.

Breaking a knuckle of pork, he said, "I've sent an osprey to your foster father, telling him you're here. It will only be a matter of days before a sept comes to fetch you."

The girl's face registered no surprise. "What? No ransom?"

"That's my business." Vaylo's voice was harsh. His teeth ached savagely, and he pushed away the tray of food. The girl was right: She would not be ransomed, just handed over as quickly as copper pennies between a trapper and his whore.

The Dog Lord owed the Surlord. Oh, Iss and his devil's helper denied the existence of any such debt. It was always *My master wants nothing in return for his assistance with the Dhoone raid,* or *We think that you're the best man to take control of the clans.* Yet the words held no truth. Vaylo had been a chief for too long not to know that all things came at a price. Iss wanted something. Vaylo wasn't sure what, but he knew enough to suspect that war in the clanholds suited the Surlord nicely. And helping the Bludd chief take the Dhooneseat was as good a way as any to start one.

Whatever the motive, the deed was done. Vaylo would not look back on his past and wish things different. He would not allow himself that weakness. He and his clan were at war, and every day that war got bigger as each and every clan was drawn into the dance of swords. Old hates resurfaced and new hates were created, and Vaylo was cold enough a man to see that if he was canny enough and moved quickly enough, there was much to be gained amid the madness. He, the Dog Lord, bastard son of Gullit Bludd, born with only half a name and half a future, might be the first Bludd chief yet to name himself Lord of the Clans.

Yet for now he had a smaller goal on his mind. Vaylo glanced at the girl. He hated being indebted to any man, most especially when that debt was as cloudy as Trenchland beer and reeked in the same foul way. Penthero Iss held his marker, and now, thanks to the keen eyes of Cluff Drybannock, Vaylo had a way to get it back.

The Surlord's daughter. Return her to Iss and all debts were paid in full. There'd be no more devil's helpers scratching at his door, upsetting his dogs, and suggesting courses of action he *might* like to take in voices more fitting to milk-maids than men. He and the Surlord would be free of each other. And that was fine with the Dog Lord. As fine as fine could be.

The day the news of the girl's capture had arrived at the Dhoonehold, Vaylo had thrown the osprey into the air himself. She was a comely bird, heavy as a newborn, trained by the cloistresses in their mountain tower, capable of flying the cold currents of dawn and twilight, and inbred with ancestral memories of Spire Vanis. She would be there now, or perhaps even on her way home, her left leg no longer burdened by the message she had carried south. The Surlord's well-manicured fingers had probably stroked her gray-and-white flight feathers as one of his helpers broke the seal.

Uncomfortable with his thoughts, Vaylo banged on the door with his fist to summon Drybone. He could look at the girl no longer. The message had been sent before he'd met her. What was done was done. So she wasn't what he had expected Iss' foster daughter to be: That was no reason to change his plans.

The girl's gaze was hot on his back as he waited for Drybone to enter. She did not speak, but he heard the malt stopper she had been holding in her hand roll to the floor. The ghosts of grandchildren lost were suddenly heavy in the room, and for a moment he expected to hear the words *Granda, don't send me away.*

Drybone entered the chief's chamber. His blue eyes met once with Vaylo's own and took from them what orders he needed. He crossed immediately to the girl, seized her wrist, and forced her to stand.

"Take the meat and see she eats it." Vaylo jerked his head toward the tray.

Drybone led the girl to the table and picked up the pork joint by the bone. His strength was such that even with one hand he could hold her. One of the dogs whined as Drybone, the girl, and more importantly the bone made their way toward the door.

The girl turned on the threshold. Holding her head high, she waited for the Dog Lord to acknowledge her. "When do you intend to kill Raif Sevrance?"

Vaylo breathed deeply. Suddenly he felt very tired and very old. The girl was exhausted, too; the corners of her mouth hung down as she waited for him to speak. "I will stay his execution until the day after you leave." His own words surprised him, yet he made both his face and his voice hard as he added, "On that you have my oath."

The girl looked at him for a moment longer, then turned and walked away.

Putting a hand against the green riverstone wall for support, Vaylo waited to hear the door latch click. He had not expected her to thank him, yet he felt her lack of response like a coldness against his heart. She would draw no more sorcery tonight, he was sure of that, yet he knew she was someone he could not control. Like the Sull that day in Cedarlode, it was a matter of superior might.

Better to have her gone. Soon.

After a time he pushed himself off from the wall and unhooked the dogs' leashes from the spit hook above the
hearth. Part of him wanted to climb up the three flights of
stairs that separated him from Nan's chamber and lose himself in her hay-scented flesh. Nan knew him well. She
would offer the kind of familiar, homely comforts he was
content with. Yet another part of him wanted to be outside,
with his dogs, walking through the sharp river-scented air of
Ganmiddich.

No one stopped or spoke to him as he crossed the entrance
hall and made his way outside. The Ganmiddich roundhouse
was high ceilinged, damp, lit by fish-oil lanterns that made
the walls slick with grease. Vaylo was glad to be free of it.
As soon as the great door closed behind him, he let the dogs
run free. Normally at such a time they would race off in all
directions, their massive lungs pulling scents of foxes, hares,
and rats from thin air. Tonight they chose to stay close to
their master. Vaylo cuffed them, told them to go and find
some supper for themselves, as *he* had no intention of feeding them, yet still they would not go. Cursing softly, he let
them stay.

He led them to the river shore, and together master and
dogs watched the Ganmiddich Tower through the dark hours
of the night.

\* \* \*

THE ASSASSIN SAT IN A CHAIR well illuminated by the amber-
burning lamp, yet Penthero Iss still found it hard to behold
her. He thought at first that the light had perhaps dimmed
owing to impurities in the fuel, yet he could detect no increase or darkening of smoke. Finally, after several minutes
of study, he was forced to conclude that Magdalena Crouch
was the sort of woman whom it was difficult to *see*.

Magdalena Crouch, or the Crouching Maiden, as she was
known to the very few people in the Northern Territories
who could afford to deal death at the rate of one hundred
golds a head, waited for Penthero Iss to speak. She was perhaps twenty, no, thirty, no, forty, years of age, with hair that
may have been either brown, red, or golden depending on

the vagaries of light. Her eyes he had given up hope on. Looking straight into them when he had opened the door, he had seen nothing but his own reflection staring back. She was slim, but somehow fleshy, small, but with the limb length and bearing of someone much taller. Or was she simply tall?

She was not attractive, yet Iss found himself attracted to her. She was not repulsive, yet he found himself repulsed.

"Did you have a good journey from . . ." Iss let the question trail away as he realized he did not know where she had journeyed from. Rumor had it that she lived within the city. But all rumors surrounding the Crouching Maiden were invariably false.

The maiden did not blink as she said, "Any journey, no matter how brief or prolonged, can tire one at this time of year."

The voice was one thing she possessed that *could* be pinned down and classified: that beautiful, honey-poured voice. Iss smiled both in acknowledgment of an answer well given and in satisfaction that he finally had something on her.

He had dealt with the Crouching Maiden before, of course, but only by proxy. Caydis Zerbina—who, with his network of liquid-eyed brothers, priests, underscribes, personal servants, bath boys, errand boys, and musicians, knew most things about most people who lived in or passed through Spire Vanis—had always taken care of the details. Meeting the assassin in places of her choosing, Caydis gave her Iss' instructions and paid her fees in gold, always gold.

This time Iss had chosen to summon her himself. It had not been an easy task, for the Crouching Maiden ill liked to be summoned by any man and valued her celebrated anonymity highly. Yet she had come. One week following the original summons, she had come.

Why? Iss could only speculate. Beforehand, he had assumed she had come because he was the Surlord of Spire Vanis and one never refused a direct request from a man such as he. Yet now, standing in the switching, blue smoke shadows of her presence, he knew that not to be so. The Crouching Maiden came only because she chose to.

"Would you care for some wine . . . a liqueur perhaps, a cup of rosewater spiked with cloves?"

"No." The word was spoken easily enough, yet the Crouching Maiden rippled her muscles like a tundra cat displaying to a rival as she spoke it.

She was a woman of business, then. Iss respected that. He found it quite delicious. "I have a problem, Magdalena," he said, fingers closing around a piece of killhound bone as he spoke. "There are people, a family, whom I would like to see . . . removed, yet I don't know the exact location of the village in which they live. I have, thanks to one of my informants, a good idea of the whereabouts of the village . . . the general area, should we say."

Iss paused, expecting to hear some small murmur of encouragement from the maiden. None came, and he was forced to continue speaking. "The family lives in a farmhouse situated a day's ride northeast from Ille Glaive. My informant named three villages which he thinks are most likely to contain them." Iss gave the names. "What *I* need is someone to move through these villages and discreetly, very discreetly, discover where the family lives, and do what is necessary to slay them."

A pause followed. Iss, who was not used to being left hanging by anyone, began to feel the first stirrings of anger in his chest. True, the Crouching Maiden was the greatest assassin in the North, her name spoken in whispered awe by those who had used, and continued to use, her services. Yet *he* was Surlord of Spire Vanis. Just as Iss' jaw moved to rebuke her, she spoke.

"Ille Glaive is nine days to the north. It will cost more."

Iss felt a measure of relief but did not show it. "Of course."

"And the family? How many are there?"

"I'm not sure. The mother, one daughter that I'm certain of, perhaps a few more."

"Uncertainty costs more."

Iss had expected it would. "I will pay whatever it costs."

The Crouching Maiden made a small movement with her mouth, flashing teeth that were dry of saliva. Iss resisted the temptation to step back. Her presence was beginning to wear on him. It took too much effort to look at her. It was like staring at a landscape through a distorted piece of glass.

Most held that the maiden's success lay in her appearance. She looked like everyone's maid. When glimpsed sideways as she made her escape from assassinations in granges, guildhouses, palaces, and private homes, all who saw her assumed she was a maid, a messenger, an ash girl, an old washerwoman, a nanny, a wet nurse, or a scullion. Unlike the handful of other female assassins who could be hired in the Northern Territories for a handful of golds or a ruby the size of a housefly, the Crouching Maiden did not look like a whore. She never seduced men, never slipped in her blade as the man slipped in his manhood, never used guile or beauty to gain access to forbidden places or hid her knife beneath a froth of lace-bound cleavage. She had no need of feminine traps. Her appearance was such that people who looked at her saw what they *expected* to see: someone who belonged in their setting.

And of course she was as subtle as a fox.

The night Sarga Veys had sent word that he had the location of the Lok farm pinpointed to a handful of villages, Iss' first thought was, *I must send for the maiden.* Sarga Veys would be no good for the job. No one would willingly pour information down the Halfman's throat, and even if they did, he had no belly for blood. The Knife had the belly, but not the guile. He would break bones for information, scare the entire population of each village he visited, and alert the very people he had come to kill.

Iss returned the piece of killhound to his desk. Besides, the Knife and the Halfman had other business to tend to. They must bring Asarhia home from Ganmiddich. She must not be lost again.

"Tell me the details," said the Crouching Maiden in her silken ribbon of a voice.

Iss thought of Angus Lok, thought of the Phage, of old hates and old worries that had preyed on his mind for sixteen years. He gave the details. The meeting lasted scant minutes after that.

# THIRTY-NINE

## *Watcher of the Dead*

RAIF BURNED. HIS SKIN was hot to the touch, wet, swollen. When he touched the broken flesh on his arms, it was like probing a roast pulled from the fire. All of him ached, yet he could barely make sense of the pain. Mostly his body plunged him into sleep. Fever thrived in the darkness, shooting out purple bloodlines along his chest and rattling his bones with shivers so intense, he felt them even as he slept.

His dreams were no longer filled with people and places he knew. Strangers spoke to him, calling him *Watcher of the Dead,* massive silver-pelted wolves chased him through forests of pale trees and across frozen lakes polished so highly they reflected the moon and stars. A pair of mated ravens flew overhead, leading him north, always north. Sometimes he glimpsed the broken walls and skeletal arches of a ruined city above the treetops. Once he looked down at his feet and saw that the hard surface he walked upon was a sea of frozen blood.

In and out of sleep, he weaved, waking for short, dizzying moments when even the effort to lift his tongue from the base of his mouth was too much to be endured.

No one beat him now. They came, once or twice a day, bringing swim bladders full of freshwater and sotted oats cooked in beer. Most spat as they made for the door, as if tending him had left a bad taste in their mouths, one they had no wish to carry home to their womenfolk and hearths. Some signed to the Stone Gods if they happened to touch him. Others swore under their breaths, calling him *the Hail Wolf's Firstborn* or other damning curses. All desired his death; Raif saw it in the cold black centers of their eyes.

*Close and unharmed.* Even now, after he had long forgotten their meaning, those words held power over him. Sometimes when he was lost in the deep well of fever bliss, his lungs hissing like war engines, the heat on his forehead raising hard, clear blisters, he would hear himself say those words.

Always they brought him back. He'd wake, dry mouthed and blinking, to find his hand at his throat and his fingers glued fast to his lore.

It was enough to keep his mind intact.

When the worst night came and he lay shivering on the stone bench, his clothes wet as a drowned man's, his mind shifting between real dreams and hallucinations the fever sent him, he felt himself slide closer to the world's edge. Death was a pale presence in the cell. Raif did not have to see her to know what she was. Like a brother parted from his sister at birth, he recognized her in an instant.

*We are alike, you and I.*

The words came from nowhere, sliding down his spine like beads of ice. Half beings, tall and distorted as children's shadows at sunset, danced in the far quarters of his vision. Raif licked lips as dry as paper. He thought he should be afraid, but neither his body nor his mind could generate the physical state of fear. He blinked, because that was one thing he could do.

*Shall I take you, Watcher?*

The voice sounded in the space beneath his jaw, causing a soft, intimate pain like a lover's bite or a sister's pinch. The shadow beings rippled and grew larger with every word.

Raif held himself still. Something brushed against his cheek. An exhaled breath condensed against his teeth and retinas. The sweet, just turned odor of sour milk filled his mouth. The scent of new death.

*Close and unharmed.* He didn't know where the words came from. They were simply *there* inside his head, tugging away like a child at his father's coattails. *Close and unharmed.* Raif strained for the memory. *Who?*

The shadow beings filled his vision, their limbs of smoke curling around his fingers and thighs, the vacant sockets of their eyes and mouths sucking the life heat from him. Cold entered through pores in his skin, sinking downward through layers of fat, muscle, membranes, and bone toward the one thing Death wanted: his soul.

Raif gasped. Something glimpsed or half glimpsed in the center of the cell stopped his heart. Death showed her wares. Raif knew terror then, knew in every particle of his being that he did not want to travel that path, did not want to visit the hell that was waiting for him in the space between her arms.

*Close and unharmed.* The words thundered through his skull. *Close and unharmed. Close and unharmed.* Raif thrashed against the stone bench. He had to know, had to remember, had to find a reason to fight back.

The shadow beings began to feed. Painless as mosquitoes drawing blood, they sank their diamond fangs into his flesh. Strings of saliva flashed like spider's silk, each one landing on his skin with a hiss of utter coldness.

Raif raised his hand toward his throat. A dozen of Death's creatures fed on his arm, weighing it down, sucking its juice, but he fought them with jaws clenched. He was Raif Sevrance, Raven Born, Oath Breaker, and Watcher of the Dead, and nothing would stop him from reaching his lore.

Anger was hot within him, pumping blood to the far reaches of his body, where necrosis had already begun. More half beings gathered, drawn to the heat that was their one stock in trade. His arm shredded their insubstance, split their death's-heads in two. *Close and unharmed.* Fingers stabbing at hollow eyes, Raif reached for his lore. As his fingertip grazed the cool black horn, Death fought him, but he was too close and too angry to let her have her way. Wrenching his arm free, he grabbed the raven's bill.

*Close and unharmed.*

A moment stretched to breaking as Raif pressed the lore against the meat of his palm. The creatures continued to feed, but he did not heed them. His heart beat, just once, as the lore spoke a name for his ears alone.

Ash.

Ash was close and unharmed. And that was reason enough to fight Death tooth and nail.

Letting the lore drop against his chest, Raif braced himself for war. He had made Ash a promise, and he would not fail her, and if he had to battle his namesake, then so be it.

As he raised his torso from the stone bench, a murmur

passed through the half beings. In an instant they were gone. Fled.

Soft laughter tinkled through the cell. Shadows grew within shadows, becoming darker and darker until it seemed as if the very substance of time collapsed under their weight. *Perhaps I won't take you yet, Watcher. You fight in my image and live in my shadow, and if I leave you where you are, I know you'll provide much fresh meat for my children.* Death smiled as she withdrew. *Kill an army for me, Raif Sevrance. Any less and I just might call you back.*

"No!" Raif screamed into the emptiness of his cell. "*NOOOOOOOOO . . .*"

A THIN KEYHOLE OF SUNLIGHT shining down upon his face woke him. Even before he opened his eyes he knew the fever had broken. Lying there motionless, enjoying the sun's warmth upon his face, he let the aches and hurts of his body occupy his mind. Memories hovered close, and he knew he could retrieve them, but first he had to deal with the pain.

Thirst made him probe the bench's ledge for the water bladder. His tongue felt large in his mouth, bloated and sore with many cuts. When he found the skin he spilled more water than he drank, letting the cool liquid run down his chin and neck. His throat stung as he swallowed, and he found he was quickly sated. He didn't have the strength to return the bladder to its place, so he let it drop into the water, where it floated for a while and then sank.

He slept for some time after that, and when he next woke the cell was dark. He missed the sun. He had not intended to sleep.

More water and a fresh bowl of sotted oats lay at his feet. Their presence reassured him: The world he had come to know remained unchanged. He drank the water—all of it this time—but had no stomach for the oats. Pain shot up his arm as he pushed the bowl away, and memories of the night before came with it. Creatures feeding on his flesh. Fangs as cold as ice. Raif shook his head, drove the images back.

He relieved himself in the corner of the cell and then let sleep take him once more.

He did not dream, or if he did, it was of simple things that had no meaning. He slept well and long, and when he next opened his eyes it was dawn.

His body moved more easily from the bench this time. His head pounded less. When he reached for the freshwater bladder, he tensed, but the pain when it came was less than expected. Having drunk his fill, he probed the cuts, bruises, and sore points on his body. A rib broken during the first of many beatings had already begun to mend. It hurt when he touched it, but the join seemed surprisingly smooth. A bruise the size and shape of a ewe's heart colored the skin above his left kidney. The organ beneath was tender, and he winced as his fingers examined it. The split stitchwork on his chest was hard with scabbed flesh, and his arms and legs were striped with cuts at various stages of healing. All of his muscles ached. When he probed the glands that lay beneath his jawline, his fingers brushed against the cord that held his lore.

Ash. Close and unharmed. He didn't even need to touch the lore itself to know it.

After that he stopped tending his wounds and lay down on the bench to rest and think of Ash. The knowledge she was safe soothed him, and he soon fell asleep.

He awoke to the awareness that he was not alone in the cell. Without opening his eyes or changing his breathing pattern, he tested the light levels through his eyelids and drew air across his tongue. It was full dark. It could have been anytime in the long winter's night, but the darkness had a weight and complexity to it that came only with many hours of nightfall. The air tasted of dogskins and rendered dog fat, and Raif knew he was in the presence of the Dog Lord.

He opened his eyes.

Moonlight silvered the cell, glinting upon the water and turning stone walls to blocks of ice. The Dog Lord was looking straight at him, his face half-hidden by shadow, his eyes the color of ink. Taking a breath, he filled his chest with air that stank of death. "They told me the fever would not take you."

Raif acknowledged the words with a small movement of his jaw. The movement annoyed the Dog Lord, and he kicked the water at his feet, sending it spraying into Raif's face. "Why is it that you live so easily when those who cross you die more quickly than newborns in a wolf's jaw?"

Shaking drops of river water from his face, Raif rose to sit upright on the bench. He made no reply. The only sound was the water sloshing against the walls of the cell.

The Dog Lord ran a large red hand over his face and his braids. For a moment he looked very old. When he spoke his voice trembled. "Tell me, what evil lies at the heart of your clan, that men such as you and the Hail Wolf are born?"

The Hail Wolf. So that's what they were calling Mace Blackhail these days. Raif said, "Do not link my name with his."

"Why? You slew in his name on the Bluddroad, then again in the snow outside Duff's."

Raif's face burned. There was nothing to say.

*"Answer me!"*

He flinched but did not speak. To answer would be a betrayal of his clan . . . of Drey. The truth had died that day on the Bluddroad. He would not be the one to resurrect it.

The Dog Lord came for him, lunging through the river water to take Raif's throat in his hands. Pressing his thumbs into Raif's windpipe, he cried, "You slew my babies. Out there, in the cold and the snow. Children, they were, just children. Scared, shivering, clutching at their mothers' skirts." His voice was terrible to hear, rough with grief so powerful that each word shook him like a fever. The image he created was so close to the truth that Raif could not meet his eyes. "And they called for their granda to help them. And their granda did not hear."

Abruptly the Dog Lord released his hold and turned away. Muscles to either side of his neck jerked powerfully, yet within a second he had stilled them.

Raif spat blood. His throat was on fire, but he made his voice hard as he said, "You slew our chief in the badlands, him and a dozen more. You started this dance of swords. You struck the first blow."

The Dog Lord lashed at air with his hand, pushing Raif's words from him. "Clan Bludd made no raid on Blackhail. It may have suited the Hail Wolf to claim it, but Dagro Blackhail did not die by my hand."

Raif stood. He knew he should be surprised at what the Dog Lord said, but he wasn't. A cold anger grew within him, and he felt his face tighten as he stared at the Dog Lord's turned back. "Why didn't you *deny* it?"

"Who would? When half of the clanholds is praising your jaw for carrying off such a raid, and the other half are so scared that it might happen to them that the piss freezes to their thighs at the sound of your name, who's going to stand up and forswear it?" The Dog Lord shook his head. "Not me."

"Who, then? *Who did it?*"

Something in Raif's voice made the Dog Lord turn to face him. His eyes were hard as sapphires, yet Raif met them with a hardness of his own. This man standing before him possessed knowledge that could have stopped a war.

The Dog Lord's braids rose and fell against his chest as he gathered breath to speak. His voice, when it came, was unrepentant. "You'll hear no answers about the badlands raid from me. I wasn't the one who rode home from a killing field and named myself a chief."

Raif felt a portion of his anger leave him. The Dog Lord had spoken his own thoughts right back to him. Struggling to find sense, Raif said, "What of the wounds? Bron Hawk was there the night you made raid on the Dhoonehouse. He said your swords entered flesh but drew no blood. I saw the same thing at the badlands camp. My father's rib cage was smashed to pieces, yet there was barely enough blood to dye his shirt."

The Dog Lord swore. Placing a hand upon the cell wall, he let the ancient stone of the Ganmiddich Tower bear a portion of his weight. "I should have known," he murmured. "The devil is playing both sides."

Hairs on Raif's arms prickled, and in the space of one second he remembered all that Death had said. *Kill an army for me, Raif Sevrance.* Raif shivered. He heard his voice say, "What do you mean?"

The Dog Lord turned on him. "What do I mean? What do I mean? You dare ask *me* what I mean? You, who have slain children in cold blood and butchered three of my warriors so badly that I could not let the widows tend their corpses." Spittle flew from his lips as he spoke, and his braids cracked against his shoulders like whips. "I will answer no questions from Watcher of the Dead. Cluff Drybannock was right. You must be finished, and quickly. Would that he and his men had cut you down where they found you, and not thought to save you for me. Would that the deed had been done, and my hands need not be stained with your blood."

Raif stood tall and silent in the face of the Dog Lord's fury. He wondered how much of it had to do with him. The Bludd chief had not known about the wounds at the badlands camp. Yet he knew now, and that knowledge had shaken him.

The Dog Lord took the three steps necessary to bring himself opposite Raif. Reaching out, he closed his hands around Raif's lore. "They said your guide had named you a raven." With one quick movement he snapped the twine. "If it wasn't for an oath spoken to the Surlord's daughter, you would be dead this night, Raif Sevrance. Know that. Think on that. And then spend the next night praying to the Stone Gods for mercy, for when the time comes you shall get none from me."

With that he turned and walked toward the door. Before he reached inside the lock hole to open it, he dropped the raven lore into the dark, greasy water at his feet.

Raif swayed, forced himself to stay upright until the Dog Lord had gone.

# FORTY

## *In the Crab Chief's Chamber*

NOTICING THAT THE SMOKE from the fish-oil lanterns irritated Sarga Veys' eyes, Vaylo Bludd ordered another two to be lit. He couldn't stand the stench of them himself—he'd been in this blasted tall roundhouse for six days now, and his clothes and braids reeked of river trout—but he'd be damned if he'd make this meeting any easier for the Halfman. They could call him the Fish Lord first!

Neither Marafice Eye nor the Halfman looked at ease. The Knife had already staked out a corner of the chief's chamber and made it his own. He walked it now, his massive body straining against his urine-softened leathers as he moved. Every now and then he would look around, his gaze alighting on blunt objects, metal pokers, and ceremonial weaponry like a prisoner contemplating escape. The Dog Lord detected a limp, carefully concealed. As for the Halfman, well, he looked no different from when Vaylo had seen him last. Despite the long ride from Ille Glaive, his white robe and kidskin boots were barely soiled, and he must have shaved on the hoof for his jaw was smoother than a purse made of silk.

They had arrived at noon. Ten men in all: the Knife, the Halfman, a sworn brother with only three fingers on his right hand, and a full Rive Watch sept. The sept's appearance upon the bluff south of the roundhouse had caused a stir among the clan. The Rive Watch, with their bloodred blades, their black leather cloaks, and the Killhound embroidered at their breasts, represented the might of Spire Vanis to the clansmen. They wore iron bird helms, which none removed until they were challenged by a dozen spearmen a hundred paces from the roundhouse door. It was an act of arrogance and hostility that Vaylo had made them pay for.

After four hours' forced wait in the ewe pen, the sept's manners seemed little improved.

It was dark now, early evening. A high wind rattled the shutters and breathed down the chimney, causing the flames in the hearth to leap into the room. The sept and the man with eight fingers had been led to the Ganmiddich kitchen, where Molo Bean had them well in hand. Vaylo almost pitied them, for Molo was an excellent hammerman and a fine cook, yet he hated city men with a vengeance. Eighteen summers ago a troop of white helms from Morning Star had killed his brother in a dawn raid upon his father's homestead in Clan Otler. The white helms had taken offense at a dam built by Shaunie Bean to direct water from the Wolf River northward to wet his fields.

Vaylo sucked on his aching teeth. The city of Morning Star was no friend to Clan Bludd. He would have to remember to send an osprey to his first son, Quarro, tell him to set more watches on the Bluddhold's southern borders. The Lord Rising and his white-helmed cockerels would get no land from Vaylo Bludd.

Troubled, the Dog Lord turned his attention to Marafice Eye and Sarga Veys. He had left them to stew for an extra hour in the chief's chamber while he fed and kenneled his dogs. It had seemed a fair idea at the time, yet now he wished he hadn't bothered. This matter was better over and done.

"Has she been given supper yet?" Sarga Veys said, his voice as high and grating as the sound of a sackpipe leaking air.

"I am not her nursemaid." Vaylo sat at the head of the chief's table, a block of green riverstone pitted with ancient fish fossils and petrified shells. A dozen horseshoe crabs, perfectly preserved, formed a circle below the Dog Lord's hand. "How would I know if she's been fed or not? What does it matter to you?" The anger was quick to come. His two remaining grandchildren were on their way home to Dhoone, escorted by Drybone and his crew. Nan had returned with them. By Vaylo's reckoning they would have reached the halfway point by now. Stone Gods protect them.

"It matters," said Sarga Veys with a sharp little jab of his chin, "because I need to drug her."

Vaylo didn't like the sound of that. "What with?"

"Nothing. A little posy to make her sleep."

"I said, *what with?*"

Marafice Eye stopped pacing and dropped his hand to his weapon's belt. It was empty, of course—the first Bluddsmen to meet the sept and its leader had ransomed their weapons until such time as they departed—yet the Knife had a way of making the gesture look threatening even when his scabbard lay slack against his thigh. He was a dangerous man, Vaylo reckoned, yet he still feared the Halfman more.

Sarga Veys sent the Knife a superior glance, one that assumed command of him by warning, *Easy with your hostilities.* Not surprisingly the Knife ignored it. No love lost between those two there.

"Very well," Sarga Veys said. "If you must know, I intend

to give Asarhia blood of the poppy and the pulverized seeds of henbane."

So he meant to carry her away from the roundhouse without her knowledge or consent. By the time those two mind-deadening drugs wore off, the Knife and the Halfman would be well away from Ganmiddich, on the far side of the Bitter Hills. And the girl herself would be left so weak, she'd be lucky if she could swallow water and sit a horse.

Vaylo took a wad of black curd from his pouch and chewed on it. He had seen for himself what the Surlord's daughter could do when she was cornered, so he understood the need for caution. Yet henbane could be poisonous in heavy doses. And that he would not have. "You will not give the girl henbane under my roof."

"Why not?" The Knife leered. "Are you smitten with the bitch, too?"

Vaylo stood. "I would have the girl delivered safely to your master. If you and your men had done your jobs properly and found the girl yourselves, you would not be dealing with me now. But you didn't, and you are here, on newly made Bluddground, and you will abide by the Bludd chief's terms."

Marafice Eye listened to Vaylo Bludd in silence.

Sarga Veys made a thin, snorting noise. "I know my master's wishes. The girl must—"

"Silence!" The Knife took a step toward Sarga Veys. "Do as he says."

Sarga Veys took five steps back and might have taken more if it hadn't been for the fact that his shoulders came in contact with the wall. His lower jaw shook violently as he said, "Very well. As you wish." Slender fingers unhooked a dun-colored pouch from his belt and retrieved a vial from within. The vial was the length of a pea pod and sealed with brown wax. Veys held it out toward the Dog Lord.

Vaylo considered knocking it onto the floor. He hated drugs and sorceries—*all* things that could play tricks with a man's mind—yet there was little choice here. Not because of the power of the two men standing before him, or even the power of their master in Mask Fortress. No, rather the power of the girl. If she were awake when they carried her away from Raif Sevrance, Vaylo did not know what she would do.

He took the vial. In a harsh voice he called to Strom Carvo, who was standing guard beyond the door. Sarga Veys gave his instructions to the dark-skinned swordsman: Use all the vial, pour it in her sotted oats and drinking water, and whip it in the butter and honey she spreads upon her bread. Vaylo spat out a wad of curd as the Halfman spoke. He had a bad taste in his mouth.

As Strom withdrew, Sarga Veys said, "I think it best if I go with him to oversee the preparations. I have some skill in such matters."

Vaylo didn't doubt it. "No. You will stay here and wait." He slammed the door shut. He would not have the Halfman walking freely about the roundhouse. With Drybone and his crew gone to Dhoone, they were short of men, and that was one fact the Dog Lord didn't want anyone to know.

Marafice Eye said, "Name your terms for the other two prisoners." His small mouth pulled tight like scar tissue as he spoke, and his hands—the largest Vaylo could recall seeing on any man—pushed against a rotten timber in the wall.

Vaylo suddenly longed for the company of his dogs. One of the bitches was in heat, and the rest were half-crazy with jealousy or lust, and he'd had little choice but to shut them away for the night in the dog cote. He ill liked being without them, but nature was one thing he knew better than to fight. Marafice Eye was another thing entirely. He said, "Angus Lok and the Hailsman are not for ransom."

The Knife smiled, his lips splitting like a sausage on a grill. "I *said*, name your terms, Dog Lord." As he pushed himself off from the wall, Vaylo marked the bulge of a hand-knife concealed above his right kidney.

"And *I* said the prisoners are not for ransom."

"You owe my master," hissed Sarga Veys. "He won't be pleased when he hears of this. I shall advise him to withdraw all assistance—"

"Tell him *do it!*" Vaylo roared. "I want no more kindness from the Spire King. Stone Gods help me, I wish I'd never given ears to him or his schemes. Tell him from me, the Dog

Lord, that once his foster daughter leaves Bluddground this night, all agreements between us are sundered. The girl is payment in full."

Sarga Veys opened his mouth to speak, but both Marafice Eye and Vaylo Bludd moved forward to stop him. For one moment the Knife and the Dog Lord locked gazes, and shared intent and shared opinions on the Halfman made passing comrades of them. He was a fighting man, Marafice Eye. He knew better than to squawk and bluster when he was outmanned and far from home.

With a mock bow, Vaylo stepped back and let him deal with his man.

Marafice Eye approached Sarga Veys, drawing so close that their shoulders touched. Putting his small lips to the cartilage of the Halfman's ear, he said, "Silence," in a voice so cold it caused the flames in the Crab Hearth to shrink.

Sarga Veys sat . . . quietly.

Vaylo poured two drams of malt liquor, keeping the first for himself and offering the second to Marafice Eye. The Knife accepted it, and the two men struck cups and drank. Any other time Vaylo might have savored the silent companionship that came with sharing a fine malt with a man he did not hate, but his mind was too agitated, and he drank his liquor fast and with little joy. When the Knife returned the empty dram cup to the stone surface of the chief's table, Vaylo said, "I'd have you take a message to your master."

The Knife raised his chin, indicating he would listen.

"Tell him to keep his fingers out of the clanholds. I know what he's doing, and if he doesn't stop, I'll gather all the clans that are loyal to me—Clan Broddic, Clan HalfBludd, Clan Otler, Clan Frees, and Clan Gray—and ride south to Mask Fortress and tear down his gates. Iss has played me for a fool once, and I'm an old man with a high opinion of myself and I'll not let him use me again.

"I know I wasn't the only chief he approached with his dirty little promises of sorcery and aid; while one of his faces was busy whispering Dhoone secrets to me, the other was talking treason to the Hail Wolf. Mace Blackhail and your master arranged the raid on the hunt party in the badlands, made it look as if Dagro and his clansmen were attacked by a troop of my men. The Hail Wolf got a chiefdom for his trouble, and Iss drew Blackhail into the war. Now I don't know which other chiefs he's approached and what other deals he struck, but I do know he'll make no more. The clanholds are no longer his business. Tell him that from me, the Dog Lord. Tell him that from this day forth all wars we wage will be of our own making."

Vaylo was shaking by the time he was finished, his throat raw. He was not one for speeches, but a warning needed to be sent. Penthero Iss had to be told that the clanholds were no longer his field of play.

Marafice Eye held Vaylo's gaze for a long moment, then said, "I'll pass your message on, Dog Lord, though I see no easy end to the Clan Wars."

He was right. Lines were too clearly drawn and hatred too deeply entrenched for any clan chief to face another over a table and speak of peace. Yet that wasn't the point. "It's a matter for the clans now."

Marafice Eye nodded, understanding immediately. Vaylo respected him for that.

They waited in silence for an hour. Marafice Eye did not sit once during that time, though Vaylo noticed that he rested his left leg from time to time and favored his right when walking. Sarga Veys sat exactly where the Knife had placed him and neither moved nor spoke. Vaylo resisted the urge to drink more. Waiting made him weary. He longed for Nan's gentle company and the closeness of his dogs. He worried about his grandchildren and wondered if Drybone had them riding through the night.

Every now and then he would glance at the southeast wall in the chamber and fix his eyes upon the window, shuttered and bolted, there. Raif Sevrance was never far from his thoughts. Even to look in the direction of the Inch brought on feelings so intense, he could taste them in his mouth. Vaylo wished Drybone had broken down just once in his self-controlled, iron-willed life and beaten the lad to death where he had found him. At least that way there would have been swift, unthinking justice. Not this slow, ever more complicated torture of truth and lies.

Vaylo pushed a hand through his braids. It had been a mistake to see him. He didn't want to see Raif Sevrance as a young yearman still protecting the honor of his clan from a cell that stank of death. He wanted to look upon a Hailsman and see a murderer instead.

Vaylo called for Strom Carvo and gave the order to check on the girl. Only when she was gone and a new dawn had come to the roundhouse could he finally put steel to the Hailsman's throat.

"She's sleeping, Chief," Strom said when he returned four minutes later. "I called her name, but she didn't respond. I shook her arm, and still she slept."

Vaylo nodded. "Bring her to me, Strom. Pull on her coat and boots as best you can—"

"And make note of how much food she has eaten."

The Dog Lord raised an eyebrow Veys' way. Hadn't anyone bothered to tell him that no one interrupted a clan chief when he was speaking? Strom's dark, storm-lined face brightened at the prospect of a verbal lashing, but Vaylo let the incident pass. He would not waste breath on the Halfman. Placing a hand on Strom's arm, he walked with the swordsman out of the chief's chamber.

When they were past earshot, Vaylo said, "Do as the Halfman says, Strom. But first, find Ranald or one of the others and tell him to search the Halfman's saddlebags and remove all powders or potions." It was little, but it was something. Henbane was scarce in winter, and Sarga Veys would not easily lay his hands on more.

Strom nodded.

"And tell Branon that I want all clansmen and clanswomen war dressed and mounted within the quarter. When Marafice Eye and his sept leave Ganmiddich I want the last thing they see to be the armed might of Bludd." Strom turned. Vaylo halted him with a final caution. "We must be careful, Strom. Marafice Eye has a soldier's mind; he'll spot our poor numbers given chance."

Strom Carvo, who was Cluff Drybannock's blood-brother and one of the finest swordsmen in the clan, simply nodded and said, "Due care has already been taken."

Vaylo felt better for hearing those words. They made the next waiting period bearable.

High winds blasted the walls of the roundhouse as the Knife, the Halfman, and the Dog Lord stood in silence and waited for Strom to bring the girl. When hail began to batter the shutters, Vaylo was neither worried nor surprised. A storm suited his feelings well enough.

When the knock came it seemed too soon. Sarga Veys' tongue came out to moisten his lips. Marafice Eye stopped pacing and shifted the massive *fact* of his body toward the door.

"Enter," called the Dog Lord.

Strom Carvo carried the girl into the room. The swordsman had taken care to wrap her tightly against the storm, and her slim body was thick with as many layers of wool and oilcloth as the remaining Bluddswomen could spare. Strom had even thought to tuck her lovely ash blond hair beneath her collar, where the wind could not find it as she rode. The girl herself was lifeless. Her head lolled back and forth with every step Strom took.

Sarga Veys moved forward. Vaylo heard the excited inhalation of his breath. It sickened him.

"Lay her on the table."

Strom obeyed his chief, yet Vaylo saw the glint of anger in his eyes. He didn't want to give her up to these men.

Sarga Veys was first to approach, pulling down the fox hood that Strom had tied in place. "Oh yes," he said. "It's her." Then to Strom: "How much food has she eaten?"

Muscles on the swordsman's face shifted with the deceptive smoothness of ice plates riding a rough sea. "Nothing. She drank only the water."

Vaylo closed his eyes. *Only water. How strong is the drug the Halfman gave her?*

As Sarga Veys plucked open her eyes and picked up her limbs and dropped them, Marafice Eye moved toward the table. His face darkened as he beheld Asarhia March, and his large hands came together to crush the air above her chest. Watching those hands, Vaylo almost said, *You cannot have her.*

Sarga Veys produced a second vial of poppy blood from his pouch. "The few drops she drank with the water are not enough. She'll wake in the night if we're not careful."

Strom looked to his chief. Vaylo said, "Take the vial from him and put two drops only upon her tongue." Strom did his bidding in silence.

When all was done and Marafice Eye was busy cracking his knuckles in readiness to bear Asarhia's weight, the Dog Lord approached the table. The girl's face was pale, her lips almost blue. Frozen. It was easy to imagine her mouth full of snow. . . .

Abruptly he turned away. "*Go!*" he commanded, chasing ghosts and men alike. "And be sure to tell your master that all debts are paid in full."

\* \* \*

RAIF WOKE.

*Ash.*

His hand clutched at his throat, seeking his lore. It wasn't there. Memory flooded back to him; the Dog Lord had cast it into the standing water at his feet. It hadn't seemed important to search for it at the time. The raven lore always came back.

Steeling himself against pain and weakness, Raif rose from the stone bench and waded through the shin-high water. Storm darkness filled the cell. He couldn't see anything, not even his hands as he plunged them into the black substance of the river and began questing for his lore.

Weeds wrapped around his fingers, slimy as uncooked meat. Other things floated by his wrists, soft things, jellylike things, bits of something smooth like hollow bone. He smelled his own filth and the filth of those who had been here before him, yet he could find nothing within him that was repulsed. He had to get to his lore.

His body was weak, *weak,* and he cursed it a dozen times in the darkness. When his legs began to tremble beneath him, he knelt in the water and continued searching. Raking his fingers along the cell floor, he probed the cracks and creases and river-worn hollows, disturbing centuries of mud and shit each time he moved a hand. The water was bitterly cold, yet he barely felt it. Outside the storm howled like a wild beast, swiping at the tower with claws of wind and hail, yet it mattered less than the hiss of his own breath. Something was wrong with Ash.

Icy water deadened his fingers, turning them into wooden sticks. Skin split and tore as he dredged through the silt. *Where is it?* Had the current carried it away? Raif shook his head. *No.* As a child he had thrown the lore from him a dozen times, yet the clan guide had always found it and brought it back.

It had to be here.

Water sloshed against the walls as he grew more frenzied. His clothes were sodden, stinking. Knife cuts on his thighs and belly burned like white fire. His rib cage felt big and swollen, the bones making unnerving creaking noises every time he took a lungful of air. He thought he heard Death laugh at him, a high, tinkling chirr that chilled him in ways no cold water could. *Ash . . .*

As he dragged his hand along the crease where the wall and floor met, a length of twine tangled in his fingers. Snatching his fist closed, he caught it in his grip and pulled it through the water. The moment his hand broke the surface, he knew his lore had come back to him.

*Here it is, Raif Sevrance. One day you may be glad of it.*

The small length of bird horn came dripping from the water. Raif held the twine, only the twine, until he had returned to the dry island of the bench. His heart beat against his rib cage with quiet force as he moved. He thought his hands might shake when he pulled the twine through his fingers, but they held steady. River water dripped from every point of his body, pooling onto the bench where he sat. He thought about signing to the Stone Gods, asking them to keep Ash safe, then decided against it. Stone Gods were clan gods, and neither he nor Ash was clan.

Forcing his lips together, he placed the lore in the palm of his right hand and closed his fist around it.

The knowledge came to him instantly, warm as his own blood, slipping into his mind like just another thought. Ash was gone. She was no longer close and unharmed. Someone had taken her away.

Spitting to clear the taste of river from his mouth, Raif rose from the stone bench. Slowly he crossed to the cell door. When he was within two paces of the oak and ironclad planking, he halted. Tensing his body for a long moment, he filled his lungs with air. Then, with a movement so fast it split the standing water in two, he sent his shoulder smashing into the wood.

Ash was gone . . . and the tower would have to fall so he could reach her.

# FORTY-ONE

## *An Object Returned*

RAIF LET THE MADNESS TAKE HIM. Hours passed as he tore at the darkness in his cell. When his right shoulder became a bruised and bloody mass, he began driving at the door with his left. When the door held firm, and whatever bar or bolts bracing it on the other side failed to crack or jump their casings, he swung himself up onto the bench and began punching the iron grating. The bars of the grate were as thick as arms, set deep into mortise holes and packed with burned lime: They did not budge under his bombardment.

He shouted until his voice was hoarse, but no one came for him to kill. He charged the walls, then kicked them, and when that failed he clawed at the green riverstone with bare hands. Blood flowed from beneath his fingernails, running along his palms and dripping from his wrists to the river below. Sweat stung his eyes and turned the clothes on his back to sopping bandages packed with salt. He wanted someone to come—*anyone.* The kill was upon him, and he imagined beating Bluddsmen senseless against the stone walls, then using their swords to carve out their hearts. Watcher of the Dead, they called him. Well, let them come and see for themselves how quickly he could take a life.

Hours passed, and still he raged. Terrible tremors shook him, making his legs bend with exhaustion and his eyes see things that could not be there. Tem was in the cell with him, lying on the stone bench, his arms burned black, and his mouth open and full of worms. When Raif looked again it was his mother, her skin all yellow and loose, her eyes sealed closed with sulfur paste. Soon his legs could no longer hold him, and he dropped into the water and began gouging rotten mortar with his lore. Ash was all that mattered. Getting to Ash.

Dimly, in some distant part of his mind that could still look ahead, he knew his best course would be to lie low until morning, wait until a Bluddsman entered the cell—one hand busy with the bolt, the other balancing a water bladder and a bowl of sotted oats—and take him as he entered. Smash the door in his face, seize his weapon, and run. Yet the idea of doing nothing until morning was unthinkable. Somehow it was all mixed up with Drey . . . he could not break another oath.

As the night wore on, he fought sleep. His mind lapsed for seconds at a time, leaving him blinking in the darkness, gripping his lore. After a time his neck could no longer support the weight of his head, and he rested his chin on his chest as he worked. His eyes closed, but he continued to jab bloody fingers against stone, using the pain to stay awake.

Eventually the pain stopped hurting, and the line between sleeping and waking began to fade. He lost seconds, then minutes, then hours. Still fighting, he fell asleep.

Clacking noises, like the sound of wooden training swords bashing together, filled his dreams. He saw Shor Gormalin parrying with Banron Lye on the court, dead men dueling with swords. *Clack! Clack! Clack!*

Raif turned in his sleep. The clacking followed him, only now it sounded different, higher, sharper, like steel meeting steel. Someone screamed. Footsteps thudded in the distance. Dogs wailed, their cries growing higher and more desperate until they stopped sounding like things bred by man and howled like wolves instead.

A mighty crash shook the tower. Raif's right arm skidded from the stone bench and fell into the water below. He opened his eyes. The pale light of winter dawn filled the cell like gray smoke. Something red and bloody lay directly in front of his face, and he stared at it for a long moment before realizing it was his own left hand. As he pulled his right free from the water, he heard a salvo of shouted orders. Sword metal clattered against stone. Footsteps drew close. Breath exploded in a violent hiss. Something, very probably a body, fell with the thud of a rolled carpet toppling onto the floor.

Even as Raif drew himself upright, the cell door burst open.

Blade metal gleamed like cut ice. A fist, gloved in black, balanced a lead-weighted sword close to a chest plated in silvered steel. A face, shadowed beneath a thorn helm of acid-blackened iron, emerged from the darkness behind the door.

*Blackhail.* Pride stabbed at Raif's heart: His clan had taken Ganmiddich back.

"On your feet."

Raif turned cold. His pride drained away as quickly as an exhaled breath. The voice behind the thorn helm was known to him. "Take off your helm."

The figure shook his head. Eyes gleamed cold beneath a mesh of iron thorns. Raising the tip of his sword, he said, "Stand."

Raif stood and faced the figure by the door. He was shaking, but the helmed man was not. The hand that gripped the sword was as solid as rock. The chest beneath the armor rose and fell with powerful, even breaths.

"Drey?"

The figure stiffened.

"Brother." It was almost, yet not quite, a question. The figure before him was barely recognizable as Drey; his voice was deeper, his shoulders broader. Even his attire was different. War dressed in tempered steel and black leathers, Drey had shed the rough hand-me-downs that were the stock of all yearmen and clan sons. He was all hard edges now.

"We are not brothers, you and I. Blood ceased flowing between us the day you broke your oath."

Raif controlled the muscles in his face. Inside, the coldness in his chest contracted to a single rigid point. Drey was not here to save him. It was a child's thought, a sudden realization that those you trusted could hurt you, and Raif felt the same sickening shock as if Drey had smacked him in the face. He knew he shouldn't have been surprised, but the habit of Drey's loyalty ran deep within him. Drey was always there to pull him out of scrapes, to conceal bloody knees from Tem and broken saplings from Longhead, and to back up incredible stories about bears fleeing over thin ice and lone elk trampling tents. Drey always waited.

Swords clashed in the chamber above. The ceiling shuddered as something heavy and metallic, like a charcoal burner or an arms rack, crashed to the floor. Drey stepped forward, jabbing the air next to Raif's throat with his sword. "Move!"

Raif cursed the reflex action that made him flinch. Fixing his gaze on what was visible of his brother's eyes through the thorn helm, he walked around the blade.

"Up the steps. One pace ahead of me, no more."

Raif climbed the spiral stair in silence. Light stung his eyes. Fresh air and new sounds made his head swim. Once he stumbled and had to put a hand upon the wall to steady himself. Drey's sword drew blood from the center of his spine, and he did not stumble or slow down again.

Two Hailsmen stood guard on the floor above. Both men's breastplates were beaten out of shape, and one man's gorget was punctured and leaking blood. Their blade edges were caked with chunks of hair and skin. Through the wire of their helms, Raif recognized Rory Cleet and Arlec Byce. As he drew closer, Raif saw that Rory's handsome face was now marred by a thick white scar running from the crease of his eye to his mouth.

"*Stone Gods!*" Rory hissed as Raif approached. "What have they *done* to him?" Rory received no answer, nor did he say anything more. Drey sent a look to silence him.

Raif kept his face hard. He could not stop them from seeing the hurts on his body, but that was *all* they would see.

"To the skiff."

Hearing his brother speak those words, Raif realized that Drey had changed more than his appearance. Arlec Byce, a full clansman of five winters, moved on his say.

They climbed through the base of the tower, past snuffed torches, unhinged doors, and a Bluddsman's decapitated corpse. Black smoke pumped from a doorway, twisting around itself to form a funneling afterbirth of soot and

fumes. Raif considered the band of darkness it created, noticed how Rory Cleet lifted his visor so he could rub his
stinging eyes and how Arlec Byce held his swordhand to his
helm to block the stench of burning flesh.

It would be so easy to take them.

*Kill an army for me, Raif Sevrance.*

Raif shook his head with quiet force. He would not slay
his clansmen. Not even for Ash.

A fourth Hailsman joined them as they filed out of the
tower into the gray stormlight that shone upon the Inch. Raif
paid him no heed, yet he knew well enough that it was Bev
Shank, kitted out in new-made plate armor and guard chains.
His sword was badly notched and would have to be sent to
Brog Widdie to be refired. Then again, perhaps his father
would buy him a new one; Orwin Shank could well afford it.
Raif was aware that Bev's gaze was upon him, yet he kept
his thoughts and his eyes upon the sword.

Spray from the river lashed his cheek as he waited to
board the skiff. High winds shaved the surface, slicing the
heads off waves and driving dark swells against the Inch.
Hailstones battered the tower, drowning out the sound of
battle to the north. On the far bank, the Ganmiddich roundhouse glowed orange and green, lit by a moat of soaring
flames. Strip fires, Raif thought, to stop the Bluddsmen from
forming lines.

The skiff rocked as he stepped into it. Gray water lay two
hands deep in the hull, yet Raif barely felt it. Compared with
the water in his cell, it was warm and fragrant. Hailstones as
big as peas bobbed on the surface.

"Tie his hands." Drey's voice was hard. His brown eyes
dared Rory Cleet to defy him.

Rory was no riverman, and when he stood to do Drey's
bidding, he sent the keel of the boat pitching into the storm-
stripped water. Bev Shank and Arlec Byce struggled to keep
the oars in their locks.

Raif held himself perfectly still as he allowed his wrists to
be tied. He thought he was going mad. He saw death everywhere he looked. It would be so easy to push Rory against
the gunwales and capsize the boat. All of them would be
thrown into the water. Some would die. Bev Shank could

swim, but his new armor must weigh two stone and a half and he'd sink straight to the bottom. All four of the Hailsmen were wearing helms and plate. The water was cold. Icy. Undertows and storm tows would pull them under in an instant, send them smashing against the Inch. Raif knew he would survive. Cold water was nothing to him . . . and there was no steel on *his* back, only rags.

Raif sat and did not move. Salt from the river burned his skin. He watched Drey yet did not seem to. He thought of death yet did not act.

It was a long journey to the shore. All four clansmen took up oars. Instead of fighting the current, Drey used it to steer the skiff to the bank, allowing the river to carry the craft downstream. Mounted figures milled upon the bank, rippling in the heat of the strip fires like demons. Hailsmen and Bluddsmen. Raif thought he saw the barrel chest and chestnut braids of Corbie Meese amid a melee of sixty men. He heard the screams of wounded horses and the furious rattle of hammermen's chains.

"Raise the oars." Drey snapped the order even though they were still some distance from the north shore, and the skiff carried them even farther downstream. By the time the skiff's keel scraped gravel, they were clear of the roundhouse and the fighting. Raif looked from face to face as the four clansmen dragged the skiff ashore. No one would meet his eyes.

Mace Blackhail. The thought came with the strength and speed of a reflex action. Mace Blackhail wanted him taken quietly, away from the fighting and the other clansmen. Far better to deal with the traitor alone, get the whole thing over and done, with no interference from the clan. Raif looked across the bank, his eyes skimming over the wooded slopes and wet meadows of Ganmiddich. Any moment he expected Mace Blackhail to ride forward on his roan.

Drey secured the skiff's lines himself and then straightened to address his men. "Rory. Arlec. Head upstream on foot, find Corbie and Hugh Bannering and tell them the Inch has been taken." He unsheathed his sword as he spoke. It was the same sword he always carried at his back along with his hammer, yet the grip was new doeskin and the blade had been oiled and whetted to a high sheen. The metal gleamed with all the colors of the storm. "Bev. You go with them. Fetch my horse and a spare pony for the prisoner. Ride them back at haste."

Arlec Byce and Rory Cleet exchanged a glance. Drey trained the tip of his sword on Raif's kneecap. "Go," he murmured, stabbing the bone. "I'll hold the prisoner until you return."

Bev Shank was first to start east. Rory Cleet and Arlec Byce were slower getting started, and Arlec looked back several times as he headed along the bank. Raif wondered what had happened to the axman's twin; the two were seldom far apart.

Drey held his position as he watched the three men scramble over the wet gravel and storm-greased rocks along the shore. Hailstones bouncing off his breastplate made ticking sounds as seconds passed.

Raif's throat was dry. He was aware of the blade point at his knee yet didn't look down to check for blood. His eyes were on his brother. Drey's face was banded by shadow. The glove that held the sword was stretched white at the seams. *I'll stand second to his oath.* Drey's words were suddenly there in Raif's head. That and the image of Drey kicking his black gelding forward on the court, one man among twenty-nine. The only one willing to back his oath.

Raif almost didn't feel the rope being cut. Drey's sword ran with light as he sliced through the horsehair twine at Raif's wrist, yet no brightness found its way to his face. Raif saw him glance east, to the grove of ancient water oaks that had hidden Rory, Arlec, and Bev from view. Slowly, not meeting his brother's eyes, Drey shifted his grip on the sword.

"Take it."

Raif blinked. Drey pushed the hilt of the sword toward him. "I said *take it.*"

Confused, Raif shook his head.

Drey sucked in breath. His eyes darted left then right. With a sudden movement he grabbed the edge of the blade and drove the pommel into Raif's chest. *"Cut me!"*

*No.* Raif took a step back. He saw where the sword edge

had bitten through Drey's glove and drawn a line of blood. Even as he watched the steel turn red, Drey moved forward, grabbing Raif's hand and forcing it around the hilt. Raif fought him, but Drey had always been stronger, and even before he could pull away, Drey stepped into the tip of the sword.

Metal punctured with a quiet hiss. Drey tensed. His eyes darkened, and his lips twisted as he fought to take the pain soundlessly . . . as Tem had taught him. Horrified, Raif pulled the sword back. Blood, shiny and nearly black, oozed from a jagged slit in Drey's breastplate. Raif lost his grip on the sword, and it clattered against the rocks, making a sound that seemed too loud.

"Go," Drey said, fingers working to release the leather straps on his breastplate. "We fought. You took my weapon from me, wounded me, then fled."

Raif moved forward to help Drey with the straps, but Drey warned him back with a single glance. His face was gray. Blood rolling down his armor pooled in the waist crease and dripped from the runnels. The wound was high in the belly, just below his ribs. How deep had the blade gone? Could it have punctured his stomach or lungs?

"GO!"

Raif's body swayed at the force of the word. *How can you expect me to leave while you are bleeding?* he wanted to scream. *We are brothers, you and I.*

Drey sucked in breath as he peeled the breastplate from his chest. Fresh blood gouted from the wound, and he forced his knuckles into the wetness. Seconds passed as he dealt with the pain.

Raif forced himself to watch. He could not believe what Drey had done. Drey Sevrance was not the sort of man to commit treason lightly. He lived for clan, like Tem before him, and his bear lore drove him hard and true.

When Drey next looked up his eyes were clouded. With hands bloody from his wound, he poked at the packages hanging from his belt. "Here," he said, snapping the horn containing his portion of guidestone from its brass hook, "take this. Inigar has hewn your memory from the guidestone. He cut a portion of stone the size and shape of a man's heart and gave it to Longhead to cart away. Mace had him smash it to dust."

Raif took a breath and held it. Excised from the guide-stone, like Ayan Blackhail, second son to Ornfel Blackhail, who killed the last of the Clan Kings, Roddie Dhoone. Ayan Blackhail had thought his father would thank him for putting an arrow in Roddie Dhoone's throat, yet Ornfel Blackhail had turned on his son and cut off both his hands. "An arrow is no way to kill a king," he had said. "You should have used your sword, or naught at all."

"You are no longer my brother or my clan," Drey said quietly, pulling Raif back. "We part here. For always. Take my portion of guidestone . . . I would not see you unprotected."

Their eyes met. Raif looked at his brother and saw a man who could be chief. He did not speak. There was no place for questions about Angus and Effie and clan. There was only enough time to look at Drey, lock his face and his presence into memory.

And in the end there wasn't even enough time for that.

A shout sounded downstream. A mounted figure crested the high bank above the river, pushing his likeness in woodsmoke before him. A wolf's head cut into his breastplate had been rubbed with acid until it burned, then worked with pure carbon so that its blackness was one of empty eye sockets, open mouths, and charred wood. Mace Blackhail. He had not spotted them yet.

For one brief moment Raif let himself imagine that Drey was coming with him, that they would ride through the Northern Territories, swords in hand, warriors and exiled clansmen alike. It wasn't to be. There was Effie and clan . . . and Ash. And days darker than night lay ahead.

Raif took the tine from his brother. He had to leave now, before Mace Blackhail saw them together. Raif had little care about himself—and there was something in him that welcomed the chance of getting close enough to kill Mace Blackhail—yet he would not endanger Drey. Not after this. Not ever.

Drey's fingers were sticky with drying blood; for a moment when he touched them, Raif felt them cleave to his own. "Go, Raif," Drey said. "I'll watch over the clan."

It was the softest Raif had heard Drey speak since he had burst into the cell what seemed like a lifetime ago. Raif looked into his brother's eyes one last time, then turned away.

As he took his first step, he felt Drey's hand capture his trailing fist. Something small and cool was pressed into his palm. Feeling it, Raif thought his heart would break.

The swearstone. Drey had kept it whole and safe until today.

Lowering his head against the storm, Raif headed west.

## FORTY-TWO

### *Ganmiddich Pass*

SARGA VEYS LAY BENEATH the overhang formed by a shelf of compressed and buckled slate. The great glacier tongues that had once reached from the Breaking Grounds to the Bitter Hills had churned up entire quarries of bedrock from the earth as they withdrew. Even now, thousands of years later, the violence of the glacier's retreat could still be observed in places. The northern slopes of the Bitter Hills, just below the Ganmiddich Pass, was one such place. A few lichen had sunk their root anchors into the hard glassy crust, yet no trees or shrubs of any kind had managed to take seed amid the rocks. The wind would have their heads off in an instant.

Wrapped in blankets spun of the softest goat's hair, Veys endured the wind now. Hood had wedged his strong, fleshy body behind Veys' back, claiming the deepest refuge—the crease directly beneath the overhang—for himself. Veys was distressed by the man's nearness, repulsed by his own physical reaction to the warm, respiring body next to his.

It did not occur to him to move. Here, lying beneath a broken plate of slate, feigning sleep in the face of a storm, he could watch both Marafice Eye and Asarhia March closely.

After taking his leave of the Dog Lord yesterday evening,

Marafice Eye had driven his party of eleven through the night. A spare pony had been purchased in Ille Glaive to carry Asarhia's drugged body back to Spire Vanis, yet the Knife had chosen to ride with the girl himself. He was determined to make the best time that he could. "Put the stench of clannish inbreeding behind me." Veys was inclined to agree with him.

A storm thundering down from the north had stopped their journey two leagues short of the pass. At first the Knife had tried to ride with it, declaring that no clannish storm could slow a brother-in-the-watch, yet when a hellish gust of wind had ripped the saddlebags from his horse's rump, he'd had little choice but to eat his words and call a halt.

Camp had been made in the deep rocky draw between two opposing ledges of slate. Veys supposed it was the best place to be found under the circumstances and had wasted no time staking out his own claim beneath the narrowest and least desirable ledge. He had assumed that no one would be willing to share space with him, yet Hood had found it amusing to force himself into the dark airless cavity at his back. "As long as I'm behind him and he's not behind me, I reckon I'll be safe." Much laughter had followed Hood's declaration, and Veys had felt his face heat in the darkness. Thoughts of revenge had followed him to sleep.

Now it was dawn, and a red and weary sun was rising in the east, and the sept that had found Hood so amusing the night before was stirring with the increase in light. Their leather cloaks were poor cover for a storm, and such lambskins that had been hastily purchased in Ille Glaive were wet and stinking. One sworn brother, a brawny giant with a slow eye, was melting a cake of elk lard in a tin cup. The smell nauseated Veys.

Marafice Eye was awake. He had relieved himself some distance from the campground and had now returned to his place by the wool-and-alcohol fueled fire. He poked the fire with a stick for a while, managing to coax some real heat from the flames, before turning his attention to Asarhia March. The girl lay on the bedroll next to his, covered by sheepskins and cloaks. Something unpleasant happened to Marafice Eye's face as he beheld her, and Veys thought it likely that he was considering the men he'd lost by the Spill. The Knife was strange like that. *My men,* he called his brothers-in-the-watch. Last night when the wind had dragged the saddlebags from his warhorse, two red swords had clattered onto the slate. Veys knew what they were in an instant: Crosshead's and Malharic's swords. The Knife meant to carry them back to the forge, heat them in that great black furnace, and return their steel to the Watch. As if *that* could do Crosshead and Malharic any good.

Veys snorted softly as he watched Asarhia March's face for signs of waking. The poppy blood the girl had been given last night in the Ganmiddich roundhouse was a strong agent of sleep. Veys had distilled it himself, turning liquid that was normally thinner than water into something that poured as slowly as cream. It was more potent than the Dog Lord knew, a fact that Veys congratulated himself on later when he found his saddlebags had been rifled and his supply of henbane seeds, so carefully concealed within the handle of his cane-and-leather horsewhip, gone.

The Dog Lord had thought to protect the girl on her journey home.

Veys smiled, allowing icy drops of rain to tap against his teeth. The small quantity of poppy blood he had on him— barely enough liquid to sauce a lamb chop—was more than enough to render Asarhia March senseless all the way to the obsidian deserts of the Far South.

The smile on Veys' face shrank as he noticed Asarhia March's gloved hand fall free of the sheepskin. Did the fingers contract?

Marafice Eye was oblivious of the movement. He was busy working on the girl's chest, whipping bodice strings through eyelets and pushing back the collar of her dress. His mouth was pulled tight like a sphincter muscle. The sworn brother heating the elk cake turned to watch.

Veys reached down beneath his blankets, questing for the vial of poppy blood. Even as his physical self was bent on the task, he probed out toward Asarhia with his mind. If she was waking, he needed to know. Normally a girl her age and size could be expected to sleep until noon on the dose of poppy blood she'd been given. Yet the more Veys learned of

the Surlord's almost-daughter, the more he realized there
was little normal about her.

Cold air buffeted his thoughts as he pushed his mind
against her skin. Quickly in and quickly out, he cautioned
himself, fear rising within his spine like cold water. A gasp
exploded from his lips as he entered Asarhia's body and ran
with her blood. Her chest cavity was riddled with opposing
forces. Hard strands of sorcery were coiled about her organs
like snakes made of glass. Wards, Veys realized, subtle ones
cast by a master. Pushing from the outside in, they exerted
control over her liver, lungs, and heart.

Yet something was pushing the other way.

Veys perceived something . . . a soft, malleable force,
shining dully like the skin that formed over cooling magma.

Pure darkness.

Externally, Veys did not move. Not one fiber on the
goat's-hair blanket shivered as he withdrew his insubstance
from the body of Asarhia March. Slowly he went, like a servant backing out of a throne room. As he slipped the last ten-
drils of self through the upper reaches of her skin, the force
that pressed from the inside out raised a finger of darkness
toward him.

Veys did not recoil. Reverence and fear tightened his
chest. Raw power, clean of emotion, filled him with the
complete opposite of light. His mouth watered. The tendons
supporting his scrotum ached with sweet pain. Here at last
was something worthy of Sarga Veys.

Too soon the connection was gone. Veys' neck strained
forward, trying to hold on to the last filament of power for as
long as he could. Yet even as he did so, he was aware of
something cold dripping through his fingers. Rain, he
thought, annoyed at such an earthly intrusion at that moment. He wanted the power back.

It was gone, though, the connection broken, and Veys had
no choice but to return to his flesh. Pain tugged at his mind
as he settled himself back into his cage of bones, and his
gaze was drawn to his hand, where a streaky pink substance,
part blood of the poppy and part blood of Sarga Veys, dribbled along his wrist. Spikes of glass were embedded in the
meat of his palm. Veys hissed. The vial had broken!

Breathless from his contact with darkness and irritated by the potential loss of such a crucial drug, Veys barely noticed what was happening at the center of the campground. More sworn brothers had gathered around Asarhia March and the Knife. One man was laughing in a hard self-conscious way, yet the others were uncharacteristically silent. Veys hardly cared. Turning his arm slowly, he let the pink emulsion roll around his wrists like honey around a jar. As long as it didn't drip into the snow or smear on his clothes or blanket, it could be saved. Once it had dried sufficiently he could scrape it off, store it like whore's rouge between two squares of waxed paper.

Veys was content to wait. The revelation of darkness filled his thoughts. So much power . . .

For the taking.

Hood shifted at Veys' back, still fast asleep and snoring softly. Sarga Veys edged minutely away.

The darkness within Asarhia March explained many things: why Penthero Iss had been so desperate to find her, why he had sent the Protector General of the Rive Watch to bring her back, and why he had isolated the girl from the sharp eyes and nails of the Spire Vanis court. The girl was dangerous . . . and powerful in ways Veys could hardly comprehend. Whoever controlled her could have that power for himself.

Veys turned his arm, allowing the last pink droplet to run flat, as he recalled the last time he and his master had spoken. The force with which Iss had taken control of his body had left Veys feeling dirty. Raped. The memory of the domination made the sweet ache in Veys' groin turn to something bitter and wanting. He glanced in the direction of Asarhia March. Iss already had one special access to power. Why should he have two?

"Strip her."

Veys' heart chilled as he heard Marafice Eye's spoken command. He looked up but could no longer see Asarhia March due to the crowd of sworn brothers that surrounded her. Marafice Eye stood in the center of the black-and-red coven, his face all shadows and hard lines.

"She killed our brothers-in-the-watch," he murmured. "Iss

wants her alive, and that's well and good, but I know one way to destroy a life without taking it."

A taut murmur of agreement united the sept. Two brothers pushed toward the girl, cheeks sucked against their teeth, eyes glinting with wind tears, hands already forming the shapes needed to hold her down.

*"No!"* Veys screamed, scrambling to his feet. He had a vision of Asarhia March waking and blasting them all to hell. The wards that shored up her body were nothing compared to that . . . *thing* that lived within her. If Marafice Eye tried to harm her in any way, there was no telling what she would do. "Stop! She'll kill us all."

Marafice Eye and his sept turned to look at him. For one moment Veys saw himself through their eyes: a narrow-shouldered figure dressed in cleric's white, with fine eyes and fine hands, clutching a blanket to his chest like a baby. Veys stood tall, let the goat blanket drop to the ground.

The Knife said something to his men. All laughed quickly. The two sworn brothers who were working on the girl straightened their bent backs. The Knife touched both men on their shoulders in turn, encouraging them to carry on. Veys caught a fleeting glimpse of the girl's body, saw pale skin peeking through wool. Raindrops fell upon her closed eyelids, gray and frothy like spit.

Marafice Eye said, "This does not concern you, Halfman. You are not one of us. If the manner of such things offends you, turn your back."

Blood colored Veys' cheeks. "Fool! Haven't you taken notice of anything I have said? The girl is dangerous. Sorcery—"

"Hood."

One word spoken by the Knife was enough to waken the eight-fingered man. Veys heard footsteps crunch wet snow. He smelled Hood's ripe breath at his back.

"Take him in hand. Mind he sees nothing that his mam wouldn't be glad to show him."

Hood slapped Veys' shoulder blade with something akin to affection. "Looks like you and me will be sitting out the storm, Halfman." Then, to Marafice Eye, "Save me a portion of the girl."

The Knife nodded. A command was spoken, and the sept turned back to their business. Marafice Eye stood and watched as Hood led Veys back to the overhang.

"The drugs have worn off," Veys cried, making a feeble attempt to break away from Hood's three-fingered grip. "She'll kill us all!"

"Hush him." Marafice Eye peeled off his black leather gloves as he spoke.

Hood punched Veys in the spine. "You heard the Knife, Halfman. No whining."

Veys tucked himself back into the space where he had slept. Pain from Hood's blow made his eyes water, yet pride kept him from crying out. Hood stood directly in front of him, his fleshy drinking-man's body blocking the view.

The wind carried the metallic snap of a belt buckle. Nervous laughter followed, then silence. Veys felt the hairs on his arm rise one by one. Through the space between Hood's legs, he watched as Marafice Eye walked a short distance from the group, found himself a section of slate to lean against, then settled down to watch the show. Of course, Veys thought, the Knife is doing this just for his men. He won't take part himself. Everyone knows he prefers to keep his own whoring private. Veys did not know why.

All thoughts except those concerned with self-protection left Sarga Veys as the first man fell upon the girl. The wind pattern changed. Gusts began swirling round and round in the space between the ledges . . . and then suddenly there was no wind at all.

*Raif!*

Veys heard the girl's cry plainly, but not in the way a man normally heard sound. The cry passed through his skin, not his eardrums, making his flesh pucker and turn cold. Hood shifted position, and Veys saw the sept standing tense, eyes focused hard upon the girl. No man among them had heard her cry.

*Stop!* Veys wanted to shout. *Can't you see what is happening? Can't you feel it?*

The stench of metal filled the air. Frost glittered on the surrounding slopes like a thousand winking eyes as the first brother fell upon the girl. Veys felt the first *push* of her power; it was nothing, a mere nudge as she struggled to wake. Yet it was enough to turn the breath in his lungs to ice.

Quietly, discreetly, he began work upon a drawing of his own. He had caught a glimpse of the darkness that was inside her, and although it fascinated and attracted him, he knew he would be a fool not to fear it. Slowly, over the course of many seconds, he drew small shavings of power to him. He could not stand against her, that much was clear, so he concentrated upon the only thing that mattered: Saving Sarga Veys' neck.

He knew the instant she became fully awake. A quarter second of pure quiet followed as she opened her eyes and gazed into the face of the man who knelt above her.

Terror threatened to crush Veys then. Sorcery had been his sole advantage for as long as he could remember, the one thing he held over every man, woman, and child he had ever met. Even Penthero Iss, magic user and Surlord of Spire Vanis, could not better Sarga Veys when it came to drawing power. It was the source of his arrogance and his pride. No matter what humiliations Marafice Eye and his like heaped upon him, Veys could always console himself with the thought that when the time came for out-and-out conflict, the advantage would be his. A man could not fight when his corneas were snapped from his eyes like badges from his chest. He could not focus his mind on winning when the air froze in his lungs like a ghost made of ice.

Now, though, sensing the terrible *pull* that Asarhia March created, the way the wind, the air, even the light itself, seemed to bend toward her person, Veys knew that his one advantage was gone.

There was no fighting the darkness inside her.

He thought of calling out one last time, warning the sept to take cover or run, but he was quick to remember their spiteful laughter, and in the end he saved his strength for himself.

"Let me go!" the girl cried, her voice high and panicky.

Veys saw pale fists pounding the sworn brother's chest, heard fabric rip, then a man's voice, low and distracted, murmur, "Shut up, bitch."

It was the last sound the man ever made. Veys had no

words for what happened next. Panic and terror reduced him to a cowering child. Light and air split, tearing open the fabric of the world. Darkness of an alien kind bled through the rents, smelling sweet and cold and wholly corrupt, rippling like black oil. A mushrooming band of air blasted into the sept, sending bodies crashing into walls of slate.

Horses squealed and thrashed, bucking their hindquarters and throwing their heads from side to side. Men screamed and screamed . . . and then fell silent. A cloud of churned snow rose high into the sky, where the storm dogs tore it to shreds.

Veys thought he was prepared, but he wasn't. Hood's body slammed into his, cracking his ribs like dry sticks. All breath left him, and the clever little drawing he had devised to save himself came out half-formed, ill timed, and without force. It was barely enough to shield his brain and his heart. His mouth and nose filled with rushing snow. He tried to keep his eyes open to see what would enter through the rents the girl's power had torn open, but ice crystals scoured his violet retinas, and in the end his eyelids were forced shut.

The force of the blast wedged him into the rear of the overhang, Hood's body pinning him in place. Fear, so complete it was like a wholly new emotion, robbed all moisture from his throat.

This was what he wanted. *This*.

His eardrums popped as air that had been moving outward began to contract. A breeze exactly the same temperature as body heat ruffled his hair, then his clothes, then the hair and clothes of Hood.

*She's pulling it back.*

Something howled, high and terrible, almost beyond hearing. Veys knew then that the creature issuing it came not from this world. No animal or beast he had ever heard of made a sound that could stop a man's heart.

Then everything ceased.

In the silence that followed Veys thought he heard something. A sound like the hiss of air escaping from a punctured water bladder. Probably the wind blowing through distant rocks. The snow that had been churned up in a great white cloud fell again, gently, floating to earth as if for the first time. Wind picked up, pushing here and there, unsure of which way to blow. Veys stole a breath. His rib cage was on fire, but he dared not move to relieve the pain. Hood's thigh was crushing his foot, and ice crystals were working their way down his throat. Still he did nothing but open his eyes.

Through a curtain of twice fallen snow, he saw the girl rise to her feet. Her dress was torn to the waist, and her breasts were bare. Her hair blew around her face, rippling as if each strand moved through water, not air. Gray eyes took in the cleared ground surrounding her, then the flopping, leaking bodies of the sept. Her lips came together. Her right hand began to shake, but she quickly gave it purpose, using it to pull at the tattered shreds of her bodice. Veys noticed the poppy blood bruises under her eyes as she turned to look his way.

If she saw him in the shadows of the overhang, she did not show it. She took a few steps his way, but only to reach for the goat's-hair blanket that he had dropped earlier. Hands shaking no longer, she wrapped the blanket around her shoulders and turned her back on Veys.

On the far side of the campground someone groaned.

Asarhia March stiffened. Veys thought she might turn and heed the cry, but she didn't, simply continued walking away from the campground in the direction of the hobbled horses.

Sarga Veys waited as quietly and silently as he knew how. The memory of the darkness he had seen eclipsed the pain of his chest and foot. It had called to him as surely as if it had spoken his name out loud.

A small movement against his foot made him realize that Hood was still alive. Hearing the muffled sound of a horse's hooves heading north, Veys pulled his foot free. "Hood?" he hissed. *"Hood?"*

Hood gurgled.

It took Veys several minutes to locate the man's knife. The tip of a broken rib pressing against his lungs made Veys wary of quick movements. To add to his difficulties, Hood had fallen awkwardly on his side, and his body had to be levered before Veys could gain access to his equipment belt and knife. Hood's tunic had ridden up, and his bare belly was in contact with icy ground. Already the rolls of flesh hanging from his gut had taken on the yellowy gray stiffness of frozen flesh.

Veys found nothing to be concerned with as he raised the knife to Hood's throat.

Frostbite was not a problem for a corpse.

# FORTY-THREE

## *Meetings*

GULL MOLER, OWNER AND sole proprietor of Drover Jack's tavern, was cleaning up the mess from last night's fight. He had a good broom in his hands, but even the stiff shire horse bristles weren't enough to scrub the dried-on vomit off the floor. Gull shook his head in exasperation. Fistfights were bad enough. But why was there always some damn fool who kicked someone else in the knackers? Guaranteed to make a man lose his supper, was a blow to the knacks. Right disrespectful to the owner of the establishment. Right disrespectful when that owner had to get down on his hands and knees and scrape rubbery, partially digested oatmeal off the floor.

It was all Desmi's fault, of course. It usually was. If that daughter of his had one talent in life it was surely for starting fights. She was just too comely for her own good. Who would have guessed that she would have turned out to be a head turner, especially with her dear departed mother looking the way she did? Not that Pegratty Moler hadn't been a good woman and an excellent wife. Heavens, no! She just wasn't known for her beauty, that was all.

Feeling a small twinge of guilt, Gull put down the broom and headed for the stove. He needed a bucket of warm water for the floor and a dram or two of malt for his soul.

Drover Jack's was a one-room tavern. Kitchen, beer cellar, dining tables, gaming tables, minstrel's stoop, and great copper bath were all crammed into an area the size of a modest vegetable garden. It had occurred to Gull that he could in all honesty remove both the stoop and the bath and suffer no ill effects to his trade. Thirty leagues northeast of Ille Glaive as he was, in the shadow of the Bitter Hills, deep in the heart of ewe country, Drover Jack's received few musicians stopping by to play for their supper. And those who did never showed an interest in performing from the stoop. Preferred to sit close to the stove, they did, or—even worse—walk among the customers while they were playing! Still, even in the face of this traitorous disinterest Gull couldn't bring himself to part with the stoop. His was the only tavern in the Three Villages that had one.

Same with the bath. Drover Jack's was strictly a tavern; it sold food, drink, and warmth. It did not sell beds for the night. Heavens, no! That was one trade Gull Moler did not want. Travelers. They were trouble, paid in foreign coin, spoke with accents Gull's one good ear had trouble deciphering, and they always started fights. True, Three Village locals had been starting enough of their own ever since Desmi came into bloom, but that was beside the point. Locals were locals; they fought in ways Gull knew and understood. They never damaged the stove, the beer taps, or the proprietor. Travelers damaged everything in sight.

Which brought Gull to the copper bath. No one except Radrow Peel had used it in the fifteen years it had been sitting in the far corner below the hung meat and drying herbs. And even then he hadn't bathed in it himself; he'd used it to thaw out a sheep. Even so, a copper bath was a copper bath, and Gull was inclined to keep it. Not only did it glow like a freshly struck penny, casting a warm, reflective light upon a corner that had once been dark, but it gave him boasting rights as well.

Drover Jack's could warm-bathe a frostbitten limb, cold-bathe a fever, and sulfur-bathe anyone with sheep ticks, scrofula, or the ghones. Overcome with feelings of affection and pride, Gull crossed to the bath and patted its curled rim. His sharp proprietor's eyes picked out telltale blue flecks around the lip. Gull Moler's soft well-fed belly jiggled in consternation.

Tarnish!

Desmi had sworn she had polished it last week, yet Gull Moler knew a month's worth of neglect when he saw it. That girl was turning out to be nothing but trouble. The fights among her suitors he could stand, the girlish tantrums he could stand, but sloppy care of Drover Jack's furnishings and fittings was where he, as owner-proprietor, drew the line. The girl needed to be talked to in the most serious terms. Her own good looks had turned her head!

"Desmi!" he called, raising his head toward the oak-and-plaster ceiling. "Come down here, daughter!"

No response. And it was already noon! Gull Moler looked from the ceiling to the bath. He could climb the steps and bring her down, but while he was doing that the tavern would not get opened, and the bath would not get scrubbed, and those hateful blue flecks would remain.

For Gull Moler it was an easy choice. From the back of his prized bloodwood serving counter, he took his basket of cloths, soft and coarse, fuller's earth, pine wax, powdered pumice, white vinegar, and lye. He loved and honored his daughter, but he treasured his bath.

He did not hear the woman enter. He was kneeling on the dark oak-plank floor, his attention given wholly to the task of removing the rust from the bath, when a voice said:

"Milk steeped in phosphorus would do the job better, and a few drops of tung oil rubbed into the surface when you're done will stop the blue scale from coming back."

Gull Moler turned his head and looked into the face of a short, no, average-size, woman of an age he guessed to be about thirty. His first reaction was one of disappointment. From the golden loveliness of her voice he had expected someone extraordinary. Yet the woman was plain of hair and face and clad in a shapeless dress of dove gray.

"I'm sorry if I distracted you," she said. "The door was open, so I let myself in."

Gull Moler looked at the door. Surely he hadn't pulled the latches yet?

"I thought of knocking, but then I said to myself, *What if a man, an owner-proprietor, is at work inside here? What right have I to pull him from his tasks?*"

Gull Moler put down his soft cloth and smoothed his collar, all thoughts of latches forgotten. He stood upright. "Such consideration does you credit, miss."

The woman, whose hair he had first thought dark and graying but now saw was a delicate shade of ash brown, nodded in a polite way. "Thank you, sir. And it's not miss, by the way, it's madam. I'm a widow."

"Oh. I am sorry to hear that, madam. Can I offer you a dram of malt?"

"I never drink."

Gull Moler began to frown. Experience told him never to trust abstainers.

"Anything stronger than fortified wine."

Gull's frown turned itself into a nod of approval. Such moderation was fitting in a widow woman.

When he returned from the counter bearing two cups of strong red wine on a limewood tray, he was greeted by the sight of the woman crouched on her hands and knees, polishing the copper bath to a glorious sheen.

"I hope you don't mind," she said, continuing to buff the metal with a wrist action so smooth and firm that watching her, Gull felt a guilty blush of sexual excitement. "But it seems to me that a busy and important owner-proprietor such as yourself must have plenty more pressing things to do than spend his time scrubbing blue scale from a copper bath."

"My daughter normally tends the polishing, but—"

"She's reached the age when she'd rather tend herself than the tavern."

Gull sighed. "Exactly."

The woman's eyes darkened. Gull could not tell what color they were, just that they darkened. "What you need is someone to work for you a few days a week. Take the strain off you and your daughter. A young girl can hardly be blamed for acting like a young girl, can she? And an owner-proprietor such as yourself should be concentrating on the higher points of his business."

Gull nodded as she spoke. He wasn't sure that a tavern like Drover Jack's *had* any higher points of business, but that didn't stop him from agreeing with her all the same.

"And a little help at the tables at night would save both your and your daughter's feet."

Suddenly catching the real meaning of the conversation, Gull laid the tray down on the nearest table. For some reason he felt as if he'd been duped. "I couldn't take you on, madam. It's just been me and my daughter since my wife died. I couldn't afford to pay another set of hands. The business doesn't warrant it."

The woman dipped her head in disappointment. "I've heard such good things about Drover Jack's. And now that I've come here and seen for myself this beautiful copper bath and the fine minstrel's stoop . . ." Abruptly the woman laid down the polishing cloth and stood. "Well, I'd best be on my way."

Gull looked from the woman to the copper bath. The metal shone more brightly than the day Rees Tanlow had brought it on his cart from Ille Glaive. Even the reliefwork around the hand rings had been scraped clean of all the gummy remainders of previous waxes and polishes. Gull glanced at the ceiling. Desmi was becoming a problem—just look at last night: Burdale Ruff had kicked Clyve Wheat in the knackers because he'd thought Clyve was looking at Desmi the wrong way.

Gull's glance came to rest upon the woman once more. She was plain enough to inspire no fights, yet not so ugly as to send customers away. And she *did* look so very honest and hardworking. "I'll pay you five coppers a week." It was a pitifully small amount, so small that Gull felt his cheeks color as he said it.

"Done." The woman, who he had first thought was of short or medium height, suddenly looked tall. "I'll get to work on those tabletops; whoever cleaned them last used too much wax. Then I'll pin on my apron, ready to serve the midday trade. Your customers come from all over the Three Village area, don't they?"

Gull nodded. "Yes, madam."

"Good." The woman smiled, displaying teeth devoid of saliva. "It wouldn't be fitting for you to call me madam anymore. I'm Maggy. Maggy Sea."

* * *

ASH RODE NORTH, THEN northwest. When she came to the banks of the Wolf River, she forced the horse into the black icy water and made him swim it. The horse was a shaggy gelding with thick legs and ears like a mule, and he had no love of moving water. Ash hardly cared. If she'd had a crop, she would have whipped him. She could not allow herself to stop and think. Stop and she might turn and ride back to the pass and take a count of the men she had killed. Think and she might slide her feet from the stirrups, push herself out of the saddle, and let the river's dark currents take her to hell.

As it was, horse and rider were buoyed by the thick black water, carried a league downstream by its force. Ash let her hand trail upon the surface as the gelding swam beneath her, watching grease and light ripple along her fingers like strange gloves. Her dress floated around her, growing ever and ever darker as it soaked up the substance of the river. Strangely, she wasn't cold. Perhaps she should be . . . but then she *should* be feeling a lot of things, yet she was feeling nothing at all.

When she reached the north bank, Ash dismounted and took the wet saddle from the horse. The gelding shook itself, thrashing its mane against its neck and kicking its hind legs into the air. Ash looked at the sky. The storm had long passed, and a late day sun sent shadows stretching for leagues. Even the wind had stilled itself, and all was quiet except for the sound of rotten ice cracking on distant ponds.

The terrain north of the river was hard. Upstream, Ash saw oaks and green meadows, apple groves and dark tilled earth. Downstream, where she was headed, lay a landscape of conifers and trap rock, spawning ponds and spider moss. On the northwest horizon, Ash saw the red and green needle foliage of resin pines, trees that held on to their seeds for a lifetime, waiting until forest fire or death to bear their young. On the southwest horizon, if she looked back, she could see the dark green finger of the Ganmiddich Tower. Night-dark smoke, the kind that was released from burning pitch and petrified wood, poured from the topmost chamber.

Blackhail. Ash had known that from the moment she

had first turned the mule-eared horse north and ridden from the camp. There were few places from which the tower could not be seen and nowhere to hide from the smoke. The red fire of Bludd had been snuffed, and now a smokestack smoldered in its place. No flames burned black, so the Hailsmen had chosen to send their message in smoke instead.

Ash wasn't sure what the taking of Ganmiddich would mean to Raif. Almost it didn't concern her. Raif had already left, that she knew, and he was somewhere west waiting to meet her. She did not question where the knowledge came from. She was a Reach. Raif had sworn to see her safely to the Cavern of Black Ice, and they were bound by that promise and the touch they had shared outside Vaingate.

She remembered calling his name while . . . while hands were *touching* her and everything was foggy and she couldn't think, and her arms had been so hard to move, like lead, and she'd heard someone say, *If she's waking, it'll make better sport.* Ash stiffened. She thought she had called Raif's name out loud, but somehow her lips wouldn't open and her tongue wouldn't move, and the cry had sounded *inside* instead. Then she'd opened her eyes and seen the face of the man kneeling above her, his breath coming all ragged and short, his eyes . . . his eyes . . .

Ash swallowed. She wouldn't think about that now. Wouldn't. She just wished she knew what she had done.

Holding the dripping saddle against her side, she led the horse downstream. The light faded slowly, over hours, and the first stars came out even before the sun had fully set. The moon shone behind her, pale and not quite full. The land surrounding the river became flatter the farther west she traveled, and from time to time she spied the square outlines of farm buildings amid the trees and freshly stamped hoofprints in the snow. Ash found herself little concerned about the possibility of being spotted by outlying clansmen or drovers. She didn't know if it was weariness or a sense of her own power that made her unafraid. Who could harm her now? Who dared?

Ash stiffened her back as she walked. They would be able to track her now, magic users, Sarga Veys, anyone else her foster father sent to fetch her. Yet next time when they came they would be wary, *prepared*. Suddenly she wished very much that she had demanded more answers from Heritas Cant. She knew nothing about her own power, couldn't even guess what she had done. *Killed men,* said a small voice inside her. *Killed them with only a thought.*

*And that might be the least of my sins.* No. Ash stopped herself dead. She hadn't reached. It wasn't possible. She had drawn power but pulled it back. Nodding firmly, she continued downstream.

Raif saw her before she saw him. Slowly, over the course of an hour, she had worked her way around a damned lake that bulged from the river like something about to burst. Now, as she returned to the main body of water, she became aware that she was drawing close to him. Gooseflesh puckered along her arms, and for the first time since she'd left the camp at dawn she felt the cold. Her stomach ached with anticipation. As she scanned the water's edge, hoping to catch sight of him in the reflected surface light, she heard her name spoken out loud. Turning her head in the direction of the sound, she saw a dark silhouette emerge from a stand of resin pines fifty paces ahead of her to the north. For an instant she was afraid. The figure was tall, distorted, the darkest object in sight. She pulled back minutely, drawing closer to the horse for reassurance.

The figure raised his hands from his side. "Ash. It's me. Raif."

Fear fled as she saw his face. Her chest tightened. The saddle slid from her grip, hitting the ground with a soft crunch. *What have they done to him?* All the quiet strength that she had filled herself with during the ride evaporated, and a wave of exhaustion made her legs shake like straw as she ran through the snow to reach him.

Raif was silent as he pressed her against his chest. He smelled like ice. Hard nubs of scarred flesh on his neck and hands scraped her cheeks, and tiny flecks of desiccated blood sifted from his hair to hers. His body was so cold. Ash had to stop herself from shivering.

He pulled away first, keeping both hands on her shoulders while he studied her. Ash saw then the leanness of his face and chest, the lack of spare fat or tissue on his body. He looked older, but something more than older as well. The raven lore at his throat glinted blue black in the moon-light . . . it was the only thing on him that looked new made.

Dark eyes searched her face. After a long moment he said, "Let's find some shelter."

His voice was weary but gentle. Ash wondered what had happened at the Inch yet dared not ask.

He went back for the horse and the saddle. Watching him, seeing how thin he was, how he moved like a wraith by the water's edge, Ash felt the slow burn of anger in her chest. She could kill the men who had done this to him, gladly and without regret.

When he fell in by her side, she offered him the blanket that covered her shoulders, yet he shook his head. In silence he led her north from the river. The moon rose higher as they climbed the bank, forming pools of blue light upon the snow.

"Do you know the area around here?" she asked after a while.

Raif shook his head. "Ganmiddich is a border clan, sworn to Dhoone. Blackhail has little use for it."

Ash thought back to the black smoke pouring from the tower. "Until now?"

"Until now."

It was the end of the conversation. Raif led them across a field of eroded slate, lately grown over by tufts of urine-colored bladdergrass and dog lichen. Snow cover was light, as the wind dried the top layers to powder and then blew them south to the Bitter Hills. Ice smoke boiled off the fields, swirling around the horses' cannons as they climbed to the high ground above the river. When they reached the top of the bluff, Ash spotted a farmhouse and half a dozen farm buildings scattered in the valley below. The farm's walls had been cut from the same green riverstone as the Ganmiddich roundhouse, and its roof was blue gray slate. Raif guided the horse toward it, crossing a series of tarred fences erected to contain sheep.

"Won't someone be living here?" Ash whispered.

"No. Blackhail would have cleared it first, before they took the roundhouse."

"Why? What threat is a farmer to an invading force?"

"When one clan takes another, it takes it wholly."

"What about the people who lived here, the clansfolk?"

Raif shrugged. "Dead. Captured. Fled to Bannen or Croser."

"What becomes of their livestock?"

"It's lost either way. If a farmer is killed or captured, his animals are taken. If he's lucky enough to escape, then most of those animals will go in Refuge Purse to the clan who takes him in."

Ash frowned. "I thought Croser was a sister clan to Ganmiddich? Wouldn't they take Ganmiddich clansmen in out of a sense of honor?"

Raif's eyes darkened at the word *honor.* "It's war. All clans must do what they must do."

The words reminded Ash that she and Raif came from different worlds. He was a clansman, grown in the windstripped spaces of the clanholds, brought up to fear nine gods who lived in stone and gloried in war. Ash frowned. Her god lived in thin air and spoke of peace—not that anyone in the Mountain Cities ever heard him. She glanced at Raif. His gods meant something to him. Hers meant almost nothing at all. She thought for a moment, then said, "If you need to stay and fight for your clan, I will not stop you."

"I have no clan."

Ash shivered at the tone of his voice. She waited, but he said no more.

The farm outbuildings consisted of a series of stone sheds and paddocks connected by walled sheep runs sunk partly underground. The main building was missing its door, and many of the shutters had been left to bang loose in the wind. As they approached the entrance, Raif stopped to pry a broken roof tile from the frozen mud. Ash tried not to look at the tattered and bloody skin on his hands, the nail turned black, the white edges of bone poking through knuckles that looked half-skinned. Hefting the slate against his chest, he bade her wait outside while he checked the building for armed men.

As the minutes passed Ash felt herself growing colder. The night was dark now, thin in substance like cold, dry nights always were. Frozen weeds crunched beneath her boots as she stamped her feet.

*So cold tonight, so cold. Warm us, mistressss, pretty mistressss. Reach for us. We're close now. We smell you, smell of warmth and blood and light . . .*

"Ash! *Ash!*"

Rough hands shook her awake. She was no longer standing by the mule-eared horse, but in the timber-framed doorway of the farmhouse. Raif stood before her, his lips tight as stretched wire, his arms supporting her weight.

"How long?"

"Seconds."

Ash looked away. She felt as sick as if she'd taken a blow to the head. Heritas Cant's wards were gone. Whatever she'd done at the campground had blasted them clean away. Nothing was standing between her and the Blind.

"Let's go inside." Raif's voice was quiet, his hand on her arm firm. "There's no one here. We'll be safe tonight."

Ash let herself be guided into the dark, strong-smelling interior of the farmhouse. Raif made her sit as he broke down a chair with his booted feet then tore a mangy sheepskin rug into strips to light a fire. The force of his actions made her flinch. She watched as he searched the black mouth of the hearth, looking for something to strike for sparks. He found an old iron pot with a rough base and built a mound of wool tufts and fabric scraps around it, then struck the base hard with a wedge of slate.

It took a lot of coaxing and blowing to turn the quick flashes of light into flames. Ash concentrated on Raif's actions, afraid that if she let her mind wander in the darkness, the voices would take her to a place she did not want to go. The muscles in her arms ached as she kept them pressed tightly against her sides.

When the fire finally took and yellow-and-white flames spilled over the broken chair spindles, releasing smoke that smelled of pines, Raif went outside to search for food. Ash did not move for a long time after he'd gone. She feared to step away from the flames. The farmhouse kitchen was a broken shell: charred timbers here, cracked masonry there. Shadows danced on walls black with soot. Ash shivered. She missed Angus . . . and Snowshoe and Moose. Where were they now? Did the Dog Lord still hold them, or had Blackhail claimed them for its own?

She closed her eyes for a moment, then set herself to working on her dress. The bodice was ripped and dirty, the hem stiff with ice. She tugged on the torn bits of fabric, tying knots and unraveling threads from the blanket to bind the bodice closed. She didn't want to have to look at her breasts for a very long time . . . not until the bruises had healed. The skirt was easier to deal with; she simply stripped it off and beat it against the wall.

Raif returned as she was feeding the fire with the last scraps of wood. He carried with him a pan packed with powdered snow, a long-leafed chicory plant with its roots still attached, and an animal carcass that was warm but not bleeding. The animal was the size of a small dog, with sharp, opaque claws, a fox's snout, and rich black-and-gold fur. At first Ash couldn't work out how Raif had killed it, as she knew he had no weapon. Then she saw the fist-size clot of blood directly above the creature's heart. Raif's eyes met hers. Ash tried to hold his gaze, but in the end she looked away.

*Even without a bow he can do it,* she thought. *Even with a jagged chunk of slate.*

Raif made short work of skinning and dressing the carcass. He told her the creature was called a fisher and its pelt was highly valued by Dhoonesmen, "for the Dhoone Kings wore cloaks of fine-spun wool, dyed as blue as thistles, with collars of fisher fur." Ash liked listening to Raif speak and was infinitely glad he didn't ask for her help in preparing the carcass for roasting. Somehow, with only a thin piece of slate, he managed to open and drain the thing, remove the organ tree, and quarter the bones. The blood he saved for gravy.

While the meat was browning on the tin platter, he stripped leaves from the chicory plant and rolled them in his fists until they were broken and leaking sap. That done, he emptied the leaves into the pot of melting snow and stirred the contents until the liquid turned green. After a few minutes he emptied the cooked blood and meat juices into the pot. The fat sizzled and spat as it hit the water, belching out steam that smelled of roasted meat and bitter licorice.

Ash's mouth began to water. "You're used to cooking, aren't you."

Raif shrugged. "Camping. Cleaning kills. In the clan-holds, before a boy takes his first yearman's oath, he's pretty much at the mercy of any sworn clansman. Clansmen hunt, bring the kills to camp, then leave the dressing and roasting to those without oaths. It's the way it's always been. Men who have sworn to die for their clan deserve respect."

Ash would have liked to ask Raif if he had spoken a year-man's oath, yet something about his movements as he spoke warned her away from the subject. Instead she said, "Do you know what's happened to Angus?"

Raif stiffened. A moment passed before his words came. "He may have been captured by Blackhail; I can't know for sure. Even if Bludd still holds him, he should be safe. He's more valuable alive than dead."

Ash wanted to believe him. "What do we do now?"

"We head west at first light."

"But we can't leave tomorrow," Ash cried. "What about Angus? And *you*. You're in no state to travel. Look at your hands, your face . . ."

Raif started shaking his head before Ash had finished speaking. "There's no time to wet-nurse wounds or look for Angus. Cant's wardings are gone. The creatures in the Blind have already begun calling you, and if Cant is to be believed, then that's not the worst of your troubles. He said you would die, remember? He said that it costs you to fight them. They've already taken you once today. What if they take you tonight or the next night or the night after that? How long will it be before I can't pull you back?"

Ash could find no words to fight with. He was right, yet she didn't want him to be. She wanted to wait, at least a day, just one day, to sit and think and put the horror of the camp-ground behind her. Unconsciously she ran a hand down the front of her dress. "What about clothing? Supplies? We've got a horse, but precious little else."

Raif gestured toward the fisher pelt hanging high above the fire, the raw face of its flesh side facing the flames. "It

should be dry enough to use tomorrow. It'll make a good pair
of mitts or a collar once I've scraped the fat. Come first light
I'll look around, see what I can find. There's bound to be
something here we can use."

"And food?"

Raif showed a cold smile. "I should be able to see to that."

Ash made her face show no reaction. For a while the only
sound was the snort of burning wood as it released small
pockets of moisture to the flames. Raif speared the roasting
heart with a stick, turned it so the side with all the veins
showed.

"What happened today at dawn?"

Ash looked up. "Why do you ask?"

"I felt something, after I left the tower. It was like the day
my father died . . . only different. The river swelled and
broke its shore ice, and I smelled metal, like when steel's
taken hot from a furnace."

"You knew it was me?"

"Yes." Raif's eyes rose to meet hers. "If anyone hurt you,
I will kill them."

A chill took her. Anyone else, and those words would
have meant nothing; but coming from Raif Sevrance they
sounded like absolute truth. She thought carefully before
speaking. "I think I was drugged. I don't remember leaving
the roundhouse. I remember feeling cold and a bit sick, and
all I wanted to do was lie down and sleep. And then I had all
these dreams . . . and they all got mixed up. And then there
were hands on me . . . and I thought it was part of the dream.
Only it wasn't." Ash found some small piece of gravel on the
floor to look at. "Then I panicked. There were all these men
around me, and I just wanted them to go away . . . and got
angrier and angrier . . ." She shook her head at the piece of
gravel.

"What happened then?"

"Do you really need to know that? Do you really need to
know what I *saw*?"

"I need to know if you reached."

Ash swallowed. Suddenly the scent of roasting meat was
enough to make her sick. When she spoke her voice was
quiet. "I felt Cant's wardings snap. And at that point, that

one point, I didn't care. I wanted those men gone. I wished them dead. I wasn't thinking about the Blind. I don't know if I reached or if I didn't; it happened so fast and my mind was on just one thing." She paused, taking a quick moment to glance at Raif's face. "Then I felt something spill out with the power. I heard a noise, high, like the sound of a knife drawn over glass. Something tore open . . . the air . . . I don't know what. There were things waiting on the other side, Raif. Terrible things. They were men, but not men, with eyes that burned black and red and bodies that were all shadow. I saw them. I knew what they were." She shivered. "And they do not fear me."

Fat hissed as it dripped onto the flames, giving off fine dark smoke. Raif moved from his place near the fire, and a moment later Ash felt a warm arm wrap around her shoulders and a second encircle her waist. She heard Raif murmur, "Stone Gods help us," and even though the clannish gods weren't her gods, she repeated the words to herself.

Quickly, before she lost nerve, she told him the last of it, how she'd panicked and pulled back, how the dark fire in the creatures' eyes had dimmed, and how they'd screamed and screamed as she'd sent them back to whatever hell they'd come from.

As she spoke, she felt the hairs on Raif's neck lift away from his skin. She counted the seconds until he pulled away from her. She thought he would turn his back, cross to the fire, and busy himself·with the cooked meat there. She did not expect him to stay and meet her eyes. But he did.

Incredibly, she saw he was smiling. The sort of gentle, crazy smile that came from shared troubles, from bad news heaped upon more bad news, and the unasked question, *What next?* His eyes were dark, but warm, too. And the fear was almost hidden. He took her hands in his, wrapping them carefully in his fists until he had covered all her flesh.

"Are you afraid of me yet?" she asked him.

"No. But I'm getting close."

Their laughter was on the edge of desperation, yet no less for it. When it was done, Raif released Ash's hands and stood. "You're not alone in this, Ash March. Know that. We will make it to the Cavern of Black Ice, and we will bring an end to this nightmare. I swear that on the faces of nine gods."

Ash nodded. She watched as he made his way to the fire, took the stock of snowmelt, meat juices, and chicory from the flames, and set it to cool on the floor. Next he moved the tin platter containing the roasted fisher carcass and its edible organs from the heat and began to section it as best he could with his sharp piece of slate. For the first time Ash noticed the silver-capped tine at his waist. It was larger than the one he normally wore, the horn darker, the tip sword bashed and peeling. She had been present when Cluff Drybannock had torn Raif's tine from his belt, yet now another hung in its place.

It meant something, yet Ash knew it wasn't the time to ask questions.

It was time to eat, then sleep.

# FORTY-FOUR

## *Something Lost*

EFFIE SEVRANCE HAD MISPLACED HER LORE.

She'd looked everywhere for it, all her secret places like the little dog cote, the space under the stairs in the great hall, and even in the strange-smelling wet cell where Longhead grew mushrooms and mold. She was certain that she'd had it yesterday when she awoke, as she clearly remembered pulling it from her neck and dropping the little gray stone in her fleece bag along with the rest of her collection. She was sure about that.

What she *wasn't* sure about was what happened next. She remembered carrying the fleece bag with her most of the morning, could almost *swear* that she'd had it with her while she ate her blood pudding at noon. Trouble was, Anwyn Bird had kept her so busy all day, running around doing all those chores that needed doing with a full half of the sworn men away, and she'd been to so many places and done so many things, that everything had got mixed up in her head. Now, thinking about it, she couldn't *really* be sure if she'd had blood pudding at supper, noonday, or dawn. Possibly she'd had it thrice. Certainly it had been cold and greasy and had to be chewed to *death* before it went down her throat.

Effie didn't mind the chores at all . . . as long as they didn't involve going outside. It was good to feel useful. Some things came easily to her, such as keeping tally of the oil and wood stores, divvying up eggs and milk quarts, and running messages word for word among Raina, Anwyn, and Orwin Shank. Sometimes whole hours went by where she forget about her lore and all the bad things it showed her. It was a good thing to walk into a room where you knew you had purpose, where people were waiting upon your message or your tally, and where they listened to what you had to say. There was less time to worry and think.

Just yesterday morning ancient, liver-spotted Gat Murdock had stopped her in the kitchen doorway and told her that she reminded him of her mother when she'd first married Da and come to live in the roundhouse. "Aye. You should've seen Meg Sevrance then," the old swordsman had said. "As clever at figuring as any man, yet comely enough so you clean forgot it and thought about her dark eyes instead."

Effie mouthed the speech to herself for the hundredth time. She did not want to forget it. Her mother had been good at figuring. Just like her.

"Effie! You wouldn't be dallying on those steps now, would you?" Anwyn Bird's voice rose up the staircase like the call of a rusty horn. Effie peered down, but the grand matron of the roundhouse was not in sight. Her graying yellow braids and barrel-shaped body were hidden by a block of bloodwood stangs. "As you know what happens to those who stop and daydream on the stairs."

Effie thought for a moment. "They get trampled if there's a fire."

Anwyn Bird's snort of indignance was enough to send roosting pigeons into flight. Effie sensed much shaking of the great yellow head. "You, my girl, are going to be a problem come the courting years. You don't say but two words a day, and when you do, you come out with something that stops all talk stone dead."

"Sorry, Anwyn."

Some distance below Effie's feet, air puffed from Anwyn's lips. "Don't sorry me, young lady. Sorry's a word for faithless husbands and bad cooks." More puffing followed. "Run along now and find Inigar Stoop. Tell him Orwin Shank's called a meeting in the Great Hearth, and his council is needed."

"Yes, Anwyn." Effie started down the steps. She knew Anwyn wasn't mad at her really, not in a special way. Anwyn was mad at most people most of the time; it was how she managed to get so much done. By the time Effie reached the final turn in the stairs, the roundhouse matron was already on her way back to the kitchen, her voice cracking orders to anyone unlucky enough to cross her path.

Effie took the stairs and headed for the small stone corridor that linked the main building to the guidehouse. It was late afternoon, not the time of day she'd normally choose to visit the guidehouse. Inigar Stoop was always there until sundown, and although Effie loved the dark smoke-filled quiet of the guidehouse very much, she always felt cold and itchy around the man who called it his home. Inigar smelled funny. Ever since the war started, he butchered hogs with his own hands and poured their blood on the smoke fires to make them burn thick and long. And his eyes were so dark they were like mirrors, and when you saw yourself in them you looked very small. Effie ducked to avoid a bloodwood beam leaking pitch. Inigar had a way of looking at you with those dark eyes that made you *sure* he knew all your secrets and bad thoughts.

The great clang and hiss of the clan forge could be heard throughout the roundhouse day and night ever since Mace Blackhail had ordered Brog Widdie and his crew to turn every bit of metal in the roundhouse into an arrow or a hammerhead, yet as Effie approached the green-stained door of the guidehouse the noise receded to the distant clamor of a kitchen at mealtime. Effie didn't like the forge. It was hot and bright, and the roughest of the tied clansmen worked there under Brog Widdie's Dhoone-blue eyes. Yet she had grown accustomed to the noise. Things seemed too quiet when it was gone.

Like many outlying parts of the roundhouse, the guide-house corridor had ceded to damp. There were no longer enough men to plaster and rechink the walls, and Raina Blackhail had forbidden any woman to spend a moment plugging leaks or repairing cracks when she could be tending to war needs instead. Supplies were the biggest problem. Even with the tied farmers and free crofters yielding their livestock and grain to the clan's keep, they were stretched for fresh eggs, butter, and milk. So many of the spring lambs had been slaughtered for meat that it was impossible to find a room in the roundhouse that was not hung with airing hides. Raina had fought many fights with the tied farmers. "Would you send your clansmen to fight on lard and oats?" she had cried when Hays Mullit threatened to drive his forty blacknecks back to his croft. Raina had shamed him and others into staying, though Effie only had to walk through the lower levels of the roundhouse to hear the sheep farmers nursing ill feeling toward the clan.

Effie frowned. Just this morning Raina had ordered one in every five yearlings slain. With no clansmen free to hunt and no migrating elk butchered and rendered this season, meat was in short supply. And yearling lambs ate their weight in hay and feed once a week.

All thoughts of war slipped from her mind as her hand came up to work the latch upon the guidehouse door. She took a breath, like a diver before entering the water. Smoke as blue as ice trickled through the opening, bearing the smells and shadows of the guidestone to Effie's nose and eyes. Instinctively she brought her hand to her chest to touch her lore. Only it wasn't there.

"Not wearing your lore, Effie Sevrance?" Inigar Stoop emerged from the shadows, his body breaking strands of smoke as he moved. Smudges of black paint beneath his eyes and in the hollows of his cheeks made him look like someone wasted by disease and ready to die. The cuffs of his pig coat were singed in recognition of the war: He was the clan guide, and he would not fight or raise a weapon in his own defense, yet every time he lit a smoke fire, guided a clansman's prayer, or chipped a warrior's portion from the guidestone, he did so with hands ringed with death. "Step inside. Close the door. Approach me."

Effie did as she was told. The smoke was stinging her eyes. Suddenly she wished very much she had not taken her lore from around her neck.

Inigar Stoop stood silent as she walked the length of the guidehouse. At one time Effie would have run her fingers along the guidestone as she passed it . . . but that was before the war. The stone was different now. Colder. Its surface was wet with pale seeping fluids that collected in ruts and hollows and hardened like tiny teeth. Even the great blocky profile of the stone had changed, and its many faces and creases were now misshapen by chisel cuts. Many clansmen had died far from home, their bodies claimed by enemy soil, leaving Inigar Stoop no choice but to cut surrogate remains from the stone. Families needed something to grieve over. Widows without bones needed stone.

A thick litter of stone dust and soot hushed Effie's footsteps as she came to stand in front of the guide. Inigar was always grinding these days, grinding and burning and speaking with the dead.

"You have not answered my question, Effie Sevrance. Why do you not wear your lore?"

Effie looked for a moment into the guide's black eyes, then thought better of it and took to studying her feet. "I have lost it."

"Did the twine break?"

"No."

"So you took it from your own neck?"

"Yes."

Inigar Stoop chose silence for his reply. Effie felt her cheeks heat. The guide's gaze was like a hand around her neck. It forced her to look up to receive the next question.

"Why?"

Effie thought of lying, but the guide's black eyes were upon her and she saw her own face reflected there. She found she could not lie to herself. "It's not always easy to wear it, not since Da died . . . and Raif left."

Inigar Stoop's shoulders stiffened at the mention of Raif's

name. "Our lores drive us hard in times of war. Why should you stand before me and claim yours drives you harder than most?"

Effie shook her head. That was not what she had meant to say.

"Does it show you things, Effie Sevrance? Does it pour the unripened juice of the future in your ear?" Inigar's bony fingers gripped her arm. "Tell me the truth, daughter of the clan. When you lie in bed at night with the lore upon your chest, are your dreams of things that will one day come to be?"

Effie yanked her arm free. Her breath was coming hard and fast, and she felt fingers of smoke clutching the insides of her lungs. "No. It's not like that. It doesn't show me anything. It never enters my dreams. It pushes me. Here—" She hit her chest. "And when I take it in my hand I know things. Small things, like . . . like . . ."

"Like what?"

Muscles in Effie's face fell slack. Her own words had trapped her. Her lore told her no small things. She had to think a moment before answering. "When Mace Blackhail came back from the badlands and he was riding his foster father's horse, and he said that no one but him had survived the raid, I knew it wasn't so. I knew Drey and Raif would come back."

The guide's eyes glinted like two pieces of coal. "What else?"

She searched for something to say. She would not speak of what had happened in the Oldwood the day she and Raina went to check on Raina's traps. Nor would she tell him of the night her lore had awakened her and told her to run away. Those things were bad secrets, and she had learned her lesson about telling those. Raising her chin, she said, "I knew Raif would leave the clan. I knew it the day that he took his oath."

"That too." The guide's face did not soften one fraction, but when he spoke again there was less anger in his voice. "It was right that your brother left us, child. There is no place for a raven in this clan."

"Will he come back?"

"Not as you know him."

Effie swallowed. She didn't understand Inigar's words, yet they made her insides ache. In all the months that Raif had been gone, she had not spoken about him to anyone. His name was no longer said in the clan. "I see him sometimes, when I hold my lore. I see ice and storms and wolves and dead men . . . and I want to warn him and tell him to be careful, but he's not here." Tears prickled in her eyes. "He's not here."

"Is that why you're not wearing your lore, child? Because it shows you things you do not want to see?"

Effie nodded. "It pushes me all the time . . . and I get frightened. I don't want to see bad things happen to Raif and Drey."

"Yet it is your lore, given to you by the man who was guide before me. No clanswoman can ever turn her back on her lore."

"I know. I only took it off for a bit. It's worst when Drey's away. Every time it pushes . . . I . . . I think—"

"Hush, child. I know you love your brother very much."

*Brothers,* Effie amended to herself.

"You must wear your lore, Effie Sevrance. Our clan is at war, and if the Stone Gods choose to send messages to you, what right do you have to turn away? Our warriors fight with fear in their bellies: How much less is their burden than yours?"

Effie had no answer for that. What Inigar said was right and true. She only had to think of Drey to know that her fears were foolish compared with his. He had to ride from clan to clan in ice and darkness, never sure when the next battle would come or what it would bring. Clansmen he had taken his yearman's oath with were dead.

"Put your lore back in its place," said the guide. "You need fear no more questions from me. You are a daughter of this clan, and you have the rock as your lore, and that means you are steadfast and silent. I trust you will speak to no others about this. There are many in the clan who would not understand the knowledge your lore brings, call it by a name which it does not deserve."

Effie nodded. She understood what Inigar meant. Mad Binny in her crannog over the lake was called bad names.

Anwyn Bird said that at one time Mad Binny was the most beautiful maid in the clan. Her name had been Birna Lorn, and Will Hawk and Orwin Shank had once fought on the graze for her hand. Orwin had won, but once the banns had been spoken and the wedding day set, rumors began to spread about Birna being a witch woman. She always knew which cows would die from grass fever and which ewes would cast their lambs before time. Clanswomen began to fear her, for all she had to do was look at a pregnant woman to tell whether or not she would give birth to a healthy child. A month before her wedding to Orwin Shank, Birna met Dagro Blackhail's first wife, Norala, in the kaleyard. According to Anwyn, Norala's belly was newly quickened with child, but not even Norala knew it. The moment Birna Lorn saw her, she said, "That bairn you're carrying will die in your womb." Three weeks later when a bloody sack was cast from Norala's belly, Birna Lorn was driven from the guidehouse by an armed and angry mob. Norala blamed her for the miscarriage of the chief's first child.

"Effie Sevrance . . ." The guide's cold, irritable voice broke through her thoughts. "See to your lore."

She shook herself. "I don't know where it is. I took it off and put it in my fleece bag with all my other stones. Only now I can't remember what I did with it afterwards."

"Your fleece bag is beneath my work bench. Fetch it now and do not leave it here again."

Too embarrassed to feel relief, Effie shuffled past Inigar Stoop and made her way to the far corner of the guidehouse, where the business of chiseling and grinding was done. She was such a fool! Of course she had come here last night! It was too cold to venture outside to the little dog cote, and she had so wanted to be somewhere quiet and alone. And safe.

As she plucked the fleece bag from the floor, Inigar said, "Do you think me a hard man, child?" She turned and shook her head, but he did not seem to notice. His eyes were focused deep within the smoke. "Mace Blackhail is the chief and he does what a chief must in times of war, yet his eyes only see so far ahead. He thinks in terms of his own lifetime; what he can gain for himself, his family, and his clan. I do not fault him for this. It is the way of all chiefs. It's not his place to think of those to come. The dark times are coming and shadows are massing in the Want. Soon the sky will burn red, and the City of Ghosts will rise from the ice, and a sword will be drawn from frozen blood. If I told this to Mace Blackhail, it would mean nothing to him. *Clan battle men, not shadows,* he would say. Yet he would be wrong. The Stone Gods will not turn their backs on this fight."

Careful not to make a sound, Effie tied the fleece bag to her belt. She didn't understand what Inigar's words had to do with her.

"It is I who must guide the clan through the long night ahead. My lore is the hawk, and I see farther than most, and that is why when your brother came to me seeking guidance, I spoke words to unbind him from this clan. My duty is to Blackhail and the gods who live in stone."

Effie breathed quietly as she listened to the guide speak. Inigar was old and wise, but she knew words alone had not sent Raif away. "Hawks do not see in the darkness," she said quietly. "Owls do."

Inigar Stoop's small, paint-smudged face turned toward her, and his gaze sought her out through the smoke. "You have the right of it, child, yet there is no owl lore amongst us. I would like to think that if you had been born two years later, after the old guide had died and his duties fell to me, I would have chosen the owl for you."

It was the nearest thing to kindness she had ever received from Inigar Stoop. Tears for herself and Raif collected in her eyes. "But guides do not choose the lores of new babies. They dream them."

"For you and Raif I would have dreamt again."

A tear slid down Effie's cheek.

"Go, child. Be sure to wear your lore day and night."

Effie moved past the guide, careful to touch neither him nor the guidestone. Only when she reached the door did she remember Anwyn's message. "Orwin Shank called a meeting in the Great Hearth. He asks for your presence there."

Inigar Stoop nodded. "Tell him I will come once I have seen to the smoke fires." His thin brown fingers caressed the burned matter at his cuffs. "And Effie, keep yourself safe."

The look he gave her almost made her speak. It would be such a relief to tell someone about the time Nellie Moss' son came for her in the middle of the night. She could not tell Drey, for his honor would leave him no choice but to go straight to Mace Blackhail and confront him. Effie's stomach twisted sharply at that thought. Drey must never know. Abruptly she dropped her hand to the fleece bag at her waist. She had her lore back now; that would warn her if Cutty Moss came again . . . if he ever did. In all the days that had passed since she'd overheard Nellie Moss speaking with Mace Blackhail outside the dog cotes, her lore hadn't once told her to flee. Perhaps she was safe. Perhaps she'd made more of the thing than it was worth. Already the details of what had been said had grown fuzzy in her mind.

"Are you all right, child?" Inigar's voice was almost gentle.

But in the end it wasn't enough. Effie tapped her fleece bag. "I'm just glad to have my lore back." Before any more questions could be asked, she slipped through the door and into the cool, damp corridor beyond. The fresher air pleased her, and with a little skip she broke into a run. She had a message to deliver to Orwin Shank, but first she would do what the guide had commanded and return her lore to its proper place. This was a thing that couldn't be done anywhere, for she was governed by her own secret rules in this matter. She needed somewhere quiet, just to hold it for a bit first, make up for time lost.

The space under the stairs in the entrance hall was a good place to sit for a while and not be noticed. It was good and dark, and there were all sorts of interesting dead spiders to look at. Once she'd tucked herself into the deepest part, where the ceiling was lowest and the stone floor was furry with dust missed by Anwyn's broom, she slipped her hand into her bag. Smooth, lifeless pebbles and chunks of rocks met her fingers. Frowning, she reached deeper and spread her hand wide, yet still could not feel her lore. Quickly she pulled the bag free from her waist and emptied the contents onto the floor.

Effie felt her face go cold as she watched the dust settle. Her lore wasn't there.

# FORTY-FIVE

## *The Iron Chamber*

THE SECRET TO BLOOD SORCERY, thought Penthero Iss as he hooked the baleen lamp to a nail hammered deep into the wall, was to remove the caul fly whole. Any fool could take a scalpel to the host's skin, make an incision above the fidgeting almond-size mass of the parasite, swiftly grip the body sac with a pair of tongs, and tug it out. Trouble was, with that method the caul fly nearly always failed to cooperate. As soon as the scalpel edge came down upon the skin, the parasite would throw itself into paroxysms. Its double-jointed legs would begin to flay. Its wings, folded over its thorax in a protective carapace until the creature was ready to leave its host, would spread and break. Its horned mouth-piece would sink into muscle flesh and its massive, articulate jaws lock in place.

It was messy, very messy. Bits of caul fly always broke off, and no matter how hard one tried to remove all the detritus, some tiny bit of matter was often overlooked. And overlooked pieces of caul fly had a nasty habit of festering and causing gangrene in the host.

Frowning, Iss turned and contemplated the iron chamber and the Bound One chained to its walls. Light seemed to shine differently here, in the very apex of the Inverted Spire, and the air was heavier and harder to breathe. The Bound One wheezed as he drew breath, the skin at his throat pulling so tight that Iss could count the veins. Iss took a step toward him. In his hand he held a pair of fine tweezers, their tips black with carbon from a whole hour spent above a flame, and a jeweler's wedge-shaped knife just in case.

A muscle as thin as trap wire contracted in the Bound One's forearm as he attempted to raise his hand toward his master. One of his eyes was as pale as milk and quite dead.

The other was cloudy, the iris stained white in places, yet he could see. Iss had long decided he could see.

Iss knelt upon the iron lip of the apex and pushed apart the loose folds of the Bound One's tunic. A small bandage, the size and shape of an eyepatch, was fixed in place on the uppermost section of the Bound One's back. One had to asphyxiate a caul fly if one wanted to remove it whole: block its airhole with a bead of fish glue, fasten a cap of bladderskin over the boil, then seal the cap edges with more glue. Eight hours was usually enough to send the caul fly to sleep.

With his fire-darkened tweezers, Iss picked at the bladderskin cap. The Bound One's skin was yellow and loose, attached to his body in very few places, and Iss had to be careful not to tear it as he worked.

When the cap was off and the glue scraped away, Iss pressed his thumb and forefinger into the flesh to either side of the boil. As he felt the hard scaly form of the caul fly rise against his fingertips, a small thrill heated his face. This one was fully formed. It had pupated in the flesh; another few days and it would have eaten its way out. It was heavy, too, gorged on blood. A perfect parasite, every organ, cilia, and membrane created by the host.

And that was the real reason why one had to withdraw it whole. Nothing, not one drop of digestive fluid, one doublejointed leg, or one hollow and serrated tooth, could be lost during the extraction. Blood sorcery could be drawn using an incomplete specimen, but it was never as potent as when the parasite was whole. It was the Bound One's creature in every way, his sorcerous child. During an eight-week incubation the caul fly had fed upon the Bound One's flesh, concentrating his power and distilling his blood. Iss had read that some men who bound sorcerers to them gained access to the sorcerer's power by using other parasites such as leeches, lice, or loa worms, but Iss found the caul flies much to his liking. They stayed close to the skin and could be easily tracked and extracted, and they lived two of their three life cycles within the host.

The caul fly was now in view, pushed to the surface by the action of Iss' fingers, its dark, segmented eye staring at Iss through the airhole. Good. It was close to death, but the tiny cilia on its body moved against the current of clear fluid that leaked from the boil. Iss flexed the tweezers, testing their bend. As he reached through the airhole, probing for the thorax, a soft gasp parted the Bound One's lips.

Iss was not disturbed. The Bound One made noises sometimes. He had no words. All speech, memories, and learning had been taken from him sixteen years earlier, during the thirty-one days of his breaking. At the end of the thirty-one days he was left with nothing but an animal's needs, and like an animal he grunted when he was afraid or in pain. A word softly spoken was all it took to calm him.

The caul fly came free with a wet *pop*. Already it had begun to darken and enlarge in preparation for attracting a mate. The carapace covering its wings was a thing of beauty: red toned, transparent, divided into angular shapes by a network of crossing sutures. Iss held it to the light.

*This one is for you, almost-daughter. That I might see how far you reached yesterday at dawn.*

The Bound One groaned as Iss withdrew his touch. Again the arm moved, and for an instant Iss thought he saw a flicker of pure hatred darken the Bound One's eye. Iss was not a man given to shivering, yet he felt his chest muscles contract all the same. Surely he was mistaken? The Bound One saw but did not *perceive*, existed but did not *feel*.

It was the way it had to be for a bound sorcerer. They had to be broken completely, both their body and their mind at the exact same instant. Iss had learned the danger of breaking the body first. Thigh bones wrenched from the pelvis, spines forced backward around a wheel, and needles inserted into the inner ear to misalign the tiny hammer-and-tong bones there, were not enough to destroy a mind. Iss knew that. He had lost two men learning *that* lesson, had the enamel burned from his teeth as a drawing leaving his mouth was forced back.

Iss snapped his head, sending the memory away. His pale hare's eyes focused upon the Bound One's face, searching for signs of sentience. The Bound One's good pupil was dull and unfocused, a black hole with nothing spilling out.

"Do you know who I am, Bound One?" Iss asked. "Do you know all that I have done?"

The Bound One's hand moved again, this time toward the package of beans sealed in waxed linen that hung from Iss' belt. Feeling a strange mixture of affection and relief, Iss nodded his head. "Hungry, eh? Of course, of course. That's the beast I've come to know."

Turning his back on the Bound One and his iron pen, Iss took a moment to still himself before he began the drawing. The close, curving walls of the iron chamber reminded him of a dry well. Even this deep the stone cutters had worked to maintain the gradual tapering of the spire's walls. Iss only had to close his eyes to imagine the spire's form: a stake into the heart of the mountain. A perfectly rounded stake.

Robb Claw, Lord of the Fourth Spire, builder of Mask Fortress, and great-grandson to Glamis Claw, was rumored to have begun excavation on the Inverted Spire five years after the Splinter was built. The city of Spire Vanis was new then, one-tenth the size it came to be. The four Bastard Lords had crossed the Ranges a hundred years earlier and wrested Mount Slain from the Sull. Robb Claw had taken the timber-and-stone stronghold the Quarterlords had erected and built a city around it. Spire Vanis was Claw's creation. The plans were his, the vision was his, and it was rumored that the curtain wall that contained the city would have been raised to twice its height if Robb Claw had lived to see an end to his work.

Iss let out a long breath. Robb Claw feared something. A man does not spend thirty-five years of a fifty-year life building a fortress unlike anything the world has ever seen if he does not believe he is in danger. Theron and Rangor Pengaron, Torny Fyfe, and Glamis Claw had no such fears. They had simply ridden north and conquered. And despite the glorious tales of impaled beasts, fields steaming with blood, and battles that lasted ninety days and ninety nights, Iss suspected they had taken Mount Slain and the Vale of Spires with ease. The Quarterlords erected their first strongwall a mere seventy days after they crossed the mountains with their warhost. *Seventy days.*

It was a tantalizing fact. The Sull, who were known throughout the settled world for yielding land to no one and defending their borders with cold fury, had barely wetted their blades in defense of Mount Slain. Oh, the historians would tell you otherwise, and Iss could name a dozen terrible and bloody battles that had supposedly taken place during the Founding Wars: battles where the sky turned as dark as night with the weight of Sull arrows, where the moon disappeared from the midnight sky, snuffed by foul Sull magic, and where dread halfbeasts walked the battlefield, their exhaled breath cold as death, their touch enough to burn the light of sanity from a fighting man's eyes. Iss had read the tales along with the rest . . . yet he wasn't sure he believed them.

Two thousand years ago the Sull had yielded Mount Slain to the Quarterlords. And a thousand years before that they had yielded the land that became known as the clanholds to the fierce, animal-skinned clansmen who were driven out of the Soft Lands by Irgar the Unchained. Historians claimed that the Sull had sanctioned the Great Settling of the clanholds because the clans were not a threat; they kept themselves to themselves, had no interest in converting or persecuting the Sull, and they took the hard, inhospitable land in the center of the continent that the Sull had no love or use for.

The reasons blew like false notes through Iss' ears. He had been reared in Trance Vor. He knew all about the Sull. He had stood by and watched as Sull warriors shot his father a dozen times in the back. Four warriors. Three arrows apiece. It was over in less than an instant.

Breath shot from Iss' throat like a pellet of white ice. His father had been a fool! Slowly encroaching on borders, stealing hair-thin slices of farmland each season, was no way to take land from the Sull. They had a sixth sense about these things, always knew the exact moment foreigners crossed into the Racklands. And they possessed deep ancestral memories of each stream, glade, heath, and wooded grove that formed their sacred borders.

Ediah Iss had acted in the same way a thousand Trance Vor farmers had before him: He saw his own marshy, ill-drained soil, then he looked in the distance and saw the soft, fertile loam of territory belonging to the Sull. "They don't work it," he had complained, using words well worn before him. "Good land laying fallow like that, while I'm out in these shit fields breaking my balls each day."

They had warned him, of course. The Sull always warned. The same four warriors who had eventually slain him rode to the Iss farm one morning at the break of dawn. Iss remembered being wakened by the sound of a metal arrowhead smashing against the claystone grate. He was eight at the time, sleeping at the foot of his parents' pallet on a dog mattress stuffed with straw. The arrow had come through a slit in the shutters no bigger than a child's mouth. Ediah Iss had been meaning to fix it since spring.

Iss stood at his mother's side as his father opened the door. Four mounted warriors dressed in lynx furs, wolverine pelts, and midnight blue suede formed an arc around the farmhouse. Seeing their black lacquered bows stamped with quarter-moons and ravens, their silver letting knives that hung on silver chains from their saddle pommels and tinkled in the wind like bells, and their arrows fletched with the snow white feathers of winter osprey, Iss learned what it was to be afraid as a man. He had known only child's fear till then.

The Sull did not speak—it was not their way—simply stood in warning for a period of time and then turned east and rode away. Iss' mother was the first to move and speak. Iss remembered her pushing her husband so hard, his forehead hit the door frame.

"You fool!" she cried. "You late-weaned fool! I told you they would know about the onion field the minute you tilled it. Run over there before they top the ridge and pull the new bulbs out."

She *hadn't* told him, Iss knew that. She had been the one who encouraged him to plant the onions in Sull soil ten days earlier, then stood over him as he spent four days turning a weed-choked meadow into a lot.

Perhaps it was anger toward his wife that made Ediah Iss leave two rows of onions undisturbed, or perhaps he believed that those two particular rows, being nearest to his

own border and hidden from the casual eye by the deep
shade thrown from a hundred-year-old milkwood, might go
unnoticed by the Sull. Either way he left forty-eight onion
bulbs in the ground. Iss knew the exact amount, as he had
pulled each one from the grainy black soil an hour after his
father's death.

It had taken the Sull less than two days to return. Iss could
still remember his mother screaming as the four warriors cut
the used strings from their bows, discarded them as if they
were soiled rags. He only had to close his eyes to see his father lying belly down on the path, a full quiver of arrows,
bristling and golden like ears of wheat, growing from his
back.

Iss sucked his lips against his cracked and discolored
teeth. It was a fool's death, foolishly invited, yet it was not
without its compensations. Iss had gained two things of
value from it. First, his mother's family had moved quickly
to be rid of him, and he was sent for fosterage to a distant
uncle in Spire Vanis who held a grangedom there; and second, he had learned a lesson about the Sull that would stay
with him for life.

"Poor Father," Iss said, turning the caul fly in the light.
"One does not take land from the Sull in small slices. One
waits until the time is right and then moves to take it all."

With a quick snap of his wrist, he drew air over the caul
fly's abdomen, shaking the creature awake. The creature's
rear legs stiffened, and deep within the red-toned carapace
four fully formed wings twitched to life. The caul fly knew it
was no longer in its host and now sought to unfold its wings
and fly in search of a mate. Iss was not displeased. The presence of such a strong and universal instinct could only add
potency to the drawing.

Iss sat in the sorcerer's seat that had been cut two thousand years earlier by masons who were later blinded and un-
tongued before they were killed so even their ghosts could
tell no secrets. The seat was little more than a hip-size depression in the chamber wall, backed with the same
pressure-formed granite that lined the entire structure of the
Inverted Spire and then plated with a sheath of dull iron.
Nothing of meaning had been stamped into the metal, no

runes or symbols or legends. The mere presence of the seat in the apex chamber was legend enough. Iss liked to imagine that it was the final refinement Robb Claw had commanded his masons to make. "Cut me a sorcerer's seat that I might sit as I do the work of gods."

Jabbing his tongue against the roof of his mouth, Iss prepared himself for the drawing. Even after all this time he was nervous. He trusted the Inverted Spire and knew the power of the Bound One as well as he knew his own, but always before taking the caul fly in his mouth, his stomach clenched as tight as a trap.

True, there was no danger from backlash. The Inverted Spire had been constructed as an insulator. The mountain's worth of rock that lagged it, the facing tiles mined from the destroyed sorcerers' tower at Linn, and the spiking iron-tipped structure itself combined to make the Inverted Spire a haven from the outside world. No outside sorcery could penetrate it. No backlash could break it. No sorcery unleashed within it could be traced to its source. Any man who drew forth power here was free to act like a god.

Iss brought the caul fly to his lips. Even as his mouth opened to accept the bloodmeal, his stomach and lungs contracted, ready to push the power out. Relaxing his grip on the tweezers, he laid the creature upon his tongue. It twitched there for just a moment until Iss bit it in two.

The Bound One screamed and screamed, his high wavering cry bashing against the walls of the chamber like a bird trapped in a well. Bitter fluids filled Iss' mouth. Stick legs scraped his teeth. Wings cracked with the soft snap of broken wafers, and then all the power of the caul fly, stolen over eight weeks of living, feeding, and shedding within its host, filled Iss' being like floodwater, pushing his insubstance out. Iss felt a moment of pure divinity as he parted from his flesh and bones. *This* was what it felt like to run with the gods.

Penthero Iss, Surlord of Spire Vanis, Lord Commander of the Rive Watch, Keeper of Mask Fortress, and Master of the Four Gates, ascended to a place where he could no longer hear the Bound One scream. Power pumped from the caul fly's body like blood from a cut vein. Iss looked down and saw his hair and robes blowing wildly below him. He took a breath with a body he no longer inhabited and tasted his own remains in the air.

Higher and higher he rose, the roar of the drawing filling his abandoned ears. The midnight blue arc of the firmament dipped to meet him, curving with the slow guile of infinity, inviting him to come and play in the cold land beyond death. Iss shrank from its gleaming edge. Follow that road and there was no going back.

As he turned inward toward himself, seeking the dark path that would lead him to the borderlands, the color of the firmament stayed within his mind. He'd seen that particular shade of blue once before . . . stretched across the bellies of the Sull the day they'd sent twelve arrows into Ediah Iss' spine.

A world and a half below him, Iss' body shivered upon its seat of iron and stone. Pushing his insubstance forward to meet the swirling gray shadows of the borderlands, Iss paid his own flesh and blood no heed.

The borderlands had many names. The Phage called it the Gray Marches, the priests in the Bone Temple called it No Man's Crossing, and the Sull had a name for it that was better left unsaid. The Listener of the Ice Trapper tribe called it nothing at all and said only that it was a place *where a man could steal dreams*. That was what Iss felt like as he approached its pale borders: a thief.

A line of light, pink as newborn flesh, marked the threshold to the borderlands like a false dawn. Smoke fingered its edges, curling and uncurling, reaching and drawing back. There was no sound or smell, yet the silence was the kind that brought no peace. Without noise or odor to divert his senses, Iss found himself looking with the same single-mindedness of heretics in the Far South, who were pegged out on the desert floor and left for dead. For the sin of disbelief, the dark-skinned priests sewed the eyes of heretics open, pinning back their eyelids against their brow bones with cross-stitches of black silk, so that the heretics might see the face of God as they died. Iss felt as if his own eyelids were sewn open. Blinking or averting his gaze was impossible. He had no choice but to *see*.

The borderlands stretched ahead of him, a landscape of gray mists, iceberg peaks, and shadow-filled troughs stretching into distant darkness. Iss knew many things about the borderlands, knew that its outskirts could be visited by a handful of people in every generation, that different people came for different reasons, and that some, like the Listener of the Ice Trappers, could see the future written here. Even with the Bound One's power fueling his journey, Iss' abilities were limited. He was a trespasser, a thief. He had no place here, not even on the threshold. If the future hung like ripe fruit around him, he could not pluck it. If he glimpsed a pathway leading inward, he had no choice but to turn away.

Asarhia March, Foundling, mountain born, spire bred, was the one person alive who could enter the borderlands without fear. It was her element. Her body was shaped for it. Her mind could perceive paths through it. Her hands could touch the Blindwall and come away unburned.

It was out there, the Blindwall, far on the other side where grayness gave way to darkness and where even the most powerful sorcerer and Listener could not tread. All worlds bordered here, all dying souls passed through on their way to final resting or ruin. Iss had once heard that people sometimes *dreamed* their way here in the dead of the night. Unlike the Listener, who made dreams his business, these people had no knowledge or ability to help them find their way. Their sleeping selves drifted here like mist, pushed by dreams filled with longing for a loved one now gone. The newly bereaved did not hold power here, only Asarhia March and the gods held that, but their loss brought them kissing close to death.

Iss floated above the threshold, held in place by power stolen from another man, and cast his gaze over all that lay below him. He did not know the borderlands well, yet he had been here a half dozen times before, and his cool Surlord's eyes saw straightaway that something had changed.

Asarhia had been here.

Leads had opened up in the smoke. Cold currents blew with the same intensity as before, but crosscurrents cut through them, creating a rippling mesh of flaws. The gray mass of the borderlands swelled and shifted, sending great lobes of matter rising above the surface and dragging other things under so quickly that they left comet tails of smoke. Beneath the surface, pockets of quiet existed as dark smudges in the grayness. And beneath them, writhing like the hide of a vast and muscular serpent, ran a river so dark that it swallowed light.

Iss shivered. Averting his gaze, he looked out across the expanse of the borderlands. The leads Asarhia had opened stretched inward toward the center of the grayness. Iss searched the visible horizon, straining to see some detail of the Blindwall beyond. *How far did you reach, almost-daughter? There is not a sorcerer in the North who did not feel your power yesterday at dawn. No one can stand against you, I know that now, not the Phage or the Sull or the First Gods themselves. For sixteen years I kept you from them, treasuring and protecting you, and now you think you can run away and leave Spire Vanis behind. Yet know this, Asarhia March. No matter how quickly you run and how far you travel, when you reach you will be doing my work.*

As Iss spoke the word *work,* a gust of wind sliced deep into the grayness. Smoke parted. For one instant his eyes focused upon a solid form. It was huge, towering, the wall of an ancient fortress, completely smooth, and dark as night. . . .

Iss gasped. Back in the apex tower, his body slumped forward as the Bound One's power wavered sharply. Iss forced his jaws together, sucking the caul fly dry. He had the Blindwall in his sights. It was vast, breathtaking, but had he seen a tiny flaw at its base? He had to know.

The Bound One screamed, higher and higher, as if he might shatter glass. Iss crushed the head of the caul fly with his teeth, releasing a broth of blood and curds. A rush of air and light stripped away all he could see. The Blindwall was gone. The borderlands were gone. The power released was not enough to hold him in place, and his flesh pulled him back.

He entered his body with a jolt. A clumsy limb banged against the wall. Teeth bit through tongue meat. The nausea that always came when he returned to his flesh hit him hard, and he spat out a wad of saliva speckled with fly parts. For some time he could do nothing but sit with his head slumped over his knees. Minutes passed before he could look up. With a gaze slower and more ungainly than the one he'd left behind, Iss contemplated the Bound One.

He lay lifeless in the iron apex, his body bathed in sweat. His eyes were open, yet his eyeballs were rolled back and nothing but white showed. Pressure sores from the manacles around his wrists were slick with blood, and the metal walls of the apex were streaked with claw marks. His chest moved . . . barely.

Iss struggled to his feet. The stench of his own body was unbearable to him. He smelled like an old man. The apex chamber reeked of urine and shit. Always when he returned to his body and took command of his five senses, it was the smells that appalled him the most. How could people live with them? Anger and disgust made him drive his fist hard into the Bound One's chest. The Bound One jerked reflexively, sliding farther down into the apex. A series of quick breaths animated his face for a few short seconds, and then he fell back into oblivion.

Iss watched him closely. What had happened here? The Bound One's power did not usually drain so quickly—even in the borderlands where such things counted for less. Iss considered aiming a second blow to test him. Could he be faking his insensibility? Had he withdrawn his power on purpose? Was it possible that he had seen the Blindwall, too? Yet what if he was sickening? He was old now, his body yellow and stiff. It was natural that his power should weaken over time. Still.

Iss returned to his sorcerer's seat and sat and watched and waited. Only when an hour had passed without the Bound One moving as much as his little finger did Iss feel satisfied enough to take his leave.

For the first time ever, the Bound One did not grieve as Iss removed the light.

# FORTY-SIX

## *A Journey Begins*

RAIF WOKE IN THE FREEZING DARKNESS before dawn. He knew he would not return to sleep, so he rose and took himself outside. He urinated against the barn wall, then scooped up a handful of snow and scoured his face. The shock of coldness passed quickly. Overhead the sky was black, but far on the eastern horizon, above the tree line and slate crags of Ganmiddich, the ice mist glowed pink with dawn.

Raif turned away. He made himself busy, binding a nick on the gelding's foreleg and then tending his own stripped and bloody skin. His hands smelled like raw beef. They burned like hot coals as he thrust them into the snow to clean and numb them before he bandaged them tightly against the cold. In winter the worst danger to broken skin was frostbite. Gat Murdock had lost his bowfinger to a dog bite no deeper than a pockmark just because he'd not thought to bandage it one night when it was icy cold. And last winter Arlec Byce had spent Godsfest with pig lard slathered over his face because he'd ridden out to the Oldwood within an hour of taking a close shave.

Hard frosts worried Raif. Ash needed to be well protected. She was underweight, and a diet of ice hares and fishers wouldn't be enough to help her fight off the cold. A person could starve on lean meat. Two summers ago Drey and Rory Cleet had returned from a ten-day hunting trip to the balds doubled up with cramps and indigestion. The hunting had been poor, and they'd lived on nothing but flat ale and rabbit meat for a week. Raif remembered standing outside the outhouse with Bitty Shank and Tull Melon, singing, *Nothing runs faster than a man with rabbit runs*, at the tops of their voices while Drey and Rory relieved themselves inside.

Raif smiled at the memory . . . and somehow, as he did so, the freezing wind brought tears to his eyes.

Drey had not waited.

Yesterday, when Raif had walked away from the shore of the Wolf River, the final thing he did before the path veered north and hid him from sight was to turn and look at his brother one last time. Only Drey wasn't there. Drey had already moved on. Raif had caught a glimpse of his slow-moving shadow slipping eastward through the rocks, on his way to meet with the Hail Wolf.

Raif stood in the snow and breathed and did not think. After a while he turned and made his way back to the farmhouse, filling his mind with the dozens of things that needed to be done before he and Ash could begin the journey west.

Ash was awake, sitting tending the fire and rewarming the remains of last night's meal. She smiled shyly at him as he entered, and he did not have the heart to tell her that he had wanted last night's stock left cold so he could skim the congealed fat from the top and use it to protect their faces from the wind. The fisher meat had been cut into strips and left to dry overnight, yet Raif could tell from the look of it that it was only partially cured. It would have to do. The pelt was stiff, but there was no time to soften it with urine, so he showed Ash how to roll it on the hearth as if it were a long piece of dough and work the stiffness out with her fists.

He left her doing that while he searched the house for clothes, knives, and food. It was bitterly cold. The few rugs and blankets he found in the storm cellar were stiff and shaggy with ice. He picked the best two blankets and beat them until they were dry. In the bottom of an old bloodwood chest he found a pair of goatskin gloves. They'd been packed away while still wet and were mottled with blue black mold, yet Raif pulled them on all the same. They were barely wearable and smelled of mange, but they fitted well enough.

By the time he returned to Ash he'd found an ancient wool cloak with a kettle burn close to the shoulder, a child's sheepskin hood, a tin cup filled with lanolin and beeswax, and a handknife with a corroded iron blade. The farmhouse had been looted with great care, possibly by both Bludd and

Hailsmen, and anything of use or value had been taken. No foodstuff of any sort remained.

Raif watched as Ash pulled on the cloak and hood. She'd been busy in his absence, wrapping the fisher meat in dock leaves, melting a new batch of snow, and airing her boots and stockings above the fire. "You haven't got a cloak for yourself," she said.

"I'll make do with a blanket. Once I put an edge to this knife, I'll cut the fisher pelt down to a hood."

Ash frowned. "I should have taken the supplies from the camp. All the saddlebags were there, scattered in the snow. I could have had whatever I wanted."

"It doesn't matter," he said, and meant it.

Her gray eyes regarded him for a short moment and then looked away.

Raif wanted to say, *If anyone touches you again, I will tear them apart with my bare hands.* Instead he said, "Pour the snowmelt on the flames and kill the fire. I'll be outside saddling the horse."

It was full light now. The rising wind smelled of glaciers. The snow underfoot was rotten in places, part melted by a midseason thaw. Raif laid the blankets over the gelding's back, then strapped the saddle in place. His hands felt big and awkward. When he gripped the handle of the knife to sharpen it against the rise of the step, pain made him gnaw his cheek.

The metal was not sound. Rot had cut deep into the untempered iron, and the blade refused to take an edge. Raif removed all visible rust and sharpened the point as best he could.

Ash came out as he was putting the finishing touches to his fisher hood, stripping fur from the two lengths of skin that would become the ties. Raif stopped what he was doing to look at her. The kettle-burned cloak was a rich rust brown and its hem skimmed snow as she walked. The wind was quick to bring color to her cheeks and a bright film of moisture to her eyes. Wisps of silver gold hair blew around the edge of her hood. The time she'd spent in Ganmiddich had improved her, and her face had a softness to it that he had not seen before.

"Did the Dog Lord treat you well?" he asked, helping her into the saddle.

Her gray eyes darkened minutely. "He couldn't wait to be rid of me."

They left the farmyard in silence. Raif led the gelding through the maze of sheep runs, pens, stone walls, and outbuildings, tasting the air as he walked. The clouds were full of snow, yet that didn't worry him as much as the stench of glaciers. When the air smelled of the Want this far south, it meant only one thing.

Raif set a hard pace. The farther west they were when the storm hit, the better. The Bitter Hills caught storms, held them between HalfBludd in the east and Bannen in the west. Their best hope was to reach the shelter of the western taiga as soon as possible, let the stone pines and black spruce bear the brunt of the storm for them.

As he padded alongside the horse, Raif searched for signs of game amid the ground birch and dogwood. The habit was deep within him. Last night had proven to him that he did not need an arrow to kill an animal with a blow to its heart. A fist of slate, heavy as iron and blue as Dhoone, was all it had taken to bring down the fisher. The fisher had been snooping around one of the sheep pens, drawn by the stench of slaughter that lingered there. It had smelled Raif with its keen nose, heard his boot heels crunching frozen mud with ears so sensitive, they could hear a red-backed vole breathing beneath two feet of snow. Raif's eyes caught its retreat. He plucked a rock from the mud, gaze still fixed upon the creature as it ran along the base of the pen wall. He warmed the rock in his fist. Ash needed food badly.

It wasn't the same as releasing an arrow. There was only the crudest sense of calling the creature to him. No moment of stillness joined him and his prey, no knowledge of the creature passed through him. Suddenly the heart was *there*, a glowing coal, in his sights. Speed was the only thing that mattered then. Without the concentrated discipline of bow eye and bowhand working in unison, he had nothing to bind the creature to him. Raif hurled the rock. Even as it left his grip, his sense of the creature's heart was fading.

He did not hear the impact. Sickness washed over him as

his throwing hand fell limp against his side. Stomach juices bubbled in his throat, and he dropped to the mud to retch and spit and clean his mouth. Minutes passed before he had strength enough to rise and claim his prey. The sickness had passed by the time he returned to the farmhouse, yet a sense of shame remained. It was no way to kill a beast.

"Aren't we going to cross the hills and enter the cityhold? I thought Angus meant to steer clear of the clans."

Ash's voice broke Raif's thoughts. He raised his head to look at her. The lanolin she wore on her face had turned waxy and opaque in the freezing wind. "We'll make better time if we keep heading west. We'd waste half a day in those hills."

"But Angus said—"

"Angus isn't here. I'm here. And I don't claim knowledge of the Glaivehold. I know the clans as far west as Orrl, and I know the route we must take to enter the Storm Margin." He spoke harshly, yet he hardly knew why. He didn't want to explain to Ash that the only reason Angus had chosen the route through the Glaivehold was to save his nephew from encountering Hailsmen. Ten days ago Raif had been glad of that consideration. Now he did not care. Blackhail had hewn his memory from the stone. If he crossed paths with a Hailsman now, he would have to kill him or be killed. And strangely he found a hard sort of comfort in that. He knew where he and his clan stood now. All dreams of homecoming were dead.

"How did you escape from the tower?"

Raif wondered why she had chosen to ask her question now. He made no answer.

"I forced a promise from the Dog Lord," she said after a moment. "He swore he would take no action against you until I was gone." He features moved through a smile as she thought on the past. "He's a fierce man. Yet I think he was more afraid of me than I of him."

"He did not take Dhoone alone."

Ash frowned. "What do you mean?"

"The Dhoonehouse is the most defensible stone keep in the clanholds, built by the first Clan King, Thornie Dhoone, with walls sixteen feet thick and a roof made of ironstone.

The night Vaylo Bludd took it, five hundred Dhoone warriors stood within its walls, and countless more manned its borders and strongwalls. Yet somehow the Dog Lord managed to breach Dhoone's defenses, raise the Thistle Gate, and slaughter three hundred men."

"It doesn't mean he had help."

"It does when every Dhoonesman who stomached a Bludd sword didn't even bleed enough to rust his plate."

"I don't understand."

"Sorcery was used on the Dhoonesmen. It slowed their hearts, made it so they couldn't raise their weapons and defend themselves. The Dog Lord rode to Dhoone knowing the Dhoonesmen would not give him battle. He claimed victory, but no honor." Raif made his voice hard. He saw the way Ash was sitting forward on her horse, ready to defend the Dog Lord. He saw and did not like it.

She looked at him as if he were speaking lies. "If he did use sorcery, as you say, then how can you be sure it came from outside? He might have had help from someone within his clan."

"Clan do not use sorcery."

"What is your point?"

"The same person who helped the Dog Lord take Dhoone killed my father, my chief, and ten other members of my clan."

A soft gasp escaped from Ash's lips.

Raif continued speaking, firming the truth in his mind. "There were fifteen of us altogether. We were camping in the badlands, along the old elk trails. Every year in the first month of winter when the elk are moving southeast, we go there to claim Blackhail's portion. This winter my brother and I were chosen to ride with the party. It was a great honor. Dagro Blackhail himself led the hunt; it was the first time he'd ridden the elk trails in five years. The hunting wasn't good. Tem said the elk knew a hard winter was coming and had moved south a month early to beat it."

"Who's Tem?" Ash asked.

"My father." It almost didn't hurt to say it. "He and Dagro Blackhail were close. Mace Blackhail had been at his foster father's heels for weeks, trying to persuade Dagro to ride north with him, but it was my father who finally convinced him to go." *Let's you and I ride north one last time, Dagro Blackhail. Let's sit our saddles until we're arse sore, drink malt until we're head sore, and shoot elk until we drown in blood.* Hearing his father's voice in his mind, Raif spoke quickly to quiet it. "The day before we were due to return, Drey and I broke bounds to shoot hares. We were having a contest to see who could shoot the farthest and take down the most game when . . . when I felt something."

"Sorcery?"

Raif nodded. Suddenly it was difficult to speak. "We rushed back, but they were dead by the time we got there. All of them. There was no blood on their weapons, not a drop of it. Twelve men dead, and not one drew a sword to defend himself."

Ash made no attempt at sympathy; he was grateful for that. They didn't speak any more about the past, and that seemed like another thing to be grateful for. There were some memories about the badlands camp he had no wish to share. In silence they traveled west along the river valley and into the territory of another clan.

At noon they came upon a stone marker, sunk deep into the snow and carved with the crossed greatswords of Bannen. Bannen was small but rich, with many well-stocked trout lakes, a series of high meadows suitable for grazing sheep, and a run of iron mines sunk hundreds of feet beneath the Bitter Hills. It was sworn to Dhoone, but it was not a long-lived oath. Past chiefs had declared themselves for Blackhail when it suited them, and Hawder Bannen had fought with Ornfel Blackhail against the Dhoone King at Mare's Rock. Bannen was known for its swordsmen. Tem had once told Raif that Bansmen trained their swordarms by moving through their positions while standing neck high in running water.

Raif glanced to the north. The Banhouse was built on low ground, with its back against a sheer sandstone cliff, and it could not be seen from the river. Raif guessed it was about ten leagues north, as he could see smoke rising above the treetops. Beyond the smoke, on the farthest reach of the horizon, stormheads rolled south from the Want.

Suddenly anxious to be gone, Raif touched Ash's boot. "Are you ready to take old Mule Ears here for a run?"

"What about you?"

"I'll be taking myself for a run. I want to reach those trees"—he pointed to the northwest, where the headland sloped down to meet a forest of oldgrowth pines—"within the hour. We'll need cover when the storm hits." He slapped the gelding hard on the rump. "Go!"

Ash had little choice but to give the mule-eared horse the reins. Snow sprayed Raif's chest as the horse took off at a fair gallop. Raif watched for a moment, satisfying himself that Ash could handle riding through snow at speed, then broke into a run himself. His body was not prepared for the shock of swift motion, and his legs trembled as they took his weight. Ribs broken and then partially mended made creaking noises as he lurched from step to step. His own weakness angered him, and he plowed through the snow, kicking up showers of blue crystals and sods of frozen earth.

Ash and the gelding pulled far ahead. Winds were already working to shift loose snow southward, and snow tails blew from ridges and high ground. Noise in the air increased, and the howling, ripping lowing of the storm buffeted Raif's ears as he ran. The Wolf River meandered due north here, where it ran shallow, feeding a dozen salmon pools, wearing riverstone down into green sand, and forming a defensible line around the Banhold's southern reach. In a way, Raif was glad of the storm. Any other day and clansmen, iron miners, and trappers would be moving back and forth between the Banhouse and the hills.

Raif's hands and face burned as he ran. Beneath the goatskin gloves, his fingers welled in a steambath of trapped sweat. By the time he caught up with Ash he'd bitten off the gloves and tucked them under his belt. Every breath he took pushed against his mending ribs as if it might snap them clean in two.

Ash had dismounted and was leaning against the spine of a thirty-year spruce. She'd reached the trees a quarter ahead of him and had had enough time to brush down the horse, shake the snow from her cloak, and hang her hood to air over the bottommost limb of the tree. She grinned as he approached. "I was found on a day like this," she said. "White weather suits me well enough."

He could not disagree with her. Her eyes sparkled like sea ice. Hunkering in the snow, he fought to catch his breath. Ash had taken one of the tin bowls from the farmhouse and packed it with fresh snow. The snow was half-melted, and he wondered where she'd nursed it for the past fifteen minutes to warm it so quickly.

"What now?" she asked.

Raif glanced through the towering spires of black spruce, up toward the sky. "We keep moving west. We can't afford to lose half a day to a storm."

She nodded briskly. "You need to ride for a while."

He would have liked to protest, to tell her that he was a clansman, and a clansman never rode when a woman walked, but his ribs were creaking and his hands were on fire, and even the *thought* of standing upright made his thighs ache. To save his pride he gave her an order. "Pull some fisher meat from the sack. We need to eat before we move on."

"I'm not hungry."

"I don't care. You can't rely on what your stomach tells you from now on. Every time we rest, you eat. You'll starve twice as quickly out here in the clanholds as you would in the walled-and-shored haven of Spire Vanis."

Ash looked at him sharply, yet she did as she was told, taking a strip of fisher meat and chewing it with venom.

Raif almost laughed, but a patch of fresh blood on the gelding's bandage caught his eye and he left her to tend to it.

Mule Ears suffered Raif's ministrations with the lethargy of an old horse who had seen and done everything before. As Raif cleaned the wound and felt for frostbite, he found himself thinking of Moose. He hoped the gray gelding was on his way home to Blackhail and Orwin Shank, not traveling north to Dhoone with the Dog Lord. He wanted that man to have nothing of his.

Ash wandered over to watch him as he rewrapped the

gelding's leg. The wind tugged at her cloak, making the rust-colored wool stream behind her like a banner. *A Clan Frees banner*, he thought senselessly.

"Earlier, when we were out in the open, you said Mace Blackhail rode to the badlands with his father. So why wasn't he killed along with the rest?"

It hadn't taken her very long to get to the heart of the matter. Tying the final knot in the gelding's bandage with double the force necessary, Raif said, "Mace claimed he was off shooting a black bear when the raiders came. Said he missed them by seconds, and that once he saw his foster father's body lying in the snow, the only thing he could think of was riding home to warn the clan." Raif was surprised at how easy it was to tell it. "By the time Drey and I got back to the roundhouse, he had everyone believing that Clan Bludd had carried out the raid. Lies. All lies. He didn't know anything about the bodies, where they lay, what wounds they'd taken. He left before the raid ever started. Rode home on his foster father's horse."

"But you and Drey must have made the clan see the truth."

Raif smiled bitterly, the skin on his face pulling tight. "You haven't met the Hail Wolf. He was born a Scarpeman. His tongue moves faster than his blade."

"If Bludd didn't carry out the raid, then why didn't the Dog Lord simply deny it?"

"You've met him. What do you think?"

Ash pushed a hand through her hair, thinking. "Pride. He liked the idea of taking credit for such a thing."

Raif tasted the bitterness in his mouth. "Spoken like the Dog Lord himself."

"He told you that?"

"Yes." Raif stood. "What did he tell you about me?"

She didn't blink, though the silver in her eyes quickened. "He said you slaughtered women and children along the Bluddroad. He called you a murderer."

Raif made no answer. He would not speak against his brother or his clan.

When it became clear to her that he was not going to deny the charge, Ash gathered her cloak about her and began to make her way west through the trees.

Raif watched her go. New snow had begun to fall, and the

wind sent the heavy white flakes swirling in the spaces between the trees. After a few minutes Ash's figure was lost to the storm, and Raif mounted the gelding and wound through the spruces to catch her.

The storm followed them deep into the taiga, dislodging snow caches from branches, bending saplings double, and roaring like a river over rocks. Riding took more concentration than walking, as ruts and sinkholes hidden beneath the snow were a constant danger to the horse. Drifts were impossible to predict in unsettled snow and forced many stops while Ash ran ahead to test the snow depth with a whip-thin stick of spruce. In the end, both he and Ash decided to walk, heads bent low against the wind.

Light faded rapidly, and the taiga shimmered blue and gray as it darkened. Raif became aware of Drey's tine banging against his hip from step to step. It seemed to weigh more than it should, and soon he could think of nothing at all except the piece of horn and the powdered guidestone within it. *Please gods, let Drey be all right*, he thought. *Let the wound heal cleanly, and let it not cause him pain.*

It was hard to turn his mind to finding shelter for the night. Part of him wanted to walk and walk and never stop. Only the thought of a warm fire, of holding his hands above yellow flames and feeling their heat upon his face, was enough to tempt him away from the storm.

No one lived in the taiga in winter. Trappers, woodsmen, and loggers spent spring and summer in the woods but retreated to the shelter of stone houses in the cold months. They often built summer huts, but Raif didn't hold out much hope of finding one in white weather. He settled upon a grove of newgrowth pines occupying a narrow flood basin and set about stripping the soft lower branches from the surrounding trees to use as thatching for the den. Ash saw to Mule Ears, then came to help him fix the crude thatch roof over the frame of bent newgrowth he'd erected. The wind drove against them as they worked, tugging whole branches from their grip. Every time Raif closed his hands around a shoot to strip it, pain made him catch his breath.

The storm was dying by the time they got the shelter to hold firm. Raif's mitts were sticky with white resin, and beneath the goatskin gloves his fingers were raw. Ash's hood was no longer protecting her head and lay against her back, filled with snow. She was breathing with quick shallow breaths so Raif ordered her to rest while he built a long fire across the entrance to the den. The fact that she didn't protest, merely sat on the pine needle floor without saying a word, worried him. The skin around her eyes looked bruised.

He packed the fire loosely in his haste. Built well, a long fire could burn through the night, with timbers packed on poles so they could drop into the flames as the poles burned down. Yet Raif was more worried about Ash than he was about a full night's warmth, and he kindled the fire quickly, blowing to make it take.

Shredding the fisher meat with the bald knife, he set about turning snowmelt into a stock. He talked to Ash as he worked, anxious that she stay awake long enough to eat and drink. It was winter and it was cold, so he spoke of spring, telling her about the Hailhold after first thaw, about the carpets of white heather that pushed up overnight and the rings of darkwood violets that flowered amid the melting snow. He told her about the birds, about the blue herons that stood as tall as men, and the horned owls that could take to the air with full-grown rabbits in their beaks, and the little dun-colored swifts that hung upside down from branches like bats.

He didn't know how long he spoke, only that once he started he kept remembering other things that seemed important to tell her. Ash listened in silence, and after a time her breathing grew shallow and her eyes began to flicker, then close. Raif took the stock from the fire. Leaning over, he touched her arm. "Here. Drink this before you sleep."

She took the bowl from him and held it to her chest, letting the steam roll over her face. After what seemed like a very long time she said, "I don't believe what the Dog Lord said about what happened on the Bluddroad. I don't think you killed anyone in cold blood."

Raif nodded. He told himself he felt no better for hearing her say it, yet it wasn't the truth.

They spoke no more after that and ate and drank in silence, the flames of the long fire dancing before them and the tail end of the storm sending gusts of winds to rattle the den. Ash fell asleep while Raif was nursing the last of the stock in his cracked and aching hands. He covered her as best he could, making sure that no part of her skin came in contact with snow, and then settled himself down before the fire.

He could not sleep. He was weary beyond telling, yet he could see the night sky through the flames. A moonless, starless night in midwinter; not the sort of night a sane man would choose to be out in. Then perhaps he wasn't sane, for Raif found himself rising from his place by the fire, pulling on his goatskin gloves and leather boots, and leaving the warmth and dryness of the den. It took him less than a minute to find a wedge of greenstone to his liking: jagged and shot with lead. Brushing it clean of snow, he entered the dark cathedral of the forest. The storm had passed and the night animals were feeding and he was Watcher of the Dead.

\* \* \*

THE LISTENER WOKE TO the hiss of the runners. His heart beat like a snow goose in his chest. His old mouth was as dry as tanned hide, and his eyes, once a dark brown color and now turned blue with snow blindness, took a very long time before they allowed him even the dimmest view of the surrounding world. The sky above the sled was dark and full of stars: The long night of winter had begun.

He'd been having the old dream again, the one where Harannaqua guided him to a dark place where the old Sull Kings were waiting. Lyan Summerled and Thay Blackdragon and Lann Swordbreaker were there, along with the Sull Queen Isane Rune. Not *his* kings, the Listener reminded himself, yet they haunted him all the same. They were not dead, not truly, for flesh still hung to their bones in places, and they moved like men, not ghosts. Isane's smile had been beautiful to behold until the instant her spread lips parted, revealing a mouth of bloody teeth. Lyan Summerled, he who had once been the most glorious and golden of all kings, had laid a skinned hand upon the Listener's shoulder and breathed a single word in his ear.

*Soon.*

Sadaluk shivered. "Nolo," he said, turning around and calling to the man who drove the sled. "We must stop and turn back. This is not a good night to ask for blessing from the god who lives beneath the sea ice."

Nolo's brown face registered not one mote of surprise; perhaps he had felt the badness, too. Calling to his team, he pulled on the standers and began driving the sled in a great turning circle on the gray shore-fast ice. Sadaluk, sitting at the front of the sled, wrapped in bearhides and wearing a squirrel cap, watched as the dogs slowed and changed their course. They were fat dogs—Nolo fed them too much—yet the Listener felt less inclined to criticize now than when he and Nolo had set off. Overfed dogs were a sign of a kind heart, and after the darkness of his unasked-for dream, the Listener found much to value in the kindness of a man who loved his dogs as if they were kin.

The sled, formed from a ladder of driftwood and horn and bound with seal sinew, skimmed to a halt as it completed its turn. The dogs, harnessed together in a line, broke formation and began worrying on their traces. The edges had been filed from their teeth, so they could do little but suck and gnaw.

Nolo pulled off his heavy sled gloves and walked to where the Listener sat. He was out of breath, and his chest rose and fell rapidly. "Are you ill, Sadaluk? You were quiet for a very long time."

The Listener shook his head. "I dreamt," he said.

Silence followed. Nolo looked guilty, as if his sled were to blame for the dream. The Listener saw no reason to argue otherwise: Perhaps if the sled *hadn't* run so smoothly and silently, he might well have stayed awake. Instead he said, "Once, many lifetimes ago when the winter lasted many seasons and the Gods Lights burned red, our people had to eat their skins and tents to survive. All the dogs were slaughtered. Mothers killed their children to relieve them of the hunger that ate from inside out. Old men like me walked out onto the sea ice and never came back. Young couples, newly wed, sealed themselves in their ice houses and starved in each other's arms.

"By the time the warm winds came and the sea ice broke, only twelve were left alive. One man, Harannaqua, who had

lost his wife and his three children, was angry at the gods for
not sending a warning. *We could have stored more food if
we had known*, he cried. *We could have eaten less at summer's end.*

"The gods listened to him, for even though they hate flesh
men pointing out their failings, they knew that he was right.
*From this day forth you shall be the warning, Harannaqua
of Four Losses*, they replied. *We will strip your body from
you and carry your soul with us, and whenever hard times
come to the Ice Trappers we will send you down to warn
them in their dreams.* And so the gods took him and kept him
and bound him to this task."

The Listener looked sharply at Nolo. A cloud of frosted
breath lay between them like a third man. "Yes, Nolo of the
Silent Sled, today I dreamt of Harannaqua, him and four
kings."

Nolo nodded slowly. He thought long before he spoke.
"What must we do, Sadaluk?"

The Listener made an impatient gesture with his hand.
"Watch ourselves. Be vigilant. Feed our fat dogs less." The
words made Nolo blush, but Sadaluk found little satisfaction
in his young friend's distress. He was afraid, and the dream
worried him, and he had spoken from fear and spite. "Run
the sled."

The dogs took much whipping and cursing before they
would re-form themselves into a line. Nolo had to put on a
harness and pull like one of them to remind the beasts what
they must do. Sadaluk drew his bearskin close as the sled
shuddered into motion.

Four Sull kings. Not *his* kings, he told himself again, as if
that could make it so. They shared blood, but that blood was
old, *old*. Blood could thin to water over the space of thirteen
thousand years. True, the Ice Trappers and the Sull came
from the same place beyond the Night Sea, but that was far
in the past. The great glaciers had receded, deserts had been
baked to glass, and iron mountains had risen from seeds of
rock and stone. All this and more had come to pass since the
Sull and the Ice Trappers had once called themselves kins-
men. Why then should their fates still be linked?

The Listener frowned at the stars, the snow, the shimmering blue landscape of sea ice. Where were the Far Riders? A raven had been sent two moons past; they should be here by now.

This was their fate unraveling, not his.

"Lash the dogs, Nolo. Lash them!" The Listener tried to set aside his dreams as he watched Nolo punish his team. Eloko had promised to show him the third secret use for whale blubber on his return and had set her stone pot to warming over the lamp even as he and Nolo packed the sled. Sadaluk had liked the first two secret uses very much, and he could think of nothing more pleasant than being introduced to the third. Yet even as he tried to conjure Eloko's wide, smooth face in his mind's eye, the face of another came to him.

Thay Blackdragon, the Night King, looked at him with eyes that were the perfect Sull blue: dark as the sky at midnight and shot with veins of ice. Strips of flesh hung from his cheeks, and the Listener could see white ridges of bone beneath. He was riding a horse that was all shadow, a dark beast made of muscle and black oil that quivered with every touch of its rider's hand. Thay Blackdragon pulled the reins, and the beast opened its mouth, revealing a bit of razored steel. The Night King smiled as Isane Rune had before him.

*Soon,* he hissed. *Our thousand years have all but passed.*

For the first time in his hundred-year life, the Listener didn't know if he was sleeping or wide awake.


# FORTY-SEVEN

## *Clothes off a Dead Man's Back*

THEY WERE ON THE MOVE before dawn, walking through the hills and valleys of snow that had formed around the bases of pines like skirts of spent wax around candles. Light came slowly, sparkling for brief moments on pine needles scored with hoarfrost and the whites of Ash's eyes and teeth. A wind, soft and cold, blew south. Somewhere beyond the horizon a ptarmigan screamed at a rival who drew too near to its roost.

Raif carried the two fox carcasses slung over his back. They were gutted but not skinned and were now freezing rapidly in the cold dry air. He would have liked to strap them to Mule Ears' cantle, but the old gelding had no liking for the smell of fox.

Ash led the horse by its reins. Uneven snow cover made riding difficult, and she had chosen to walk instead. Raif did not like the look of the dark patches beneath her eyes and the yellowish cast to her skin. Gradually he was leading her to the taiga's southwestern edge, where settled snow would make riding easier.

He suspected that they might already be in the Scarpehold, yet any markers that might have proclaimed that fact were buried deep beneath the white. Bannen and Scarpe were close neighbors, though there was little love lost between the two. Scarpe was sworn to Blackhail, yet its oath did not prevent it from encroaching on Blackhail's southern reach. Its chief was Yelma Scarpe, and in the ten years she had led the clan she had annexed land from Bannen and Dregg and taken control of an escarpment that Clan Orrl had held for eight decades and was a prime site for hunting and spotting wild sheep. The Scarpe badge was a black weasel with a mouse in its jaws. The Scarpe boast was, *Our words cut as sharply as our swords*. Yelma Scarpe had fought no battles with Bannen, Dregg, and Orrl. No. She had simply *talked* them out of their land.

And now one of her clan was Blackhail's chief.

Raif almost smiled. Inside his mitts, skin split as he bunched his hands into fists.

"Look!" Ash said, pointing to the northwest sky above the treetops. "Smoke."

Raif followed her gaze. Smoke, greasy and thick with burned matter, billowed up in great clouds several leagues north of their position. The Scarpehouse. It had to be. Scarpe's roundhouse was situated close to the Bannen border, on a greenstone bluff surrounded by a moat of poison pines.

Unease cooled Raif's face. Who would attack Scarpe? Bludd had pushed no farther west than Ganmiddich, and now they were in retreat. Blackhail would not attack one of its own war-sworn clans, most especially when that clan was birthplace to the Hail Wolf. Was it Bannen or Gnash, then? Or dispossessed Ganmiddich? Or was it dispossessed Dhoone?

None of the possibilities were good. Any one of them meant an escalation in the Clan Wars. And for someone to attack a clan sworn to Blackhail meant Blackhail itself must respond.

"Raif! Stop! Why are you heading north?"

Raif had to glance over his shoulder to see Ash. She was many paces below him, on the trail they had been walking since dawn. He stared at his own footprints in the snow, following their course as they cleaved north away from the path. He shook himself hard. *What am I doing? The torching of the Scarpehouse means nothing to me.* Angry at himself, he headed down the slope and back onto the trail.

He set a grim pace after that. They emerged from the taiga at noon and traveled west along the frost fields north of the river. To the south, the rocky balds and escarpments that formed the tail end of the Bitter Hills cast dark, shifting shadows upon the water. The Iron Caves lay somewhere beneath them, excavated by Mordrag Blackhail, the Mole Chief, and seized by the Forsworn some hundred years later when all the iron seams had been mined out. According to Tem, the walls of the Iron Caves were black and sparkling, and no man could carry a knife there for fear of it flying from his hand. The Forsworn claimed the caves as a holy place. They believed the One True God had slept there the night after he Remade the World. It took Aran Blackhail, Mordrag's grandson, twenty years to drive them out.

Directly ahead the pale blue peaks of the Coastal Ranges rode the western horizon like ships made of ice. Raif found himself staring at them for much of the day. It was easier to look forward than back.

From time to time they passed bits of freestanding wall, broken arches, and blocks of stone. Ruins. And they had stood in the clanholds longer than any roundhouse. Raif had seen such things on the Hailhold, made of the same milky blue stone that always felt cool to the touch, even on the hottest day. Tem had said that in the great white forests of Dhoone and Bludd whole cities stood buried beneath the snow. Clan Castlemilk was rumored to have taken its name from one such place.

Raif farmed the landscape as he walked, searching the grassbeds and shrub groves for bearberries frozen on the vine, rosehips, field mint, and the little wood ear mushrooms that grew on rotting logs. They had meat, but foxes were musty on the tongue, and Raif didn't much like the thought of eating them on their own. Once or twice he spotted a glossy white ptarmigan hiding in the snow, yet he left the birds undisturbed. Ash knew he could kill game with a rock, she *knew*, but it didn't mean he wanted her to see him do it.

When they came upon a grove of old willows, Raif called a halt while he cut himself a staff. The knife he'd taken from the Ganmiddich farmhouse was little use against the hard, finely grained wood, and it took many long minutes of sawing and twisting to cut a branch free. Ash, who had been riding since they'd broken free of the taiga, did not dismount as he stripped the stave of side suckers. She slouched in the saddle, her chin almost touching her chest. When she noticed Raif looking at her, she straightened her spine and made an effort to smile. Raif could not smile back. He was remembering what Heritas Cant had said about her, about how the power within her would press against her organs until they leaked.

Perhaps she read the thoughts on his face, for she said, "I'm fine. Just a bit tired, that's all."

"And the voices?"

"I fight them." Her clear gray eyes met his, and Raif suddenly wished the voices were real men he could fight and kill, not shadowy nothings he could not see.

"You need to eat," he said after a while. "Here. Take these." He handed her a stem of frozen bearberries and a few of the rosehips he had collected. All clansmen who rode to the badlands for a season's hunting carried a pouch of dried rosehips in their packs. The hard pink fruits stopped the shaking sickness from coming, even when there were no fresh greens to eat.

Ash grimaced as she bit into one of the buds.

"You'll get used to them quicker than fox meat," he promised. The smile she gave him warmed something deep and very cold inside his chest. "Let's get going. There's still an hour of daylight left."

That night they camped in the lee of a hill, digging a burrow into old drifted snow. Raif hunted while Ash slept, bagging an ice hare he flushed from its den and a fat white ptarmigan who burst into flight when Raif stumbled upon its roost. Feeling pleased with his prizes, he returned to the dugout with plans for a midnight roast. The fox supper he'd prepared by boiling the dark, purplish meat in snowmelt had not been a great success.

He sensed something was wrong when he topped the hill. The night seemed suddenly dark and small, as if it had shrunk to half its size. The dugout looked the same as when he'd left it, and the fire was burning as well as an unattended fire could, yet something had changed. The air was colder. A nearby grove of aspens rustled and clicked as a gust of wind drove their trunks together like wooden sticks. Suddenly the night's kills felt like ghost weight against Raif's back, and he let them drop to the snow.

*Ash.*

Clutching the cold ivory of his raven lore, he raced the short distance to the dugout. The snow surrounding the entrance was clean except for his own footprints, yet even though no man or animal had entered the shelter he knew Ash was gone. Her body lay on the mat of willow switches he had spread to protect her from the cold. Muscles in her shoulders and upper arms were convulsing, causing her body to buck against the dugout's floor. Her mouth was open, and something dark and tarlike moved within it. *Oh, gods.*

Raif squeezed his lore. An instinct he wasn't prepared for made him want to run. He could smell the power inside her the way a dog smelled disease. Heritas Cant was right: It was something that wasn't meant to be.

*Kill an army for me, Raif Sevrance.*

Raif shook his head, alarmed at how quickly the thought of killing her entered his mind. *It would be a mercy*, a small voice said. *The world would thank you for it in the end.*

"No." Raif spoke the word out loud. He had no brother, no clan, and no memories stored in stone. But he had Ash, and he had sworn to protect her. And who was he to judge the value of another's life?

Thinking of Angus, imagining what he would do if he were here in the river valley west of Scarpe, Raif stripped off his gloves and knelt by Ash's side. Angus had thrust a wad of wool in her mouth whenever she began to draw sorcery, so that's what *he* would do. Swiftly Raif cut a handful of wool from Ash's cloak and packed it in his fist. He tried to be gentle as he pushed the wad of fabric into her mouth, but his hands shook, and the desire to be rid of the dark thing on her tongue made him thrust the gag deep into her throat. Her stomach sucked into a hollow the moment the gag was in place, and he laid a hand on her rib cage and pushed hard to counter the reflex action to vomit. Despite the coldness of the dugout, droplets of sweat rose like blisters on Raif's face.

Ash's legs jerked. Cords of muscle in her neck rose as she fought the muzzle. Raif held her down, hard as he could, until her muscles fell slack under his hands. He stayed pressing her long after, his breaths ragged and his heart hammering against his ribs. Finally he released his grip, but only so he could tear the foxhides into strips to bind her. There was a taste in his mouth that might have been fear. He kept seeing the rippling blackness of the thing upon her tongue . . . the way it shifted and ran like liquid metal.

He was not gentle as he bound her.

Later, when he sat at the entrance to the dugout, turning the fire over with the tip of his willow staff, he wondered what would have happened if he had not returned when he had. Ash was silent now, her arms resting easy in their sheathing of blankets and rope. A Reach, Cant had named her. Yet Raif did not know what that meant. He had heard Cant's words, yet they seemed like shadowy things, concealing more than they showed.

Raif put down the staff and held his hands above the

flames to warm them. He tried to send his mind elsewhere, to the ice hare and ptarmigan that were lying unclaimed in the snow, to the dwindling stock of firewood, to clothes that needed airing, yet he made no move to start any of those tasks. Better that he stay here and watch over Ash.

Time passed and the fire burned low, sending little red flames to eat the insides of logs. Raif thought he would not sleep. The pain in his ribs ran deeper tonight than any other night, and his hands ached and wept. Still, his eyes closed and his thoughts stopped coming and he slipped into a deep, dreamless sleep.

He awoke in darkness hours later, sore all over but strangely well rested. Before he stepped outside to relieve himself or feed the fire, he cut the lashings that held Ash's arms to her side. The gag was drenched with saliva, and he had to force her teeth apart to pull out the expanded wool.

She opened her eyes as he removed his hand from her jaw.

Raif slid the gag behind his back.

Ash lifted her right arm and rubbed the section where the ties had dug deep. "How long?"

"Overnight. Just overnight."

She looked away from him. He thought he saw her lip tremble, but a fraction of a moment later it was still.

He helped her to sit up. Already he was counting days. Another two to reach the Storm Margin. A week to reach the base of Mount Flood. "How are you feeling?"

"Tired. My arms are aching." She made a face. "And something tastes bad in my mouth."

"I'll fetch some water."

"Raif."

He turned to look at her.

"Do you think we'll make it? I was lucky this time . . . I woke." She shook her head softly, her eyes darkening as memories filled them. "They're so hard to fight. They're stronger now. That day at the pass changed them. They came so close to breaking through they could taste it."

Raif didn't know how to reply. Ash needed to be told that she would make it to the Cavern of Black Ice alive and well. Yet Tem had not taught him how to lie. In the end he said, "I will slaughter the horse for blood and meat, carry you on my back, and walk until my feet turn yellow with ice before I give up or turn back."

He bowed his head and walked outside to a frost so hard, each breath stung like acid in his throat.

They left the dugout while it was still dark. If there had been a moon, it had long set, yet the ground snow glimmered blue and gray as if light from some distant source shone upon it. On Raif's insistence Ash rode the gelding at a trot. Raif ran for short bursts to keep pace. Often he fell behind, as his mending ribs would allow him to take only so much air. When the sun rose in a brilliant blue sky, the granite peaks of the Coastal Ranges seemed close enough to touch. The winter sun made Raif nervous, especially when he saw Ash tugging at the collar of her cloak as if she were warm and needed air. It *wasn't* warm. It was cold enough to freeze tears. And there were men and women in Clan Blackhail who could tell you all about the danger of believing that sun-*shine* meant warmth. As many clan ears had been lost beneath a blue sky as in the deepest, darkest night.

Raif monitored his own body closely. His hands ached constantly . . . but at least they weren't numb. "It's when you *can't* feel them there's a problem," Tem would always say, "not when you can."

The terrain changed gradually over the course of the day. The great dark body of the taiga extended all the way to the Coastal Ranges, but the trees living within it altered as they neared the divide. They were smaller now, stunted by late spring frosts, midwinter thaws, and the black blight of snow mold. Hemlocks and spruce gave way to the twisted bones of whitebark and limber pines. The ground underfoot grew harder, and giant boulders riven with frost cracks studded the valley floor. Scraggy beards of bladdergrass and yellow moss occupied niches in the rocks, and prostrate willow hugged the ground like something spilled, not grown. The snow underfoot was as hard and dry as white sand.

The area reminded Raif of the badlands. He felt the same sense of cold drought.

By the time the sun reached its highest point he was no longer sure which clan's territory he was in. He guessed they might be traveling through the Orrlhold, which was the most westerly of the border clans, but he also knew that a small creek named the Red Run lay somewhere out here, beyond whose banks Blackhail claimed all land west to the Ranges.

The Wolf River flowed to the south here, and Raif glimpsed its black oily surface at intervals throughout the day. Most of its tributaries were dry or frozen, and its mass remained unchanged as it flowed toward the sea. The Wolf River and its valley cut straight through the Ranges, and Raif knew it would provide the quickest, safest route to the Storm Margin.

They stopped briefly at midday and ate the last of the roasted bird. Raif watched Ash closely. Her skin was markedly yellow now, and there was something wrong with her face. The change was subtle, yet Raif recognized it for what it was straightaway. The tiny crinkles around her eyes and mouth were gone. Fluid beneath her skin was filling out wrinkles and depressions and making her cheeks swell. He had seen symptoms like these before, on Braida Tanner, elder sister to Lansa and Hailly, whose body had been laid in a hollowed-out basswood the month Drey took his yearman's oath. It was poison, Inigar Stoop had said. The girl's body had poisoned itself.

Raif made Ash ride the gelding at a gallop for long periods during the afternoon. He ran behind her, his feet pounding over frozen earth, his ears burning in the rushing air. At sunset she surprised him by calling a halt. He was some distance behind her, catching his breath against a massive snout of limestone, when he heard her call his name. By the time he reached the horse she had dismounted and was approaching a crop of rocks that lay on a ridge north of the path.

A small movement of Ash's body turned him cold. She continued walking forward, yet she drew her arms to her sides and closed her mouth. Raif took a second look at the rocks. They were colored a delicate shade of blue gray, coated with hoarfrost and granules of snow, and they were not rocks at all. They were corpses. Six of them. Orrlsmen, judging from the strips of white willow plaited into their braids, and the pale, shimmering fabric of their cloaks. From the depth and condition of the surrounding snow, Raif guessed they had been here for less than two weeks, yet already the cold dry air had begun to mummify their remains.

Raif took Ash's hand. His gaze was drawn to the dark shadows beneath the hoarfrost crust: a blue eye, perfectly preserved, a mouth open wide enough to show the pink hump of a frozen tongue, a fist clenched around a column of air.

"What should we do?" Ash's voice was a whisper.

As she spoke, Raif noticed a cap of beaten silver discarded a short distance from the bodies. "Nothing."

"But shouldn't they be blessed, buried, *something*?"

He could tell she was upset, yet he still shook his head. "My clan brought this death. It's not for me to deal with the corpses they left behind."

"How do you know it was Blackhail who did this?"

"That piece of silver over there belongs to Blackhail and no other. They killed these men, and when they were done, one of their number flicked the cap off his tine and drew a circle in the frost."

"To honor the dead men's memories?"

"No. You do not honor the memory of a man you've just killed. The circle was made to draw the eyes of the Stone Gods, so they may know there are souls to be claimed."

Ash pulled free of Raif's grip. "Why kill these men *here*, where no one lives?"

"Because we are on Blackhail land, and a state of war exists in the clanholds, and something has happened to make the Hail wolf angry or nervous, or both."

Raif dragged his hands over his face. Orrl was sworn to Blackhail. The two clans had shared borders for two thousand years, and for as far back as he could remember all disputes between them had been settled at the hearth. Now this. What was Mace Blackhail doing? What had happened to make him order such a killing? Orrl's chief, Spynie Orrl, was no fool. He was the oldest living chief in the clanholds, outliving four wives, two sons, and a daughter. Dagro Blackhail had liked him well enough to invite him to hear vows at both his weddings, and when Spynie's first great-granddaughter had been born five years back, Spynie had sent Dagro ten head of blackneck sheep in celebration. Raif could not imagine Spynie Orrl attacking Blackhail. No man lived as long as he did by taking chances.

Clan Scarpe. The memory of smoke rising above the Scarpe tree line cooled Raif's face as quickly as if it had been stroked with ice. If something had happened to bring the two clans into dispute, and Clan Orrl had crossed swords with Clan Scarpe, then Mace Blackhail would make sure that it was Orrl that paid the highest price. He might call himself the Hail Wolf, but he was a Scarpeman through and through.

Raif closed his eyes. He felt tired enough to lie on the frozen ground and sleep with the dead.

He knew there was no way of knowing for certain if the torching of the Scarpehouse was connected to the mummified bodies on the ridge—Scarpe collected enemies like flat roofs collected rain. Yet even if the two events were unrelated, there was still a hard truth to be learned here. The Clan Wars were spiraling out of control. Mace Blackhail had ordered the killing of Orrlsmen. The Scarpe roundhouse had been torched. Ganmiddich had been taken first by Bludd, then by Blackhail. Dhoone survivors were still unhoused and scattered, yet it was only a matter of time before they massed for a strike against Bludd. When would it end? When every guidestone was smashed to rubble and every clansman dead?

Raif looked northeast toward Blackhail. After a few minutes the lines around his mouth hardened, and he went to strip clothes from the corpses.

HE FOUND NO GAME to kill that night. The thought of Ash sitting alone while he hunted kept him close to the camp. The night was dark, and there was no moon showing, and the sky seemed close enough to touch. Wind moving down from the mountains froze the saliva on his teeth and made his eyes stream with stinging tears. His breath glaciated upon his fisher hood within minutes.

He returned to the camp dragging numb feet in the snow. They had not traveled far from the Orrlsmen, just enough to put the sight of death behind them. Camp was a dry storm channel thatched with willow switches and laid with willow leaves and moss. The clothes Raif had stripped from the Orrlsmen had been beaten free of ice and were now laid over the gelding's back so they would be warm and dry by morning. Ash had offered to help, but he had set her the task of building the fire and preparing the dried fox supper instead. Skin had peeled off with the dead men's clothes, and although it bore little resemblance to living flesh, Raif had not wanted her to see it.

Ash was awake when he entered the shelter, sitting with her knees tucked close to her chest. Smoke choked the air—too much to escape easily from the smoke hole—and Raif could tell by the length and fierceness of the flames that Ash had been feeding the fire.

He stripped off his gloves and came to kneel beside her. She was shaking as violently as if she'd been pulled from freezing water. "Here," he said, tucking the blankets around her shoulders. "You need to cover yourself properly."

She smiled weakly. "No kill tonight?"

"No." His gaze took in the pile of willow branches he'd collected for firewood; there was no longer enough to last the night. Ash had burned more than half their stock. "Did the voices come again?"

She lowered her head as she nodded. "They never leave me now. Sometimes they're not strong, and I can push them back. Other times it's as if they're standing right beside me . . . and I can smell them . . . and they're cold and their eyes are black and dead. *It's so easy*, they say. *So easy. All you have to do is reach.*"

"Do you know what they are?"

"Men. At least they once were men . . . it's as if the shadows on the outside have found a way in." Ash swallowed hard. "They hate us, Raif. They've been shut away for so long, and all they can do is imagine what it's like to be free. It's cold there, and no light ever touches them . . . and they're in chains, and the chains are made of blood. They call me *mistress* and say they love me, but their words are all lies. There's thousands of them, thousands upon thousands, and each and every one of them is waiting for me to reach."

Raif leaned over and fed more willow to the fire. He understood her need for warmth now.

As yellow flames dripped onto the new wood and the frozen clay walls of the shelter shivered in the changing light, Ash said, "Why do I exist, Raif? If what I can do is so terrible, why was I born?"

Her eyes were bright in the firelight. A patch on her bottom lip was red and tattered where she had chewed on it. Raif wanted to take her in his arms and crush her until she was warm and safe and unafraid. He wanted to say, *It doesn't matter what you are capable of. If you breached the Blind-wall this night and let loose an army from the Blind, I would stay by your side and protect you. You are clan to me now.* Instead he said, "All of us are born with the ability to bring death and suffering. Some of us have to fight harder than others to cause no harm."

It was not the answer Ash wanted, yet he could see her thinking as she pushed smoke away from her face. "You fight it too, don't you?"

"Yes."

She edged closer to him, so that their shoulders and arms were touching, yet kept her gaze on the fire as she said, "Why do you stay with me, Raif? You don't want anything from me. There's no reward for taking me to the cavern. We could both die in the cold and the snow, and by the time someone came upon our bodies we'd be like those Orrlsmen on the ridge, blue and white and frozen."

Raif sat still and did not speak. How could he answer? Staying with Ash was all he had, yet he could not let her know that. She might pity him . . . and that was something he had no need for. After a time he leaned forward and stoked the fire with his staff. "I think we'd better sleep."

Ash looked at him without blinking, yet he pretended not to notice as he shouldered down beneath his blanket, closed his eyes, and waited for sleep to take him.

The screaming of the wind woke him before dawn. The fire was long dead, and the temperature in the shelter had dropped below freezing. Ice smoke hung in the air above Raif's body, like a small piece of his soul. He lay still for a while and listened to the wind, as Tem had taught him. The high-pitched whistling told of air forced through mountain passes and needle-thin fissures in rocks. The undertone of white noise, a sound as soft as a mother *shss*ing a baby to sleep, spoke of ice. The wind was full of ice.

Although he didn't much feel like it, Raif rose. Pain shot through his hands as he contracted muscles locked by cold. His left eye was frozen shut, and when he rubbed his beard, dead skin and ice crystals flaked into his hand. He needed to heat water and render the last drops of fat from the fox, yet the idea of going outside and collecting more fuel for the fire rested like an undigested meal in his belly. He rubbed his left eye until it ached and scarlet colors bloomed against the inside of his eyelid, and then pried the eye open. Some portion of ice held fast, and as he forced back the lid a handful of eyelashes were plucked clean.

Raif damned the cold.

Gathering his blanket around him like a cloak, he crossed to where Ash lay sleeping against the back wall of the shelter. Breaths so shallow they hardly raised her chest exited her mouth with little scraping noises. Raif spoke her name, loudly, afraid she might not wake.

Her eyes blinked open.

Raif concealed his relief. "It's morning. We must be ready to leave within the quarter. Wrap up well. There's ice on the wind today."

He left her alone then, as he always did, aware that women needed time for themselves after waking. Breaking up the roof thatch, he pulled himself free of the shelter and entered the ice storm beyond. The land was white and shifting, driven by winds that could be seen and touched. Great webs of ice hung from bent and crippled pines, and hoarfrost grew on everything that lived like a plague. The snow underfoot was so hard and dry it snapped like panes of glass beneath Raif's feet.

Head down, arms crossed over his chest, he made his way toward the prostrate willow where he had tethered the horse.

The gelding was in a bad way. It had not fed during the night. Veins around its mouth and eyes were chilblained and broken, and despite the many blankets and articles of clothing spread over its back, it was shivering violently. As soon as it heard Raif, it whickered softly and came toward him on uncertain legs. Raif stroked the old horse's nose, oddly touched by its desire to be near him.

Ash came out to join them sometime later, huddled in every scrap of skin and wool she could find. The harsh, shadowless light showed up the yellow tones in her skin and made her lips look the same color as her face. She smiled weakly. "I see now why they call this land the Storm Margin."

Raif hardly knew how he managed to smile back. He didn't have the heart to tell her that the Storm Margin didn't begin true until they'd crossed the mountains and entered the strip of land that ran the length of the coast.

Ash motioned to the pile of clothes tucked beneath the gelding's blanket. "You need to put on some of those things, the ones you took from the . . ." She let her words trail away.

*Dead men*, he finished the sentence for her in his mind. Ash shivered as if he had spoken the words out loud. Raif felt like shivering too, but he turned and began unloading the horse instead.

They fitted well, the dead men's clothes, sitting over his back like garments tailored for him alone. The Orrl cloak he had taken was the same white blue color of snow, and Raif found some small measure of satisfaction in being rendered invisible in the storm. Orrlsmen were famous white-weather hunters, able to feast on fresh meat in the dead of winter when all other clans were grinding their teeth on cured elk. Their badge was the ice hare, and Tem said that no one moved as swiftly and silently through snow as an Orrlsman. Raif touched the cap of his tine out of respect for their skills. Orrl was a hard clan, with a hard clanhold, and it had been loyal to Blackhail for a thousand years.

He pushed the thought away. What Blackhail did, what any clan did, was not his business now. Forcing his mind into the present, forcing his senses to deal with the storm, he saddled the gelding and prepared for the journey west.

The dead men's clothes warmed his back.

# FORTY-EIGHT

## *A Night at Drover Jack's*

THAT NEW GIRL OF YOURS is a witch," said Clyve Wheat.

"No. An angel," corrected Burdale Ruff. "The ability to know what a man wants before he knows it himself comes from the heavens, not the twelve sheepless hells." Burdale Ruff spoiled the eloquence of his words somewhat by belching with great satisfaction at the end of them. With a smile made sloppy by drink, the great hairy eweman apologized, then belched again.

Gull Moler could appreciate the compliment inherent in a goodly belch as much as the next man, but the current subject of discussion was of too great an interest to him to risk being diverted by one of Burdale Ruff's infamous after-supper performances. Before blond-eyebrowed Clyve Wheat and little rat-faced Silas Craw could spoil the conversation by snickering at Burdale's antics, Gull said hotly, "I'd hardly call Maggy a girl. She's long past the days of pink ribbons and shoes that pinch. She's a widow, you know. A widow."

Clyve Wheat, who was not as drunk as Burdale Ruff yet no cleverer for it, nudged Silas Craw with such force that the little eweman nearly fell from the beer cask he had taken to sitting upon in light of the shortage of chairs. "A widow, he says! A widow! Well, all I can say to that is she must have wed before she was weaned from the teat. For I tell you now that woman is no older than my sister Bell."

Silas Craw, who had righted himself with the quick, ferrety action of a man well used to being pushed, grunted in agreement. "Bell!" he said with feeling. Everyone waited, but he said no more.

Gull Moler frowned as he looked from man to man. They were blind stinking drunk, the lot of them. What did they know about women and women's ages? With a sniff he judged fitting to his position as owner-proprietor, Gull squeezed his well-fed body between Burdale Ruff's and Clyve Wheat's chairs and began rounding up the empty tankards, pitchers, and serving bowls sitting on the table.

Burdale Ruff caught his arm as he withdrew. "Taken a fancy to our Maggy, have ye, Gull?"

Having been owner and sole proprietor of Drover Jack's for fourteen years, Gull Moler was well accustomed to drunks and drunken talk. Experience told him the best way to deal with a man who was overpotted and overopinionated was to purse your lips in deep thought and then proclaim loudly, "Aye! You might well be right." Nothing took the fight from a man like agreement. Yet in this instance Gull could not bring himself to agree. Not about Maggy. It just wasn't right.

He cleared his throat. "Maggy's a decent woman, Burdale Ruff. Keeps herself to herself. I won't have you upsetting her with drunken comments and low talk." As he spoke, Gull tried to keep his voice low, but as always happened in taverns when conflict between men erupted, wind of it passed from patron to patron like the scent of a good pork pie. By the time he'd finished his last sentence, he was speaking in a silent room. Gull was suddenly aware he was hot. The three dozen patrons of Drover Jack's, many of them still wet and steaming from exposure to the storm that raged outside, waited to see what Burdale Ruff would do.

Burdale Ruff was not the largest man in the Three Villages—that honor went to dim-witted Brod Haunch, who broke rocks for a living—but by far he was the most feared. He was an unpredictable drunk: the worst kind. He could switch from jest to threat in less time than it took to draw a pint. Gull could feel Burdale's big, sausage-shaped fingers pressing into his arm. The eweman's small eyes shrank to pinpoints, and suddenly he did not look drunk. Without releasing his grip on Gull's arm, he kicked out the table to give himself space to stand.

Gull spared a thought for the table legs; they would need to be sanded then polished. Burdale Ruff's wet, peaty-smelling breath brushed Gull's cheeks. The knuckles on Burdale's free hands cracked one by one as he curled a fist.

Gull feared broken chairs and broken tables. Blood on his fine oak floor. Bent pewter. Spilled beer. Patrons who might leave without paying full due. It was only as Burdale Ruff's right arm—muscled like a bull's throat from the machinelike action of shearing sheep—made the small retraction necessary for a big punch that it occurred to Gull Moler to fear for himself.

He closed his eyes. Prayed to the spirits of tavernkeepers past to save his chairs, his tankards, his hide.

With eyes closed he did not see what happened next. Footsteps tapped across the wood floor, their rhythm coming to an abrupt end with a woman's cry of pain. A chair toppled with a mighty crack. A clamor of noise followed as metal tankards bounced off tables and hard objects dropped to the floor. Clyve Wheat hissed loudly, "Damn it!"

Gull risked opening his eyes. Maggy Sea stood to the side of him, bending over to rub her ankle, an empty tray pressed to her chest. "Forgive me, gentle sirs," she said in her most golden-toned voice. "I twisted my ankle on Farmer's Lane this morning. I never thought it would betray me tonight."

Gull followed her gaze to where Clyve Wheat and Silas Craw sat at Burdale Ruff's table, soaked to their skins and dripping ale. Their hair was plastered to their heads, their eweman's mustaches dangled over their lips like limp bits of rope, and puddles were forming where their elbows touched table wood. Gull blinked in astonishment. Maggy Sea had flung a whole tray's worth of beer at them. Miraculously, it would occur to him only later, without spilling one drop on Burdale Ruff.

Gull's attention snapped back to Burdale as a queer puff of sound exited the eweman's lips. Burdale was not looking at Gull. Burdale was looking at his two drinking companions. His fist was still clenched, but there was air between his fingers. For one frozen moment all was still. None of the thirty-six patrons in the tavern moved or spoke. Burdale Ruff stood, breathed, deliberated.

Then laughed. It was like watching a volcano erupt. Burdale's large mouth flew open, his nostrils flared, his head came back, and a sound like rocks exploding from a summit came forth from his lips. Most importantly to Gull, he released his grip on Gull's arm and slapped his fist on his own large belly as he rocked back and forth in merriment. Within seconds everyone in the tavern was laughing. Tears came to one man's eyes. Another laughed until he choked, and another still fell under the table, where he laughed until his wife put her boot to his throat.

Gull Moler never laughed at customers; it wasn't good for business. Instead he frowned at the puddles of ale on the table and floor, while attempting to work out his losses. For some reason, though, the sums that usually came so easily to him got muddled in his head, and all he could think of was Burdale Ruff's fist.

Maggy Sea wasn't laughing, either. She had put down her tray and was now, very discreetly, mopping up the mess. In the ten days she had worked at Drover Jack's, Gull had never known her to spill as much as a thimble's worth of ale. Now this. Gull looked at her more sharply. Had she done it on purpose to divert Burdale Ruff's attention?

"Aye! Maggy," said Burdale Ruff. "Let me give ye a hand with that. You need to rest that ankle. I was on Farmer's Lane myself two days back, and it's as potholed as my father's arse. It's a wonder you didn't break a leg."

Gull Moler watched in astonishment as Burdale Ruff bent down on all fours and began collecting the pewter tankards that had rolled to the floor. The small speech he had made marked the end of the entertainment, and patrons turned back to their own tables with the swiftness of rats bailing ship. Gull, suddenly realizing he had been standing and staring for far too long, shook himself and headed to the back to fetch towels.

Ten days Maggy Sea had been here. Ten days without a single fight. Business had never been better or run smoother. The beer taps were clean enough to pump mother's milk. The oak floor shone like a serving platter, and the wick oil in the lanterns had been forced through a wire cloth so fine that it burned almost entirely free of smoke. All Maggy's doing. She had improved the quality of food served, rising before dawn each day to cook fresh beans, pea and bacon soup, and lamb shanks crusted with mint—she even baked her own bread! She had cleaned and varnished the Drover Jack's

sign, unclogged the storm drains, located an old and myste-
rious leak in the roof and mended it with cordage as a sailor
would a ship, and even taken to distilling the barrel dregs
and making a rough but surprisingly palatable wheat liquor
from them that she had christened Moler's Brew. All in all
the woman was a wonder.

Why then did Gull feel an itch of unease as he took the
warm towels from the kettle and turned to face the tavern
once more?

She was so quiet; that was the thing. The words she had
spoken just now to Clyve Wheat and Silas Craw were the
most she'd said all night. And then there was the queer business of her appearance. Fancy Clyve Wheat calling her a
girl! Why, she was at least as old as Clyve Wheat's mother
and very probably older than Gull himself. Or was she? It
was so very hard to tell.

Her plain face inspired no male admirers, but her skill at
hearth and beer keg was becoming something of a local
myth. It was already drawing patrons from the Ewe's Feet.
Good ones, mind. Men with trades. The kind who brought
their wives and elder daughters with them and always paid in
coin there and then.

Gull Moler only had to look around his tavern to see the
way things were changing for the better. Maggy was a trea-
sure. Just tonight she'd stopped a fight that had threatened not
only his tables and chairs, but his own good health as well.
And looking down upon the puddles of spilled ale, Gull saw
that it was yellow-oat: the least expensive brew that Drover
Jack's offered. Unease forgotten, Gull congratulated his own
good luck. Maggy Sea even spilled ale with good sense!

As he handed over warm towels to Clyve Wheat and Silas
Craw, he noticed that Maggy was speaking to a patron who
had just walked through the door. The fact that it was clearly
Maggy who was doing the talking, not the newcomer, took
Gull by surprise. A small twinge of possessiveness bent
muscles in his chest as he watched Maggy's lip graze the
newcomer's ear.

A hand came down upon Gull's shoulder with considerable force. "Gull! Friends, eh? I canna say what came over
me, great fool that I am. I wouldna hit ye, ye know that. And

if I had, I surely would've missed." Burdale Ruff stepped into Gull's line of vision, grinning like a charming and very naughty child. He pressed coins into Gull's hand. "For beer lost, my friend. Better that than friendship, eh?"

Gull pulled himself together. Burdale Ruff was a trouble-maker, yet where he drank all the other ewemen in the Three Villages drank, too. Gull made a show of refusing the coins but ultimately accepted them: When a man offered you a gift it was an insult not to accept it. Gull knew this. He also knew that Burdale Ruff *would* have hit him and *would not* have missed. Yet he was owner-proprietor of Drover Jack's and as such could afford to bear no grudges. He made an effort. "Aye, Bear. You're a good man to think of my loss. Step over to the counter wi' me and let's share a dram of malt." The malt would cost him more than Burdale Ruff's coins, but that was the way of things in tavern life.

Only when he had filled two wooden thumb-cups with liquor did he remember Maggy and the man she had been speaking with. He glanced toward the door. The man was sit-ting with a crew. Now that his face was better situated to catch light, Gull recognized him as one of the patrons newly come from the Ewe's Feet. Thurlo Pike. Tradesman. A roofer, if Gull remembered rightly, one with fat pockets and a mouth to match. Gull struck cups with Burdale Ruff. Thurlo Pike was speaking with another of the Ewe's Feet crew, laughing loudly at a jest of his own making.

"That Thurlo Pike's in for a good season," Burdale Ruff said, following Gull's gaze.

Gull finished his malt before striking an expression of mild interest. "How's that, Bear?"

"Roofer, ain't he? What with the winds and late thaws we've been having around here, he'll be lining his pockets with master's gold. Near everyone's roof is rotted or missing tiles. Take me own roof—leaks like a woman on the rag. 'Cording to Silas, Thurlo's the only roofer in the Three Vil-lages who has a ladder tall enough to reach anything higher than an outhouse. And he's known for his tools. When his mother died and left him four gold pieces, he buried the poor woman in an apple crate and spent the money saved on a good set of hand chisels and a lathe. Never looked back since. 'Cept to watch for his mother's vengeful spirit, o' course."

Smiling in appreciation of the jest, Gull sat and waited for Burdale to finish his measure of malt. Idle tavern talk was exchanged, and much nodding and agreement passed between the two. Then, when Gull judged the mutual show of goodwill sufficient, he poured Burdale a second dram of malt and bade him sit and savor it while he rose and tended to business.

Burdale surprised Gull by catching his arm for the second time that night. "You're a good man, Gull Moler. And you run a good tavern. If I ever take a strike at you again, may the door of the dark house come tumbling down and the wralls ride out and take me."

Gull felt ice slide down his spine. Burdale's words were old ones, said by people of the Three Villages for generations. Gull did not know where they came from or what they meant, but to hear them sworn in oath in his tavern made him afraid. Words had power, everyone knew that, and once something was spoken it could not be unsaid.

It cost Gull much to hold his smile as he disengaged his arm from Burdale's grip. The malt rested as uneasy as sour vinegar upon his stomach, and even the knowledge that Burdale Ruff and his crew were more closely bound to Drover Jack's than ever before did little to repair his spirits.

When he came upon Maggy Sea by the soup kettle, where she was skimming the fat, he spoke more harshly than was his wont. "Maggy. Run upstairs and fetch me my wool coat. It's passing cold in here tonight."

Maggy Sea regarded him with eyes that might have been green or gray. With fingers that were never dirty despite the hard nature of her work, she rubbed the faintest sheen of sweat from her brow. Gull felt his cheeks color. Yet even though her actions demonstrated the warmth of the kitchen area, she simply nodded and said, "Aye. 'Tis a bite cold near the door."

*Where Thurlo Pike is sitting*, added Gull to himself with a second guilty flush. He looked up, half expecting Maggy Sea's knowing gaze to be resting on the Ewe's Feet roofer, but she had already turned for the stairs. Gull felt a tiny bit of relief. He did not like deception and knew quite well he was not good at it, yet his position as owner-proprietor often called for small lies. A man could not manage thirty-six drunken patrons on truth alone. Still. This was different. Gull knew that, yet it did not stop him from hastening toward Thurlo Pike the moment Maggy Sea's small neatly shod feet disappeared from view.

"Gentlemen! May I take the liberty of welcoming you to Drover Jack's on this bleak and stormy night." As Gull spoke, the small crew of Ewe's Feet regulars ceased speaking among themselves and turned to look at him. Gull smiled warmly and then continued. "I'm Gull Moler, owner-proprietor of this humble establishment, and if there's anything I can do to increase your comfort or your bellies' girth, speak up and let me know."

Thurlo Pike leaned back in his chair. "Aye! You can tell us where Drover Jack is!" A hard burst of laughter united the Ewe's Feet crew. Thurlo Pike, who was dressed in expensive fabric cheaply dyed and wore a beaver collar to warm his red and pimpled neck, smirked in satisfaction at his own wit.

Gull was well used to such teasing about the name of his establishment, yet for some reason he found it difficult to retain his normal good humor. "There never was a Drover Jack, gentlemen. 'Tis but a name my late departed wife picked on account of its favorable sound." *Back in the days when me and Peg still hoped of having a son and dreamt of naming the two the same.*

Thurlo Pike sucked air until his cheeks hollowed. "Let me get this settled. Your name's not Jack, and no offense, friend, but you look too well fed to be a drover. So what you're really saying is that there's no truth to the sign above your door." One of the Ewe's Feet crew snickered. Thurlo polished his fingernails on his beaver collar as he delivered his final sting. "How then can we be sure that when we ask for best dark stout we're getting it? And not last night's slops instead."

Gull had to force his teeth together to stop himself from crying, *"Outside!"* Jests about his tavern's name he could stand. Comments about his girth were something that pained him less with each passing year. But when someone brought into question his integrity as owner-proprietor of Drover

Jack's, it was like a dagger in his heart. He was not by nature a violent man, but for an instant he entertained the wild image of smashing Thurlo Pike in the teeth. Drover Jack's was an honest tavern, where a man could purchase an honest beer and an honest supper and take warmth from the hearth for free. And its owner-proprietor had never topped a barrel in his life. Now this roofer from the Ewe's Feet was sitting before him, as cocky as a trapper with a mink in his snare, suggesting just that.

Gull cleared his throat. "I'd never take it upon myself to thatch a roof, Thurlo Pike, and unless you fancy stoking my fire and cleaning my taps, then I suggest you leave the business of tavernkeeping to me."

A murmur of approval rose from the Ewe's Feet crew. The crewman who had snickered moments earlier—a small but muscular apprentice potter named Slip—said, "Aye, Thurlo. The man has the right of it."

Thurlo Pike said nothing. Gull watched as he finished his ale with slow insolence, wiped the foam from his lips, then stood. "I think I'll be heading back to the Ewe's Feet. At least there a man's free to make a jest without worry that the help may take offense." With that, he flicked over his pewter tankard, sending it rolling across the table toward Gull, and stalked out the door.

Gull stood and suffered the blast of wind and snow that accompanied the man's exit. What was wrong with him tonight? In less time than it took to bake a loaf of bread he'd nearly talked himself into two separate fights. It was all very upsetting. Very upsetting indeed. As a reflex action, Gull righted the upturned tankard and wiped away the spilled droplets with his sleeve.

"Don't mind him," said the apprentice potter, wagging his head toward the door. "He's not much loved wherever he goes. Dorri May over at the Ewe's Feet won't be thanking you for sending him back. Thought she'd got rid of him for the night, she did."

Gull made a noise.

"Besides, you wouldn't want him getting too friendly with your new girl. What with her being so highly spoke of and all. He'd only bring trouble to you both."

"Oh."

"Aye. Thurlo's got his eye on her all right. Boasting away, he was. Telling her how he's working all the local roofs, making enough money to buy himself a horse and cart. He mentioned one job up near the oldgrowth forest, you know, on the far side of Buck Stream. Said there's a house full of women up there. Last week's storms pulled part of their chimney down, and Thurlo's planning on making them pay through the nose, what with them being women and all."

Gull found his wits. "And Maggy was interested in this?"

The apprentice potter shrugged. Particles of clay dust sifted from his sleeves onto the table. "With women who can tell? I think she only asked the family's name out of politeness."

It was tavern talk then—a man bragging and a woman listening—the kind of thing that Gull Moler saw and heard every day of his life. He should have felt better for knowing it, but the memory of Maggy Sea's dry flinty teeth near Thurlo Pike's ear disturbed him in a way he had no words for. Gull suddenly wished the night were over. He was tired, and his legs felt shaky beneath him. He put a hand on the table to steady himself. Even now he found himself unable to set aside his owner-proprietor obligation of providing congenial conversation. A man, a *patron*, sat before him, having just said something that required a reply. Gull searched for a way to turn the conversation away from Maggy Sea. "And who might this family who lives in the woods be?"

The apprentice potter ran a gray and powdery hand across the table, wiping away his own dust. "I don't think Thurlo knew. To be honest, I think it upset him that Maggy asked a question he had no answer for—you know how some men are. Should have seen his chest get all bloated up as he tried to tell her something else of interest instead. To listen to him tell it, the womenfolk who work the farm are all of passing beauty, and with the husband away for the season on a whaler, the wife and eldest daughter are desperate for a man."

Gull's expression let the apprentice potter know what he thought of *that*. Reaching beyond the man, he collected more tankards in readiness to withdraw. "Well. Houseful of women or not, Thurlo Pike will be hard put to practice his trade in this weather. Burdale Ruff reckons the storms won't clear for a week."

"Aye. Well, that won't bother Thurlo. He told the women he was full pressed for the next five days. It's one of his tricks . . . makes himself seem busier and more in demand than he actually is. You know how these things go: *For an extra silver piece I'll fit you in between jobs.*"

Gull frowned. And this from the same man who had dared question the honesty of Drover Jack's! Moving away from the table, he raised his voice to address all the remaining Ewe's Feet crew. "Well, I'll be off now to tend the stove. Can't risk it burning out on a night like this. Nay, gentlemen. Keep your seats. I'll send Maggy with a round." Gull glanced at the empty cups in his hands, his expert eyes discerning the exact quality of ales drunk from the scum of froth around each rim. He made a quick calculation. "On the house."

That ensured him a fond farewell. It was such a relief to have patrons feeling nothing but goodwill toward him that Gull almost didn't care about the cost. Besides, only one of them had been drinking his best stout.

"Gull."

Gull turned and came face-to-face with Maggy Sea. She was so close, he could smell her. She smelled of ice and stone and other hard things.

"Your coat."

"Oh. Yes. Thank you, Maggy." For some reason Gull found himself fumbling. Maggy Sea was just so. . . . *intense.* That was the word. Her eyes seemed to focus more deeply than most, and she possessed no capacity for gaiety or humor. She smiled when conversation called for it, yet Gull had never heard her laugh.

Her deeply set eyes never left him for a moment as she handed over the coat. The material was as cool as if it had not been handled, merely picked straight up from the floor. "Should I see to the fire?" she asked, her teeth making little biting actions as she spoke.

Gull collected himself. "No, Maggy. See to the Ewe's

Feet crew over there. I've promised them a round on the house."

Maggy Sea nodded. "Gull, I'd like half a day to myself next week. I need to go to market and purchase some good winter boots. I should be back in time for the evening trade." Teeth, dry as fingernails, flashed in the firelight. "I'll expect my wages to be duly docked."

So put, Gull Moler had no choice but to consent.

# FORTY-NINE

## Ice Wolves

THE MULE-EARED HORSE COLLAPSED on the fifth day. Without a sharp knife or a stout length of rope, it was not going to be easy to destroy it.

Freezing winds blasted Raif's face as he stroked the animal's neck. The high mountain valley they had come to was choked with compacted ridges of ice. It was not a glacier, for the field was not deep or old enough to be named so, but the creak and rumble of grinding ice filled the air. Directly below, the Wolf River ran slow and narrow beneath a partially frozen crust. The sheets of ice floating upon its surface were as black as night, smoothed to glass by the continuous movements of river currents and wind. Overhead, the sky was white with suspended snow.

Raif met eyes with Ash. She sat with her body pressed against the gelding's naked belly, sharing what little warmth she had with the dying horse. The journey through the mountains had visibly weakened her, and she could not hold Raif's gaze for long without dropping her head and looking down. Raif searched his mind for some new way to help her, to keep her warm and protected and out of reach of the voices that hounded her. Yet there was nothing to do but deliver her swiftly to the Cavern of Black Ice.

Abruptly he bit on the tip of his mitt to remove it and then pulled the elkhide belt from his waist. With a twist of his wrist he tied a hard knot beneath the velvety flesh of the animal's chin, binding its jaw closed. The old horse jerked its head in protest, but the frozen snow beneath its flank was leeching away its will to fight, and it did not strain for long. Raif filled his fist with snow and began packing it around the gelding's nose. Gradually, over the course of many minutes, he blocked the creature's nostrils, running his scarred hands over the snow until meltwater glistened on the surface. Within seconds it hard-froze to ice.

The effort of drawing air through the ice pack proved too great for the failing horse, and it died within the quarter. Raif watched its huge dark eye turn dull and gelid, then rose to fetch his knife from his pack.

As his hand closed around the limewood hilt, he heard Ash's boots crunching snow at his back. "No, Raif. Don't butcher him. Not with that dull knife. Not like that."

Raif turned to face her. "Look away. I have not made a kill in three days. We have no food save for a few berries and a scrap of smoked meat."

*"Please."* The light in Ash's eyes wavered as she spoke, and for a moment he was reminded sharply of the dying horse.

Relaxing muscles in his hand, he let the knife drop. He had not intended to butcher the horse—his blade was not keen enough for that—but he had wanted to bleed the animal while it was still warm and collect its blood in a skin. Horse blood was rich in goodness and fat.

"Let's just leave him here. He was a good horse." Ash made a small motion with her hand. "It wouldn't be right to open him."

*No*, he thought. *We'll leave the wolves to do that.* Aloud he said, "We should be moving on. It'll be dark soon. I want to camp by the river tonight."

She looked at him for a moment, trying to decide if there was anger in his voice, then nodded slowly. "I'll fetch the blankets from the horse."

Raif spared no time wondering if she considered his actions cruel. It was too cold for thought. Any clansman would butcher a fallen animal in the same conditions. There was tragedy in eating one's own horse, but no shame.

Pulling his mitts over the hard chilblained flesh of his hands, he watched as Ash moved around the gelding. The voices might take her at any time. Twice in the night he'd had to shake her until bones in her neck cracked. It was becoming harder to wake her, and he lived in fear of the day when no amount of shaking would bring her back.

Stooping as he walked into the wind, he went to reclaim his belt from the horse. Ash was sitting in the snow. She had begun the work of unleashing the blankets but had stopped short of pulling them free. When he approached her she smiled like a sleepy child. Gently he helped her to stand. In a soft voice he bade her stamp her feet until he was done with the horse. His face betrayed no worry to her, yet he recognized the first symptoms of cold sickness. The smile she had given him was one of contentment. Left on her own, she would have curled up by the horse's corpse and slept.

Keeping an ear to the sound of her stamping feet, he rethreaded his belt and hung his antler tine in place.

Cold sickness could kill a man as surely as a fall through broken ice yet keep a smile on his face as it did so. *Sleep, it said. Rest for a bit, just here in this soft bank of snow, and I promise all your hurts will pass.* With the sickness upon him a man could swear to the Stone Gods that he was warm, believe it so completely that he loosened his collar and tugged down his hood. And all the while his heart was slowing like a failing clock and his feet were turning yellow with ice. "Cold sickness is like a whore with a knife," Gat Murdock was fond of saying. "Drugs you with sweet words and sweet feelings and then stabs you with her knife."

Raif stayed at Ash's side during the descent from the high meadow. He asked her questions about her life in Mask Fortress, the city itself, Penthero Iss. She was too tired to speak for long on any subject, yet he pressed her for details, forced her to remember, think. He considered laying one of the horse blankets over her back for extra warmth, but he wasn't sure she could bear the weight. Many times she slowed and asked to rest, yet he shook his head and told her, "Just a little more."

Whenever they came upon a wide expanse of snow, Raif tested its depth with his willow staff. One fall and they would both be done.

The ascent to the pass had been easy up to a point. The Wolf River retained walkable gravel banks for a fair portion of the way, until a hundred-foot wall of granite rose from its waters, sheer as the tallest cliff. They had been forced to climb for half a day to reach the top of the wind-carved bluff and take the pass. The west side of the pass was a breaking ground of split rock, frozen waterfalls, gravel beds, and drifted snow. Most surfaces were stippled with hoarfrost. All edges had been scoured by the wind.

Raif fought hard to keep his mind in the now. Ash was weaker than he; the sickness that poisoned her blood and robbed the color from her skin made her more susceptible to the altitude and the cold. But that did not mean he was immune. Several times he caught himself drifting away from the present on the wave of a collapsing thought. So far he had managed to pull himself back, but the fear of lethargy was present and real. He could not afford to let his mind drift.

Ash was what mattered. Keeping Ash safe.

A path of sorts, a game track used by horned sheep in high summer, wound down through the cliff to the river and the Storm Margin below. Through chinks in the clouds, Raif spotted the dark body of a bloodwood forest far to the south. The mighty red-barked trees were the tallest living things in the Territories, and they grew only in the wet, foggy slopes of the southern margin. Every summer men and women from the clanholds made the journey west and then south to purchase timber from the Cold Axes who lived in their high timber halls amid the trees. Croser was the only clan that had riverboats capable of hauling the raw timber upstream. All other clans paid freightage to the Master of Ille Glaive.

When Raif turned his gaze north, he saw nothing but white snow clouds. Mount Flood and the Hollow River were out there, yet he could not be sure where either of them lay. Clan knowledge ended here.

"I miss Angus," Ash said. "I wish he were here with us."

Raif dragged his hand over his face. Her words robbed a portion of his strength. "We've come so far without him. We'll manage the rest of the way."

"He will be all right, won't he?"

Raif forced himself to reassure her. How could she know that the mention of Angus' name cut him—she who had no kin?

The last hour of the descent was undertaken during a long bloody sunset that turned the surrounding mist pink and made west-facing snowbanks look like killing fields. The Wolf River ran dark and silent, unaffected by the failing light. The wind died and the air cooled, and the first wolf cries rose above the grinding of the ice. Raif wondered how long it would take the pack to find the horse.

He and Ash did not speak much after the words about Angus. They were a good two hundred feet below the high meadow, and the risk of cold and altitude sickness was now less, despite the drop in the temperature. Besides, the final descent was tricky, pitted with bog holes and wet ice, and concentrating on avoiding falls seemed mental exercise enough.

Raif watched Ash every second. Her cloak was weighted with frost, and the fur around her hood was stiff and white. Every so often she swayed with the wind, and Raif would reach over and steady her, disguising the gesture as a casual touch or a gentle reminder to stay on the path. Toward the end of the descent her legs began to buckle and she started missing steps, and it seemed natural to put his arm around her shoulder and take her weight as his own.

By the time they reached the river, ice smoke steaming off the surface made it difficult to see more than a few feet ahead. The air was colder than the black, oily water, and the river would steam through the night. Raif could not find the will to search for a proper campsite and settled upon the first bluff that afforded shelter from the wind. Ash slipped in and out of consciousness as he hacked at the resin-preserved remains of a frost-killed willow. The only thing that kept him from stopping what he was doing and tending her was the cold certainty that she needed heat from the fire more than any words of comfort from him.

It took forever for the fire to catch. Raif couldn't stop his hands from shaking as he cupped and blew on the pine needle kindling. When the fire finally took and bright little fingers of light shivered around the wood, he set snow to melt over the hottest part of the flames, then turned his attention to Ash. She had fallen fast asleep, bundled up in the roughest horse blanket, her hooded head resting against the smooth belly of a basalt boulder. He meant to wake her; she needed to drink, to eat, to take off her boots and beat the ice from her stockings and the inside of her collar and hood. Yet somehow he didn't. She was resting easy, and for the first time that day the muscles in her face were fully relaxed. Quietly he set about securing the camp for the night. The fire would warm her soon enough.

After a portion of the night had passed, he wrapped himself in the second blanket and slept.

When he woke Ash the next morning, she did not know who he was. Her eyes were as dull as gray clay. Skin around her mouth was shedding, and the yellowing of her flesh had spread to her tongue and gums.

Raif felt the fear rise within him. He shook her. *"Ash!"*

Her eyes flickered at the sound of her name. Raif fought the desire to shake her harder. Instead he pulled her up by her shoulders and spoke in a firm voice. "You must ready yourself to leave now. We have to make our way north, to Mount Flood."

Lips shrunk by dehydration mouthed the word, "Flood."

Raif's breath drained out of him. She was standing, that would have to be enough. Holding on to her with one hand, he reached back until his fingers found the warmth of the tin bowl that contained the snowmelt. "Drink this."

She took the bowl from him and drank it dry. Water spilled down her chin, but she didn't seem to notice and made no effort to wipe it away when she was done.

"Stay here while I roll the blankets and store my pack." Raif guided her back to the basalt boulder where she'd slept. He could feel the heat of her body through a double layer of wool. "If you need to relieve yourself, do it here in the warmth. . . ." Heat of a different kind burned his face. "I won't look."

He did not know if she understood him. Her eyes were focused somewhere else.

When all was done and the fire was kicked cold, its remains buried beneath the snow, he came for her again. She was sitting with her chin slumped against her chest. Her hands were dropped against her thighs, mitted fingers curled tight. He took her arm. "Ash. We've got to go now. Remember?"

It was like leading a ghost from the grave.

The day began like the last one had ended: with ice mist peeling off the river and the hidden sun turning everything red. The wind was sharp but not unbearable, breaking up grease ice on the river's surface and shifting drifts back and forth between the trees and raised ground. The air stank of snow. Raif kept an eye to the thick featureless clouds as he traveled: This was no time for a storm.

Ash walked, in a manner. She shivered uncontrollably, her body too weak to counter the reflex action, yet somehow she retained the will to keep moving. Raif wrapped an arm around her waist and took as much of her weight as he could, but it was her own determination that placed one foot in front of the other and made her walk.

Raif wondered how much she was aware of. He spoke to her, but she made no reply. He looked into her eyes, but the shadows he saw living there soon made him look away.

Within an hour of breaking camp, they parted company with the river that had led them this far. The great channel of black water headed west toward the sea, where choked ice in its channel formed a delta each spring. Raif was sorry to leave its banks, but his route took him northward, and there was no time to spare on sentiment for the river that was known throughout the clanholds as the Sum of All Streams.

Mist lifted over the course of the morning to reveal a landscape of black basalt spires, sheared cliffs, valleys pocked with frost boils and hummocks, floodways blocked with ice rubble, and dead and calcified pines sunk half into the ground like beached whales. No bloodwoods grew this far north, or if they did they were no longer recognizable as the sure and towering trees that were more highly valued than livestock in the clanholds. The trees that *did* grow were beaten to their knees by the wind, their trunks smooth as polished stone, their limbs webbed with mistletoe, whose pale fruits shone like opals and were poisonous to man.

Hard granite mountains rode the east and northern horizons, and Raif's gaze traveled from peak to peak, looking for the glacier-pressed form of Mount Flood. The wind stung tears from his eyes, and inside his gloves his hands hurt like all the hells. According to Angus and Heritas Cant, the Hollow River lay at the base of Mount Flood, fed each spring by a flow of snow and glacier melt so great that it broke mountains. Raif wasn't sure what state the river would be in now. Rivers fed by a single source often froze or ran dry by midwinter, but nothing was certain this far north. Sudden changes in the weather, hot springs, or swift currents could keep a river flowing through to spring.

Raif stripped off his gloves and massaged his hands. The cold made his eyes slow to change focus from the distant mountains to the nearness of his fingers. Weariness tugged him down. If he could just rest for a little while . . . *sleep* . . .

He snapped back with a start, suddenly aware that Ash's weight was no longer upon him. She had slid to the ground and was now kneeling in the snow. Raif cursed his own weakness. How could he have been stupid enough to close his eyes for even a moment? Anger made him rough with himself, and he thrust his gloves over fingers that were shadowed yellow and gray with early frostbite.

"Ash." His throat was raw as he spoke her name. Crouching, he touched flesh as cold and rigid as tent hide pegged out in a storm. A chill took him, and he placed a hand upon the back of her neck and drew her head against his. Her eyes were closed, and her throat muscles were pumping, and he smelled the sorcery upon her like liquor.

The coolness of her skin was slowly replaced with something else. Raif heard the murmur of voices. *Reach, mistresses,* they whispered. *So dark here, so cold. Reach.*

He could not help but pull back. Clan had no word for the sound of those voices. They were the hissings of insane things. What sort of men were they, these creatures who lived in the Blind? Heritas Cant had spoken about shadows and other vague things, but it seemed to Raif that he'd left too much unsaid. Shadows could not hold a sword and kill a man, yet why did he think these things could?

Raif let the thought go. He could not think about that now. Forcing numb hands to grapple with his pack, he searched for something to use as a gag. Wind howled, rushing under Ash's cloak and whipping it hard against her back. Suddenly rocks and trees grew shadows, gliding across the snow like living things. Ash's lips parted, and the power massed upon her tongue turned day into night.

*No.* Raif moved so quickly he crashed into her, sending them both falling back into the snow. He had a whole blanket in his hand, and he pushed what he could of it into her mouth, shoving the pool of blackness back. When he could no longer fit any more wool into her mouth, he spread his weight full out upon her, pinning her arms and legs.

Raif did not know how long they lay there, their bodies forming a cross in the snow. He knew only that his breath slowed and his body cooled, and when the first snowflakes fell upon his eyelids they roused him to a world where day and night had merged into the grayness of a false dawn. Ash's hood had slipped during the fall, and pale strands of hair blew around her face. Raif spoke her name, knowing that she would not respond yet unable to stop himself. He rolled off her, brushing ice crystals from his shoulders and elbows. Working cold cramps from his muscles, he fixed his pack to his back, jammed his willow staff under his belt, and settled his dead man's cloak in place. A lone wolf howled beyond the horizon.

When he was ready, Raif knelt in the snow and lifted Ash to his chest . . . then continued the journey north.

\* \* \*

MAGDALENA CROUCH WAITED in shadows the color of slate. Thurlo Pike had told her to meet him *inside* the Ewe's Feet, not outside in the storm-darkened street, but for reasons of her own she chose not to enter the tavern at this time. Besides, no one ever *told* the Crouching Maiden what to do.

She knew him from his footsteps. The man spent money on clothes, not shoes, and the uneven tread of mismatched

soles, poorly mended, gave him away before he turned into
the street. The maiden was ready for him with a soft word
sure to please: "Thurlo."

All men liked the sound of their own names, but some especially so. Thurlo Pike was one of the latter, and turned his
head so quickly that for a moment the pale skin around his
neck was bared, ready to take a knife. The maiden smacked
her lips so softly it sounded like a kiss. She waited a moment, for she knew nothing interested a man more than mystery, then stepped into the light. "Over here." A slim finger,
closely sheathed in leather so highly polished it looked wet,
beckoned him forth.

Thurlo Pike, roofer, joiner, and rogue, recognized Maggy
Sea, then frowned. "Get inside, Maggy. It's cold enough to
freeze arse hair."

Magdalena took a step forward, but only because she
wanted to. "I can't go in there, Thurlo. Gull would send me
packing if I did. You saw what he's like."

Though in fact all Thurlo Pike had seen of Gull Moler was
a man mildly affronted when the good name of his tavern
was brought into question, he was quick to nod his head.
Men always made monsters of their enemies; Magdalena
knew that. It was one of her tricks. Thurlo snorted air. "All
right. All right. But you'd better make this quick. If you had
balls swinging beneath that skirt of yours, not fresh air, you
wouldn't be so quick to do business outside on a day like
this."

The maiden smiled, but it did not reach her eyes. As the
roofer approached she moved farther back into the dark
space between buildings. The walls of the Ewe's Feet were
dry-laid flint, and it was a testament to the man who'd built
them that even without aid of mortar or sand he'd managed
to construct such flat, ice-resistant plains. Magdalena
Crouch appreciated good workmanship, no matter what the
trade. She continued edging back until Thurlo Pike's beaver
pelt mitts caught and held her arm.

"What you playing at? I'm not going no further than this."

Magdalena Crouch had killed many times, but only once
out of anger. It was something she wished never to do again.
With a quick, almost powerless movement, she moved her

arm toward the roofer's chest, causing his wrist to twist to such a degree that he was forced to let her go. After he released her, she continued flaying her arms in panic, as if unaware of what she had done. "Very well," she said. "Tell me your secrets here."

As she spoke, she glanced into the street. All was quiet. The hour of gray light that occurred before a storm was in some ways better than true darkness itself. Smugglers, thieves, prostitutes, unfaithful husbands, and procurers all came out at night. No one ventured out in a storm.

"Have you got the means?"

The maiden tapped a bulge in her loom-woven coat. "Tell me what you've found out."

Thurlo Pike's eyes ranged from the bulge, to the storm clouds, to Magdalena's face. He was dressed in a brown wool coat edged with beaver fur and fastened with pewter buckles. Sweat and dirt had caused the fur around the collar to clump and shed, and it looked as if a mangy cat had the roofer by the throat. "There's four of them all right. The mother. A daughter about sixteen—all plump and ready for splitting. 'Nother girl, young. No tits. Then the baby."

A single droplet of saliva wetted the dark desert of the maiden's mouth. "Did you catch their names?"

"Real close, they were. The mother bundled the children into a back room the moment she saw me coming. 'Course you know what children are. Specially young-uns. The baby starts crying for its mother, and the oldest daughter tries to hush it. Then the middle daughter starts up. Well, all the while I'm talking to the mother about stone struts and what backing she'd prefer on the flue, I'm listening to this wi' my second ear. Then I hear the middle daughter cry out as plain as day. Calls her sister Cassy. *You're hurting me, Cassy. Let me go!*" Thurlo Pike wagged his head. "Should have seen the mother's face. Couldn't wait to be rid of me. In her haste she agreed to two layers of baked brick on the stack. Two layers! That'll cost her a master's penny." The roofer showed his teeth. "And who's to say *what's* beneath that first layer of brick."

The maiden whispered the word, "Aye." She disliked petty crimes and the people who committed them. She was not the kind of woman who sought to justify her own actions. She was an assassin, and she knew her place in hell was assured. Yet she also knew that there was more honesty to be found in killing a man swiftly than in duping him and continuing to smile in his face. The world was full of Thurlo Pikes; Magdalena Crouch depended on it. Their greed made them easy to use.

She maintained eye contact with the roofer as she said, "Where exactly does this farmhouse lie?"

Thurlo Pike rubbed his thumb against his mitted fingers. "Means, Maggy. Means."

She took out the dogskin bag containing salt she had ground to a powder with her own hands. Pulling apart the drawstring, she showed the contents to the light. Thurlo's hand came out to grab it, but the maiden snatched it away. "Where's the farm?"

Thurlo's hazel eyes darkened. "How do I know it will do as you say?"

"How do I know you have told me the truth?"

Thurlo Pike had no answer to that. With a dissatisfied shrug, he gave the details of the farmhouse location. Magdalena watched his eyes as he spoke.

When he was done, she weighed the dogskin bag in her hand. "Follow me. A deal is a deal." Without waiting for his response she headed down the alleyway to the back of the building.

"Hey! Where d'you think you're off to? Give me that now." Thurlo snatched at her arm but found himself grabbing air instead.

The maiden continued walking, increasing her pace from step to step. This was the point where any other female assassin would use the promise of sex. A downcast glance, a lick of the lips, perhaps even a handful of soft flesh pressed into a waiting hand. *Let's do it out of sight. I'd be beaten if my father saw us.* Magdalena raked her tongue over teeth that were perfectly dry. Seduction was not her stock in trade. She said, "I have to show you how the drug works. I need water for that."

This statement intrigued him; she could tell from the subtle change in his breath. "Wait here, then. I'll get a pitcher from the Feet."

Magdalena shook her head. She was free of the building now, in what had once been the Ewe's Feet courtyard but was now no more than a paved square with broken-down walls, littered with beer kegs, iron hoops, chairs with missing legs, women's underthings, crates, and several dead crows. It stank of semen and sour ale. Magdalena headed for a break in the walls.

"Where you going? There's no damn water out there."

"Yes there is. In the pond, behind the basswoods."

"That pisshole! It'll be frozen hard as brass balls until spring."

"No it's not. I passed there along the way." The maiden hiked over the rubble of stone blocks that had once been the courtyard wall, forcing Thurlo to keep up with her if he wanted his voice heard.

"Why'd you be passing there?" Suspicion was clear in his voice.

"Children," she said. "I heard one of them crying as I crossed the road in front of the Feet. I ran to the back, quick as I could. They'd been playing on the pond when the ice cracked. One of them got a soaking."

"Brats!" Thurlo said with feeling.

The maiden was facing away from him, striking out toward the stand of stout-trunked basswoods that surrounded the pond, so he was unaware of the shift in the color of her eyes. There *were* no children, and if he had thought to look at the snow as he trod it, he would have seen that no footprints led to or from the courtyard and the pond. Magdalena had been at the pond an hour earlier, but she had come and gone from a different route. The ice pick and hammer she had used to break the ice were two items she had no wish to be seen with.

It had not been a pleasant job, making the first crack in the ice. She'd had to lie with her lower body on the bank and upper body over the ice as she'd hammered down the pick until it hit water. The pond was small, and its water was frozen to the depth of half a foot. Magdalena had blackened her

knuckles in the process. After the initial crack had been
made, she'd bellied her way back to the bank and worked on
the shore ice there. By the time she'd finished, the armpits of
her good widow's dress had become a pulp of wool and
sweat. After throwing the pick and hammer into the body of
open water she had created, she'd brushed the ice from her
coat and hood and left the way she'd come.

Preparation was *everything* to the Crouching Maiden.

"You'd best not be playing games with me, Maggy Sea."

Magdalena looked back. Thurlo Pike was crab-walking
down the slope, his arms held stubbornly at his sides. He did
not look happy. To make him feel better she feigned a stumble. "Come on. We're nearly there." For good measure she
tapped the dogskin bag.

He was out of breath and red-faced by the time he cleared
the trees. The maiden positioned herself on the bank of the
pond, directly in front of the break. Water exposed to the air
an hour earlier was already quickening with ice.

The roofer wiped his nose on his sleeve. "Right. Show me
how it's done then, and let's get the piss out of here before
the storm hits and blows that skirt of yours up around your
neck."

From a pouch sewn inside her coat, Magdalena produced
a soft leather cup. It did not hold water well, having being
waxed in haste and tarred only around the stitching, but that
mattered little to the maiden. She bent over the water and
scooped it full of the icy gray slush. As she stood she slipped
two other items from her coat. The first was the dogskin bag.
With a gloved finger she agitated the cup water. "See, you
have to get the water moving before you add the powder.
And it must be very cold. Like this." Magdalena did not look
up as she spoke, but every hair on her body was aware of the
roofer drawing closer to the bank. "Now, you must add only
enough powder to salt a roast. Too much and the women will
sleep like dead dogs for days."

"Will it harm 'em?"

Magdalena almost smiled. "No. But there are degrees of
sleep. You want the entire family insensible, yes?" Again,
she did not need to look at Thurlo Pike to feel the air he dis-
placed with his nod. "Then you have to be careful with the

dosage, for what's enough to lay a full-grown woman on her back might prove too much for a baby or a child. You wouldn't want the two young girls to sleep too long past the waking of their mother and elder sister."

Thurlo Pike grunted. He was so close now Magdalena could smell the excitement on his breath. "I want 'em all asleep until I'm finished and gone."

"One cup of this in the well before they wake and draw water for the day will be enough for that." Magdalena added a pinch of salt to the cup. "You should have at least three hours to do what you will. A man could uncover much hidden gold and precious stones in that time."

Thurlo shifted his weight. When he spoke his voice was low and tight. "Aye."

Magdalena's distaste for him deepened. Profit was not his motive here. He did not seek to drug the family in the woods to rob them, though he wouldn't be above poking around teakettles and forcing locks when he was done. He had seen a household of women and girls and now had rape on his mind. She had read the desire in him three nights ago in Drover Jack's, when he spoke with bright eyes and a mouth wetted by saliva and ale. All she had done was offer him the means: drugs to render the family senseless in exchange for information. Now the deal was nearly done, and Magdalena Crouch was eager to be parted from this man.

She raised the cup. "Taste it, so that you may know the strength of the drug."

Thurlo Pike thought himself no one's fool. "You taste it first."

The maiden was more than happy to do so. The taste of salt was not unpleasant to her, but she still made a face. "Here," she said, thrusting it toward him. "I didn't promise it would taste like mother's milk."

Thurlo Pike took the last step he would ever take. As he raised the cup to his lips and sniffed, the Crouching Maiden warmed her knife.

It was over in less than an instant: a blade thrust through the rib cage, lungs, and heart, in that order. Magdalena preferred to do her killing from behind. The back bled so much less

than the soft flesh of the abdomen and chest. The cup rolled
into the water with a *plop* as a gust of wind shook the basswoods and ruffled the roofer's collar. Magdalena held the
body upright until she felt the soft slump of unsouled flesh,
then yanked her knife free and let him go the way of the cup.
The hole she had made in the ice fit him perfectly, and he
slipped through to the cold black waters below. Within an
hour the surface would be completely refrozen, and an hour
after that the storm would dust it with snow. Thurlo Pike
wouldn't be found until spring.

Magdalena sincerely doubted he'd be missed.

Turning her back on the pond, she cleaned her knife, not
with water or snow, but with a soft rag moistened with tung
oil. She was particular about such things, and although her
knife was plainly wrought and of little value, she had no
wish to replace it. Its steel carried the sum of lives she had
taken.

With a small movement she removed the blade from sight
before her own reflection had chance to settle there and
catch her eye, then started up the slope. If she was lucky she
would arrive at Drover Jack's one step ahead of the storm.

* * *

THE WOLVES WERE DRAWN by the smell of sickness. Raif
heard them call to each other, long notes that wailed in the
darkness like the calls of children lost, then dropped away
with the wind. Once, when he had looked back, he had seen
one—high upon the basalt ridge, its eyes burning like blue
fire. An ice wolf.

They smelled Ash: the wrongness in her body, the blood
that had rolled from her nose to her mouth and had now
dried to a black crust on her lips. She stank of weakness to
them, like a lame elk, or an aging moose, or a horned sheep
riddled with lasp worms. The smell meant easy prey. Raif
tried not to think about it, tried to force every last bit of his
strength into carrying Ash across the barren, snow-dressed
valley he had entered. But the howling of the wolves took
something from him. The creatures hunted, and as Raif
stepped from a trench onto a shelf of hard rock and saw a

second pair of ice blue eyes watching from the shadows, he knew they were sizing their prey.

There was nothing for Raif to do but continue walking. "Wolves will not attack a full-grown man," Tem had said more times than Raif had fingers to count. "They know men from the scent they leave on carcasses and traps, and wolves learn quickly to pair this scent with death." Raif held on to these words as he trekked through the falling snow. Sometimes his lips moved as his mind repeated them.

Ash lay motionless against his chest, her breathing so shallow that it hardly seemed as if she were alive at all. Raif watched her face. Air continued to whiten as it left her mouth: *That* was what kept him moving. He could not tell how many hours he had walked or what sights he had seen since Ash fell unconscious. He knew only that he couldn't stop. The cold was something he no longer gave mind to. Within his gloves his hands were numb, their circulation slowed by the weight of Ash's body upon his arms and chest. Another time it would have mattered; he would have paused to wrap them in a second layer or tuck them in the warm pockets of flesh beneath his arms. Now he thought only of walking until he could walk no more.

He had broken First Oath and failed his brother. He would not break the second and fail Ash.

Exhaustion was something he could not give in to. He kept his spine rigid as he walked, his mind farming the pain it caused, using it to keep him awake. He could not feel his feet and could not recall the last time he had been aware of the slow-working coldness of snow around his boots. His lips were dry to the point that to stretch them in a smile would draw blood. Good thing he had nothing to smile about.

Good thing too that he had passed no tree or rock formation tall enough to supply south-facing shelter. He did not know what he would do when faced with the decision between continuing on and halting for the long night of darkness to come. Halting would help him, but it would not help Ash.

Raif thrust the thought from him. Glancing up, he saw snow clouds the color of furnace metal. *Good. There's still an hour of daylight left*. His mind was quick to allow the lie.

On he walked, forcing his body into the wind. He stumbled often, stepping into snowdrifts whose true depths were hidden by shadows or uneven ground or placing his weight on a prostrate tree only to find its dead bark turn beneath his feet. Ice was a constant danger. Clan had no knowledge of this valley, and the thick snow cover made reading the land for frozen streams, muskegs, and ponds near impossible. Sometimes Raif would spot a line of willows closely following a depression in the valley floor. *Stream*, he said to himself with little satisfaction. Knowing that was as good as knowing nothing at all. Mostly he kept to head ground: basalt plateaus, rocks, and moraines. The many small climbs were hard on his legs.

He had reached the midway point in the valley when he first heard the sound of wolf paws breaking snow. It was silvery dark now, with midnight blue shadows crouching behind pines and on the east side of rocks. Snow continued to fall, but a drop in the wind slowed its descent. Already newly settled flakes were hardening to ice. The wolf cracked this frozen crust as it padded downwind of Raif. Raif stiffened for an instant, then continued walking. The desire to increase his pace ran like heat through his body, and it cost him dear to control it. The massacre on the Bluddroad had taught him all he needed to know about predators and their prey. Like men, wolves preferred their victims on the run.

He could not resist glancing back. Three pairs of ice blue eyes glowed from the darkness behind him. Two other shadows moved far to his flank: long-legged, loping, their great shaggy necks thicker than their heads. Aware the eyes of their prey were upon them, the pack hesitated, drawing their forelegs beneath their bodies and lowering their heads. They wanted him to run.

Raif cracked his lips in a grim smile. He was so far past running, he doubted if he could manage to break into a trot if the devil himself were at his heels.

Slowly he brought his head forward and continued on. A crop of rocks, blunt as cornerstones and half-sunk into the snow, broke the line of the valley floor ahead. The tallest was perhaps as high as Raif's chest. It would do.

The pack began to close distance.

Raif thought of nothing but reaching the rocks. He was too exhausted to feel fear. His arms were numb to the elbows, and his thigh muscles ached with the kind of pain that only sleep could cure. As he neared the rocks, he prepared himself to face the pack. Slowly, over the course of many steps, he turned a half circle in the snow so that his back was against the rocks and his eyes met gazes with the pack. The wolves were close now, and Raif could see the black guard hairs that ringed their eyes and their muzzles and the snow white fleece of their throats. The hackles on the first wolf rose as Raif looked at it, and its ears dropped flat against its skull. The second wolf bared yellow teeth. Another growled, a long, vibrating rumble that skimmed the snow. All slowed . . . waiting to see what the pack leader would do.

Keeping his gaze fixed upon Pack Leader, Raif dropped slowly to his knees. The wolves were nervous, excited by the smell of blood and weakness, but fearful of the creature who would turn and look them in the eyes. Raif suspected fear would hold them only so long. Pack Leader's belly was narrow beneath its coat of silver fur, its cheeks sunk to the depth of its eyes. Watching it, Raif knew with cold certainty that his father was wrong. This one would attack a man.

The wind drove a flurry of snow into Raif's face as he lowered Ash's body to the ground. Her weight had been a part of him for so long it was as if he were peeling away his skin. She sank motionless into the foot-deep snow, her chest sinking to the lowest point. Raif risked glancing down to check that the bare skin of her nose and cheeks was not in contact with snow or ice. The pain in his freed arms made his eyes tear as he reached out to draw the hood around her face.

Pack Leader snarled, its blue eyes shrinking to slits. Lowering its neck, it pounced forward and snapped its jaws at the air.

Raif flinched. The wolves saw it, and the air thickened with their calls.

Rising, Raif reached back and pulled the willow staff from his belt. His hands felt huge and numb, and the wood hardly registered in his grip. It nearly rolled from his glove as he stepped over Ash's body and put himself between her and the pack.

The wolves were claiming space. Teeth bared, they charged forward, making swift imaginary strikes. The two wolves bringing up the rear were now only a short distance behind the lead three, and Raif saw dark patches of matted hair, a white ridge of scar tissue on a foreleg, and a torn and bloody snout.

Pack Leader ran at Raif. It was all snout and teeth and maw. Strings of saliva shivered between its fangs as its eyes winked out to darkness. Raif cursed the aching stiffness in his arms that made them move so slowly. He barely had time to draw the staff across his chest and no moment to brace for a blow. The heat of wolf breath pumped against his throat as Pack Leader charged at his belly. Raif wheeled back, trusting in the strength of his legs more than his arms. The wolf's teeth hit wood and the shock of impact caused both predator and prey to jump back.

The two guard wolves moved forward as Pack Leader shook its great head and edged back into the pack.

Raif barely had time to curse the dead flesh of his arms. A second animal came for him, launching its long gray snout at the unboned flesh at Raif's waist. Again Raif had no choice but to step back. His nostrils filled with the rangy aroma of wolf musk. Gagging, he forced his arms to raise the staff. The *clack* of teeth meeting wood split the night.

Angry at his own weakness, Raif forced the cold meat of his hands to buttress the staff. The second wolf retreated, and this time Raif made a show of chasing after it, sending every wolf except Pack Leader scampering back.

*Kill an army for me, Raif Sevrance.* Raif's jaw tightened. What was one wolf compared to that?

He made his stand twenty paces from the rocks. Stripping off his gloves, he bared hands mottled blue and yellow to the night. Swiftly he closed his fingers in a new arrangement around the butt of the staff. All around him wolves' eyes burned with sliver blue light that looked borrowed from the moon. Raif had mind for only one pair. Pack Leader stood at the head of the formation, its snout bunched, its lips pulled back revealing the hard purple substance of its gums.

Raif dropped his gaze from its eyes to the muscled bow of its chest . . . and within an instant sighted its heart. Big as a man's, but beating twice as quickly, it rested against the wolf's ribs: a fist of gristle and meat. Blood heat and blood stench mingled in Raif's mouth, and he had no way of knowing if they were his own or the wolf's. Pack Leader's heart was his, and it was all dancing after that.

Snarling, the wolf hunkered for an attack. Raif raised the butt of the staff high above his head. As the animal pounced he waited . . . *waited* . . . until the darkness at the center of its open maw was all that he could see. And then thrust the staff down its throat. Bone crunched. Breath hissed like steam. Blood shot from the cavity in a fine mist that wetted the upside of Raif's face. Down the staff went, down the gullet to the heart.

The wolf hung there, its paws no longer touching earth, spitted upon a branch of willow like a suckling pig ready for the hearth. Raif watched as the blue ice in its eyes melted and the curled bullwhip of its tail fell flat. *Watcher of the Dead*. Abruptly he threw the staff from him.

The wolf's body slumped into the snow, raising a cloud of white ice. Blood seeping from its mouth and the break in its chest fed the frost a meal of scarlet. The other wolves padded forward nervously, haunches low to the ground, nostrils twitching as they pulled knowledge from thin air. Raif ran at them, roaring.

It was enough to scatter the pack. One by one they turned and ran, leaving their leader to the cold embrace of death. None looked back.

Shivering, Raif turned. His strength was gone. He could not lift his feet free of the snow and had to force his way through it to return to Ash. Wolf blood drying on his face tightened like a mask as he approached her.

She was still, perfectly still. Her hood was twisted back behind her neck. Dark liquid rolled from her nose, ears, and mouth. Streams of it. And her head now rested in a pool of red ice.

Madness came swiftly to Raif. Thought shedded from him like old skin. Sense and understanding drained away as quickly as water down a slope, and all that was left was Ash, the darkness, and the faces of nine gods.

She could not die.

He would not let her.

With hands long past feeling, he plucked Drey's tine from his belt. The elk horn was as smooth as teeth, cold as the night itself. The silver cap popped softly as he flicked it free with his thumb. A thin stream of powder blew free with the wind, the color of ashes and stone. Turning the tine on its side, Raif walked a circle in the snow.

*Ganolith, Hammada, Ione, Loss, Uthred, Oban, Larannyde, Malweg, Behathmus*, Raif so named the Stone Gods. Powdered guidestone trailed behind him like a plume of dark smoke, scattering a line of charcoal upon the ice. The night deepened and hollowed like a pit, and Raif felt himself falling, falling, falling . . .

Circle completed, he stepped inside it. And howled like the wolf he had just slain.

# FIFTY

## *Far Riders and Old Men*

MAL NAYSAYER AND ARK VEINSPLITTER were riding in silence through a valley of smooth snow when they heard the call of the gods. The two warriors had known each other for so long that they had little need for talk. Ark could tell what the Naysayer was thinking from the slightest shrinking of his pale ice eyes. A moment before the cry, Ark had considered calling a halt, but Mal's eyes had warned him off. They were overlate as it was.

A dead raven had called them north. Meeda Longwalker, heartborn daughter of the Sull and mother of He Who Leads, had excavated the frozen carcass from the snow. By her reckoning it had been there eleven days . . . which made Mal Naysayer and Ark Veinsplitter eleven days out of time. Normally such considerations were nothing to Far Riders— they were Sull, and all men waited upon them—but a summons from the Listener was different. It carried the compulsion of blood and gods shared. Ice Trappers were Old Blood, like the Sull.

Ark Veinsplitter barely had time to thrust his hands into the ashes of the Heart Fire before the summons had come. Blood from his horse was still wet upon his letting knife, as He Who Leads had pointed his opal-tipped arrow north. "The Listener calls us north to speak of war and darkness. Staunch the wounds of your horses and ride forth. You speak in my voice and act in my image, and the sons and daughters of the Sull will fast from dawn to moonrise to mark the sacrifices you must make. May you find a bright moon to guide you."

Mal Naysayer and Ark Veinsplitter had drunk their horses' blood and left. Neither had kin to see them off, yet even so when they halted that first night on high ground above the Heart Fires, they found freshly fletched arrows in their cases of wolverine and bone, and new-roasted caribou tongues in the packs that rode their horses' rumps. Hungry as they were, they honored the fast and did not eat until the blind eye of the moon rose high above the trees.

They were Sull. The blood of their horses was enough.

Winter was too deeply set to head north and ride through the Want. The Want was a wasteland of frozen ground. Its pocked and broken earth bore the scars of ancient magic and ancient battles. And even the Sull's ancestral tellings of its terrain were sparsely worded in parts. The Want *was* Sull land. They had won and claimed it at the cost of a whole generation of warrior sons and daughters, yet still it remained an unknowable place. Things older than the Sull had lived there in the Time Before.

Instead the Far Riders had headed west through the clanholds, weaving a path through the territories of twelve separate clans, seen by few save old cragsmen, drovers, and clanswomen tending their traps. The Far Riders skirted the margins, traveling in the mists created by open waters, in the troughs left by dry streams, in the shadows raised by tree lines, and over ice, frozen marshes, and wetlands that no clan horse could dance. The clanholds had once been Sullholds, and the memories of the land still burned with cold fire in their blood.

The pass they had taken west through the Ranges was known to none save the Sull. The path slipped beneath the rock in places, and both Ark and Mal had to unmount. The tunnel walls had been chiseled smooth by Sull hands, and ravens and the moon in all its phases were drawn there in silver and midnight blue so dark it looked almost black. The Far Riders gave thanks to the stonecutters who had formed the tunnel and paid a toll of hair and blood.

That was in the final hour of daylight last night. This morning they had awakened from their cold camp on the west face of the mountain and made good pace to the Storm Margin below. The thick snows that were born in the Wrecking Sea and held within the margin by mountains that would allow none but the highest clouds to pass did little to slow them down. The blue and the gray were bred for white weather and their dams had birthed them upon ice. Even with a day of hard travel behind them, the two stallions and the packhorse showed no sign of tiring, and their heads were erect and alert.

Both stallions responded to the cold howl that seemed to crack the very substance of time. Ark's gray shook its head and fought the bit. Mal's blue lowered its ears so they touched the back of its skull and snorted a great cloud of air. Ark spoke a word to calm his stallion. All about, snow swirled in whirlwind forms, rising and flickering like white flames. The wind murmured softly through the lynx fur at Ark's ears and throat, and for the first time since journey's start the Far Rider felt fear.

He turned to face Mal. The Naysayer was a large man, made huge by the bulk of his furs. His face was hardened by white-weather travel and white-weather fights. He could use more weapons than any other living man, and his eyes were the color of ice. He had needed no word to calm his horse.

*You speak in my voice and act in my image. . . .* Ark Veinsplitter counted those words through his head like prayer beads as he decided what to say to his *hass*. The howl of a creature who was not a wolf had broken their journey, and every scar on his body where blood had been let ached with the knowledge of God.

The Naysayer waited, his pale eyes blinking only when

snowflakes touched them. He could be patient, this man whose anger when stirred was enough to stampede caribou herds and send entire villages inside to lock their doors.

Ark breathed deeply, then spoke. "What think you, Mal Naysayer? Should we continue our journey as if we have not heard the cry that halted us, and ride north sure in the knowledge that what we do is right in the eyes of moon and God?"

Mal Naysayer made a move that caused his lynx furs to ripple, a move that anyone else but Ark Veinsplitter might easily have mistaken for a shrug. He said just one word: "Nay."

It was enough to turn the two men west, and change the course of fate.

\* \* \*

SPYNIE ORRL, THE ANCIENT chief of Clan Orrl, faced the Dog Lord over the chief's table at Dhoone. A storm pushed clouds and snow against the Dhoonehouse's blue sandstone walls, but inside the chief's chamber all was still. The dogs were chained to their rat hooks by the hearth, but harsh words from Vaylo Bludd moments earlier had forestalled the normal hostilities they showed to uninvited guests.

The Dog Lord poured malt in silence, giving the amber-colored liquid the respect it was due. Two wood cups, plainly turned with neither handles nor embellishment, were filled to the exact same mark. Pushing the first in the Orrl chief's direction, Vaylo said, "What brings a Blackhail-sworn chief to Dhoone this night?"

Spynie Orrl made no response, save to retrieve his cup and drink. He was an old man, the oldest chief in the clanholds, and his body was all knots and bone. A few white hairs clung to his scalp, but apart from that he was bald in the way newborns were bald: eyebrowless, pink, and shiny. His eyes were dark and shrunken, but they were still as sharp as picks. Placing his wooden cup on the table, he nodded toward it. "Good malt. I've tasted Bludd liquor before now, and no offense to your malters and distillers, but this stuff must belong to the Dhoone."

"So you think ill of our Bludd's own brew?"

"Ill's not the word. Let's just say I wouldn't feed it to my sheep."

Vaylo Bludd snorted with laughter, slapping his hand on the table and stamping his booted feet. At the hearth, his dogs tugged nervously on their leashes. They had not heard their master laugh in months, and the sound disturbed them deeply. Vaylo reached for Spynie's cup. "Well, coming from an Orrlsman, I'll consider both myself and my clan reprimanded. Here. Let's drink to brewers with nimble fingers and distillers with surgeon's hands."

Spynie Orrl was more than happy to drink to that.

When the second cup had been drunk and an agreeable silence had settled between the two chiefs, Vaylo decided to try his hand again. He had been too arrogant the first time; he saw that now. This man before him might be a chief from a lesser clan, but he had lorded that clan for fifty years, and for that alone he demanded respect. "I hear there's trouble between you and Scarpe."

The Orrl chief nodded absently, the gooseflesh on his neck continuing to wobble after the movement stopped. "Aye. And trouble with Blackhail as well."

The Dog Lord knew this, but he also knew it was better to let a man tell his own story in his own words. So he nodded and said nothing and let the Orrl chief speak.

"It's Mace Blackhail. The Hail Wolf, they call him now. Any other man or woman in that clan would have been a better choice to lead it. His foster father was a good man. I say that because I knew and respected him, and named a grandson in his honor. But Mace Blackhail shares neither blood nor mettle with the man who fostered him from Scarpe. Mace is a Scarpeman. Yelma Scarpe is his mother's cousin. He can't help but favor her claims. When she came to him asking for his help against us, he should have done what Dagro always did. Told the sharp-toothed bitch he never so much as pissed between his war-sworn clans." Spynie Orrl wagged his ancient head. "Of course, Dagro would have used words sweeter than those. But then sweet words didn't save him in the end."

He looked at the Dog Lord sharply, and Vaylo got the distinct feeling that the old chief had long since guessed that

Clan Bludd wasn't responsible for Dagro Blackhail's death. Vaylo was too much of an old dog himself to allow his face to betray him, but his dogs picked up on the change in his scent and growled accordingly at Spynie Orrl.

The Orrl chief tipped his head in their direction. "Nice dogs. When you're done with them send them to me. I've got some sheep I'd like to scare hairless. Not to mention a few of my wife's kin." Before Vaylo had chance to react, Spynie leaned across the table and said, "Mace Blackhail has as good as declared war on our clan. Twelve Scarpemen were slain on our border, and it suited Yelma Scarpe to point her finger our way. She's always wanted that borderland. My hunters take down a hundred head of elk there each season. It's good ranging land, and Yelma Scarpe went running to Mace Blackhail to get it. You know how Scarpes are: She didn't want to fight. There's more muscles in their tongues than their guts. *We'll pardon you for the killing of our men if you relinquish the land they died on.*" Spynie Orrl's breath exploded from his mouth. "And Mace Blackhail thought this fair! *Take the land*, he said, quick as if it were his Stone God-given right to grant it. *I'll send a score of hammermen to keep the peace.*"

Vaylo frowned. No Bludd, Dhoone, or Blackhail chief had any business intervening in conflicts between their war-sworn clans.

Spynie Orrl continued, his head shaking softly as he spoke. "I had no choice but to defend my borders against Scarpe- and Hailsmen. Orrl against Blackhail, I never thought to see it in my lifetime. Before they rode north, I warned my axmen to slay only those men showing the colors and badges of Scarpe. But even then I knew I was giving an order that could not be obeyed. You cannot order men to cherry-pick their foe." He sighed heavily. "Two Hailsmen were slain along with a score of Scarpemen. All men of mine who venture outside the Orrlhold now risk death. I've lost two border patrols, and a party I sent east to treat with the Crab chief." There was a pause. "And I'm waiting on the return of my firstborn grandson and the five men who traveled west with him for the hunt."

The Dog Lord stood and turned his face toward his dogs. He

knew all about grandchildren and their loss. When he spoke he kept his voice hard. "Yet you torched the Scarpehouse."

"Aye. And I'd torch it again if I could. We are Orrl, we hunt our enemies and our game alike."

The Orrl boast. Vaylo had never thought much of it until now. Bending joints that creaked like old wood, Vaylo reached down to handle the dogs he had left. The wolf dog forced its large streamlined head into his hand, demanding to be scratched and tussled first. The burns on its ear and scalp were dry now, but the healed flesh was hard and raised, and fur would never grow there again. Not for the first time, Vaylo found himself thinking back to that last night in Ganmiddich. If the dogs had not been shackled and housed, they would have provided fair warning of the Blackhail attack. As it was, Vaylo had barely had time to assemble his men and raise an attack on Blackhail lines. Strom Carvo was dead, his skull smashed by a Blackhail hammer. Molo Bean was dead, his arms hacked off at the elbows, his face burned black by the flames that had rained from the sky. Others were gone. Good men, who all took pieces of the Dog Lord's heart to the Stone Halls beyond. Two of his dogs were burned beyond recognition. One made it as far as Withy before Vaylo broke its neck.

The sight of his two grandchildren, running toward him across the courtyard at Dhoone, nearly made his hurts go away. Cluff Drybannock had taken them north two days ahead of the raid, and they and Nan were safe. Drybone didn't say it but both he and the Dog Lord knew that if half the Bludd force hadn't been sent north from Ganmiddich to escort the children home, Blackhail would have won nothing but death that day.

"You know the Hail Wolf refused to relinquish control of the Ganmiddich roundhouse until the Crab forswore his oath to Dhoone, and gave word to Blackhail instead?" Spynie Orrl's dark eyes glinted like pieces of coal. Could he read thoughts? Vaylo wondered.

"I have heard that. 'Tis a bad business. Ganmiddich has been sworn to Dhoone for as long—"

"As Orrl's been sworn to Blackhail," Spynie finished for

him. The old clan chief met and held the Dog Lord's gaze. Silence in the room deepened and stretched, and Vaylo felt it press against each of his seventeen teeth.

Why had he come here, this chief from an enemy clan? Why had he risked the lives of eleven of his best men by riding east through territory that encompassed three separate warring clans? And then there was the greatest risk of all: presenting himself at the Dhoone border and demanding an audience with the Dog Lord himself. It took jaw to do that. Vaylo almost smiled to think of it. Spynie Orrl was as tough as a mountain goat.

"I haven't come here to offer my clan to Bludd," the Orrl chief said, once again snatching the thoughts straight from Vaylo's head. "Only a fool would do that. I've got Blackhail-sworn clans on two sides, and playing piggy-in-the-middle suits me about as much as a truss made of ice. No. I'll keep my oath to Blackhail as best I can. A thousand years of loyalty should not be easily set aside."

The look in Spynie's eyes left no doubt as to what he thought of oath breakers. Suddenly angry, the Dog Lord said, "Say what you came here for, Orrl chief. I will not be preached at. The Stone Gods bred war into us, and I would not be a clansman if I did not see an advantage and take it. Battle is in my blood."

Spynie Orrl was not ruffled in the slightest. Before he spoke he winked at the wolf dog. "Aye, I don't deny it. But I did stop to wonder what you saw when you reached the top of the Ganmiddich Tower and turned your gaze north. There have always been wars in the clanholds, but can you honestly say you have ever known or heard of one like this? Bludd against Dhoone, Blackhail against Bludd, war-sworn clans fighting amongst themselves. And now that the Hail Wolf has forced a Dhoone-sworn clan to turn, Blackhail will have to cross axes with Dhoone." The ancient pink-skinned clan chief clicked his tongue against the roof of his mouth. "There are outside forces at work here, Bludd chief. I know it. You know it. And the question that now remains is, Are you content to let it be?"

Vaylo Bludd breathed deeply. Knowing he needed a moment to think, he fished in his belt pouch and pulled out a chunk of chewing curd, tough and black as Nan could make it. As he pushed it into his mouth, he was aware of Spynie's eyes upon him. Vaylo hated scrutiny. "Why come to me with these words? Why not search out the Dhoone chief in exile, or the Hail Wolf himself?"

"You know why, Bludd chief. We are the oldest chiefs in the clanholds, you and I. Together we have close to ninety years of chiefdom between us, and that cannot be lightly said. We come from the two opposite ends of the clanholds, and today we meet here, in its heart.

"I know you're an ambitious man, and no one can fault you for that, but I wonder if you sleep well at night. You're cut from different timber than the Hail Wolf. Oh, I know you both fancy yourselves Lord of the Clans, but you've led Bludd for thirty-five years and he's led Blackhail for less than one. His ambition is blind. He has not learned what it is to be a chief in the true sense of the word, to put his clan, not himself, first. You *have*. No one stays chief for as long as you have without learning that sword strength alone is not enough." Spynie Orrl paused for a long moment, and when he spoke again he sounded tired and very old.

"The cities are planning to take the clanholds. They're behind this war, stirring the pot, keeping it on the boil until such a time that so many of our clansmen are dead, they can just hike straight over the Bitter Hills and shatter our guide-stones to dust. We're waging the war *for* them. And unless we shake ourselves out of this senseless slaying, we'll destroy ourselves for them, too."

Vaylo Bludd took breath to speak, but Spynie waved him to silence. The Orrl chief wasn't done yet.

"And there's one last thing for you to think on, Bludd chief, you whose clan boasts, *We are Clan Bludd, chosen by the Stone Gods to guard their borders. Death is our companion. A hard life long lived is our reward.* The Sull are preparing for war."

The words hung in the air like dragon smoke, heavy and black and scented with the fragrance of old myths. When the Dog Lord breathed he took them in. Deep inside his lungs they worked on him, stirring memories so old he wondered if they belonged to his father, or the man who had fathered him. Fear touched him like the swift nick of a knife. *No,* he told himself, quick to turn fear into anger. *Gullit Bludd passed no memories to me. He barely spoke five words to me in all the years I grew to manhood at his hearth.*

"How do you know this to be so?"

"I'm an old man. I do little these days but listen and watch."

It was no answer, but seeing the hardness in Spynie Orrl's eyes, Vaylo knew it was the best he was going to get. "Do they mean to make war on the cities or the clanholds?"

The Orrl chief raised the ridges of pink skin where his eyebrows had once grown. "They're Sull. Who's to say who or what they will fight?"

Again, fear pricked at Vaylo's neck. "Are you playing games with me, old man?"

"Perhaps if you had wintered at your own roundhouse and not blue Dhoone's, you might have seen the signs yourself."

Vaylo spat his wad of curd onto the floor. "Damn you, Orrl chief. Speak plainly. If you know more, *say it!*"

"I know only that while the clans are busy butchering themselves, the Sull are cleansing and fasting and growing their proudlocks for war. Five nights back one of my cragsmen saw two Far Riders passing west. The week before that an Ille Glaive trader came and purchased all my stocks of opal and jet. Opal and jet. Moon and night sky. The Sull use both in their bows." Spynie Orrl let out a thin breath as he waited for the Dog Lord to meet his eyes. "Tell me, Bludd chief, have you ever wondered what your clan boast means?"

The question disturbed Vaylo deeply. He said nothing rather than speak a lie.

Spynie Orrl watched the Dog Lord's face for a long moment, his eyes pulling, *pulling,* at Vaylo's thoughts. Abruptly he stood. "It's time I started my journey back. Send for my escort. I trust you *didn't* order their slaying. It would be quite an inconvenience to me to have to war against Bludd as well as Blackhail and Scarpe."

Vaylo did not take the bait. Unease was too deep upon him. "They have been treated as guests. Their weapons were ransomed but not removed from their sight."

"Aye. I thank you for that courtesy." Spynie Orrl reached the door. Standing, the Dog Lord towered over him, a bear beside a goat. "You must not let your hatred of the Hail Wolf poison you against Blackhail. There are good people in that clan. Raina Blackhail, Corbie Meese, Ballic the Red, Drey Sevrance—"

The word *Sevrance* was too much for Vaylo Bludd, and he shook his head until his braids whipped against his face. "Say no more, Orrl chief. You come close to crossing bounds."

Surprisingly, Spynie Orrl nodded. "Aye. Perhaps I do, but you cannot blame a man for the actions of his brother."

Vaylo growled. The noise was so low and terrible, the dogs shrank back in the hearth.

Spynie Orrl shrugged. "Think on what I have said, Bludd chief. When an old man travels through the darkness of four nights and three warring clans to see you, you'd be a fool to take note of what he said." With that the old man left.

It would be a full five days before Vaylo received word of his death.

\* \* \*

THE NAYSAYER SPOTTED the clansman first. He was crouching in the shelter of granite rocks, his back bent over a bundle of bloody rags. Ark named him an Orrlsman, as he was wearing the shifting, snow-colored cloak of a hunter from that clan. Well before they reached him, the two Far Riders dismounted and entered the ground he had claimed on foot.

Neither Mal nor Ark drew weapons. They were Far Riders, and both knew that while there was much to fear here, the clansman was unarmed and in no state to fight. Ark watched as the clansman became aware of them, as his head rose and his eyes long focused and his expression shifted between anger and fear.

Ark Veinsplitter, Son of the Sull and chosen Far Rider, was well used to being the object of fear. He had ridden these lands for twenty years, fought battles with men and beasts, borne messages across frozen seas, iron mountains, and desert floors baked as hard as glass: Fear was his due. What he didn't expect was his own fear, fluid as liquid mercury, rising in the back of his throat. The clansman's eyes pinned him with a look he would remember for always. And a question he would ask himself for the rest of his life murmured in his ears like the wind: *Have I done the will of the gods?*

The clansman stood to meet them, his cloak spreading in the wind, his bare hands yellow and frozen. Ark's whole being was so completely focused upon him, he nearly missed the carcass embedded in the snow. A full-grown wolf, big as a black bear, with two feet of willow jammed down its throat. "Heart-killed," said the Naysayer, the words dropping like stones from his mouth.

Ark closed his eyes and sent a prayer to the Sender of Storms. When he opened them he knew the world he lived in had changed. A clansman had heart-killed a wolf.

"Help her." The clansman spoke Common with a clannish lilt. As he spoke he jerked his right hand in the direction of the bloody rags. No greeting. No questions. No fear.

At Ark's side, Mal Naysayer reached for one of his wolverine-skin packs. With a tiny jolt of realization, Ark understood that the clansman was not alone and that the bloody bundle of rags he stood over was a person . . . a girl. And Mal meant to tend her, because that was the nature of Mal Naysayer. He would not turn his back on a cry for help.

Ark almost cried for him to stop. Too late he saw the pale circle of powder in the snow, too late he realized that blood should be let and a price paid *now*, not later, for entry into territory that had been marked by clannish gods. Transfixed, Ark Veinsplitter watched Mal Naysayer break the circle and drop to his knees by the girl. Already he had a sable blanket bunched in his hands, ready to place under her.

There was nothing for Ark to do but raise the tents and build a fire.

# FIFTY-ONE

## *Snow Ghosts*

EFFIE STAYED AWAKE UNTIL her eyes were sore, but there was still no sign of Drey. Anwyn Bird had sworn he would return from Ganmiddich today, but it was long past midnight now and the roundhouse was dark and creaking, and Bitty Shank was drawing the iron bar across the greatdoor and securing the pullstone in place.

"Hey, little one. You should go to bed. The storm's slowed Drey down, that's all. He'll be here in the morning, I promise." Bitty Shank tied greased rope as thick as his wrist around the brass claws that were sunk deep into the stonework on either side of the door. "I spoke to him myself only ten days ago. Said as soon as the Crab chief reclaims that tall green roundhouse of his, he'll be back to scrub your face and pull your hair."

Despite herself, Effie smiled. Bitty Shank was funny. Like all the Shanks, he had a shiny red face and pale hair. And he loved Drey. All the Shanks loved Drey.

Done with sealing the great roundhouse door, Bitty turned to look at Effie, who was sitting at the foot of the stairs. Bitty was the second youngest of the Shank boys, a yearman of two winters who'd lost one ear to a Bluddsman's sword and the tip of two fingers to the 'bite. His blond hair was already thinning, though he swore that since he'd lost his ear it had started growing back of its own accord. Effie didn't see it herself, but she never offered opinions unasked.

"So. Would m'lady care for an escort to her chamber?" Bitty flourished his arm in the air and then bowed with exaggerated grace. "Though I do say it myself, I have a sword forged for guarding maidens and the kind of walk that scatters rats."

Effie giggled. Part of her felt bad doing so, but Bitty *was* so very funny, and she was wound up so tightly inside with worry and fear that it sort of broke out on its own. Like wind. *That* thought made Effie giggle even more. All the while Bitty stood by the door, smiling and then laughing right back. It felt good to laugh. It banished the blindness for a while.

"Come on, little one. I best get you off to bed 'fore you wake Anwyn and get us both spoon-bled and kettle-whipped."

Effie didn't think such a thing as spoon-bleeding existed, and she knew for a fact that no amount of laughing in the entrance hall would rouse Anwyn, because the barrel-shaped matron slept in the game room at the rear of the building, guarding her butchered meat. Still, she stopped laughing and rose to her feet. Bitty Shank was a yearman, wounded in battle, and he deserved her respect.

He put out his good hand for her to take, but Effie ignored it and took his frostbitten one instead. Effie Sevrance was not squeamish. The two stubs, with their shiny pink flesh and smooth, nailless tips, were things of wonder to her. Bitty, first embarrassed and then pleased with her interest, demonstrated his range of movements as he led her downstairs. "See," he said, pausing a third of the way down to waggle his fingers in the light of a burning lunt. "I can still hold a halfsword and draw a full bow."

Effie nodded gravely: She was clan; she knew that no matter how casual his voice sounded, nothing mattered more.

Bitty was one of a dozen yearmen and sworn clansmen who made it their business to watch over Drey Sevrance's little sister while Drey was away from home. Effie knew what they were up to and guessed that Drey asked everyone he rode with to keep an eye on her when he was gone. Oh, they thought they were being as clever as grown men could be, always arranging to bump into her late at night when it was long past her bedtime, or checking in on her when they thought she was asleep, or sometimes even sleeping right outside her door and claiming drunkenness had made them pass out then and there.

The proud part of Effie knew she should resent it; she was nearly grown-up now, a full eight years of age, and certainly didn't need any old clansman watching over her. But ever since she'd lost her lore, only the sight of men such as Bitty,

Corbie Meese, Rory Cleet, and Bullhammer could make her feel safe inside.

She was blind without her lore. *Blind*.

No one had seen it or knew where it was. Anwyn Bird had ordered some of the older children to search the roundhouse from wet cell to dovecote; Raina Blackhail had addressed the clan and commanded the person who had taken it to drop it outside her door, no questions asked. Even Inigar Stoop had fallen down on his hands and knees and raked through the ash, rock dust, and gravel that had accumulated on the guidehouse floor. Losing one's lore was bad luck of the worst kind. Effie knew it. Inigar knew it, and that's why when the guide found nothing the first time he searched, he went back and searched again.

Trouble was, she hadn't known how much she relied upon the little ear-shaped chunk of granite until it was gone. Always when she was worried or afraid, she reached up and touched her lore. It didn't always show her things—not proper things, not things that she could make sense of—but it always made her *feel* something. In the past, when Drey was late home from scouting or raids, all she had to do was take her lore in her fist and *think* of him. As long as it didn't push, it meant he was safe. Bad things only happened with her knowledge . . . like Da, like Raina, like Cutty Moss. Now bad things could happen and she would know nothing at all.

Three loud thuds broke Effie's thoughts. "Open up! Open up! Clansmen wounded!" The call of returning war parties.

Effie looked at Bitty, and before she knew it the blond-haired yearman had grabbed her by the waist and swung her over his back. For the first time in her life Effie saw the ceiling above the staircase close up. Green-and-black mildew grew there, in the fuzzy bits between stones. "Drey and the Ganmiddich eleven are back!" Bitty cried as he raced up the stairs, Effie bouncing like an animal hide on his shoulders. "They're back! They're back!"

Effie wasn't sure what she felt about heights, but at that moment she supposed she wouldn't have minded if the entire Shank family had stood shoulder upon shoulder and balanced her right on top. Drey was back. *Drey*.

The hue and cry at the door roused the roundhouse, and all those clansfolk who had waited with Effie most of the night but given up and gone to bed before her suddenly came rushing into the hall. Effie hardly spared a thought for the river of clansmen descending from the Great Hearth, their leather-and-metal armor jouncing loose against their chests, or the miraculous appearance of Anwyn Bird, who was suddenly *there* at the top of the stairs, a tray of fried bread in her hands and a barrel of hearth-warmed ale at her feet.

Effie's mind was on the door. Bitty had set her down on two feet and then appointed her the most important task of unraveling the cords of rope that bound the bar securely in its iron cradle. Effie's heart swelled with pride as she worked. She was helping a yearman open the door. Even when Orwin Shank, Bitty's father, came to help with the pullstone, Bitty made space for Effie's hand upon it, and together the three of them dragged the quarter-ton weight of sandstone on its greased tracks across the floor.

Then the bar was raised and the door swung open, revealing its waxed and metal-studded exterior face to the hall, and there, standing in the doorway like dark gods, bodies steaming, iron armor blue with frost, mud-stained faces set into grim lines, were the first of the Ganmiddich eleven. They were the men who had held the Ganmiddich roundhouse while Mace Blackhail had ridden to treat with the Crab chief at Croser. Now the Crab was war-sworn to Blackhail and newly returned to his roundhouse and Drey and the eleven were back.

Like everyone in the clan, Effie had heard the story of how Raif had been taken at the tower, only to escape that same night by wounding Drey so deeply with Drey's own sword that the bleeding persisted for two days. Effie didn't waste a single moment believing it. She didn't need her lore to tell her that Raif would never raise a hand against Drey. *Ever.*

Corbie Meese was the first through the door. Effie called to him, "Where's Drey?" but her voice was small and Corbie's eyes were on his wife, Sarolyn, who was heavy with child and paler than either Anwyn or Raina liked, and the great dent-headed hammerman pushed past Effie without once glancing down. Mull Shank came next, and Effie meant to ask her question to him, but Orwin Shank stepped right in front of her, sweeping his eldest son in a hug so brutal, it almost looked as if they were fighting.

Effie stepped outside into the cold. She spied Cleg Trotter, son of crofter Paille Trotter, and headed toward him, clearing her throat. Bodies smelling of horses, leather, and frost drove against her, sweeping her sideways and then back. She lost sight of Cleg Trotter, and when she saw him again his father's arm was around his shoulder, and the two great bear-size men were talking head-to-head. There was no room for an eight-year-old girl to come between them.

All around, clansmen and clanswomen were pouring onto the court. A light snow was falling, and apart from the wedge of orange light spilling from the doorway, it was as dark as a winter night could be. Sounds of laughter and private whisperings filled Effie's ears, promises of lovemaking, special potions for easing chilblains, and favorite foods steaming on the hearth. To either side of her, bodies came together violently, mud and ice from boots and cloak tails dropping in heavy clods to the earth. Horses shook their heads and snorted streams of white mist into the air. Clansmen came from the stables to tend them, and soon it was impossible to tell the Ganmiddich eleven from any of the dozens of clansmen who had invaded the court.

"Drey?" Effie asked time and time again. "Drey?" No one heard, or if they did hear, they soon forgot when a loved one of their own came into sight.

Effie walked farther away from the roundhouse. Ahead she spied a lone clansman tending a horse. He was tall enough for Drey . . . it was so very difficult to tell in the dark. Shivering, she made her way toward him. By the time she got close enough to see his face, she knew it wasn't Drey. He was dressed in the gray leathers and moose felt of Bannen, and his braids were tied close to his head. Shivering, Effie changed course. He wasn't even a Hailsman. He wouldn't even know who Drey was.

Cold stole slowly over Effie's body, rising up from her feet like tidewater. Crossing her hands over her rib cage, she looked out over the graze. Her heart moved in her chest.

There. On the slope, a shadow within the shadows, a man-size shape standing watch. *Drey*.

She ran. Icy air roared against her cheeks as she scrambled over ground frozen to the hardness of stone. Her breath came in shallow bursts, her chest too tight to breathe deeply. The figure waited. It *waited*. It had to be Drey.

When she reached the bottom of the slope, the figure shuddered. Suddenly she saw he was dressed in white. She stopped. "Drey?" Even to her own ears her voice sounded weak and uncertain. In response, the wind carried the smell of resin to her nostrils, and with a cold shock she realized her mistake. The figure wasn't a man at all. It was a snow ghost, a pine sapling completely encased within fallen snow.

*Should have known*, she told herself harshly. *Any fool knows the difference between a snow ghost and a grown man.*

The snow ghost swayed and creaked with the wind, its middle branches beckoning obscenely. Effie felt tiny pinches of fear tighten the skin around her face. Quickly she turned away . . . and saw how far she had come.

The roundhouse was a monstrous black dome against a charcoal sky. The square of orange light that marked the door was no bigger than a speck in Effie's sights. As she stood and watched, it slimmed to a hairline, then disappeared completely. Shut. Effie's heartbeat increased. Purposely she kept her gaze on the roundhouse, her eyes searching for the stable block and more light. Only the stable doors faced *toward* the roundhouse, not away from it, and all she saw was a pale corona of light glowing around the stable door.

Effie started toward it. She tried not to look at the dark curves of the roundhouse or the land that spread out in all directions around it. But it was hard. There were no walls to block the view. Shadows surrounded her, not small shadows, not people shadows, but shadows of slopes and hills and great black bodies of trees. And it was cold, so cold.

"*Ah!*" Effie sucked in breath as something whipped across her cheek. She jumped out of its way, her eyes searching the darkness for monsters. In her mind she conjured up gray worms as big as men, with teeth like glass spikes and limbs made of the same wet substance as eyes. What she saw was a thin birch branch extending from the snow, a flag of red felt flying from its tip. It was one of Longhead's graze posts; once the snow reached a certain depth it was his only way of knowing where the graze ended and the court began.

Shaken, Effie quickened her pace.

She barely heard the first footsteps. The thin film of light that marked the stable was growing dimmer, and all of Effie's attention was upon it. They couldn't close the stable doors, too. *Not yet*. Panic swirled like thick fog in her head. Could she make it before they locked the doors if she ran? What if she fell in the snow? What if there were *things* lying beneath the snow, tree root things that curled around her ankles and trapped her? Her heart was beating so fast that it was many seconds before she realized that the soft crunching noise she kept hearing in between her footsteps wasn't the sound of her own rushing blood.

Slowly the realization dawned on her. Someone was walking behind her. All the exposed skin on Effie's face cooled. It wasn't Drey. He wouldn't do anything to scare her. No. It was a monster, or a cowlman, or Mace Blackhail come to . . .

*Crunch, crunch, crunch*. The footsteps quickened. Effie looked ahead at the roundhouse, but now the stable light had gone out and she had nowhere to head for. With a little cry, she broke into a run.

*Crunch, crunch, crunch*. The footsteps were right at her back. Effie imagined a monster dressed in cowlman's robes, with tree roots for fingers and Mace Blackhail's yellow eyes. Faster, she ran. *Faster*.

Snow was everywhere: in her hair, in her dress, in her boots. The monster's breath was hot on her scalp, his footsteps close enough to be her own. Effie was dizzy with fear, no longer paying any attention to where she ran. She heard the footsteps change rhythm, and then a hand jerked viciously at her hair. White pain exploded in Effie's scalp. Night turned to day and then back again as she felt herself being dragged down into the snow. Suddenly she didn't know which way was up or down. Her head hurt *so*.

". . . teach you, little bitch. Run crying to the roundhouse."

It took Effie a moment to realize that the monster was talking . . . *in a normal clansman's voice*. She twisted around and came face-to-face with Cutty Moss. No monster, just a clansman with one blue and one hazel eye.

"Bitch."

Effie tried pulling away from him, but he had wound a thick coil of her hair once around his wrist and held the length tightly in his hand. Feeling her resistance, he jerked her back. The pain made white dots of daytime dance before her eyes.

"Not got your little witch's stone this time, eh?" Cutty Moss tapped his throat. Effie's vision was fuzzy, but she saw enough to realize that the twine suspended there was the exact same reverse-twist cord she had spun to hold her lore. Cutty laughed softly, his mouth splitting into two red strips. "Didn't see that one coming, did yer?"

Effie didn't move. Cutty's lips were wet with spittle, his eyes two greasy stones that glittered on his face. The ties that held his braids had come undone, and his hair blew unchecked around his face in filthy kinks. Calmly he took out a knife. "Reckon a cowlman's going to get you. Right here in the snow." He jabbed the snow with its tip.

Quick as a flash the blade was at Effie's throat. Effie saw the trail of blue light it carved in the air, felt air puff against her skin, then something warm bit muscle in her neck. No pain, just a pinprick, then warmness. She jerked back, snapping her head away from the knife. Cutty swore. Pulling on her hair, he yanked her back down into the snow. Effie smelled the sour sweetness of his breath and the urine and man-stench on his clothes. Warm liquid trickled down her throat. Frightened more by the liquid and what it meant than by Cutty Moss, she bucked and struggled against the clansman, kicking up clouds of snow.

"Sevrance witch." Cutty Moss kept sticking her with his knife, and Effie felt the tip enter her cheek, her arm, her chest. Hot blood was everywhere, sliding across her teeth and the whites of her eyes. Still she struggled. She didn't want to think about what would happen if she stopped.

Cutty Moss shifted the grip on his knife so that he was holding it only with a finger and thumb, and then he slapped her face with what was left of his hand. *"Bitch!"*

At that moment Effie's feet found hard ground beneath

the snow. Hands slamming down on the packed white surface, she vaulted into the air. For one breathtaking moment she thought her hair was coming with her. Cutty had been so focused on slapping her that he had slackened his hold on her locks. Effie felt her hair unraveling from his wrist like wool from a reel. Then he yanked her back. This time Effie snapped *against* him, throwing the entire weight of her body in the opposite direction. The pain was like a thousand white-hot razors slicing her scalp. Her skin ripped, making a wet sucking sound like chicken skin pulled from a bird. She lost vision, but not balance. She lost all sense of direction, but no sense of purpose.

Blood running in a river down her scalp, she ran. And ran. And ran.

Cutty was only seconds behind her, but she was lighter in the snow than he and she was burning with animal fear. She heard him curse and grab at her, but now she had an instinct for keeping to deep snow where she could run and he would sink. It did not occur to her to scream; screaming was not something Effie Sevrance did. She needed all her breath to run and think.

Twice she felt Cutty's hands clutching at her hair and dress, but both times she was merciless with hair and fabric and helped him tear both from her by pulling violently away. Her scalp was on fire, raw flesh stinging in air cold enough to freeze breath. The hurts on other parts of her body hardly mattered; the blood seeping from the cuts warmed her skin.

When she rounded the far corner of the stable block, she saw a figure step out of the shadows. Even before her eyes could focus properly, a deeper part of her brain responded to the figure's shape—the sunken chest, the bony shoulders, the man-set jaw: Nellie Moss. The luntwoman ran toward her, calling words in some foul mother's tongue to her son. Effie understood few words, but she felt the luntwoman's sense of rage against a son who had failed to carry out his appointed task swiftly and with little fuss.

Effie ran wide of Nellie Moss and her clutching tar-blackened fingers, careful to keep to deep snow. As she glanced ahead into the landscape of shadows and open spaces, a shiver of recognition passed along her spine. She knew the profiles of those stone pines and the mound of packed earth behind them. She *knew* them, and suddenly the darkness made sense. Kicking her heels through the snow, she altered her course. She had a place to run to now.

Nellie Moss was lighter on her feet than her son, and Effie heard her gaining. A hand clutched at her collar, but Effie's hair and dress were slick with blood, and it was easy to pull away from an unclosed grip. Too tired to feel relief, she continued running. Her legs were weakening beneath her, and it was becoming difficult to think. She was so tired . . . her eyelids were as heavy as stones . . . she knew she had to run . . . but it was so very hard to think . . .

The howl and clamor of the shankshounds cut through the haze of Effie's thoughts like a light through a storm. Shaking herself, she saw the little dog cote straight ahead. The shankshounds knew she was coming. They *knew*. And they were guiding her home.

Tears prickled Effie's eyes. She heard the deep bass rumble of Darknose, the excited howls of Cally and Teeth, the angry snarl of Cat, the low roar of Old Scratch, and the bloodcurdling growl of Lady Bee—Lady Bee, who thought Effie was one of her pups.

Behind her, Effie heard Nellie Moss and her son hesitate. Their footstep rhythm wavered. Angry words were exchanged. Nellie Moss called her son foul names. Effie tried not to hear them, but the wind carried them straight to her ears. They stung like the coldest air in the middle of the night. Darknose began howling frantically, and suddenly she couldn't hear mother and son anymore. Footsteps quickened, and two sets of hands began grabbing at her dress and hair.

The shankshounds shrieked and wailed like madmen trapped in a burning house. The plank door of the little dog cote rattled and strained as the weight of six dogs came against it. Tears and blood rolled in pink streams down Effie's face as hands pulled her down into the snow. She tasted ice as Nellie Moss began hauling her back. The door was so close that she could see the grain of the heartwood and the orange rust on the latch. If only she could get her arm to work properly . . . if only it didn't hurt so. There was a *hole* at the top of her shoulder, a dark red pit where Cutty Moss had stuck her with his knife.

She threw the useless arm toward the door. Pain made her teeth come down upon her tongue. Nellie Moss' hands were around her waist, pulling, *pulling*. Effie's hand slid down the planks. Her fingers caught on the latch. Cutty Moss gripped her thighs. Effie stiffened her fingers around the latch, and as the clansman hauled her body through the snow, the metal bar jumped its cradle.

And the night of dogs began.

Dark beasts exploded from the cote, sleek nightmare forms, all snout and teeth and neck. Their growls shook the air like thunder, raising hair on Effie's back and neck. She heard terrible, terrible screams and the word *No* stretched over seconds until it ceased having meaning and became the sound of pure terror instead. A neck snapped with the wet crunch of a rotten log, fingers scratched at snow, something tore with a twisting-wrenching kind of sound, and then Effie knew no more.

Later, when it was over, Corbie Meese and others found her lying in the center of a killing ground of blood, bones, viscera, and human hair, protected by a circle of dogs. The dogs had licked her clean of blood and were keeping her broken body warm by pressing their bellies against it. Orwin Shank had to be roused from the Great Hearth, for the dogs would release her to no one but him, and it wasn't until many hours later that the first whisper of the word *witch* was heard.

## FIFTY-TWO

### *The Sull*

Drink this, Orrlsman. It will thicken your blood."

Raif heard the words, but he had just woken from a deep sleep and it took him a moment to understand them. The dark-haired warrior was cupping in his hands a brass bowl decorated with midnight blue enamel. Raif could not see what the contents were, only that they were hot enough to cause steam to rise above the rim. Pink steam. He shifted his position beneath the wolfskin blanket, then tested moving his right hand. Pain made him bare his teeth. The hand that emerged from the blanket was thickly swaddled in some kind of birdskin and greased with shale oil scented with a sharp, smoky fragrance he could not name. Underneath, his fingers felt swollen and stiff, and he was suddenly glad he could not see them. Frostbite was seldom pretty to look at.

It took him a while to shift his sore and aching body into a sitting position and even longer to align both hands in a position suitable for holding the enamel bowl. The Sull warrior waited in silence, his hard ice-tanned face giving nothing away. Raif kept his own face still when he took the cup, though its weight and heat caused him pain. In silence he drank the red liquid, realizing as he did so that horse blood was the main ingredient. Its taste was not unpleasant, but it was strangely spiced, and some of the blood had congealed in long strings that clung to his tongue and teeth. When he had finished, he placed the bowl into the Sull warrior's waiting hands and gave his thanks.

The warrior bowed his head. He had stripped off his outer clothes and was now dressed in fluid furs and soft midnight blue suedes inlaid with horn sliced so thinly, it rippled like dragon's scales. On first glance Raif had thought his hair braided, but now he saw that although it was held in thick strands by a series of opal and white metal rings, the hair itself was not woven in any way. Both men's features were somehow *different* from clannish features: their eye color more vivid, their lips and brows more finely shaped, and their cheekbones harder, with more obvious bone mass beneath.

The tent they had erected was made of hides and caribou felt, and it was lined with a dark fishskinlike substance that cut the wind dead. The floor was laid with an exquisitely woven carpet, showing the moon in all its phases against a field of night blue silk. A firestone formed the center of the tent, and although Raif had memories of seeing timber burned over the course of the past two nights, chunks of dark stone were now alight, burning with smokeless amethyst flames. Ash lay on the opposite side of the tent, her body entirely covered with white fox blankets, her face turned toward the wall. Her hair had been washed, and it now shone the exact same color of the white metal the Sull warriors hung in their hair and at their throats.

Raif made a small movement toward her. "How is she?"

The Sull warrior brought a hand to his chin, and as he did so the sleeve of his lynx coat fell back, revealing dozens of bloodletting scars on his forearm and wrist. *So they bleed themselves as well as their horses.* Raif wasn't sure if he was fascinated or disturbed.

"The one who sleeps grows stronger, Orrlsman. Today she woke and drank broth and asked words about you."

Raif saw no reason to correct the Sull warrior's assumption he was an Orrlsman. "When will she be able to get up?"

"You mean, when will she be able to travel?"

Raif nodded. The Sull warrior spoke Common with only the faintest hint of an accent to betray the fact that it was not his first-spoken language. The first night when they had ridden out of the darkness, seeming to Raif's eyes to have stepped straight from a legend of blood and war, they had spoken to each other in foreign tongue. Raif had never encountered Sull before in his life, yet he knew them for what they were the moment his eyes fell upon them. Sull. The warriors who rode the vast forests of the Boreal Sway, lived in cities built from icewood and cold hard milkstone, and carried arrowheads so fine and sharp, they could penetrate a man's brain through the orb of his eye. Their blades were a swordsman's dream, layered and folded and pale as ghosts, wrought from metals that fell from the stars. Clansmen whispered that their hard shimmering edges could take a man's soul as well as his life.

"It would depend upon where she must travel and why." The Sull warrior did not blink as he spoke. His letting scars glowed like broken veins in the amethyst light.

Raif had not yet decided how much to tell the Sull. "We travel north on a matter of urgency."

The Sull warrior nodded slowly, as if he had heard and understood a lot more than the small thing Raif had said. His sable-colored eyes glanced to the tent slit. "The Naysayer will have answers better than mine. He has tended the girl day and night. Her life is now a weight upon his own."

A speck of fear rested in Raif's chest. "What do you mean?"

"The Naysayer has spilt his own blood to save her."

"Why?"

"That is not my question to answer, Orrlsman." The warrior's voice tightened with something that might have been anger. He stood, the horn scales on his coat snapping like teeth. Although he was neither large nor tall like his companion, his presence filled the space of two men.

"Why did he let his blood?" Raif persisted, unable to shake off his unease.

The Sull warrior turned and looked at Raif as if he were some bit of dirt he had scraped from under his boot. "When we make sacrifice or pay toll, we settle in the highest currency we have. And nothing in this world of cold moons and sharp arrows comes dearer than Sull blood." Thrusting aside the tent slit, he stepped into the darkness beyond.

Raif breathed deeply. Beneath the bandages his hands felt like raw meat. Pain had made him twist and sweat in his blankets for two nights. It was almost as if his flesh had been burned, not frozen. In his dreams he envisaged tearing off the bandages and thrusting the scorched flesh in snow. The worst time had been sunset on the second night, when the Sull warrior called the Naysayer had stripped off the first set of bandages and cleaned the black flesh. Bits of tissue had come away in his cloth. Raif had looked down and not recognized the wet sticks of flesh as his fingers. When he'd asked the Sull warrior if he would lose any of them, the man had said simply, "Nay."

He'd used the same word later, in the middle of the night, when Ash had cried out in her sleep. Raif had watched as the great bear of a man had laid his hand on her head and said, "Nay, silver-haired one. No demons will reach you here."

The care the warrior had taken of Ash was beyond Raif's knowledge as a clansman. The Naysayer had taken dried blackroot and barberry leaves and made a hot tea from them, which he woke Ash every few hours to drink. When asked, he'd said that the tea would take the yellow poison from her blood. There had been tinctures made from the leafy twigs of mistletoe and the golden resin of a tree unknown to Raif. Her body had been cleaned and massaged with fragrant oils, the chilblains on her face washed with witch hazel, and the cuts and frost sores dressed with purified fox grease and native moss.

Raif slept through much of what the Naysayer had done. Exhaustion made it impossible for him to stay awake for long periods of time. By the time the two Sull warriors stepped into the circle he had drawn in the snow, it took everything he had to meet them standing. Raif smiled grimly at the memory. He was paying the cost of that clannish pride now.

It took him an unacceptable amount of time to struggle to his feet. He could not use his bandaged hands to lever his weight, so his legs were forced to do all the work. The more his muscles labored, the more determined he became to stand and walk. The Sull warriors had helped him and Ash, and he was grateful for that, but the thought of being dependent upon them for one moment longer than necessary stiffened his jaw. They were Sull. He was clan. For three thousand years they had shared borders, nothing else.

By the time he reached Ash, she was beginning to stir. He called her name softly, and it was enough to cause her eyes to open. "Raif."

He sent thanks to the Stone Gods . . . and the Sull gods, whose names he did not know. "Morning, sleepy."

She yawned a great big yawn, then smiled up at him apologetically. "Sorry. That's not very ladylike, is it?"

He didn't care. Whatever the Naysayer had done, it had worked. The skin on her face was now pink and translucent, and no sign of jaundice or swelling remained. He risked kneeling so he could be nearer to her. "How do you feel?"

"Sore. Tired." Her gaze had followed his hands as he knelt. "What happened?"

He shrugged. "I killed a wolf bare-handed."

She smiled nervously, unsure whether or not he was joking. Switching the subject, he said, "I need to ask the two Sull—"

"Sull?"

He nodded. "The two men who found us in the valley and took us in are Sull."

Absently Ash touched the moss patch on her cheek. "I didn't realize . . . I just felt warm hands touching me . . . voices asking me to drink." Her gray eyes suddenly took on the amethyst light from the fire. "How long have I . . ."

"We're two days north of the pass. On the morning of the second day you lost consciousness and I carried you until it grew dark."

"Carried me." Ash repeated the words in a small voice. "What happened then?"

Raif looked down. He hardly knew the answer to that himself and wasn't sure he really wanted to know. For the first time in days he felt for his lore. It was tucked deep beneath his wool shirt, the twine that held it half-rotted with sweat. Abruptly he tucked it away. As quickly as he could he told his story.

When he had finished, Ash said, "So you drew a guide circle and the two Sull warriors came?"

"The sound of the wolves may have drawn them."

"You don't believe that, do you?"

"I don't know what I believe anymore." His voice was harder than he meant it to be.

Ash looked at him for a long moment before saying, "How long will it take us to reach Mount Flood?"

He was grateful to her for changing the subject. He refused to think about what possible reasons the Stone Gods might have for protecting him. "That's what I meant to ask you. I may need to tell the Sull warriors where we're headed. There's a mountain peak to the north of here, a great blue thing choked with glaciers, and I'm pretty sure it's Mount Flood. But what I don't know is where the Hollow River lies in relation to the base. We could lose a week just searching for running water."

Ash thought for a while before answering. Raif could hear the rough catch of her breath, and he reminded himself that she was still very weak. Finally she said, "You trusted these men with both our lives. At any point over the past two days they could have caused us harm, but they didn't. I think they came because you summoned them, and both you and they know it, and somehow that binds them to you." Raif opened his mouth to protest, but she headed him off with a question. "Do you think the Stone Gods brought them here merely to bandage our wounds and send us on our way, like surgeons on a battlefield?"

Raif frowned. By speaking so, she was brushing too close to issues no clansman would ever dare to question. Stone Gods were not like the One God who watched over the city-holds: They did not concern themselves with the day-to-day lives of their followers. And they answered no small prayers. Suddenly aware of the pain in his hands, he said, "I will tell them only of our destination. Nothing more."

Ash nodded.

Raif shifted his body toward the fire and set his mind on finding warm food and liquid for her to take.

The lip of the firepit was ringed with stone carvings that were meant to be held in the hand. All were the color of the night sky or the moon. Objects carved from obsidian, opal, white mica, blue black iron, and rock crystal shot with silver had all collected so much heat from the fire that they were warm to the touch. The carvings were very old, and much of the detail had been lost, but their round edges and heavy weight made them pleasing to hold. Raif had watched as the smaller of the two Sull warriors had placed one carving in a copper bowl packed with snow, then set it aside until the carving's heat had rendered the snow liquid. He had not drunk the snowmelt, Raif recalled. Instead he had used it to moisten a cloth that both he and his companion had cleansed their hands with.

Raif returned the carvings to their place and reached down to take a small copper kettle from the fire's edge.

"The man who cared for me," Ash said, "he reminded me of one of the Bluddsmen."

"Cluff Drybannock." Raif could not keep the hardness from his voice. "He's a Trench-born bastard."

"So he's part Sull?"

Raif winced as his fingers dealt with the weight of the kettle. "Yes. Trenchlanders haven't called themselves Sull for centuries, but no matter how many children they sire with clan and city men, the Sull still protect them as their own."

"Why?"

"I'm not sure. Trenchlanders trade with the clans and the Mountain Cities. Sull don't; they trade only with Trenchlanders."

"So the Sull need the Trenchlanders for trade, and the Trenchlanders need the Sull for protection?"

Raif shrugged. "Something like that." As he spoke a giant pair of hands parted the tent flap and the warrior named Naysayer stepped into the tent in a flurry of wind and snow. The second warrior stepped after him, carrying an iced-up chunk of meat in his fist. While the Naysayer brushed ice from his hair and furs, the second warrior dropped the meat at Raif's feet.

"I cut the heart from the beast, Clansman. It is yours to eat."

Raif didn't have to look at it to know that it was Pack Leader's heart. He shook his head. "Clan do not eat wolf."

The two warriors exchanged glances. "So you do not heart-kill for meat?"

Realizing the object of discussion was no longer the wolf, but the man who had killed it, Raif said, "I did what I had to, to protect Ash and myself. If you want the carcass, take it. I have nothing else to offer you in payment."

The Sull warrior made no reply. After a moment he said, "The Naysayer believes you wear the cloak of a false clan. He says you are a Hailsman. Is this true?"

*So they have found the silver cap from Drey's tine.* Aloud Raif said, "I have no clan."

"Do you have no name also?"

"I am Raif Sevrance." *Watcher of the Dead.*

The Sull warrior nodded slowly. "I am Ark Veinsplitter, Son of the Sull and chosen Far Rider. My *hass* is Mal Naysayer, son and Far Rider also."

The two warriors stood still, awaiting a response. Raif hesitated, unsure what to do. It was Ash who broke the silence. "I am Ash March, Foundling, born in the shadow of Vaingate. I thank you, Ark Veinsplitter and Mal Naysayer, for the gifts of care and shelter you have given. As Raif said, we have no gifts to repay you, but know this: I shall carry the knowledge of Sull kindness with me always."

The expressions of the two Sull warriors did not alter as Ash spoke, but something within their eyes changed. The Naysayer was the first to come forward and bow to her, the lynx fur at his throat still shedding snow. Ark Veinsplitter watched his companion, the firelight casting fingers of shadow on his face, then came and bowed no less deeply. "You have spoken well, Ash March, Foundling. May the moon always light your way in darkness and your arrows always find the heart."

Food was cooked and eaten after that. Ark Veinsplitter pulled a partially butchered goat carcass in from the snow, while the Naysayer fed dead wood to the fire to make it hot enough for cooking. After he had gutted the carcass and presented Ash with the raw liver to strengthen her blood, Ark rubbed the meat with dark spices and sourwood and set it to roast. Within minutes the tent was filled with the fatty, briny aroma of roasted goat.

"No wolf?" Raif said when it was obvious that no other meat was to be added to the fire.

Ark Veinsplitter cracked his first smile. "Sull do not eat wolf, either. If we want tough meat we eat our saddles instead." He reached down and picked up Pack Leader's heart. The heat in the tent had thawed it, and now Raif could clearly see where the willow staff had split it in two. "Of course, the Naysayer has been known to chew on their bones. What say you, *hass*?"

"Wolf bones! Nay! You speak with false memories, Veinsplitter. Perhaps you have spilt too much blood today."

Laughing softly, Ark Veinsplitter slipped from the tent. After a moment Raif pulled on his cloak and followed him out.

The wind was shocking after the stillness of the tent. Snow had stopped falling, but dry powder blew close to the ground like shifting sand. Beneath his bandages, Raif felt his hands burning as if they had been doused in pure alcohol and set alight. He watched as the Sull warrior threw the wolf heart onto the ground and pushed it deep beneath the snow with the sole of his boot.

"That mountain ahead, the dark wall on the horizon, is it Mount Flood?"

If the Sull warrior was surprised he was not alone, he did not show it. "It is one name for it." He did not turn around as he spoke.

"And do you know from which face the Hollow River flows?"

Ark Veinsplitter's body stiffened. "I do."

Raif waited. Minutes passed, and still he waited, and finally the Sull warrior spoke.

"The Hollow River runs from the southwest face of Mount Flood. It is easily found by the dark mass of spruce that grow on its banks, and the glacier tongue that points down from the mountain toward it."

"And caverns. Do you know of any that lie close to the river?"

The Sull warrior breathed so softly his breath failed to whiten in the air. Raif saw that he had pulled on no gloves, yet he held his hands unclenched. Without a word he moved around the tent to a sheltered place where the three Sull horses had been stabled beneath a canvas of caribou hide stretched on poles. All three horses wore lamb's-wool blankets, and the metal on their bits and harnesses was wrapped with fleece. They were huge animals, with deep chests, thick coats, and feathered skirts around each hoof. Their intelligent, sculpted heads reminded Raif of Angus' bay.

Ark Veinsplitter rubbed the gray's nose. "The caverns lie beneath the river, not beside it."

The blue sniffed Raif, looking for contact or treats. With his hands bandaged and aching, Raif could offer neither, yet for some reason the horse chose to stay. "I don't understand."

"*Kith Masso*. The Hollow River. The Sull named it so."

"Why?"

Finally Ark Veinsplitter turned and looked at him, his ice-tanned hands on his horse's bridle. Strangely, he was smiling. "I had forgotten you were a clansman," he said. There was no malice in his words, just a deep and terrible sadness that made Raif afraid for all of them: the Sull warriors, Ash, himself.

Looking into Ark Veinsplitter's night-dark eyes, Raif knew he had not made a mistake by asking about the river and its caverns, but there was something here that he did not understand. When the Sull warrior spoke, each word seemed to come at a cost.

"*Kith Masso* is fed by the snow and glacier melt of Mount Flood. During the moons of spring it is a deep river, fast moving with water the color of sapphires and the scent of wildflowers and iron ore. Beneath later moons its waters slow and stiffen, and a great crust of ice forms upon the surface, while the river runs silent beneath. Then the headwaters freeze. There is no more snow or glacier melt, and the fountainhead of the spring that births the river becomes blocked with gravel and ice. So the waters of *Kith Masso* drain.

"This happens to a handful of other rivers in the Storm Margin, but all except *Kith Masso* are broad and shallow. Their ice crusts collapse, and their headwaters find ways round the ice. *Kith Masso* is different. It runs deep and narrow through a canyon of its own making. When its waters drain, its ice crust stays in place."

"The Hollow River." Raif could not keep the wonder from his voice.

"So we named it." The Sull warrior sounded tired now. The horn and metal rings in his hair clicked softly in the wind. "To reach the cavern you seek, you must break through the ice crust and walk along the riverbed toward the mountain. Soon you will come to a tributary that feeds the river to the west. Take it. It is the only entrance to the Cavern of Black Ice."

Ark Veinsplitter met eyes with Raif Sevrance. Snow whipped and swirled between them like clouds of tiny insects, each one delivering a sting of pure frost. Raif's heart was pounding in his chest. He wanted to ask the warrior how he had known their destination, but something warned him the answer was best left unsaid. *Later. There will be time for questions later, when Ash has visited the cavern and everything is done.*

"The cavern can only be reached in winter when the waters that flow around it have drained. You are fortunate to have come when you did, Raif Sevrance of No Clan." The tone of the warrior's voice didn't make Raif feel fortunate at all. Before he could speak, Ark said, "Come. We have stood too long under this cold, moonless sky. My scars ache like new wounds tonight."

Raif followed him into the tent. Mal Naysayer was spreading fresh goose grease on the snowburns on Ash's face. The Sull warrior with eyes the color of ice turned to look at his companion as he entered. An unspoken communication passed between the two, and Mal Naysayer stood and left Ash. Unlike Ark Veinsplitter, who had laid his weapons in arrangement around his sleeping mat, the Naysayer had a six-foot longsword couched in a harness at his back. Raif could not see the blade, but the hilt was cast from white metal, and its two-handed grip was wrapped with leather one shade lighter than black. The pommel was shaped like a raven's head.

Raif let his dead man's cloak slide to the floor. It was the first time he had seen a raven's likeness stamped on anything used by a man. All clans and cities had their badges, and many, like Croser and Spire Vanis, chose birds of prey, but none had claimed a raven for their own. Raif did not know what ravens meant in the Mountain Cities, but in the clanholds they meant just one thing: death. A ghost smile crossed Raif's face. Perhaps it wasn't such a bad thing to have on a sword after all.

"Raif Sevrance of No Clan, and Ash March, Foundling."

Raif looked up as Ark Veinsplitter addressed him. The two Sull warriors were standing behind the firepit, the light from the flames glancing off the down-facing planes of their faces. They had spoken briefly in their own tongue, but Raif's thoughts had been on Mal Naysayer's weapon, and he had paid scant attention to the rough catch of their voices. Now, though, he saw that they had been discussing him and Ash, and they had come to a decision on something.

Instinctively Raif crossed to Ash, and the two parties faced each other across the smoke and flames of the firepit.

Ark Veinsplitter spoke. "My *hass* and I have spoken of your journey. Like us, you travel north, and like us also, your path leads beneath the shadows of Mount Flood. The Naysayer tells me that the new moon which rides tomorrow brings storms. He says that those burned once by the frost will likely burn again. And he ill likes the thought of the Foundling treading snow. To this end we offer to travel with you and take our axes to *Kith Masso*'s ice."

"Ash March shall have my mount for the journey," said the Naysayer in a voice so deep it made the air in the tent vibrate.

"And Raif Sevrance shall have mine."

Raif looked from warrior to warrior, and finally to Ash. In the bright light of the wood fire her face looked paler and more drawn than before. It was too much to ask that she walk tomorrow; he knew that. But it didn't stop him from wishing that she would turn their offer down.

"What say you, Raif? You think me incapable of walking on my own two feet?" Although Ash made both her eyes and her face strong as she spoke, it wasn't nearly enough.

He loved that she had tried, though. Crouching down, he felt for her hand through the blanket. "I know how capable you are of walking, but it would ease my mind if you rode." He waited until she nodded before giving his answer to the Sull.

"So it is settled." Ark Veinsplitter's face was grim. "What say you, Naysayer? Is two days' hard travel enough to reach the *kith*?"

"Nay," Mal Naysayer said. "More like three."

## FIFTY-THREE

### *Marafice One Eye*

"SO THE HALFMAN IS GONE?"

"Yes, and God and the devil help him if he ever returns."

"Are you sure he murdered Hood?"

"Do not question me like one of your flunkies, Surlord. I know what I saw. Seven dead men cannot slit a live one's throat."

Penthero Iss studied the Protector General of the Rive Watch carefully as they walked side by side in the black limestone vault below the Cask. Something would have to be done about his eye. He had been back only one full day, yet already the whispers had started. Marafice One Eye, they called him now. It was not a sight to warm a mother's heart; the spur he had fallen on had punctured his left eyeball and raised great welts of flesh in a sunburst around the socket. Little doctoring had been done, and Iss suspected that the Knife had simply plucked out the deflated eyeball, pressed his fist into the cavity to stanch the bleeding, doused the entire thing with alcohol, and then got thoroughly and disgustingly drunk. Iss smiled faintly as he stepped into shadow. This would certainly add to the Knife's reputation. The Protector General of the Rive Watch might become a legend yet.

Marafice Eye had returned from Ganmiddich alone, telling a tale of how Asarhia had blasted his sept with sorcery in the slate fields below Ganmiddich Pass. All the sept had died, their spines snapped like sticks, their ribs smashed to pieces and driven like nails into their hearts. Marafice Eye claimed that although he was flung with equal force to the others, the soft body of one his brothers-in-the-watch broke his fall. Regrettably, that brother's boots had been kitted with steel spurs.

"I will not be sent on any more of your petty errands, Surlord. If you want that cursed daughter of yours brought back find another fool to do it."

Penthero Iss nodded. It was obvious now that no one could get near Asarhia until she reached. Better to wait until it was done and collect her then. Besides, he needed his Knife here, with him. "You know the Master of Ille Glaive has doubled the number of his Tear Guard, and has turned no Forsworn from his gates all winter?"

The Knife grunted. "He swells his numbers, as all the Mountain Cities do. The clanholds at war is a tempting target to one and all."

"No doubt. But if anyone is going to make first claim upon the southern clans, it will be the armies and grangelords of Spire Vanis. Not the Master of the City on the Lake."

"There is good land beyond the Bitter Hills. Swift rivers. Fine grazing. Roundhouses with proper battlements and defenses, not like those stone turds they build up north."

So the Knife had liked what he had seen of Ganmiddich. Perhaps the journey north hadn't been an utter failure after all. Penthero Iss came to a halt by a limestone column carved with the image of a three-headed warhorse impaled upon a spire and turned to look the Knife in his one remaining eye. "A dozen grangelords are massing armies as we speak. Lord of the Straw Granges, Lord of Almsgate, and the Lady of the East Granges and her son the Whitehog are just a few who have been calling their hideclads to arms. They see the time coming when they will ride north and claim portions of the clanholds for themselves."

"Lord of the Straw Granges! That fool couldn't piss out of his own bed, let alone lead an army north." Marafice Eye punched the column with the heel of his hand. "And as for that tub of lard Ballon Troak, who now styles himself Lord of Almsgate . . ." Words failed the Knife, and he punched the column again. "I'd sooner follow the bitch of the East Granges into battle. At least she knows how to ride a man then leave him for dead."

Penthero Iss smiled thinly. Marafice Eye's assessment of the three grangelords might be crude, but it was entirely true. He was clever in low ways, the Knife. It was easy to forget that. "Whatever their faults may be, meekness isn't one of them. They want land. All the grangelords do. They have sons and fosterlings and bastards and nephews, and the cityhold of Spire Vanis is hemmed in by mountains and barren rocks. North is the only way to expand. North, into those fat border clans."

Aware that his voice was growing louder, Iss worked to control it. The thick walls of the Blackvault created echoes, and broken bits of his own words floated back. "The world is about to change, Knife. Land will be won and lost. A thousand years ago Haldor Hews rode out with a warhost and claimed the ranging ground south of the Spill and all land west of the Skagway. A thousand years before that Theron Pengaron marched north across the Ranges and founded the city where we stand today. Now another thousand years have passed, and it's time to take more. War is coming, make no mistake about it. Houses and reputations will be made. *Men* will be made. Fortunes will be brought home and divided amongst brothers and kin. And the only question that really matters is, Will Spire Vanis move first to claim her portion, or will we wait until it's too late and let the Glaive, the Star, and the Vor take it all?"

Iss met eyes with Marafice Eye. "What say you, Knife? It's been a hundred years since an army rode forth from Spire Vanis. The grangelords will raise their own forces and carry their own banners, but one man alone must lead them." He stopped there, knowing he had said enough. It was always better to leave a man enough room to reason things out on his own.

Marafice Eye's face was hideous in the candlelight. His missing eye needed stitching, and weeks of white-weather travel had turned his skin to hide. Earlier Iss had detected a limp, and even now, as the Knife stood silent and still, he clearly favored his right leg. When he spoke his voice was harsh. "So you would give me an army, Surlord? Send me to wet-nurse the grangelords and their armies and claim land in the names of their soft-arsed sons?"

Iss shook his head. "You will ride at the head of all armies. First claims and first plunder will be yours."

"Not enough, Surlord. If I wanted land, don't you think I would have armed myself and taken some by now?"

"But what of your brothers-in-the-watch? Would they turn such an offer down? Clan land and clan plunder would mean riches to them."

*That* made him think. It wasn't as easy to turn down wealth for his sworn brothers as it was for himself. The Knife was deeply loyal to his men. Just this morning, the first thing he had done upon entering the fortress was walk to the Red Forge and tell his brothers-in-the-watch how he had lost eight of their men. Fool that he was, he had brought back all the dead men's weapons, and they had fired up the forge then and there. The mercury-treated metal was cooling even as they spoke. New swords had been cast. The refiring deepened the red taint and set the memories of brothers lost in steel. It was the closest the Rive Watch came to belief.

"Ganmiddich is fine land," Iss murmured, echoing the Knife's own words. "They say in spring the hunting is so good that a man just has to ride with his spear sticking out, and elk and deer simply run themselves upon the tip."

Marafice Eye snorted. Still, Iss could see the gleam of interest in his one blue eye. "Who would watch the city if the Rive Watch rode to war?"

Careful now, Iss reminded himself. "He who leads an army must also raise one Almstown must be smashed. Able bodies must be recruited and trained. Every man in this city who *can* fight must be made to do so. The grangelords can do only so much. They are known and feared only in their granges. You, Knife, are known from Wrathgate to Vaingate and the grangeholds beyond. You could raise an army and a safekeeping force single-handed."

"The Rive Watch has defended the city and the surlord for twelve hundred years."

"The Rive Watch was birthed in war. Thomas Mar forged the first red swords with the blood of his brothers-in-arms. When he and his last twelve men took them up, they wrested the northern passage from Ille Glaive."

Marafice Eye could not deny it. Nor could he deny that it was the Rive Watch who smashed the city of High Rood, slaying the settlers and masons who had come from the Soft Lands to build a rival to Spire Vanis one hundred leagues to the east. The Rive Watch rode forth when it suited them; both Iss and the Knife knew it. And the only question that now remained was, Would they ride forth with Marafice Eye come spring?

Iss needed them. The grangelords and their hideclads were not enough to take on the clans. Oh, they *thought* they were, with their swords of patterned steel and their horses bred as tough and ugly as moose stags, but the Surlord knew differently. Without a hard man behind them, they would crumble as easily as oatcakes in the hands of a child. "What say you, Knife? Will you lead the army north to crush the clans?"

"My men will be given first claim on all land?"

"And titles of holdlords as soon as roofs are raised over land held in their names."

The Knife stroked the dagger at his belt, his small lips pressed so tightly together that it hardly looked as if he had a mouth at all. "There is risk here, Surlord."

"Name what else you would have."

"Your title when you're dead and gone."

If the branch of candles lighting the Blackvault had been nearer to the two men, the Knife would have seen Iss' pupils shrink to specks. Always there was someone who wanted his place. It wasn't enough to be surlord, not when any man with land and power could arm himself and unman you. Here, in this very chamber, Connad Hews had been held captive for thirty days of his hundred-day rule. His brother Rannock had stormed the fortress to free him, but he'd come seven hours too late. Trant Gryphon had already put a broad-blade through his heart. Hews of the Hundred Days they called him now. And Penthero Iss could name a dozen other surlords who had ruled less than a year.

It was a thought that brought him no peace. Quietly he said, "No surlord can name his own successor; you know that as well as any man. I had to seize power from Borhis Horgo. If you want power, you must seize it yourself."

"Don't think I haven't thought about it, Surlord." Marafice Eye was suddenly close, his dead socket inches from Iss' face. "I have lost three septs to your daughter. Three septs. One eye. And the skin off my ankle and foot. There's witchery here, and there's more to come—I can smell it like a dog on a bitch. I know you, Penthero Iss, and I know you're clever enough to take the clanholds with or without me, but I also know your interest doesn't end with the clans. You have those pale, drowned-man's hands of yours in meals bloodier than clanmeat. And I don't want to find myself in a position where me and my men are sent forth to battle only to be abandoned when a brighter prize catches your eye."

He was so close to the truth, Iss wondered if losing an eye hadn't endowed him with second sight. Clanholds first, Sull second: That had always been the plan. Strike hard while their attention was diverted. Strike hard, claim land for Spire Vanis . . . and a crown for himself. Surlord wasn't enough. He hadn't come this far, pulled himself up from farmer's son to ruler, spent ten years as a grangelord's fosterling, put to work as a retainer rather than the kin that he was, then another twelve years in the Watch, working his way up, always up, until Borhis Horgo named him Protector General and made him his right hand, to have it all taken away from him by some usurper with a blade. He had worked too hard and planned too long for that.

Keeping his face still, he said, "You are crucial to me in all things, Knife. As I rise so do you."

"Name me as your successor."

"If I did it would mean nothing. A surlord must have the support of the Rive Watch *and* the grangelords. If I named you as my successor, the grangelords would laugh at both of us. 'Who do Iss and the Knife think they are,' they would say, 'the Spire King and his son?'"

"They say the Lord of Trance Vor has taken to calling himself the Vor King."

"Yes, and they also say his brain is addled with *ivysh* and he takes pleasure in little boys."

Marafice Eye sneered. "I want to be named, Surlord. It's my business if the grangelords laugh or plot death behind my back. Today they think of me only as your creature, your *Knife*. Name me as your successor, and before this war is over I'll make them think again."

Iss stepped back from Marafice Eye. He reeked of meat and horses, and he suddenly seemed dangerous in the way that wounded animals were. The journey home had taken eleven days. Eleven days alone with a blind and stinking eye and the memory of eight men's deaths. Iss shivered. He did not like this new and subtle Knife. What he proposed was unheard of—a Surlord naming his *own* successor—but Iss could understand the Knife's motives and even recognize the sense behind them.

Marafice Eye was nothing to the grangelords, a cutthroat with a red-tainted sword. He was not born to land as they were; he was a hog butcher's son who spoke with the words and accent of Hoargate. While grangelords' sons were learning swordplay in their wind-sheltered courtyards, Marafice Eye was learning to cut the hands off anyone who stole sausages or pork belly from the front of his father's shop. He had joined the Rive Watch when he was fourteen, after his father began to suspect that not all the thieves his son maimed had actually thieved. Marafice Eye would have their hands for just a *look*.

As far as Iss knew, the Knife had spent his first three years in the Watch being bullied in the usual brutal way. Perhaps it had done him some good: Iss did not know. What he *did* know was that by the time the Knife turned seventeen he had won himself the right to wear the red-tainted sword. Marafice Eye, a hog butcher's son from Hoargate, wearing the red alongside grangelords' bastards and third sons.

Iss had always assumed that the Knife had joined the Rive Watch thinking he would become one of the Lower Watch: those men who were bound without oaths and could not wear the red and patrolled only those parts of the city where no one but the poor and starving lived. Now Iss found himself wondering if ambition hadn't been within the Knife from the start.

As Protector General he had risen as high as any baseborn man could. Now, by publicly declaring his intent to become surlord, he sought to take the final step. Oh, he knew the grangelords would be incensed—they'd shake their well-manicured fists and swear they'd *never* accept a commoner as a surlord—but that wasn't really the point. Slowly he was going to get them accustomed to the idea. In five years' time what had once seemed so outrageous would have mellowed to plain fact: *So Marafice Eye wants to become surlord . . . well, even Iss himself thinks him fit for it.*

Iss breathed thinly. There was gain here, but danger also. *Your title when you're dead and gone*, the Knife had said. Yet would he be content to wait that long? It was easy to imagine him seizing control of Mask Fortress, sealing the Cask, and taking his surlord's life. The Rive Watch was his and his alone; if he commanded them to march through the Want in midwinter, they would do it. And yet . . . The Knife was no fool. He needed legitimacy, and he would not get that by murdering his surlord. He needed time to remake himself as grangelord and warlord, and leading Spire Vanis to victory against the clans would be half of it. Iss' resolve stiffened. Far better to have Marafice Eye close, let him have a vested interest in this war—he would fight better and longer for it—and later, when it was over and done . . . well, who could say what might become of a general on his long march home? The Northern Territories were about to become an extremely dangerous place.

Comforted by that thought, Iss said, "You do know you will have to acquire yourself a grangedom by fair means or foul?"

The Knife shrugged. "There's a lot of ugly grangelords' daughters out there." His mouth was too narrow for grinning, but he managed a fair semblance of a leer. "Or mayhap I'll find some old fart willing to foster me, just as you did when you first came to the Vanis. I heard tell that the land you were born to was some sodden piece of farmland on the poor side of the Vor, not some fine castle-held estate."

Iss ignored the gibe. Land was land, and his father may have been a farmer, but his great-grandfather had been born Lord of the Sundered Granges. There was a world of difference between Marafice Eye and himself, and if the Knife didn't know that, then he was a fool. No commonborn man had ever ruled Spire Vanis. Never had. Never would.

Stepping toward the candle branch, Iss turned so the light limned his shoulders and shone through his fingertips and hair. "Tomorrow I will begin spreading the word that I see you as my natural successor. My word alone cannot make a surlord of you, but I will do what I can to change minds. In return you will form an army for me and lead the Rive Watch and the grangelords north."

Marafice Eye nodded. "'Tis agreed."

Iss looked at the Knife's ruined face and trembled at what he had done.

*　*　*

THE CROUCHING MAIDEN crouched in the shadows at the rear of the house. It was a pleasant building, its faded yellow stonework glowing warmly in the noonday sun. The wind-damaged chimney stack leaked smoke near the base, and all the surrounding roof snow had turned black with soot and ash.

The door and windows were especially interesting to the maiden, for while first glance showed the usual oak and basswood frames and rusted iron latches, second and third glances revealed other details to the eye. The windows were equipped with two sets of shutters, and although the inner ones had been painted in the same dark color as pitch-soaked wood and certainly *looked* like wood from a distance, they had the smooth texture of cast iron. Similarly, the door itself was a great hunk of weathered and peeling oak that apparently hung on two horse-head hinges that were crusted with black rot. Magdalena had been studying the door for quite a while and had come to admire the subtle *untruth* of the thing. It would take more than two rusted potiron hinges to support a block of oak a foot thick.

The thickness of the door was not in question. An hour earlier a young girl with fair hair had stepped from it, revealing the true width of the wood. The girl, whom Magdalena thought to be about seven winters old, had moved no farther than the front step. "It's freezing," she had called to someone inside, "but the sun's shining as if it were spring." A woman's voice had replied, telling her to shut and bar the door before all the heat fell out.

Magdalena pursed lips few living had ever kissed. Shut *and* bar the door. The Lok farmhouse was built like a fort. Oh, it didn't look it, and the maiden was full of admiration for the person who had modified the original structure in such a way as to fool the casual eye, but the simple fact was that all the entrances and exits could be sealed. It was *that* fact more than anything said by the roofer Thurlo Pike that made the maiden certain she had found the right place.

"The Lok family will be living in seclusion," Iss had said. "Angus Lok trusts no one with their whereabouts, not even his close-lipped brothers in the Phage."

Magdalena knew several assassins who refused to take commissions against any man or woman who was believed to be associated with a Steep House, as the Phage named their secret lodges. But she had looked deep within herself and found little fear of sorcery or those who wielded it. She had been born in the Cloistered Tower, raised by the green-robed sisters there, and she had known a man once who had sworn she wielded a brand of sorcery all her own. Magdalena bared dry teeth. She had killed the man, of course, but his accusations still tugged at her from the grave. She was the Crouching Maiden; all the power she needed lay within her own two hands.

Suddenly uncomfortable with her position in the dogwood that grew beneath the stripped canopy of oldgrowth at the back of the house, Magdalena stood and stretched her legs. Shadows followed her like small children, and although she had little fear of being spotted by anything more troublesome than rabbits and birds, she still moved no closer to the house.

Gaining access was going to be a problem. Obviously the women took due care with their own safety, and at night the door and the windows would be barred. Breaking locks and hinges was noisy and troublesome and not the maiden's way. Also, if there were defenses in place on the outside of the house, it was fair to assume that there would be arms close at hand within. Iss had offered no insight into the characters of the Lok womenfolk, but Magdalena suspected that the mother and oldest daughter would likely know their way around a knife. By all accounts Angus Lok was a swordsman of high order, and it would take a foolish man not to see the sense of passing along some small portion of those skills to his daughters and his wife.

No. Magdalena shook her head. It would be too dangerous to break into the house and chance being caught in darkness by people who might be armed. It was a risk the Crouching Maiden would not take.

Assassination was all about reducing risk. Those who didn't know about such things assumed all an assassin did was stalk her mark down a dark alley, slit the mark's throat, then flee by some secret route. Truth was, Magdalena had killed only one man in an alleyway, and it had been one of the most dangerous commissions she had ever taken. She had been young then, her fee a mere sparrow's weight in gold, and she hadn't realized how difficult it was to approach an unknown man and simply kill him. This particular man had lived through four other assassination attempts, and even though the maiden had approached him quietly and from behind, he had caught wind of her intent even before moonlight found her blade. He was large and brutal and had broken two of her fingers before she finally located his windpipe with her knife. His blood was all over her arms and face, and his cries had alerted people in nearby streets. It had taken all her maiden's skills to return to her safe house undetected.

She had since learned to arrange situations more carefully, to use lures and props as means to insinuate herself into others' lives and create little "death plays" where she was playwright, player, and stagehand in one. Take Thurlo Pike: The man had been so taken with the thought of a drug that knocked women senseless, he had walked right into his grave.

And that was another thing few gave proper thought to: the arrangement of the bodies later. Not all assassinations called for a corpse spread-eagled on a bed. Most called for greater subtlety than that; patrons asked that the means of death be disguised as natural illness, a rogue attack by thieves, an accidental fall into cold water, suicide, or murder by a third party's hand. And quite a number of patrons requested that the corpse be permanently lost, so that no record of death remained.

Magdalena stripped off her thin leather gloves and massaged the deepening chill from her hands. As the Lok girl had said, it was bitterly cold, yet the sun shone with all the absurdity of a king at a beggar's feast. The maiden was sensitive to the cold. She worried about her hands yet could not bring herself to wear thick woolen mitts. Touch was everything to an assassin.

With a small animal sound, Magdalena turned her attention back to the house. Iss had left all decisions concerning the Lok women's deaths to her, as was proper in such cases, and had asked only for "discretion." This suited the maiden well enough. Whenever she took the trouble of placing herself in a tightly knit community like that of the Three Villages, she preferred to leave blameless once the commission was over and done. Thurlo Pike's death would actually help her in this regard, as it was quite possible that blame would fall upon him. If indeed there *was* blame to portion out.

Magdalena still hadn't made a decision about that yet. She might make the deaths look like an accident.

Slowly she began to work her way around the side of the house, moving in a wide-turning circle around farm buildings, stone pens, rusted plow bits, a covered well, a grove of winter-withered apple trees, and a retaining ward built in the crease where the slope of a neighboring hillside met level ground.

The front entrance was not well used; the maiden saw that straightaway. Not one pair of footsteps were stamped upon the path, and a wedge of drifted snow lay undisturbed against the door. No one ever came or went this way, and Magdalena suspected that the door was sealed permanently closed. She saw no evidence to suggest this, but she had seen enough of the farmhouse defenses for her mind to work in the same way as the person who had constructed them. A second door was an unnecessary risk; far better to board it up and perhaps the front windows as well and so leave only the back of the house vulnerable to invasion.

Magdalena suppressed the cold wave of curiosity that rose within her. Why Angus Lok chose to keep his family in protected seclusion was not her affair. He feared *something*, that she knew, and the fact that she was here now, an assassin crouching in the shadows at the side of his house, was proof that he feared correctly . . . but nowhere near deeply enough.

She studied the door, its frame, jamb, and pitch weatherproofing for only a minute longer before heading back to the woods. It was her last night working at Drover Jack's, and she saw no reason to be late. She had worked under many taskmasters in her time, and Gull Moler was kinder than most. The fact that he had fallen a little in love with her was reason enough to be moving on.

Tomorrow. She would leave the Three Villages tomorrow, under cover of darkness, once her commission here was done. She had made her decision about the deaths: By the time she had finished with the bodies it would look as if a terrible tragedy had taken place.

Fire was always good for that.

# FIFTY-FOUR

## *The Hollow River*

THE WIND HOWLED as the Sull warriors took their axes to the ice. Great bear-shaped Mal Naysayer put the full force of his body behind each blow, sending a battery of sharp white splinters into the air. Ark Veinsplitter worked on the dimple holes he had created, chipping away at weak points, thaw edges, and cracks. The river ice smelled of belowground places, of pine roots and iron ore and cooled magma. It rang like a great and ancient bell as the Naysayer's pick found its heart.

Raif was standing on a raised bank that was heavily forested with stick-thin black spruce. Above him towered the massive, glaciated west face of Mount Flood. Boulders as big as barns rose above the snow cover at the mountain's base, towering over fields of rubble and dead, frost-riven trees. All surrounding land sloped down toward the river in a great misshapen bowl. Rock walls plunged beneath the surface, sheer as cliffs. A frozen waterfall hung like a monstrous white chandelier above a bend in the river's course, and countless dry streambeds funneled wind along the ice.

The Hollow River itself ran through a granite canyon and into the maze of knife-edge ridges that formed the mountain's skirt. Raif raised his bandaged fingers to his face and blew on them. From where he stood by the horses, the river looked like a sea of blue glass.

It had taken them three days of hard travel to reach here, as the Naysayer had promised it would. The two Sull warriors chose paths Raif would never have dared to take: across fields of loose shale, past seepage meadows bogged with melt holes, and over lakes fast with ice. Always they trusted their horses. Even when neither Ark nor the Naysayer was riding, they let the blue and the gray lead the way. Ash had ridden a Sull horse before, and it was easy for her to hand her stallion the reins and allow it the freedom to choose its own path. Raif found himself constantly pulling his stallion back the first day, the reins held so tightly around his wrists that for once his fingers went numb from lack of blood, not cold. The state of his hands did not help, as it was difficult to fine-guide a horse without fingers on the reins.

The pain was excruciating. Raif had dreams that his hands had been skinned, and turned and sweated in his blankets as his dream-self watched Death and her creatures pick the last scraps of meat from his bones. Raif woke shivering and filled with fear. Once he had torn off the bandages, just to see for himself that there was living flesh beneath. Straightaway he wished he hadn't. There *was* living flesh, pink flesh lying beneath a black-and-red jelly of blisters and cast skin, but the sight was almost as bad as the pared fingers in his dreams, and he couldn't get the Naysayer to rebandage them quickly enough.

Mal Naysayer saw nothing in the blistered, shedding skin to be alarmed about. In one of the few long speeches Raif had ever heard him speak in Common, he said, "They will work again, I promise you that. I've seen worse in my time and doubtless caused worse, too. This hand here will be capable of holding a drawn bow, and this finger here able to hold and release a string at tension. They will not look pretty, and they'll be frost shy from now on and must be tended like newborns in the cold, but that is the price you pay for killing wolves."

It did not occur to Raif until much later that Mal Naysayer had no way of knowing that the bow was Raif's first-chosen weapon and had simply assumed it was so.

Both warriors carried fine recurve longbows made of horn and sinew, with lacquered risers and wet-spun string. The Naysayer hunted on foot as he traveled alongside the packhorse and managed to flush a few ptarmigan and marten from their lairs. Whenever he made a kill, he plucked the lacquered arrow shaft from the carcass, slipped it back into his case, and then drained the blood into a lacquered bowl and served it, still steaming, to Ash.

Ash remained weak, but she insisted on walking for increasingly long periods each day. The Naysayer had given her a coat that was so long it dragged behind her as she tramped through the snow. It was a thing of alien beauty, combining lynx fur and woven fabric in a way that Raif had never seen before. Ash refused to have it cut to fit her and cinched a leather belt around her waist to raise the hem by less destructive means. She looked, Raif had to admit, just as he imagined a Sull princess would look: tall, pale, and covered from head to toe in the silvery pelts of predatory beasts.

Ark Veinsplitter had offered gifts to Raif: mitts made from flying squirrel pelts that had the softest, richest fur Raif had ever touched, a hood of wolverine fur that shed even breath ice with just a shrug, and a padded inner coat that was woven from lamb's wool and stuffed with shredded silk. Raif had refused them. He had no wish to be further beholden to the Sull.

Ark Veinsplitter had nodded his head at the refusal and said something that Raif did not understand. "To Sull, a gift is given in the offering, not the accepting, and I will hold them for you until such a time comes when you need them, or the Sender of Storms claims my soul."

Raif had thought a lot about that over the past three days. At first he had assumed it was just a way for the Sull to claim a debt even when a proffered gift had been refused, yet now he thought differently. Ark Veinsplitter had separated the mitts, hood, and inner coat from his other possessions and made a parcel of them, which he placed in the bottom of his least-used pack. And Raif believed with growing certainty that the parcel would be opened again only on *his* say.

The Sull were a different race. They thought in different ways. Raif found himself thinking back to what Angus had said about them, how it had taken Mors Stormyielder fourteen years to breed a horse to repay a debt. He understood that now. It was quite possible that Ark Veinsplitter would carry that package with him, unopened, until the day he died.

"We're through!" The cry came from Ark Veinsplitter, and it broke through Raif's thoughts like a whip cracked against his cheek. Both he and Ash looked down to the riverbank where the two Sull warriors continued to chip at the ice. Ark

Veinsplitter's bent back was turned toward them. They waited, but he said no more.

Raif glanced at Ash. "Are you ready?"

"Yes." Her gray eyes flickered with snowlight as she spoke. "It's time this was over and done."

He let her walk ahead of him to the bank, glad for a few moments to settle his mind in place. He waited to feel fear, *expected* to feel fear, but there was nothing but emptiness inside him. Their journey was coming to an end.

Readying himself as he walked, he pulled on his gloves and packed the spaces between his fingers with dried moss as the Naysayer had taught him. He had no weapon or guidestone to weigh his belt, yet he tugged on the buckle to check its hold as if it were loaded down with gear. The hard edges of his dead man's cloak curled in the wind as he approached the river's edge.

The two warriors stepped back, their faces reddened by exertion, their axes sparkling with ice. No one spoke. Ash shivered as she looked down upon the hole they had created. The ice was nearly two feet thick, carpeted by an uneven layer of dry snow. The hole was roughly circular in shape, its blue and jagged edges creating a trap for the light. Score lines caused by ax strokes drew Raif's gaze down through the shadowless rim to the utter darkness at its center. It was impossible to see the riverbed or anything else that lay beyond.

"How deep is it?" Ash's voice was a whisper.

"Let us see." Ark Veinsplitter unhooked the coil of rope that was attached to his belt by a white metal dog hook. Swiftly he fed the weighted end of the rope into the hole and let it run through his half-closed fist until it halted of its own accord. He pulled up close to fifteen feet of rope. "It will be deeper near the middle."

Raif looked out across the ice. "I'll go first."

The two warriors exchanged a glance. Ark said, "Blood must be spilt before you enter. This is a place of sacrifice to the Sull." Almost instantly the warrior's letting knife appeared in his hand, the silver chain that linked the crosshilt to his belt chiming softly like struck glass. With his free hand he pulled back his sleeve and bared his forearm.

Raif's hand shot out to stop him. "No. If anyone must pay

a toll for this journey, it will be me." Biting the end of his glove, he stripped it off. "Here. Cut the wrist."

Muscles in Ark Veinsplitter's face tightened. When he spoke his voice was dangerously low. "Your blood is not Sull blood. It comes at a cheaper price."

"That may be so, Far Rider, but Ash and I will be the ones who make this journey, not you."

"I don't understand," Ash said. "I thought—"

"Nay, Ash March," the Naysayer said, his gruff voice almost gentle. "We travel with you only this far."

"But you will wait for us?" Ash glanced from Raif to Ark to the Naysayer. The fear in her voice was barely masked. "You *will* wait for us?"

The Naysayer's ice blue eyes held hers without blinking. "We cannot stay here, Ash March. We must pay a toll for the passage we have opened and ride north before moonlight strikes the ice. We are Far Riders. *Kith Masso* is no place for us."

Ash looked at him, the plea slowly slipping from her face. After a long moment she matched his unblinking gaze. "So be it."

Raif held his face still as he listened to her speak. The hollow place inside him ached for her, and he wanted nothing more than to lift her from the ice and crush her against his chest. Instead he thrust his wrist toward Ark Veinsplitter. "Cut it."

The Sull warrior's eyes darkened, and Raif saw himself reflected in the black oil of his irises. Slowly Ark raised the letting knife to his mouth and breathed upon the razor-thin edge. His breath condensed upon the metal, then cooled to form a rime of ice. With a circle of wool dyed midnight blue, he wiped the edge. That done, he grasped Raif's forearm and jabbed his fingers hard into the flesh. Raif could feel him searching for, and finding, veins. With a movement so fast it could not be followed with the eye, Ark Veinsplitter slashed Raif's wrist.

Raif felt the shock of cold metal, but no pain. Blood oozed quickly to the surface, rolling in a wide band along his wrist.

Only when the first red drops landed in the snow above

the river's surface did the Sull warrior release his grip. "There. Clan blood has been spilt upon Sull ice. Let us hope for all our sakes that this angers no gods." Ark Veinsplitter turned and made his way to his horse.

Raif breathed deeply and then jammed his knuckles into the wound. The pain in both his hands was blinding, and it made him wonder if he'd lost his mind. What had he been thinking, letting Ark Veinsplitter spill his blood? He counted seconds as he continued to press against the cut vein. Truth was, he *knew* what he had been thinking; it just didn't make much sense, that was all. He didn't want the Sull paying for his journey. Not this part, the last part, after he and Ash had come this far.

"Here."

Raif looked up. Mal Naysayer held something out for him to take: a broad leaf, deep green in color and covered with rough hairs. Recognizing it for what it was and what it did, Raif thanked the Naysayer and took it from him. Bracing himself, he laid the leaf flat in his palm and then pressed it against the cut vein. Comfrey or, as some called it, wound heal: Clans used it like the Sull to stop the bleeding of small wounds.

As the Naysayer walked a small distance to retrieve the pack he had left on the bank, Ash turned to Raif. "You knew they wouldn't come under the ice with us." It was not a question.

"I thought they wouldn't, but I wasn't sure until I saw their faces when we first reached here this morning." Raif adjusted his grip on the comfrey leaf; a thin trail of blood was still leaking from the wound. "They know this place, Ash. I think—" He stopped himself before the words *they even fear it* left his lips.

"You think what?"

He shrugged. "It means something to them, that's all."

Ash gave him a look that made him feel like a liar. She was so pale and thin, he wondered how she stood against the wind. After a moment she nodded toward his wrist and said, "He cut you pretty deeply, didn't he?"

Raif couldn't deny it. "It'll heal," was all he said.

As if by unspoken agreement, the two Sull warriors picked

that moment to converge upon the hole in the ice. Both held packs in their hand, and Ark Veinsplitter held a length of stout rope woven from flax that Raif had seen him use to raise the tent. The dark-eyed warrior handed his pack to the Naysayer. No words passed between the two men, yet Raif knew and understood what was happening. It shamed him.

The Naysayer held out both packs toward Ash. "Here, Ash March, Foundling, I offer you these gifts for the journey. There is a stone lamp and what oil we can spare, food and blankets and herbs to ward off sickness, and other such things as one who travels beneath ice might need."

Ash's eyes filled with tears as the great bear-size warrior spoke. With a small movement she tugged down her hood so he could see her face wholly. When she spoke her words were as formal as his, and the wind dried her tears before they fell. "I thank you, Mal Naysayer, Son of the Sull and chosen Far Rider, for these gifts that you have given. Without them I would have neither light nor warmth along the way. You have saved my life, yet claimed no debt, and for that I owe you, and give you, a piece of my heart. May all the moons you travel beneath be full ones."

The Naysayer stood still, his ice eyes unblinking, his back straight as a black spruce, his lynx hood shedding snow, and studied Ash without speaking. His face looked carved from stone. After a moment he laid both packages in the snow, then bowed so low to Ash that the crown of his hood touched river ice. He bowed again to Raif and then walked away, and Raif knew he would not come back.

Ark Veinsplitter knelt on the river surface and hammered an iron stake into shore-fast ice three feet from the hole. Raif watched his bent back, feeling nothing but shame. The Sull warrior had not wanted his gifts refused a second time, so he had passed them to his *hass*, who had given them to Ash.

"There. It is done." Ark secured the rope to the fixed stake and then tested its strength by tugging on it. "It will hold well enough."

Raif pushed his mitt over his hand, covering the bloody bandage and the letting wound, and stepped forward. Ark Veinsplitter's eyes met his. Raif knew it wasn't his place to thank the Sull warrior for the gifts he had given to another, so he said only, "Thank you for heeding my call in the darkness."

Ark Veinsplitter nodded slowly, the flat plains of muscle on his face suddenly looking worn. "It was Mal who gave the word to aid you."

"That may be so, but I've only known Mal Naysayer to give one answer to any question he is asked." Raif held his gaze firm, and both men stood in silence, feet apart, the wind blowing their clothes separate ways. After a moment Raif held out his hand. "I thank you, Ark Veinsplitter, for asking the right question."

The Sull warrior clasped Raif's arm, his face grave. "Do not thank me for something we both may come to regret, Raif Sevrance of No Clan. Thank me instead for the use of my horse, and my tent, and my rope." He smiled roughly. "Perhaps we can both live with that."

Raif nodded. He found he could not speak.

Together he and Ark Veinsplitter secured the rope around his chest. The Sull warrior rechecked all knots and took care to thread the rope in such a way that it removed all possible strain from Raif's hands during the drop. Fifteen feet was not a great drop, but a bad landing on hard rock could break bones. Raif had walked on dry riverbeds before, but he had no idea what he would find beneath *Kith Masso*'s frozen crust.

Ark Veinsplitter pinned Raif's arms flat against the ice as Raif eased his legs and lower body into the hole. Muscles bunched beneath the Sull warrior's lynx coat as he transferred Raif's weight to the rope. Raif thought he was ready for the pain as his gloved hands closed around the flax, but he wasn't. Streaks of white fire shot up his arms to his heart. The letting wound on his wrist suddenly seemed deep enough to sever his hand, and as his fingers sprang from the rope in fear, his body dropped.

The world he entered was as cool and still as a guidehouse. The blue glow of icelight closed around his body, like water around a sinking stone. All was quiet. Raif heard his own heart beating. The sharp tang of air trapped beneath ice stole into his nose and mouth. Above him, Ark Veinsplitter lowered the rope. The flax ticked with strain, the free swinging of Raif's body making it saw against the ice edge. Wincing, Raif forced both hands around the rope and guided his body down.

His feet hit bottom with a jolt. Quickly he worked himself free of the makeshift hoist and called for Ark to pull it back. As the rope disappeared above his head, Raif pressed his mitted hands against his jaw. He hated being weak. Hearing the soft catch of Ash's voice above him, he turned his attention to the icy blue tunnel that surrounded him. He did not want to hear what words passed between her and Ark Veinsplitter.

To his left, the granite bank glittered with lenses of ice. Flecks of iron ore shone darkly within the wall like pieces of ossified bone. Beneath his feet the riverbed was a rough valley of rock, frozen pools, and desiccated litter of fish carcasses and caribou antlers, pine needles and algae. A white scum of frosted minerals lay over everything; salts and rock silt condensed as the river drained. Above it all stretched the ice ceiling. It was like nothing Raif had ever seen before: warped, folded, jagged and then smooth like a wall of transparent rock. Light and color *poured* from it, creating a waterfall of sea greens and silver grays and dark midnight blues. Raif felt as if he were standing in the underbelly of a glacier, in the place where ice and shadow met.

Dry matter crunched beneath his boots as he stepped aside to make way for Ash's descent. To either side of him darkness pooled beyond the light.

Ash came down smoothly, both hands feeding rope. Raif caught her before she hit the riverbed and pulled her free of the hoist. She was shivering. The blue light reflecting off her face looked like moonlight. When he pulled his hand free of her waist, she made a small movement as if to hold it there. As they waited for Ark Veinsplitter to lower the two packs, Raif watched Ash closely. Since the night of the wolves she had not lapsed into unconsciousness, but he didn't know if she was still fighting the voices. By unspoken agreement, neither had mentioned them in front of the Sull.

By the time the packs were lowered, Raif could already perceive a darkening above the ice. This day was the shortest winter had shown him so far. He wondered what Drey and

Effie would be doing now, then closed the thought off from his mind.

"You will need to remember this place," Ark Veinsplitter called as he let the rope drop for the final time. "This may be your only way out, save for picking a new hole in the ice."

Raif nodded; he had already thought of that.

"From here you head upriver until you come upon the tributary that branches west. That may be frozen, too." Ark's ice-tanned face finally appeared above them. "You must take due care, Raif Sevrance of No Clan and Ash March, Foundling. The Naysayer says the riding moon will bring no thaw, but that which is cold and brittle may collapse."

"Then we will dance ice," Ash said, looking up at him, "as all your horses do."

Raif thought perhaps the Sull warrior would smile, but his lips barely stretched against his teeth. "The Naysayer and I head north. We will leave such a trail as can be followed by a clansman, if you choose to take our path." He left them then, with no word of farewell save the sound of his footsteps beating a cold rhythm upon the ice.

"Come," Raif said when all was still. "We need to use the last hour of daylight as best we can." He picked up both packs from the floor and slung them over his back. One was a lot heavier than the other, and metal items jingled dully within.

Ash did not move or speak. She stood in the circle of diminishing daylight directly below the hole in the ice. Raif did not like the quick manner in which she was breathing. He touched her lightly on the arm. "Let's go," he said, his voice as gentle as he could make it. "We've come too far to stop now."

Slowly her gaze turned upon him. Her eyes were made brilliant by reflections of ice, and he almost didn't see the fear that shone through them like light from a second, weaker source. "They know I'm here," she said. "They know . . . and terror grows within them."

RAIF FOUND HIMSELF WATCHING the ice ceiling as they walked. The mass of frozen and suspended water weighed upon his thoughts. It was a slice of the river, frozen from the surface down; smooth above, where he could no longer see; and roughly coved below, like the roof of a cave. The ice was thickest nearest the bank, where frozen white piles rested against granite and cantilevered the great weight of ice. Raif had already decided that he and Ash were safer close to the bank, yet as darkness fell and the air around them cooled, the ice supports began to creak and rumble like a round-house in a storm.

Ash carried the soapstone lamp the Naysayer had given her, cupping it in both hands for warmth. Raif wasn't sure what kind of oil fueled it, for it burned with a silver flame and trailed the sweet, musky, not-quite-human odor of whale yeast in its smoke. The single flame produced was housed in a protective guard of mica, but it was more than enough to light the way.

"Do you think Mal and Ark know what I am?"

Raif was surprised to hear Ash speak. She had been silent since she had lit the lamp. Switching his gaze from the blue glass of the ice ceiling to her face, he said, "Perhaps. Tem once told me that the Sull know more than any other race. He said they pass knowledge from generation to generation and some even inherit memories, like clansfolk inherit the will to fight."

Ash hugged the lamp closer. Above the cuff of her mitt, Raif could see the white stick of bone and flesh that was her wrist. "I think Mal gave me something that first night to make the voices go away."

"A warding, like the one Heritas Cant set?"

"No. Something different . . . I can't explain." She shrugged. "It's gone now."

Raif glanced into the tunnel of shadows ahead. Even in the far distance light from the lamp created a corona of blue light around the ice. "Perhaps we should stop here for the night. Build a camp. Sleep."

Ash shook her head even before he had finished speaking. "No. They'd have me the moment I shut my eyes. They're desperate now. And so close . . ." She swallowed. "So close I can smell them."

A spark of anger flared within Raif as she spoke. Sud-denly he hated everyone who had helped her come this far:

Ark Veinsplitter and Mal Naysayer, Heritas Cant, even Angus. None of them were clan. No clansman would have forced a sick girl to travel north in full winter. Tem Sevrance would have kept her warm by the stove and taken his hammer to any shadows or dark beasts who approached her.

Abruptly Raif stopped. Emptying the contents of both packs onto the riverbed, he searched for something to use as a weapon. Amid the pouches of lamp oil, cured salmon, and wax, he found a slender spike of steel the length of his forearm. An ice pick. He weighed it in his hand, forced his fingers around the squared-off butt. It would do. It would have to do.

Ash frowned at him. "You can't fight what isn't here."

Raif thought of a reply but didn't say it. Instead he began scooping the spilled contents back into the packs. Bits of river litter stuck to his mitts like frost, and deep beneath the fur he felt blood trickle along his wrist as the scab that had formed over the letting wound stretched to breaking. When he was done, he slid the pick through his belt. "We'll travel through the night."

Hours passed in silence. No wind disturbed the air in the tunnel, and the only sound was the shifting of the ice and their own booted feet grinding dried and frozen pine needles to dust. The riverbed rose steadily as they moved upriver, and the ice ceiling grew closer with every step. Raif was constantly aware of the fragile mass above him. Tons upon tons of frozen water, suspended above his head. After a time it became impossible to walk near the bank, and Raif set a course close to the river's middle, where the ice crust was at its thinnest.

From time to time the dark, gaping holes of tributaries breached the granite wall of the bank. Most channels were choked with clumps of gray ice that spilled out onto the riverbed in rubble heaps several feet high. Pools of frozen water lying flat beneath the rubble told of late-season thaws and water running *after* the channel had hard-froze. Raif dismissed each channel as he came upon it; the one he was looking for had to run from the west and be clear enough to let a man and woman pass.

The passage of time was difficult to gauge. Raif felt his

body growing colder and his mind moving slowly from thought to thought. He forced Ash to eat some strips of cured salmon, but he had no stomach for food himself. The air in the drained riverbed was becoming thicker and more condensed. The river itself was shrinking, and soon Raif found himself walking with his back and neck partially bent. The ice crust was so close he could reach up and touch the hard glassy surface, see the flaw lines and pressure whorls within. Tiny bubbles of trapped air shone like pearls.

On and on they walked, following the bends and bow curves of *Kith Masso* as it skirted the mountain's base. Raif watched Ash constantly, finding a dozen excuses to touch her in small unassuming ways. Her face was gray and tightly drawn. Too often her eyes were focused in a place he tried to but could not see. At some point she had stripped off her mitts, and her bare hands were now closed around the lamp so tightly it looked as if she were trying to crush it. Her knuckles showed white and jagged like teeth.

He spoke to her little, and received few responses, yet he feared to do much more. She was fighting the voices, and even Tem's hammer would have proven useless against those.

Eventually they entered a stretch of the river where the granite walls were jagged and twisted as if something had been wrenched from them at force. Stone ledges broke through the ice crust. Great piers of black iron rock jutted from the walls, and troughs gouged deep into the riverbed were filled with dark ice. Raif turned his head sharply as a cry that came from nothing human ripped through the tunnel like a blast of cold air. The flame within the soapstone lamp wavered. Ash inhaled sharply. Her eyes met Raif's and she nodded, once. "They draw nearer," she said. "Their world touches ours in this place."

Raif closed his eyes. He had used up a lifetime's worth of prayers the night the ice wolves had attacked him, and he knew better than to ask the Stone Gods for more.

In silence they continued walking. Ash could no longer stand fully upright, and Raif wondered how long it would be before they'd have to get down on their hands and knees and crawl. Time passed. Progress was slow over the warped and concertinaed granite that formed the river's floor. Fear grew in Raif slowly, filling the hollow places in his chest. A second cry came: high and terrible, almost beyond hearing. Listening to it, Raif wished he were back on the snow plains, facing wolves. Other sounds followed: hisses and broken whispers and the wet snarls of things with snouts. As he rounded a bend in the river's course, Raif breathed in the faint odor of charred meat and singed hair. When he breathed again it was gone.

*Nooooooooooo.*

The hairs on Raif's neck pricked up all at once. Something *other* had spoken, yet it reminded him of another time and place. When he realized what it was it made him sick. The Bluddroad. The Bludd women and children. The sound of desperation was the same in both worlds.

With his back bent almost double and his stomach heaving, he almost missed the gash in the far bank. He thought at first it was just shadows, as there was no telltale gleam of ice on the surrounding riverbed, but the darkness ran too deeply, and the surrounding rocks were too flat to cast shadows of any depth.

"Ash. Bring the lamp." He waited until she reached his side before crossing the riverbed. The river was barely the length of three horses now, and the ice ceiling dipped to chest height in parts. Light in the tunnel dimmed noticeably as Ash crouched to set down the lamp.

The gash in the rock was bell shaped, tall as Ash's shoulders, and completely clean of ice. Raif stepped through to check the way. Here the air was different: colder, drier, shot with the smell of iron ore. No ice ceiling stretched overhead, just a barrel curve of rock. The tunnel led west into the mountain, disappearing into darkness so complete, it gave Raif a chill to see it.

"Raif. Here."

Raif backed out of the gash. Ash was crouching by the lamp, her right arm extending outward, her hand flat upon the riverwall.

"Look."

Raif quested for his lore. A raven etched in stone marked the way.

# FIFTY-FIVE

## A Cavern of Black Ice

CASSY LOK WOKE to the smell of smoke. *Beth*, came the thought straightaway. *She's been up making honey cakes again and forgotten how many she put on the fire.* Cassy huffed in her pillow, determined to go back to sleep. *I'm not saving her this time. I don't care how many honey cakes have fallen through the griddle and caught light . . . and I hope she gets fat from eating the ones that turned out. Fat and spotty with big rot holes in her teeth.*

Cassy closed her eyes as tightly as she could, then scrunched up her face for good measure. Just this morning she'd caught Beth trying on the good blue dress Father had brought back with him from Ille Glaive. *Her* dress. And she wouldn't have minded much—well, not *that* much—if it hadn't been for the fact that Beth was prancing in front of the looking glass at the time, pretending to be a fine court-bred maiden, nibbling on sweetmeats rolled in gold leaf and sipping wine through a crust of rose-scented ice. For sweetmeats Beth had used hazelnuts coated in cinnamon. For wine she had used plum juice. *Plum juice!* Cassy gritted her teeth. And when this fine court-bred maiden had found herself caught in the act, the first thing she'd done was twirl around to face her elder sister, *holding the cup of plum juice in her hand!*

It didn't bear thinking about. Mother said the stain would come out. And Beth *had* spent the rest of the day following her around with a kicked-dog expression on her face. But still. Father had bought her that dress, and it fitted so well, and it was a grown-up dress, without any of those silly girlish frills that Father knew she hated, and it didn't really matter that she had nowhere special to wear it until spring.

"I'll take you dancing in it when I return from the North, Casilyn Lok," Father had said as he'd handed her the package. "And that's a promise as binding as I've made to any man."

Cassy unscrunched her face. Perhaps she'd been a bit harsh on Beth earlier. The smell of burning was growing worse, and if she didn't know better, she'd imagine a whole tray of honey cakes had fallen onto the fire.

The *chimney*. Cassy sat bolt upright. What if more bricks had caved in and blocked the flue? It was windy enough for it. And the roofer hadn't come today, as he was supposed to, and the whole stack was held up by only a couple of pinewood struts.

Quickly and in complete darkness, Cassy found her slippers and shawl. As she stepped toward the door, a sleepy voice spoke out from the deep shadows at the far side of the room. "Cassy? Is that you?" Beth.

A small shift took place in Cassy's chest: not fear exactly, but the first stirrings of it. There *were* no honey cakes on the fire. "Beth, put your coat and slippers on. Quick now."

Sheets rustled in the darkness. "You're not still mad at me, Cassy?"

Cassy shook her head. Then, realizing her younger sister couldn't see her, she said, "No. Not much," out loud.

"What's burning?"

"I think the chimney's caved in."

"But—"

"No buts, Beth. Do as I say." Cassy was surprised at how sharp her voice sounded. Bare feet thudded onto the floor. More rustling followed. A moment later she felt Beth's shoulders knock against her arm. "Here. Take my hand." Beth's hand was warm and sweaty: She always fell asleep with her fists clenched. Cassy led her toward the door. "You didn't put anything to cook on the hearth tonight, did you?"

"No, Cassy."

"Good girl." Cassy lifted the latch and opened the door. A wave of smoke and heat puffed through the room, making the shutters rattle behind their backs. "Come on. Let's wake Mother and Little Moo." This time she made sure her voice sounded calm.

"It's hot."

Cassy felt her way through the darkness, her hand now

closed tightly around her sister's. "I know. Let's just get to Mother's room and you can tell her how you found your way in the dark." Even as she spoke, Cassy felt heat push against her face. A cracking noise sounded from the floor below. Beth flinched. Cassy pulled her sister firmly in the direction of their mother's room.

Mother and Little Moo slept in the room directly above the kitchen. Heat from the fire warmed the floor through the cold months of winter, and two large windows let in great squares of sunlight in summer and spring. Cassy felt a wave of relief roll over her as she saw the pale corona of light around the door: Mother had kept a lamp lit. Little Moo didn't like to sleep in the dark. She said something called *beemies* lived under her bed. No one but Little Moo knew what beemies were. Cassy suspected that Beth had frightened Little Moo with tales of beasties and monsters and other fey things, and Little Moo had taken this information and invented a whole new class of baby peril from it.

Cassy's fingers found the latch on first try. Warm air rushed past her as the door opened, pressing her nightgown flat against the backs of her legs. Light stung her eyes. Smoke rolled into the room, greasy and nearly black. Cassy felt its hot little fingers slip around her ankles, grasping like hands without bone. Beth began to cough.

"Cassy?" Darra Lok sat up in bed. The beautiful honey-colored hair that she normally kept pinned in a simple knot spilled over her shoulders like dark fire. For the first time ever, Cassy noticed gray strands within the gold.

"Mother. I—"

Darra Lok nodded her eldest daughter into silence, her eyes on the smoke. Reaching over, she plucked the sleeping form of Little Moo from the opposite side of the bed. Little Moo's head rolled onto her mother's shoulder, and she made a soft gurgling noise but did not wake. Darra spoke soft words to her anyway as she kicked the blankets from the bed and rose to her feet. Beth tugged on Cassy's arm, wanting to go to her mother, but Cassy held her firm. Darra Lok sent her eldest daughter a look that said many things. Cassy nodded.

"Come on, Beth. Let's go downstairs." It was easier to sound calm now that Mother was here. As she pulled Beth from the room, she heard Darra Lok take the lamp from the washstand and follow behind with Little Moo.

Beth shivered as Cassy guided her into the smoke that rolled up the stairs like a wave of black foam. Cassy felt like shivering too, but Mother had sent her a look saying, *Be strong now, for Beth and yourself*. So instead of shivering she tugged her younger sister forward and said, "This is no worse than looking for mushrooms in the mist. Remember that time you found those big brown ones under the dogwood, and everyone else had already looked, but you were the only who could see them? Remember that?"

Beth nodded. Her small face looked pinched.

Cassy continued guiding her down the stairs, one step at a time. "And you said that no one could spot mushrooms better than you, and even Father agreed."

"He said we couldn't eat them. Said they were rabbits bane."

Cassy managed a dim smile. She could clearly hear the low roar of fire now, coming from the front of the house. Wood snapped and popped as it burned, and Cassy imagined fang-shaped flames eating away at the house.

"Cassy. We're going to the back of the house, to the kitchen." Darra Lok's voice was firm but calm. "Can you see the way ahead?"

"I can! I can!" cried Beth.

"Good. Stay close to your sister and help her find the way."

Smoke was gouting along the corridor that linked the front entrance to the kitchen. Scorched bits of matter sailed on the warm currents of air that blew around the house. Flaming embers, ducking and darting like little red fishes, floated past Cassy's face. The fire sounded like one long continuous roll of thunder now, a storm bearing down on the house. Still she could see no flames. Perhaps the fire was burning from the outside *in*. Perhaps the chimney flue had collapsed and the wind had showered sparks over the roof.

Little Moo woke as Cassy and Beth made their way through the chest-high smoke in the corridor. The baby made a frightened, snuffling sound and cried the words, "*Mize. Mize.*" Cassy hoped her eyes weren't stinging.

Mother hushed her, and she was quiet for a while, but her breaths came in hard little wheezes.

Beth was first to reach the kitchen. There was less smoke here than on the stairs and in the hallways, and the hardwood embers glowing in the hearth provided a second source of light. As Darra and Little Moo entered the room, a mighty crack shook the house. Hot air beat against Cassy's back. The stench of burning wood sharpened, and when she sucked in breath, crispy little cinders caught in the back of her throat.

"Cassy. Beth. Get the door." Darra rocked Little Moo on her hip. "Hurry now."

Cassy and Beth ran to the door. By unspoken agreement, Cassy pulled the top bolts while Beth took care of those at the bottom. Cassy's hands felt like clumps of clay. Stupidly she found herself thinking about the blue dress. Father would never take her dancing in it now.

The heavy door needed a good shove to start it swinging, and when the final bolt was drawn both sisters put their shoulders to the wood. It gave a little, then jerked back suddenly as if something were blocking its way. They tried again, but the door would open only so far. Cassy glanced at her mother. "It's jammed."

"There's enough room to squeeze through, though," cried Beth.

"One by one," Cassy added in small voice.

Darra Lok looked from the door to the encroaching tide of smoke at her back. Little Moo began to cry. "Beth. Squeeze through and see if you can find what's blocking it."

Beth sucked in her chest much farther than it needed to be sucked. Cassy could see the outline of her ribs beneath her nightgown as she forced her way through the foot-wide opening. Her eyes were sparkling; this was now an adventure to her. "It's so dark I can't see anything," were the last words she said.

Darra called to her, but the roar and crackle of the fire drowned out any reply. They waited, but Beth did not return. Cassy went to follow her out.

"No," Darra said sharply. "Here. You take Moo. I'll go after her."

Little Moo did not want to leave her mother's arms. Her pudgy fingers clutched at the fabric of Darra's dress, raising little nubs of wool as Cassy pulled her away. It was very hot now, and a great quantity of thick black smoke was pouring into the kitchen. Cassy moved so her back was to it, shielding Little Moo.

Darra took the three steps toward the door, hooked the lamp on a nail hammered into the frame, then turned to look at her daughters. The lines around her mouth were the deepest Cassy had ever known them to be. Her eyes had stopped being blue and were as gray as steel. She looked strong and utterly beautiful to her eldest daughter. "I'll be back in just a moment," she said.

Cassy almost called her back. She would remember that afterward, and it would tear her apart. She almost said, *Mother, please don't go.* But she didn't, and Darra Lok forced her way through the opening, and Cassy never saw her again.

There was an intake of breath, sharp, as if Darra meant to scream, then silence. "Mother!" Cassy called, rocking Little Moo against her chest. *"Mother!"*

Somewhere inside the house hot air exploded, punching out shutters and glass. A low ripping noise sounded, as hot plaster peeled off the corridor walls. Suddenly Cassy could no longer see the glow of orange light that marked the hearth. She jigged Little Moo against her chest, saying nonsense things to her in a voice that was ragged with fear.

Quickly she glanced at the door. The foot-wide opening was dark with shadows, and strings of smoke poured into it like water into a ditch.

*One by one.* Cassy shivered as her own words came back to her. Hardly aware of what she was doing or why, she moved from the door to the nearest window. Both sets of shutters were barred and bolted, and she had to set Little Moo down on the floor while she dealt with them. *Why were there so many bolts?* Frustration made her careless with her fingers, and she gouged her knuckles on a raised nailhead as she pulled back the first set of shutters. The pain was surprisingly easy to ignore. The second set of shutters proved easier, and she had them done in less than an instant. Cool, clean air wafted against her face. Outside in the farmyard all was dark and still. Shaking with relief, she bent to pick up Little Moo.

Only Little Moo wasn't there. Cassy turned her head. A wave of sickness and fear rose in her throat. *No!*

Little Moo had crawled to the door. Her fat little fist was in the opening, and she was calling softly, *"Mama? Mama?"*

Cassy moved faster than she had ever moved in her life. Her hands reached out for Little Moo's blue-socked feet, but other hands beyond the door found her first. Little Moo was *pulled* through the opening. Cassy clutched . . . and clutched. . . . touched the soft wool of Little Moo's socks . . . and then nothing but cold air.

Cassy stared at the space her sister had left behind. Stupidly, ridiculously, she couldn't stop clutching at thin air. Her heart was dead inside her chest.

*Mother gave the baby to me.*

She breathed in that thought, took it deep inside herself, deep into the place where her heart had ceased to be. And then she stood and stepped away from the door. Someone on the other side wished her dead. Someone had lit a fire at the front of the house and then dragged something heavy like a stone or a piece of timber in front of the back door, so the Lok family would escape one by one.

Like a ghost Cassy moved through the smoke. Sweat was pouring down her face, turning the neck of her dress black and making it steam. The silver chain she wore at her throat burned like hot wire. Touching the lamp was like touching a hot coal. The little copper disk that covered the opening to the oil chamber swung back with a single flick. As she pulled a nearby chair under the window and stepped onto it, droplets of pine oil sprinkled the floor. She made no effort to disguise her movements as she hefted her body onto the windowsill: Let those hands that pulled Little Moo come for *her*. Let them burn in hell.

She saw the shadow moving toward her as she pushed her body clear of the frame. Dark and fluid it came, moving like spilled ink. The hands were gloved in shiny leather, and they held the plainest sort of knife. The blade was immaculate, but Cassy wasn't fooled. She had skinned rabbits and spring lambs before now. She knew how easily blood wiped clean. Time slowed as the blade slid through air. A second stretched to an impossibly thin line as Cassy swung the lamp. The knife touched her, and she was glad of it, glad because the lamp and its free-spilling oil crashed into those gloved hands.

Fire *whooshed* into existence, creating a wall of blazing light. Suddenly there was no air to breathe, only hot, stinking gas. Cassy heard her hair crackle like dry twigs as smolder fell upon it, yet she hardly cared. The gloved hands were burning in a cauldron of bloodred flames.

\* \* \*

FINALLY THEY CAME TO A PLACE where the walls were planed smooth. The corridor of rock widened and heightened, and they could pick themselves off the ground they had crawled over and stand erect on two feet. Raif pulled Ash up. The lynx coat she was wearing had shed fur at the elbows and knees, and it was matted with a greasy spume of mineral oil and ice. The palm sides of both her mitts were bald. One was torn, and there was blood around the frayed edges. There was blood on her cheek, too; sometime earlier she had stumbled into a spur of rock that had sliced a thumbnail's worth of skin from her face.

Raif had lost all sense of time's passage. He no longer knew if it was day or night. How many hours had passed since they had left the Hollow River was something he would never know. If someone had told him he had spent thirty hours on his hands and knees, crawling through openings no bigger than a doghouse door and along passages so jagged that they had torn his dead man's cloak to shreds, he would have nodded and taken it as truth. His hands burned. Once during the journey he had made the mistake of biting off his gloves and probing the bandaged flesh. It was like prodding a waterskin; fluid oozed around his fingers, lukewarm and yellow as beaten eggs. He had pulled the mitts back on and not looked since. Pain alone was easier to live with.

As he worked the soreness out of his legs, he looked at the

smoothly planed corridor ahead. A vision of the night sky had been tattooed into the rock. Stars and constellations glittered overhead, and night herons and great horned owls soared the cold currents beneath a moon of pure ice. Shadow creatures with fingers of charred bone and eyes as black as hell rode wraith horses from a rift cut deep into the stone. Raif switched his gaze to another section of rock, only to see a second rift with things that had no place in the world of men spilling out like maggots from an old kill.

*Kill an army for me, Raif Sevrance.*

Softly Raif said to Ash, "Dim the light."

She did, and when he took her hand in his it was warm with the lantern's heat. He knew she had seen the same things he had, and his heart ached at her strength. Never once during the journey had she stopped and rested. Never once had she spoken about fear. He loved her completely and could no longer imagine a world where she was not at his side. He had to protect her for always. She was clan.

In this smooth new corridor there was enough room for them to walk side by side. Briefly Raif let himself imagine a future where he and Ash lived on a croft in some distant corner of the clanholds. Effie would be there too, and Ash would love her like a sister, and he would teach them both how to fight and hunt, and together they would plant a good bed of oats and another of onions and keep six head of sheep for wool and milk. And Drey . . . Drey would ride there twice a week and be closer than a brother to them all.

Raif breathed hard. Bit by bit he shredded the dream in his mind until there was nothing but torn bits left. It was a childish fantasy, and he was a fool to imagine it, and the only thing that mattered was the Cavern of Black Ice.

*Noooooooo.*

Ash flinched as the scream ripped along the corridor. The voices had been quiet for some time, and Raif had hoped against hope they had gone. Yet even as the tail end of the scream faded into freezing air, a second scream came, and then another. And then the wailing began.

*Please, mistresss, no, mistressss . . .*
*So cold, mistresss, share the light . . .*
*Want it, give it, reach. . . .*

Raif's skin crawled. He could hear the click of fingernails against stone and smell the stench of burned things. Everything that was within him told him this was no place for a clansman to be. He had seen the moon and the night sky on the wall: This was the domain of the Sull.

And yet. There was a raven too, and it had been guiding the way, and there had to be something in that.

Setting his mouth in a grim line, he tightened his hold on Ash's hand and led her through the keening of insane things to the cavern that awaited her at the end.

There wasn't far to go, not really. The voices had known she was close. Suddenly there were no more decorations on the walls, only symbols carved in a foreign hand. An archway cut from mountain rock marked the end of the journey. It was another Sull-made thing, dark and shaded with moonlight, with night-blooming flowers at its base and silver-winged moths suspended in the stone. A roughly carved figure leaped over the cantle of the arch, his features turned toward the rock so his face was unknowable, a sword of shadows in his hand.

As they passed beneath the arch Raif noticed a mated pair of ravens had been carved within the deepest recesses of the rock. Their bills were open as if frozen in midcall, and their clawed feet danced a jig upon the stone. Without thought, he raised his hand to his neck and pulled out his lore. Touching it, he entered the Cavern of Black Ice.

Clan had no words for this place. The world of the clan-holds was one of daylight and hunting and white ice; it had boundaries and borders—dozens of ways to separate one clanhold from another and one clansman's holdings from his neighbor's. This place was thin around the edges, like a sword turned side on. Its boundaries bled into another world, and Raif doubted they were true boundaries at all. It hardly seemed to exist before his eyes, like something conjured up out of moonlight and rain, yet even as he thought that, he was aware of the weight and the sheer *mass* of the place.

The ice steamed like a great black dragon emerging from a frozen lake. It glittered with every color ever seen at night. Once, many summers ago, Effie had gone trapping with Raina. She was only a baby at the time, barely able to walk on her own two feet, yet somehow she had returned home with an egg-size granite pebble in her fist. She was excited about it in her own quiet way, and to please her, Inigar Stoop had taken it to his mill-saw and broken it in two. Raif could remember watching the cooling water spill over the granite as the saw bit sliced into stone. He remembered frowning at the waste of a good skimmer. Then it had split in two, and inside was a heart of pure quartz. Dark and smoky and flashing like the brightest jewel, encased in a rime of hard rock. Raif thought about that now as he looked upon the cavern. It was like standing in the center of such a stone.

He could not begin to guess what liquid had cooled to form the ice. Slabs of it, some so smooth he could see his own face reflected there, and some as jagged as spinal cords, lined every portion of the cave. He walked upon it as he entered, heard it tick and fracture as his weight came down upon it, felt the entire structure *shudder* as stresses spread around it like whispers around a room.

The cavern soared three stories high and was as wide as any cave he'd ever seen. It was massive and utterly cold: a boundary between worlds. When he looked into the ice he saw shapes shifting and undulating in the place where the cave wall should have lain. Black fire burned within. He saw the shades of hooded things, of beasts with many heads and wolves with thrashing tails, and things that were not men, not quite. He saw nightmares and shadows and darkly craven things, yet when he looked again the ice was still.

The voices were hysterical now. They pleaded with their mistress, begging her to turn back, to flee the cavern, to reach in another place.

Raif felt Ash pulling her hand free of his, and he hated to let it go. She felt his resistance and turned to face him, and already he could see that she was changing. Her eyes were taking on the colors of the Sull. No longer gray, they shone silver and midnight blue. Her jaw was hard set, and her chin was raised, but her lips were red where she had chewed on them. Looking at her, he realized one thing: He could not help her in this.

The ice pick he had jammed through his belt was no use here. Tem, Drey, Corbie Meese: No clansman could do more than stand and watch. There was nothing of flesh and blood to fight, no necks or soft stomachs that would yield to an ax. Just shadows and black ice. When Ash reached she would do so alone.

Unbidden, the image of the women and children fleeing Hailsmen on the Bluddroad came to him. He had stood and watched then, too.

*Watcher of the Dead.* A shudder began at the base of his spine, but he made himself rigid and stopped it. He would show nothing but strength to Ash.

She looked at him for a long moment, pinning him where he stood. Slowly she stripped off her gloves and let them fall to the floor. Her coat slipped off with a single shrug, and suddenly she was standing in the cavern wearing a plain gray dress, with her silver gold hair flowing loose over her shoulders. Gently she smiled at him, and gently she spoke. "It's all right," she said. "I'm here, and I know what I must do. It's just dancing ice from now on."

He did not smile. Fear for her consumed him. She knew he could heart-kill beasts—she had seen him do so with her own two eyes—yet she did not know he was Watcher of the Dead. He should have told her sooner . . . for he could not tell her now.

"You must let me go, Raif."

He did not know he had taken hold of her arm until she pulled it back. She began to turn from him, and dread rose in his belly at the thought of her standing alone. He had to protect her. He, who had watched Bludd women and children die on the Bluddroad, seen Shor Gormalin brought home over the back of his horse, and killed three Bluddsmen in the snow outside Duff's, had to keep her from harm.

In his frustration, he tugged at the cord that held his lore. The hard, black piece of bird ivory jabbed against his gloved hands. Raven lore. He took it and weighed it in his fist. It had warded him all along. And perhaps it warded the Sull, too. And perhaps the ravens he had passed on the archway and on the riverwall had been *guarding*, not showing, the way.

Swiftly he plucked it from him. "Ash."

She turned her head toward him.

"Wear this." He held out his lore.

"I can't. It's part of your clan."

"You are my clan. And you have no lore to protect you." *And ravens always survive to the end.* "Take it."

Something in his voice compelled her, and she took it from him and fastened it about her neck. It looked dark and savage there, on its cord of sweat-rotted twine. Yet something deep within him eased at the sight of it lying flat against her skin. He could let her go now.

She walked from him in silence, the hem of her skirt trailing across the ice. The cavern shuddered with every step she took and the voices hounded her like dogs.

*Hate you, mistressss, slash your pretty face.*

*Pull you down with us, make you burn.*

Ash's chin stayed high, though the threats were terrible in their violence and hatred, and the black ice was colder than a tomb. He felt the power cumulating in her, felt her *pull* what she needed from the air. Her belly swelled, and her breasts rose and fell, and muscles in her shoulders began to work.

The cavern glittered like dark fire, its borders and knife edges flickering between worlds. Into its center walked the Reach. Firmly she stepped, ice winds blowing her hair and the sleeves of her dress, the corner of her lip moving as she bit down upon it. The air around her thickened and warped, and slowly, very slowly, a fine nimbus of blue light grew about her shoulders and arms. Raif felt his face burn with coldness. He had seen light like that before, on the blades of clansmen making kills in moonlight and in the cold inner hearts of flames.

As black ice creaked and shivered around her, Ash March *reached*. Later Raif would remember her beauty as she stood there limned in blue light, her fingers rising first, then her hands and her arms, as she reached out toward a place that he would never, ever, know firsthand. Later he would remember that . . . but for now he felt only fear.

Up came her arms, spreading wide to encompass a world beyond his own. Her mouth fell open and a terrible dark substance poured from her tongue and blasted against the ice. The cavern shook. The mountain rumbled with a deep bass note that sounded like the Stone Gods shattering the world. Yet the black ice remained intact. The walls *bent* to her power, yielding like saltwater ice, yet they did not let it pass. The ice stretched and contorted, forming grotesque black bulges and pressure sores where the ice was stretched so thinly it was almost white. The cavern hummed with tension. And the voices screamed, higher and higher, wailing a song of terror and damnation that rose from a place far deeper than any hell.

On and on the power flowed, exiting Ash's body with the force of steam venting under pressure and bursting against the cavern walls. The black ice flashed under the bombardment, turning as transparent as polished glass. Within it, Raif saw things he wished never to see again.

A charred landscape. A nightmare world. A slithering, jerking mass of dark souls.

Ash stood against them all. He saw that now, clearly; he also saw that the change that had begun the moment she'd entered the cavern was still taking place within her. She was becoming what had been only a word to Raif before. A Reach. It would never be over for her, not truly, even after she left this place. Heritas Cant had said as much, yet Raif had not wanted to understand. He had wanted to believe that the Cavern of Black Ice marked the end. Now, seeing the air rippling with heat from her power and the skin of black ice *straining* to contain what she unleashed, he knew it was just the start.

Ash's eyes were focused on some far distant point beyond the ice. Briefly he glimpsed a sea of shifting gray waters . . . or was it clouds or smoke? Heritas Cant had called it the borderlands and said that Ash was the only person living who could walk there without fear.

Sobered, Raif watched her face. He wanted it to end.

The cavern walls ground against each other as Ash's power continued to drain. Sweat ran in rivulets down her neck and the high curves of her breasts, and wet hair clung like chains to her face. Words had failed the voices now, and all that was left to them was the awful bleating of herd animals penned for the kill. Raif hated to hear them. He thought they would drive him insane.

Finally the noises faded to grunts and whimpers, then died completely. The air stilled. Dust drifted to earth as the milling of the cavern walls ground to a halt. The black ice glowed silver for a moment and then faded to matt black. It was used up now. Raif imagined that one quick stab with a pickax would be enough to shatter it like glass.

Raif's sense of what lay beyond had gone. Fled. Yet something about his last glimpse of the nightmare world pricked a new kind of fear. He barely understood it, and even as he tried to seize upon the image that disturbed him it disappeared. Had there been a crack in the blindwall? It wasn't possible. Ash had released her power safely here. That he knew.

Ash stood in the center of the cavern, her arms held wide before her, the light surrounding her body dimming into thin air.

Nothing moved for the longest moment. Raif felt as if he were alone in the cavern; it hardly seemed as if Ash were there at all. Her back was rigid, and her eyes were far focused, and even the bit of lip she had chewed on had paled. The only thing upon her that seemed wholly in this world was the ugly piece of raven around her neck. *That* was solid: dark with oils from Raif's skin, worn thin in the places where he handled it, its ivory as cracked and flawed as an old man's fingernail. It belonged in the earth or in the remains of a burned-out fire. It did not belong in the land beyond the ice.

Raif waited. He wanted to smash the ice to splinters with his fists and snatch Ash away like a man kidnapping a child. Yet he did not want to hurt her. She was so thin, like Effie almost; if he handled her roughly, he could break her bones.

Slowly, breath by breath, she returned to him.

Her mouth closed, and after many minutes she blinked, and when her gaze refocused it came to rest on something that both of them could see. It seemed difficult for her to relax her arms, and she made awkward little movements as she drew them to her sides. After a moment she raised her hand to her throat and touched the raven lore. She looked at it with her new silver blue eyes, brought it to her lips, and kissed it. "It guided me back," she said in a voice drained of all strength. "I was lost and it guided me back."

Raif closed his eyes. His heart had been so long without joy, he did not know what it was that filled him. He just knew he had to go to her and take her from this place.

## Heart of Darkness

RETAINING THE THOUGHT was the hardest thing of all. He
could wait in silence, unmoving, barely breathing, betraying
not the slightest reaction as the caul flies fed on his flesh.
That was easy. Such was the measure of his life. It was the
nursing of the thought that took it from him.

*When he is gone I will return to the place where I took
him. And this time I go there alone.*

The Nameless One ran the words through his head, sounding each slowly, testing their meaning, afraid that at any moment he might lose the sense of one or all. Words were as water
to him. He grasped and cupped, yet he still could not hold them
in mind. He had waited here before, in his iron chamber, feigning senselessness or fatigue. Yet though his body served him as
well as a wheel-broken body could, the words always left him
in the end. Without words he had no intent. Without intent he
was every bit as senseless as he feigned.

This time would be different, though. *This time I go there
alone.*

The Light Bearer watched him, suspicion sharp as needles
in his eyes. He had not liked being yanked back from that
place. Anger and exhaustion made him shake. The Nameless
One smelled urine that was not his own. The Light Bearer
was weak in many ways.

The blow when it came was hardly a surprise. "Wake,
damn you! I know you can see and hear me. I know you
brought me back too soon."

The Nameless One allowed his head to slump back
against the iron wall. His rotted chains rustled like dry
sticks.

The Light Bearer watched his every breath. "You think to
play games with me? You, who exist only on my say?" Silk

slithered over metal as he drew closer. "Perhaps I have left you untouched for too long. Perhaps I should have Caydis warm his hooks."

The Nameless One did not fall into the trap of fear. Fear lost him words. Unblinking, he focused his gaze upon the Light Bearer's left shoulder and the image of the Killhound emblazoned there.

Time passed. The Light Bearer felt it more keenly than he, shifting his weight from foot to foot, breathing harshly, and finally pushing himself away from the iron chamber. He was not satisfied, but what more could he do? He could hardly beat the creature who was the source of all his power.

"I will be back tomorrow," he warned as he retrieved his stone lamp and headed up the stairs. "And next time I will pull two flies from your back." With the last of his words the light faded and darkness came to the apex chamber, rising from the ground to the ceiling as always.

The Nameless One did not move. When a measure of time satisfying to him had passed, he closed his eyes. *This time I go there alone.*

It was easy, really. The Light Bearer had shown him the way. Power enough he had, for he had learned the ways to keep a poor man's portion for himself. The Light Bearer suspected this, but truth was hard to extract from one who had lost all fear of pain.

With the soft clack of bones dropped in a pot, the Nameless One forsook his flesh. Up he traveled through layers of rock and surface tiles, up through the Inverted Spire. Pushing his insubstance forward to meet the night sky, he tested his attitude to freedom. It was dark here, and cold as ice smoke, and the horizon stretched and curved, stretched and curved, as far as the eyes could see. He could not say it pleased him. He was still one man alone with a broken body and no name; a blue firmament above him made no difference. Fleeing his despair, he journeyed to the place where the Light Bearer had taken him.

*This time I go there alone.*

The gray landscape of the borderlands was still in turmoil, roiling and steaming like a sea settling down from a storm.

In his excitement the Light Bearer had sucked the caul fly dry, wanting to go deeper, farther, see if he could find the source. The Nameless One took some small portion of pleasure in recalling how he had wrenched his master back. It had been worth the examination and the rage. And now . . . well, now he had the power to search this place himself.

Vast continents of ether floated before his eyes, great cliffs and headlands of dust, yet he spared them little but a passing thought. The Dark River was here; he knew it, he smelled it, and within it lived his name. Deeper and deeper he traveled, skimming the cold peaks and fathomless troughs, until finally he saw it in the distance. A line of utter darkness. He sought not to allow himself hope, yet it rose in his throat like a hard bright thing, and suddenly he felt like a child.

He could not reach the river soon enough. Cold were its waters and strong was its current, so strong that it pulled him downstream. Knowledge came to him in tantalizing glimpses; he remembered a man's face and a night full of stars and the heat of yellow flames against his cheek. He did not remember his name. Straining, he swam deeper, giving himself wholly to the current, and when an undertow seized him with an icy hand he did not struggle against it.

*Heart of Darknessss, you have come.*

A voice spoke a name that was not his own, yet he answered to it all the same. If he had possessed a body to shiver, he would have done so upon hearing the voice's reply.

*We have waited such a long time, Heart of Darknessss.*

Suddenly the Nameless One was no longer in the river, he was standing on a shore, and before him rose a wall that stretched to the ends of the world. He had seen this place once before when he had journeyed here with the Light Bearer, and that time, as this time, he perceived the same fault. It was new-made, still raw around the edges, and it smelled strangely sweet. Almost female.

*Push against it, Heart of Darknessss, and in return we will give you your name.*

It was an offer he could not refuse.

The substance of the wall burned him as he touched it, burned with a coldness so deep and so ungodly, he knew his flesh hands would pay a price. It mattered not. For when the world shuddered and the wall cracked and the cry of something not human rose from the breach, the Nameless One received a thought.

It was his name, and he spoke it out loud.

*"Baralis."*

# ABOUT THE AUTHOR

J. V. Jones is the author of the bestselling Book of Words trilogy, *The Barbed Coil*, and *A Fortress of Grey Ice*, the second book of the Sword of Shadows series. Born in England, she has lived in San Diego, California, and now lives in New York State where she's working on the third Sword of Shadows novel, *A Sword from Red Ice*.